GEORGE GISSING

NEW GRUB STREET

Edited with an introduction by
Bernard Bergonzi

PENGUIN BOOKS

Penguin Books Ltd, Harmondsworth, Middlesex, England
Penguin Books Inc., 3300 Clipper Mill Road, Baltimore, Md 21211, U.S.A.
Penguin Books Australia Ltd, Ringwood, Victoria, Australia

—

First published 1891
Published in Penguin English Library 1968
Copyright Introduction and Notes © Bernard Bergonzi, 1968

—

Made and printed in Great Britain
by Hazell Watson & Viney Ltd,
Aylesbury, Bucks
Set in Linotype Juliana

CONTENTS

GEORGE ROBERT GISSING

GEORGE ROBERT GISSING was born in Wakefield in 1857. His academic career at Owen's College, Manchester, was abruptly terminated in 1876 when he was imprisoned for theft. He spent a year in the United States, 1876–7, then returned and embarked on a literary career in London. In 1879 he married Helen Harrison, who died in 1888. He married his second wife, Edith Underwood, in 1891, and in 1898 he met Gabrielle Fleury, with whom he spent the rest of his life. Gissing's literary reputation was slowly established during the eighteen-nineties, and in 1896 he met H. G. Wells, who became a close friend. He died in 1903 at St Jean Pied de Port in the Pyrenees.

Gissing's principal works are: *Workers in the Dawn* (1880), *The Unclassed* (1884), *Isabel Clarendon* (1886), *Demos* (1886), *Thyrza* (1887), *A Life's Mourning* (1888), *The Nether World* (1889), *The Emancipated* (1890), *New Grub Street* (1891), *Denzil Quarrier* (1892), *Born in Exile* (1892), *The Odd Women* (1893), *In the Year of Jubilee* (1894), *Eve's Ransom* (1895), *The Paying Guest* (1895), *Sleeping Fires* (1895), *The Whirlpool* (1897), *Human Odds and Ends* (1898), *Charles Dickens: A Critical Study* (1898), *The Town Traveller* (1898), *The Crown of Life* (1899), *Our Friend the Charlatan* (1901), *By the Ionian Sea* (1901), *The Private Papers of Henry Ryecroft* (1903), *Veranilda* (1904), *Will Warburton* (1905), *The House of Cobwebs* (1906).

B. B.

INTRODUCTION

I

MOST novels deal with leisure rather than with work, with the margins of life, where the human personality is free to expand and enter into interesting relationships, rather than with the quotidian toil which, for the greater part of humanity, both defines and limits existence. Even novels that are overtly about industrial life present the factory or the mine as a menacing shape in the background influencing the lives of the characters, but do not dwell for long on the actual industrial processes. This is natural, even inevitable; many forms of work – or at least the more mechanical forms that Hannah Arendt describes as 'labour' in distinction to 'work' – are basically dehumanizing, and the novelist is bound to be interested in people when they are most fully and articulately human, even if, at the same time, they may be crushed by adversity. New Grub Street is one of the few exceptions, and this fact should, I think, be recognized initially, before one passes on to make the more familiar point that it is the most explicit fictional study of literary life ever written in English. Granted, the 'work' involved – the writing of novels – is, in the eyes of most people, at the furthest possible extreme from mere 'labour', and might even be considered so delightful and rewarding an activity as scarcely to deserve the name of work at all. Such an assumption is likely to be supported by those works of popular fiction where the 'novelist' who appears as a character is a glamorized, tweedy figure, with infinite time at his disposal and subject to little apparent necessity to spend long hours at his desk or typewriter.

Gissing presents a very different picture – of a society where literature has become a commodity, and where the writing of fiction does not differ radically from any other form of commercial or industrial production: 'After all, there came a day when Edwin Reardon found himself regularly at work once more, ticking off his stipulated quantum of manuscript each four-and-twenty hours'. The splendid freedom of creativity has become,

quite literally, a mechanical process. Gissing relentlessly in-
volves the reader in Edwin Reardon's attempts to write as a professional whilst desperately preserving some vestige of literary
integrity, culminating in the brutal forcing of his exhausted
imagination as he tries to meet the demands of the three-volume
novel convention.

In one sense, New Grub Street is a remarkably self-contained
book: a reader quite ignorant of Gissing's life and the literary
climate of the eighteen-eighties will learn enough from the novel
to be able both to enjoy the story and grasp its larger implica-
tions; indeed, New Grub Street is far more directly informative
in a social-historical way than most Victorian novels, and contains a mass of material about such things as the cost of living
among the shabby-genteel population of London in the eighties.
And yet the reader who is fairly sure that Edwin Reardon is a
direct autobiographical portrait of Gissing himself, might still
find it illuminating to learn, from Gissing's letters and other
biographical sources, just how faithful the rendering is, and
how exactly the mode of composition described in New Grub
Street corresponded to Gissing's own practice. Thus, Edwin
Reardon is shown as habitually writing about 4,000 words a
day when engaged on a novel. Gissing himself wrote New
Grub Street in exactly two months in the autumn of 1890, and
since it is a book of over 220,000 words, a simple calculation
shows that it must have been written at a daily rate not
far short of Edwin Reardon's. The principal difference, however, between Gissing's work and that of his character is that
whereas Reardon, who is not at heart a novelist at all, suffers
disastrously from this cruel rate of composition and produces
work of increasingly little merit, in New Grub Street Gissing
drew on a unique source of strength, in writing so immediately out of his personal predicament, and the result was
a singular if not flawless masterpiece. In the words of Mrs Q. D.
Leavis:

But when he took as the subject of a novel his most vital interest –
the problem of how to live as a man of letters, the literary world
being what it is, without sacrificing your integrity of purpose – he
produced his one permanent contribution to the English novel. I

think it can be shown to be a major contribution. The subject was both inside and outside him.*

When he began work on New Grub Street, Gissing was approaching his thirty-third birthday. He had already published eight novels, which had achieved for him the kind of modest, limited reputation that must be very trying for the aspiring novelist, falling as it does between the clear catastrophe of total literary failure and the clear success of wide and unequivocal critical recognition. After ten years of such disappointment and genteel poverty, Gissing was approaching a personal crisis, and it is his encounter with it that gives New Grub Street so much of its peculiar distinction, and which helps to explain the barely restrained bitterness with which it treats literary life. Nevertheless, it would be too simple to regard Gissing as a mere victim of circumstances, whose fate was entirely out of his own control. There is ample biographical evidence that he had a marked self-destructive streak that led him often to embrace tribulations that might have been avoided, and to exaggerate the nature of those that he had undergone. In 1880, the philosopher Frederic Harrison had read the young Gissing's first novel, Workers in the Dawn, with considerable enthusiasm; as a result, Gissing became a protégé of Harrison's. He was introduced to John Morley, then editor of the Pall Mall Gazette, who professed admiration for his work and pressed him to write for the paper. Gissing contributed a couple of articles but was disinclined to write more. Here is an account of the refusal by Frederic Harrison's son, Austin, to whom Gissing had been tutor:

We implored him to write again. But Gissing refused. He hated editors; he was no journalist, he said; he could not degrade himself by such 'trash'. In truth, at any time after 1882 Gissing could have obtained a place as critic or writer on some journal, which could have enabled him to write at leisure. But he would never hear of such a thing. My father begged him to accept some post, but Gissing declined to 'serve'. Gissing positively chose to live in strife.†

---

* Q. D. Leavis, 'Gissing and the English Novel', Scrutiny, VII, June 1938, pp. 73–81.

† Austin Harrison, 'George Gissing', Nineteenth Century and After, LX, September 1906, pp. 453–63.

In addition to tutoring Harrison's two sons Gissing was found other pupils, but he was determined to earn a living solely by writing novels, and in 1884 he courteously declined Harrison's offer of more pupils, wishing to devote his whole time to fiction. The payment he could expect was meagre, since his reputation was scarcely established, but, Austin Harrison insisted, 'if he remained poor it was largely because he chose to.'

Integrity and perversity were inextricably interwoven in Gissing's make-up, and his life seems to have been dominated by the myth of the artist who *must* subject himself to intense suffering if he is to produce work of any value. Austin Harrison's final summary of his character emphasizes this aspect :

He deliberately regarded himself as a sort of social outlaw, making a virtue of self indulgence and self-concentration, fostering the hunger of querulous self-pity. He gloried in the vanity of self-compassion. In literature he thought of poverty in avoirdupois. He revelled in the gloom of London's misery. Every fibre of him betrayed the artist, and because he was an artist he was also an aristocrat. His delight in poverty, in misery, and in vice was purely literary and consciously egotistical.

Even though this outline may seem unsympathetic to Gissing, one must admit that it gives a good impression of the characteristic atmosphere of much of his fiction. It also helps to place him in a larger cultural context, for the collocation of 'outlaw' and 'artist' and 'aristocrat' is familiar in late nineteenth-century life and letters, and has been usefully discussed by Frank Kermode in *Romantic Image*.

At the beginning of his adult life Gissing had been an 'outlaw' in a painfully literal sense : his brilliant academic career at Owen's College, Manchester, was cut short when he was discovered in an act of theft. He was tried, convicted, and briefly imprisoned, and Gissing felt that his whole life had been branded by this experience. He had stolen in order to obtain money to help a young prostitute, Helen Harrison, whom he subsequently married and with whom he endured several years of totally miserable married life before she finally drank herself to death. Gissing felt that life without a partner was impossible, but he was convinced that his lack of financial prospects made it impossible for him to marry an educated, middle-class girl, and early in 1891, whilst New Grub Street was in the press, Gissing married another working-class girl, Edith Underwood, a match which was to prove no less disastrous for a man of his sensitive and fastidious temperament. Here, more than anywhere, one sees evidence of Gissing's self-destructive tendencies, for there is no evidence that he was passionately in love with Edith, and in New Grub Street, he had described with great lucidity the unhappy situation of Alfred Yule, a man of letters married to an ignorant wife, who is quite unable to share his interests and aspirations. And Mrs Yule was at least a woman of placid and amenable temperament, which, by all accounts, the second Mrs Gissing was not. Jacob Korg, Gissing's biographer, remarks that Gissing must have been aware of the likely consequences of his second marriage, but adds:

It is difficult to escape the obvious conclusion that he married Edith in spite of his foreknowledge because a part of him wanted to suffer those consequences. Apparently, the marriage was another of those acts of self-mortification that Gissing committed from time to time with the subconscious motive of putting himself at a disadvantage.*

It was, then, at a crucial period in his life that Gissing embarked on New Grub Street, a book which seems to have been regarded during the frenzied process of composition as merely one more piece of competent routine fiction, and whose outstanding quality he was slow to realize. Whilst correcting the proofs in February 1891, he wrote to his brother: 'I am astonished to find how well it reads. There are savage truths in it.' When the novel appeared it was generally admired, both by his family and by his German friend Eduard Bertz, to whom he wrote:

Well now, it is unnecessary for me to say how your remarks on New Grub Street rejoice me. As all my acquaintances agree in loud praise of the book, I suppose it is not bad. I wrote it in utter prostration of spirit; no book of mine was regarded so hopelessly in the production. This experience encourages me; if I could write tolerably

---

* Jacob Korg, George Gissing: A Critical Biography, Seattle, 1963, p. 153.

then, I am pretty sure to be able to produce under any circumstances likely to befall me.*

Gissing's last encouraging assumption was plausible but false: it was precisely the fact that it had been wrung out of 'utter prostration of spirit' that gave *New Grub Street* its unique character. With a few reservations, the critics shared the favourable opinion of *New Grub Street* expressed by his intimates, and within a month the novel went into a second impression, being the first of his books to achieve this distinction. Nevertheless, this general approval, though encouraging, was not marked enough to bring Gissing's reputation to the decisive take-off point that he had hoped for, and the book's sales could have no effect on his financial position, since he had sold it outright to Smith, Elder & Co. for £150.

II

The pressure of Gissing's predicament is everywhere apparent in *New Grub Street*. Nevertheless, it would be a mistake to see the novel as exclusively concerned with the unhappy situation of Edwin Reardon. He forms part of a complex of personal and literary relationships; almost as important is Jasper Milvain, the thrusting and ambitious young journalist, who represents the new-style, exploitative view of the literary profession, as opposed to Reardon's gentle, old-fashioned integrity. We meet Jasper on the first page of the novel and again on the last, and his rise to fame and wealth is set against the decline of Reardon to failure and final disaster. Gissing presents a society in miniature, a microcosm of the literary world as he had experienced it, whose significance is symbolized by the novel's title. He explained it in a letter to Bertz:

Grub Street actually existed in London some hundred and fifty years ago. In Pope and his contemporaries the name has become synonymous for wretched-authordom. In Hogarth's 'Distressed Author' there is 'Grub Street' somewhere inscribed. Poverty and meanness of spirit being naturally associated, the street came to denote an abode, not merely of poor, but of insignificant, writers.†

---

* Arthur C. Young (ed.), *The Letters of George Gissing to Eduard Bertz 1887–1903*, London, 1961, p. 121.
  † ibid., p. 122.

The Grub Street of the eighteen-eighties was still homogeneous enough to include within its confines types who today would have little point of contact. In addition to Reardon, who at heart is a classical scholar but who is determined to make a respectable name and living by writing novels, we have the ageing, embittered critic Alfred Yule and his clever daughter Marian, who earns a living by ghost-writing and devilling for her father. Nowadays, since the rise of English as a university subject, both of them would be more at home as academics; Alfred Yule's conversation provides some choice examples of the shop-talk of Eng. Lit. professionals. On the other hand, Jasper Milvain – who thinks of marrying Marian, until he sets his sights higher – would probably be destined for a job in advertising or public relations. Grouped around these central figures are the lesser occupants of the picture, like Reardon's pathetic friend, Biffen, an exponent of what he calls 'an absolute realism in the sphere of the ignobly decent', toiling with Flaubertian concentration at a novel called *Mr Bailey, Grocer*; or Whelpdale, a failed writer who shows considerable ingenuity at exploiting the commercial fringes of literature: he dabbles in the lowest forms of the new popular journalism, runs a fiction-writing course, and launches a literary agency.

In Gissing's novel all natural human relations are affected by the claims of 'literature', which forms a thin disguise for basic economic pressures, since literature is itself no more than a commodity. Jasper Milvain, who is the sole support of his family, successfully sets his two sisters to work at writing children's stories (a better alternative, as he reasonably argues, than taking employment as governess, which was the only other possibility for middle-class girls at that period). The relationship between Alfred Yule and Marian has dwindled to one entirely defined by the literary hack work she does for him, until she receives a legacy, when Alfred subjects her to intolerable pressures to use it to finance a new literary magazine which he will edit. Above all, the relationship between Edwin Reardon and his wife Amy is eroded by his lack of literary success.

Gissing presents his vision of literature as a commodity in a powerful passage in Chapter 8. Marian Yule is in the British Museum Reading Room:

One day at the end of the month she sat with books open before her, but by no effort could she fix her attention upon them. It was gloomy, and one could scarcely see to read; a taste of fog grew perceptible in the warm, headachy air. Such profound discouragement possessed her that she could not even maintain the pretence of study; heedless whether anyone observed her, she let her hands fall and her head droop. She kept asking herself what was the use and purpose of such a life as she was condemned to lead. When already there was more good literature in the world than any mortal could cope with in his lifetime, here was she exhausting herself in the manufacture of printed stuff which no one even pretended to be more than a commodity for the day's market. What unspeakable folly! To write – was not that the joy and the privilege of one who had an urgent message for the world? Her father, she knew well, had no such message; he had abandoned all thought of original production, and only wrote about writing. She herself would throw away her pen with joy but for the need of earning money. And all these people about her, what aim had they save to make new books out of those already existing, that yet newer books might in turn be made out of them? This huge library, growing into unwieldiness, threatening to become a trackless desert of print – how intolerably it weighed upon the spirit.

Marian's reflection about 'the manufacture of printed stuff' is subsequently echoed when Reardon is shown as 'ticking off his stipulated quantum of manuscript each four-and-twenty hours': writing is, in such conditions, reduced to a purely mechanical process. In Marian's dismal conception of the endless superfetation of works of unnecessary literature, Gissing catches something of Pope's vision of the original Grub Street in the *Dunciad*. He develops her reverie in a paragraph which has, for Gissing, an unusual intensity of metaphoric life:

The fog grew thicker; she looked up at the windows beneath the dome and saw that they were a dusky yellow. Then her eye discerned an official walking along the upper gallery, and in pursuance of her grotesque humour, her mocking misery, she likened him to a black, lost soul, doomed to wander in an eternity of vain research along endless shelves. Or again, the readers who sat here at these radiating lines of desks, what were they but hapless flies caught in a huge web, its nucleus the great circle of the Catalogue? Darker, darker. From the towering wall of volumes seemed to emanate visible motes, intensifying the obscurity; in a moment the book-lined circumference of the room would be but a featureless prison-limit.

The image of the reading room as a great spider's web is very apt, and so is its transformation, in the final phrase, into a panopticon or circular prison. It is in passages such as this, as well as in many incidental felicities of characterization, that we see Gissing's basic debt to Dickens. Gissing is sometimes spoken of in literary histories as an English disciple of the Continental naturalists, and particularly as one whose immersion in grim realism owed much to Zola. In point of fact, although Gissing came increasingly to admire Zola in the latter part of his life, during the eighteen-eighties, when his fiction was at its most unrelentingly naturalistic, he shared the customary English distaste for Zola as a morally subversive writer. It is more appropriate to see him as a novelist whose realism, particularly his awareness of the darker side of London life, derives very largely from Dickens, though without the Dickensian exuberance and pervading fantasy.

In such a world, where literature has become a commodity and its production a mechanical business, one may either accept the prevalent standards and try to succeed by them, which is the role freely adopted by Jasper Milvain, or one can vainly struggle against them in the interests of a nobler ideal of literature, as does Edwin Reardon. But Edwin's struggle is undermined, not merely by his weak and faltering temperament, but by a radical scepticism about values of any kind, which, as an up-to-date positivist of the eighties, he is unable to repress:

'And yet,' he continued, 'of course it isn't only for the sake of reputation that one tries to do uncommon work. There's the shrinking from conscious insincerity of workmanship – which most of the writers nowadays seem never to feel. "It's good enough for the market"; that satisfies them. And perhaps they are justified. I can't pretend that I rule my life by absolute ideals; I admit that everything is relative. There is no such thing as goodness or badness, in the absolute sense, of course. Perhaps I am absurdly inconsistent when – though knowing my work can't be first-rate – I strive to make it as good as possible. I don't say this in irony, Amy; I really mean it. It may very well be that I am just as foolish as the people I ridicule for moral and religious superstition.'

This was not the spirit that inspired Pope or Dr Johnson, and it is scarcely surprising that Reardon is constantly unable to overcome the obstacles of his environment. Yet he is sufficiently distanced and integrated into the fictional pattern to be more than a mere vehicle for Gissing's own self-pity and special-pleading.

In his relations with his wife, Reardon illustrates Gissing's life-long contention that girls of middle-class background could not make suitable wives for poor and struggling writers, since they were used to high material standards and could not bring themselves to sacrifice them. Amy has married Reardon in the hope and expectation that he is on the verge of a distinguished career as a novelist, and she becomes less and less sympathetic to his failure. Following the passage quoted above there is a painful scene in which Reardon tells his wife that they are living above their means and that they must move to a cheaper flat; she receives this news with cold incomprehension. The scene is curiously reminiscent of the exchanges between Lydgate and Rosamund in *Middlemarch*, when the conflict between Lydgate's lack of means and his wife's extravagant habits finally explodes. This theme of the inevitable conflict between masculine aspiration and feminine materialism was common in the fiction of the final decades of the nineteenth century and the early years of the twentieth. The pitfalls of marriage for the ambitious male are dwelt on by Hardy in *Jude the Obscure* and by Wells in *Love and Mr Lewisham* and *Tono-Bungay*. The ideal of masculine exclusiveness and self-sufficiency as a viable alternative to marriage was frequently manifested, and was expressed in scenes evoking the cosy male companionship of the club or smoking room, such as we find, for instance, in Kipling or Conan Doyle. Their humble equivalent in *New Grub Street* is in the evenings that Reardon and Biffen spend together discussing the metrics of Greek poetry.

Set against Reardon and Biffen, who try to preserve their integrity and resist the pressures of the environment, are Amy and Milvain, who accept the fact that literature is a commodity, and the literary world a system, whose workings must be mastered by the would-be author. Amy realizes this very thoroughly, and early in the novel she coldly and shrewdly tells Reardon:

'Art must be practised as a trade, at all events in our time. This is the age of trade. Of course if one refuses to be of one's time, and yet hasn't the means to live independently, what can result but break-down and wretchedness?'

Gissing is very fair-minded, even sympathetic, towards Amy and Jasper. For most of the novel Amy, a clearly intelligent and attractive girl, is treated ironically but not unkindly; Gissing makes it apparent that she could have made a good wife for a successful novelist, and her inability to share Edwin's ideals and sacrifice herself with him is as much a hall-mark of her class and upbringing as a personal fault. Nevertheless, in a rather shocking fashion, Gissing seems to withdraw all sympathy from Amy towards the end of the novel, and to regard her with open dislike; and this at a point – after she has experienced the death, within a day or so, of her husband and her only child – when even a wholly disagreeable character might be entitled to a modicum of tenderness. It is as if the death of Reardon, his fictional persona, had aroused in Gissing something of the self-pity and bitterness that, for most of the novel, are successfully kept in check.

The conclusion of the novel is heavily ironical, with Jasper and Amy, who speak the same language and understand the world in the same way, joined in marriage and 'dreamy bliss'. Mrs Leavis has remarked that 'when any nineteenth-century novelist names a character Jasper, I think we may safely conclude that that character is intended to be the villain'. Nevertheless, Jasper Milvain is not presented as emphatically villainous. If he is ruthlessly calculating in his careerism, he also has an attractive energy, a Stendhalian quality which is rare in Gissing's work. He is seen in this light by Marian Yule, who loves him; she thinks of Jasper as a

man who aimed with frank energy at the joys of life . . . She did not ask for high intellect or great attainments; but vivacity, courage, determination to succeed were delightful to her senses.

In the event, Jasper's determination to succeed causes him to jilt Marian, and shows him at his least agreeable. Yet, for the most part, Jasper's moral faults, like Amy's, are seen as arising from his deliberate decision to accept the prevalent system of values. In this context, the close and necessary relationship between Jasper

and Edwin becomes intelligible. If Edwin's poverty and wretchedness serve as a constant warning to Jasper of the results of a 'pure'
dedication to literature, then conversely Jasper's brutal careerism
and incessant pursuit of the main chance repel Edwin from any
idea of writing for the market, since, it seems, to do so will
inevitably turn one into a Milvain. On his part, Jasper respects
the values that he is unable to pursue, and has a real admiration
for Edwin's fiction, whilst lamenting Edwin's inability or refusal
to operate the system in such a way as to ensure the maximum
advantage for his reputation. Early in the novel Jasper points
this out to Marian:

'There's a friend of mine who writes novels,' Jasper pursued. 'His
books are not works of genius, but they are glaringly distinct from
the ordinary circulating novel. Well, after one or two attempts, he
made half a success; that is to say, the publishers brought out a
second edition of the book in a few months. There was his opportunity. But he couldn't use it; he had no friends, because he had no
money. A book of half that merit if written by a man in the position
of Warbury when he started would have established the reputation
of a lifetime. His influential friends would have referred to it in
leaders, in magazine articles, in speeches, in sermons. It would have
run through numerous editions, and the author would have had
nothing to do but to write another book and demand his price. But
the novel I'm speaking of was practically forgotten a year after its
appearance; it was whelmed beneath the flood of next season's
literature.'

The ironic counterpointing of the two men's careers is brought
to its culmination when, after Edwin's death, Milvain writes a
respectful article called 'The Novels of Edwin Reardon', which
arouses a grateful response from the widowed Amy; she is by
now well-off, as she has received a convenient legacy, and the
nuptials of Jasper and Amy follow with smooth inevitability.

If the system is the ultimate villain of New Grub Street,
rather than the individuals who live by its demands, the novel
certainly cannot be seen as striking any very severe blow against
the system. For Gissing is writing a novel of resentment rather
than of protest. Although no one knew better the evils of industrial capitalism and the wretchedness of the poor, Gissing was
the reverse of a reformer. His resentment was fed by his convic-

tion that nothing could be done about the evils of modern society, and that all attempts at political reform were folly, or worse. In his combination of a profound immersion in misery with an engrained conservatism he has some affinity with Dostoyevsky, even though his range is infinitely narrower. Gissing's social attitudes are made clear in *Demos* (1886), where he writes movingly about the plight of the London poor, and at the same time makes a violent onslaught on the socialist movement. And yet there is a strong streak of primitive Marxism implicit in *New Grub Street*, with its insistence that so-called intellectual values are merely a concealment for economic realities, that money underlies most forms of social and cultural attainment, and that literature has become reified into a market commodity. (One sees much the same attitudes apparent in George Orwell's *Keep the Aspidistra Flying* [1936], a novel which reads rather like a pastiche of *New Grub Street* transplanted to the London of the early nineteen-thirties.)

There are no hints for reform or improvement in *New Grub Street*, and it is implied that the cultural scene so bitterly anatomized is changing rapidly for the worse, and that there must once have been a period when things were better. In this area there is very little conclusive evidence, and one must be cautious about accepting Gissing's implicit valuations. The eighteen-eighties were certainly a time when the commercial possibilities of the printed word were being vigorously exploited, and there are many references to this in the novel, particularly to the rise of cheap sensational magazines, and to Whelpdale's manifold other activities. Twentieth-century cultural criticism has been possessed with myths of catastrophe, and *New Grub Street* lends itself with dangerous ease to such readings, with its suggestion that there had once been the possibility of a decent standard of literary endeavour, but that now the world has fallen into the hands of the Milvains and the Whelpdales. Raymond Williams, in *The Long Revolution*, provides material to offset any easy assumption of a sudden disastrous decline in standards, as opposed to a long, slow and exceedingly complex process of cultural change. If Gissing, writing about the eighteen-eighties, formulated the complaint that literature had been turned into a commodity, then it is salutary to remember that Defoe, a long time before, had described writing as a 'very considerable Branch of the English Commerce'. Even in specific practices, what seemed objectionable in the eighteen-eighties had been equally prevalent fifty years before. Thus, the puffing of books, which Jasper Milvain claimed to be essential for a soundly established reputation, had been a great feature of literary life in the eighteen-thirties, as Royal A. Gettmann has shown in his invaluable study of the Bentley papers, *A Victorian Publisher* (1961). And Edwin Reardon's struggles to spin out his story to fill the space required by the three-volume novel seem to have been anticipated much earlier in the century.

New Grub Street is an absorbing volume for the social historian, but it also has its dangers, since Gissing was consumed by his own highly personal myth of catastrophe, which effectively coloured his view of reality. In this novel he has outlined for us a *romancier maudit* who has affinities with the *poète maudit* of much late nineteenth-century literature, though Gissing's mythopoeic tendencies are controlled and balanced by his infinitely scrupulous narrative realism (also, in a different way, so characteristic of its time), and his infallible patience before the surface of life. This balance, or tension, between opposites gives *New Grub Street* some of its essential quality. Although Edwin Reardon seems very much like an example of the modern oversensitive, exacerbated consciousness, he is not presented in stark isolation, as such figures tend to be in twentieth-century fiction. He is very much part of a social context, which is defined in considerable detail, and the interest arises from his feeble attempts to assert his independence from its demands. Again, there is the skilfully handled tension between the rising Milvain and the falling Reardon. One should also mention the blend of sympathy and judgement with which we are invited to regard Milvain and – at least until the last part of the novel – Amy Reardon. Finally, and least specifically, there is the reconciliation of opposites in the pervasive but unobtrusive irony with which Gissing conducts his narrative, and which occasionally becomes memorable in such phrases as 'They had had three children; all were happily buried.' (If, like Gissing, one believes that life is both intolerable and irredeemable, one will have frequent recourse to some form of defensive irony.)

Gissing has several qualities in common with the great Victorian novelists: the ability to fill a broad canvas, skill in characterization, and in the evocation of atmosphere. But he lacks their energy and inventiveness, and there are various *longueurs* in *New Grub Street* that clearly arise from the desperate processes of its composition, so vividly described in the novel itself. If *New Grub Street* cannot claim a place in the very front rank of English fiction, it certainly deserves a prominent and permanent place in the second rank.

III

I have referred in passing to Edwin Reardon's bitter struggles with the three-volume novel form, or three-decker; indeed the three-decker assumes the role of a major though silent character in *New Grub Street*, and I should like, finally, to devote some space to this phenomenon, which is both an important element in the content of *New Grub Street* and the formal vehicle by which Gissing's novel came into the world. During the eighteenth century novels had been published in any number of volumes, but early in the nineteenth the three-volume variety became dominant, and was to remain so for seventy years. Professor Gettmann has described it thus: 'In the simplest physical terms the three-decker may be described as a work of prose fiction in three post-octavo volumes, with a list price of 31s. 6d.' Price and format remained stable for a remarkably long time, at least for as long as the circulating libraries found this kind of book a profitable commodity. It is true that the three-decker was never totally dominant: novels in one or two volumes continued to appear, although the libraries did not care for them, and a novelist like Dickens could reach a wide audience through serialization in monthly parts. Nevertheless, for several decades the three-decker was pre-eminent, and the circulating libraries maintained pressure on publishers to ensure that most novels came out in that form (since subscribers could take out only one volume at a time, a reader who wanted all three volumes at once had to take out three subscriptions). Publishers in turn put pressure on their authors by offering much higher payment for the three-decker than for novels in one or two volumes.

The dimensions of the three-decker were clearly defined and limited: each volume had to consist of about three hundred pages, with something over twenty lines to the page. Sometimes these specifications could be extraordinarily detailed, as Mr Gettmann points out: 'In a letter written in 1883 George Bentley informed an author that a novel consisted of 920 pages with twenty-one and a half lines on each page and nine and a half words in each line.' In point of fact, the composition of the three-decker was not always so minutely laid down as this, and books could be stretched to fit the three-volume format in ways suggested by Gissing's description of Edwin Reardon at work:

> He wrote a very small hand; sixty written slips of the kind of paper he habitually used would represent – thanks to the astonishing system which prevails in such matters: large type, wide spacing, frequency of blank pages – a passable three-hundred-page volume. On an average he could write four such slips a day; so here we have fifteen days for the volume, and forty-five for the completed book.

Reardon's resentment at the mechanical demands of the three-decker forms a prominent motif in New Grub Street:

> The second volume ought to have been much easier work than the first; it proved far harder. Messieurs and mesdames the critics are wont to point out the weakness of second volumes; they are generally right, simply because a story which would have made a tolerable book (the common run of stories) refuses to fill three books.

In his desperation to fill out the space Reardon – like many real-life novelists – resorts to the most patent forms of padding:

> Description of locality, deliberate analysis of character or motive, demanded far too great an effort for his present condition. He kept as much as possible to dialogue; the space is filled so much more quickly, and at a pinch one can make people talk about the paltriest incidents of life.

New Grub Street itself is undoubtedly marred by an excess of thinly spun conversation, as Gissing himself realized, for when the book was translated into French in 1898 he made radical cuts in the conversational material.

At times Reardon vows he will have no more to do with the accursed three-decker, and takes heart from a suggestion that 'numbers of authors were abandoning that procrustean system'. But in an important conversation with Milvain in Chapter 15, Reardon makes clear the precise nature of his dependence on the library-supported three-decker; publishers, assured of a steady sale to the libraries, could take the risk of paying their authors a fairly substantial sum in outright purchase of copyright:

'For anyone in my position,' said Reardon, 'how is it possible to abandon the three volumes? It is a question of payment. An author of moderate repute may live on a yearly three-volume novel – I mean the man who is obliged to sell his book out and out, and who gets from one to two hundred pounds for it. But he would have to produce four one-volume novels to obtain the same income; and I doubt whether he could get so many published within the twelve months. And here comes in the benefit of the libraries; from the commercial point of view the libraries are indispensable. Do you suppose the public would support the present number of novelists if each book had to be purchased? A sudden change to that system would throw three-fourths of the novelists out of work.'

The curiously Luddite note in the last sentence is significant. In the eighties it was evidently possible for the not very successful novelist to scratch a modest living, just like, say, a not very successful barrister. It was the system of outright purchase that made this possible. This system is often spoken of as unfair to authors and so it is in principle, particularly if a book sells very well and the author reaps no benefit at all from its success. But it did at least mean that a man of mediocre reputation could still live as a professional novelist, even if in a straitened fashion. Since the general switch to the royalty system, an author's rewards have been related to his book's sales, and only unusually successful writers can hope to make a living exclusively from novels. Arnold Bennett recalls that his first novel, written when he was a full-time journalist, made the net sum of precisely one guinea when it appeared in 1898.

The change in the system, which was discussed in *New Grub Street*, in fact came about in the mid-nineties, when the circulating libraries, which for so long had buttressed the three-decker, turned abruptly against it, and informed publishers that they would no longer be ordering it. Publishers had been following up the traditional three-volume edition of a novel at 31s. 6d. with a

cheap one-volume edition at 6s., and this had badly undermined
the libraries' dependence on the former. In retaliation they
wrecked the three-decker altogether: in 1894, 184 three-volume
novels appeared, in 1897 only four. The change was abrupt and
decisive: novels became shorter and cheaper, and outright purchase gave way to the royalty system. The way of life so memor-
ably described in *New Grub Street* would no longer be possible.

Bernard Bergonzi
University of Warwick

SUGGESTED FURTHER READING

TWO early essays on Gissing are of biographical value, 'George Gissing' by Austin Harrison, *Nineteenth Century and After*, LX, September 1906, and 'George Gissing, An Impression' by H. G. Wells, *Monthly Review*, XVI, August 1904, reprinted in *George Gissing and H. G. Wells*, 1961. Morley Roberts' *The Private Life of Henry Maitland*, 1912, revised edition, 1958, is a fictionalized biography of Gissing, by his oldest friend; it is excessively sensational in places, but remains a useful source of biographical information. The standard modern biography is by Jacob Korg, *George Gissing: A Critical Biography*, 1963. Frank Swinnerton's *George Gissing, A Critical Study*, 1912, remains an excellent introduction. Gissing's letters are of considerable interest and have appeared in three volumes: *Letters of George Gissing to Members of His Family*, edited by A. and E. Gissing, 1927; *George Gissing and H. G. Wells: Their Friendship and Correspondence*, edited by Royal A. Gettmann, 1961; *The Letters of George Gissing to Eduard Bertz 1887–1903*, edited by Arthur C. Young, 1961. Recommended essays on Gissing include 'George Gissing' by Virginia Woolf, *The Common Reader*, *Second Series*, 1932, which is also available in Virginia Woolf, *Collected Essays* I, 1966; and 'Gissing and the English Novel' by Q. D. Leavis, *Scrutiny*, VII, June 1938.

THE TEXT

The text of this book reproduces that of the first edition of *New Grub Street*, issued in three volumes in 1891. It was not revised during Gissing's lifetime.

Facsimile of title-page of Volume I
of the first edition, 1891

NEW GRUB STREET

A NOVEL

BY

GEORGE GISSING

AUTHOR OF 'THE NETHER WORLD' 'DEMOS' ETC.

IN THREE VOLUMES

VOL. I.

LONDON

SMITH, ELDER, & CO., 15 WATERLOO PLACE

1891

CONTENTS

OF

THE FIRST VOLUME

CONTENTS

OF

THE SECOND VOLUME

CONTENTS
OF
THE THIRD VOLUME

NEW GRUB STREET

Volume 1

Chapter 1

A MAN OF HIS DAY

As the Milvains sat down to breakfast the clock of Wattle-borough parish church struck eight; it was two miles away, but the strokes were borne very distinctly on the west wind this autumn morning. Jasper, listening before he cracked an egg, remarked with cheerfulness:

'There's a man being hanged in London at this moment.'

'Surely it isn't necessary to let us know that,' said his sister Maud, coldly.

'And in such a tone, too!' protested his sister Dora.

'Who is it?' inquired Mrs Milvain, looking at her son with pained forehead.

'I don't know. It happened to catch my eye in the paper yesterday that someone was to be hanged at Newgate this morning. There's a certain satisfaction in reflecting that it is not oneself.'

'That's your selfish way of looking at things,' said Maud.

'Well,' returned Jasper, 'seeing that the fact came into my head, what better use could I make of it? I could curse the brutality of an age that sanctioned such things; or I could grow doleful over the misery of the poor – fellow. But those emotions would be as little profitable to others as to myself. It just happened that I saw the thing in a light of consolation. Things are bad with me, but not so bad as *that*. I might be going out between Jack Ketch and the Chaplain to be hanged; instead of that, I am eating a really fresh egg, and very excellent buttered toast, with coffee as good as can be reasonably expected in this part of the world. – (Do try boiling the milk, mother.) – The tone in which I spoke was spontaneous; being so, it needs no justification.'

He was a young man of five-and-twenty, well built, though a trifle meagre, and of pale complexion. He had hair that was very nearly black, and a clean-shaven face, best described, perhaps, as of bureaucratic type. The clothes he wore were of expensive material, but had seen a good deal of service. His stand-up collar curled over at the corners, and his necktie was lilac-sprigged.

Of the two sisters, Dora, aged twenty, was the more like him in visage, but she spoke with a gentleness which seemed to indicate a different character. Maud, who was twenty-two, had bold, handsome features, and very beautiful hair of russet tinge; hers was not a face that readily smiled. Their mother had the look and manners of an invalid, though she sat at table in the ordinary way. All were dressed as ladies, though very simply. The room, which looked upon a small patch of garden, was furnished with old-fashioned comfort, only one or two objects suggesting the decorative spirit of 1882.

'A man who comes to be hanged,' pursued Jasper, impartially, 'has the satisfaction of knowing that he has brought society to its last resource. He is a man of such fatal importance that nothing will serve against him but the supreme effort of law. In a way, you know, that is success.'

'In a way,' repeated Maud, scornfully.

'Suppose we talk of something else,' suggested Dora, who seemed to fear a conflict between her sister and Jasper.

Almost at the same moment a diversion was afforded by the arrival of the post. There was a letter for Mrs Milvain, a letter and newspaper for her son. Whilst the girls and their mother talked of unimportant news communicated by the one correspondent, Jasper read the missive addressed to himself.

'This is from Reardon,' he remarked to the younger girl. 'Things are going badly with him. He is just the kind of fellow to end by poisoning or shooting himself.'

'But why?'

'Can't get anything done; and begins to be sore troubled on his wife's account.'

'Is he ill?'

'Overworked, I suppose. But it's just what I foresaw. He isn't the kind of man to keep up literary production as a paying business. In favourable circumstances he might write a fairly good book once every two or three years. The failure of his last depressed him, and now he is struggling hopelessly to get another done before the winter season. Those people will come to grief.'

'The enjoyment with which he anticipates it!' murmured Maud, looking at her mother.

'Not at all,' said Jasper. 'It's true I envied the fellow, because he persuaded a handsome girl to believe in him and share his risks, but I shall be very sorry if he goes to the – to the dogs. He's my one serious friend. But it irritates me to see a man making such large demands upon fortune. One must be more modest – as I am. Because one book had a sort of success he imagined his struggles were over. He got a hundred pounds for "On Neutral Ground," [1] and at once counted on a continuance of payments in geometrical proportion. I hinted to him that he couldn't keep it up, and he smiled with tolerance, no doubt thinking "He judges me by himself." But I didn't do anything of the kind. – (Toast, please, Dora.) – I'm a stronger man than Reardon; I can keep my eyes open, and wait.'

'Is his wife the kind of person to grumble?' asked Mrs Milvain.

'Well, yes, I suspect that she is. The girl wasn't content to go into modest rooms – they must furnish a flat. I rather wonder he didn't start a carriage for her. Well, his next book brought only another hundred, and now, even if he finishes this one, it's very doubtful if he'll get as much. "The Optimist" was practically a failure.'

'Mr Yule may leave them some money,' said Dora.

'Yes. But he may live another ten years, and he would see them both in Marylebone Workhouse before he advanced sixpence, or I'm much mistaken in him. Her mother has only just enough to live upon; can't possibly help them. Her brother wouldn't give or lend twopence halfpenny.'

'Has Mr Reardon no relatives?' asked Maud.

'I never heard him make mention of a single one. No, he has done the fatal thing. A man in his position, if he marry at all, must take either a work-girl or an heiress, [2] and in many ways the work-girl is preferable.'

'How can you say that?' asked Dora. 'You never cease talking about the advantages of money.'

'Oh, I don't mean that for *me* the work-girl would be preferable; by no means; but for a man like Reardon. He is absurd enough to be conscientious, likes to be called an "artist," and so on. He might possibly earn a hundred and fifty a year if his mind were at rest, and that would be enough if he had married a decent little dressmaker. He wouldn't desire superfluities, and the quality of his work would be its own reward. As it is, he's ruined.'

'And I repeat,' said Maud, 'that you enjoy the prospect.'

'Nothing of the kind. If I seem to speak exultantly it's only because my intellect enjoys the clear perception of a fact. — A little marmalade, Dora; the home-made, please.'

'But this is very sad, Jasper,' said Mrs Milvain, in her half-absent way. 'I suppose they can't even go for a holiday?'

'Quite out of the question.'

'Not even if you invited them to come here for a week?'

'Now, mother,' urged Maud, '*that's* impossible, you know very well.'

'I thought we might make an effort, dear. A holiday might mean everything to him.'

'No, no,' fell from Jasper, thoughtfully. 'I don't think you'd get along very well with Mrs Reardon; and then, if her uncle is coming to Mr Yule's, you know, that would be awkward.'

'I suppose it would; though those people would only stay a day or two, Miss Harrow said.'

'Why can't Mr Yule make them friends, those two lots of people?' asked Dora. 'You say he's on good terms with both.'

'I suppose he thinks it's no business of his.'

Jasper mused over the letter from his friend.

'Ten years hence,' he said, 'if Reardon is still alive, I shall be lending him five-pound notes.'

A smile of irony rose to Maud's lips. Dora laughed.

'To be sure! To be sure!' exclaimed their brother. 'You have no faith. But just understand the difference between a man like Reardon and a man like me. He is the old type of unpractical artist; I am the literary man of 1882. He won't make concessions, or rather, he can't make them; he can't supply the market. I — well, you may say that at present I do nothing; but that's a great mistake, I am learning my business. Literature nowadays is a trade. Putting aside men of genius, who may succeed by mere cosmic force, your successful man of letters is your skilful trades-man. He thinks first and foremost of the markets; when one kind of goods begins to go off slackly, he is ready with something new and appetising. He knows perfectly all the possible sources of income. Whatever he has to sell he'll get payment for it from all sorts of various quarters; none of your unpractical selling for a lump sum to a middleman who will make six distinct profits. Now, look you: if I had been in Reardon's place, I'd have made four hundred at least out of "The Optimist"; I should have gone shrewdly to work with magazines and newspapers and foreign publishers, and – all sorts of people. Reardon can't do that kind of thing, he's behind his age; he sells a manuscript as if he lived in Sam Johnson's Grub Street. But our Grub Street of to-day is quite a different place: it is supplied with telegraphic communication, it knows what literary fare is in demand in every part of the world, its inhabitants are men of business, however seedy.'

'It sounds ignoble,' said Maud.

'I have nothing to do with that, my dear girl. Now, as I tell you, I am slowly, but surely, learning the business. My line won't be novels; I have failed in that direction, I'm not cut out for the work. It's a pity, of course; there's a great deal of money in it. But I have plenty of scope. In ten years, I repeat, I shall be making my thousand a year.'

'I don't remember that you stated the exact sum before,' Maud observed.

'Let it pass. And to those who have shall be given. When I have a decent income of my own, I shall marry a woman with an income somewhat larger, so that casualties may be provided for.'

Dora exclaimed, laughing:

'It would amuse me very much if the Reardons got a lot of money at Mr Yule's death – and that can't be ten years off, I'm sure.'

'I don't see that there's any chance of their getting much,' replied Jasper, meditatively. 'Mrs Reardon is only his niece. The man's brother and sister will have the first helping, I suppose. And then, if it comes to the second generation, the literary Yule has a daughter, and by her being invited here I should think she's the favourite niece. No, no; depend upon it they won't get anything at all.'

Having finished his breakfast, he leaned back and began to unfold the London paper that had come by post.

'Had Mr Reardon any hopes of that kind at the time of his marriage, do you think?' inquired Mrs Milvain.

'Reardon? Good heavens, no! Would he were capable of such forethought!'

In a few minutes Jasper was left alone in the room. When the servant came to clear the table he strolled slowly away, humming a tune.

The house was pleasantly situated by the roadside in a little village named Finden. Opposite stood the church, a plain, low, square-towered building. As it was cattle-market to-day in the town of Wattleborough, droves of beasts and sheep occasionally went by, or the rattle of a grazier's cart sounded for a moment. On ordinary days the road saw few vehicles, and pedestrians were rare.

Mrs Milvain and her daughters had lived here for the last seven years, since the death of the father, who was a veterinary surgeon. The widow enjoyed an annuity of two hundred and forty pounds, terminable with her life; the children had nothing of their own. Maud acted irregularly as a teacher of music; Dora had an engagement as visiting governess in a Wattleborough family. Twice a year, as a rule, Jasper came down from London to spend a fortnight with them; to-day marked the middle of his autumn visit, and the strained relations between him and his sisters which invariably made the second week rather trying for all in the house had already become noticeable.

In the course of the morning Jasper had half an hour's private talk with his mother, after which he set off to roam in the sunshine. Shortly after he had left the house, Maud, her domestic duties dismissed for the time, came into the parlour where Mrs Milvain was reclining on the sofa.

'Jasper wants more money,' said the mother, when Maud had sat in meditation for a few minutes.

'Of course. I knew that. I hope you told him he couldn't have it.'

'I really didn't know what to say,' returned Mrs Milvain, in a feeble tone of worry.

'Then you must leave the matter to me, that's all. There's no money for him, and there's an end of it.'

Maud set her features in sullen determination. There was a brief silence.

'What's he to do, Maud?'

'To do? How do other people do? What do Dora and I do?'

'You don't earn enough for your support, my dear.'

'Oh, well!' broke from the girl. 'Of course if you grudge us our food and lodging —'

'Don't be so quick-tempered. You know very well I am far from grudging you anything, dear. But I only meant to say that Jasper does earn something, you know.'

'It's a disgraceful thing that he doesn't earn as much as he needs. We are sacrificed to him, as we always have been. Why should we be pinching and stinting to keep him in idleness?'

'But you really can't call it idleness, Maud. He is studying his profession.'

'Pray call it trade; he prefers it. How do I know that he's studying anything? What does he mean by "studying"? And to hear him speak scornfully of his friend Mr Reardon, who seems to work hard all through the year! It's disgusting, mother. At this rate, he will *never* earn his own living. Who hasn't seen or heard of such men? If we had another hundred a year, I would say nothing. But we can't live on what he leaves us, and I'm not going to let you try. I shall tell Jasper plainly that he's got to work for his own support.'

Another silence, and a longer one. Mrs Milvain furtively wiped a tear from her cheek.

'It seems very cruel to refuse,' she said at length, 'when another year may give him the opportunity he's waiting for.'

'Opportunity? What does he mean by his opportunity?'

'He says that it always comes, if a man knows how to wait.'

'And the people who support him may starve meanwhile! Now just think a bit, mother. Suppose anything were to happen to you, what becomes of Dora and me? And what becomes of Jasper, too? It's the truest kindness to him to compel him to earn a living. He gets more and more incapable of it.'

'You can't say that, Maud. He earns a little more each year. But for that, I should have my doubts. He has made thirty pounds already this year, and he only made about twenty-five the whole of last. We must be fair to him, you know. I can't help feeling that he knows what he's about. And if he does succeed, he'll pay us all back.'

Maud began to gnaw her fingers, a disagreeable habit she had in privacy.

'Then why doesn't he live more economically?'

'I really don't see how he can live on less than a hundred and fifty a year. London, you know –'

'The cheapest place in the world.'

'Nonsense, Maud !'

'But I know what I'm saying. I've read quite enough about such things. He might live very well indeed on thirty shillings a week, even buying his clothes out of it.'

'But he has told us so often that it's no *use* to him to live like that. He is obliged to go to places where he must spend a little, or he makes no progress.'

'Well, all I can say is,' exclaimed the girl impatiently, 'it's very lucky for him that he's got a mother who willingly sacrifices her daughters to him.'

'That's how you always break out. You don't care what unkindness you say !'

'It's a simple truth.'

'Dora never speaks like that.'

'Because she's afraid to be honest.'

'No, because she has too much love for her mother. I can't bear to talk to you, Maud. The older I get, and the weaker I get, the more unfeeling you are to me.'

Scenes of this kind were no uncommon thing. The clash of tempers lasted for several minutes, then Maud flung out of the room. An hour later, at dinner-time, she was rather more caustic in her remarks than usual, but this was the only sign that remained of the stormy mood.

Jasper renewed the breakfast-table conversation.

'Look here,' he began, 'why don't you girls write something? I'm convinced you could make money if you tried. There's a tremendous sale for religious stories; why not patch one together? I am quite serious.'

'Why don't you do it yourself?' retorted Maud.

'I can't manage stories, as I have told you; but I think you

could. In your place, I'd make a speciality of Sunday-school
prize-books; you know the kind of thing I mean. They sell like
hot cakes. And there's so deuced little enterprise in the business.
If you'd give your mind to it, you might make hundreds a year.'

'Better say "abandon your mind to it."'

'Why, there you are! You're a sharp enough girl. You can
quote as well as anyone I know.'

'And please, why am I to take up an inferior kind of work?'

'Inferior? Oh, if you can be a George Eliot, begin at the earliest opportunity. I merely suggested what seemed practicable.
But I don't think you have genius, Maud. People have got that
ancient prejudice so firmly rooted in their heads – that one mustn't
write save at the dictation of the Holy Spirit. I tell you, writing
is a business. Get together half a dozen fair specimens of the
Sunday-school prize; study them; discover the essential points
of such composition; hit upon new attractions; then go to
work methodically, so many pages a day. There's no question of
the divine afflatus; that belongs to another sphere of life. We
talk of literature as a trade, not of Homer, Dante, and Shakspeare.
If I could only get that into poor Reardon's head. He thinks me a
gross beast, often enough. What the devil – I mean what on
earth is there in typography to make everything it deals with
sacred? I don't advocate the propagation of vicious literature; I
speak only of good, coarse, marketable stuff for the world's
vulgar. You just give it a thought, Maud; talk it over with
Dora.'

He resumed presently:

'I maintain that we people of brains are justified in supplying
the mob with the food it likes. We are not geniuses, and if we sit
down in a spirit of long-eared gravity we shall produce only
commonplace stuff. Let us use our wits to earn money, and make
the best we can of our lives. If only I had the skill, I would
produce novels out-trashing the trashiest that ever sold fifty
thousand copies. But it needs skill, mind you; and to deny it is a
gross error of the literary pedants. To please the vulgar you
must, one way or another, incarnate the genius of vulgarity. For
my own part, I shan't be able to address the bulkiest multitude;
my talent doesn't lend itself to that form. I shall write for the
upper middle-class of intellect, the people who like to feel that

what they are reading has some special cleverness, but who can't distinguish between stones and paste. That's why I'm so slow in warming to the work. Every month I feel surer of myself, however. That last thing of mine in *The West End* distinctly hit the mark; it wasn't too flashy, it wasn't too solid. I heard fellows speak of it in the train.'

Mrs Milvain kept glancing at Maud, with eyes which desired her attention to these utterances. None the less, half an hour after dinner, Jasper found himself encountered by his sister in the garden, on her face a look which warned him of what was coming.

'I want you to tell me something, Jasper. How much longer shall you look to mother for support? I mean it literally; let me have an idea of how much longer it will be.'

He looked away, and reflected.

'To leave a margin,' was his reply, 'let us say twelve months.'

'Better say your favourite "ten years" at once.'

'No. I speak by the card. In twelve months' time, if not before, I shall begin to pay my debts. My dear girl, I have the honour to be a tolerably long-headed individual. I know what I'm about.'

'And let us suppose mother were to die within half a year?'

'I should make shift to do very well.'

'You? And please – what of Dora and me?'

'You would write Sunday-school prizes.'

Maud turned away and left him.

He knocked the dust out of the pipe he had been smoking, and again set off for a stroll along the lanes. On his countenance was just a trace of solicitude, but for the most part he wore a thoughtful smile. Now and then he stroked his smoothly-shaven jaws with thumb and fingers. Occasionally he became observant of wayside details – of the colour of a maple leaf, the shape of a tall thistle, the consistency of a fungus. At the few people who passed he looked keenly, surveying them from head to foot.

On turning, at the limit of his walk, he found himself almost face to face with two persons, who were coming along in silent companionship; their appearance interested him. The one was a man of fifty, grizzled, hard featured, slightly bowed in the shoulders; he wore a grey felt hat with a broad brim, and a decent suit of broadcloth. With him was a girl of perhaps two-

and-twenty, in a slate-coloured dress with very little ornament, and a yellow-straw hat of the shape originally appropriated to males; her dark hair was cut short, and lay in innumerable crisp curls. Father and daughter, obviously. The girl, to a casual eye, was neither pretty nor beautiful, but she had a grave and impressive face, with a complexion of ivory tone; her walk was gracefully modest, and she seemed to be enjoying the country air.

Jasper mused concerning them. When he had walked a few yards, he looked back; at the same moment the unknown man also turned his head.

'Where the deuce have I seen them – him and the girl too?' Milvain asked himself.

And before he reached home the recollection he sought flashed upon his mind.

'The Museum Reading-room, of course!'

Chapter 2

THE HOUSE OF YULE

'I THINK,' said Jasper, as he entered the room where his mother and Maud were busy with plain needlework, 'I must have met Alfred Yule and his daughter.'

'How did you recognise them?' Mrs Milvain inquired.

'I passed an old buffer and a pale-faced girl whom I know by sight at the British Museum. It wasn't near Yule's house, but they were taking a walk.'

'They may have come already. When Miss Harrow was here last, she said "in about a fortnight."'

'No mistaking them for people of these parts, even if I hadn't remembered their faces. Both of them are obvious dwellers in the valley of the shadow of books.' [3]

'Is Miss Yule such a fright then?' asked Maud.

'A fright! Not at all. A good example of the modern literary girl. I suppose you have the oldest old-fashioned ideas of such people. No, I rather liked the look of her. *Simpatica*, I should think, as that ass Whelpdale would say. A very delicate, pure complexion, though morbid; nice eyes; figure not spoilt yet. But of course I may be wrong about their identity.'

Later in the afternoon Jasper's conjecture was rendered a certainty. Maud had walked to Wattleborough, where she would meet Dora on the latter's return from her teaching, and Mrs Milvain sat alone, in a mood of depression; there was a ring at the door-bell, and the servant admitted Miss Harrow.

This lady acted as housekeeper to Mr John Yule, a wealthy resident in this neighbourhood; she was the sister of his deceased wife – a thin, soft-speaking, kindly woman of forty-five. The greater part of her life she had spent as a governess; her position now was more agreeable, and the removal of her anxiety about the future had developed qualities of cheerfulness which formerly no one would have suspected her to possess. The acquaintance between Mrs Milvain and her was only of twelve months' standing; prior to that, Mr Yule had inhabited a house at the end of Wattleborough remote from Finden.

'Our London visitors came yesterday,' she began by saying.

Mrs Milvain mentioned her son's encounter an hour or two ago.

'No doubt it was they,' said the visitor. 'Mrs Yule hasn't come; I hardly expected she would, you know. So very unfortunate when there are difficulties of that kind, isn't it?'

She smiled confidentially.

'The poor girl must feel it,' said Mrs Milvain.

'I'm afraid she does. Of course it narrows the circle of her friends at home. She's a sweet girl, and I should so like you to meet her. Do come and have tea with us to-morrow afternoon, will you? Or would it be too much for you just now?'

'Will you let the girls call? And then perhaps Miss Yule will be so good as to come and see me?'

'I wonder whether Mr Milvain would like to meet her father? I have thought that perhaps it might be some advantage to him. Alfred is so closely connected with literary people, you know.'

'I feel sure he would be glad,' replied Mrs Milvain. 'But – what of Jasper's friendship with Mrs Edmund Yule and the Reardons? Mightn't it be a little awkward?'

'Oh, I don't think so, unless he himself felt it so. There would be no need to mention that, I should say. And, really, it would be so much better if those estrangements came to an end. John makes no scruple of speaking freely about everyone, and I don't think Alfred regards Mrs Edmund with any serious unkindness. If Mr Milvain would walk over with the young ladies to-morrow, it would be very pleasant.'

'Then I think I may promise that he will. I'm sure I don't know where he is at this moment. We don't see very much of him, except at meals.'

'He won't be with you much longer, I suppose?'

'Perhaps a week.'

Before Miss Harrow's departure Maud and Dora reached home. They were curious to see the young lady from the valley of the shadow of books, and gladly accepted the invitation offered them.

They set out on the following afternoon in their brother's company. It was only a quarter of an hour's walk to Mr Yule's habitation, a small house in a large garden. Jasper was coming hither for the first time; his sisters now and then visited Miss Harrow, but very rarely saw Mr Yule himself, who made no secret of the fact that he cared little for female society. In Wattleborough and the neighbourhood opinions varied greatly as to this gentleman's character, but women seldom spoke very favourably of him. Miss Harrow was reticent concerning her brother-in-law; no one, however, had any reason to believe that she found life under his roof disagreeable. That she lived with him at all was of course occasionally matter for comment, certain Wattleborough ladies having their doubts regarding the position of a deceased wife's sister under such circumstances; but no one was seriously exercised about the relations between this sober lady of forty-five and a man of sixty-three in broken health.

A word of the family history.

John, Alfred, and Edmund Yule were the sons of a Wattleborough stationer. Each was well educated, up to the age of seventeen, at the town's grammar school. The eldest, who was a hot-headed lad, but showed capacities for business, worked at first with his father, endeavouring to add a bookselling department to the trade in stationery; but the life of home was not much to his taste, and at one-and-twenty he obtained a clerk's place in the office of a London newspaper. Three years after, his father died, and the small patrimony which fell to him he used in making himself practically acquainted with the details of paper manufacture, his aim being to establish himself in partnership with an acquaintance who had started a small paper-mill in Hertfordshire. His speculation succeeded, and as years went on he became a thriving manufacturer. His brother Alfred, in the meantime, had drifted from work at a London bookseller's into the modern Grub Street, his adventures in which region will concern us hereafter. Edmund carried on the Wattleborough business, but with small success. Between him and his eldest brother existed a good deal of affection, and in the end John

offered him a share in his flourishing paper-works; whereupon
Edmund married, deeming himself well established for life. But
John's temper was a difficult one; Edmund and he quarrelled,
parted; and when the younger died, aged about forty, he left but
moderate provision for his widow and two children.

Only when he had reached middle age did John marry; the
experiment could not be called successful, and Mrs Yule died
three years later, childless.

At fifty-four John Yule retired from active business; he came
back to the scenes of his early life, and began to take an important
part in the municipal affairs of Wattleborough. He was then a
remarkably robust man, fond of out-of-door exercise; he made it
one of his chief efforts to encourage the local Volunteer movement, the cricket and football clubs, public sports of every kind,
showing no sympathy whatever with those persons who wished
to establish free libraries, lectures, and the like. At his own expense he built for the Volunteers a handsome drill-shed; he
founded a public gymnasium; and finally he allowed it to be
rumoured that he was going to present the town with a park. But
by presuming too far upon the bodily vigour which prompted
these activities, he passed of a sudden into the state of a confirmed invalid. On an autumn expedition in the Hebrides, he
slept one night under the open sky, with the result that he had
an all but fatal attack of rheumatic fever. After that, though the
direction of his interests was unchanged, he could no longer set
the example to Wattleborough youth of muscular manliness.
The infliction did not improve his temper; for the next year or
two he was constantly at warfare with one or other of his colleagues and friends, ill brooking that the familiar control of
various local interests should fall out of his hands. But before
long he appeared to resign himself to his fate, and at present
Wattleborough saw little of him. It seemed likely that he might
still found the park which was to bear his name; but perhaps it
would only be done in consequence of directions in his will. It
was believed that he could not live much longer.

With his kinsfolk he held very little communication. Alfred
Yule, a battered man of letters, had visited Wattleborough only
twice (including the present occasion) since John's return hither.
Mrs Edmund Yule, with her daughter – now Mrs Reardon – had

been only once, three years ago. These two families, as you have heard, were not on terms of amity with each other, owing to difficulties between Mrs Alfred and Mrs Edmund; but John seemed to regard both impartially. Perhaps the only real warmth of feeling he had ever known was bestowed upon Edmund, and Miss Harrow had remarked that he spoke with somewhat more interest of Edmund's daughter, Amy, than of Alfred's daughter, Marian. But it was doubtful whether the sudden disappearance from the earth of all his relatives would greatly have troubled him. He lived a life of curious self-absorption, reading newspapers (little else), and talking with old friends who had stuck to him in spite of his irascibility.

Miss Harrow received her visitors in a small and soberly furnished drawing-room. She was nervous, probably because of Jasper Milvain, whom she had met but once – last spring – and who on that occasion had struck her as an alarmingly modern young man. In the shadow of a window-curtain sat a slight, simply-dressed girl, whose short curly hair and thoughtful countenance Jasper again recognised. When it was his turn to be presented to Miss Yule, he saw that she doubted for an instant whether or not to give her hand; yet she decided to do so, and there was something very pleasant to him in its warm softness. She smiled with a slight embarrassment, meeting his look only for a second.

'I have seen you several times, Miss Yule,' he said in a friendly way, 'though without knowing your name. It was under the great dome.'

She laughed, readily understanding his phrase.

'I am there very often,' was her reply.

'What great dome?' asked Miss Harrow, with surprise.

'That of the British Museum Reading-room,' explained Jasper; 'known to some of us as the valley of the shadow of books. People who often work there necessarily get to know each other by sight. In the same way I knew Miss Yule's father when I happened to pass him in the road yesterday.'

The three girls began to converse together, perforce of trivialities. Marian Yule spoke in rather slow tones, thoughtfully, gently; she had linked her fingers, and laid her hands, palms downwards, upon her lap – a nervous action. Her accent was pure, unpretentious; and she used none of the fashionable turns of speech which would have suggested the habit of intercourse with distinctly metropolitan society.

'You must wonder how we exist in this out-of-the-way place,' remarked Maud.

'Rather, I envy you,' Marian answered, with a slight emphasis.

The door opened, and Alfred Yule presented himself. He was tall, and his head seemed a disproportionate culmination to his meagre body, it was so large and massively featured. Intellect and uncertainty of temper were equally marked upon his visage; his brows were knitted in a permanent expression of severity. He had thin, smooth hair, grizzled whiskers, a shaven chin. In the multitudinous wrinkles of his face lay a history of laborious and stormy life; one readily divined in him a struggling and embittered man. Though he looked older than his years, he had by no means the appearance of being beyond the ripeness of his mental vigour.

'It pleases me to meet you, Mr Milvain,' he said, as he stretched out his bony hand. 'Your name reminds me of a paper in *The Wayside* a month or two ago, which you will perhaps allow a veteran to say was not ill done.'

'I am grateful to you for noticing it,' replied Jasper.

There was positively a touch of visible warmth upon his cheek. The allusion had come so unexpectedly that it caused him keen pleasure.

Mr Yule seated himself awkwardly, crossed his legs, and began to stroke the back of his left hand, which lay on his knee. He seemed to have nothing more to say at present, and allowed Miss Harrow and the girls to support conversation. Jasper listened with a smile for a minute or two, then he addressed the veteran.

'Have you seen *The Study* this week, Mr Yule?'

'Yes.'

'Did you notice that it contains a very favourable review of a novel which was tremendously abused in the same columns three weeks ago?'

Mr Yule started, but Jasper could perceive at once that his emotion was not disagreeable.

'You don't say so?'

'Yes. The novel is Miss Hawk's "On the Boards." How will the editor get out of this?'

'H'm! Of course Mr Fadge is not immediately responsible; but it'll be unpleasant for him, decidedly unpleasant.' He smiled grimly. 'You hear this, Marian?'

'How is it explained, father?'

'May be accident, of course; but – well, there's no knowing. I think it very likely this will be the end of Mr Fadge's tenure of office. Rackett, the proprietor, only wants a plausible excuse for making a change. The paper has been going downhill for the last year; I know of two publishing houses who have withdrawn their advertising from it, and who never send their books for review. Everyone foresaw that kind of thing from the day Mr Fadge became editor. The tone of his paragraphs has been detestable. Two reviews of the same novel, eh? And diametrically opposed? Ha! ha!'

Gradually he had passed from quiet appreciation of the joke to undisguised mirth and pleasure. His utterance of the name 'Mr Fadge' sufficiently intimated that he had some cause of personal discontent with the editor of *The Study.*

'The author,' remarked Milvain, 'ought to make a good thing out of this.'

'Will, no doubt. Ought to write at once to the papers calling attention to this sample of critical impartiality. Ha! ha!'

He rose and went to the window, where for several minutes he stood gazing at vacancy, the same grim smile still on his face. Jasper in the meantime amused the ladies (his sisters had heard him on this subject already) with a description of the two antagonistic notices. But he did not trust himself to express so freely as he had done at home his opinion of reviewing in general; it was more than probable that both Yule and his daughter did a good deal of such work.

'Suppose we go into the garden,' suggested Miss Harrow, presently. 'It seems a shame to sit indoors on such a lovely afternoon.'

Hitherto there had been no mention of the master of the house. But Mr Yule now remarked to Jasper:

'My brother would be glad if you would come and have a

word with him. He isn't quite well enough to leave his room to-day.'

So, as the ladies went gardenwards, Jasper followed the man of letters upstairs to a room on the first floor. Here, in a deep cane chair, which was placed by the open window, sat John Yule. He was completely dressed, save that instead of a coat he wore a dressing-gown. The facial likeness between him and his brother was very strong, but John's would universally have been judged the finer countenance; illness notwithstanding, he had a complexion which contrasted in its pure colour with Alfred's parchmenty skin, and there was more finish about his features. His abundant hair was reddish, his long moustache and trimmed beard a lighter shade of the same hue.

'So you too are in league with the doctors,' was his bluff greeting, as he held a hand to the young man and inspected him with a look of slighting good-nature.

'Well, that certainly is one way of regarding the literary profession,' admitted Jasper, who had heard enough of John's way of thinking to understand the remark.

'A young fellow with all the world before him, too. Hang it, Mr Milvain, is there no less pernicious work you can turn your hand to?'

'I'm afraid not, Mr Yule. After all, you know, you must be held in a measure responsible for my depravity.'

'How's that?'

'I understand that you have devoted most of your life to the making of paper. If that article were not so cheap and so abundant, people wouldn't have so much temptation to scribble.'

Alfred Yule uttered a short laugh.

'I think you are cornered, John.'

'I wish,' answered John, 'that you were both condemned to write on such paper as I chiefly made; it was a special kind of whitey-brown, used by shopkeepers.'

He chuckled inwardly, and at the same time reached out for a box of cigarettes on a table near him. His brother and Jasper each took one as he offered them, and began to smoke.

'You would like to see literary production come entirely to an end?' said Milvain.

'I should like to see the business of literature abolished.'

'There's a distinction, of course. But, on the whole, I should say that even the business serves a good purpose.'

'What purpose?'

'It helps to spread civilisation.'

'Civilisation!' exclaimed John, scornfully. 'What do you mean by civilisation? Do you call it civilising men to make them weak, flabby creatures, with ruined eyes and dyspeptic stomachs? Who is it that reads most of the stuff that's poured out daily by the ton from the printing-press? Just the men and women who ought to spend their leisure hours in open-air exercise; the people who earn their bread by sedentary pursuits, and who need to *live* as soon as they are free from the desk or the counter, not to moon over small print. Your Board schools, your popular press, your spread of education! Machinery for ruining the country, that's what I call it.'

'You have done a good deal, I think, to counteract those influences in Wattleborough.'

'I hope so; and if only I had kept the use of my limbs I'd have done a good deal more. I have an idea of offering substantial prizes to men and women engaged in sedentary work who take an oath to abstain from all reading, and keep it for a certain number of years. There's a good deal more need for that than for abstinence from strong liquor. If I could have had my way I would have revived prize-fighting.'

His brother laughed with contemptuous impatience.

'You would doubtless like to see military conscription introduced into England?' said Jasper.

'Of course I should! You talk of civilising; there's no such way of civilising the masses of the people as by fixed military service. Before mental training must come training of the body.[4] Go about the Continent, and see the effect of military service on loutish peasants and the lowest classes of town population. Do you know why it isn't even more successful? Because the damnable education movement interferes. If Germany would shut up her schools and universities for the next quarter of a century and go ahead like blazes with military training there'd be a nation such as the world has never seen. After that, they might begin a little book-teaching again – say an hour and a half a day for everyone above nine years old. Do you suppose, Mr Milvain, that society is going to be reformed by you people who write for money? Why, you are the very first class that will be swept from the face of the earth as soon as the reformation really begins!'

Alfred puffed at his cigarette. His thoughts were occupied with Mr Fadge and *The Study*. He was considering whether he could aid in bringing public contempt upon that literary organ and its editor. Milvain listened to the elder man's diatribe with much amusement.

'You, now,' pursued John, 'what do you write about?'

'Nothing in particular. I make a saleable page or two out of whatever strikes my fancy.'

'Exactly! You don't even pretend that you've got anything to say. You live by inducing people to give themselves mental indigestion – and bodily, too, for that matter.'

'Do you know, Mr Yule, that you have suggested a capital idea to me? If I were to take up your views, I think it isn't at all unlikely that I might make a good thing of writing against writing. It should be my literary specialty to rail against literature. The reading public should pay me for telling them that they oughtn't to read. I must think it over.'

'Carlyle [5] has anticipated you,' threw in Alfred.

'Yes, but in an antiquated way. I would base my polemic on the newest philosophy.'

He developed the idea facetiously, whilst John regarded him as he might have watched a performing monkey.

'There again! your new philosophy!' exclaimed the invalid. 'Why, it isn't even wholesome stuff, the kind of reading that most of you force on the public. Now there's the man who has married one of my nieces – poor lass! Reardon, his name is. You know him, I dare say. Just for curiosity I had a look at one of his books; it was called "The Optimist." Of all the morbid trash I ever saw, that beat everything. I thought of writing him a letter, advising a couple of antibilious pills before bedtime for a few weeks.'

Jasper glanced at Alfred Yule, who wore a look of indifference.

'That man deserves penal servitude, in my opinion,' pursued John. 'I'm not sure that it isn't my duty to offer him a couple of hundred a year on condition that he writes no more.'

Milvain, with a clear vision of his friend in London, burst into laughter. But at that point Alfred rose from his chair.

'Shall we rejoin the ladies?' he said, with a certain pedantry of phrase and manner which often characterised him.

'Think over your ways whilst you're still young,' said John as he shook hands with his visitor.

'Your brother speaks quite seriously, I suppose?' Jasper remarked when he was in the garden with Alfred.

'I think so. It's amusing now and then, but gets rather tiresome when you hear it often. By-the-by, you are not personally acquainted with Mr Fadge?'

'I didn't even know his name until you mentioned it.'

'The most malicious man in the literary world. There's no uncharitableness in feeling a certain pleasure when he gets into a scrape. I could tell you incredible stories about him; but that kind of thing is probably as little to your taste as it is to mine.'

Miss Harrow and her companions, having caught sight of the pair, came towards them. Tea was to be brought out into the garden.

'So you can sit with us and smoke, if you like,' said Miss Harrow to Alfred. 'You are never quite at your ease, I think, without a pipe.'

But the man of letters was too preoccupied for society. In a few minutes he begged that the ladies would excuse his withdrawing; he had two or three letters to write before post-time, which was early at Finden.

Jasper, relieved by the veteran's departure, began at once to make himself very agreeable company. When he chose to lay aside the topic of his own difficulties and ambitions, he could converse with a spontaneous gaiety which readily won the good-will of listeners. Naturally he addressed himself very often to Marian Yule, whose attention complimented him. She said little, and evidently was at no time a free talker, but the smile on her face indicated a mood of quiet enjoyment. When her eyes wandered, it was to rest on the beauties of the garden, the moving patches of golden sunshine, the forms of gleaming cloud. Jasper liked to observe her as she turned her head: there seemed to him a particular grace in the movement; her head and neck were admirably formed, and the short hair drew attention to this.

It was agreed that Miss Harrow and Marian should come on the second day after to have tea with the Milvains. And when Jasper took leave of Alfred Yule, the latter expressed a wish that they might have a walk together one of these mornings.

Chapter 3

HOLIDAY

JASPER'S favourite walk led him to a spot distant perhaps a mile and a half from home. From a tract of common he turned into a short lane which crossed the Great Western railway, and thence by a stile into certain meadows forming a compact little valley. One recommendation of this retreat was that it lay sheltered from all winds; to Jasper a wind was objectionable. Along the bottom ran a clear, shallow stream, overhung with elder and hawthorn bushes; and close by the wooden bridge which spanned it was a great ash tree, making shadow for cows and sheep when the sun lay hot upon the open field. It was rare for anyone to come along this path, save farm labourers morning and evening.

But to-day – the afternoon that followed his visit to John Yule's house – he saw from a distance that his lounging place on the wooden bridge was occupied. Someone else had discovered the pleasure there was in watching the sun-flecked sparkle of the water as it flowed over the clean sand and stones. A girl in a yellow straw hat; yes, and precisely the person he had hoped, at the first glance, that it might be. He made no haste as he drew nearer on the descending path. At length his footstep was heard; Marian Yule turned her head and clearly recognized him.

She assumed an upright position, letting one of her hands rest upon the rail. After the exchange of ordinary greetings, Jasper leaned back against the same support and showed himself disposed for talk.

'When I was here late in the spring,' he said, 'this ash was only just budding, though everything else seemed in full leaf.'

'An ash, is it?' murmured Marian. 'I didn't know. I think an oak is the only tree I can distinguish. Yet,' she added quickly, 'I knew that the ash was late; some lines of Tennyson[6] come to my memory.'

'Which are those?'

'Delaying, as the tender ash delays
To clothe herself, when all the woods are green,

somewhere in the "Idylls."'

'I don't remember; so I won't pretend to – though I should do so as a rule.'

She looked at him oddly, and seemed about to laugh, yet did not.

'You have had little experience of the country?' Jasper continued.

'Very little. You, I think, have known it from childhood?'

'In a sort of way. I was born in Wattleborough, and my people have always lived here. But I am not very rural in temperament. I have really no friends here; either they have lost interest in me, or I in them. What do you think of the girls, my sisters?'

The question, though put with perfect simplicity, was embarrassing.

'They are tolerably intellectual,' Jasper went on, when he saw that it would be difficult for her to answer. 'I want to persuade them to try their hands at literary work of some kind or other. They give lessons, and both hate it.'

'Would literary work be less – burdensome?' said Marian, without looking at him.

'Rather more so, you think?'

She hesitated.

'It depends, of course, on – on several things.'

'To be sure,' Jasper agreed. 'I don't think they have any marked faculty for such work; but as they certainly haven't for teaching, that doesn't matter. It's a question of learning a business. I am going through my apprenticeship, and find it a long affair. Money would shorten it, and, unfortunately, I have none.'

'Yes,' said Marian, turning her eyes upon the stream, 'money is a help in everything.'

'Without it, one spends the best part of one's life in toiling for that first foothold which money could at once purchase. To have money is becoming of more and more importance in a literary career; principally because to have money is to have friends. Year by year, such influence grows of more account. A lucky man will still occasionally succeed by dint of his own honest perseverance, but the chances are dead against anyone who can't make private interest with influential people; his work is simply overwhelmed by that of the men who have better opportunities.'

'Don't you think that, even to-day, really good work will sooner or later be recognised?'

'Later, rather than sooner; and very likely the man can't wait; he starves in the meantime. You understand that I am not speaking of genius; I mean marketable literary work. The quantity turned out is so great that there's no hope for the special attention of the public unless one can afford to advertise hugely. Take the instance of a successful all-round man of letters; take Ralph Warbury, whose name you'll see in the first magazine you happen to open. But perhaps he is a friend of yours?'

'Oh, no!'

'Well, I wasn't going to abuse him. I was only going to ask: Is there any quality which distinguishes his work from that of twenty struggling writers one could name? Of course not. He's a clever, prolific man; so are they. But he began with money and friends; he came from Oxford into the thick of advertised people; his name was mentioned in print six times a week before he had written a dozen articles. This kind of thing will become the rule. Men won't succeed in literature that they may get into society, but will get into society that they may succeed in literature.'

'Yes, I know it is true,' said Marian, in a low voice.

'There's a friend of mine who writes novels,' Jasper pursued. 'His books are not works of genius, but they are glaringly distinct from the ordinary circulating novel. Well, after one or two attempts, he made half a success; that is to say, the publishers brought out a second edition of the book in a few months. There was his opportunity. But he couldn't use it; he had no friends, because he had no money. A book of half that merit if written by a man in the position of Warbury when he started would have established the reputation of a lifetime. His influential friends would have referred to it in leaders, in magazine articles, in speeches, in sermons. It would have run through numerous editions, and the author would have had nothing to do but to write another book and demand his price. But the novel I'm speaking of was practically forgotten a year after its appearance; it was whelmed beneath the flood of next season's literature.'

Marian urged a hesitating objection.

'But, under the circumstances, wasn't it in the author's power to make friends? Was money really indispensable?'

'Why, yes – because he chose to marry. As a bachelor he might possibly have got into the right circles, though his character would in any case have made it difficult for him to curry favour. But as a married man, without means, the situation was hopeless. Once married, you must live up to the standard of the society you frequent; you can't be entertained without entertaining in return. Now if his wife had brought him only a couple of thousand pounds all might have been well. I should have advised him, in sober seriousness, to live for two years at the rate of a thousand a year. At the end of that time he would have been earning enough to continue at pretty much the same rate of expenditure.'

'Perhaps.'

'Well, I ought rather to say that the average man of letters would be able to do that. As for Reardon –'

He stopped. The name had escaped him unawares.

'Reardon?' said Marian, looking up. 'You are speaking of him?'

'I have betrayed myself, Miss Yule.'

'But what does it matter? You have only spoken in his favour.'

'I feared the name might affect you disagreeably.'

Marian delayed her reply.

'It is true,' she said, 'we are not on friendly terms with my cousin's family. I have never met Mr Reardon. But I shouldn't like you to think that the mention of his name is disagreeable to me.'

'It made me slightly uncomfortable yesterday – the fact that I am well acquainted with Mrs Edmund Yule, and that Reardon is my friend. Yet I didn't see why that should prevent my making your father's acquaintance.'

'Surely not. I shall say nothing about it; I mean, as you uttered the name unintentionally.'

There was a pause in the dialogue. They had been speaking almost confidentially, and Marian seemed to become suddenly aware of an oddness in the situation. She turned towards the uphill path, as if thinking of resuming her walk.

'You are tired of standing still,' said Jasper. 'May I walk back a part of the way with you?'

'Thank you; I shall be glad.'

They went on for a few minutes in silence.

'Have you published anything with your signature, Miss Yule?' Jasper at length inquired.

'Nothing. I only help father a little.'

The silence that again followed was broken this time by Marian.

'When you chanced to mention Mr Reardon's name,' she said, with a diffident smile in which lay that suggestion of humour so delightful upon a woman's face, 'you were going to say something more about him?'

'Only that –' he broke off and laughed. 'Now, how boyish it was, wasn't it? I remember doing just the same thing once when I came home from school and had an exciting story to tell, with preservation of anonymities. Of course I blurted out a name in the first minute or two, to my father's great amusement. He told me that I hadn't the diplomatic character. I have been trying to acquire it ever since.'

'But why?'

'It's one of the essentials of success in any kind of public life. And I mean to succeed, you know. I feel that I am one of the men who do succeed. But I beg your pardon; you asked me a question. Really, I was only going to say of Reardon what I had said before: that he hasn't the tact requisite for acquiring popularity.'

'Then I may hope that it isn't his marriage with my cousin which has proved a fatal misfortune?'

'In no case,' replied Milvain, averting his look, 'would he have used his advantages.'

'And now? Do you think he has but poor prospects?'

'I wish I could see any chance of his being estimated at his right value. It's very hard to say what is before him.'

'I knew my cousin Amy when we were children,' said Marian, presently. 'She gave promise of beauty.'

'Yes, she is beautiful.'

'And – the kind of woman to be of help to such a husband?'

'I hardly know how to answer, Miss Yule,' said Jasper, looking frankly at her. 'Perhaps I had better say that it's unfortunate they are poor.'

Marian cast down her eyes.

'To whom isn't it a misfortune?' pursued her companion. 'Poverty is the root of all social ills; its existence accounts even for the ills that arise from wealth. The poor man is a man labouring in fetters. I declare there is no word in our language which sounds so hideous to me as "Poverty."'

Shortly after this they came to the bridge over the railway line. Jasper looked at his watch.

'Will you indulge me in a piece of childishness?' he said. 'In less than five minutes a London express goes by; I have often watched it here, and it amuses me. Would it weary you to wait?'

'I should like to,' she replied with a laugh.

The line ran along a deep cutting, from either side of which grew hazel bushes and a few larger trees. Leaning upon the parapet of the bridge, Jasper kept his eye in the westward direction, where the gleaming rails were visible for more than a mile. Suddenly he raised his finger.

'You hear?'

Marian had just caught the far-off sound of the train. She looked eagerly, and in a few moments saw it approaching. The front of the engine blackened nearer and nearer, coming on with dread force and speed. A blinding rush, and there burst against the bridge a great volley of sunlit steam. Milvain and his companion ran to the opposite parapet, but already the whole train had emerged, and in a few seconds it had disappeared round a sharp curve. The leafy branches that grew out over the line swayed violently backwards and forwards in the perturbed air.

'If I were ten years younger,' said Jasper, laughing, 'I should say that was jolly! It inspirits me. It makes me feel eager to go back and plunge into the fight again.'

'Upon me it has just the opposite effect,' fell from Marian, in very low tones.

'Oh, don't say that! Well, it only means that you haven't had enough holiday yet. I have been in the country more than a week; a few days more and I must be off. How long do you think of staying?'

'Not much more than a week, I think.'

'By-the-by, you are coming to have tea with us to-morrow,' Jasper remarked *à propos* of nothing. Then he returned to another subject that was in his thoughts.

'It was by a train like that that I first went up to London. Not really the first time; I mean when I went to live there, seven years ago. What spirits I was in! A boy of eighteen going to live independently in London; think of it!'

'You went straight from school?'

'I was for two years at Redmayne College after leaving Wattleborough Grammar School. Then my father died, and I spent nearly half a year at home. I was meant to be a teacher, but the prospect of entering a school by no means appealed to me. A friend of mine was studying in London for some Civil Service exam., so I declared that I would go and do the same thing.'

'Did you succeed?'

'Not I! I never worked properly for that kind of thing. I read voraciously, and got to know London. I might have gone to the dogs, you know; but by when I had been in London a year a pretty clear purpose began to form in me. Strange to think that you were growing up there all the time. I may have passed you in the street now and then.'

Marian laughed.

'And I did at length see you at the British Museum, you know.'

They turned a corner of the road, and came full upon Marian's father, who was walking in this direction with eyes fixed upon the ground.

'So here you are!' he exclaimed, looking at the girl, and for the moment paying no attention to Jasper. 'I wondered whether I should meet you.' Then, more dryly, 'How do you do, Mr Milvain?'

In a tone of easy indifference Jasper explained how he came to be accompanying Miss Yule.

'Shall I walk on with you, father?' Marian asked, scrutinising his rugged features.

'Just as you please; I don't know that I should have gone much further. But we might take another way back.'

Jasper readily adapted himself to the wish he discerned in Mr Yule; at once he offered leave-taking in the most natural way. Nothing was said on either side about another meeting.

The young man proceeded homewards, but, on arriving, did not at once enter the house. Behind the garden was a field used for the grazing of horses; he entered it by the unfastened gate, and strolled idly hither and thither, now and then standing to observe a poor worn-out beast, all skin and bone, which had presumably been sent here in the hope that a little more labour might still be exacted from it if it were suffered to repose for a few weeks. There were sores upon its back and legs; it stood in a fixed attitude of despondency, just flicking away troublesome flies with its grizzled tail.

It was tea-time when he went in. Maud was not at home, and Mrs Milvain, tormented by a familiar headache, kept her room; so Jasper and Dora sat down together. Each had an open book on the table; throughout the meal they exchanged only a few words.

'Going to play a little?' Jasper suggested when they had gone into the sitting-room.

'If you like.'

She sat down at the piano, whilst her brother lay on the sofa, his hands clasped beneath his head. Dora did not play badly, but an absent-mindedness which was commonly observable in her had its effect upon the music. She at length broke off idly in the middle of a passage, and began to linger on careless chords. Then, without turning her head, she asked:

'Were you serious in what you said about writing story-books?'

'Quite. I see no reason why you shouldn't do something in that way. But I tell you what; when I get back, I'll inquire into the state of the market. I know a man who was once engaged at Jolly & Monk's – the chief publishers of that kind of thing, you know; I must look him up – what a mistake it is to neglect *any* acquaintance! – and get some information out of him. But it's obvious what an immense field there is for anyone who can just hit the taste of the new generation of Board school children. Mustn't be too goody-goody; that kind of thing is falling out of date. But you'd have to cultivate a particular kind of vulgarity. There's an idea, by-the-by. I'll write a paper on the characteristics of that new generation; it may bring me a few guineas, and it would be a help to you.'

'But what do you know about the subject?' asked Dora doubtfully.

'What a comical question! It is my business to know something about every subject – or to know where to get the knowledge.'

'Well,' said Dora, after a pause, 'there's no doubt Maud and I ought to think very seriously about the future. You are aware, Jasper, that mother has not been able to save a penny of her income.'

'I don't see how she could have done. Of course I know what you're thinking; but for me, it would have been possible. I don't mind confessing to you that the thought troubles me a little now and then; I shouldn't like to see you two going off governessing in strangers' houses. All I can say is, that I am very honestly working for the end which I am convinced will be most profitable. I shall not desert you; you needn't fear that. But just put your heads together, and cultivate your writing faculty. Suppose you could both together earn about a hundred a year in Grub Street, it would be better than governessing; wouldn't it?'

'You say you don't know what Miss Yule writes?'

'Well, I know a little more about her than I did yesterday. I've had an hour's talk with her this afternoon.'

'Indeed?'

'Met her down in the Leggatt fields. I find she doesn't write independently; just helps her father. What the help amounts to I can't say. There's something very attractive about her. She quoted a line or two of Tennyson; the first time I ever heard a woman speak blank verse with any kind of decency.'

'She was walking alone?'

'Yes. On the way back we met old Yule; he seemed rather grumpy, I thought. I don't think she's the kind of girl to make a paying business of literature. Her qualities are personal. And it's pretty clear to me that the valley of the shadow of books by no means agrees with her disposition. Possibly old Yule is something of a tyrant.'

'He doesn't impress me very favourably. Do you think you will keep up their acquaintance in London?'

'Can't say. I wonder what sort of a woman that mother really is? Can't be so very gross, I should think.'

'Miss Harrow knows nothing about her, except that she was a quite uneducated girl.'

'But, dash it! by this time she must have got decent manners. Of course there may be other objections. Mrs Reardon knows nothing against her.'

Midway in the following morning, as Jasper sat with a book in the garden, he was surprised to see Alfred Yule enter by the gate.

'I thought,' began the visitor, who seemed in high spirits, 'that you might like to see something I received this morning.'

He unfolded a London evening paper, and indicated a long letter from a casual correspondent. It was written by the authoress of 'On the Boards,' and drew attention, with much expenditure of witticism, to the conflicting notices of that book which had appeared in *The Study*. Jasper read the thing with laughing appreciation.

'Just what one expected!'

'And I have private letters on the subject,' added Mr Yule. 'There has been something like a personal conflict between Fadge and the man who looks after the minor notices. Fadge, *more suo*, charged the other man with a design to damage him and the paper. There's talk of legal proceedings. An immense joke!'

He laughed in his peculiar croaking way.

'Do you feel disposed for a turn along the lanes, Mr Milvain?'

'By all means. – There's my mother at the window; will you come in for a moment?'

With a step of quite unusual sprightliness Mr Yule entered the house. He could talk of but one subject, and Mrs Milvain had to listen to a laboured account of the blunder just committed by *The Study*. It was Alfred Yule's characteristic that he could do nothing light-handedly. He seemed always to converse with effort; he took a seat with stiff ungainliness; he walked with a stumbling or sprawling gait.

When he and Jasper set out for their ramble, his loquacity was in strong contrast with the taciturn mood he had exhibited yesterday and the day before. He fell upon the general aspects of contemporary literature.

'... The evil of the time is the multiplication of ephemerides. Hence a demand for essays, descriptive articles, fragments of criticism, out of all proportion to the supply of even tolerable work. The men who have an aptitude for turning out this kind of thing in vast quantities are enlisted by every new periodical, with the result that their productions are ultimately watered down into worthlessness. ... Well now, there's Fadge. Years ago some of Fadge's work was not without a certain – a certain conditional promise of – of comparative merit; but now his writing, in my opinion, is altogether beneath consideration; how Rackett could be so benighted as to give him *The Study* – especially after a man like Henry Hawkridge – passes my comprehension. Did you read a paper of his, a few months back, in *The Wayside*, a preposterous rehabilitation of Elkanah Settle?[7] Ha! ha! That's what such men are driven to. Elkanah Settle! And he hadn't even a competent acquaintance with his paltry subject. Will you credit that he twice or thrice referred to Settle's reply to "Absalom and Achitophel" by the title of "Absalom Transposed," when every schoolgirl knows that the thing was called "Achitophel Transposed"! This was monstrous enough, but there was something still more contemptible. He positively, I assure you, attributed the play of "Epsom Wells" to Crowne! I should have presumed that every student of even the most trivial primer of literature was aware that "Epsom Wells" was written by Shadwell. ... Now, if one were to take Shadwell for the subject of a paper, one might very well show how unjustly his name has fallen into contempt. It has often occurred to me to do this. "But Shadwell never deviates into sense." The sneer, in my opinion, is entirely unmerited. For my own part, I put Shadwell very high among the dramatists of his time, and I think I could show that his absolute worth is by no means inconsiderable. Shadwell has distinct vigour of dramatic conception; his dialogue. ...'

And as he talked the man kept describing imaginary geometrical figures with the end of his walking-stick; he very seldom raised his eyes from the ground, and the stoop in his shoulders grew more and more pronounced, until at a little distance one might have taken him for a hunchback. At one point Jasper made a pause to speak of the pleasant wooded prospect that lay before them; his companion regarded it absently, and in a moment or two asked:

'Did you ever come across Cottle's poem[8] on the Malvern Hills? No? It contains a couple of the richest lines ever put into print:

> It needs the evidence of close deduction
> To know that I shall ever reach the top.

Perfectly serious poetry, mind you!'

He barked in laughter. Impossible to interest him in anything apart from literature; yet one saw him to be a man of solid understanding, and not without perception of humour. He had read vastly; his memory was a literary cyclopædia. His failings, obvious enough, were the results of a strong and somewhat pedantic individuality ceaselessly at conflict with unpropitious circumstances.

Towards the young man his demeanour varied between a shy cordiality and a dignified reserve which was in danger of seeming pretentious. On the homeward part of the walk, he made a few discreet inquiries regarding Milvain's literary achievements and prospects, and the frank self-confidence of the replies appeared to interest him. But he expressed no desire to number Jasper among his acquaintances in town, and of his own professional or private concerns he said not a word.

'Whether he could be any use to me or not, I don't exactly know,' Jasper remarked to his mother and sisters at dinner. 'I suspect it's as much as he can do to keep a footing among the younger tradesmen. But I think he might have said he was willing to help me if he could.'

'Perhaps,' replied Maud, 'your large way of talking made him think any such offer superfluous.'

'You have still to learn,' said Jasper, 'that modesty helps a man in no department of modern life. People take you at your own valuation. It's the men who declare boldly that they need no help to whom practical help comes from all sides. As likely as not Yule will mention my name to someone. "A young fellow who seems to see his way pretty clear before him." The other man will repeat it to somebody else, "A young fellow whose way is clear before him," and so I come to the ears of a man who thinks "Just the fellow I want; I must look him up and ask him if he'll do such-and-such a thing." But I should like to see these Yules at home; I must fish for an invitation.'

In the afternoon, Miss Harrow and Marian came at the expected hour. Jasper purposely kept out of the way until he was summoned to the tea-table.

The Milvain girls were so far from effusive, even towards old acquaintances, that even the people who knew them best spoke of them as rather cold and perhaps a trifle condescending; there were people in Wattleborough who declared their airs of superiority ridiculous and insufferable. The truth was that nature had endowed them with a larger share of brains than was common in their circle, and had added that touch of pride which harmonised so ill with the restrictions of poverty. Their life had a tone of melancholy, the painful reserve which characterises a certain clearly defined class in the present day. Had they been born twenty years earlier, the children of that veterinary surgeon would have grown up to a very different, and in all probability a much happier, existence, for their education would have been limited to the strictly needful, and – certainly in the case of the girls – nothing would have encouraged them to look beyond the simple life possible to a poor man's offspring. But whilst Maud and Dora were still with their homely schoolmistress, Wattleborough saw fit to establish a Girls' High School, and the moderateness of the fees enabled these sisters to receive an intellectual training wholly incompatible with the material conditions of their life. To the relatively poor (who are so much worse off than the poor absolutely) education is in most cases a mocking cruelty. The burden of their brother's support made it very difficult for Maud and Dora even to dress as became their intellectual station; amusements, holidays, the purchase of such simple luxuries as were all but indispensable to them, could not be thought of. It resulted that they held apart from the society which would have welcomed them, for they could not bear to receive without offering in turn. The necessity of giving lessons galled them; they felt – and with every reason – that it made their position ambiguous. So that, though they could not help knowing many people, they had no intimates; they encouraged no one to visit them, and visited other houses as little as might be.

In Marian Yule they divined a sympathetic nature. She was unlike any girl with whom they had hitherto associated, and it was the impulse of both to receive her with unusual friendliness. The habit of reticence could not be at once overcome, and Marian's own timidity was an obstacle in the way of free intercourse, but Jasper's conversation at tea helped to smooth the course of things.

'I wish you lived anywhere near us,' Dora said to their visitor, as the three girls walked in the garden afterwards, and Maud echoed the wish.

'It would be very nice,' was Marian's reply. 'I have no friends of my own age in London.'

'None?'

'Not one!'

She was about to add something, but in the end kept silence.

'You seem to get along with Miss Yule pretty well, after all,' said Jasper, when the family were alone again.

'Did you anticipate anything else?' Maud asked.

'It seemed doubtful, up at Yule's house. Well, get her to come here again before I go. But it's a pity she doesn't play the piano,' he added, musingly.

For two days nothing was seen of the Yules. Jasper went each afternoon to the stream in the valley, but did not again meet Marian. In the meanwhile, he was growing restless. A fortnight always exhausted his capacity for enjoying the companionship of his mother and sisters, and this time he seemed anxious to get to the end of his holiday. For all that, there was no continuance of the domestic bickering which had begun. Whatever the reason, Maud behaved with unusual mildness to her brother, and Jasper in turn was gently disposed to both the girls.

On the morning of the third day – it was Saturday – he kept silence through breakfast, and just as all were about to rise from the table, he made a sudden announcement.

'I shall go to London this afternoon.'

'This afternoon?' all exclaimed. 'But Monday is your day.'

'No, I shall go this afternoon, by the 2.45.'

And he left the room. Mrs Milvain and the girls exchanged looks.

'I suppose he thinks the Sunday will be too wearisome,' said the mother.

'Perhaps so,' Maud agreed, carelessly.

Half an hour later, just as Dora was ready to leave the house for her engagements in Wattleborough, her brother came into the hall and took his hat, saying:

'I'll walk a little way with you, if you don't mind.'

When they were in the road, he asked her in an off-hand manner:

'Do you think I ought to say good-bye to the Yules? Or won't it signify?'

'I should have thought you would wish to.'

'I don't care about it. And, you see, there's been no hint of a wish on their part that I should see them in London. No, I'll just leave you to say good-bye for me.'

'But they expect to see us to-day or to-morrow. You told them you were not going till Monday, and you don't know but Mr Yule might mean to say something yet.'

'Well, I had rather he didn't,' replied Jasper, with a laugh.

'Oh, indeed?'

'I don't mind telling you,' he laughed again. 'I'm afraid of that girl. No, it won't do! You understand that I'm a practical man, and I shall keep clear of dangers. These days of holiday idleness put all sorts of nonsense into one's head.'

Dora kept her eyes down, and smiled ambiguously.

'You must act as you think fit,' she remarked at length.

'Exactly. Now I'll turn back. You'll be with us at dinner?'

They parted. But Jasper did not keep to the straight way home. First of all, he loitered to watch a reaping-machine at work; then he turned into a lane which led up the hill on which was John Yule's house. Even if he had purposed making a farewell call, it was still far too early; all he wanted to do was to pass an hour of the morning, which threatened to lie heavy on his hands. So he rambled on, and went past the house, and took the field-path which would lead him circuitously home again.

His mother desired to speak to him. She was in the dining-room; in the parlour Maud was practising music.

'I think I ought to tell you of something I did yesterday, Jasper,' Mrs Milvain began. 'You see, my dear, we have been rather straitened lately, and my health, you know, grows so uncertain, and, all things considered, I have been feeling very anxious about the girls. So I wrote to your uncle William, and told him that I must positively have that money. I must think of my own children before his.'

The matter referred to was this. The deceased Mr Milvain had a brother who was a struggling shopkeeper in a Midland town. Some ten years ago, William Milvain, on the point of bankruptcy, had borrowed a hundred and seventy pounds from his brother in Wattleborough, and this debt was still unpaid; for on the death of Jasper's father repayment of the loan was impossible for William, and since then it had seemed hopeless that the sum would ever be recovered. The poor shopkeeper had a large family, and Mrs Milvain, notwithstanding her own position, had never felt able to press him; her relative, however, often spoke of the business, and declared his intention of paying whenever he could.

'You can't recover by law now, you know,' said Jasper.

'But we have a *right* to the money, law or no law. He must pay it.'

'He will simply refuse – and be justified. Poverty doesn't allow of honourable feeling, any more than of compassion. I'm sorry you wrote like that. You won't get anything, and you might as well have enjoyed the reputation of forbearance.'

Mrs Milvain was not able to appreciate this characteristic remark. Anxiety weighed upon her, and she became irritable.

'I am obliged to say, Jasper, that you seem rather thoughtless. If it were only myself, I would make any sacrifice for you; but you must remember –'

'Now listen, mother,' he interrupted, laying a hand on her shoulder; 'I have been thinking about all this, and the fact of the matter is, I shall do my best to ask you for no more money. It may or may not be practicable, but I'll have a try. So don't worry. If uncle writes that he can't pay, just explain why you wrote, and keep him gently in mind of the thing, that's all. One doesn't like to do brutal things if one can avoid them, you know.'

The young man went to the parlour, and listened to Maud's music for a while. But restlessness again drove him forth. Towards eleven o'clock, he was again ascending in the direction of John Yule's house. Again he had no intention of calling, but when he reached the iron gates, he lingered.

'I will, by Jove!' he said within himself at last. 'Just to prove I have complete command of myself. It's to be a display of strength, not weakness.'

At the house door he inquired for Mr Alfred Yule. That gentleman had gone in the carriage to Wattleborough, half an hour ago, with his brother.

'Miss Yule?'

Yes, she was within. Jasper entered the sitting-room, waited a few moments, and Marian appeared. She wore a dress in which Milvain had not yet seen her, and it had the effect of making him regard her attentively. The smile with which she had come towards him passed from her face, which was perchance a little warmer of hue than commonly.

'I'm sorry your father is away, Miss Yule,' Jasper began, in an animated voice. 'I wanted to say good-bye to him. I return to London in a few hours.'

'You are going sooner than you intended?'

'Yes, I feel I mustn't waste any more time. I think the country air is doing you good; you certainly look better than when I passed you that first day.'

'I feel better, much.'

'My sisters are anxious to see you again. I shouldn't wonder if they come up this afternoon.'

Marian had seated herself on the sofa, and her hands were linked upon her lap in the same way as when Jasper spoke with her here before, the palms downward. The beautiful outline of her bent head was relieved against a broad strip of sunlight on the wall behind her.

'They deplore,' he continued in a moment, 'that they should come to know you only to lose you again so soon.'

'I have quite as much reason to be sorry,' she answered, looking at him with the slightest possible smile. 'But perhaps they will let me write to them, and hear from them now and then.'

'They would think it an honour. Country girls are not often invited to correspond with literary ladies in London.'

He said it with as much jocoseness as civility allowed, then at once rose.

'Father will be very sorry,' Marian began, with one quick

glance towards the window and then another towards the door. 'Perhaps he might possibly be able to see you before you go?'

Jasper stood in hesitation. There was a look on the girl's face which, under other circumstances, would have suggested a ready answer.

'I mean,' she added, hastily, 'he might just call, or even see you at the station?'

'Oh, I shouldn't like to give Mr Yule any trouble. It's my own fault, for deciding to go to-day. I shall leave by the 2.45.'

He offered his hand.

'I shall look for your name in the magazines, Miss Yule.'

'Oh, I don't think you will ever find it there.'

He laughed incredulously, shook hands with her a second time, and strode out of the room, head erect – feeling proud of himself.

When Dora came home at dinner-time, he informed her of what he had done.

'A very interesting girl,' he added, impartially. 'I advise you to make a friend of her. Who knows but you may live in London some day, and then she might be valuable – morally, I mean. For myself, I shall do my best not to see her again for a long time; she's dangerous.'

Jasper was unaccompanied when he went to the station. Whilst waiting on the platform, he suffered from apprehension lest Alfred Yule's seamed visage should present itself; but no acquaintance approached him. Safe in the corner of his third-class carriage, he smiled at the last glimpse of the familiar fields, and began to think of something he had decided to write for *The West End*.

Chapter 4

AN AUTHOR AND HIS WIFE

EIGHT flights of stairs, consisting alternately of eight and nine steps. Amy had made the calculation, and wondered what was the cause of this arrangement. The ascent was trying, but then no one could contest the respectability of the abode. In the flat immediately beneath resided a successful musician, whose carriage and pair came at a regular hour each afternoon to take him and his wife for a most respectable drive. In this special building no one else seemed at present to keep a carriage, but all the tenants were gentlefolk.

And as to living up at the very top, why, there were distinct advantages – as so many people of moderate income are nowadays hastening to discover. The noise from the street was diminished at this height; no possible tramplers could establish themselves above your head; the air was bound to be purer than that of inferior strata; finally, one had the flat roof whereon to sit or expatiate in sunny weather. True that a gentle rain of soot was wont to interfere with one's comfort out there in the open, but such minutiæ are easily forgotten in the fervour of domestic description. It was undeniable that on a fine day one enjoyed extensive views. The green ridge from Hampstead to Highgate, with Primrose Hill and the foliage of Regent's Park in the foreground; the suburban spaces of St John's Wood, Maida Vale, Kilburn; Westminster Abbey and the Houses of Parliament, lying low by the side of the hidden river, and a glassy gleam on far-off hills which meant the Crystal Palace; then the clouded majesty of eastern London, crowned by St Paul's dome. These things one's friends were expected to admire. Sunset often afforded rich effects, but they were for solitary musing.

A sitting-room, a bedroom, a kitchen. But the kitchen was called dining-room, or even parlour at need; for the cooking range lent itself to concealment behind an ornamental screen, the walls displayed pictures and bookcases, and a tiny scullery which lay apart sufficed for the coarser domestic operations. This was Amy's territory during the hours when her husband was working, or endeavouring to work. Of necessity, Edwin Reardon used the front room as his study. His writing-table stood against the window; each wall had its shelves of serried literature; vases, busts, engravings (all of the inexpensive kind) served for ornaments.

A maid-servant, recently emancipated from the Board school, came at half-past seven each morning, and remained until two o'clock, by which time the Reardons had dined; on special occasions, her services were enlisted for later hours. But it was Reardon's habit to begin the serious work of the day at about three o'clock, and to continue with brief interruptions until ten or eleven; in many respects an awkward arrangement, but enforced by the man's temperament and his poverty.

One evening he sat at his desk with a slip of manuscript paper before him. It was the hour of sunset. His outlook was upon the backs of certain large houses skirting Regent's Park, and lights had begun to show here and there in the windows: in one room a man was discoverable dressing for dinner, he had not thought it worth while to lower the blind; in another, some people were playing billiards. The higher windows reflected a rich glow from the western sky.

For two or three hours Reardon had been seated in much the same attitude. Occasionally he dipped his pen into the ink, and seemed about to write: but each time the effort was abortive. At the head of the paper was inscribed 'Chapter III,' but that was all. And now the sky was dusking over; darkness would soon fall.

He looked something older than his years, which were two-and-thirty; on his face was the pallor of mental suffering. Often he fell into a fit of absence, and gazed at vacancy with wide, miserable eyes. Returning to consciousness, he fidgeted nervously on his chair, dipped his pen for the hundredth time, bent forward in feverish determination to work. Useless; he scarcely knew what he wished to put into words, and his brain refused to construct the simplest sentence.

The colours faded from the sky, and night came quickly. Reardon threw his arms upon the desk, let his head fall forward, and remained so, as if asleep.

Presently the door opened, and a young, clear voice made inquiry:

'Don't you want the lamp, Edwin?'

The man roused himself, turned his chair a little, and looked towards the open door.

'Come here, Amy.'

His wife approached. It was not quite dark in the room, for a glimmer came from the opposite houses.

'What's the matter? Can't you do anything?'

'I haven't written a word to-day. At this rate, one goes crazy. Come and sit by me a minute, dearest.'

'I'll get the lamp.'

'No; come and talk to me; we can understand each other better.'

'Nonsense; you have such morbid ideas. I can't bear to sit in the gloom.'

At once she went away, and quickly reappeared with a reading-lamp, which she placed on the square table in the middle of the room.

'Draw down the blind, Edwin.'

She was a slender girl, but not very tall; her shoulders seemed rather broad in proportion to her waist and the part of her figure below it. The hue of her hair was ruddy gold; loosely arranged tresses made a superb crown to the beauty of her small, refined head. Yet the face was not of distinctly feminine type; with short hair and appropriate clothing, she would have passed unquestioned as a handsome boy of seventeen, a spirited boy too, and one much in the habit of giving orders to inferiors. Her nose would have been perfect but for ever so slight a crook which made it preferable to view her in full face than in profile; her lips curved sharply out, and when she straightened them of a sudden, the effect was not reassuring to anyone who had counted upon her for facile humour. In harmony with the broad shoulders, she had a strong neck; as she bore the lamp into the room a slight turn of her head showed splendid muscles from the ear downward. It was a magnificently clear-cut bust; one thought, in looking at her, of the newly-finished head which some honest sculptor has wrought with his own hand from the marble block; there was a suggestion of 'planes' and of the chisel. The atmosphere was cold; ruddiness would have been quite out of place on her cheeks, and a flush must have been the rarest thing there.

Her age was not quite two-and-twenty; she had been wedded nearly two years, and had a child ten months old.

As for her dress, it was unpretending in fashion and colour, but of admirable fit. Every detail of her appearance denoted scrupulous personal refinement. She walked well; you saw that the foot, however gently, was firmly planted. When she seated herself, her posture was instantly graceful, and that of one who is indifferent about the support for the back.

'What is the matter?' she began. 'Why can't you get on with the story?'

It was the tone of friendly remonstrance, not exactly of affection, not at all of tender solicitude.

Reardon had risen and wished to approach her, but could not do so directly. He moved to another part of the room, then came round to the back of her chair, and bent his face upon her shoulder.

'Amy – '

'Well.'

'I think it's all over with me. I don't think I shall write any more.'

'Don't be so foolish, dear. What is to prevent your writing?'

'Perhaps I am only out of sorts. But I begin to be horribly afraid. My will seems to be fatally weakened. I can't see my way to the end of anything; if I get hold of an idea which seems good, all the sap has gone out of it before I have got it into working shape. In these last few months, I must have begun a dozen different books; I have been ashamed to tell you of each new beginning. I write twenty pages, perhaps, and then my courage fails. I am disgusted with the thing, and *can't* go on with it – *can't*! My fingers refuse to hold the pen. In mere writing, I have done enough to make much more than three volumes; but it's all destroyed.'

'Because of your morbid conscientiousness. There was no need to destroy what you had written. It was all good enough for the market.'

'Don't use that word, Amy. I hate it!'

'You can't afford to hate it,' was her rejoinder, in very practical tones. 'However it was before, you *must* write for the market now. You have admitted that yourself.'

He kept silence.

'Where are you?' she went on to ask. 'What have you actually done?'

'Two short chapters of a story I can't go on with. The three volumes lie before me like an interminable desert. Impossible to get through them. The idea is stupidly artificial, and I haven't a living character in it.'

'The public don't care whether the characters are living or not. – Don't stand behind me, like that; it's such an awkward way of talking. Come and sit down.'

He drew away, and came to a position whence he could see her face, but kept at a distance.

'Yes,' he said, in a different way, 'that's the worst of it.'

'What is?'

'That you – well, it's no use.'

'That I – what?'

She did not look at him; her lips, after she had spoken, drew in a little.

'That your disposition towards me is being affected by this miserable failure. You keep saying to yourself that I am not what you thought me. Perhaps you even feel that I have been guilty of a sort of deception. I don't blame you; it's natural enough.'

'I'll tell you quite honestly what I do think,' she replied, after a short silence. 'You are much weaker than I imagined. Difficulties crush you, instead of rousing you to struggle.'

'True. It has always been my fault.'

'But don't you feel it's rather unmanly, this state of things? You say you love me, and I try to believe it. But whilst you are saying so, you let me get nearer and nearer to miserable, hateful poverty. What is to become of me – of us? Shall you sit here day after day until our last shilling is spent?'

'No; of course I *must* do something.'

'When shall you begin in earnest? In a day or two you must pay this quarter's rent, and that will leave us just about fifteen pounds in the world. Where is the rent at Christmas to come from? What are we to live upon? There's all sorts of clothing to be bought; there'll be all the extra expenses of winter. Surely it's bad enough that we have had to stay here all the summer; no holiday of any kind. I have done my best not to grumble about it, but I begin to think that it would be very much wiser if I did grumble.'

She squared her shoulders, and gave her head just a little shake, as if a fly had troubled her.

'You bear everything very well and kindly,' said Reardon. 'My behaviour is contemptible; I know that. Good heavens! if I only had some business to go to, something I could work at in any state of mind, and make money out of! Given this chance, I would work myself to death rather than you should lack anything you desire. But I am at the mercy of my brain; it is dry and powerless. How I envy those clerks who go by to their offices in the morning! There's the day's work cut out for them; no question of mood and feeling; they have just to work at something, and when the evening comes, they have earned their wages, they are free to rest and enjoy themselves. What an insane thing it is to make literature one's only means of support! When the most trivial accident may at any time prove fatal to one's power of work for weeks or months. No, that is the unpardonable sin! To make a trade of an art! I am rightly served for attempting such a brutal folly.'

He turned away in a passion of misery.

'How very silly it is to talk like this!' came in Amy's voice, clearly critical. 'Art must be practised as a trade, at all events in our time. This is the age of trade. Of course if one refuses to be of one's time, and yet hasn't the means to live independently, what can result but break-down and wretchedness? The fact of the matter is, you could do fairly good work, and work which would sell, if only you would bring yourself to look at things in a more practical way. It's what Mr Milvain is always saying, you know.'

'Milvain's temperament is very different from mine. He is naturally light-hearted and hopeful; I am naturally the opposite. What you and he say is true enough; the misfortune is that I can't act upon it. I am no uncompromising artistic pedant; I am quite willing to try and do the kind of work that will sell; under the circumstances, it would be a kind of insanity if I refused. But power doesn't answer to the will. My efforts are utterly vain; I suppose the prospect of pennilessness is itself a hindrance; the fear haunts me. With such terrible real things pressing upon me, my imagination can shape nothing substantial. When I have laboured out a story, I suddenly see it in a light of such contemptible triviality that to work at it is an impossible thing.'

'You are ill, that's the fact of the matter. You ought to have had a holiday. I think even now you had better go away for a week or two. Do, Edwin !'

'Impossible ! It would be the merest pretence of holiday. To go away and leave you here – no !'

'Shall I ask mother or Jack to lend us some money?'

'That would be intolerable.'

'But *this* state of things is intolerable !'

Reardon walked the length of the room and back again.

'Your mother has no money to lend, dear, and your brother would do it so unwillingly that we can't lay ourselves under such an obligation.'

'Yet it will come to that, you know,' remarked Amy, calmly.

'No; it shall not come to that. I must and will get something done long before Christmas. If only you –'

He came and took one of her hands.

'If only you will give me more sympathy, dearest. You see, that's one side of my weakness. I am utterly dependent upon you. Your kindness is the breath of life to me. Don't refuse it !'

'But I have done nothing of the kind.'

'You begin to speak very coldly. And I understand your feeling of disappointment. The mere fact of your urging me to do anything that will sell is a proof of bitter disappointment. You would have looked with scorn at anyone who talked to me like that two years ago. You were proud of me because my work wasn't altogether common, and because I had never written a line that was meant to attract the vulgar. All that's over now. If you knew how dreadful it is to see that you have lost your hopes of me !'

'Well, but I haven't – altogether,' Amy replied, meditatively. 'I know very well that, if you had a lot of money, you would do better things than ever.'

'Thank you a thousand times for saying that, my dearest.'

'But, you see, we haven't money, and there's little chance of our getting any. That scrubby old uncle won't leave anything to us; I feel too sure of it. I often feel disposed to go and beg him on my knees to think of us in his will.' She laughed. 'I suppose it's impossible, and would be useless; but I should be capable of it if I knew it would bring money.'

Reardon said nothing.

'I didn't think so much of money when we were married,' Amy continued. 'I had never seriously felt the want of it, you know. I did think – there's no harm in confessing it – that you were sure to be rich some day; but I should have married you all the same if I had known that you would win only reputation.'

'You are sure of that?'

'Well, I think so. But I know the value of money better now. I know it is the most powerful thing in the world. If I had to choose between a glorious reputation with poverty and a contemptible popularity with wealth, I should choose the latter.'

'No!'

'I should.'

'Perhaps you are right.'

He turned away with a sigh.

'Yes, you are right. What is reputation? If it is deserved, it originates with a few score of people among the many millions who would never have recognised the merit they at last applaud. That's the lot of a great genius. As for a mediocrity like me – what ludicrous absurdity to fret myself in the hope that half a dozen folks will say I am "above the average!" After all, is there sillier vanity than this? A year after I have published my last book, I shall be practically forgotten; ten years later, I shall be as absolutely forgotten as one of those novelists of the early part of this century, whose names one doesn't even recognise. What fatuous posing!'

Amy looked askance at him, but replied nothing.

'And yet,' he continued, 'of course it isn't only for the sake of reputation that one tries to do uncommon work. There's the shrinking from conscious insincerity of workmanship – which most of the writers nowadays seem never to feel. "It's good enough for the market"; that satisfies them. And perhaps they are justi-fied. I can't pretend that I rule my life by absolute ideals; I admit that everything is relative. There is no such thing as goodness or badness, in the absolute sense, of course. Perhaps I am absurdly inconsistent when – though knowing my work can't be first-rate – I strive to make it as good as possible. I don't say this in irony, Amy; I really mean it. It may very well be that I am just as foolish as the people I ridicule for moral and religious superstition. This habit of mine is superstitious. How well I can imagine the answer of some popular novelist if he heard me speak scornfully of his books. "My dear fellow," he might say, "do you suppose I am not aware that my books are rubbish? I know it just as well as you do. But my vocation is to live comfortably. I have a luxurious house, a wife and children who are happy and grateful to me for their happiness. If you choose to live in a garret, and, what's worse, make your wife and children share it with you, that's your concern." The man would be abundantly right.'

'But,' said Amy, 'why should you assume that his books are rubbish? Good work succeeds – now and then.'

'I speak of the common kind of success, which is never due to literary merit. And if I speak bitterly, well, I am suffering from my powerlessness. I am a failure, my poor girl, and it isn't easy for me to look with charity on the success of men who deserved it far less than I did, when I was still able to work.'

'Of course, Edwin, if you make up your mind that you are a failure, you will end by being so. But I'm convinced there's no reason that you should fail to make a living with your pen. Now let me advise you; put aside all your strict ideas about what is worthy and what is unworthy, and just act upon my advice. It's impossible for you to write a three-volume novel; very well, then do a short story of a kind that's likely to be popular. You know Mr Milvain is always saying that the long novel has had its day, and that in future people will write shilling books. Why not try? Give yourself a week to invent a sensational plot, and then a fortnight for the writing. Have it ready for the new season at the end of October. If you like, don't put your name to it; your name certainly would have no weight with this sort of public. Just make it a matter of business, as Mr Milvain says, and see if you can't earn some money.'

He stood and regarded her. His expression was one of pained perplexity.

'You mustn't forget, Amy, that it needs a particular kind of faculty to write stories of this sort. The invention of a plot is just the thing I find most difficult.'

'But the plot may be as silly as you like, providing it holds the attention of vulgar readers. Think of "The Hollow Statue"; what could be more idiotic? Yet it sells by thousands.'

'I don't think I can bring myself to that,' Reardon said, in a low voice.

'Very well, then will you tell me what you propose to do?'

'I might perhaps manage a novel in two volumes, instead of three.'

He seated himself at the writing-table, and stared at the blank sheets of paper in an anguish of hopelessness.

'It will take you till Christmas,' said Amy, 'and then you will get perhaps fifty pounds for it.'

'I must do my best. I'll go out and try to get some ideas. I –'

He broke off, and looked steadily at his wife.

'What is it?' she asked.

'Suppose I were to propose to you to leave this flat and take cheaper rooms?'

He uttered it in a shamefaced way, his eyes falling. Amy kept silence.

'We might sublet it,' he continued, in the same tone, 'for the last year of the lease.'

'And where do you propose to live?' Amy inquired, coldly.

'There's no need to be in such a dear neighbourhood. We could go to one of the outer districts. One might find three unfurnished rooms for about eight and sixpence a week – less than half our rent here.'

'You must do as seems good to you.'

'For Heaven's sake, Amy, don't speak to me in that way! I can't stand that! Surely you can see that I am driven to think of every possible resource. To speak like that is to abandon me. Say you can't or won't do it, but don't treat me as if you had no share in my miseries!'

She was touched for the moment.

'I didn't mean to speak unkindly, dear. But think what it means, to give up our home and position. That is open confession of failure. It would be horrible.'

'I won't think of it. I have three months before Christmas, and I *will* finish a book!'

'I really can't see why you shouldn't. Just do a certain number of pages every day. Good or bad, never mind; let the pages be finished. Now you have got two chapters –'

'No; that won't do. I must think of a better subject.'

Amy made a gesture of impatience.

'There you are! What *does* the subject matter? Get this book finished and sold, and then do something better next time.'

'Give me to-night, just to think. Perhaps one of the old stories I have thrown aside will come back in a clearer light. I'll go out for an hour; you don't mind being left alone?'

'You mustn't think of such trifles as that.'

'But nothing that concerns you in the slightest way is a trifle to me – nothing! I can't bear that you should forget that. Have patience with me, darling, a little longer.'

He knelt by her, and looked up into her face.

'Say only one or two kind words – like you used to!'

She passed her hand lightly over his hair, and murmured something with a faint smile.

Then Reardon took his hat and stick and descended the eight flights of stone steps, and walked in the darkness round the outer circle of Regent's Park, racking his fagged brain in a hopeless search for characters, situations, motives.

Chapter 5

THE WAY HITHER

EVEN in mid-rapture of his marriage month he had foreseen this possibility; but fate had hitherto rescued him in sudden ways when he was on the brink of self-abandonment, and it was hard to imagine that this culmination of triumphant joy could be a preface to base miseries.

He was the son of a man who had followed many different pursuits, and in none had done much more than earn a livelihood. At the age of forty – when Edwin, his only child, was ten years old – Mr Reardon established himself in the town of Hereford as a photographer, and there he abode until his death, nine years after, occasionally risking some speculation not inconsistent with the photographic business, but always with the result of losing the little capital he ventured. Mrs Reardon died when Edwin had reached his fifteenth year. In breeding and education she was superior to her husband, to whom, moreover, she had brought something between four and five hundred pounds; her temper was passionate in both senses of the word, and the marriage could hardly be called a happy one, though it was never disturbed by serious discord. The photographer was a man of whims and idealisms; his wife had a strong vein of worldly ambition. They made few friends, and it was Mrs Reardon's frequently expressed desire to go and live in London, where fortune, she thought, might be kinder to them. Reardon had all but made up his mind to try this venture when he suddenly became a widower; after that he never summoned energy to embark on new enterprises.

The boy was educated at an excellent local school; at eighteen he had a far better acquaintance with the ancient classics than most lads who have been expressly prepared for a university, and, thanks to an anglicised Swiss who acted as an assistant in Mr Reardon's business, he not only read French, but could talk it with a certain haphazard fluency. These attainments, however, were not of much practical use; the best that could be done for

Edwin was to place him in the office of an estate agent. His health was indifferent, and it seemed likely that open-air exercise, of which he would have a good deal under the particular circumstances of the case, might counteract the effects of study too closely pursued.

At his father's death he came into possession (practically it was put at his disposal at once, though he was little more than nineteen) of about two hundred pounds – a life-insurance for five hundred had been sacrificed to exigencies not very long before. He had no difficulty in deciding how to use this money. His mother's desire to live in London had in him the force of an inherited motive; as soon as possible he released himself from his uncongenial occupations, converted into money all the possessions of which he had not immediate need, and betook himself to the metropolis.

To become a literary man, of course.

His capital lasted him nearly four years, for, notwithstanding his age, he lived with painful economy. The strangest life, of almost absolute loneliness. From a certain point of Tottenham Court Road [9] there is visible a certain garret window in a certain street which runs parallel with that thoroughfare; for the greater part of these four years the garret in question was Reardon's home. He paid only three-and-sixpence a week for the privilege of living there; his food cost him about a shilling a day; on clothing and other unavoidable expenses he laid out some five pounds yearly. Then he bought books – volumes which cost anything between twopence and two shillings; further than that he durst not go. A strange time, I assure you.

When he had completed his twenty-first year, he desired to procure a reader's ticket for the British Museum. Now this was not such a simple matter as you may suppose; it was necessary to obtain the signature of some respectable householder, and Reardon was acquainted with no such person. His landlady was a decent woman enough, and a payer of rates and taxes, but it would look odd, to say the least of it, to present oneself in Great Russell Street armed with this person's recommendation. There was nothing for it but to take a bold step, to force himself upon the attention of a stranger – the thing from which his pride had always shrunk. He wrote to a well-known novelist – a man with whose works he had some sympathy. 'I am trying to prepare myself for a literary career. I wish to study in the Reading-room of the British Museum, but have no acquaintance to whom I can refer in the ordinary way. Will you help me – I mean, in this particular only?' That was the substance of his letter. For reply came an invitation to a house in the West-end. With fear and trembling Reardon answered the summons. He was so shabbily attired; he was so diffident from the habit of living quite alone; he was horribly afraid lest it should be supposed that he looked for other assistance than he had requested. Well, the novelist was a rotund and jovial man; his dwelling and his person smelt of money; he was so happy himself that he could afford to be kind to others.

'Have you published anything?' he inquired, for the young man's letter had left this uncertain.

'Nothing. I have tried the magazines, but as yet without success.'

'But what do you write?'

'Chiefly essays on literary subjects.'

'I can understand that you would find a difficulty in disposing of them. That kind of thing is supplied either by men of established reputation, or by anonymous writers who have a regular engagement on papers and magazines. Give me an example of your topics.'

'I have written something lately about Tibullus.'

'Oh, dear! Oh, dear! – Forgive me, Mr Reardon; my feelings were too much for me; those names have been my horror ever since I was a schoolboy. Far be it from me to discourage you, if your line is to be solid literary criticism; I will only mention, as a matter of fact, that such work is indifferently paid and in very small demand. It hasn't occurred to you to try your hand at fiction?'

In uttering the word he beamed; to him it meant a thousand or so a year.

'I am afraid I have no talent for that.'

The novelist could do no more than grant his genial signature for the specified purpose, and add good wishes in abundance. Reardon went home with his brain in a whirl. He had had his first glimpse of what was meant by literary success. That luxurious study, with its shelves of handsomely-bound books, its beautiful pictures, its warm, fragrant air – great heavens! what might not a man do who sat at his ease amid such surroundings!

He began to work at the Reading-room, but at the same time he thought often of the novelist's suggestion, and before long had written two or three short stories. No editor would accept them; but he continued to practise himself in that art, and by degrees came to fancy that, after all, perhaps he *had* some talent for fiction. It was significant, however, that no native impulse had directed him to novel-writing. His intellectual temper was that of the student, the scholar, but strongly blended with a love of independence which had always made him think with distaste of a teacher's life. The stories he wrote were scraps of immature psychology – the last thing a magazine would accept from an unknown man.

His money dwindled, and there came a winter during which he suffered much from cold and hunger. What a blessed refuge it was, there under the great dome, when he must else have sat in his windy garret with the mere pretence of a fire! The Reading-room was his true home; its warmth enwrapped him kindly; the peculiar odour of its atmosphere – at first a cause of headache – grew dear and delightful to him. But he could not sit here until his last penny should be spent. Something practical must be done, and practicality was not his strong point.

Friends in London he had none; but for an occasional conversation with his landlady he would scarcely have spoken a dozen words in a week. His disposition was the reverse of democratic, and he could not make acquaintances below his own intellectual level. Solitude fostered a sensitiveness which to begin with was extreme; the lack of stated occupation encouraged his natural tendency to dream and procrastinate and hope for the improbable. He was a recluse in the midst of millions, and viewed with dread the necessity of going forth to fight for daily food.

Little by little he had ceased to hold any correspondence with his former friends at Hereford. The only person to whom he still wrote and from whom he still heard was his mother's father – an old man who lived at Derby, retired from the business of a draper, and spending his last years pleasantly enough with a daughter who had remained single. Edwin had always been a favourite with his grandfather, though they had met only once or twice during the past eight years. But in writing he did not allow it to be understood that he was in actual want, and he felt that he must come to dire extremities before he could bring himself to beg assistance.

He had begun to answer advertisements, but the state of his wardrobe forbade his applying for any but humble positions. Once or twice he presented himself personally at offices, but his reception was so mortifying that death by hunger seemed preferable to a continuance of such experiences. The injury to his pride made him savagely arrogant; for days after the last rejection he hid himself in his garret, hating the world.

He sold his little collection of books, and of course they brought only a trifling sum. That exhausted, he must begin to sell his clothes. And then – ?

But help was at hand. One day he saw it advertised in a newspaper that the secretary of a hospital in the north of London was in need of a clerk; application was to be made by letter. He wrote, and two days later, to his astonishment, received a reply asking him to wait upon the secretary at a certain hour. In a fever of agitation he kept the appointment, and found that his business was with a young man in the very highest spirits, who walked up and down a little office (the hospital was of the "special" order, a house of no great size), and treated the matter in hand as an excellent joke.

'I thought, you know, of engaging someone much younger – quite a lad, in fact. But look there! Those are the replies to my advertisement.'

He pointed to a heap of five or six hundred letters, and laughed consumedly.

'Impossible to read them all, you know. It seemed to me that the fairest thing would be to shake them together, stick my hand in, and take out one by chance. If it didn't seem very promising, I would try a second time. But the first letter was yours, and I thought the fair thing to do was at all events to see you, you know. The fact is, I am only able to offer a pound a week.'

'I shall be very glad indeed to take that,' said Reardon, who was bathed in perspiration.

'Then what about references, and so on?' proceeded the young man, chuckling and rubbing his hands together.

The applicant was engaged. He had barely strength to walk home; the sudden relief from his miseries made him, for the first time, sensible of the extreme physical weakness into which he had sunk. For the next week he was very ill, but he did not allow this to interfere with his new work, which was easily learnt and not burdensome.

He held this position for three years, and during that time important things happened. When he had recovered from his state of semi-starvation, and was living in comfort (a pound a week is a very large sum if you have previously had to live on ten shillings), Reardon found that the impulse to literary production awoke in him more strongly than ever. He generally got home from the hospital about six o'clock, and the evening was his own. In this leisure time he wrote a novel in two volumes; one publisher refused it, but a second offered to bring it out on the terms of half profits[10] to the author. The book appeared, and was well spoken of in one or two papers; but profits there were none to divide. In the third year of his clerkship he wrote a novel in three volumes; for this his publishers gave him twenty-five pounds, with again a promise of half the profits after deduction of the sum advanced. Again there was no pecuniary success. He had just got to work upon a third book, when his grandfather at Derby died and left him four hundred pounds.

He could not resist the temptation to recover his freedom. Four hundred pounds, at the rate of eighty pounds a year, meant five years of literary endeavour. In that period he could certainly determine whether or not it was his destiny to live by the pen.

In the meantime his relations with the secretary of the hospital, Carter by name, had grown very friendly. When Reardon began to publish books, the high-spirited Mr Carter looked upon him with something of awe; and when the literary man ceased to be a clerk, there was nothing to prevent association on equal terms between him and his former employer. They continued to see a good deal of each other, and Carter made Reardon acquainted with certain of his friends, among whom was one John Yule, an easy-going, selfish, semi-intellectual young man who had a place in a Government office. The time of solitude had gone by for Reardon. He began to develop the power that was in him.

Those two books of his were not of a kind to win popularity. They dealt with no particular class of society (unless one makes a distinct class of people who have brains), and they lacked local colour. Their interest was almost purely psychological. It was clear that the author had no faculty for constructing a story, and that pictures of active life were not to be expected of him; he could never appeal to the multitude. But strong characterisation was within his scope, and an intellectual fervour, appetising to a small section of refined readers, marked all his best pages.

He was the kind of man who cannot struggle against adverse conditions, but whom prosperity warms to the exercise of his powers. Anything like the cares of responsibility would sooner or later harass him into unproductiveness. That he should produce much was in any case out of the question; possibly a book every two or three years might not prove too great a strain upon his delicate mental organism, but for him to attempt more than that would certainly be fatal to the peculiar merit of his work. Of this he was dimly conscious, and, on receiving his legacy, he put aside for nearly twelve months the new novel he had begun. To give his mind a rest he wrote several essays, much maturer than those which had formerly failed to find acceptance, and two of these appeared in magazines.

The money thus earned he spent – at a tailor's. His friend Carter ventured to suggest this mode of outlay.

His third book sold for fifty pounds. It was a great improvement on its predecessors, and the reviews were generally favourable. For the story which followed, 'On Neutral Ground,' he received a hundred pounds. On the strength of that he spent six months travelling in the south of Europe.

He returned to London at mid-June, and on the second day after his arrival befell an incident which was to control the rest of his life. Busy with the pictures in the Grosvenor Gallery, he heard himself addressed in a familiar voice, and on turning he was aware of Mr Carter, resplendent in fashionable summer attire, and accompanied by a young lady of some charms. Reardon had formerly feared encounters of this kind, too conscious of the defects of his attire; but at present there was no reason why he should shirk social intercourse. He was passably dressed, and the half-year of travel had benefited his appearance in no slight degree. Carter presented him to the young lady, of whom the novelist had already heard as affianced to his friend.

Whilst they stood conversing, there approached two ladies, evidently mother and daughter, whose attendant was another of Reardon's acquaintances, Mr John Yule. This gentleman stepped briskly forward and welcomed the returned wanderer.

'Let me introduce you,' he said, 'to my mother and sister. Your fame has made them anxious to know you.'

Reardon found himself in a position of which the novelty was embarrassing, but scarcely disagreeable. Here were five people grouped around him, all of whom regarded him unaffectedly as a man of importance; for though, strictly speaking, he had no 'fame' at all, these persons had kept up with the progress of his small repute, and were all distinctly glad to number among their acquaintances an unmistakable author, one, too, who was fresh from Italy and Greece. Mrs Yule, a lady rather too pretentious in her tone to be attractive to a man of Reardon's refinement, hastened to assure him how well his books were known in her house, 'though for the run of ordinary novels we don't care much.' Miss Yule, not at all pretentious in speech, and seemingly reserved of disposition, was good enough to show frank interest in the author. As for the poor author himself, well, he merely fell in love with Miss Yule at first sight, and there was an end of the matter.

A day or two later he made a call at their house, in the region of Westbourne Park. It was a small house, and rather showily than handsomely furnished; no one after visiting it would be astonished to hear that Mrs Edmund Yule had but a small income, and that she was often put to desperate expedients to keep up the gloss of easy circumstances. In the gauzy and fluffy and varnishy little drawing-room Reardon found a youngish gentleman already in conversation with the widow and her daughter. This proved to be one Mr Jasper Milvain, also a man of letters. Mr Milvain was glad to meet Reardon, whose books he had read with decided interest.

'Really,' exclaimed Mrs Yule, 'I don't know how it is that we have had to wait so long for the pleasure of knowing you, Mr

Reardon. If John were not so selfish he would have allowed us a share in your acquaintance long ago.'

Ten weeks thereafter, Miss Yule became Mrs Reardon.

It was a time of frantic exultation with the poor fellow. He had always regarded the winning of a beautiful and intellectual wife as the crown of a successful literary career, but he had not dared hope that such a triumph would be his. Life had been too hard with him on the whole. He, who hungered for sympathy, who thought of a woman's love as the prize of mortals supremely blessed, had spent the fresh years of his youth in monkish solitude. Now of a sudden came friends and flattery, aye, and love itself. He was rapt to the seventh heaven.

Indeed, it seemed that the girl loved him. She knew that he had but a hundred pounds or so left over from that little inheritance, that his books sold for a trifle, that he had no wealthy relatives from whom he could expect anything; yet she hesitated not a moment when he asked her to marry him.

'I have loved you from the first.'

'How is that possible?' he urged. 'What is there lovable in me? I am afraid of waking up and finding myself in my old garret, cold and hungry.'

'You will be a great man.'

'I implore you not to count on that! In many ways I am wretchedly weak. I have no such confidence in myself.'

'Then I will have confidence for both.'

'But can you love me for my own sake – love me as a man?'

'I love you!'

And the words sang about him, filled the air with a mad pulsing of intolerable joy, made him desire to fling himself in passionate humility at her feet, to weep hot tears, to cry to her in insane worship. He thought her beautiful beyond anything his heart had imagined; her warm gold hair was the rapture of his eyes and of his reverent hand. Though slenderly fashioned, she was so gloriously strong. 'Not a day of illness in her life,' said Mrs Yule, and one could readily believe it.

She spoke with such a sweet decision. Her 'I love you!' was a bond with eternity. In the simplest as in the greatest things she saw his wish and acted frankly upon it. No pretty petulance, no affectation of silly-sweet languishing, none of the weaknesses of woman. And so exquisitely fresh in her twenty years of maiden-hood, with bright young eyes that seemed to bid defiance to all the years to come.

He went about like one dazzled with excessive light. He talked as he had never talked before, recklessly, exultantly, insolently – in the nobler sense. He made friends on every hand; he wel-comed all the world to his bosom; he felt the benevolence of a God.

'I love you!' It breathed like music at his ears when he fell asleep in weariness of joy; it awakened him on the morrow as with a glorious ringing summons to renewed life.

Delay? Why should there be delay? Amy wished nothing but to become his wife. Idle to think of his doing any more work until he sat down in the home of which she was mistress. His brain burned with visions of the books he would henceforth write, but his hand was incapable of anything but a love-letter. And what letters! Reardon never published anything equal to those. 'I have received your poem,' Amy replied to one of them. And she was right; not a letter, but a poem he had sent her, with every word on fire.

The hours of talk! It enraptured him to find how much she had read, and with what clearness of understanding. Latin and Greek, no. Ah! but she should learn them both, that there might be nothing wanting in the communion between his thought and hers. For he loved the old writers with all his heart; they had been such strength to him in his days of misery.

They would go together to the charmed lands of the South. No, not now for their marriage holiday – Amy said that would be an imprudent expense; but as soon as he had got a good price for a book. Will not the publishers be kind? If they knew what happi-ness lurked in embryo within their foolish cheque-books!

He woke of a sudden in the early hours of one morning, a week before the wedding-day. You know that kind of awaking, so complete in an instant, caused by the pressure of some trouble-some thought upon the dreaming brain. 'Suppose I should not succeed henceforth? Suppose I could never get more than this poor hundred pounds for one of the long books which cost me so much labour? I shall perhaps have children to support; and Amy – how would Amy bear poverty?'

He knew what poverty means. The chilling of brain and heart, the unnerving of the hands, the slow gathering about one of fear and shame and impotent wrath, the dread feeling of helplessness, of the world's base indifference. Poverty! Poverty!

And for hours he could not sleep. His eyes kept filling with tears, the beating of his heart was low; and in his solitude he called upon Amy with pitiful entreaty: 'Do not forsake me! I love you! I love you!'

But that went by. Six days, five days, four days – will one's heart burst with happiness? The flat is taken, is furnished, up there towards the sky, eight flights of stone steps.

'You're a confoundedly lucky fellow, Reardon,' remarked Milvain, who had already become very intimate with his new friend. 'A good fellow, too, and you deserve it.'

'But at first I had a horrible suspicion.'

'I guess what you mean. No; I wasn't even in love with her, though I admired her. She would never have cared for me in any case; I am not sentimental enough.'

'The deuce!'

'I mean it in an inoffensive sense. She and I are rather too much alike, I fancy.'

'How do you mean?' asked Reardon, puzzled, and not very well pleased.

'There's a great deal of pure intellect about Miss Yule, you know. She was sure to choose a man of the passionate kind.'

'I think you are talking nonsense, my dear fellow.'

'Well, perhaps I am. To tell you the truth, I have by no means completed my study of women yet. It is one of the things in which I hope to be a specialist some day, though I don't think I shall ever make use of it in novels – rather, perhaps, in life.'

Three days – two days – one day.

Now let every joyous sound which the great globe can utter ring forth in one burst of harmony! Is it not well done to make the village-bells chant merrily when a marriage is over? Here in London we can have no such music; but for us, my dear one, all the roaring life of the great city is wedding-hymn. Sweet, pure face under its bridal-veil! The face which shall, if fate spare it, be as dear to me many a long year hence as now at the culminating moment of my life!

As he trudged on in the dark, his tortured memory was living through that time again. The images forced themselves upon him, however much he tried to think of quite other things – of some fictitious story on which he might set to work. In the case of his earlier books he had waited quietly until some suggestive 'situation', some group of congenial characters, came with sudden delightfulness before his mind and urged him to write; but nothing so spontaneous could now be hoped for. His brain was too weary with months of fruitless, harassing endeavour; moreover, he was trying to devise a 'plot,' the kind of literary Jack-in-the-box which might excite interest in the mass of readers, and this was alien to the natural working of his imagination. He suffered the torments of nightmare – an oppression of the brain and heart which must soon be intolerable.

Chapter 6
THE PRACTICAL FRIEND

WHEN her husband had set forth, Amy seated herself in the study and took up a new library volume, as if to read. But she had no real intention of doing so; it was always disagreeable to her to sit in the manner of one totally unoccupied, with hands on lap, and even when she consciously gave herself up to musing an open book was generally before her. She did not, in truth, read much nowadays; since the birth of her child she had seemed to care less than before for disinterested study. If a new novel that had succeeded came into her hands she perused it in a very practical spirit, commenting to Reardon on the features of the work which had made it popular; formerly, she would have thought much more of its purely literary merits, for which her eye was very keen. How often she had given her husband a thrill of exquisite pleasure by pointing to some merit or defect of which the common reader would be totally insensible! Now she spoke less frequently on such subjects. Her interests were becoming more personal; she liked to hear details of the success of popular authors – about their wives or husbands, as the case might be, their arrangements with publishers, their methods of work. The gossip columns of literary papers – and of some that were not literary – had an attraction for her. She talked of questions such as international copyright, was anxious to get an insight into the practical conduct of journals and magazines, liked to know who 'read' for the publishing-houses. To an impartial observer it might have appeared that her intellect was growing more active and mature.

More than half an hour passed. It was not a pleasant train of thought that now occupied her. Her lips were drawn together, her brows were slightly wrinkled; the self-control which at other times was agreeably expressed upon her features had become rather too cold and decided. At one moment it seemed to her that she heard a sound in the bedroom – the doors were purposely left ajar – and her head turned quickly to listen, the look in her eyes instantaneously softening; but all remained quiet. The street would have been silent but for a cab that now and then passed – the swing of a hansom or the roll of a four-wheeler – and within the buildings nothing whatever was audible.

Yes, a footstep, briskly mounting the stone stairs. Not like that of the postman. A visitor, perhaps, to the other flat on the top-most landing. But the final pause was in this direction, and then came a sharp rat-tat at the door. Amy rose immediately and went to open.

Jasper Milvain raised his urban silk hat, then held out his hand with the greeting of frank friendship. His inquiries were in so loud a voice that Amy checked him with a forbidding gesture.

'You'll wake Willie!'

'By Jove! I always forget,' he exclaimed in subdued tones. 'Does the infant flourish?'

'Oh, yes!'

'Reardon out? I got back on Saturday evening, but couldn't come round before this.' It was Monday. 'How close it is in here! I suppose the roof gets so heated during the day. Glorious weather in the country! And I've no end of things to tell you. He won't be long, I suppose?'

'I think not.'

He left his hat and stick in the passage, came into the study, and glanced about as if he expected to see some change since he was last here, three weeks ago.

'So you have been enjoying yourself?' said Amy as, after listening for a moment at the door, she took a seat.

'Oh, a little freshening of the faculties. But whose acquaintance do you think I have made?'

'Down there?'

'Yes. Your uncle Alfred and his daughter were staying at John Yule's, and I saw something of them. I was invited to the house.'

'Did you speak of us?'

'To Miss Yule only. I happened to meet her on a walk, and in a blundering way I mentioned Reardon's name. But of course it didn't matter in the least. She inquired about you with a good deal of interest – asked if you were as beautiful as you promised to be years ago.'

Amy laughed.

'Doesn't that proceed from your fertile invention, Mr Milvain?'

'Not a bit of it! By-the-by, what would be your natural question concerning *her*? Do you think she gave promise of good looks?'

'I'm afraid I can't say that she did. She had a good face, but – rather plain.'

'I see.' Jasper threw back his head and seemed to contemplate an object in memory. 'Well, I shouldn't wonder if most people called her a trifle plain even now; and yet – no, that's hardly possible, after all. She has no colour. Wears her hair short.'

'Short?'

'Oh, I don't mean the smooth, boyish hair with a parting – not the kind of hair that would be lank if it grew long. Curly all over. Looks uncommonly well, I assure you. She has a capital head. Odd girl; very odd girl! Quiet, thoughtful – not very happy, I'm afraid. Seems to think with dread of a return to books.'

'Indeed! But I had understood that she was a reader.'

'Reading enough for six people, probably. Perhaps her health is not very robust. Oh, I knew her by sight quite well – had seen her at the Reading-room. She's the kind of girl that gets into one's head, you know – suggestive; much more in her than comes out until one knows her very well.'

'Well, I should hope so,' remarked Amy, with a peculiar smile.

'But that's by no means a matter of course. They didn't invite me to come and see them in London.'

'I suppose Marian mentioned your acquaintance with this branch of the family?'

'I think not. At all events, she promised me she wouldn't.'

Amy looked at him inquiringly, in a puzzled way.

'She promised you?'

'Voluntarily. We got rather sympathetic. Your uncle – Alfred, I mean – is a remarkable man; but I think he regarded me as a youth of no particular importance. Well, how do things go?'

Amy shook her head.

'No progress?'

'None whatever. He can't work; I begin to be afraid that he is really ill. He *must* go away before the fine weather is over. Do persuade him to-night! I wish you could have had a holiday with him.'

'Out of the question now, I'm sorry to say. I must work savagely. But can't you all manage a fortnight somewhere – Hastings, Eastbourne?'

'It would be simply rash. One goes on saying "What does a pound or two matter?" – but it begins at length to matter a great deal.'

'I know, confound it all! Think how it would amuse some rich grocer's son who pitches his half-sovereign to the waiter when he has dined himself into good humour! But I tell you what it is: you must really try to influence him towards practicality. Don't you think – ?'

He paused, and Amy sat looking at her hands.

'I have made an attempt,' she said at length, in a distant undertone.

'You really have?'

Jasper leaned forward, his clasped hands hanging between his knees. He was scrutinising her face, and Amy, conscious of the too fixed regard, at length moved her head uneasily.

'It seems very clear to me,' she said, 'that a long book is out of the question for him at present. He writes so slowly, and is so fastidious. It would be a fatal thing to hurry through something weaker even than the last.'

'You think "The Optimist" weak?' Jasper asked, half absently.

'I don't think it worthy of Edwin; I don't see how anyone can.'

'I have wondered what your opinion was. Yes, he ought to try a new tack, I think.'

Just then there came the sound of a latch-key opening the outer door. Jasper lay back in his chair and waited with a smile for his expected friend's appearance; Amy made no movement.

'Oh, there you are!' said Reardon, presenting himself with the dazzled eyes of one who has been in darkness; he spoke in a voice of genial welcome, though it still had the note of depression. 'When did you get back?'

Milvain began to recount what he had told in the first part of his conversation with Amy. As he did so, the latter withdrew, and was absent for five minutes; on reappearing she said:

'You'll have some supper with us, Mr Milvain?'

'I think I will, please.'

Shortly after, all repaired to the eating room, where conversation had to be carried on in a low tone because of the proximity of the bedchamber in which lay the sleeping child. Jasper began to tell of certain things that had happened to him since his arrival in town.

'It was a curious coincidence – but, by-the-by, have you heard of what *The Study* has been doing?'

'I should rather think so,' replied Reardon, his face lighting up. 'With no small satisfaction.'

'Delicious, isn't it?' exclaimed his wife. 'I thought it too good to be true when Edwin heard of it from Mr Biffen.'

All three laughed in subdued chorus. For the moment, Reardon became a new man in his exultation over the contradictory reviewers.

'Oh, Biffen told you, did he? Well,' continued Jasper, 'it was an odd thing, but when I reached my lodgings on Saturday evening there lay a note from Horace Barlow, inviting me to go and see him on Sunday afternoon out at Wimbledon, the special reason being that the editor of *The Study* would be there, and Barlow thought I might like to meet him. Now this letter gave me a fit of laughter; not only because of those precious reviews, but because Alfred Yule had been telling me all about this same editor, who rejoices in the name of Fadge. Your uncle, Mrs Reardon, declares that Fadge is the most malicious man in the literary profession; though that's saying such a very great deal – well, never mind! Of course I was delighted to go and meet Fadge. At Barlow's I found the queerest collection of people, most of them women of the inkiest description. The great Fadge himself surprised me; I expected to see a gaunt, bilious man, and he was the rosiest and dumpiest little dandy you can imagine; a fellow of forty-five, I dare say, with thin yellow hair and blue eyes and a manner of extreme innocence. Fadge flattered me with confidential chat, and I discovered at length why Barlow had asked me to meet him; it's Fadge that is going to edit Culpepper's new monthly – you've heard about it? – and he had actually thought it worth while to enlist me among contributors! Now, how's that for a piece of news?'

The speaker looked from Reardon to Amy with a smile of vast significance.

'I rejoice to hear it !' said Reardon, fervently.

'You see ! you see !' cried Jasper, forgetting all about the infant in the next room, 'all things come to the man who knows how to wait. But I'm hanged if I expected a thing of this kind to come so soon ! Why, I'm a man of distinction ! My doings have been noted; the admirable qualities of my style have drawn attention; I'm looked upon as one of the coming men ! Thanks, I confess, in some measure, to old Barlow; he seems to have amused himself with cracking me up to all and sundry. That last thing of mine in *The West End* has done me a vast amount of good, it seems. And Alfred Yule himself had noticed that paper in *The Wayside*. That's how things work, you know; reputation comes with a burst, just when you're not looking for anything of the kind.'

'What's the new magazine to be called?' asked Amy.

'Why, they propose *The Current*. Not bad, in a way; though you imagine a fellow saying "Have you seen the current *Current*?" At all events, the tone is to be up to date, and the articles are to be short; no padding, *merum sel* [11] from cover to cover. What do you think I have undertaken to do, for a start? A paper consisting of sketches of typical readers of each of the principal daily and weekly papers. A deuced good idea, you know – my own, of course – but deucedly hard to carry out. I shall rise to the occasion, see if I don't. I'll rival Fadge himself in maliciousness – though I must confess I discovered no particular malice in the fellow's way of talking. The article shall make a sensation. I'll spend a whole month on it, and make it a perfect piece of satire.'

'Now that's the kind of thing that inspires me with awe and envy,' said Reardon. 'I could no more write such a paper than an article on Fluxions.'

' 'Tis my vocation, Hal ! You might think I hadn't experience enough, to begin with. But my intuition is so strong that I can make a little experience go an immense way. Most people would imagine I had been wasting my time these last few years, just sauntering about, reading nothing but periodicals, making acquaintance with loafers of every description. The truth is, I have been collecting ideas, and ideas that are convertible into coin of the realm, my boy; I have the special faculty of an extempore writer. Never in my life shall I do anything of solid literary value; I shall always despise the people I write for. But my path will be that of success. I have always said it, and now I'm sure of it.'

'Does Fadge retire from *The Study*, then?' inquired Reardon, when he had received this tirade with a friendly laugh.

'Yes, he does. Was going to, it seems, in any case. Of course I heard nothing about the two reviews, and I was almost afraid to smile whilst Fadge was talking with me, lest I should betray my thought. Did you know anything about the fellow before?'

'Not I. Didn't know who edited *The Study*.'

'Nor I either. Remarkable what a number of illustrious obscure are going about. But I still have something else to tell you. I'm going to set my sisters afloat in literature.'

'How?'

'Well, I don't see why they shouldn't try their hands at a little writing, instead of giving lessons, which doesn't suit them a bit. Last night, when I got back from Wimbledon, I went to look up Davies. Perhaps you don't remember my mentioning him; a fellow who was at Jolly and Monk's, the publishers, up to a year ago. He edits a trade journal now, and I see very little of him. However, I found him at home, and had a long practical talk with him. I wanted to find out the state of the market as to such wares as Jolly and Monk dispose of. He gave me some very useful hints, and the result was that I went off this morning and saw Monk himself – no Jolly exists at present. "Mr Monk," I began, in my blandest tone – you know it – "I am requested to call upon you by a lady who thinks of preparing a little volume to be called 'A Child's History of the English Parliament.' Her idea is, that" – and so on. Well, I got on admirably with Monk, especially when he learnt that I was to be connected with Culpepper's new venture; he smiled upon the project, and said he should be very glad to see a specimen chapter; if that pleased him, we could then discuss terms.'

'But has one of your sisters really begun such a book?' inquired Amy.

'Neither of them knows anything of the matter, but they are certainly capable of doing the kind of thing I have in mind, which will consist largely of anecdotes of prominent statesmen. I myself shall write the specimen chapter, and send it to the girls to show them what I propose. I shouldn't wonder if they make some fifty pounds out of it. The few books that will be necessary they can either get at a Wattleborough library, or I can send them.'

'Your energy is remarkable, all of a sudden,' said Reardon.

'Yes. The hour has come, I find. "There is a tide" [12]– to quote something that has the charm of freshness.'

The supper – which consisted of bread and butter, cheese, sardines, cocoa – was now over, and Jasper, still enlarging on his recent experiences and future prospects, led the way back to the sitting-room. Not very long after this, Amy left the two friends to their pipes; she was anxious that her husband should discuss his affairs privately with Milvain, and give ear to the practical advice which she knew would be tendered him.

'I hear that you are still stuck fast,' began Jasper, when they had smoked awhile in silence.

'Yes.'

'Getting rather serious, I should fear, isn't it?'

'Yes,' repeated Reardon, in a low voice.

'Come, come, old man, you can't go on in this way. Would it, or wouldn't it, be any use if you took a seaside holiday?'

'Not the least. I am incapable of holiday, if the opportunity were offered. Do something I must, or I shall fret myself into imbecility.'

'Very well. What is it to be?'

'I shall try to manufacture two volumes. They needn't run to more than about two hundred and seventy pages, and those well spaced out.'

'This is refreshing. This is practical. But look now: let it be something rather sensational. Couldn't we invent a good title – something to catch eye and ear? The title would suggest the story, you know.'

Reardon laughed contemptuously, but the scorn was directed rather against himself than Milvain.

'Let's try,' he muttered.

Both appeared to exercise their minds on the problem for a few minutes. Then Jasper slapped his knee.

'How would this do: "The Weird Sisters"? Devilish good, eh?

Suggests all sorts of things, both to the vulgar and the educated. Nothing brutally clap-trap about it, you know.'

'But – what does it suggest to you?'

'Oh, witch-like, mysterious girls or women. Think it over.'

There was another long silence. Reardon's face was that of a man in blank misery.

'I have been trying,' he said at length, after an attempt to speak which was checked by a huskiness in his throat, 'to explain to myself how this state of things has come about. I almost think I can do so.'

'How?'

'That half-year abroad, and the extraordinary shock of happiness which followed at once upon it, have disturbed the balance of my nature. It was adjusted to circumstances of hardship, privation, struggle. A temperament like mine can't pass through such a violent change of conditions without being greatly affected; I have never since been the man I was before I left England. The stage I had then reached was the result of a slow and elaborate building up; I could look back and see the processes by which I had grown from the boy who was a mere bookworm to the man who had all but succeeded as a novelist. It was a perfectly natural, sober development. But in the last two years and a half I can distinguish no order. In living through it, I have imagined from time to time that my powers were coming to their ripest; but that was mere delusion. Intellectually, I have fallen back. The probability is that this wouldn't matter, if only I could live on in peace of mind; I should recover my equilibrium, and perhaps once more understand myself. But the due course of things is troubled by my poverty.'

He spoke in a slow, meditative way, in a monotonous voice, and without raising his eyes from the ground.

'I can understand,' put in Jasper, 'that there may be philosophical truth in all this. All the same, it's a great pity that you should occupy your mind with such thoughts.'

'A pity – no! I must remain a reasoning creature. Disaster may end by driving me out of my wits, but till then I won't abandon my heritage of thought.'

'Let us have it out, then. You think it was a mistake to spend those months abroad?'

'A mistake from the practical point of view. That vast broadening of my horizon lost me the command of my literary resources. I lived in Italy and Greece as a student, concerned especially with the old civilisations; I read little but Greek and Latin. That brought me out of the track I had laboriously made for myself; I often thought with disgust of the kind of work I had been doing; my novels seemed vapid stuff, so wretchedly and shallowly modern. If I had had the means, I should have devoted myself to the life of a scholar. That, I quite believe, is my natural life; it's only the influence of recent circumstances that has made me a writer of novels. A man who can't journalise, yet must earn his bread by literature, nowadays inevitably turns to fiction, as the Elizabethan men turned to the drama. Well, but I should have got back, I think, into the old line of work. It was my marriage that completed what the time abroad had begun.'

He looked up suddenly, and added:

'I am speaking as if to myself. You, of course, don't misunderstand me, and think I am accusing my wife.'

'No, I don't take you to mean that, by any means.'

'No, no; of course not. All that's wrong is my accursed want of money. But that threatens to be such a fearful wrong, that I begin to wish I had died before my marriage day. Then Amy would have been saved. The Philistines are right: a man has no business to marry unless he has a secured income equal to all natural demands. I behaved with the grossest selfishness. I might have known that such happiness was never meant for me.'

'Do you mean by all this that you seriously doubt whether you will ever be able to write again?'

'In awful seriousness, I doubt it,' replied Reardon, with haggard face.

'It strikes me as extraordinary. In your position I should work as I never had done before.'

'Because you are the kind of man who is roused by necessity. I am overcome by it. My nature is feeble and luxurious. I never in my life encountered and overcame a practical difficulty.'

'Yes; when you got the work at the hospital.'

'All I did was to write a letter, and chance made it effective.'

'My view of the case, Reardon, is that you are simply ill.'

'Certainly, I am; but the ailment is desperately complicated.

Tell me: do you think I might possibly get any kind of stated work to do? Should I be fit for any place in a newspaper office, for instance?'

'I fear not. You are the last man to have anything to do with journalism.'

'If I appealed to my publishers, could they help me?'

'I don't see how. They would simply say: Write a book and we'll buy it.'

'Yes, there's no help but that.'

'If only you were able to write short stories, Fadge might be useful.'

'But what's the use? I suppose I might get ten guineas, at most, for such a story. I need a couple of hundred pounds at least. Even if I could finish a three-volume book, I doubt if they would give me a hundred again, after the failure of "The Optimist"; no, they wouldn't.'

'But to sit and look forward in this way is absolutely fatal, my dear fellow. Get to work at your two-volume story. Call it "The Weird Sisters," or anything better that you can devise; but get it done, so many pages a day. If I go ahead as I begin to think I shall, I shall soon be able to assure you good notices in a lot of papers. Your misfortune has been that you had no influential friends. By-the-by, how has *The Study* been in the habit of treating you?'

'Scrubbily.'

'I'll make an opportunity of talking about your books to Fadge. I think Fadge and I shall get on pretty well together. Alfred Yule hates the man fiercely, for some reason or other. By the way, I may as well tell you that I broke short off with the Yules on purpose.'

'Oh?'

'I had begun to think far too much about the girl. Wouldn't do, you know. I must marry someone with money, and a good deal of it. That's a settled point with me.'

'Then you are not at all likely to meet them in London?'

'Not at all. And if I get allied with Fadge, no doubt Yule will involve me in his savage feeling. You see how wisely I acted. I have a scent for the prudent course.'

They talked for a long time, but again chiefly of Milvain's

affairs. Reardon, indeed, cared little to say anything more about
his own. Talk was mere vanity and vexation of spirit, for the
spring of his volition seemed to be broken, and, whatever resolve
he might utter, he knew that everything depended on influences
he could not even foresee.

Chapter 7

MARIAN'S HOME

THREE weeks after her return from the country – which took place a week later than that of Jasper Milvain – Marian Yule was working one afternoon at her usual place in the Museum Reading-room. It was three o'clock, and with the interval of half an hour at midday, when she went away for a cup of tea and a sandwich, she had been closely occupied since half-past nine. Her task at present was to collect materials for a paper on 'French Authoresses of the Seventeenth Century,' the kind of thing which her father supplied on stipulated terms for anonymous publication. Marian was by this time almost able to complete such a piece of manufacture herself, and her father's share in it was limited to a few hints and corrections. The greater part of the work by which Yule earned his moderate income was anonymous: volumes and articles which bore his signature dealt with much the same subjects as his unsigned matter, but the writing was laboured with a conscientiousness unusual in men of his position. The result, unhappily, was not correspondent with the efforts. Alfred Yule had made a recognisable name among the critical writers of the day; seeing him in the title-lists of a periodical, most people knew what to expect, but not a few forbore the cutting open of the pages he occupied. He was learned, copious, occasionally mordant in style; but grace had been denied to him. He had of late begun to perceive the fact that those passages of Marian's writing which were printed just as they came from her pen had merit of a kind quite distinct from anything of which he himself was capable, and it began to be a question with him whether it would not be advantageous to let the girl sign these compositions. A matter of business, to be sure – at all events in the first instance.

For a long time Marian had scarcely looked up from the desk, but at this moment she found it necessary to refer to the invaluable Larousse. As so often happened, the particular volume of which she had need was not upon the shelf; she turned away, and looked about her with a gaze of weary disappointment. At a little distance were standing two young men, engaged, as their faces showed, in facetious colloquy; as soon as she observed them, Marian's eyes fell, but the next moment she looked again in that direction. Her face had wholly changed; she wore a look of timid expectancy.

The men were moving towards her, still talking and laughing. She turned to the shelves, and affected to search for a book. The voices drew near, and one of them was well known to her; now she could hear every word; now the speakers were gone by. Was it possible that Mr Milvain had not recognised her? She followed him with her eyes, and saw him take a seat not far off; he must have passed without even being aware of her.

She went back to her place and for some minutes sat trifling with a pen. When she made a show of resuming work, it was evident that she could no longer apply herself as before. Every now and then she glanced at people who were passing; there were intervals when she wholly lost herself in reverie. She was tired, and had even a slight headache. When the hand of the clock pointed to half-past three, she closed the volume from which she had been copying extracts, and began to collect her papers.

A voice spoke close behind her.

'Where's your father, Miss Yule?'

The speaker was a man of sixty, short, stout, tonsured by the hand of time. He had a broad, flabby face, the colour of an ancient turnip, save where one of the cheeks was marked with a mulberry stain; his eyes, grey-orbed in a yellow setting, glared with good-humoured inquisitiveness, and his mouth was that of the confirmed gossip. For eyebrows he had two little patches of reddish stubble; for moustache, what looked like a bit of discoloured tow, and scraps of similar material hanging beneath his creasy chin represented a beard. His garb must have seen a great deal of Museum service; it consisted of a jacket, something between brown and blue, hanging in capacious shapelessness, a waistcoat half open for lack of buttons and with one of the pockets coming unsewn, a pair of bronze-hued trousers which had all run to knee. Necktie he had none, and his linen made distinct appeal to the laundress.

Marian shook hands with him.

'He went away at half-past two,' was her reply to his question.

'How annoying! I wanted particularly to see him. I have been running about all day, and couldn't get here before. Something important – most important. At all events, I can tell you. But I entreat that you won't breathe a word save to your father.'

Mr Quarmby – that was his name – had taken a vacant chair and drawn it close to Marian's. He was in a state of joyous excitement, and talked in thick, rather pompous tones, with a pant at the end of a sentence. To emphasize the extremely confidential nature of his remarks, he brought his head almost in contact with the girl's, and one of her thin, delicate hands was covered with his red, podgy fingers.

'I've had a talk with Nathaniel Walker,' he continued; 'a long talk – a talk of vast importance. You know Walker? No, no; how should you? He's a man of business; close friend of Rackett's – Rackett, you know, the owner of *The Study*.'

Upon this he made a grave pause, and glared more excitedly than ever.

'I have heard of Mr Rackett,' said Marian.

'Of course, of course. And you must also have heard that Fadge leaves *The Study* at the end of this year, eh?'

'Father told me it was probable.'

'Rackett and he have done nothing but quarrel for months; the paper is falling off seriously. Well, now, when I came across Nat Walker this afternoon, the first thing he said to me was, "You know Alfred Yule pretty well, I think?" "Pretty well," I answered; "why?" "I'll tell you," he said, "but it's between you and me, you understand. Rackett is thinking about him in connection with *The Study*." "I'm delighted to hear it." "To tell you the truth," went on Nat, "I shouldn't wonder if Yule gets the editorship; but you understand that it would be altogether premature to talk about it." Now what do you think of this, eh?'

'It's very good news,' answered Marian.

'I should think so! Ho, ho!'

Mr Quarmby laughed in a peculiar way, which was the result of long years of mirth-subdual in the Reading-room.

'But not a breath to anyone but your father. He'll be here

tomorrow? Break it gently to him, you know; he's an excitable
man; can't take things quietly, like I do. Ho, ho!'

His suppressed laugh ended in a fit of coughing – the Reading-
room cough. When he had recovered from it, he pressed Marian's
hand with paternal fervour, and waddled off to chatter with
someone else.

Marian replaced several books on the reference shelves, returned others to the central desk, and was just leaving the room,
when again a voice made demand upon her attention.

'Miss Yule! One moment, if you please!'

It was a tall, meagre, dry-featured man, dressed with the painful neatness of self-respecting poverty: the edges of his coat-
sleeves were carefully darned; his black necktie and a skull-cap
which covered his baldness were evidently of home manufacture.
He smiled softly and timidly with blue, rheumy eyes. Two or
three recent cuts on his chin and neck were the result of conscientious shaving with an unsteady hand.

'I have been looking for your father,' he said, as Marian turned.
'Isn't he here?'

'He has gone, Mr Hinks.'

'Ah, then would you do me the kindness to take a book for
him? In fact, it's my little "Essay on the Historical Drama," just
out.'

He spoke with nervous hesitation, and in a tone which seemed
to make apology for his existence.

'Oh, father will be very glad to have it.'

'If you will kindly wait *one* minute, Miss Yule. It's at my
place over there.'

He went off with long strides, and speedily came back panting, in his hand a thin new volume.

'My kind regards to him, Miss Yule. You are quite well, I
hope? I won't detain you.'

And he backed into a man who was coming inobservantly this
way.

Marian went to the ladies' cloak-room, put on her hat and
jacket, and left the Museum. Some one passed out through the
swing-door a moment before her, and as soon as she had issued
beneath the portico, she saw that it was Jasper Milvain; she must
have followed him through the hall, but her eyes had been cast

down. The young man was now alone; as he descended the steps he looked to left and right, but not behind him. Marian followed at a distance of two or three yards. Nearing the gateway, she quickened her pace a little, so as to pass out into the street almost at the same moment as Milvain. But he did not turn his head.

He took to the right. Marian had fallen back again, but she still followed at a very little distance. His walk was slow, and she might easily have passed him in quite a natural way; in that case he could not help seeing her. But there was an uneasy suspicion in her mind that he really must have noticed her in the Reading-room. This was the first time she had seen him since their parting at Finden. Had he any reason for avoiding her? Did he take it ill that her father had shown no desire to keep up his acquaintance?

She allowed the interval between them to become greater. In a minute or two Milvain turned up Charlotte Street, and so she lost sight of him.

In Tottenham Court Road she waited for an omnibus that would take her to the remoter part of Camden Town; obtaining a corner seat, she drew as far back as possible, and paid no attention to her fellow-passengers. At a point in Camden Road she at length alighted, and after ten minutes' walk reached her destination in a quiet by-way called St Paul's Crescent, consisting of small, decent houses. That at which she paused had an exterior promising comfort within; the windows were clean and neatly curtained, and the polishable appurtenances of the door gleamed to perfection. She admitted herself with a latch-key, and went straight upstairs without encountering anyone.

Descending again in a few moments, she entered the front room on the ground-floor. This served both as parlour and dining-room; it was comfortably furnished, without much attempt at adornment. On the walls were a few autotypes and old engravings. A recess between fireplace and window was fitted with shelves, which supported hundreds of volumes, the overflow of Yule's library. The table was laid for a meal. It best suited the convenience of the family to dine at five o'clock; a long evening, so necessary to most literary people, was thus assured. Marian, as always when she had spent a day at the Museum, was faint with weariness and hunger; she cut a small piece of bread from a loaf on the table, and sat down in an easy chair.

Presently appeared a short, slight woman of middle age, plainly dressed in serviceable grey. Her face could never have been very comely, and it expressed but moderate intelligence; its lines, however, were those of gentleness and good feeling. She had the look of one who is making a painful effort to understand something; this was fixed upon her features, and probably resulted from the peculiar conditions of her life.

'Rather early, aren't you, Marian?' she said, as she closed the door and came forward to take a seat.

'Yes; I have a little headache.'

'Oh, dear! Is that beginning again?'

Mrs Yule's speech was seldom ungrammatical, and her intonation was not flagrantly vulgar, but the accent of the London poor, which brands as with hereditary baseness, still clung to her words, rendering futile such propriety of phrase as she owed to years of association with educated people. In the same degree did her bearing fall short of that which distinguishes a lady. The London work-girl is rarely capable of raising herself, or being raised, to a place in life above that to which she was born; she cannot learn how to stand and sit and move like a woman bred to refinement, any more than she can fashion her tongue to graceful speech. Mrs Yule's behaviour to Marian was marked with a singular diffidence; she looked and spoke affectionately, but not with a mother's freedom; one might have taken her for a trusted servant waiting upon her mistress. Whenever opportunity offered, she watched the girl in a curiously furtive way, that puzzled look on her face becoming very noticeable. Her consciousness was never able to accept as a familiar and unimportant fact the vast difference between herself and her daughter. Marian's superiority in native powers, in delicacy of feeling, in the results of education, could never be lost sight of. Under ordinary circumstances she addressed the girl as if tentatively; however sure of anything from her own point of view, she knew that Marian, as often as not, had quite a different criterion. She understood that the girl frequently expressed an opinion by mere reticence, and hence the carefulness with which, when conversing, she tried to discover the real effect of her words in Marian's features.

'Hungry, too,' she said, seeing the crust Marian was nibbling.

'You really must have more lunch, dear. It isn't right to go so long; you'll make yourself ill.'

'Have you been out?' Marian asked.

'Yes; I went to Holloway.'

Mrs Yule sighed and looked very unhappy. By 'going to Holloway' was always meant a visit to her own relatives – a married sister with three children, and a brother who inhabited the same house. To her husband she scarcely ever ventured to speak of these persons; Yule had no intercourse with them. But Marian was always willing to listen sympathetically, and her mother often exhibited a touching gratitude for this condescension – as she deemed it.

'Are things no better?' the girl inquired.

'Worse, as far as I can see. John has begun his drinking again, and him and Tom quarrel every night; there's no peace in the 'ouse.'

If ever Mrs Yule lapsed into gross errors of pronunciation or phrase, it was when she spoke of her kinsfolk. The subject seemed to throw her back into a former condition.

'He ought to go and live by himself,' said Marian, referring to her mother's brother, the thirsty John.

'So he ought, to be sure. I'm always telling them so. But there! you don't seem to be able to persuade them, they're that silly and obstinate. And Susan, she only gets angry with me, and tells me not to talk in a stuck-up way. I'm sure I never say a word that could offend her; I'm too careful for that. And there's Annie; no doing anything with her! She's about the streets at all hours, and what'll be the end of it no one can say. They're getting that ragged, all of them. It isn't Susan's fault; indeed it isn't. She does all that woman can. But Tom hasn't brought home ten shillings the last month, and it seems to me as if he was getting careless. I gave her half a crown; it was all I could do. And the worst of it is, they think I could do so much more if I liked. They're always hinting that we are rich people, and it's no good my trying to persuade them. They think I'm telling falsehoods, and it's very hard to be looked at in that way; it is, indeed, Marian.'

'You can't help it, mother. I suppose their suffering makes them unkind and unjust.'

'That's just what it does, my dear; you never said anything truer. Poverty will make the best people bad, if it gets hard enough. Why there's so much of it in the world, I'm sure I can't see.'

'I suppose father will be back soon?'

'He said dinner-time.'

'Mr Quarmby has been telling me something which is wonderfully good news if it's really true; but I can't help feeling doubtful. He says that father may perhaps be made editor of *The Study* at the end of this year.'

Mrs Yule, of course, understood, in outline, these affairs of the literary world; she thought of them only from the pecuniary point of view, but that made no essential distinction between her and the mass of literary people.

'My word!' she exclaimed. 'What a thing that would be for us!'

Marian had begun to explain her reluctance to base any hopes on Mr Quarmby's prediction, when the sound of a postman's knock at the house-door caused her mother to disappear for a moment.

'It's for you,' said Mrs Yule, returning. 'From the country.'

Marian took the letter and examined its address with interest.

'It must be one of the Miss Milvains. Yes; Dora Milvain.'

After Jasper's departure from Finden his sisters had seen Marian several times, and the mutual liking between her and them had been confirmed by opportunity of conversation. The promise of correspondence had hitherto waited for fulfilment. It seemed natural to Marian that the younger of the two girls should write; Maud was attractive and agreeable, and probably clever, but Dora had more spontaneity in friendship.

'It will amuse you to hear,' wrote Dora, 'that the literary project our brother mentioned in a letter whilst you were still here is really to come to something. He has sent us a specimen chapter, written by himself, of the "Child's History of Parliament," and Maud thinks she could carry it on in that style, if there's no hurry. She and I have both set to work on English histories, and we shall be authorities before long. Jolly and Monk offer thirty pounds for the little book, if it suits them when finished, with certain possible profits in the future. Trust Jasper for making a bargain! So perhaps our literary career will be something more than a joke, after all. I hope it may; anything rather than a life of teaching. We shall be so glad to hear from you, if you still care to trouble about country girls.'

And so on. Marian read with a pleased smile, then acquainted her mother with the contents.

'I'm very glad,' said Mrs Yule; 'it's so seldom you get a letter.'

'Yes.'

Marian seemed desirous of saying something more, and her mother had a thoughtful look, suggestive of sympathetic curiosity.

'Is their brother likely to call here?' Mrs Yule asked, with misgiving.

'No one has invited him to,' was the girl's quiet reply.

'He wouldn't come without that?'

'It's not likely that he even knows the address.'

'Your father won't be seeing him, I suppose?'

'By chance, perhaps. I don't know.'

It was very rare indeed for these two to touch upon any subject save those of everyday interest. In spite of the affection between them, their exchange of confidence did not go very far; Mrs Yule, who had never exercised maternal authority since Marian's earliest childhood, claimed no maternal privileges, and Marian's natural reserve had been strengthened by her mother's respectful aloofness. The English fault of domestic reticence could scarcely go further than it did in their case; its exaggeration is, of course, one of the characteristics of those unhappy families severed by differences of education between the old and young.

'I think,' said Marian, in a forced tone, 'that father hasn't much liking for Mr Milvain.'

She wished to know if her mother had heard any private remarks on this subject, but she could not bring herself to ask directly.

'I'm sure I don't know,' replied Mrs Yule, smoothing her dress. 'He hasn't said anything to me, Marian.'

An awkward silence. The mother had fixed her eyes on the mantelpiece, and was thinking hard.

'Otherwise,' said Marian, 'he would have said something, I should think, about meeting in London.'

'But is there anything in – this gentleman that he wouldn't like?'

'I don't know of anything.'

Impossible to pursue the dialogue; Marian moved uneasily, then rose, said something about putting the letter away, and left the room.

Shortly after, Alfred Yule entered the house. It was no uncommon thing for him to come home in a mood of silent moroseness, and this evening the first glimpse of his face was sufficient warning. He entered the dining-room and stood on the hearthrug reading an evening paper. His wife made a pretence of straightening things upon the table.

'Well?' he exclaimed irritably. 'It's after five; why isn't dinner served?'

'It's just coming, Alfred.'

Even the average man of a certain age is an alarming creature when dinner delays itself; the literary man in such a moment goes beyond all parallel. If there be added the fact that he has just returned from a very unsatisfactory interview with a publisher, wife and daughter may indeed regard the situation as appalling. Marian came in, and at once observed her mother's frightened face.

'Father,' she said, hoping to make a diversion, 'Mr Hinks has sent you his new book, and wishes –'

'Then take Mr Hinks's new book back to him, and tell him that I have quite enough to do without reading tedious trash. He needn't expect that I'm going to write a notice of it. The simpleton pesters me beyond endurance. I wish to know, if you please,' he added with savage calm, 'when dinner will be ready. If there's time to write a few letters, just tell me at once, that I mayn't waste half an hour.'

Marian resented this unreasonable anger, but she durst not reply. At that moment the servant appeared with a smoking joint, and Mrs Yule followed carrying dishes of vegetables. The man of letters seated himself and carved angrily. He began his meal by drinking half a glass of ale; then he ate a few mouthfuls in a quick, hungry way, his head bent closely over the plate. It happened commonly enough that dinner passed without a word of conversation, and that seemed likely to be the case this evening. To his wife Yule seldom addressed anything but a curt inquiry or caustic comment; if he spoke humanly at table it was to Marian.

Ten minutes passed; then Marian resolved to try any means of clearing the atmosphere.

'Mr Quarmby gave me a message for you,' she said. 'A friend of his, Nathaniel Walker, has told him that Mr Rackett will very likely offer you the editorship of *The Study*.'

Yule stopped in the act of mastication. He fixed his eyes intently on the sirloin for half a minute; then, by way of the beer-jug and the salt-cellar, turned them upon Marian's face.

'Walker told him that? Pooh!'

'It was a great secret. I wasn't to breathe a word to anyone but you.'

'Walker's a fool and Quarmby's an ass,' remarked her father.

But there was a tremulousness in his bushy eyebrows; his forehead half unwreathed itself; he continued to eat more slowly, and as if with appreciation of the viands.

'What did he say? Repeat it to me in his words.'

Marian did so, as nearly as possible. He listened with a scoffing expression, but still his features relaxed.

'I don't credit Rackett with enough good sense for such a proposal,' he said deliberately. 'And I'm not very sure that I should accept it if it were made. That fellow Fadge has all but ruined the paper. It will amuse me to see how long it takes him to make Culpepper's new magazine a distinct failure.'

A silence of five minutes ensued; then Yule said of a sudden:

'Where is Hinks's book?'

Marian reached it from a side table; under this roof, literature was regarded almost as a necessary part of table garnishing.

'I thought it would be bigger than this,' Yule muttered, as he opened the volume in a way peculiar to bookish men.

A page was turned down, as if to draw attention to some passage. Yule put on his eyeglasses, and soon made a discovery which had the effect of completing the transformation of his visage. His eyes glinted, his chin worked in pleasurable emotion. In a moment he handed the book to Marian, indicating the small

type of a foot-note; it embodied an effusive eulogy – introduced
à propos of some literary discussion – of 'Mr Alfred Yule's critical acumen, scholarly research, lucid style,' and sundry other
distinguished merits.

'That is kind of him,' said Marian.

'Good old Hinks ! I suppose I must try to get him half a dozen
readers.'

'May I see?' asked Mrs Yule, under her breath, bending to
Marian.

Her daughter passed on the volume, and Mrs Yule read the
foot-note with that look of slow apprehension which is so pathetic when it signifies the heart's good-will thwarted by the mind's
defect.

'That'll be good for you, Alfred, won't it?' she said, glancing
at her husband.

'Certainly,' he replied, with a smile of contemptuous irony. 'If
Hinks goes on, he'll establish my reputation.'

And he took a draught of ale, like one who is reinvigorated for
the battle of life. Marian, regarding him askance, mused on what
seemed to her a strange anomaly in his character; it had often
surprised her that a man of his temperament and powers should
be so dependent upon the praise and blame of people whom he
justly deemed his inferiors.

Yule was glancing over the pages of the work.

'A pity the man can't write English. What a vocabulary !
Obstruent – *reliable* – *particularization* – *fabulosity* – *different*
to – *averse to* – did one ever come across such a mixture of an-
tique pedantry and modern vulgarism ! Surely he has his name
from the German *hinken* [13] – eh, Marian?'

With a laugh he tossed the book away again. His mood was
wholly changed. He gave various evidences of enjoying the meal,
and began to talk freely with his daughter.

'Finished the authoresses?'

'Not quite.'

'No hurry. When you have time I want you to read Ditchley's
new book, and jot down a selection of his worst sentences. I'll
use them for an article on contemporary style; it occurred to
me this afternoon.'

He smiled grimly. Mrs Yule's face exhibited much contentment, which became radiant joy when her husband remarked casually that the custard was very well made to-day. Dinner over, he rose without ceremony and went off to his study.

The man had suffered much and toiled stupendously. It was not inexplicable that dyspepsia, and many another ill that literary flesh is heir to, racked him sore.

Go back to the days when he was an assistant at a bookseller's in Holborn. Already ambition devoured him, and the genuine love of knowledge goaded his brain. He allowed himself but three or four hours of sleep; he wrought doggedly at languages, ancient and modern; he tried his hand at metrical translations; he planned tragedies. Practically he was living in a past age; his literary ideals were formed on the study of Boswell.

The head assistant in the shop went away to pursue a business which had come into his hands on the death of a relative; it was a small publishing concern, housed in an alley off the Strand, and Mr Polo (a singular name, to become well known in the course of time) had his ideas about its possible extension. Among other instances of activity he started a penny weekly paper, called *All Sorts*, and in the pages of this periodical Alfred Yule first appeared as an author. Before long he became sub-editor of *All Sorts*, then actual director of the paper. He said good-bye to the bookseller, and his literary career fairly began.

Mr Polo used to say that he never knew a man who could work so many consecutive hours as Alfred Yule. A faithful account of all that the young man learnt and wrote from 1855 to 1860 – that is, from his twenty-fifth to his thirtieth year – would have the look of burlesque exaggeration. He had set it before him to become a celebrated man, and he was not unaware that the attainment of that end would cost him quite exceptional labour, seeing that nature had not favoured him with brilliant parts. No matter; his name should be spoken among men – unless he killed himself in the struggle for success.

In the meantime he married. Living in a garret, and supplying himself with the materials of his scanty meals, he was in the habit of making purchases at a little chandler's shop, where he was waited upon by a young girl of no beauty, but, as it seemed to him, of amiable disposition. One holiday he met this girl as she was walking with a younger sister in the streets; he made her nearer acquaintance, and before long she consented to be his wife and share his garret. His brothers, John and Edmund, cried out that he had made an unpardonable fool of himself in marrying so much beneath him; that he might well have waited until his income improved. This was all very well, but they might just as reasonably have bidden him reject plain food because a few years hence he would be able to purchase luxuries; he could not do without nourishment of some sort, and the time had come when he could not do without a wife. Many a man with brains but no money has been compelled to the same step. Educated girls have a pronounced distaste for London garrets; not one in fifty thousands would share poverty with the brightest genius ever born. Seeing that marriage is so often indispensable to that very success which would enable a man of parts to mate equally, there is nothing for it but to look below one's own level, and be grateful to the untaught woman who has pity on one's loneliness.

Unfortunately, Alfred Yule was not so grateful as he might have been. His marriage proved far from unsuccessful; he might have found himself united to a vulgar shrew, whereas the girl had the great virtues of humility and kindliness. She endeavoured to learn of him, but her dulness and his impatience made this attempt a failure; her human qualities had to suffice. And they did, until Yule began to lift his head above the literary mob. Previously, he often lost his temper with her, but never expressed or felt repentance of his marriage; now he began to see only the disadvantages of his position, and, forgetting the facts of the case, to imagine that he might well have waited for a wife who could share his intellectual existence. Mrs Yule had to pass through a few years of much bitterness. Already a martyr to dyspepsia, and often suffering from bilious headaches of extreme violence, her husband now and then lost all control of his temper, all sense of kind feeling, even of decency, and reproached the poor woman with her ignorance, her stupidity, her low origin. Naturally enough she defended herself with such weapons as a sense of cruel injustice supplied. More than once the two all but parted. It did not come to an actual rupture, chiefly because Yule could not do without his wife; her tendance had become indispensable. And then there was the child to consider.

From the first it was Yule's dread lest Marian should be in-
fected with her mother's faults of speech and behaviour. He
would scarcely permit his wife to talk to the child. At the earliest
possible moment Marian was sent to a day-school, and in her
tenth year she went as weekly boarder to an establishment at
Fulham; any sacrifice of money to insure her growing up with
the tongue and manners of a lady. It can scarcely have been a
light trial to the mother to know that contact with her was regarded as her child's greatest danger; but in her humility and her
love for Marian she offered no resistance. And so it came to pass
that one day the little girl, hearing her mother make some flagrant grammatical error, turned to the other parent and asked
gravely: 'Why doesn't mother speak as properly as we do?'
Well, that is one of the results of such marriages, one of the
myriad miseries that result from poverty.

The end was gained at all hazards. Marian grew up everything that her father desired. Not only had she the bearing of refinement, but it early became obvious that nature had well endowed her with brains. From the nursery her talk was of books,
and at the age of twelve she was already able to give her father
some assistance as an amanuensis.

At that time Edmund Yule was still living; he had overcome
his prejudices, and there was intercourse between his household
and that of the literary man. Intimacy it could not be called, for
Mrs Edmund (who was the daughter of a law-stationer) had
much difficulty in behaving to Mrs Alfred with show of suavity.
Still, the cousins Amy and Marian from time to time saw each
other, and were not unsuitable companions. It was the death of
Amy's father that brought these relations to an end; left to the
control of her own affairs Mrs Edmund was not long in giving
offence to Mrs Alfred, and so to Alfred himself. The man of
letters might be inconsiderate enough in his behaviour to his
wife, but as soon as anyone else treated her with disrespect that
was quite another matter. Purely on this account he quarrelled
violently with his brother's widow, and from that day the two
families kept apart.

The chapter of quarrels was one of no small importance in
Alfred's life; his difficult temper, and an ever increasing sense of
neglected merit, frequently put him at war with publishers,

editors, fellow authors, and he had an unhappy trick of exciting the hostility of men who were most likely to be useful to him. With Mr Polo, for instance, who held him in esteem, and whose commercial success made him a valuable connection, Alfred ultimately broke on a trifling matter of personal dignity. Later came the great quarrel with Clement Fadge, an affair of considerable advantage in the way of advertisement to both the men concerned. It happened in the year 1873. At that time Yule was editor of a weekly paper called *The Balance*, a literary organ which aimed high, and failed to hit the circulation essential to its existence. Fadge, a younger man, did reviewing for *The Balance*; he was in needy circumstances, and had wrought himself into Yule's good opinion by judicious flattery. But with a clear eye for the main chance Mr Fadge soon perceived that Yule could only be of temporary use to him, and that the editor of a well-established weekly which lost no opportunity of throwing scorn upon Yule and all his works would be a much more profitable conquest. He succeeded in transferring his services to the more flourishing paper, and struck out a special line of work by the free exercise of a malicious flippancy which was then without rival in the periodical press. When he had thoroughly got his hand in, it fell to Mr Fadge, in the mere way of business, to review a volume of his old editor's, a rather pretentious and long-winded but far from worthless essay 'On Imagination as a National Characteristic.' The notice was a masterpiece; its exquisite virulence set the literary circles chuckling. Concerning the authorship there was no mystery, and Alfred Yule had the indiscretion to make a violent reply, a savage assault upon Fadge, in the columns of *The Balance*. Fadge desired nothing better; the uproar which arose – chaff, fury, grave comments, sneering spite – could only result in drawing universal attention to his anonymous cleverness, and throwing ridicule upon the heavy, conscientious man. Well, you probably remember all about it. It ended in the disappearance of Yule's struggling paper, and the establishment on a firm basis of Fadge's reputation.

It would be difficult to mention any department of literary endeavour in which Yule did not, at one time or another, try his fortune. Turn to his name in the Museum Catalogue; the list of works appended to it will amuse you. In his thirtieth year he published a novel; it failed completely, and the same result awaited a similar experiment five years later. He wrote a drama of modern life, and for some years strove to get it acted, but in vain; finally it appeared 'for the closet' – giving Clement Fadge such an opportunity as he seldom enjoyed. The one noteworthy thing about these productions, and about others of equally mistaken direction, was the sincerity of their workmanship. Had Yule been content to manufacture a novel or a play with due disregard for literary honour, he might perchance have made a mercantile success; but the poor fellow had not pliancy enough for this. He took his efforts *au grand sérieux*; thought he was producing works of art; pursued his ambition in a spirit of fierce conscientiousness. In spite of all, he remained only a journeyman. The kind of work he did best was poorly paid, and could bring no fame. At the age of fifty he was still living in a poor house, in an obscure quarter. He earned enough for his actual needs, and was under no pressing fear for the morrow, so long as his faculties remained unimpaired; but there was no disguising from himself that his life had been a failure. And the thought tormented him.

Now there had come unexpectedly a gleam of hope. If, indeed, the man Rackett thought of offering him the editorship of *The Study* he might even yet taste the triumphs for which he had so vehemently longed. *The Study* was a weekly paper of fair repute. Fadge had harmed it, no doubt of that, by giving it a tone which did not suit the majority of its readers – serious people, who thought that the criticism of contemporary writing offered an opportunity for something better than a display of malevolent wit. But a return to the old earnestness would doubtless set all right again. And the joy of sitting in that dictatorial chair! The delight of having his own organ once more, of making himself a power in the world of letters, of emphasising to a large audience his developed methods of criticism!

An embittered man is a man beset by evil temptations. *The Study* contained each week certain columns of flying gossip, and when he thought of this, Yule also thought of Clement Fadge and sundry other of his worst enemies. How the gossip column can be used for hostile purposes, yet without the least overt

offence, he had learnt only too well. Sometimes the mere omission of a man's name from a list of authors can mortify and
injure. In our day the manipulation of such paragraphs has become a fine art; but you recall numerous illustrations. Alfred
knew well enough how incessantly the tempter would be at his
ear; he said to himself that in certain instances yielding would
be no dishonour. He himself had many a time been mercilessly
treated; in the very interest of the public it was good that certain
men should suffer a snubbing, and his fingers itched to have hold
of the editorial pen. Ha, ha! Like the war-horse he snuffed the
battle afar off.

No work this evening, though there were tasks which pressed
for completion. His study – the only room on the ground level
except the dining-room – was small, and even a good deal of the
floor was encumbered with books, but he found space for walking nervously hither and thither. He was doing this when,
about half-past nine, his wife appeared at the door, bringing him
a cup of coffee and some biscuits, his wonted supper. Marian
generally waited upon him at this time, and he asked why she had
not come.

'She has one of her headaches again, I'm sorry to say,' Mrs
Yule replied. 'I persuaded her to go to bed early.'

Having placed the tray upon the table – books had to be
pushed aside – she did not seem disposed to withdraw.

'Are you busy, Alfred?'

'Why?'

'I thought I should like just to speak of something.'

She was using the opportunity of his good humour. Yule
spoke to her with the usual carelessness, but not forbiddingly.

'What is it? Those Holloway people, I'll warrant.'

'No, no! It's about Marian. She had a letter from one of those
young ladies this afternoon.'

'What young ladies?' asked Yule, with impatience of this cir-
cuitous approach.

'The Miss Milvains.'

'Well there's no harm that I know of. They're decent
people.'

'Yes; so you told me. But she began to speak about their
brother, and –'

'What about him? Do say what you want to say, and have done with it!'

'I can't help thinking, Alfred, that she's disappointed you didn't ask him to come here.'

Yule stared at her in slight surprise. He was still not angry, and seemed quite willing to consider this matter suggested to him so timorously.

'Oh, you think so? Well, I don't know. Why should I have asked him? It was only because Miss Harrow seemed to wish it that I saw him down there. I have no particular interest in him. And as for –'

He broke off and seated himself. Mrs Yule stood at a distance.

'We must remember her age,' she said.

'Why yes, of course.'

He mused, and began to nibble a biscuit.

'And you know, Alfred, she never does meet any young men. I've often thought it wasn't right to her.'

'H'm! But this lad Milvain is a very doubtful sort of customer. To begin with, he has nothing, and they tell me his mother for the most part supports him. I don't quite approve of that. She isn't well off, and he ought to have been making a living by now. He has a kind of cleverness, may do something; but there's no being sure of that.'

These thoughts were not coming into his mind for the first time. On the occasion when he met Milvain and Marian together in the country road he had necessarily reflected upon the possibilities of such intercourse, and with the issue that he did not care to give any particular encouragement to its continuance. He of course heard of Milvain's leave-taking call, and he purposely refrained from seeing the young man after that. The matter took no very clear shape in his meditations; he saw no likelihood that either of the young people would think much of the other after their parting, and time enough to trouble one's head with such subjects when they could no longer be postponed. It would not have been pleasant to him to foresee a life of spinsterhood for his daughter; but she was young, and – she was a valuable assistant.

How far did that latter consideration weigh with him? He put the question pretty distinctly to himself now that his wife had broached the matter thus unexpectedly. Was he prepared to behave with deliberate selfishness? Never yet had any conflict been manifested between his interests and Marian's; practically he was in the habit of counting upon her aid for an indefinite period.

If indeed he became editor of *The Study*, why, in that case her assistance would be less needful. And indeed it seemed probable that young Milvain had a future before him.

'But, in any case,' he said aloud, partly continuing his thoughts, partly replying to a look of disappointment on his wife's face, 'how do you know that he has any wish to come and see Marian?'

'I don't know anything about it, of course.'

'And you may have made a mistake about her. What made you think she – had him in mind?'

'Well, it was her way of speaking, you know. And then, she asked if you had got a dislike to him.'

'She did? H'm! Well, I don't think Milvain is any good to Marian. He's just the kind of man to make himself agreeable to a girl for the fun of the thing.'

Mrs Yule looked alarmed.

'Oh, if you really think that, don't let him come. I wouldn't for anything.'

'I don't say it for certain.' He took a sip of his coffee. 'I have had no opportunity of observing him with much attention. But he's not the *kind* of man I care for.'

'Then no doubt it's better as it is.'

'Yes. I don't see that anything could be done now. We shall see whether he gets on. I advise you not to mention him to her.'

'Oh no, I won't.'

She moved as if to go away, but her heart had been made uneasy by that short conversation which followed on Marian's reading the letter, and there were still things she wished to put into words.

'If those young ladies go on writing to her, I dare say they'll often speak about their brother.'

'Yes, it's rather unfortunate.'

'And you know, Alfred, he may have asked them to do it.'

'I suppose there's one subject on which all women can be subtle,' muttered Yule, smiling. The remark was not a kind one, but he did not make it worse by his tone.

The listener failed to understand him, and looked with her familiar expression of mental effort.

'We can't help that,' he added, with reference to her suggestion. 'If he has any serious thoughts, well, let him go on and wait for opportunities.'

'It's a great pity, isn't it, that she can't see more people – of the right kind?'

'No use talking about it. Things are as they are. I can't see that her life is unhappy.'

'It isn't very happy.'

'You think not?'

'I'm sure it isn't.'

'If I get *The Study* things may be different. Though – But it's no use talking about what can't be helped. Now don't you go encouraging her to think herself lonely, and so on. It's best for her to keep close to work, I'm sure of that.'

'Perhaps it is.'

'I'll think it over.'

Mrs Yule silently left the room, and went back to her sewing.

She had understood that 'Though –' and the 'what can't be helped.' Such allusions reminded her of a time unhappier than the present, when she had been wont to hear plainer language. She knew too well that, had she been a woman of education, her daughter would not now be suffering from loneliness.

It was her own choice that she did not go with her husband and Marian to John Yule's. She made an excuse that the house could not be left to one servant; but in any case she would have remained at home, for her presence must needs be an embarrassment both to father and daughter. Alfred was always ashamed of her before strangers; he could not conceal his feeling, either from her or from other people who had reason for observing him. Marian was not perhaps ashamed, but such companionship put restraint upon her freedom. And would it not always be the same? Supposing Mr Milvain were to come to this house, would it not repel him when he found what sort of person Marian's mother was?

She shed a few tears over her needlework.

At midnight the study door opened. Yule came to the dining-room to see that all was right, and it surprised him to find his wife still sitting there.

'Why are you so late?'

'I've forgot the time.'

'Forgotten, forgotten. Don't go back to that kind of language again. Come, put the light out.'

Chapter 8

TO THE WINNING SIDE

O F the acquaintances Yule had retained from his earlier years several were in the well-defined category of men with unpresentable wives. There was Hinks, for instance, whom, though in anger he spoke of him as a bore, Alfred held in some genuine regard. Hinks made perhaps a hundred a year out of a kind of writing which only certain publishers can get rid of, and of this income he spent about a third on books. His wife was the daughter of a laundress, in whose house he had lodged thirty years ago, when new to London but already long-acquainted with hunger; they lived in complete harmony, but Mrs Hinks, who was four years the elder, still spoke the laundress tongue, unmitigated and immitigable. Another pair were Mr and Mrs Gorbutt. In this case there were no narrow circumstances to contend with, for the wife, originally a nursemaid, not long after her marriage inherited house property from a relative. Mr Gorbutt deemed himself a poet; since his accession to an income he had published, at his own expense, a yearly volume of verses; the only result being to keep alive rancour in his wife, who was both parsimonious and vain. Making no secret of it, Mrs Gorbutt rued the day on which she had wedded a man of letters, when by waiting so short a time she would have been enabled to aim at a prosperous tradesman, who kept his gig and had everything handsome about him. Mrs Yule suspected, not without reason, that this lady had an inclination to strong liquors. Thirdly came Mr and Mrs Christopherson, who were poor as church mice. Even in a friend's house they wrangled incessantly, and made tragi-comical revelations of their home life. The husband worked casually at irresponsible journalism, but his chosen study was metaphysics; for many years he had had a huge and profound book on hand, which he believed would bring him fame, though he was not so unsettled in mind as to hope for anything else. When an article or two had earned enough money for immediate necessities he went off to the British Museum, and then the difficulty was to recall him to profitable exertions. Yet husband and wife had an affection for each other. Mrs Christopherson came from Camberwell, where her father, once upon a time, was the smallest of small butchers. Disagreeable stories were whispered concerning her earlier life, and probably the metaphysician did not care to look back in that direction. They had had three children; all were happily buried.

These men were capable of better things than they had done or would ever do; in each case their failure to fulfil youthful promise was largely explained by the unpresentable wife. They should have waited; they might have married a social equal at something between fifty and sixty.

Another old friend was Mr Quarmby. Unwedded, he, and perpetually exultant over men who, as he phrased it, had noosed themselves. He made a fair living, but, like Dr Johnson, had no passion for clean linen.

Yule was not disdainful of these old companions, and the fact that all had a habit of looking up to him increased his pleasure in their occasional society. If, as happened once or twice in half a year, several of them were gathered together at his house, he tasted a sham kind of social and intellectual authority which he could not help relishing. On such occasions he threw off his habitual gloom and talked vigorously, making natural display of his learning and critical ability. The topic, sooner or later, was that which is inevitable in such a circle – the demerits, the pretentiousness, the personal weaknesses of prominent contemporaries in the world of letters. Then did the room ring with scornful laughter, with boisterous satire, with shouted irony, with fierce invective. After an evening of that kind Yule was unwell and miserable for several days.

It was not to be expected that Mr Quarmby, inveterate chatterbox of the Reading-room and other resorts, should keep silence concerning what he had heard of Mr Rackett's intentions. The rumour soon spread that Alfred Yule was to succeed Fadge in the direction of *The Study*, with the necessary consequence that Yule found himself an object of affectionate interest to a great many people of whom he knew little or nothing. At the same time the genuine old friends pressed warmly about him, with congratulations, with hints of their sincere readiness to assist in filling the columns of the paper. All this was not disagreeable, but in the meantime Yule had heard nothing whatever from Mr Rackett himself, and his doubts did not diminish as week after week went by.

The event justified him. At the end of October appeared an authoritative announcement that Fadge's successor would be – not Alfred Yule, but a gentleman who till of late had been quietly working as a sub-editor in the provinces, and who had neither friendships nor enmities among the people of the London literary press. A young man, comparatively fresh from the university, and said to be strong in pure scholarship. The choice, as you are aware, proved a good one, and The Study became an organ of more repute than ever.

Yule had been secretly conscious that it was not to men such as he that positions of this kind are nowadays entrusted. He tried to persuade himself that he was not disappointed. But when Mr Quarmby approached him with blank face, he spoke certain wrathful words which long rankled in that worthy's mind. At home he kept sullen silence.

No, not to such men as he – poor, and without social recommendations. Besides, he was growing too old. In literature, as in most other pursuits, the press of energetic young men was making it very hard for a veteran even to hold the little grazing-plot he had won by hard fighting. Still, Quarmby's story had not been without foundation; it was true that the proprietor of The Study had for a moment thought of Alfred Yule, doubtless as the natural contrast to Clement Fadge, whom he would have liked to mortify if the thing were possible. But counsellors had proved to Mr Rackett the disadvantages of such a choice.

Mrs Yule and her daughter foresaw but too well the results of this disappointment, notwithstanding that Alfred announced it to them with dry indifference. The month that followed was a time of misery for all in the house. Day after day Yule sat at his meals in sullen muteness; to his wife he scarcely spoke at all, and his conversation with Marian did not go beyond necessary questions and remarks on topics of business. His face became so strange a colour that one would have thought him suffering from an attack of jaundice; bilious headaches exasperated his savage mood. Mrs Yule knew from long experience how worse than useless it was for her to attempt consolation; in silence was her only safety. Nor did Marian venture to speak directly of what had happened. But one evening, when she had been engaged in the study and was now saying 'Good-night,' she laid her cheek against her father's, an unwonted caress which had a strange effect upon him. The expression of sympathy caused his thoughts to reveal themselves as they never yet had done before his daughter.

'It might have been very different with me,' he exclaimed abruptly, as if they had already been conversing on the subject. 'When you think of my failures – and you must often do so now you are grown up and understand things – don't forget the obstacles that have been in my way. I don't like you to look upon your father as a thickhead who couldn't be expected to succeed. Look at Fadge. He married a woman of good social position; she brought him friends and influence. But for that, he would never have been editor of *The Study*, a place for which he wasn't in the least fit. But he was able to give dinners; he and his wife went into society; everybody knew him and talked of him. How has it been with me? I live here like an animal in its hole, and go blinking about if by chance I find myself among the people with whom I ought naturally to associate. If I had been able to come in direct contact with Rackett and other men of that kind, to dine with them, and have them to dine with me, to belong to a club, and so on, I shouldn't be what I am at my age. My one opportunity – when I edited *The Balance* – wasn't worth much; there was no money behind the paper; we couldn't hold out long enough. But even then, if I could have assumed my proper social standing, if I could have opened my house freely to the right kind of people – How was it possible?'

Marian could not raise her head. She recognised the portion of truth in what he said, but it shocked her that he should allow himself to speak thus. Her silence seemed to remind him how painful it must be to her to hear these accusations of her mother, and with a sudden 'Good-night' he dismissed her.

She went up to her room, and wept over the wretchedness of all their lives. Her loneliness had seemed harder to bear than ever since that last holiday. For a moment, in the lanes about Finden, there had come to her a vision of joy such as fate owed her youth; but it had faded, and she could no longer hope for its return. She was not a woman, but a mere machine for reading and writing. Did her father never think of this? He was not the only one to suffer from the circumstances in which poverty had involved him.

She had no friends to whom she could utter her thoughts. Dora Milvain had written a second time, and more recently had come a letter from Maud; but in replying to them she could not give a true account of herself. Impossible, to them. From what she wrote they would imagine her contentedly busy, absorbed in the affairs of literature. To no one could she make known the aching sadness of her heart, the dreariness of life as it lay before her.

That beginning of half-confidence between her and her mother had led to nothing. Mrs Yule found no second opportunity of speaking to her husband about Jasper Milvain, and purposely she refrained from any further hint or question to Marian. Everything must go on as hitherto.

The days darkened. Through November rains and fogs Marian went her usual way to the Museum, and toiled there among the other toilers. Perhaps once a week she allowed herself to stray about the alleys of the Reading-room, scanning furtively those who sat at the desks, but the face she might perchance have discovered was not there.

One day at the end of the month she sat with books open before her, but by no effort could fix her attention upon them. It was gloomy, and one could scarcely see to read; a taste of fog grew perceptible in the warm, headachy air. Such profound discouragement possessed her that she could not even maintain the pretence of study; heedless whether anyone observed her, she let her hands fall and her head droop. She kept asking herself what was the use and purpose of such a life as she was condemned to lead. When already there was more good literature in the world than any mortal could cope with in his lifetime, here was she exhausting herself in the manufacture of printed stuff which no one even pretended to be more than a commodity for the day's market. What unspeakable folly! To write – was not that the joy and the privilege of one who had an urgent message for the world? Her father, she knew well, had no such message; he had abandoned all thought of original production, and only wrote about writing.

She herself would throw away her pen with joy but for the need of earning money. And all these people about her, what aim had they save to make new books out of those already existing, that yet newer books might in turn be made out of theirs? This huge library, growing into unwieldiness, threatening to become a trackless desert of print – how intolerably it weighed upon the spirit!

Oh, to go forth and labour with one's hands, to do any poorest, commonest work of which the world had truly need! It was ignoble to sit here and support the paltry pretence of intellectual dignity. A few days ago her startled eye had caught an advertisement in the newspaper, headed 'Literary Machine'; had it then been invented at last, some automaton to supply the place of such poor creatures as herself, to turn out books and articles? Alas! the machine was only one for holding volumes conveniently, that the work of literary manufacture might be physically lightened. But surely before long some Edison would make the true automaton; the problem must be comparatively such a simple one. Only to throw in a given number of old books, and have them reduced, blended, modernised into a single one for to-day's consumption.

The fog grew thicker; she looked up at the windows beneath the dome and saw that they were a dusky yellow. Then her eye discerned an official walking along the upper gallery, and in pursuance of her grotesque humour, her mocking misery, she likened him to a black, lost soul, doomed to wander in an eternity of vain research along endless shelves. Or again, the readers who sat here at these radiating lines of desks, what were they but hapless flies caught in a huge web, its nucleus the great circle of the Catalogue? Darker, darker. From the towering wall of volumes seemed to emanate visible motes, intensifying the obscurity; in a moment the book-lined circumference of the room would be but a featureless prison-limit.

But then flashed forth the sputtering whiteness of the electric light, and its ceaseless hum was henceforth a new source of headache. It reminded her how little work she had done to-day; she must, she must, force herself to think of the task in hand. A machine has no business to refuse its duty. But the pages were blue and green and yellow before her eyes; the uncertainty of the light was intolerable. Right or wrong she would go home, and hide herself, and let her heart unburden itself of tears.

On her way to return books she encountered Jasper Milvain. Face to face; no possibility of his avoiding her.

And indeed he seemed to have no such wish. His countenance lighted up with unmistakable pleasure.

'At last we meet, as they say in the melodramas. Oh, do let me help you with those volumes, which won't even let you shake hands. How do you do? How do you like this weather? And how do you like this light?'

'It's very bad.'

'That'll do both for weather and light, but not for yourself. How glad I am to see you! Are you just going?'

'Yes.'

'I have scarcely been here half a dozen times since I came back to London.'

'But you are writing still?'

'Oh yes! But I draw upon my genius, and my stores of observation, and the living world.'

Marian received her vouchers for the volumes, and turned to face Jasper again. There was a smile on her lips.

'The fog is terrible,' Milvain went on. 'How do you get home?'

'By omnibus from Tottenham Court Road.'

'Then do let me go a part of the way with you. I live in Mornington Road – up yonder, you know. I have only just come in to waste half an hour, and after all I think I should be better at home. Your father is all right, I hope?'

'He is not quite well.'

'I'm sorry to hear that. You are not exactly up to the mark, either. What weather! What a place to live in, this London, in winter! It would be a little better down at Finden.'

'A good deal better, I should think. If the weather were bad, it would be bad in a natural way; but this is artificial misery.'

'I don't let it affect me much,' said Milvain. 'Just of late I have been in remarkably good spirits. I'm doing a lot of work. No end of work – more than I've ever done.'

'I am very glad.'

'Where are your out-of-door things? I think there's a ladies' vestry somewhere, isn't there?'

'Oh yes.'

'Then will you go and get ready? I'll wait for you in the hall. But, by-the-by, I am taking it for granted that you were going alone.'

'I was, quite alone.'

The 'quite' seemed excessive; it made Jasper smile.

'And also,' he added, 'that I shall not annoy you by offering my company?'

'Why should it annoy me?'

'Good!'

Milvain had only to wait a minute or two. He surveyed Marian from head to foot when she appeared – an impertinence as unintentional as that occasionally noticeable in his speech – and smiled approval. They went out into the fog, which was not one of London's densest, but made walking disagreeable enough.

'You have heard from the girls, I think?' Jasper resumed.

'Your sisters? Yes; they have been so kind as to write to me.'

'Told you all about their great work? I hope it'll be finished by the end of the year. The bits they have sent me will do very well indeed. I knew they had it in them to put sentences together. Now I want them to think of patching up something or other for *The English Girl*; you know the paper?'

'I have heard of it.'

'I happen to know Mrs Boston Wright, who edits it. Met her at a house the other day, and told her frankly that she would have to give my sisters something to do. It's the only way to get on; one has to take it for granted that people are willing to help you. I have made a host of new acquaintances just lately.'

'I'm glad to hear it,' said Marian.

'Do you know – but how should you? I am going to write for the new magazine, *The Current*.'

'Indeed!'

'Edited by that man Fadge.'

'Yes.'

'Your father has no affection for him, I know.'

'He has no reason to have, Mr Milvain.'

'No, no. Fadge is an offensive fellow, when he likes; and I fancy he very often does like. Well, I must make what use of him I can. You won't think worse of me because I write for him?'

'I know that one can't exercise choice in such things.'

'True. I shouldn't like to think that you regard me as a Fadge-like individual, a natural Fadgeite.'

Marian laughed.

'There's no danger of my thinking that.'

But the fog was making their eyes water and getting into their throats. By when they reached Tottenham Court Road they were both thoroughly uncomfortable. The 'bus had to be waited for, and in the meantime they talked scrappily, coughily. In the vehicle things were a little better, but here one could not converse with freedom.

'What pestilent conditions of life!' exclaimed Jasper, putting his face rather near to Marian's. 'I wish to goodness we were back in those quiet fields – you remember? – with the September sun warm about us. Shall you go to Finden again before long?'

'I really don't know.'

'I'm sorry to say my mother is far from well. In any case I must go at Christmas, but I'm afraid it won't be a cheerful visit.'

Arrived in Hampstead Road he offered his hand for good-bye.

'I wanted to talk about all sorts of things. But perhaps I shall find you again some day.'

He jumped out, and waved his hat in the lurid fog.

Shortly before the end of December appeared the first number of *The Current*. Yule had once or twice referred to the forth-coming magazine with acrid contempt, and of course he did not purchase a copy.

'So young Milvain has joined Fadge's hopeful standard,' he remarked, a day or two later, at breakfast. 'They say his paper is remarkably clever; I could wish it had appeared anywhere else. Evil communications, &c.'

'But I shouldn't think there's any personal connection,' said Marian.

'Very likely not. But Milvain has been invited to contribute, you see.'

'Do you think he ought to have refused?'

'Oh no. It's nothing to me; nothing whatever.'

Mrs Yule glanced at her daughter, but Marian seemed uncon-cerned. The subject was dismissed. In introducing it Yule had

had his purpose; there had always been an unnatural avoidance of
Milvain's name in conversation, and he wished to have an end of
this. Hitherto he had felt a troublesome uncertainty regarding his
position in the matter. From what his wife had told him it
seemed pretty certain that Marian was disappointed by the
abrupt closing of her brief acquaintance with the young man, and
Yule's affection for his daughter caused him to feel uneasy in the
thought that perhaps he had deprived her of a chance of happiness. His conscience readily took hold of an excuse for justifying
the course he had followed. Milvain had gone over to the enemy.
Whether or not the young man understood how relentless the
hostility was between Yule and Fadge mattered little; the probability was that he knew all about it. In any case intimate relations
with him could not have survived this alliance with Fadge, so
that, after all, there had been wisdom in letting the acquaintance
lapse. To be sure, nothing could have come of it. Milvain was the
kind of man who weighed opportunities; every step he took
would be regulated by consideration of advantage; at all events
that was the impression his character had made upon Yule. Any
hopes that Marian might have been induced to form would
assuredly have ended in disappointment. It was kindness to interpose before things had gone so far.

Henceforth, if Milvain's name was unavoidable, it should be
mentioned just like that of any other literary man. It seemed very
unlikely indeed that Marian would continue to think of him with
any special and personal interest. The fact of her having got into
correspondence with his sisters was unfortunate, but this kind of
thing rarely went on for very long.

Yule spoke of the matter with his wife that evening.

'By-the-by, has Marian heard from those girls at Finden
lately?'

'She had a letter one afternoon last week.'

'Do you see these letters?'

'No; she told me what was in them at first, but now she
doesn't.'

'She hasn't spoken to you again of Milvain?'

'Not a word.'

'Well, I understood what I was about,' Yule remarked, with the
confident air of one who doesn't wish to remember that he had

ever felt doubtful. 'There was no good in having the fellow here. He has got in with a set that I don't care at all for. If she ever says anything – you understand – you can just let me know.'

Marian had already procured a copy of *The Current*, and read it privately. Of the cleverness of Milvain's contribution there could be no two opinions; it drew the attention of the public, and all notices of the new magazine made special reference to this article. With keen interest Marian sought after comments of the press; when it was possible she cut them out and put them carefully away.

January passed, and February. She saw nothing of Jasper. A letter from Dora in the first week of March made announcement that the 'Child's History of the English Parliament' would be published very shortly; it told her, too, that Mrs Milvain had been very ill indeed, but that she seemed to recover a little strength as the weather improved. Of Jasper there was no mention.

A week later came the news that Mrs Milvain had suddenly died.

This letter was received at breakfast-time. The envelope was an ordinary one, and so little did Marian anticipate the nature of its contents that at the first sight of the words she uttered an exclamation of pain. Her father, who had turned from the table to the fireside with his newspaper, looked round and asked what was the matter.

'Mrs Milvain died the day before yesterday.'

'Indeed !'

He averted his face again and seemed disposed to say no more. But in a few moments he inquired :

'What are her daughters likely to do?'

'I have no idea.'

'Do you know anything of their circumstances?'

'I believe they will have to depend upon themselves.'

Nothing more was said. Afterwards Mrs Yule made a few sympathetic inquiries, but Marian was very brief in her replies.

Ten days after that, on a Sunday afternoon when Marian and her mother were alone in the sitting-room, they heard the knock of a visitor at the front door. Yule was out, and there was no likelihood of the visitor's wishing to see any one but him. They listened; the servant went to the door, and, after a murmur of voices, came to speak to her mistress.

'It's a gentleman called Mr Milvain,' the girl reported, in a way that proved how seldom callers presented themselves. 'He asked for Mr Yule, and when I said he was out, then he asked for Miss Yule.'

Mother and daughter looked anxiously at each other. Mrs Yule was nervous and helpless.

'Show Mr Milvain into the study,' said Marian with sudden decision.

'Are you going to see him there?' asked her mother in a hurried whisper.

'I thought you would prefer that to his coming in here.'

'Yes – yes. But suppose father comes back before he's gone?'

'What will it matter? You forget that he asked for father first.'

'Oh yes! Then don't wait.'

Marian, scarcely less agitated than her mother, was just leaving the room, when she turned back again.

'If father comes in, you will tell him before he goes into the study?'

'Yes, I will.'

The fire in the study was on the point of extinction; this was the first thing Marian's eye perceived on entering, and it gave her assurance that her father would not be back for some hours. Evidently he had intended it to go out; small economies of this kind, unintelligible to people who have always lived at ease, had been the life-long rule with him. With a sensation of gladness at having free time before her, Marian turned to where Milvain was standing, in front of one of the bookcases. He wore no symbol of mourning, but his countenance was far graver than usual, and rather paler. They shook hands in silence.

'I am so grieved –' Marian began with broken voice.

'Thank you. I know the girls have told you all about it. We knew for the last month that it must come before long, though there was a deceptive improvement just before the end.'

'Please to sit down, Mr Milvain. Father went out not long ago, and I don't think he will be back very soon.'

'It was not really Mr Yule I wished to see,' said Jasper, frankly.

'If he had been at home I should have spoken with him about what I have in mind, but if you will kindly give me a few minutes it will be much better.'

Marian glanced at the expiring fire. Her curiosity as to what Milvain had to say was mingled with an anxious doubt whether it was not too late to put on fresh coals; already the room was growing very chill, and this appearance of inhospitality troubled her.

'Do you wish to save it?' Jasper asked, understanding her look and movement.

'I'm afraid it has got too low.'

'I think not. Life in lodgings has made me skilful at this kind of thing; let me try my hand.'

He took the tongs and carefully disposed small pieces of coal upon the glow that remained. Marian stood apart with a feeling of shame and annoyance. But it is so seldom that situations in life arrange themselves with dramatic propriety; and, after all, this vulgar necessity made the beginning of the conversation easier.

'That will be all right now,' said Jasper at length, as little tongues of flame began to shoot here and there.

Marian said nothing, but seated herself and waited.

'I came up to town yesterday,' Jasper began. 'Of course we have had a great deal to do and think about. Miss Harrow has been very kind indeed to the girls; so have several of our old friends in Wattleborough. It was necessary to decide at once what Maud and Dora are going to do, and it is on their account that I have come to see you.'

The listener kept silence, with a face of sympathetic attention.

'We have made up our minds that they may as well come to London. It's a bold step; I'm by no means sure that the result will justify it. But I think they are perhaps right in wishing to try it.'

'They will go on with literary work?'

'Well, it's our hope that they may be able to. Of course there's no chance of their earning enough to live upon for some time. But the matter stands like this. They have a trifling sum of money, on which, at a pinch, they could live in London for perhaps a year and a half. In that time they *may* find their way to a sort of income; at all events, the chances are that a year and a half hence I shall be able to help them to keep body and soul together.'

The money of which he spoke was the debt owed to their father by William Milvain. In consequence of Mrs Milvain's pressing application half of this sum had at length been paid, and the remainder was promised in a year's time, greatly to Jasper's astonishment. In addition, there would be the trifle realised by the sale of furniture, though most of this might have to go in payment of rent unless the house could be relet immediately.

'They have made a good beginning,' said Marian.

She spoke mechanically, for it was impossible to keep her thoughts under control. If Maud and Dora came to live in London it might bring about a most important change in her life; she could scarcely imagine the happiness of having two such friends always near. On the other hand, how would it be regarded by her father? She was at a loss amid conflicting emotions.

'It's better than if they had done nothing at all,' Jasper replied to her remark. 'And the way they knocked that trifle together promises well. They did it very quickly, and in a far more work-manlike way than I should have thought possible.'

'No doubt they share your own talent.'

'Perhaps so. Of course I know that I have talent of a kind, though I don't rate it very high. We shall have to see whether they can do anything more than mere bookseller's work; they are both very young, you know. I think they may be able to write something that'll do for The English Girl, and no doubt I can hit upon a second idea that will appeal to Jolly and Monk. At all events they'll have books within reach, and better opportunities every way than at Finden.'

'How do their friends in the country think of it?'

'Very dubiously; but then what else was to be expected? Of course, the respectable and intelligible path marked out for both of them points to a lifetime of governessing. But the girls have no relish for that; they'd rather do almost anything. We talked over all the aspects of the situation seriously enough – it is desperately serious, no doubt of that. I told them fairly all the hardships they would have to face – described the typical London lodgings, and so on. Still, there's an adventurous vein in them, and they decided for the risk. If it came to the worst I suppose they could still find governess work.'

'Let us hope better things.'

'Yes. But now, I should have felt far more reluctant to let them come here in this way hadn't it been that they regard you as a friend. To-morrow morning you will probably hear from one or both of them. Perhaps it would have been better if I had left them to tell you all this, but I felt I should like to see you and – put it in my own way. I think you'll understand this feeling, Miss Yule. I wanted, in fact, to hear from yourself that you would be a friend to the poor girls.'

'Oh, you already know that! I shall be so very glad to see them often.'

Marian's voice lent itself very naturally and sweetly to the expression of warm feeling. Emphasis was not her habit; it only needed that she should put off her ordinary reserve, utter quietly the emotional thought which so seldom might declare itself, and her tones had an exquisite womanliness.

Jasper looked full into her face.

'In that case they won't miss the comfort of home so much. Of course they will have to go into very modest lodgings indeed. I have already been looking about. I should like to find rooms for them somewhere near my own place; it's a decent neighbourhood, and the park is at hand, and then they wouldn't be very far from you. They thought it might be possible to make a joint establishment with me, but I'm afraid that's out of the question. The lodgings we should want in that case, everything considered, would cost more than the sum of our expenses if we live apart. Besides, there's no harm in saying that I don't think we should get along very well together. We're all of us rather quarrelsome, to tell the truth, and we try each other's tempers.'

Marian smiled and looked puzzled.

'Shouldn't you have thought that?'

'I have seen no signs of quarrelsomeness.'

'I'm not sure that the worst fault is on my side. Why should one condemn oneself against conscience? Maud is perhaps the hardest to get along with. She has a sort of arrogance, an exaggeration of something I am quite aware of in myself. You have noticed that trait in me?'

'Arrogance – I think not. You have self-confidence.'

'Which goes into extremes now and then. But, putting myself aside, I feel pretty sure that the girls won't seem quarrelsome to *you*; they would have to be very fractious indeed before that were possible.'

'We shall continue to be friends, I am sure.'

Jasper let his eyes wander about the room.

'This is your father's study?'

'Yes.'

'Perhaps it would have seemed odd to Mr Yule if I had come in and begun to talk to him about these purely private affairs. He knows me so very slightly. But, in calling here for the first time –'

An unusual embarrassment checked him.

'I will explain to father your very natural wish to speak of these things,' said Marian, with tact.

She thought uneasily of her mother in the next room. To her there appeared no reason whatever why Jasper should not be introduced to Mrs Yule, yet she could not venture to propose it. Remembering her father's last remarks about Milvain in connection with Fadge's magazine, she must wait for distinct permission before offering the young man encouragement to repeat his visit. Perhaps there was complicated trouble in store for her; impossible to say how her father's deep-rooted and rankling antipathies might affect her intercourse even with the two girls. But she was of independent years, she must be allowed the choice of her own friends. The pleasure she had in seeing Jasper under this roof, in hearing him talk with such intimate friendliness, strengthened her to resist timid thoughts.

'When will your sisters arrive?' she asked.

'I think in a very few days. When I have fixed upon lodgings for them I must go back to Finden; then they will return with me as soon as we can get the house emptied. It's rather miserable selling things one has lived among from childhood. A friend in Wattleborough will house for us what we really can't bear to part with.'

'It must be very sad,' Marian murmured.

'You know,' said the other suddenly, 'that it's my fault the girls are left in such a hard position?'

Marian looked at him with startled eyes. His tone was quite unfamiliar to her.

'Mother had an annuity,' he continued. 'It ended with her life, but if it hadn't been for me she could have saved a good deal out of it. Until the last year or two I have earned nothing, and I have spent more than was strictly necessary. Well, I didn't live like that in mere recklessness; I knew I was preparing myself for remunerative work. But it seems too bad now. I'm sorry for it. I wish I had found some way of supporting myself. The end of mother's life was made far more unhappy than it need have been. I should like you to understand all this.'

The listener kept her eyes on the ground.

'Perhaps the girls have hinted it to you?' Jasper added.

'No.'

'Selfishness – that's one of my faults. It isn't a brutal kind of selfishness; the thought of it often enough troubles me. If I were rich, I should be a generous and good man; I know I should. So would many another poor fellow whose worst features come out under hardship. This isn't a heroic type; of course not. I am a civilised man, that's all.'

Marian could say nothing.

'You wonder why I am so impertinent as to talk about myself like this. I have gone through a good deal of mental pain these last few weeks, and somehow I can't help showing you something of my real thoughts. Just because you are one of the few people I regard with sincere respect. I don't know you very well, but quite well enough to respect you. My sisters think of you in the same way. I shall do many a base thing in life, just to get money and reputation; I tell you this that you mayn't be surprised if anything of that kind comes to your ears. I can't afford to live as I should like to.'

She looked up at him with a smile.

'People who are going to live unworthily don't declare it in this way.'

'I oughtn't to; a few minutes ago I had no intention of saying such things. It means I am rather overstrung, I suppose; but it's all true, unfortunately.'

He rose, and began to run his eye along the shelves nearest to him.

'Well, now I will go, Miss Yule.'

Marian stood up as he approached.

'It's all very well,' he said smiling, 'for me to encourage my sisters in the hope that they may earn a living; but suppose I can't even do it myself? It's by no means certain that I shall make ends meet this year.'

'You have every reason to hope, I think.'

'I like to hear people say that, but it'll mean savage work. When we were all at Finden last year, I told the girls that it would be another twelve months before I could support myself. Now I am forced to do it. And I don't like work; my nature is lazy. I shall never write for writing's sake, only to make money. All my plans and efforts will have money in view – all. I shan't allow *anything* to come in the way of my material advancement.'

'I wish you every success,' said Marian, without looking at him, and without a smile.

'Thank you. But that sounds too much like good-bye. I trust we are to be friends, for all that?'

'Indeed, I hope we may be.'

They shook hands, and he went towards the door. But before opening it, he asked:

'Did you read that thing of mine in *The Current*?'

'Yes, I did.'

'It wasn't bad, I think?'

'It seemed to me very clever.'

'Clever – yes, that's the word. It had a success, too. I have as good a thing half done for the April number, but I've felt too heavy-hearted to go on with it. The girls shall let you know when they are in town.'

Marian followed him into the passage, and watched him as he opened the front door. When it had closed, she went back into the study for a few moments before rejoining her mother.

Chapter 9

INVITA MINERVA

AFTER all, there came a day when Edwin Reardon found himself regularly at work once more, ticking off his stipulated quantum of manuscript each four-and-twenty hours. He wrote a very small hand; sixty written slips of the kind of paper he habitually used would represent – thanks to the astonishing system which prevails in such matters: large type, wide spacing, frequency of blank pages – a passable three-hundred-page volume. On an average he could write four such slips a day; so here we have fifteen days for the volume, and forty-five for the completed book.

Forty-five days; an eternity in the looking forward. Yet the calculation gave him a faint-hearted encouragement. At that rate he might have his book sold by Christmas. It would certainly not bring him a hundred pounds; seventy-five perhaps. But even that small sum would enable him to pay the quarter's rent, and then give him a short time, if only two or three weeks, of mental rest. If such rest could not be obtained all was at an end with him. He must either find some new means of supporting himself and his family, or – have done with life and its responsibilities altogether.

The latter alternative was often enough before him. He seldom slept for more than two or three consecutive hours in the night, and the time of wakefulness was often terrible. The various sounds which marked the stages from midnight to dawn had grown miserably familiar to him; worst torture to his mind was the chiming and striking of clocks. Two of these were in general audible, that of Marylebone parish church, and that of the adjoining workhouse; the latter always sounded several minutes after its ecclesiastical neighbour, and with a difference of note which seemed to Reardon very appropriate – a thin, querulous voice, reminding one of the community it represented. After lying awake for awhile he would hear quarters sounding; if they ceased before the fourth he was glad, for he feared to know what time it was. If the hour was complete, he waited anxiously for its number. Two, three, even four, were grateful; there was still a long time before he need rise and face the dreaded task, the horrible four blank slips of paper that had to be filled ere he might sleep again. But such restfulness was only for a moment; no sooner had the workhouse bell become silent than he began to toil in his weary imagination, or else, incapable of that, to vision fearful hazards of the future. The soft breathing of Amy at his side, the contact of her warm limbs, often filled him with intolerable dread. Even now he did not believe that Amy loved him with the old love, and the suspicion was like a cold weight at his heart that to retain even her wifely sympathy, her wedded tenderness, he must achieve the impossible.

The impossible; for he could no longer deceive himself with a hope of genuine success. If he earned a bare living, that would be the utmost. And with bare livelihood Amy would not, could not, be content.

If he were to die a natural death it would be well for all. His wife and the child would be looked after; they could live with Mrs Edmund Yule, and certainly it would not be long before Amy married again, this time a man of whose competency to maintain her there would be no doubt. His own behaviour had been cowardly selfishness. Oh yes, she had loved him, had been eager to believe in him. But there was always that voice of warning in his mind; he foresaw – he knew –

And if he killed himself? Not here; no lurid horrors for that poor girl and her relatives; but somewhere at a distance, under circumstances which would render the recovery of his body difficult, yet would leave no doubt of his death. Would that, again, be cowardly? The opposite, when once it was certain that to live meant poverty and wretchedness. Amy's grief, however sincere, would be but a short trial compared with what else might lie before her. The burden of supporting her and Willie would be a very slight one if she went to live in her mother's house. He considered the whole matter night after night, until perchance it happened that sleep had pity upon him for an hour before the time of rising.

Autumn was passing into winter. Dark days, which were always an oppression to his mind, began to be frequent, and would soon succeed each other remorselessly. Well if only each of them represented four written slips.

Milvain's advice to him had of course proved useless. The sensational title suggested nothing, or only ragged shapes of incomplete humanity that fluttered mockingly when he strove to fix them. But he had decided upon a story of the kind natural to him; a 'thin' story, and one which it would be difficult to spin into three volumes. His own, at all events. The title was always a matter for head-racking when the book was finished; he had never yet chosen it before beginning.

For a week he got on at the desired rate; then came once more the crisis he had anticipated.

A familiar symptom of the malady which falls upon outwearied imagination. There were floating in his mind five or six possible subjects for a book, all dating back to the time when he first began novel-writing, when ideas came freshly to him. If he grasped desperately at one of these, and did his best to develop it, for a day or two he could almost content himself; characters, situations, lines of motive, were laboriously schemed, and he felt ready to begin writing. But scarcely had he done a chapter or two when all the structure fell into flatness. He had made a mistake. Not this story, but that other one, was what he should have taken. The other one in question, left out of mind for a time, had come back with a face of new possibility; it invited him, tempted him to throw aside what he had already written. Good; now he was in more hopeful train. But a few days, and the experience repeated itself. No, not this story, but that third one, of which he had not thought for a long time. How could he have rejected so hopeful a subject?

For months he had been living in this way; endless circling, perpetual beginning, followed by frustration. A sign of exhaustion, it of course made exhaustion more complete. At times he was on the border-land of imbecility; his mind looked into a cloudy chaos, a shapeless whirl of nothings. He talked aloud to himself, not knowing that he did so. Little phrases which indicated dolorously the subject of his preoccupation often escaped him in the street: 'What could I make of that, now?' 'Well, suppose I made him –?' 'But no, that wouldn't do,' and so on. It had happened that he caught the eye of some one passing fixed in surprise upon him; so young a man to be talking to himself in evident distress!

The expected crisis came, even now that he was savagely determined to go on at any cost, to write, let the result be what it would. His will prevailed. A day or two of anguish such as there is no describing to the inexperienced, and again he was dismissing slip after slip, a sigh of thankfulness at the completion of each one. It was a fraction of the whole, a fraction, a fraction.

The ordering of his day was thus. At nine, after breakfast, he sat down to his desk, and worked till one. Then came dinner, followed by a walk. As a rule he could not allow Amy to walk with him, for he had to think over the remainder of the day's toil, and companionship would have been fatal. At about half-past three he again seated himself, and wrote until half-past six, when he had a meal. Then once more to work from half-past seven to ten. Numberless were the experiments he had tried for the day's division. The slightest interruption of the order for the time being put him out of gear; Amy durst not open his door to ask however necessary a question.

Sometimes the three hours' labour of a morning resulted in half a dozen lines, corrected into illegibility. His brain would not work; he could not recall the simplest synonyms; intolerable faults of composition drove him mad. He would write a sentence beginning thus: 'She took a book with a look of – ;' or thus: 'A revision of this decision would have made him an object of derision.' Or, if the period were otherwise inoffensive, it ran in a rhythmic gallop which was torment to the ear. All this, in spite of the fact that his former books had been noticeably good in style. He had an appreciation of shapely prose which made him scorn himself for the kind of stuff he was now turning out. 'I can't help it; it must go; the time is passing.'

Things were better, as a rule, in the evening. Occasionally he wrote a page with fluency which recalled his fortunate years; and then his heart gladdened, his hand trembled with joy.

Description of locality, deliberate analysis of character or motive, demanded far too great an effort for his present condition. He kept as much as possible to dialogue; the space is filled so much more quickly, and at a pinch one can make people talk about the paltriest incidents of life.

There came an evening when he opened the door and called to Amy.

'What is it?' she answered from the bedroom. 'I'm busy with Willie.'

'Come as soon as you are free.'

In ten minutes she appeared. There was apprehension on her face; she feared he was going to lament his inability to work. Instead of that, he told her joyfully that the first volume was finished.

'Thank goodness!' she exclaimed. 'Are you going to do any more to-night?'

'I think not – if you will come and sit with me.'

'Willie doesn't seem very well. He can't get to sleep.'

'You would like to stay with him?'

'A little while. I'll come presently.'

She closed the door. Reardon brought a high-backed chair to the fireside, and allowed himself to forget the two volumes that had still to be struggled through, in a grateful sense of the portion that was achieved. In a few minutes it occurred to him that it would be delightful to read a scrap of the 'Odyssey'; he went to the shelves on which were his classical books, took the desired volume, and opened it where Odysseus speaks to Nausicaa:

'For never yet did I behold one of mortals like to thee, neither man nor woman; I am awed as I look upon thee. In Delos once, hard by the altar of Apollo, I saw a young palm-tree shooting up with even such a grace.'

Yes, yes; *that* was not written at so many pages a day, with a workhouse clock clanging its admonition at the poet's ear. How it freshened the soul! How the eyes grew dim with a rare joy in the sounding of those nobly sweet hexameters!

Amy came into the room again.

'Listen,' said Reardon, looking up at her with a bright smile. 'Do you remember the first time that I read you this?'

And he turned the speech into free prose. Amy laughed.

'I remember it well enough. We were alone in the drawing-room; I had told the others that they must make shift with the dining-room for that evening. And you pulled the book out of your pocket unexpectedly. I laughed at your habit of always carrying little books about.'

The cheerful news had brightened her. If she had been summoned to hear lamentations her voice would not have rippled thus soothingly. Reardon thought of this, and it made him silent for a minute.

'The habit was ominous,' he said, looking at her with an uncertain smile. 'A practical literary man doesn't do such things.'

'Milvain, for instance. No.'

With curious frequency she mentioned the name of Milvain. Her unconsciousness in doing so prevented Reardon from thinking about the fact; still, he had noted it.

'Did you understand the phrase slightingly?' he asked.

'Slightingly? Yes, a little, of course. It always has that sense on your lips, I think.'

In the light of this answer he mused upon her readily-offered instance. True, he had occasionally spoken of Jasper with something less than respect, but Amy was not in the habit of doing so.

'I hadn't any such meaning just then,' he said. 'I meant quite simply that my bookish habits didn't promise much for my success as a novelist.'

'I see. But you didn't think of it in that way at the time.'

He sighed.

'No. At least – no.'

'At least what?'

'Well, no; on the whole I had good hope.'

Amy twisted her fingers together impatiently.

'Edwin, let me tell you something. You are getting too fond of speaking in a discouraging way. Now, why should you do so? I don't like it. It has one disagreeable effect on me, and that is, when people ask me about you, how you are getting on, I don't quite know how to answer. They can't help seeing that I am uneasy. I speak so differently from what I used to.'

'Do you, really?'

'Indeed I can't help it. As I say, it's very much your own fault.'

'Well, but granted that I am not of a very sanguine nature, and that I easily fall into gloomy ways of talk, what is Amy here for?'

'Yes, yes. But –'

'But?'

'I am not here only to try and keep you in good spirits, am I?'

She asked it prettily, with a smile like that of maidenhood.

'Heaven forbid! I oughtn't to have put it in that absolute way. I was half joking, you know. But unfortunately it's true that I can't be as light-spirited as I could wish. Does that make you impatient with me?'

'A little. I can't help the feeling, and I ought to try to overcome it. But you must try on your side as well. Why should you have said that thing just now?'

'You're quite right. It was needless.'

'A few weeks ago I didn't expect you to be cheerful. Things began to look about as bad as they could. But now that you've got a volume finished, there's hope once more.'

Hope? Of what quality? Reardon durst not say what rose in his thoughts. 'A very small, poor hope. Hope of money enough to struggle through another half year, if indeed enough for that.' He had learnt that Amy was not to be told the whole truth about anything as he himself saw it. It was a pity. To the ideal wife a man speaks out all that is in him; she had infinitely rather share his full conviction than be treated as one from whom facts must be disguised. She says: 'Let us face the worst and talk of it together, you and I.' No, Amy was not the ideal wife from that point of view. But the moment after this half-reproach had traversed his consciousness he condemned himself, and looked with the joy of love into her clear eyes.

'Yes, there's hope once more, my dearest. No more gloomy talk to-night! I have read you something, now you shall read something to me; it is a long time since I delighted myself with listening to you. What shall it be?'

'I feel rather too tired to-night.'

'Do you?'

'I have had to look after Willie so much. But read me some more Homer; I shall be very glad to listen.'

Reardon reached for the book again, but not readily. His face showed disappointment. Their evenings together had never been the same since the birth of the child; Willie was always an excuse – valid enough – for Amy's feeling tired. The little boy had come between him and the mother, as must always be the case in poor homes, most of all where the poverty is relative. Reardon could not pass the subject without a remark, but he tried to speak humorously.

'There ought to be huge public *crèche* in London. It's monstrous that an educated mother should have to be nursemaid.'

'But you know very well I think nothing of that. A *crèche*, indeed! No child of mine should go to any such place.'

There it was. She grudged no trouble on behalf of the child. That was love; whereas – But then maternal love was a mere matter of course.

'As soon as you get two or three hundred pounds for a book,' she added laughing, 'there'll be no need for me to give so much time.'

'Two or three hundred pounds!' He repeated it with a shake of the head. 'Ah, if that were possible!'

'But that's really a paltry sum. What would fifty novelists you could name say if they were offered three hundred pounds for a book? How much do you suppose even Markland got for his last?'

'Didn't sell it at all, ten to one. Gets a royalty.' [14]

'Which will bring him five or six hundred pounds before the book ceases to be talked of.'

'Never mind. I'm sick of the word "pounds."'

'So am I.'

She sighed, commenting thus on her acquiescence.

'But look, Amy. If I try to be cheerful in spite of natural dumps, wouldn't it be fair for you to put aside thoughts of money?'

'Yes. Read some Homer, dear. Let us have Odysseus down in Hades, and Ajax stalking past him. Oh, I like that!'

So he read, rather coldly at first, but soon warming. Amy sat with folded arms, a smile on her lips, her brows knitted to the epic humour. In a few minutes it was as if no difficulties threatened their life. Every now and then Reardon looked up from his translating with a delighted laugh, in which Amy joined.

When he had returned the book to the shelf he stepped behind his wife's chair, leaned upon it, and put his cheek against hers.

'Amy!'

'Yes, dear?'

'Do you still love me a little?'

'Much more than a little.'

'Though I am sunk to writing a wretched pot-boiler?'

'Is it so bad as all that?'

'Confoundedly bad. I shall be ashamed to see it in print; the proofs will be a martyrdom.'

'Oh, but why? why?'

'It's the best I can do, dearest. So you don't love me enough to hear that calmly.'

'If I *didn't* love you, I might be calmer about it, Edwin. It's dreadful to me to think of what they will say in the reviews.'

'Curse the reviews!'

His mood had changed on the instant. He stood up with darkened face, trembling angrily.

'I want you to promise me something, Amy. You won't read a single one of the notices unless it is forced upon your attention. Now, promise me that. Neglect them absolutely, as I do. They're not worth a glance of your eyes. And I shan't be able to bear it if I know you read all the contempt that will be poured on me.'

'I'm sure I shall be glad enough to avoid it; but other people, our friends, read it. That's the worst.'

'You know that their praise would be valueless, so have strength to disregard the blame. Let our friends read and talk as much as they like. Can't you console yourself with the thought that I am not contemptible, though I may have been forced to do poor work?'

'People don't look at it in that way.'

'But, darling,' he took her hands strongly in his own, 'I want you to disregard other people. You and I are surely everything to each other? Are you ashamed of me, of me myself?'

'No, not ashamed of you. But I am sensitive to people's talk and opinions.'

'But that means they *make* you feel ashamed of me. What else?'

There was silence.

'Edwin, if you find you are unable to do good work, you mustn't do bad. We must think of some other way of making a living.'

'Have you forgotten that you urged me to write a trashy sensational story?'

She coloured and looked annoyed.

'You misunderstood me. A sensational story needn't be trash. And then, you know, if you had tried something entirely unlike your usual work that would have been excuse enough if people had called it a failure.'

'People! People!'

'We can't live in solitude, Edwin, though really we are not far from it.'

He did not dare to make any reply to this. Amy was so exasperatingly womanlike in avoiding the important issue to which he tried to confine her; another moment, and his tone would be that of irritation. So he turned away and sat down to his desk, as if he had some thought of resuming work.

'Will you come and have some supper?' Amy asked, rising.

'I have been forgetting that to-morrow morning's chapter has still to be thought out.'

'Edwin, I can't think this book will really be so poor. You couldn't possibly give all this toil for no result.'

'No; not if I were in sound health. But I am far from it.'

'Come and have supper with me, dear, and think afterwards.'

He turned and smiled at her.

'I hope I shall never be able to resist an invitation from you, sweet.'

The result of all this was, of course, that he sat down in anything but the right mood to his work next morning. Amy's anticipation of criticism had made it harder than ever for him to labour at what he knew to be bad. And, as ill-luck would have it, in a day or two he caught his first winter's cold. For several years a succession of influenzas, sore throats, lumbagoes, had tormented him from October to May; in planning his present work, and telling himself that it must be finished before Christmas, he had not lost sight of these possible interruptions. But he said to himself: 'Other men have worked hard in seasons of illness; I must do the same.' All very well, but Reardon did not belong to the heroic class. A feverish cold now put his powers and resolution to the test. Through one hideous day he nailed himself to the desk – and wrote a quarter of a page. The next day Amy would not let him rise from bed; he was wretchedly ill. In the night he had talked about his work deliriously, causing her no slight alarm.

'If this goes on,' she said to him in the morning, 'you'll have brain fever. You must rest for two or three days.'

'Teach me how to. I wish I could.'

Rest had indeed become out of the question. For two days he could not write, but the result upon his mind was far worse than if he had been at the desk. He looked a haggard creature when he again sat down with the accustomed blank slip before him.

The second volume ought to have been much easier work than the first; it proved far harder. Messieurs and mesdames the critics are wont to point out the weakness of second volumes; they are generally right, simply because a story which would have made a tolerable book (the common run of stories) refuses to fill three books. Reardon's story was in itself weak, and this second volume had to consist almost entirely of laborious padding. If he wrote three slips a day he did well.

And the money was melting, melting, despite Amy's efforts at economy. She spent as little as she could; not a luxury came into their home; articles of clothing all but indispensable were left unpurchased. But to what purpose was all this? Impossible, now, that the book should be finished and sold before the money had all run out.

At the end of November, Reardon said to his wife one morning:

'To-morrow I finish the second volume.'

'And in a week,' she replied, 'we shan't have a shilling left.'

He had refrained from making inquiries, and Amy had forborne to tell him the state of things, lest it should bring him to a dead stop in his writing. But now they must needs discuss their position.

'In three weeks I can get to the end,' said Reardon, with unnatural calmness. 'Then I will go personally to the publishers, and beg them to advance me something on the manuscript before they have read it.'

'Couldn't you do that with the first two volumes?'

'No, I can't; indeed I can't. The other thing will be bad enough; but to beg on an incomplete book, and *such* a book – I can't!'

There were drops on his forehead.

'They would help you if they knew,' said Amy in a low voice.

'Perhaps; I can't say. They can't help every poor devil. No; I

will sell some books. I can pick out fifty or sixty that I shan't
much miss.'

Amy knew what a wrench this would be. The imminence of
distress seemed to have softened her.

'Edwin, let *me* take those two volumes to the publishers, and
ask –'

'Heavens! no. That's impossible. Ten to one you will be told
that my work is of such doubtful value that they can't offer even
a guinea till the whole book has been considered. I can't allow you
to go, dearest. This morning I'll choose some books that I can
spare, and after dinner I'll ask a man to come and look at them.
Don't worry yourself; I can finish in three weeks, I'm sure I can.
If I can get you three or four pounds you could make it do,
couldn't you?'

'Yes.'

She averted her face as she spoke.

'You shall have that.' He still spoke very quietly. 'If the books
won't bring enough there's my watch – oh, lots of things.'

He turned abruptly away, and Amy went on with her household work.

Chapter 10

THE FRIENDS OF THE FAMILY

IT was natural that Amy should hint dissatisfaction with the loneliness in which her days were mostly spent. She had never lived in a large circle of acquaintances; the narrowness of her mother's means restricted the family to intercourse with a few old friends and such new ones as were content with tea-cup entertainment; but her tastes were social, and the maturing process which followed upon her marriage made her more conscious of this than she had been before. Already she had allowed her husband to understand that one of her strongest motives in marrying him was the belief that he would achieve distinction. At the time she doubtless thought of his coming fame only – or principally – as it concerned their relations to each other; her pride in him was to be one phase of her love. Now she was well aware that no degree of distinction in her husband would be of much value to her unless she had the pleasure of witnessing its effect upon others; she must shine with reflected light before an admiring assembly.

The more conscious she became of this requirement of her nature the more clearly did she perceive that her hopes had been founded on an error. Reardon would never be a great man; he would never even occupy a prominent place in the estimation of the public. The two things, Amy knew, might be as different as light and darkness; but in the grief of her disappointment she would rather have had him flare into a worthless popularity than flicker down into total extinction, which it almost seemed was to be his fate. She knew so well how 'people' were talking of him and her. Even her unliterary acquaintances understood that Reardon's last novel had been anything but successful, and they must of course ask each other how the Reardons were going to live if the business of novel-writing proved unremunerative. Her pride took offence at the mere thought of such conversations. Presently she would become an object of pity; there would be talk of 'poor Mrs Reardon.' It was intolerable.

So during the last half year she had withheld as much as

possible from the intercourse which might have been one of her
chief pleasures. And to disguise the true cause she made pretences
which were a satire upon her state of mind – alleging that she had
devoted herself to a serious course of studies, that the care of
house and child occupied all the time she could spare from her
intellectual pursuits. The worst of it was, she had little faith in
the efficacy of these fictions; in uttering them she felt an unpleasant warmth upon her cheeks, and it was not difficult to
detect a look of doubt in the eyes of the listener. She grew angry
with herself for being dishonest, and with her husband for
making such dishonesty needful.

The female friend with whom she had most trouble was Mrs
Carter. You remember that on the occasion of Reardon's first
meeting with his future wife, at the Grosvenor Gallery, there
were present his friend Carter and a young lady who was shortly
to bear the name of that spirited young man. The Carters had
now been married about a year; they lived in Bayswater, and saw
much of a certain world which imitates on a lower plane the
amusements and affectations of society proper. Mr Carter was
still secretary to the hospital where Reardon had once earned
his twenty shillings a week, but by voyaging in the seas of charitable enterprise he had come upon supplementary sources of
income; for instance, he held the post of secretary to the Barclay
Trust, a charity whose moderate funds were largely devoted to
the support of gentlemen engaged in administering it. This
young man, with his air of pleasing vivacity, had early ingratiated
himself with the kind of people who were likely to be of use to
him; he had his reward in the shape of offices which are only
procured through private influence. His wife was a good-natured,
lively, and rather clever girl; she had a genuine regard for
Amy, and much respect for Reardon. Her ambition was to form
a circle of distinctly intellectual acquaintances, and she was
constantly inviting the Reardons to her house; a real live
novelist is not easily drawn into the world where Mrs Carter had
her being, and it annoyed her that all attempts to secure Amy
and her husband for five o'clock teas and small parties had of
late failed.

On the afternoon when Reardon had visited a second-hand
bookseller with a view of raising money – he was again shut up in

his study, dolorously at work – Amy was disturbed by the sound of a visitor's rat-tat; the little servant went to the door, and returned followed by Mrs Carter.

Under the best of circumstances it was awkward to receive any but intimate friends during the hours when Reardon sat at his desk. The little dining-room (with its screen to conceal the kitchen range) offered nothing more than homely comfort; and then the servant had to be disposed of by sending her into the bedroom to take care of Willie. Privacy, in the strict sense, was impossible, for the servant might listen at the door (one room led out of the other) to all the conversation that went on; yet Amy could not request her visitors to speak in a low tone. For the first year these difficulties had not been felt; Reardon made a point of leaving the front room at his wife's disposal from three to six; it was only when dread of the future began to press upon him that he sat in the study all day long. You see how complicated were the miseries of the situation; one torment involved another, and in every quarter subjects of discontent were multiplied.

Mrs Carter would have taken it ill had she known that Amy did not regard her as strictly an intimate. They addressed each other by their Christian names, and conversed without ceremony; but Amy was always dissatisfied when the well-dressed young woman burst with laughter and animated talk into this abode of concealed poverty. Edith was not the kind of person with whom one can quarrel; she had a kind heart, and was never disagreeably pretentious. Had circumstances allowed it, Amy would have given frank welcome to such friendship; she would have been glad to accept as many invitations as Edith chose to offer. But at present it did her harm to come in contact with Mrs Carter; it made her envious, cold to her husband, resentful against fate.

'Why can't she leave me alone?' was the thought that rose in her mind as Edith entered. 'I shall let her see that I don't want her here.'

'Your husband at work?' Edith asked, with a glance in the direction of the study, as soon as they had exchanged kisses and greetings.

'Yes, he is busy.'

'And you are sitting alone, as usual. I feared you might be out;

an afternoon of sunshine isn't to be neglected at this time of year.'

'Is there sunshine?' Amy inquired coldly.

'Why, look! Do you mean to say you haven't noticed it? What a comical person you are sometimes! I suppose you have been over head and ears in books all day. How is Willie?'

'Very well, thank you.'

'Mayn't I see him?'

'If you like.'

Amy stepped to the bedroom door and bade the servant bring Willie for exhibition. Edith, who as yet had no child of her own, always showed the most flattering admiration of this infant; it was so manifestly sincere that the mother could not but be moved to a grateful friendliness whenever she listened to its expression. Even this afternoon the usual effect followed when Edith had made a pretty and tender fool of herself for several minutes. Amy bade the servant make tea.

At this moment the door from the passage opened, and Reardon looked in.

'Well, if this isn't marvellous!' cried Edith. 'I should as soon have expected the heavens to fall!'

'As what?' asked Reardon, with a pale smile.

'As you to show yourself when I am here.'

'I should like to say that I came on purpose to see you, Mrs Carter, but it wouldn't be true. I'm going out for an hour, so that you can take possession of the other room if you like, Amy.'

'Going out?' said Amy, with a look of surprise.

'Nothing – nothing. I mustn't stay.'

He just inquired of Mrs Carter how her husband was, and withdrew. The door of the flat was heard to close after him.

'Let us go into the study, then,' said Amy, again in rather a cold voice.

On Reardon's desk were lying slips of blank paper. Edith, approaching on tiptoe with what was partly make-believe, partly genuine, awe, looked at the literary apparatus, then turned with a laugh to her friend.

'How delightful it must be to sit down and write about people one has invented! Ever since I have known you and Mr Reardon I have been tempted to try if I couldn't write a story.'

'Have you?'

'And I'm sure I don't know how *you* can resist the temptation. I feel sure you could write books almost as clever as your husband's.'

'I have no intention of trying.'

'You don't seem very well to-day, Amy.'

'Oh, I think I am as well as usual.'

She guessed that her husband was once more brought to a stand-still, and this darkened her humour again.

'One of my reasons for coming,' said Edith, 'was to beg and entreat and implore you and Mr Reardon to dine with us next Wednesday. Now don't put on such a severe face! Are you engaged that evening?'

'Yes; in the ordinary way. Edwin can't possibly leave his work.'

'But for one poor evening! It's such ages since we saw you.'

'I'm very sorry. I don't think we shall ever be able to accept invitations in future.'

Amy spoke thus at the prompting of a sudden impulse. A minute ago, no such definite declaration was in her mind.

'Never?' exclaimed Edith. 'But why? Whatever do you mean?'

'We find that social engagements consume too much time,' Amy replied, her explanation just as much of an impromptu as the announcement had been. 'You see, one must either belong to society or not. Married people can't accept an occasional invitation from friends and never do their social duty in return. We have decided to withdraw altogether – at all events for the present. I shall see no one except my relatives.'

Edith listened with a face of astonishment.

'You won't even see *me*?' she exclaimed.

'Indeed I have no wish to lose your friendship. Yet I am ashamed to ask you to come here when I can never return your visits.'

'Oh, please don't put it in that way! But it seems so very strange.'

Edith could not help conjecturing the true significance of this resolve. But, as is commonly the case with people in easy circumstances, she found it hard to believe that her friends were so straitened as to have a difficulty in supporting the ordinary obligations of a civilised state.

'I know how precious your husband's time is,' she added, as if to remove the effect of her last remark. 'Surely there's no harm in my saying – we know each other well enough – you wouldn't think it necessary to devote an evening to entertaining us just because you had given us the pleasure of your company. I put it very stupidly, but I'm sure you understand me, Amy. Don't refuse just to come to our house now and then.'

'I'm afraid we shall have to be consistent, Edith.'

'But do you think this is a *wise* thing to do?'

'Wise?'

'You know what you once told me, about how necessary it was for a novelist to study all sorts of people. How can Mr Reardon do this if he shuts himself up in the house? I should have thought he would find it necessary to make new acquaintances.'

'As I said,' returned Amy, 'it won't be always like this. For the present, Edwin has quite enough "material."'

She spoke distantly; it irritated her to have to invent excuses for the sacrifice she had just imposed on herself. Edith sipped the tea which had been offered her, and for a minute kept silence.

'When will Mr Reardon's next book be published?' she asked at length.

'I'm sure I don't know. Not before the spring.'

'I shall look so anxiously for it. Whenever I meet new people I always turn the conversation to novels, just for the sake of asking them if they know your husband's books.'

She laughed merrily.

'Which is seldom the case, I should think,' said Amy with a smile of indifference.

'Well, my dear, you don't expect ordinary novel-readers to know about Mr Reardon. I wish my acquaintances were a better kind of people; then, of course, I should hear of his books more often. But one has to make the best of such society as offers. If you and your husband forsake me, I shall feel it a sad loss; I shall indeed.'

Amy gave a quick glance at the speaker's face.

'Oh, we must be friends just the same,' she said, more naturally than she had spoken hitherto. 'But don't ask us to come and dine just now. All through this winter we shall be very busy, both of us. Indeed, we have decided not to accept any invitations at all.'

'Then, so long as you let me come here now and then, I must give in. I promise not to trouble you with any more complaining. But how you can live such a life I don't know. I consider myself more of a reader than women generally are, and I should be mortally offended if anyone called me frivolous; but I must have a good deal of society. Really and truly, I can't live without it.'

'No?' said Amy, with a smile which meant more than Edith could interpret. It seemed slightly condescending.

'There's no knowing; perhaps if I had married a literary man –' She paused, smiling and musing. 'But then I haven't, you see.' She laughed. 'Albert is anything but a bookworm, as you know.'

'You wouldn't wish him to be.'

'Oh no! Not a bookworm. To be sure, we suit each other very well indeed. He likes society just as much as I do. It would be the death of him if he didn't spend three-quarters of every day with lively people.'

'That's rather a large portion. But then you count yourself among the lively ones.'

They exchanged looks, and laughed together.

'Of course you think me rather silly to want to talk so much with silly people,' Edith went on. 'But then there's generally some amusement to be got, you know. I don't take life quite so seriously as you do. People are people after all; it's good fun to see how they live and hear how they talk.'

Amy felt that she was playing a sorry part. She thought of sour grapes, and of the fox who had lost his tail. Worst of all, perhaps Edith suspected the truth. She began to make inquiries about common acquaintances, and fell into an easier current of gossip.

A quarter of an hour after the visitor's departure Reardon came back. Amy had guessed aright; the necessity of selling his books weighed upon him so that for the present he could do nothing. The evening was spent gloomily, with very little conversation.

Next day came the bookseller to make his inspection. Reardon had chosen out and ranged upon a table nearly a hundred volumes. With a few exceptions they had been purchased secondhand. The tradesman examined them rapidly.

'What do you ask?' he inquired, putting his head aside.

'I prefer that you should make an offer,' Reardon replied, with the helplessness of one who lives remote from traffic.

'I can't say more than two pounds ten.'

'That is at the rate of sixpence a volume –?'

'To me that's about the average value of books like these.'

Perhaps the offer was a fair one; perhaps it was not. Reardon had neither time nor spirit to test the possibilities of the market; he was ashamed to betray his need by higgling.

'I'll take it,' he said, in a matter-of-fact voice.

A messenger was sent for the books that afternoon. He stowed them skilfully in two bags, and carried them downstairs to a cart that was waiting.

Reardon looked at the gaps left on his shelves. Many of those vanished volumes were dear old friends to him; he could have told you where he had picked them up and when; to open them recalled a past moment of intellectual growth, a mood of hope or despondency, a stage of struggle. In most of them his name was written, and there were often pencilled notes in the margin. Of course he had chosen from among the most valuable he possessed; such a multitude must else have been sold to make this sum of two pounds ten. Books are cheap, you know. At need, one can buy a Homer for fourpence, a Sophocles for sixpence. It was not rubbish that he had accumulated at so small expenditure, but the library of a poor student – battered bindings, stained pages, supplanted editions. He loved his books, but there was something he loved more, and when Amy glanced at him with eyes of sympathy he broke into a cheerful laugh.

'I'm only sorry they have gone for so little. Tell me when the money is nearly at an end again, and you shall have more. It's all right; the novel will be done soon.'

And that night he worked until twelve o'clock, doggedly, fiercely.

The next day was Sunday. As a rule he made it a day of rest, and almost perforce, for the depressing influence of Sunday in London made work too difficult. Then, it was the day on which he either went to see his own particular friends or was visited by them.

'Do you expect anyone this evening?' Amy inquired.

'Biffen will look in, I dare say. Perhaps Milvain.'

'I think I shall take Willie to mother's. I shall be back before eight.'

'Amy, don't say anything about the books.'

'No, no.'

'I suppose they always ask you when we think of removing over the way?'

He pointed in a direction that suggested Marylebone Workhouse. Amy tried to laugh, but a woman with a child in her arms has no keen relish for such jokes.

'I don't talk to them about our affairs,' she said.

'That's best.'

She left home about three o'clock, the servant going with her to carry the child.

At five a familiar knock sounded through the flat; it was a heavy rap followed by half a dozen light ones, like a reverberating echo, the last stroke scarcely audible. Reardon laid down his book, but kept his pipe in his mouth, and went to the door. A tall, thin man stood there, with a slouch hat and long grey overcoat. He shook hands silently, hung his hat in the passage, and came forward into the study.

His name was Harold Biffen, and, to judge from his appearance, he did not belong to the race of common mortals. His excessive meagreness would all but have qualified him to enter an exhibition in the capacity of living skeleton, and the garments which hung upon this framework would perhaps have sold for three and sixpence at an old-clothes dealer's. But the man was superior to these accidents of flesh and raiment. He had a fine face: large, gentle eyes, nose slightly aquiline, small and delicate mouth. Thick black hair fell to his coat-collar; he wore a heavy moustache and a full beard. In his gait there was a singular dignity; only a man of cultivated mind and graceful character could move and stand as he did.

His first act on entering the room was to take from his pocket a pipe, a pouch, a little tobacco-stopper, and a box of matches, all of which he arranged carefully on a corner of the central table. Then he drew forward a chair and seated himself.

'Take your top-coat off,' said Reardon.

'Thanks, not this evening.'

'Why the deuce not?'

'Not this evening, thanks.'

The reason, as soon as Reardon sought for it, was obvious. Biffen had no ordinary coat beneath the other. To have referred to this fact would have been indelicate; the novelist of course understood it, and smiled, but with no mirth.

'Let me have your Sophocles,' were the visitor's next words.

Reardon offered him a volume of the Oxford Pocket Classics.

'I prefer the Wunder, please.'

'It's gone, my boy.'

'Gone?'

'Wanted a little cash.'

Biffen uttered a sound in which remonstrance and sympathy were blended.

'I'm sorry to hear that; very sorry. Well, this must do. Now, I want to know how you scan this chorus in the "Œdipus Rex."'

Reardon took the volume, considered, and began to read aloud with metric emphasis.

'Choriambics, eh?' cried the other. 'Possible, of course; but treat them as Ionics a minore with an anacrusis, and see if they don't go better.'

He involved himself in terms of pedantry, and with such delight that his eyes gleamed. Having delivered a technical lecture, he began to read in illustration, producing quite a different effect from that of the rhythm as given by his friend. And the reading was by no means that of a pedant, rather of a poet.

For half an hour the two men talked Greek metres as if they lived in a world where the only hunger known could be satisfied by grand or sweet cadences.

They had first met in an amusing way. Not long after the publication of his book 'On Neutral Ground' Reardon was spending a week at Hastings. A rainy day drove him to the circulating library, and as he was looking along the shelves for something readable a voice near at hand asked the attendant if he had anything 'by Edwin Reardon.' The novelist turned in astonishment; that any casual mortal should inquire for his books seemed incredible. Of course there was nothing by that author in the library, and he who had asked the question walked out again. On the morrow Reardon encountered this same man at a lonely part of the shore; he looked at him, and spoke a word or two of common civility; they got into conversation, with the result that Edwin told the story of yesterday. The stranger introduced himself as Harold Biffen, an author in a small way, and a teacher whenever he could get pupils; an abusive review had interested him in Reardon's novels, but as yet he knew nothing of them but the names.

Their tastes were found to be in many respects sympathetic, and after returning to London they saw each other frequently. Biffen was always in dire poverty, and lived in the oddest places; he had seen harder trials than even Reardon himself. The teaching by which he partly lived was of a kind quite unknown to the respectable tutorial world. In these days of examinations, numbers of men in a poor position – clerks chiefly – conceive a hope that by 'passing' this, that, or the other formal test they may open for themselves a new career. Not a few such persons nourish preposterous ambitions; there are warehouse clerks privately preparing (without any means or prospect of them) for a call to the Bar, drapers' assistants who 'go in' for the preliminary examination of the College of Surgeons, and untaught men innumerable who desire to procure enough show of education to be eligible for a curacy. Candidates of this stamp frequently advertise in the newspapers for cheap tuition, or answer advertisements which are intended to appeal to them; they pay from sixpence to half a crown an hour – rarely as much as the latter sum. Occasionally it happened that Harold Biffen had three or four such pupils in hand, and extraordinary stories he could draw from his large experience in this sphere.

Then as to his authorship. – But shortly after the discussion of Greek metres he fell upon the subject of his literary projects, and, by no means for the first time, developed the theory on which he worked.

'I have thought of a new way of putting it. What I really aim at is an absolute realism in the sphere of the ignobly decent. The field, as I understand it, is a new one; I don't know any writer who has treated ordinary vulgar-life with fidelity and seriousness. Zola writes deliberate tragedies; his vilest figures become heroic from the place they fill in a strongly imagined drama. I want to deal with the essentially unheroic, with the day-to-day life of that vast majority of people who are at the mercy of paltry circumstance. Dickens understood the possibility of such work, but his tendency to melodrama on the one hand, and his humour on the other, prevented him from thinking of it. An instance, now. As I came along by Regent's Park half an hour ago a man and a girl were walking close in front of me, love-making; I passed them slowly and heard a good deal of their talk – it was part of the situation that they should pay no heed to a stranger's proximity. Now, such a love-scene as that has absolutely never been written down; it was entirely decent, yet vulgar to the nth power. Dickens would have made it ludicrous – a gross injustice. Other men who deal with low-class life would perhaps have preferred idealising it – an absurdity. For my own part, I am going to reproduce it verbatim, without one single impertinent suggestion of any point of view save that of honest reporting. The result will be something unutterably tedious. Precisely. That is the stamp of the ignobly decent life. If it were anything *but* tedious it would be untrue. I speak, of course, of its effect upon the ordinary reader.'

'I couldn't do it,' said Reardon.

'Certainly you couldn't. You – well, you are a psychological realist in the sphere of culture. You are impatient of vulgar circumstances.'

'In a great measure because my life has been martyred by them.'

'And for that very same reason I delight in them,' cried Biffen. 'You are repelled by what has injured you; I am attracted by it. This divergence is very interesting; but for that, we should have resembled each other so closely. You know that by temper we are rabid idealists, both of us.'

'I suppose so.'

'But let me go on. I want, among other things, to insist upon the fateful power of trivial incidents. No one has yet dared to do this seriously. It has often been done in farce, and that's why farcical writing so often makes one melancholy. You know my stock instances of the kind of thing I mean. There was poor Allen, who lost the most valuable opportunity of his life because he hadn't a clean shirt to put on; and Williamson, who would probably have married that rich girl but for the grain of dust that got into his eye and made him unable to say or do anything at the critical moment.'

Reardon burst into a roar of laughter.

'There you are!' cried Biffen, with friendly annoyance. 'You take the conventional view. If you wrote of these things you would represent them as laughable.'

'They *are* laughable,' asserted the other, 'however serious to the persons concerned. The mere fact of grave issues in life depending on such paltry things is monstrously ludicrous. Life is a huge farce, and the advantage of possessing a sense of humour is that it enables one to defy with mocking laughter.'

'That's all very well, but it isn't an original view. I am not lacking in sense of humour, but I prefer to treat these aspects of life from an impartial standpoint. The man who laughs takes the side of a cruel omnipotence, if one can imagine such a thing. I want to take no side at all; simply to say, Look, this is the kind of thing that happens.'

'I admire your honesty, Biffen,' said Reardon, sighing. 'You will never sell work of this kind, yet you have the courage to go on with it because you believe in it.'

'I don't know; I may perhaps sell it some day.'

'In the meantime,' said Reardon, laying down his pipe, 'suppose we eat a morsel of something. I'm rather hungry.'

In the early days of his marriage Reardon was wont to offer the friends who looked in on Sunday evening a substantial supper; by degrees the meal had grown simpler, until now, in the depth of his poverty, he made no pretence of hospitable entertainment. It was only because he knew that Biffen as often as not had nothing whatever to eat that he did not hesitate to offer him a slice of bread and butter and a cup of tea. They went into the back room, and over the Spartan fare continued to discuss aspects of fiction.

'I shall never,' said Biffen, 'write anything like a dramatic scene. Such things do happen in life, but so very rarely that they are nothing to my purpose. Even when they happen, by-the-by, it is in a shape that would be useless to the ordinary novelist; he would have to cut away this circumstance, and add that. Why? I should like to know. Such conventionalism results from stage necessities. Fiction hasn't yet outgrown the influence of the stage on which it originated. Whatever a man writes *for effect* is wrong and bad.'

'Only in your view. There may surely exist such a thing as the *art* of fiction.'

'It is worked out. We must have a rest from it. You, now – the best things you have done are altogether in conflict with novelistic conventionalities. It was because that blackguard review of "On Neutral Ground" clumsily hinted this that I first thought of you with interest. No, no; let us copy life. When the man and woman are to meet for a great scene of passion, let it all be frustrated by one or other of them having a bad cold in the head, and so on. Let the pretty girl get a disfiguring pimple on her nose just before the ball at which she is going to shine. Show the numberless repulsive features of common decent life. Seriously, coldly; not a hint of facetiousness, or the thing becomes different.'

About eight o'clock Reardon heard his wife's knock at the door. On opening, he saw not only Amy and the servant, the latter holding Willie in her arms, but with them Jasper Milvain.

'I have been at Mrs Yule's,' Jasper explained as he came in. 'Have you anyone here?'

'Biffen.'

'Ah, then we'll discuss realism.'

'That's over for the evening. Greek metres also.'

'Thank Heaven!'

The three men seated themselves with joking and laughter, and the smoke of their pipes gathered thickly in the little room. It was half an hour before Amy joined them. Tobacco was no disturbance to her, and she enjoyed the kind of talk that was held on these occasions; but it annoyed her that she could no longer play the hostess at a merry supper-table.

'Why ever are you sitting in your overcoat, Mr Biffen?' were her first words when she entered.

'Please excuse me, Mrs Reardon. It happens to be more convenient this evening.'

She was puzzled but a glance from her husband warned her not to pursue the subject.

Biffen always behaved to Amy with a sincerity of respect which had made him a favourite with her. To him, poor fellow, Reardon seemed supremely blessed. That a struggling man of letters should have been able to marry, and *such* a wife, was miraculous in Biffen's eyes. A woman's love was to him the unattainable ideal; already thirty-five years old, he had no prospect of ever being rich enough to assure himself a daily dinner; marriage was wildly out of the question. Sitting here, he found it very difficult not to gaze at Amy with uncivil persistency. Seldom in his life had he conversed with educated women, and the sound of this clear voice was always more delightful to him than any music.

Amy took a place near to him, and talked in her most charming way of such things as she knew interested him. Biffen's deferential attitude as he listened and replied was in strong contrast with the careless ease which marked Jasper Milvain. The realist would never smoke in Amy's presence, but Jasper puffed jovial clouds even while she was conversing with him.

'Whelpdale came to see me last night,' remarked Milvain, presently. 'His novel is refused on all hands. He talks of earning a living as a commission agent for some sewing-machine people.'

'I can't understand how his book should be positively refused,' said Reardon. 'The last wasn't altogether a failure.'

'Very nearly. And this one consists of nothing but a series of conversations between two people. It is really a dialogue, not a novel at all. He read me some twenty pages, and I no longer wondered that he couldn't sell it.'

'Oh, but it has considerable merit,' put in Biffen. 'The talk is remarkably true.'

'But what's the good of talk that leads to nothing?' protested Jasper.

'It's a bit of real life.'

'Yes, but it has no market value. You may write what you like so long as people are willing to read you. Whelpdale's a clever fellow, but he can't hit a practical line.'

'Like some other people I have heard of,' said Reardon, laughing.

'But the odd thing is, that he always strikes one as practical-minded. Don't you feel that, Mrs Reardon?'

He and Amy talked for a few minutes, and Reardon, seemingly lost in meditation, now and then observed them from the corner of his eye.

At eleven o'clock husband and wife were alone again.

'You don't mean to say,' exclaimed Amy, 'that Biffen has sold his coat?'

'Or pawned it.'

'But why not the overcoat?'

'Partly, I should think, because it's the warmer of the two; partly, perhaps, because the other would fetch more.'

'That poor man will die of starvation some day, Edwin.'

'I think it not impossible.'

'I hope you gave him something to eat?'

'Oh yes. But I could see he didn't like to take as much as he wanted. I don't think of him with so much pity as I used to; that's a result of suffering oneself.'

Amy set her lips and sighed.

Chapter 11

RESPITE

THE last volume was written in fourteen days. In this achieve-
ment Reardon rose almost to heroic pitch, for he had much to
contend with beyond the mere labour of composition. Scarcely
had he begun when a sharp attack of lumbago fell upon him; for
two or three days it was torture to support himself at the desk,
and he moved about like a cripple. Upon this ensued headaches,
sore-throat, general enfeeblement. And before the end of the
fortnight it was necessary to think of raising another small sum
of money; he took his watch to the pawnbroker's (you can imagine that it would not stand as security for much), and sold a few
more books. All this notwithstanding, here was the novel at
length finished. When he had written 'The End' he lay back,
closed his eyes, and let time pass in blankness for a quarter of an
hour.

It remained to determine the title. But his brain refused another effort; after a few minutes' feeble search he simply took the
name of the chief female character,[15] Margaret Home. That
must do for the book. Already, with the penning of the last
word, all its scenes, personages, dialogues had slipped away into
oblivion; he knew and cared nothing more about them.

'Amy, you will have to correct the proofs for me. Never as long
as I live will I look upon a page of this accursed novel. It has all
but killed me.'

'The point is,' replied Amy, 'that here we have it complete.
Pack it up and take it to the publishers' to-morrow morning.'

'I will.'

'And – you will ask them to advance you a few pounds?'

'I must.'

But that undertaking was almost as hard to face as a re-writing
of the last volume would have been. Reardon had such super-
fluity of sensitiveness that, for his own part, he would far rather
have gone hungry than ask for money not legally his due. To-day
there was no choice. In the ordinary course of business it would
be certainly a month before he heard the publishers' terms, and

perhaps the Christmas season might cause yet more delay. Without borrowing, he could not provide for the expenses of more than another week or two.

His parcel under his arm, he entered the ground-floor office, and desired to see that member of the firm with whom he had previously had personal relations. This gentleman was not in town; he would be away for a few days. Reardon left the manuscript, and came out into the street again.

He crossed, and looked up at the publishers' windows from the opposite pavement. 'Do they suspect in what wretched circumstances I am? Would it surprise them to know all that depends upon that budget of paltry scribbling? I suppose not; it must be a daily experience with them. Well, I must write a begging letter.'

It was raining and windy. He went slowly homewards, and was on the point of entering the public door of the flats when his uneasiness became so great that he turned and walked past. If he went in, he must at once write his appeal for money, and he felt that he *could* not. The degradation seemed too great.

Was there no way of getting over the next few weeks? Rent, of course, would be due at Christmas, but that payment might be postponed; it was only a question of buying food and fuel. Amy had offered to ask her mother for a few pounds; it would be cowardly to put this task upon her now that he had promised to meet the difficulty himself. What man in all London could and would lend him money? He reviewed the list of his acquaintances, but there was only one to whom he could appeal with the slightest hope – that was Carter.

Half an hour later he entered that same hospital door through which, some years ago, he had passed as a half-starved applicant for work. The matron met him.

'Is Mr Carter here?'

'No, sir. But we expect him any minute. Will you wait?'

He entered the familiar office, and sat down. At the table where he had been wont to work, a young clerk was writing. If only all the events of the last few years could be undone, and he, with no soul dependent upon him, be once more earning his pound a week in this room! What a happy man he was in those days!

Nearly half an hour passed. It is the common experience of

beggars to have to wait. Then Carter came in with quick step; he wore a heavy ulster of the latest fashion, new gloves, a resplendent silk hat; his cheeks were rosy from the east wind.

'Ha, Reardon! How do? how do? Delighted to see you!'

'Are you very busy?'

'Well, no, not particularly. A few cheques to sign, and we're just getting out our Christmas appeals. You remember?'

He laughed gaily. There was a remarkable freedom from snobbishness in this young man; the fact of Reardon's intellectual superiority had long ago counteracted Carter's social prejudices.

'I should like to have a word with you.'

'Right you are!'

They went into a small inner room. Reardon's pulse beat at fever-rate; his tongue was cleaving to his palate.

'What is it, old man?' asked the secretary, seating himself and flinging one of his legs over the other. 'You look rather seedy, do you know. Why the deuce don't you and your wife look us up now and then?'

'I've had a hard pull to finish my novel.'

'Finished, is it? I'm glad to hear that. When'll it be out? I'll send scores of people to Mudie's after it.' [16]

'Thanks; but I don't think much of it, to tell you the truth.'

'Oh, we know what that means.'

Reardon was talking like an automaton. It seemed to him that he turned screws and pressed levers for the utterance of his next words.

'I may as well say at once what I have come for. Could you lend me ten pounds for a month – in fact, until I get the money for my book?'

The secretary's countenance fell, though not to that expression of utter coldness which would have come naturally under the circumstances to a great many vivacious men. He seemed genuinely embarrassed.

'By Jove! I – confound it! To tell you the truth, I haven't ten pounds to lend. Upon my word I haven't, Reardon! These infernal housekeeping expenses! I don't mind telling you, old man, that Edith and I have been pushing the pace rather.' He laughed, and thrust his hands down into his trousers-pockets. 'We pay such a darned rent, you know – hundred and twenty-five. We've only just been saying we should have to draw it mild for the rest of the winter. But I'm infernally sorry; upon my word I am.'

'And I am sorry to have annoyed you by the unseasonable request.'

'Devilish seasonable, Reardon, I assure you!' cried the secretary, and roared at his joke. It put him into a better temper than ever, and he said at length: 'I suppose a fiver wouldn't be much use? – For a month, you say? – I might manage a fiver, I think.'

'It would be very useful. But on no account if –'

'No, no; I *could* manage a fiver, for a month. Shall I give you a cheque?'

'I'm ashamed –'

'Not a bit of it! I'll go and write the cheque.'

Reardon's face was burning. Of the conversation that followed when Carter again presented himself he never recalled a word. The bit of paper was crushed together in his hand. Out in the street again, he all but threw it away, dreaming for the moment that it was a 'bus ticket or a patent medicine bill.

He reached home much after the dinner hour. Amy was surprised at his long absence.

'Got any thing?' she asked.

'Yes.'

It was half his intention to deceive her, to say that the publishers had advanced him five pounds. But that would be his first word of untruth to Amy, and why should he be guilty of it? He told her all that had happened. The result of this frankness was something that he had not anticipated; Amy exhibited profound vexation.

'Oh, you *shouldn't* have done that!' she exclaimed. 'Why didn't you come home and tell me? I would have gone to mother at once.'

'But does it matter?'

'Of course it does,' she replied sharply. 'Mr Carter will tell his wife, and how pleasant that is!'

'I never thought of that. And perhaps it wouldn't have seemed to me so annoying as it does to you.'

'Very likely not.'

She turned abruptly away, and stood at a distance in gloomy muteness.

'Well,' she said at length, 'there's no helping it now. Come and have your dinner.'

'You have taken away my appetite.'

'Nonsense! I suppose you're dying of hunger.'

They had a very uncomfortable meal, exchanging few words. On Amy's face was a look more resembling bad temper than anything Reardon had ever seen there. After dinner he went and sat alone in the study. Amy did not come near him. He grew stubbornly angry; remembering the pain he had gone through he felt that Amy's behaviour to him was cruel. She must come and speak when she would.

At six o'clock she showed her face in the doorway and asked if he would come to tea.

'Thank you,' he replied, 'I had rather stay here.'

'As you please.'

And he sat alone until about nine. It was only then he recollected that he must send a note to the publishers, calling their attention to the parcel he had left. He wrote it, and closed with a request that they would let him hear as soon as they conveniently could. As he was putting on his hat and coat to go out and post the letter Amy opened the dining-room door.

'You're going out?'

'Yes.'

'Shall you be long?'

'I think not.'

He was away only a few minutes. On returning he went first of all into the study, but the thought of Amy alone in the other room would not let him rest. He looked in and saw that she was sitting without a fire.

'You can't stay here in the cold, Amy.'

'I'm afraid I must get used to it,' she replied, affecting to be closely engaged upon some sewing.

That strength of character which it had always delighted him to read in her features was become an ominous hardness. He felt his heart sink as he looked at her.

'Is poverty going to have the usual result in our case?' he asked, drawing nearer.

'I never pretended that I could be indifferent to it.'

'Still, don't you care to try and resist it?'

She gave no answer. As usual in conversation with an ag-
grieved woman it was necessary to go back from the general to
the particular.

'I'm afraid,' he said, 'that the Carters already knew pretty well
how things were going with us.'

'That's a very different thing. But when it comes to asking
them for money –'

'I'm very sorry. I would rather have done anything if I had
known how it would annoy you.'

'If we have to wait a month, five pounds will be very little use
to us.'

She detailed all manner of expenses that had to be met – outlay
there was no possibility of avoiding so long as their life was maintained on its present basis.

'However, you needn't trouble any more about it. I'll see to it.
Now you are free from your book try to rest.'

'Come and sit by the fire. There's small chance of rest for me if
we are thinking unkindly of each other.'

A doleful Christmas. Week after week went by and Reardon
knew that Amy must have exhausted the money he had given to
her. But she made no more demands upon him, and necessaries
were paid for in the usual way. He suffered from a sense of
humiliation; sometimes he found it difficult to look in his wife's
face.

When the publishers' letter came it contained an offer of
seventy-five pounds for the copyright of 'Margaret Home,'
twenty-five more to be paid if the sale in three-volume form
should reach a certain number of copies.

Here was failure put into unmistakable figures. Reardon said
to himself that it was all over with his profession of authorship.
The book could not possibly succeed even to the point of completing his hundred pounds; it would meet with universal contempt, and indeed deserved nothing better.

'Shall you accept this?' asked Amy, after dreary silence.

'No one else would offer terms as good.'

'Will they pay you at once?'

'I must ask them to.'

Well, it was seventy-five pounds in hand. The cheque came as

soon as it was requested, and Reardon's face brightened for the
moment. Blessed money! root of all good, until the world invent
some saner economy.

'How much do you owe your mother?' he inquired, without
looking at Amy.

'Six pounds,' she answered coldly.

'And five to Carter; and rent, twelve pounds ten. We shall
have a matter of fifty pounds to go on with.'

Chapter 12

WORK WITHOUT HOPE

THE prudent course was so obvious that he marvelled at Amy's failing to suggest it. For people in their circumstances to be paying a rent of fifty pounds when a home could be found for half the money was recklessness; there would be no difficulty in letting the flat for this last year of their lease, and the cost of removal would be trifling. The mental relief of such a change might enable him to front with courage a problem in any case very difficult, and, as things were, desperate. Three months ago, in a moment of profoundest misery, he had proposed this step; courage failed him to speak of it again, Amy's look and voice were too vivid in his memory. Was she not capable of such a sacrifice for his sake? Did she prefer to let him bear all the responsibility of whatever might result from a futile struggle to keep up appearances?

Between him and her there was no longer perfect confidence. Her silence meant reproach, and – whatever might have been the case before – there was no doubt that she now discussed him with her mother, possibly with other people. It was not likely that she concealed his own opinion of the book he had just finished; all their acquaintances would be prepared to greet its publication with private scoffing or with mournful shaking of the head. His feeling towards Amy entered upon a new phase. The stability of his love was a source of pain; condemning himself, he felt at the same time that he was wronged. A coldness which was far from representing the truth began to affect his manner and speech, and Amy did not seem to notice it, at all events she made no kind of protest. They no longer talked of the old subjects, but of those mean concerns of material life which formerly they had agreed to dismiss as quickly as possible. Their relations to each other – not long ago an inexhaustible topic – would not bear spoken comment; both were too conscious of the danger-signal when they looked that way.

In the time of waiting for the publishers' offer, and now again when he was asking himself how he should use the respite granted him, Reardon spent his days at the British Museum. He could not read to much purpose, but it was better to sit here among strangers than seem to be idling under Amy's glance. Sick of imaginative writing, he turned to the studies which had always been most congenial, and tried to shape out a paper or two like those he had formerly disposed of to editors. Among his unused material lay a mass of notes he had made in a reading of Diogenes Laertius,[17] and it seemed to him now that he might make something saleable out of these anecdotes of the philosophers. In a happier mood he could have written delightfully on such a subject – not learnedly, but in the strain of a modern man whose humour and sensibility find free play among the classic ghosts; even now he was able to recover something of the light touch which had given value to his published essays.

Meanwhile the first number of *The Current* had appeared, and Jasper Milvain had made a palpable hit. Amy spoke very often of the article called 'Typical Readers,' and her interest in its author was freely manifested. Whenever a mention of Jasper came under her notice she read it out to her husband. Reardon smiled and appeared glad, but he did not care to discuss Milvain with the same frankness as formerly.

One evening at the end of January he told Amy what he had been writing at the Museum, and asked her if she would care to hear it read.

'I began to wonder what you were doing,' she replied.

'Then why didn't you ask me?'

'I was rather afraid to.'

'Why afraid?'

'It would have seemed like reminding you that – you know what I mean.'

'That a month or two more will see us at the same crisis again. Still, I had rather you had shown an interest in my doings.'

After a pause Amy asked :

'Do you think you can get a paper of this kind accepted?'

'It isn't impossible. I think it's rather well done. Let me read you a page –'

'Where will you send it?' she interrupted.

'To *The Wayside*.'

'Why not try *The Current*? Ask Milvain to introduce you to Mr Fadge. They pay much better, you know.'

'But this isn't so well suited for Fadge. And I much prefer to be independent, as long as it's possible.'

'That's one of your faults, Edwin,' remarked his wife, mildly. 'It's only the strongest men that can make their way independently. You ought to use every means that offers.'

'Seeing that I am so weak?'

'I didn't think it would offend you. I only meant –'

'No, no; you are quite right. Certainly, I am one of the men who need all the help they can get. But I assure you, this thing won't do for *The Current*.'

'What a pity you will go back to those musty old times! Now think of that article of Milvain's. If only you could do something of that kind! What *do* people care about Diogenes and his tub and his lantern?'

'My dear girl, Diogenes Laertius had neither tub nor lantern, that I know of. You are making a mistake; but it doesn't matter.'

'No, I don't think it does.' The caustic note was not very pleasant on Amy's lips. 'Whoever he was, the mass of readers will be frightened by his name.'

'Well, we have to recognise that the mass of readers will never care for anything I do.'

'You will never convince me that you couldn't write in a popular way if you tried. I'm sure you are quite as clever as Milvain –'

Reardon made an impatient gesture.

'Do leave Milvain aside for a little! He and I are as unlike as two men could be. What's the use of constantly comparing us?'

Amy looked at him. He had never spoken to her so brusquely.

'How can you say that I am constantly comparing you?'

'If not in spoken words, then in your thoughts.'

'That's not a very nice thing to say, Edwin.'

'You make it so unmistakable, Amy. What I mean is, that you are always regretting the difference between him and me. You lament that I can't write in that attractive way. Well, I lament it myself – for your sake. I wish I had Milvain's peculiar talent, so that I could get reputation and money. But I haven't, and there's an end of it. It irritates a man to be perpetually told of his disadvantages.'

'I will never mention Milvain's name again,' said Amy, coldly.

'Now that's ridiculous, and you know it.'

'I feel the same about your irritation. I can't see that I have given any cause for it.'

'Then we'll talk no more of the matter.'

Reardon threw his manuscript aside, and opened a book. Amy never asked him to resume his intention of reading what he had written.

However, the paper was accepted. It came out in *The Wayside* for March, and Reardon received seven pounds ten for it. By that time he had written another thing of the same gossipy kind, suggested by Pliny's Letters. The pleasant occupation did him good, but there was no possibility of pursuing this course. 'Margaret Home' would be published in April; he *might* get the five-and-twenty pounds contingent upon a certain sale, yet that could in no case be paid until the middle of the year, and long before then he would be penniless. His respite drew to an end.

But now he took counsel of no one; as far as it was possible he lived in solitude, never seeing those of his acquaintances who were outside the literary world, and seldom even his colleagues. Milvain was so busy that he had only been able to look in twice or thrice since Christmas, and Reardon nowadays never went to Jasper's lodgings.

He had the conviction that all was over with the happiness of his married life, though how the events which were to express this ruin would shape themselves he could not foresee. Amy was revealing that aspect of her character to which he had been blind, though a practical man would have perceived it from the first; so far from helping him to support poverty, she perhaps would even refuse to share it with him. He knew that she was slowly drawing apart; already there was a divorce between their minds, and he tortured himself in uncertainty as to how far he retained her affections. A word of tenderness, a caress, no longer met with response from her; her softest mood was that of mere comradeship. All the warmth of her nature was expended upon the child; Reardon learnt how easy it is for a mother to forget that both parents have a share in her offspring.

He was beginning to dislike the child. But for Willie's existence Amy would still love him with undivided heart; not, perhaps, so passionately as once, but still with lover's love. And Amy understood – or, at all events, remarked – this change in him. She was aware that he seldom asked a question about Willie, and that he listened with indifference when she spoke of the little fellow's progress. In part offended, she was also in part pleased.

But for the child, mere poverty, he said to himself, should never have sundered them. In the strength of his passion he could have overcome all her disappointments; and, indeed, but for that new care, he would most likely never have fallen to this extremity of helplessness. It is natural in a weak and sensitive man to dream of possibilities disturbed by the force of circumstance. For one hour which he gave to conflict with his present difficulties, Reardon spent many in contemplation of the happiness that might have been.

Even yet, it needed but a little money to redeem all. Amy had no extravagant aspirations; a home of simple refinement and freedom from anxiety would restore her to her nobler self. How could he find fault with her? She knew nothing of such sordid life as *he* had gone through, and to lack money for necessities seemed to her degrading beyond endurance. Why, even the ordinary artisan's wife does not suffer such privations as hers at the end of the past year. For lack of that little money his life must be ruined. Of late he had often thought about the rich uncle, John Yule, who might perhaps leave something to Amy; but the hope was so uncertain. And supposing such a thing were to happen; would it be perfectly easy to live upon his wife's bounty – perhaps exhausting a small capital, so that, some years hence, their position would be no better than before? Not long ago, he could have taken anything from Amy's hand; would it be so simple since the change that had come between them?

Having written his second magazine-article (it was rejected by two editors, and he had no choice but to hold it over until sufficient time had elapsed to allow of his again trying *The Wayside*), he saw that he must perforce plan another novel. But this time he was resolute not to undertake three volumes. The advertisements informed him that numbers of authors were abandoning that procrustean system; hopeless as he was, he might as well try his chance with a book which could be written in a few weeks. And why not a glaringly artificial story with a sensational title? It could not be worse than what he had last written.

So, without a word to Amy, he put aside his purely intellectual work and began once more the search for a 'plot.' This was towards the end of February. The proofs of 'Margaret Home' were coming in day by day; Amy had offered to correct them, but after all he preferred to keep his shame to himself as long as possible, and with a hurried reading he dismissed sheet after sheet. His imagination did not work the more happily for this repugnant task; still, he hit at length upon a conception which seemed absurd enough for the purpose before him. Whether he could persevere with it even to the extent of one volume was very doubtful. But it should not be said of him that he abandoned his wife and child to penury without one effort of the kind that Milvain and Amy herself had recommended.

Writing a page or two of manuscript daily, and with several holocausts to retard him, he had done nearly a quarter of the story when there came a note from Jasper telling of Mrs Milvain's death. He handed it across the breakfast table to Amy, and watched her as she read it.

'I suppose it doesn't alter his position,' Amy remarked, without much interest.

'I suppose not appreciably. He told me once his mother had a sufficient income; but whatever she leaves will go to his sisters, I should think. He has never said much to me.'

Nearly three weeks passed before they heard anything more from Jasper himself; then he wrote, again from the country, saying that he purposed bringing his sisters to live in London. Another week, and one evening he appeared at the door.

A want of heartiness in Reardon's reception of him might have been explained as gravity natural under the circumstances. But Jasper had before this become conscious that he was not welcomed here quite so cheerily as in the old days. He remarked it distinctly on that evening when he accompanied Amy home from Mrs Yule's; since then he had allowed his pressing occupations to be an excuse for the paucity of his visits. It seemed to him perfectly intelligible that Reardon, sinking into literary insignificance, should grow cool to a man entering upon a successful career; the vein of cynicism in Jasper enabled him to pardon a weakness of this kind, which in some measure flattered him. But he both liked and respected Reardon, and at present he was in the mood to give expression to his warmer feelings.

'Your book is announced, I see,' he said with an accent of pleasure, as soon as he had seated himself.

'I didn't know it.'

'Yes. "New novel by the author of 'On Neutral Ground.'"' Down for the sixteenth of April. And I have a proposal to make about it. Will you let me ask Fadge to have it noticed in "Books of the Month," in the May *Current*?'

'I strongly advise you to let it take its chance. The book isn't worth special notice, and whoever undertook to review it for Fadge would either have to lie, or stultify the magazine.'

Jasper turned to Amy.

'Now what is to be done with a man like this? What is one to say to him, Mrs Reardon?'

'Edwin dislikes the book,' Amy replied, carelessly.

'That has nothing to do with the matter. We know quite well that in anything he writes there'll be something for a well-disposed reviewer to make a good deal of. If Fadge will let me, I should do the thing myself.'

Neither Reardon nor his wife spoke.

'Of course,' went on Milvain, looking at the former, 'if you had rather I left it alone –'

'I had much rather. Please don't say anything about it.'

There was an awkward silence. Amy broke it by saying:

'Are your sisters in town, Mr Milvain?'

'Yes. We came up two days ago. I found lodgings for them not far from Mornington Road. Poor girls! they don't quite know where they are, yet. Of course they will keep very quiet for a time, then I must try to get friends for them. Well, they have one already – your cousin, Miss Yule. She has already been to see them.'

'I'm very glad of that.'

Amy took an opportunity of studying his face. There was again a silence as if of constraint. Reardon, glancing at his wife, said with hesitation:

'When they care to see other visitors, I'm sure Amy would be very glad –'

'Certainly!' his wife added.

'Thank you very much. Of course I knew I could depend on Mrs Reardon to show them kindness in that way. But let me speak frankly of something. My sisters have made quite a friend of Miss Yule, since she was down there last year. Wouldn't that' – he turned to Amy – 'cause you a little awkwardness?'

Amy had difficulty in replying. She kept her eyes on the ground.

'You have no quarrel with your cousin,' remarked Reardon.

'None whatever. It's only my mother and my uncle.'

'I can't imagine Miss Yule having a quarrel with anyone,' said Jasper. Then he added quickly: 'Well, things must shape themselves naturally. We shall see. For the present they will be fully occupied. Of course it's best that they should be. I shall see them every day, and Miss Yule will come pretty often, I dare say.'

Reardon caught Amy's eye, but at once looked away again.

'My word!' exclaimed Milvain, after a moment's meditation. 'It's well this didn't happen a year ago. The girls have no income; only a little cash to go on with. We shall have our work set. It's a precious lucky thing that I have just got a sort of footing.'

Reardon muttered an assent.

'And what are you doing now?' Jasper inquired suddenly.

'Writing a one-volume story.'

'I'm glad to hear that. Any special plan for its publication?'

'No.'

'Then why not offer it to Jedwood? He's publishing a series of one-volume novels. You know of Jedwood, don't you? He was Culpepper's manager; started business about half a year ago, and it looks as if he would do well. He married that woman – what's her name? – Who wrote "Mr Henderson's Wives"?'

'Never heard of it.'

'Nonsense! – Miss Wilkes, of course. Well, she married this fellow Jedwood, and there was a great row about something or other between him and her publishers. Mrs Boston Wright told me all about it. An astonishing woman that; a cyclopædia of the day's small talk. I'm quite a favourite with her; she's promised to help the girls all she can. Well, but I was talking about Jedwood. Why not offer him this book of yours? He's eager to get hold of the new writers. Advertises hugely; he has the whole back page of *The Study* about every other week. I suppose Miss Wilkes's profits are paying for it. He has just given Markland two hundred pounds for a paltry little tale that would scarcely swell out to a volume. Markland told me himself. You know that I've scraped an acquaintance with him? Oh! I suppose I haven't seen you since then. He's a dwarfish fellow with only one eye. Mrs Boston Wright cries him up at every opportunity.'

'Who *is* Mrs Boston Wright?' asked Reardon, laughing impatiently.

'Edits *The English Girl*, you know. She's had an extraordinary life. Was born in Mauritius – no, Ceylon – I forget; some such place. Married a sailor at fifteen. Was shipwrecked somewhere, and only restored to life after terrific efforts; – her story leaves it all rather vague. Then she turns up as a newspaper correspondent at the Cape. Gave up that, and took to some kind of farming, I forget where. Married again (first husband lost in aforementioned shipwreck), this time a Baptist minister, and began to devote herself to soup-kitchens in Liverpool. Husband burned to death, somewhere. She's next discovered in the thick of literary society in London. A wonderful woman, I assure you. Must be nearly fifty, but she looks twenty-five.'

He paused, then added impulsively:

'Let me take you to one of her evenings – nine on Thursday. Do persuade him, Mrs Reardon?'

Reardon shook his head.

'No, no. I should be horribly out of my element.'

'I can't see why. You would meet all sorts of well-known people; those you ought to have met long ago. Better still, let me ask her to send an invitation for both of you. I'm sure you'd like her, Mrs Reardon. There's a good deal of humbug about her, it's true, but some solid qualities as well. No one has a word to say against her. And it's a splendid advertisement to have her for a friend. She'll talk about your books and articles till all is blue.'

Amy gave a questioning look at her husband. But Reardon moved in an uncomfortable way.

'We'll see about it,' he said. 'Some day, perhaps.'

'Let me know whenever you feel disposed. But about Jedwood: I happen to know a man who reads for him.'

'Heavens!' cried Reardon. 'Who *don't* you know?'

'The simplest thing in the world. At present it's a large part of my business to make acquaintances. Why, look you; a man who has to live by miscellaneous writing couldn't get on without a vast variety of acquaintances. One's own brain would soon run dry; a clever fellow knows how to use the brains of other people.'

Amy listened with an unconscious smile which expressed keen interest.

'Oh,' pursued Jasper, 'when did you see Whelpdale last?'

'Haven't seen him for a long time.'

'You don't know what he's doing? The fellow has set up as a "literary adviser." He has an advertisement in *The Study* every week. "To Young Authors and Literary Aspirants" – something of the kind. "Advice given on choice of subjects, MSS. read, corrected, and recommended to publishers. Moderate terms." A fact! And what's more, he made six guineas in the first fortnight; so he says, at all events. Now that's one of the finest jokes I ever heard. A man who can't get anyone to publish his own books makes a living by telling other people how to write!'

'But it's a confounded swindle!'

'Oh, I don't know. He's capable of correcting the grammar of "literary aspirants," and as for recommending to publishers – well, anyone can recommend, I suppose.'

Reardon's indignation yielded to laughter.

'It's not impossible that he may thrive by this kind of thing.'

'Not at all,' assented Jasper.

Shortly after this, he looked at his watch.

'I must be off, my friends. I have something to write before I can go to my truckle-bed, and it'll take me three hours at least. Good-bye, old man. Let me know when your story's finished, and we'll talk about it. And think about Mrs Boston Wright; oh, and about that review in *The Current*. I wish you'd let me do it. Talk it over with your guide, philosopher, and friend.'

He indicated Amy, who laughed in a forced way.

When he was gone, the two sat without speaking for several minutes.

'Do you care to make friends with those girls?' asked Reardon at length.

'I suppose in decency I must call upon them?'

'I suppose so.'

'You may find them very agreeable.'

'Oh yes.'

They conversed with their own thoughts for a while. Then Reardon burst out laughing.

'Well, there's the successful man, you see. Some day he'll live in a mansion, and dictate literary opinions to the universe.'

'How has he offended you?'

'Offended me? Not at all. I am glad of his cheerful prospects.'

'Why should you refuse to go among those people? It might be good for you in several ways.'

'If the chance had come when I was publishing my best work, I dare say I shouldn't have refused. But I certainly shall not present myself as the author of "Margaret Home," and the rubbish I'm now writing.'

'Then you must cease to write rubbish.'

'Yes. I must cease to write altogether.'

'And do what?'

'I wish to Heaven I knew!'

END OF THE FIRST VOLUME

NEW GRUB STREET

Volume 2

Chapter 13

A WARNING

IN the spring list of Mr Jedwood's publications, announcement was made of a new work by Alfred Yule. It was called 'English Prose in the Nineteenth Century,' and consisted of a number of essays (several of which had already seen the light in periodicals) strung into continuity. The final chapter dealt with contemporary writers, more especially those who served to illustrate the author's theme – that journalism is the destruction of prose style: on certain popular writers of the day there was an outpouring of gall which was not likely to be received as though it were sweet ointment. The book met with rather severe treatment in critical columns; it could scarcely be ignored (the safest mode of attack when one's author has no expectant public), and only the most skilful could write of it in a hostile spirit without betraying that some of its strokes had told. An evening newspaper which piqued itself on independence indulged in laughing appreciation of the polemical chapter, and the next day printed a scornful letter from a thinly-disguised correspondent who assailed both book and reviewer. For the moment people talked more of Alfred Yule than they had done since his memorable conflict with Clement Fadge.

The publisher had hoped for this. Mr Jedwood was an energetic and sanguine man, who had entered upon his business with a determination to rival in a year or so the houses which had slowly risen into commanding stability. He had no great capital, but the stroke of fortune which had wedded him to a popular novelist enabled him to count on steady profit from one source, and boundless faith in his own judgment urged him to an initial outlay which made the prudent shake their heads. He talked much of 'the new era,' foresaw revolutions in publishing and bookselling, planned every week a score of untried ventures which should appeal to the democratic generation just maturing; in the meantime, was ready to publish anything which seemed likely to get talked about.

The May number of *The Current*, in its article headed 'Books of the Month,' devoted about half a page to 'English Prose in the Nineteenth Century.' This notice was a consummate example of the flippant style of attack. Flippancy, the most hopeless form of intellectual vice, was a characterising note of Mr Fadge's periodical; his monthly comments on publications were already looked for with eagerness by that growing class of readers who care for nothing but what can be made matter of ridicule. The hostility of other reviewers was awkward and ineffectual compared with this venomous banter, which entertained by showing that in the book under notice there was neither entertainment nor any other kind of interest. To assail an author without increasing the number of his readers is the perfection of journalistic skill, and The Current, had it stood alone, would fully have achieved this end. As it was, silence might have been better tactics. But Mr Fadge knew that his enemy would smart under the poisoned pin-points, and that was something gained.

On the day that The Current appeared, its treatment of Alfred Yule was discussed in Mr Jedwood's private office. Mr Quarmby, who had intimate relations with the publisher, happened to look in just as a young man (one of Mr Jedwood's 'readers') was expressing a doubt whether Fadge himself was the author of the review.

'But there's Fadge's thumb-mark all down the page,' cried Mr Quarmby.

'He inspired the thing, of course; but I rather think it was written by that fellow Milvain.'

'Think so?' asked the publisher.

'Well, I know with certainty that the notice of Markland's novel is his writing, and I have reasons for suspecting that he did Yule's book as well.'

'Smart youngster, that,' remarked Mr Jedwood. 'Who is he, by-the-by?'

'Somebody's illegitimate son, I believe,' replied the source of trustworthy information, with a laugh. 'Denham says he met him in New York a year or two ago, under another name.'

'Excuse me,' interposed Mr Quarmby, 'there's some mistake in all that.'

He went on to state what he knew, from Yule himself, concerning Milvain's history. Though in this instance a corrector,

Mr Quarmby took an opportunity, a few hours later, of inform-
ing Mr Hinks that the attack on Yule in *The Current* was almost
certainly written by young Milvain, with the result that when
the rumour reached Yule's ears it was delivered as an undoubted
and well-known fact.

It was a month prior to this that Milvain made his call upon
Marian Yule, on the Sunday when her father was absent. When
told of the visit, Yule assumed a manner of indifference, but his
daughter understood that he was annoyed. With regard to the
sisters who would shortly be living in London, he merely said
that Marian must behave as discretion directed her. If she wished
to invite the Miss Milvains to St Paul's Crescent, he only
begged that the times and seasons of the household might not be
disturbed.

As her habit was, Marian took refuge in silence. Nothing could
have been more welcome to her than the proximity of Maud and
Dora, but she foresaw that her own home would not be freely
open to them; perhaps it might be necessary to behave with
simple frankness, and let her friends know the embarrassments
of the situation. But that could not be done in the first instance;
the unkindness would seem too great. A day after the arrival of
the girls, she received a note from Dora, and almost at once replied to it by calling at her friends' lodgings. A week after that,
Maud and Dora came to St Paul's Crescent; it was Sunday, and
Mr Yule purposely kept away from home. They had only been once
to the house since then, again without meeting Mr Yule. Marian,
however, visited them at their lodgings frequently; now and then
she met Jasper there. The latter never spoke of her father, and
there was no question of inviting him to repeat his call.

In the end, Marian was obliged to speak on the subject with
her mother. Mrs Yule offered an occasion by asking when the
Miss Milvains were coming again.

'I don't think I shall ever ask them again,' Marian replied.

Her mother understood, and looked troubled.

'I must tell them how it is, that's all,' the girl went on. 'They
are sensible; they won't be offended with me.'

'But your father has never had anything to say against them,'
urged Mrs Yule. 'Not a word to me, Marian. I'd tell you the
truth if he had.'

'It's too disagreeable, all the same. I can't invite them here with pleasure. Father has grown prejudiced against them all, and he won't change. No, I shall just tell them.'

'It's very hard for you,' sighed her mother. 'If I thought I could do any good by speaking – but I can't, my dear.'

'I know it, mother. Let us go on as we did before.'

The day after this, when Yule came home about the hour of dinner, he called Marian's name from within the study. Marian had not left the house to-day; her work had been set, in the shape of a long task of copying from disorderly manuscript. She left the sitting-room in obedience to her father's summons.

'Here's something that will afford you amusement,' he said, holding to her the new number of *The Current*, and indicating the notice of his book.

She read a few lines, then threw the thing on to the table.

'That kind of writing sickens me,' she exclaimed, with anger in her eyes. 'Only base and heartless people can write in that way. You surely won't let it trouble you?'

'Oh, not for a moment,' her father answered, with exaggerated show of calm. 'But I am surprised that you don't see the literary merit of the work. I thought it would distinctly appeal to you.'

There was a strangeness in his voice, as well as in the words, which caused her to look at him inquiringly. She knew him well enough to understand that such a notice would irritate him profoundly; but why should he go out of his way to show it her, and with this peculiar acerbity of manner?

'Why do you say that, father?'

'It doesn't occur to you who may probably have written it?'

She could not miss his meaning; astonishment held her mute for a moment, then she said :

'Surely Mr Fadge wrote it himself?'

'I am told not. I am informed on very good authority that one of his young gentlemen has the credit of it.'

'You refer, of course, to Mr Milvain,' she replied quietly. 'But I think that can't be true.'

He looked keenly at her. He had expected a more decided protest.

'I see no reason for disbelieving it.'

'I see every reason, until I have your evidence.'

This was not at all Marian's natural tone in argument with him. She was wont to be submissive.

'I was told,' he continued, hardening face and voice, 'by someone who had it from Jedwood.'

Yule was conscious of untruth in this statement, but his mood would not allow him to speak ingenuously, and he wished to note the effect upon Marian of what he said. There were two beliefs in him: on the one hand, he recognised Fadge in every line of the writing; on the other, he had a perverse satisfaction in convincing himself that it was Milvain who had caught so successfully the master's manner. He was not the kind of man who can resist an opportunity of justifying, to himself and others, a course into which he has been led by mingled feelings, all more or less unjustifiable.

'How should Jedwood know?' asked Marian.

Yule shrugged his shoulders.

'As if these things didn't get about among editors and publishers!'

'In this case, there's a mistake.'

'And why, pray?' His voice trembled with choler. 'Why need there be a mistake?'

'Because Mr Milvain is quite incapable of reviewing your book in such a spirit.'

'There is *your* mistake, my girl. Milvain will do anything that's asked of him, provided he's well enough paid.'

Marian reflected. When she raised her eyes again they were perfectly calm.

'What has led you to think that?'

'Don't I know the type of man? *Noscitur ex sociis* [18] – have you Latin enough for that?'

'You'll find that you are misinformed,' Marian replied, and therewith went from the room.

She could not trust herself to converse longer. A resentment such as her father had never yet excited in her – such, indeed, as she seldom, if ever, conceived – threatened to force utterance for itself in words which would change the current of her whole life. She saw her father in his worst aspect, and her heart was shaken by an unnatural revolt from him. Let his assurance of what he reported be ever so firm, what right had he to make this use of it? His behaviour was spiteful. Suppose he entertained suspicions which seemed to make it his duty to warn her against Milvain, this was not the way to go about it. A father actuated by simple motives of affection would never speak and look thus.

It was the hateful spirit of literary rancour that ruled him; the spirit that made people eager to believe all evil, that blinded and maddened. Never had she felt so strongly the unworthiness of the existence to which she was condemned. That contemptible review, and now her father's ignoble passion – such things were enough to make all literature appear a morbid excrescence upon human life.

Forgetful of the time, she sat in her bedroom until a knock at the door, and her mother's voice, admonished her that dinner was waiting. An impulse all but caused her to say that she would rather not go down for the meal, that she wished to be left alone. But this would be weak peevishness. She just looked at the glass to see that her face bore no unwonted signs, and descended to take her place as usual.

Throughout the dinner there passed no word of conversation. Yule was at his blackest; he gobbled a few mouthfuls, then occupied himself with the evening paper. On rising, he said to Marian:

'Have you copied the whole of that?'

The tone would have been uncivil if addressed to an impertinent servant.

'Not much more than half,' was the cold reply.

'Can you finish it to-night?'

'I'm afraid not. I am going out.'

'Then I must do it myself.'

And he went to the study.

Mrs Yule was in an anguish of nervousness.

'What is it, dear?' she asked of Marian, in a pleading whisper. 'Oh, don't quarrel with your father! Don't!'

'I can't be a slave, mother, and I can't be treated unjustly.'

'What is it? Let me go and speak to him.'

'It's no use. We can't live in terror.'

For Mrs Yule this was unimaginable disaster. She had never

dreamt that Marian, the still, gentle Marian, could be driven to revolt. And it had come with the suddenness of a thunder-clap. She wished to ask what had taken place between father and daughter in the brief interview before dinner; but Marian gave her no chance, quitting the room upon those last trembling words.

The girl had resolved to visit her friends, the sisters, and tell them that in future they must never come to see her at home. But it was no easy thing for her to stifle her conscience, and leave her father to toil over that copying which had need of being finished. Not her will, but her exasperated feeling, had replied to him that she would not do the work; already it astonished her that she had really spoken such words. And as the throbbing of her pulses subsided, she saw more clearly into the motives of this wretched tumult which possessed her. Her mind was harassed with a fear lest in defending Milvain she had spoken foolishly. Had he not himself said to her that he might be guilty of base things, just to make his way? Perhaps it was the intolerable pain of imagining that he had already made good his words, which robbed her of self-control and made her meet her father's rudeness with defiance.

Impossible to carry out her purpose; she could not deliberately leave the house and spend some hours away with the thought of such wrath and misery left behind her. Gradually she was return-ing to her natural self; fear and penitence were chill at her heart.

She went down to the study, tapped, and entered.

'Father, I said something that I did not really mean. Of course I shall go on with the copying and finish it as soon as possible.'

'You will do nothing of the kind, my girl.' He was in his usual place, already working at Marian's task; he spoke in a low, thick voice. 'Spend your evening as you choose, I have no need of you.'

'I behaved very ill-temperedly. Forgive me, father.'

'Have the goodness to go away. You hear me?'

His eyes were inflamed, and his discoloured teeth showed themselves savagely. Marian durst not, really durst not approach him. She hesitated, but once more a sense of hateful injustice moved within her, and she went away as quietly as she had entered.

She said to herself that now it was her perfect right to go whither she would. But the freedom was only in theory; her submissive and timid nature kept her at home – and upstairs in her own room : for, if she went to sit with her mother, of necessity she must talk about what had happened, and that she felt unable to do. Some friend to whom she could unbosom all her sufferings would now have been very precious to her, but Maud and Dora were her only intimates, and to them she might not make the full confession which gives solace.

Mrs Yule did not venture to intrude upon her daughter's privacy. That Marian neither went out nor showed herself in the house proved her troubled state, but the mother had no confidence in her power to comfort. At the usual time she presented herself in the study with her husband's coffee; the face which was for an instant turned to her did not invite conversation, but distress obliged her to speak.

'Why are you cross with Marian, Alfred?'

'You had better ask what she means by her extraordinary behaviour.'

A word of harsh rebuff was the most she had expected. Thus encouraged, she timidly put another question.

'How has she behaved?'

'I suppose you have ears?'

'But wasn't there something before that? You spoke so angry to her.'

'Spoke so angry, did I? She is out, I suppose?'

'No, she hasn't gone out.'

'That'll do. Don't disturb me any longer.'

She did not venture to linger.

The breakfast next morning seemed likely to pass without any interchange of words. But when Yule was pushing back his chair, Marian – who looked pale and ill – addressed a question to him about the work she would ordinarily have pursued to-day at the Reading-room. He answered in a matter-of-fact tone, and for a few minutes they talked on the subject much as at any other time. Half an hour after, Marian set forth for the Museum in the usual way. Her father stayed at home.

It was the end of the episode for the present. Marian felt that the best thing would be to ignore what had happened, as her father evidently purposed doing. She had asked his forgiveness, and it was harsh in him to have repelled her; but by now she was able once more to take into consideration all his trials and toils, his embittered temper and the new wound he had received. That he should resume his wonted manner was sufficient evidence of regret on his part. Gladly she would have unsaid her resentful words; she had been guilty of a childish outburst of temper, and perhaps had prepared worse sufferings for the future.

And yet, perhaps it was as well that her father should be warned. She was not all submission, he might try her beyond endurance; there might come a day when perforce she must stand face to face with him, and make it known she had her own claims upon life. It was as well he should hold that possibility in view.

This evening no work was expected of her. Not long after dinner she prepared for going out; to her mother she mentioned she should be back about ten o'clock.

'Give my regards to them, dear – if you like to,' said Mrs Yule just above her breath.

'Certainly I will.'

Chapter 14

RECRUITS

MARIAN walked to the nearest point of Camden Road, and there waited for an omnibus, which conveyed her to within easy reach of the Street where Maud and Dora Milvain had their lodgings. This was at the north-east of Regent's Park and no great distance from Mornington Road, where Jasper still dwelt.

On learning that the young ladies were at home and alone, she ascended to the second floor and knocked.

'That's right!' exclaimed Dora's pleasant voice, as the door opened and the visitor showed herself. And then came the friendly greeting which warmed Marian's heart, the greeting which until lately no house in London could afford her.

The girls looked oddly out of place in this second-floor sitting-room, with its vulgar furniture and paltry ornaments. Maud especially so, for her fine figure was well displayed by the dress of mourning, and her pale, handsome face had as little congruence as possible with a background of humble circumstances. Dora impressed one as a simpler nature, but she too had distinctly the note of refinement which was out of harmony with these surroundings. They occupied only two rooms, the sleeping-chamber being double-bedded; they purchased food for themselves and prepared their own meals, excepting dinner. During the first week a good many tears were shed by both of them; it was not easy to transfer themselves from the comfortable country home to this bare corner of lodgers' London. Maud, as appeared at the first glance, was less disposed than her sister to make the best of things; her countenance wore an expression rather of discontent than of sorrow, and she did not talk with the same readiness as Dora.

On the round table lay a number of books; when disturbed, the sisters had been engaged in studious reading.

'I'm not sure that I do right in coming again so soon,' said Marian as she took off her things. 'Your time is precious.'

'So are you,' replied Dora, laughing. 'It's only under protest that we work in the evening when we have been hard at it all day.'

'We have news for you, too,' said Maud, who sat languidly on an uneasy chair.

'Good, I hope?'

'Someone called to see us yesterday. I dare say you can guess who it was.'

'Amy, perhaps?'

'Yes.'

'And how did you like her?'

The sisters seemed to have a difficulty in answering. Dora was the first to speak.

'We thought she was sadly out of spirits. Indeed she told us that she hasn't been very well lately. But I think we shall like her if we come to know her better.'

'It was rather awkward, Marian,' the elder sister explained. 'We felt obliged to say something about Mr Reardon's books, but we haven't read any of them yet, you know, so I just said that I hoped soon to read his new novel. "I suppose you have seen reviews of it?" she asked at once. Of course I ought to have had the courage to say no, but I admitted that I had seen one or two – Jasper showed us them. She looked very much annoyed, and after that we didn't find much to talk about.'

'The reviews are very disagreeable,' said Marian with a troubled face. 'I have read the book since I saw you the other day, and I'm afraid it isn't any good, but I have seen many worse novels more kindly reviewed.'

'Jasper says it's because Mr Reardon has no friends among the journalists.'

'Still,' replied Marian, 'I'm afraid they couldn't have given the book much praise, if they wrote honestly. Did Amy ask you to go and see her?'

'Yes, but she said it was uncertain how long they would be living at their present address. And really we can't feel sure whether we should be welcome or not just now.'

Marian listened with bent head. She too had to make known to her friends that they were not welcome in her own home; but she knew not how to utter words which would sound so unkind.

'Your brother,' she said after a pause, 'will soon find suitable friends for you.'

'Before long,' replied Dora, with a look of amusement, 'he's going to take us to call on Mrs Boston Wright. I hardly thought he was serious at first, but he says he really means it.'

Marian grew more and more silent. At home she had felt that it would not be difficult to explain her troubles to these sympathetic girls, but now the time had come for speaking, she was oppressed by shame and anxiety. True, there was no absolute necessity for making the confession this evening, and if she chose to resist her father's prejudice, things might even go on in a seemingly natural way. But the loneliness of her life had developed in her a sensitiveness which could not endure situations such as the present; difficulties which are of small account to people who take their part in active social life, harassed her to the destruction of all peace. Dora was not long in noticing the dejected mood which had come upon her friend.

'What's troubling you, Marian?'

'Something I can hardly bear to speak of. Perhaps it will be the end of your friendship for me, and I should find it very hard to go back to my old solitude.'

The girls gazed at her, in doubt at first whether she spoke seriously.

'What *can* you mean?' Dora exclaimed. 'What crime have you been committing?'

Maud, who leaned with her elbows on the table, searched Marian's face curiously, but said nothing.

'Has Mr Milvain shown you the new number of *The Current*?' Marian went on to ask.

They replied with a negative, and Maud added:

'He has nothing in it this month, except a review.'

'A review?' repeated Marian in a low voice.

'Yes; of somebody's novel.'

'Markland's,' supplied Dora.

Marian drew a breath, but remained for a moment with her eyes cast down.

'Do go on, dear,' urged Dora. 'What ever are you going to tell us?'

'There's a notice of father's book,' continued the other, 'a

very ill-natured one; it's written by the editor, Mr Fadge. Father
and he have been very unfriendly for a long time. Perhaps Mr
Milvain has told you something about it?'

Dora replied that he had.

'I don't know how it is in other professions,' Marian resumed,
'but I hope there is less envy, hatred and malice than in this of
ours. The name of literature is often made hateful to me by the
things I hear and read. My father has never been very fortunate,
and many things have happened to make him bitter against the
men who succeed; he has often quarrelled with people who were
at first his friends, but never so seriously with anyone as with Mr
Fadge. His feeling of enmity goes so far that it includes even
those who are in any way associated with Mr Fadge. I am sorry
to say' – she looked with painful anxiety from one to the other of
her hearers – 'this has turned him against your brother, and –'

Her voice was checked by agitation.

'We were afraid of this,' said Dora, in a tone of sympathy.

'Jasper feared it might be the case,' added Maud, more coldly,
though with friendliness.

'Why I speak of it at all,' Marian hastened to say, 'is because I
am so afraid it should make a difference between yourselves and
me.'

'Oh! don't think that!' Dora exclaimed.

'I am so ashamed,' Marian went on in an uncertain tone, 'but I
think it will be better if I don't ask you to come and see me. It
sounds ridiculous; it is ridiculous and shameful. I couldn't complain if you refused to have anything more to do with me.'

'Don't let it trouble you,' urged Maud, with perhaps a trifle
more of magnanimity in her voice than was needful. 'We quite
understand. Indeed, it shan't make any difference to us.'

But Marian had averted her face, and could not meet these
assurances with any show of pleasure. Now that the step was
taken she felt that her behaviour had been very weak. Unreasonable harshness such as her father's ought to have been met
more steadily; she had no right to make it an excuse for such
incivility to her friends. Yet only in some such way as this could
she make known to Jasper Milvain how her father regarded him,
which she felt it necessary to do. Now his sisters would tell him,
and henceforth there would be a clear understanding on both

sides. That state of things was painful to her, but it was better than ambiguous relations.

'Jasper is very sorry about it,' said Dora, glancing rapidly at Marian.

'But his connection with Mr Fadge came about in such a natural way,' added the eldest sister. 'And it was impossible for him to refuse opportunities.'

'Impossible; I know,' Marian replied earnestly. 'Don't think that I wish to justify my father. But I can understand him, and it must be very difficult for you to do so. You can't know, as I do, how intensely he has suffered in these wretched, ignoble quarrels. If only you will let me come here still, in the same way, and still be as friendly to me. My home has never been a place to which I could have invited friends with any comfort, even if I had had any to invite. There were always reasons – but I can't speak of them.'

'My dear Marian,' appealed Dora, 'don't distress yourself so ! Do believe that nothing whatever has happened to change our feeling to you. Has there, Maud?'

'Nothing whatever. We are not unreasonable girls, Marian.'

'I am more grateful to you than I can say.'

It had seemed as if Marian must give way to the emotions which all but choked her voice; she overcame them, however, and presently was able to talk in pretty much her usual way, though when she smiled it was but faintly. Maud tried to lead her thoughts in another direction by speaking of work in which she and Dora were engaged. Already the sisters were doing a new piece of compilation for Messrs Jolly and Monk; it was more exacting than their initial task for the book-market, and would take a much longer time.

A couple of hours went by, and Marian had just spoken of taking her leave, when a man's step was heard rapidly ascending the nearest flight of stairs.

'Here's Jasper,' remarked Dora, and in a moment there sounded a short, sharp summons at the door.

Jasper it was; he came in with radiant face, his eyes blinking before the lamp-light.

'Well, girls ! Ha ! how do you do, Miss Yule? I had just the vaguest sort of expectation that you might be here. It seemed a likely night; I don't know why. I say, Dora, we really must get two or three decent easy-chairs for your room. I've seen some outside a second-hand furniture shop in Hampstead Road, about six shillings apiece. There's no sitting on chairs such as these.'

That on which he tried to dispose himself, when he had flung aside his trappings, creaked and shivered ominously.

'You hear? I shall come plump on to the floor, if I don't mind. My word, what a day I have had! I've just been trying what I really could do in one day if I worked my hardest. Now just listen; it deserves to be chronicled for the encouragement of aspiring youth. I got up at 7.30, and whilst I breakfasted I read through a volume I had to review. By 10.30 the review was written – three-quarters of a column of the *Evening Budget*.'

'Who is the unfortunate author?' interrupted Maud, caustically.

'Not unfortunate at all. I had to crack him up; otherwise I couldn't have done the job so quickly. It's the easiest thing in the world to write laudation; only an inexperienced grumbler would declare it was easier to find fault. The book was Billington's "Vagaries"; pompous idiocy, of course, but he lives in a big house and gives dinners. Well, from 10.30 to 11, I smoked a cigar and reflected, feeling that the day wasn't badly begun. At eleven, I was ready to write my Saturday *causerie* for the *Will o' the Wisp*; it took me till close upon one o'clock, which was rather too long. I can't afford more than an hour and a half for that job. At one, I rushed out to a dirty little eating-house in Hampstead Road. Was back again by a quarter to two, having in the meantime sketched a paper for *The West End*. Pipe in mouth, I sat down to leisurely artistic work; by five, half the paper was done; the other half remains for to-morrow. From five to half-past I read four newspapers and two magazines, and from half-past to a quarter to six I jotted down several ideas that had come to me whilst reading. At six I was again in the dirty eating-house, satisfying a ferocious hunger. Home once more at 6.45, and for two hours wrote steadily at a long affair I have in hand for *The Current*. Then I came here, thinking hard all the way. What say you to this? Have I earned a night's repose?'

'And what's the value of it all?' asked Maud.

'Probably from ten to twelve guineas, if I calculated.'

'I meant, what was the literary value of it,' said his sister, with a smile.

'Equal to that of the contents of a mouldy nut.'

'Pretty much what I thought.'

'Oh, but it answers the purpose,' urged Dora, 'and it does no one any harm.'

'Honest journey-work!' cried Jasper. 'There are few men in London capable of such a feat. Many a fellow could write more in quantity, but they couldn't command my market. It's rubbish, but rubbish of a very special kind, of fine quality.'

Marian had not yet spoken, save a word or two in reply to Jasper's greeting; now and then she just glanced at him, but for the most part her eyes were cast down. Now Jasper addressed her.

'A year ago, Miss Yule, I shouldn't have believed myself capable of such activity. In fact, I wasn't capable of it then.'

'You think such work won't be too great a strain upon you?' she asked.

'Oh, this isn't a specimen day, you know. To-morrow I shall very likely do nothing but finish my *West End* article, in an easy two or three hours. There's no knowing; I might perhaps keep up the high pressure if I tried. But then I couldn't dispose of all the work. Little by little – or perhaps rather quicker than that – I shall extend my scope. For instance, I should like to do two or three leaders a week for one of the big dailies. I can't attain unto that just yet.'

'Not political leaders?'

'By no means. That's not my line. The kind of thing in which one makes a column out of what would fill six lines of respectable prose. You call a cigar a "convoluted weed," and so on, you know; that passes for facetiousness. I've never really tried my hand at that style yet; I shouldn't wonder if I managed it brilliantly. Some day I'll write a few exercises; just take two lines of some good prose-writer, and expand them into twenty, in half a dozen different ways. Excellent mental gymnastics!'

Marian listened to his flow of talk for a few minutes longer, then took the opportunity of a brief silence to rise and put on her hat. Jasper observed her, but without rising; he looked at his sisters in a hesitating way. At length he stood up, and declared that he too must be off. This coincidence had happened once before when he met Marian here in the evening.

'At all events, you won't do any more work to-night,' said Dora.

'No; I shall read a page of something or other over a glass of whisky, and seek the sleep of a man who has done his duty.'

'Why the whisky?' asked Maud.

'Do you grudge me such poor solace?'

'I don't see the need of it.'

'Nonsense, Maud!' exclaimed her sister. 'He needs a little stimulant when he works so hard.'

Each of the girls gave Marian's hand a significant pressure as she took leave of them, and begged her to come again as soon as she had a free evening. There was gratitude in her eyes.

The evening was clear, and not very cold.

'It's rather late for you to go home,' said Jasper, as they left the house. 'May I walk part of the way with you?'

Marian replied with a low 'Thank you.'

'I think you get on pretty well with the girls, don't you?'

'I hope they are as glad of my friendship as I am of theirs.'

'Pity to see them in a place like that, isn't it? They ought to have a good house, with plenty of servants. It's bad enough for a civilised man to have to rough it, but I hate to see women living in a sordid way. Don't you think they could both play their part in a drawing-room, with a little experience?'

'Surely there's no doubt of it.'

'Maud would look really superb if she were handsomely dressed. She hasn't a common face, by any means. And Dora is pretty, I think. Well, they shall go and see some people before long. The difficulty is, one doesn't like it to be known that they live in such a crib; but I daren't advise them to go in for expense. One can't be sure that it would repay them, though – Now, in my own case, if I could get hold of a few thousand pounds I should know how to use it with the certainty of return; it would save me, probably, a clear ten years of life; I mean, I should go at a jump to what I shall be ten years hence without the help of money. But they have such a miserable little bit of capital, and everything is still so uncertain. One daren't speculate under the circumstances.'

Marian made no reply.

'You think I talk of nothing but money?' Jasper said suddenly, looking down into her face.

'I know too well what it means to be without money.'

'Yes, but – you do just a little despise me?'

'Indeed, I don't, Mr Milvain.'

'If that is sincere, I'm very glad. I take it in a friendly sense. I *am* rather despicable, you know; it's part of my business to be so. But a friend needn't regard that. There is the man apart from his necessities.'

The silence was then unbroken till they came to the lower end of Park Street, the junction of roads which lead to Hampstead, to Highgate, and to Holloway.

'Shall you take an omnibus?' Jasper asked.

She hesitated.

'Or will you give me the pleasure of walking on with you? You are tired, perhaps?'

'Not the least.'

For the rest of her answer she moved forward, and they crossed into the obscurity of Camden Road.

'Shall I be doing wrong, Mr Milvain,' Marian began in a very low voice, 'if I ask you about the authorship of something in this month's *Current*?'

'I'm afraid I know what you refer to. There's no reason why I shouldn't answer a question of the kind.'

'It was Mr Fadge himself who reviewed my father's book?'

'It was – confound him ! I don't know another man who could have done the thing so vilely well.'

'I suppose he was only replying to my father's attack upon him and his friends.'

'Your father's attack is honest and straightforward and justifiable and well put. I read that chapter of his book with huge satisfaction. But has anyone suggested that another than Fadge was capable of that masterpiece?'

'Yes. I am told that Mr Jedwood, the publisher, has somehow made a mistake.'

'Jedwood? And what mistake?'

'Father heard that you were the writer.'

'I?' Jasper stopped short. They were in the rays of a

street-lamp, and could see each other's faces. 'And he believes that?'

'I'm afraid so.'

'And *you* believe – believed it?'

'Not for a moment.'

'I shall write a note to Mr Yule.'

Marian was silent a while, then said:

'Wouldn't it be better if you found a way of letting Mr Jedwood know the truth?'

'Perhaps you are right.'

Jasper was very grateful for the suggestion. In that moment he had reflected how rash it would be to write to Alfred Yule on such a subject, with whatever prudence in expressing himself. Such a letter, coming under the notice of the great Fadge, might do its writer serious harm.

'Yes, you are right,' he repeated. 'I'll stop that rumour at its source. I can't guess how it started; for aught I know, some enemy hath done this, though I don't quite discern the motive. Thank you very much for telling me, and still more for refusing to believe that I could treat Mr Yule in that way, even as a matter of business. When I said that I was despicable, I didn't mean that I could sink quite to such a point as that. If only because it was your father –'

He checked himself, and they walked on for several yards without speaking.

'In that case,' Jasper resumed at length, 'your father doesn't think of me in a very friendly way?'

'He scarcely could –'

'No, no. And I quite understand that the mere fact of my working for Fadge would prejudice him against me. But that's no reason, I hope, why you and I shouldn't be friends?'

'I hope not.'

'I don't know that my friendship is worth much,' Jasper continued, talking into the upper air, a habit of his when he discussed his own character. 'I shall go on as I have begun and fight for some of the good things of life. But *your* friendship is valuable. If I am sure of it, I shall be at all events within sight of the better ideals.'

Marian walked on with her eyes upon the ground. To her

surprise she discovered presently that they had all but reached St Paul's Crescent.

'Thank you for having come so far,' she said pausing.

'Ah, you are nearly home. Why, it seems only a few minutes since we left the girls. Now I'll run back to the whisky of which Maud disapproves.'

'May it do you good !' said Marian with a laugh.

A speech of this kind seemed unusual upon her lips. Jasper smiled as he held her hand and regarded her.

'Then you *can* speak in a joking way ?'

'Do I seem so very dull ?'

'Dull, by no means. But sage and sober and reticent – and exactly what I like in my friend, because it contrasts with my own habits. All the better that merriment lies below it. Goodnight, Miss Yule.'

He strode off, and in a minute or two turned his head to look at the slight figure passing into darkness.

Marian's hand trembled as she tried to insert her latchkey. When she had closed the door very quietly behind her she went to the sitting-room; Mrs Yule was just laying aside the sewing on which she had occupied herself throughout the lonely evening.

'I'm rather late,' said the girl, in a voice of subdued joyousness.

'Yes; I was getting a little uneasy, dear.'

'Oh, there's no danger.'

'You have been enjoying yourself, I can see.'

'I have had a pleasant evening.'

In the retrospect it seemed the pleasantest she had yet spent with her friends, though she had set out in such a different mood. Her mind was relieved of two anxieties; she felt sure that the girls had not taken ill what she told them, and there was no longer the least doubt concerning the authorship of that review in *The Current*.

She could confess to herself now that the assurance from Jasper's lips was not superfluous. He *might* have weighed profit against other considerations, and have written in that way of her father; she had not felt that absolute confidence which defies every argument from human frailty. And now she asked herself if faith of that unassailable kind is ever possible; is it not only the poet's dream, the far ideal?

Marian often went thus far in her speculation. Her candour was allied with clear insight into the possibilities of falsehood; she was not readily the victim of illusion; thinking much, and speaking little, she had not come to her twenty-third year without perceiving what a distance lay between a girl's dream of life as it might be and life as it is. Had she invariably disclosed her thoughts, she would have earned the repute of a very sceptical and slightly cynical person.

But with what rapturous tumult of the heart she could abandon herself to a belief in human virtues when their suggestion seemed to promise her a future of happiness!

Alone in her room she sat down only to think of Jasper Milvain, and extract from the memory of his words, his looks, new sustenance for her hungry heart. Jasper was the first man who had ever evinced a man's interest in her. Until she met him she had not known a look of compliment or a word addressed to her emotions. He was as far as possible from representing the lover of her imagination, but from the day of that long talk in the fields near Wattleborough the thought of him had supplanted dreams. On that day she said to herself: I could love him if he cared to seek my love. Premature, perhaps; why yes, but one who is starving is not wont to feel reluctance at the suggestion of food. The first man who had approached her with display of feeling and energy and youthful self-confidence; handsome too, it seemed to her. Her womanhood went eagerly to meet him.

Since then she had made careful study of his faults. Each conversation had revealed to her new weakness and follies. With the result that her love had grown to a reality.

He was so human, and a youth of all but monastic seclusion had prepared her to love the man who aimed with frank energy at the joys of life. A taint of pedantry would have repelled her. She did not ask for high intellect or great attainments; but vivacity, courage, determination to succeed were delightful to her senses. Her ideal would not have been a literary man at all; certainly not a man likely to be prominent in journalism; rather a man of action, one who had no restraints of commerce or official routine. But in Jasper she saw the qualities that attracted her apart from the accidents of his position. Ideal personages do not descend to girls who have to labour at the British Museum; it seemed a marvel to her, and of good augury, that even such a man as Jasper should have crossed her path.

It was as though years had passed since their first meeting. Upon her return to London had followed such long periods of hopelessness. Yet whenever they encountered each other he had look and speech for her with which surely he did not greet every woman. From the first his way of regarding her had shown frank interest. And at length had come the confession of his 'respect,' his desire to be something more to her than a mere acquaintance. It was scarcely possible that he should speak as he several times had of late if he did not wish to draw her towards him.

That was the hopeful side of her thoughts. It was easy to forget for a time those words of his which one might think were spoken as distinct warning; but they crept into the memory, unwelcome, importunate, as soon as imagination had built its palace of joy. Why did he always recur to the subject of money? 'I shall allow nothing to come in my way;' he once said that as if meaning, 'certainly not a love affair with a girl who is penniless.' He emphasised the word 'friend,' as if to explain that he offered and asked nothing more than friendship.

But it only meant that he would not be in haste to declare himself. Of a certainty there was conflict between his ambition and his love, but she recognised her power over him and exulted in it. She had observed his hesitancy this evening, before he rose to accompany her from the house; her heart laughed within her as the desire drew him. And henceforth such meetings would be frequent, with each one her influence would increase. How kindly fate had dealt with her in bringing Maud and Dora to London!

It was within his reach to marry a woman who would bring him wealth. He had that in mind; she understood it too well. But not one moment's advantage would she relinquish. He must choose her in her poverty, and be content with what his talents could earn for him. Her love gave her the right to demand this sacrifice; let him ask for her love, and the sacrifice would no longer seem one, so passionately would she reward him.

He would ask it. To-night she was full of a rich confidence, partly, no doubt, the result of reaction from her miseries. He had said at parting that her character was so well suited to his; that he liked her. And then he had pressed her hand so warmly. Before long he would ask her love.

The unhoped was all but granted her. She could labour on in the valley of the shadow of books, for a ray of dazzling sunshine might at any moment strike into its musty gloom.

Chapter 15

THE LAST RESOURCE

THE past twelve months had added several years to Edwin Reardon's seeming age; at thirty-three he would generally have been taken for forty. His bearing, his personal habits, were no longer those of a young man; he walked with a stoop and pressed noticeably on the stick he carried; it was rare for him to show the countenance which tells of present cheerfulness or glad onward-looking; there was no spring in his step; his voice had fallen to a lower key, and often he spoke with that hesitation in choice of words which may be noticed in persons whom defeat has made self-distrustful. Ceaseless perplexity and dread gave a wandering, sometimes, a wild, expression to his eyes.

He seldom slept, in the proper sense of the word; as a rule, he was conscious all through the night of 'a kind of fighting' [19] between physical weariness and wakeful toil of the mind. It often happened that some wholly imaginary obstacle in the story he was writing kept him under a sense of effort throughout the dark hours; now and again he woke, reasoned with himself, and remembered clearly that the torment was without cause, but the short relief thus afforded soon passed in the recollection of real distress. In his unsoothing slumber he talked aloud, frequently wakening Amy; generally he seemed to be holding a dialogue with someone who had imposed an intolerable task upon him; he protested passionately, appealed, argued in the strangest way about the injustice of what was demanded. Once Amy heard him begging for money – positively begging, like some poor wretch in the street; it was horrible, and made her shed tears; when he asked what he had been saying, she could not bring herself to tell him.

When the striking clocks summoned him remorselessly to rise and work he often reeled with dizziness. It seemed to him that the greatest happiness attainable would be to creep into some dark, warm corner, out of sight and memory of men, and lie there torpid, with a blessed half-consciousness that death was slowly overcoming him. Of all the sufferings collected into each four-and-twenty hours this of rising to a new day was the worst.

The one-volume story which he had calculated would take him four or five weeks was with difficulty finished in two months. March winds made an invalid of him; at one time he was threatened with bronchitis, and for several days had to abandon even the effort to work. In previous winters he had been wont to undergo a good deal of martyrdom from the London climate, but never in such a degree as now; mental illness seemed to have enfeebled his body.

It was strange that he succeeded in doing work of any kind, for he had no hope from the result. This one last effort he would make, just to complete the undeniableness of his failure, and then literature should be thrown behind him; what other pursuit was possible to him he knew not, but perhaps he might discover some mode of earning a livelihood. Had it been a question of gaining a pound a week, as in the old days, he might have hoped to obtain some clerkship like that at the hospital, where no commercial experience or aptitude was demanded; but in his present position such an income would be useless. Could he take Amy and the child to live in a garret? On less than a hundred a year it was scarcely possible to maintain outward decency. Already his own clothing began to declare him poverty-stricken, and but for gifts from her mother Amy would have reached the like pass. They lived in dread of the pettiest casual expense, for the day of pennilessness was again approaching.

Amy was oftener from home than had been her custom. Occasionally she went away soon after breakfast, and spent the whole day at her mother's house. 'It saves food,' she said with a bitter laugh, when Reardon once expressed surprise that she should be going again so soon.

'And gives you an opportunity of bewailing your hard fate,' he returned coldly.

The reproach was ignoble, and he could not be surprised that Amy left the house without another word to him. Yet he resented that, as he had resented her sorrowful jest. The feeling of unmanliness in his own position tortured him into a mood of perversity. Through the day he wrote only a few lines, and on Amy's return he resolved not to speak to her. There was a sense of repose in this change of attitude; he encouraged himself in the view that Amy was treating him with cruel neglect. She, surprised that her friendly questions elicited no answer, looked into his face and saw a sullen anger of which hitherto Reardon had never seemed capable. Her indignation took fire, and she left him to himself.

For a day or two he persevered in his muteness, uttering a word only when it could not be avoided. Amy was at first so resentful that she contemplated leaving him to his ill-temper and dwelling at her mother's house until he chose to recall her. But his face grew so haggard in fixed misery that compassion at length prevailed over her injured pride. Late in the evening she went to the study, and found him sitting unoccupied.

'Edwin –'

'What do you want?' he asked indifferently.

'Why are you behaving to me like this?'

'Surely it makes no difference to you how I behave? You can easily forget that I exist, and live your own life.'

'What have I done to make this change in you?'

'Is it a change?'

'You know it is.'

'How did I behave before?' he asked, glancing at her.

'Like yourself – kindly and gently.'

'If I always did so, in spite of things that might have embittered another man's temper, I think it deserved some return of kindness from you.'

'What "things" do you mean?'

'Circumstances for which neither of us is to blame.'

'I am not conscious of having failed in kindness,' said Amy, distantly.

'Then that only shows that you have forgotten your old self, and utterly changed in your feeling to me. When we first came to live here could you have imagined yourself leaving me alone for long, miserable days, just because I was suffering under misfortunes? You have shown too plainly that you don't care to give me the help even of a kind word. You get away from me as often as you can, as if to remind me that we have no longer any interests in common. Other people are your confidants; you speak of me to them as if I were purposely dragging you down into a mean condition.'

'How can you know what I say about you?'

'Isn't it true?' he asked, flashing an angry glance at her.

'It is not true. Of course I have talked to mother about our difficulties; how could I help it?'

'And to other people.'

'Not in a way that you could find fault with.'

'In a way that makes me seem contemptible to them. You show them that I have made you poor and unhappy, and you are glad to have their sympathy.'

'What you mean is, that I oughtn't to see anyone. There's no other way of avoiding such a reproach as this. So long as I don't laugh and sing before people, and assure them that things couldn't be more hopeful, I shall be asking for their sympathy, and against you. I can't understand your unreasonableness.'

'I'm afraid there is very little in me that you can understand. So long as my prospects seemed bright, you could sympathise readily enough; as soon as ever they darkened, something came between us. Amy, you haven't done your duty. Your love hasn't stood the test as it should have done. You have given me no help; besides the burden of cheerless work I have had to bear that of your growing coldness. I can't remember one instance when you have spoken to me as a wife might – a wife who was something more than a man's housekeeper.'

The passion in his voice and the harshness of the accusation made her unable to reply.

'You said rightly,' he went on, 'that I have always been kind and gentle. I never thought I could speak to you, or feel to you, in any other way. But I have undergone too much, and you have deserted me. Surely it was too soon to do that. So long as I endeavoured my utmost, and loved you the same as ever, you might have remembered all you once said to me. You might have given me help, but you haven't cared to.'

The impulses which had part in this outbreak were numerous and complex. He felt all that he expressed, but at the same time it seemed to him that he had the choice between two ways of uttering his emotion, the tenderly appealing and the sternly reproachful; he took the latter course because it was less natural to him than the former. His desire was to impress Amy with the bitter intensity of his sufferings; pathos and loving words seemed to have lost their power upon her, but perhaps if he yielded to that other form of passion she would be shaken out of her coldness. The stress of injured love is always tempted to speech which seems its contradiction. Reardon had the strangest mixture of pain and pleasure in flinging out these first words of wrath that he had ever addressed to Amy; they consoled him under the humiliating sense of his weakness, and yet he watched with dread his wife's countenance as she listened to him. He hoped to cause her pain equal to his own, for then it would be in his power at once to throw off this disguise, and soothe her with every softest word his heart could suggest. That she had really ceased to love him he could not, durst not, believe; but his nature demanded frequent assurance of affection. Amy had abandoned too soon the caresses of their ardent time; she was absorbed in her maternity, and thought it enough to be her husband's friend. Ashamed to make appeal directly for the tenderness she no longer offered, he accused her of utter indifference, of abandoning him and all but betraying him, that in self-defence she might show what really was in her heart.

But Amy made no movement towards him.

'How can you say that I have deserted you?' she returned, with cold indignation. 'When did I refuse to share your poverty? When did I grumble at what we have had to go through?'

'Ever since the troubles really began you have let me know what your thoughts were, even if you didn't speak them. You have never shared my lot willingly. I can't recall one word of encouragement from you, but many, many which made the struggle harder for me.'

'Then it would be better for you if I went away altogether, and left you free to do the best for yourself. If that is what you mean by all this, why not say it plainly? I won't be a burden to you. Someone will give me a home.'

'And you would leave me without regret? Your only care would be that you were still bound to me?'

'You must think of me what you like. I don't care to defend myself.'

'You won't admit, then, that I have anything to complain of? I seem to you simply in a bad temper without a cause?'

'To tell you the truth, that's just what I do think. I came here to ask what I had done that you were angry with me, and you break out furiously with all sorts of vague reproaches. You have much to endure, I know that, but it's no reason why you should turn against me. I have never neglected my duty. Is the duty all on my side? I believe there are very few wives who would be as patient as I have been.'

Reardon gazed at her for a moment, then turned away. The distance between them was greater than he had thought, and now he repented of having given way to an impulse so alien to his true feelings; anger only estranged her, whereas by speech of a different kind he might have won the caress for which he hungered.

Amy, seeing that he would say nothing more, left him to himself.

It grew late in the night. The fire had gone out, but Reardon still sat in the cold room. Thoughts of self-destruction were again haunting him, as they had done during the black months of last year. If he had lost Amy's love, and all through the mental impotence which would make it hard for him even to earn bread, why should he still live? Affection for his child had no weight with him; it was Amy's child rather than his, and he had more fear than pleasure in the prospect of Willie's growing to manhood.

He had just heard the workhouse clock strike two when, without the warning of a footstep, the door opened. Amy came in; she wore her dressing-gown, and her hair was arranged for the night.

'Why do you stay here?' she asked.

It was not the same voice as before. He saw that her eyes were red and swollen.

'Have you been crying, Amy?'

'Never mind. Do you know what time it is?'

He went towards her.

'Why have you been crying?'

'There are many things to cry for.'

'Amy, have you any love for me still, or has poverty robbed me of it all?'

'I have never said that I didn't love you. Why do you accuse me of such things?'

He took her in his arms and held her passionately and kissed
her face again and again. Amy's tears broke forth anew.

'Why should we come to such utter ruin?' she sobbed. 'Oh,
try, try if you can't save us even yet! You know without my
saying it that I do love you; it's dreadful to me to think all our
happy life should be at an end, when we thought of such a future
together. Is it impossible? Can't you work as you used to and
succeed as we felt confident you would? Don't despair yet,
Edwin; do, do try, whilst there's still time!'

'Darling, darling – if only I *could* !'

'I have thought of something, dearest. Do as you proposed
last year; find a tenant for the flat whilst we still have a little
money, and then go away into some quiet country place, where
you can get back your health and live for very little, and write
another book – a good book, that'll bring you reputation again.
I and Willie can go and live at mother's for the summer months.
Do this! It would cost you so little, living alone, wouldn't it?
You would know that I was well cared for; mother would be
willing to have me for a few months, and it's easy to explain
that your health has failed, that you're obliged to go away for a
time.'

'But why shouldn't you go with me, if we are to let this
place?'

'We shouldn't have enough money. I want to free your mind
from the burden whilst you are writing. And what is before us if
we go on in this way? You don't think you will get much for
what you're writing now, do you?'

Reardon shook his head.

'Then how can we live even to the end of the year? Something *must* be done, you know. If we go into poor lodgings,
what hope is there that you'll be able to write anything
good?'

'But, Amy, I have no faith in my power of –'

'Oh, it would be different ! A few days – a week or a fortnight
of real holiday in this spring weather. Go to some seaside place.
How is it possible that all your talents should have left you? It's
only that you have been so anxious and in such poor health. You
say I don't love you, but I have thought and thought what would
be best for you to do, how you could save yourself. How can

you sink down to the position of a poor clerk in some office? That *can't* be your fate, Edwin; it's incredible. Oh, after such bright hopes, make one more effort! Have you forgotten that we were to go to the South together – you were to take me to Italy and Greece? How can that ever be if you fail utterly in literature? How can you ever hope to earn more than bare sustenance at any other kind of work?'

He all but lost consciousness of her words in gazing at the face she held up to his.

'You love me? Say again that you love me!'

'Dear, I love you with all my heart. But I am so afraid of the future. I can't bear poverty; I have found that I can't bear it. And I dread to think of your becoming only an ordinary man –'

Reardon laughed.

'But I am *not* "only an ordinary man," Amy! If I never write another line, that won't undo what I have done. It's little enough, to be sure; but you know what I *am*. Do you only love the author in me? Don't you think of me apart from all that I may do or not do? If I had to earn my living as a clerk, would that make me a clerk in soul?'

'You shall not fall to that! It would be too bitter a shame to lose all you have gained in these long years of work. Let me plan for you; do as I wish. You are to be what we hoped from the first. Take all the summer months. How long will it be before you can finish this short book?'

'A week or two.'

'Then finish it, and see what you can get for it. And try at once to find a tenant to take this place off our hands; that would be twenty-five pounds saved for the rest of the year. You could live on so little by yourself, couldn't you?'

'Oh, on ten shillings a week, if need be.'

'But not to starve yourself, you know. Don't you feel that my plan is a good one? When I came to you to-night I meant to speak of this, but you were so cruel –'

'Forgive me, dearest love! I was half a madman. You have been so cold to me for a long time.'

'I have been distracted. It was as if we were drawing nearer and nearer to the edge of a cataract.'

'Have you spoken to your mother about this?' he asked uneasily.

'No – not exactly this. But I know she will help us in this way.'

He had seated himself, and was holding her in his arms, his face laid against hers.

'I shall dread to part from you, Amy. That's such a dangerous thing to do. It may mean that we are never to live as husband and wife again.'

'But how could it? It's just to prevent that danger. If we go on here till we have no money – what's before us then? Wretched lodgings at the best. And I am afraid to think of that. I can't trust myself if that should come to pass.'

'What do you mean?' he asked anxiously.

'I hate poverty so. It brings out all the worst things in me; you know I have told you that before, Edwin?'

'But you would never forget that you are my wife?'

'I hope not. But – I can't think of it; I can't face it! That would be the very worst that can befall us, and we are going to try our utmost to escape from it. Was there ever a man who did as much as you have done in literature and then sank into hopeless poverty?'

'Oh, many!'

'But at your age, I mean. Surely not at your age?'

'I'm afraid there have been such poor fellows. Think how often one hears of hopeful beginnings, new reputations, and then – you hear no more. Of course it generally means that the man has gone into a different career; but sometimes, sometimes –'

'What?'

'The abyss.' He pointed downward. 'Penury and despair and a miserable death.'

'Oh, but those men haven't a wife and child! They would struggle –'

'Darling, they do struggle. But it's as if an ever increasing weight were round their necks; it drags them lower and lower. The world has no pity on a man who can't do or produce something it thinks worth money. You may be a divine poet, and if some good fellow doesn't take pity on you you will starve by the roadside. Society is as blind and brutal as fate. I have no right to complain of my own ill-fortune; it's my own fault (in a sense) that I can't continue as well as I began; if I could write books as good as the early ones I should earn money. For all that, it's hard that I must be kicked aside as worthless just because I don't know a trade.'

'It shan't be! I have only to look into your face to know that you will succeed after all. Yours is the kind of face that people come to know in portraits.'

He kissed her hair, and her eyes, and her mouth.

'How well I remember your saying that before! Why have you grown so good to me all at once, my Amy? Hearing you speak like that I feel there's nothing beyond my reach. But I dread to go away from you. If I find that it is hopeless; if I am alone somewhere, and know that the effort is all vain –'

'Then?'

'Well, I can leave you free. If I can't support you, it will be only just that I should give you back your freedom.'

'I don't understand –'

She raised herself, and looked into his eyes.

'We won't talk of that. If you bid me go on with the struggle, I shall do so.'

Amy had hidden her face, and lay silently in his arms for a minute or two. Then she murmured:

'It is so cold here, and so late. Come!'

'So early. There goes three o'clock.'

The next day they talked much of this new project. As there was sunshine Amy accompanied her husband for his walk in the afternoon; it was long since they had been out together. An open carriage that passed, followed by two young girls on horseback, gave a familiar direction to Reardon's thoughts.

'If one were as rich as those people! They pass so close to us; they see us, and we see them; but the distance between is infinity. They don't belong to the same world as we poor wretches. They see everything in a different light; they have powers which would seem supernatural if we were suddenly endowed with them.'

'Of course,' assented his companion with a sigh.

'Just fancy, if one got up in the morning with the thought

that no reasonable desire that occurred to one throughout the day need remain ungratified! And that it would be the same, any day and every day, to the end of one's life! Look at those houses; every detail, within and without, luxurious. To have such a home as that!'

'And they are empty creatures who live there.'

'They do *live*, Amy, at all events. Whatever may be their faculties, they all have free scope. I have often stood staring at houses like these until I couldn't believe that the people owning them were mere human beings like myself. The power of money is so hard to realise; one who has never had it marvels at the completeness with which it transforms every detail of life. Compare what we call our home with that of rich people; it moves one to scornful laughter. I have no sympathy with the stoical point of view; between wealth and poverty is just the difference between the whole man and the maimed. If my lower limbs are paralysed I may still be able to think, but then there is such a thing in life as walking. As a poor devil I may live nobly; but one happens to be made with faculties of enjoyment, and those have to fall into atrophy. To be sure, most rich people don't understand their happiness; if they did, they would move and talk like gods – which indeed they are.'

Amy's brow was shadowed. A wise man, in Reardon's position, would not have chosen this subject to dilate upon.

'The difference,' he went on, 'between the man with money and the man without is simply this: the one thinks, "How shall I use my life?" and the other, "How shall I keep myself alive?" A physiologist ought to be able to discover some curious distinction between the brain of a person who has never given a thought to the means of subsistence, and that of one who has never known a day free from such cares. There must be some special cerebral development representing the mental anguish kept up by poverty.'

'I should say,' put in Amy, 'that it affects every function of the brain. It isn't a special point of suffering, but a misery that colours every thought.'

'True. Can I think of a single subject in all the sphere of my experience without the consciousness that I see it through the medium of poverty? I have no enjoyment which isn't tainted by that thought, and I can suffer no pain which it doesn't increase. The curse of poverty is to the modern world just what that of slavery was to the ancient. Rich and destitute stand to each other as free man and bond. You remember the line of Homer I have often quoted about the demoralising effect of enslavement; poverty degrades in the same way.'

'It has had its effect upon me – I know that too well,' said Amy, with bitter frankness.

Reardon glanced at her, and wished to make some reply, but he could not say what was in his thoughts.

He worked on at his story. Before he had reached the end of it, 'Margaret Home' was published, and one day arrived a parcel containing the six copies to which an author is traditionally entitled. Reardon was not so old in authorship that he could open the packet without a slight flutter of his pulse. The book was tastefully got up; Amy exclaimed with pleasure as she caught sight of the cover and lettering.

'It may succeed, Edwin. It doesn't look like a book that fails, does it?'

She laughed at her own childishness. But Reardon had opened one of the volumes, and was glancing over the beginning of a chapter.

'Good God!' he cried. 'What hellish torment it was to write that page! I did it one morning when the fog was so thick that I had to light the lamp. It brings cold sweat to my forehead to read the words. And to think that people will skim over it without a suspicion of what it cost the writer! – What execrable style! A potboy could write better narrative.'

'Who are to have copies?'

'No one, if I could help it. But I suppose your mother will expect one?'

'And – Milvain?'

'I suppose so,' he replied, indifferently. 'But not unless he asks for it. Poor old Biffen, of course; though it'll make him despise me. Then one for ourselves. That leaves two – to light the fire with. We have been rather short of fire-paper since we couldn't afford our daily newspaper.'

'Will you let me give one to Mrs Carter?'

'As you please.'

He took one set and added it to the row of his productions which stood on a topmost shelf. Amy laid her hand upon his shoulder, and contemplated the effect of this addition.

'The works of Edwin Reardon,' she said, with a smile.

'The work, at all events – rather a different thing, unfortunately. Amy, if only I were back at the time when I wrote "On Neutral Ground," and yet had you with me! How full my mind was in those days! Then I had only to look, and I *saw* something; now I strain my eyes, but can make out nothing more than nebulous grotesques. I used to sit down knowing so well what I had to say; now I strive to invent, and never come at anything. Suppose you pick up a needle with warm, supple fingers; try to do it when your hand is stiff and numb with cold; there's the difference between my manner of work in those days and what it is now.'

'But you are going to get back your health. You will write better than ever.'

'We shall see. Of course there was a great deal of miserable struggle even then, but I remember it as insignificant compared with the hours of contented work. I seldom did anything in the mornings except think and prepare; towards evening I felt myself getting ready, and at last I sat down with the first lines buzzing in my head. And I used to read a great deal at the same time. Whilst I was writing "On Neutral Ground" I went solidly through the "Divina Commedia," a canto each day. Very often I wrote till after midnight, but occasionally I got my quantum finished much earlier, and then I used to treat myself to a ramble about the streets. I can recall exactly the places where some of my best ideas came to me. You remember the scene in Prendergast's lodgings? That flashed on me late one night as I was turning out of Leicester Square into the slum that leads to Clare Market; ah, how well I remember! And I went home to my garret in a state of delightful fever, and scribbled notes furiously before going to bed.'

'Don't trouble; it'll all come back to you.'

'But in those days I hadn't to think of money. I could look forward and see provision for my needs. I never asked myself what I should get for the book; I assure you, that never came into my head – never. The work was done for its own sake. No hurry to finish it; if I felt that I wasn't up to the mark, I just waited till the better mood returned. "On Neutral Ground" took me seven months; now I have to write three volumes in nine weeks, with the lash stinging on my back if I miss a day.'

He brooded for a little.

'I suppose there must be some rich man somewhere who has read one or two of my books with a certain interest. If only I could encounter him and tell him plainly what a cursed state I am in, perhaps he would help me to some means of earning a couple of pounds a week. One has heard of such things.'

'In the old days.'

'Yes. I doubt if it ever happens now. Coleridge wouldn't so easily meet with his Gillman nowadays. Well, I am not a Coleridge,[20] and I don't ask to be lodged under any man's roof; but if I could earn money enough to leave me good long evenings unspoilt by fear of the workhouse –'

Amy turned away, and presently went to look after her little boy.

A few days after this they had a visit from Milvain. He came about ten o'clock in the evening.

'I'm not going to stay,' he announced. 'But where's my copy of "Margaret Home"? I am to have one, I suppose?'

'I have no particular desire that you should read it,' returned Reardon.

'But I *have* read it, my dear fellow. Got it from the library on the day of publication; I had a suspicion that you wouldn't send me a copy. But I must possess your *opera omnia*.'[21]

'Here it is. Hide it away somewhere. – You may as well sit down for a few minutes.'

'I confess I should like to talk about the book, if you don't mind. It isn't so utterly and damnably bad as you make out, you know. The misfortune was that you had to make three volumes of it. If I had leave to cut it down to one, it would do you credit. The motive is good enough.'

'Yes. Just good enough to show how badly it's managed.'

Milvain began to expatiate on that well-worn topic, the evils of the three-volume system.

'A triple-headed monster, sucking the blood of English novelist. One might design an allegorical cartoon for a comic literary paper. By-the-by, why doesn't such a thing exist? – a weekly paper treating of things and people literary in a facetious spirit. It would be caviare to the general, but might be supported, I should think. The editor would probably be assassinated, though.'

'For anyone in my position,' said Reardon, 'how is it possible to abandon the three volumes? It is a question of payment. An author of moderate repute may live on a yearly three-volume novel – I mean the man who is obliged to sell his book out and out, and who gets from one to two hundred pounds for it. But he would have to produce four one-volume novels to obtain the same income; and I doubt whether he could get so many published within the twelve months. And here comes in the benefit of the libraries; from the commercial point of view the libraries are indispensable. Do you suppose the public would support the present number of novelists if each book had to be purchased? A sudden change to that system would throw three-fourths of the novelists out of work.'

'But there's no reason why the libraries shouldn't circulate novels in one volume.'

'Profits would be less, I suppose. People would take the minimum subscription.'

'Well, to go to the concrete, what about your own one-volume?'

'All but done.'

'And you'll offer it to Jedwood? Go and see him personally. He's a very decent fellow, I believe.'

Milvain stayed only half an hour. The days when he was wont to sit and talk at large through a whole evening were no more; partly because of his diminished leisure, but also for a less simple reason – the growth of something like estrangement between him and Reardon.

'You didn't mention your plans,' said Amy, when the visitor had been gone some time.

'No.'

Reardon was content with the negative, and his wife made no further remark.

The result of advertising the flat was that two or three persons called to make inspection. One of them, a man of military appearance, showed himself anxious to come to terms; he was willing to take the tenement from next quarter-day (June), but wished, if possible, to enter upon possession sooner than that.

'Nothing could be better,' said Amy in colloquy with her husband. 'If he will pay for the extra time, we shall be only too glad.'

Reardon mused and looked gloomy. He could not bring himself to regard the experiment before him with hopefulness, and his heart sank at the thought of parting from Amy.

'You are very anxious to get rid of me,' he answered, trying to smile.

'Yes, I am,' she exclaimed; 'but simply for your own good, as you know very well.'

'Suppose I can't sell this book?'

'You will have a few pounds. Send your "Pliny" article to *The Wayside*. If you come to an end of all your money, mother shall lend you some.'

'I am not very likely to do much work in *that* case.'

'Oh, but you will sell the book. You'll get twenty pounds for it, and that alone would keep you for three months. Think – three months of the best part of the year at the seaside! Oh, you will do wonders!'

The furniture was to be housed at Mrs Yule's. Neither of them durst speak of selling it; that would have sounded too ominous. As for the locality of Reardon's retreat, Amy herself had suggested Worthing, which she knew from a visit a few years ago; the advantages were its proximity to London, and the likelihood that very cheap lodgings could be found either in the town or near it. One room would suffice for the hapless author, and his expenses, beyond a trifling rent, would be confined to mere food. Oh yes, he might manage on considerably less than a pound a week.

Amy was in much better spirits than for a long time; she appeared to have convinced herself that there was no doubt of the issue of this perilous scheme; that her husband would write a notable book, receive a satisfactory price for it, and so re-establish their home. Yet her moods varied greatly. After all, there was delay in the letting of the flat, and this caused her annoyance. It was whilst the negotiations were still pending that she made her call upon Maud and Dora Milvain; Reardon did not know of her intention to visit them until it had been carried out. She mentioned what she had done in almost a casual manner.

'I had to get it over,' she said, when Reardon exhibited surprise, 'and I don't think I made a very favourable impression.'

'You told them, I suppose, what we are going to do?'

'No; I didn't say a word of it.'

'But why not? It can't be kept a secret. Milvain will have heard of it already, I should think, from your mother.'

'From mother? But it's the rarest thing for him to go there. Do you imagine he is a constant visitor? I thought it better to say nothing until the thing is actually done. Who knows what may happen?'

She was in a strange, nervous state, and Reardon regarded her uneasily. He talked very little in these days, and passed hours in dark reverie. His book was finished, and he awaited the publisher's decision.

Chapter 16

REJECTION

ONE of Reardon's minor worries at this time was the fear that by chance he might come upon a review of 'Margaret Home.' Since the publication of his first book he had avoided as far as possible all knowledge of what the critics had to say about him; his nervous temperament could not bear the agitation of reading these remarks, which, however inept, define an author and his work to so many people incapable of judging for themselves. No man or woman could tell him anything in the way of praise or blame which he did not already know quite well; commendation was pleasant, but it so often aimed amiss, and censure was for the most part so unintelligent. In the case of this latest novel he dreaded the sight of a review as he would have done a gash from a rusty knife. The judgments could not but be damnatory, and their expression in journalistic phrase would disturb his mind with evil rancour. No one would have insight enough to appreciate the nature and cause of his book's demerits; every comment would be wide of the mark; sneer, ridicule, trite objection, would but madden him with a sense of injustice.

His position was illogical – one result of the moral weakness which was allied with his aesthetic sensibility. Putting aside the worthlessness of current reviewing, the critic of an isolated book has of course nothing to do with its author's state of mind and body any more than with the condition of his purse. Reardon would have granted this, but he could not command his emotions. He was in passionate revolt against the base necessities which compelled him to put forth work in no way representing his healthy powers, his artistic criterion. Not he had written this book, but his accursed poverty. To assail him as the author was, in his feeling, to be guilty of brutal insult. When by ill-hap a notice in one of the daily papers came under his eyes, it made his blood boil with a fierceness of hatred only possible to him in a profoundly morbid condition; he could not steady his hand for half an hour after. Yet this particular critic only said what was quite true – that the novel contained not a single striking scene and not one living character; Reardon had expressed himself about it in almost identical terms. But he saw himself in the position of one sickly and all but destitute man against a relentless world, and every blow directed against him appeared dastardly. He could have cried 'Coward!' to the writer who wounded him.

The would-be sensational story which was now in Mr Jedwood's hands had perhaps more merit than 'Margaret Home'; its brevity, and the fact that nothing more was aimed at than a concatenation of brisk events, made it not unreadable. But Reardon thought of it with humiliation. If it were published as his next work it would afford final proof to such sympathetic readers as he might still retain that he had hopelessly written himself out, and was now endeavouring to adapt himself to an inferior public. In spite of his dire necessities he now and then hoped that Jedwood might refuse the thing.

At moments he looked with sanguine eagerness to the three or four months he was about to spend in retirement, but such impulses were the mere outcome of his nervous disease. He had no faith in himself under present conditions; the permanence of his sufferings would mean the sure destruction of powers he still possessed, though they were not at his command. Yet he believed that his mind was made up as to the advisability of trying this last resource; he was impatient for the day of departure, and in the interval merely killed time as best he might. He could not read, and did not attempt to gather ideas for his next book; the delusion that his mind was resting made an excuse to him for the barrenness of day after day. His 'Pliny' article had been despatched to The Wayside, and would possibly be accepted. But he did not trouble himself about this or other details; it was as though his mind could do nothing more than grasp the bald fact of impending destitution; with the steps towards that final stage he seemed to have little concern.

One evening he set forth to make a call upon Harold Biffen, whom he had not seen since the realist called to acknowledge the receipt of a copy of 'Margaret Home' left at his lodgings when he was out. Biffen resided in Clipstone Street, a thoroughfare discoverable in the dim district which lies between Portland Place and Tottenham Court Road. On knocking at the door of the

lodging-house, Reardon learnt that his friend was at home. He
ascended to the third storey and tapped at a door which allowed
rays of lamplight to issue from great gaps above and below. A
sound of voices came from within, and on entering he perceived
that Biffen was engaged with a pupil.

'They didn't tell me you had a visitor,' he said. 'I'll call again
later.'

'No need to go away,' replied Biffen, coming forward to shake
hands. 'Take a book for a few minutes. Mr Baker won't mind.'

It was a very small room, with a ceiling so low that the tall
lodger could only just stand upright with safety; perhaps three
inches intervened between his head and the plaster, which was
cracked, grimy, cobwebby. A small scrap of weedy carpet lay in
front of the fireplace; elsewhere the chinky boards were uncon-
cealed. The furniture consisted of a round table, which kept such
imperfect balance on its central support that the lamp entrusted
to it looked in a dangerous position, of three small cane-bot-
tomed chairs, a small wash-hand-stand with sundry rude appurtenances, and a chair-bedstead which the tenant opened at the
hour of repose and spread with certain primitive trappings at
present kept in a cupboard. There was no bookcase, but a few
hundred battered volumes were arranged some on the floor and
some on a rough chest. The weather was too characteristic of an
English spring to make an empty grate agreeable to the eye, but
Biffen held it an axiom that fires were unseasonable after the first
of May.

The individual referred to as Mr Baker, who sat at the table in
the attitude of a student, was a robust, hard-featured, black-
haired young man of two or three-and-twenty; judging from
his weather-beaten cheeks and huge hands, as well as from the
garb he wore, one would have presumed that study was not his
normal occupation. There was something of the riverside about
him; he might be a dockman, or even a bargeman. He looked
intelligent, however, and bore himself with much modesty.

'Now do endeavour to write in shorter sentences,' said Biffen,
who sat down by him and resumed the lesson, Reardon having
taken up a volume. 'This isn't bad – it isn't bad at all, I assure
you; but you have put all you had to say into three appalling
periods, whereas you ought to have made about a dozen.'

'There it is, sir; there it is!' exclaimed the man, smoothing his wiry hair. 'I can't break it up. The thoughts come in a lump, if I may say so. To break it up – there's the art of compersition.'

Reardon could not refrain from a glance at the speaker, and Biffen, whose manner was very grave and kindly, turned to his friend with an explanation of the difficulties with which the student was struggling.

'Mr Baker is preparing for the examination of the Outdoor Customs Department. One of the subjects is English composition, and really, you know, that isn't quite such a simple matter as some people think.'

Baker beamed upon the visitor with a homely, good-natured smile.

'I can make headway with the other things, sir,' he said, striking the table lightly with his clenched fist. 'There's handwriting, there's orthography, there's arithmetic; I'm not afraid of one of 'em, as Mr Biffen 'll tell you, sir. But when it comes to compersition, that brings out the sweat on my forehead, I do assure you.'

'You're not the only man in that case, Mr Baker,' replied Reardon.

'It's thought a tough job in general, is it, sir?'

'It is indeed.'

'Two hundred marks for compersition,' continued the man. 'Now how many would they have given me for this bit of a try, Mr Biffen?'

'Well, well; I can't exactly say. But you improve; you improve, decidedly. Peg away for another week or two.'

'Oh, don't fear me, sir! I'm not easily beaten when I've set my mind on a thing, and I'll break up the compersition yet, see if I don't!'

Again his fist descended upon the table in a way that reminded one of the steam-hammer cracking a nut.

The lesson proceeded for about ten minutes, Reardon, under pretence of reading, following it with as much amusement as anything could excite in him nowadays. At length Mr Baker stood up, collected his papers and books, and seemed about to depart; but, after certain uneasy movements and glances, he said to Biffen in a subdued voice:

'Perhaps I might speak to you outside the door a minute, sir?'

He and the teacher went out, the door closed, and Reardon heard sounds of muffled conversation. In a minute or two a heavy footstep descended the stairs, and Biffen re-entered the room.

'Now that's a good, honest fellow,' he said, in an amused tone. 'It's my pay-night, but he didn't like to fork out money before you. A very unusual delicacy in a man of that standing. He pays me sixpence for an hour's lesson; that brings me two shillings a week. I sometimes feel a little ashamed to take his money, but then the fact is he's a good deal better off than I am.'

'Will he get a place in the Customs, do you think?'

'Oh, I've no doubt of it. If it seemed unlikely, I should have told him so before this. To be sure, that's a point I have often to consider, and once or twice my delicacy has asserted itself at the expense of my pocket. There was a poor consumptive lad came to me not long ago and wanted Latin lessons; talked about going in for the London Matric., on his way to the pulpit. I couldn't stand it. After a lesson or two I told him his cough was too bad, and he had no right to study until he got into better health; that was better, I think, than saying plainly he had no chance on earth. But the food I bought with his money was choking me. Oh yes, Baker will make his way right enough. A good, modest fellow. You noticed how respectfully he spoke to me? It doesn't make any difference to him that I live in a garret like this; I'm a man of education, and he can separate this fact from my surroundings.'

'Biffen, why don't you get some decent position? Surely you might.'

'What position? No school would take me; I have neither credentials nor conventional clothing. For the same reason I couldn't get a private tutorship in a rich family. No, no; it's all right. I keep myself alive, and I get on with my work. – By-the-by, I've decided to write a book called "Mr Bailey, Grocer."'

'What's the idea?'

'An objectionable word, that. Better say : "What's the reality?" Well, Mr Bailey is a grocer in a little street by here. I have dealt with him for a long time, and as he's a talkative fellow I've come to know a good deal about him and his history. He's fond of talking about the struggle he had in his first year of business. He had no money of his own, but he married a woman who had saved forty-five pounds out of a cat's-meat business. You should see that woman! A big, coarse, squinting creature; at the time of the marriage she was a widow and forty-two years old. Now I'm going to tell the true story of Mr Bailey's marriage and of his progress as a grocer. It'll be a great book – a great book!'

He walked up and down the room, fervid with his conception.

'There'll be nothing bestial in it, you know. The decently ignoble – as I've so often said. The thing'll take me a year at least. I shall do it slowly, lovingly. One volume, of course; the length of the ordinary French novel. There's something fine in the title, don't you think? "Mr Bailey, Grocer"!'

'I envy you, old fellow,' said Reardon, sighing. 'You have the right fire in you; you have zeal and energy. Well, what do you think I have decided to do?'

'I should like to hear.'

Reardon gave an account of his project. The other listened gravely, seated across a chair with his arms on the back.

'Your wife is in agreement with this?'

'Oh yes.' He could not bring himself to say that Amy had suggested it. 'She has great hopes that the change will be just what I need.'

'I should say so too – if you were going to rest. But if you have to set to work at once it seems to me very doubtful.'

'Never mind. For Heaven's sake don't discourage me! If this fails I think – upon my soul, I think I shall kill myself.'

'Pooh!' exclaimed Biffen, gently. 'With a wife like yours?'

'Just because of that.'

'No, no; there'll be some way out of it. By-the-by, I passed Mrs Reardon this morning, but she didn't see me. It was in Tottenham Court Road, and Milvain was with her. I felt myself too seedy in appearance to stop and speak.'

'In Tottenham Court Road?'

That was not the detail of the story which chiefly held Reardon's attention, yet he did not purposely make a misleading remark. His mind involuntarily played this trick.

'I only saw them just as they were passing,' pursued Biffen. 'Oh, I knew I had something to tell you! Have you heard that Whelpdale is going to be married?'

Reardon shook his head in a preoccupied way.

'I had a note from him this morning, telling me. He asked me to look him up to-night, and he'd let me know all about it. Let's go together, shall we?'

'I don't feel much in the humour for Whelpdale. I'll walk with you, and go on home.'

'No, no; come and see him. It'll do you good to talk a little. – But I must positively eat a mouthful before we go. I'm afraid you won't care to join?'

He opened his cupboard, and brought out a loaf of bread and a saucer of dripping, with salt and pepper.

'Better dripping this than I've had for a long time. I get it at Mr Bailey's – that isn't his real name, of course. He assures me it comes from a large hotel where his wife's sister is a kitchen-maid, and that it's perfectly pure; they very often mix flour with it, you know, and perhaps more obnoxious things that an econo-mical man doesn't care to reflect upon. Now, with a little pepper and salt, this bread and dripping is as appetising food as I know. I often make a dinner of it.'

'I have done the same myself before now. Do you ever buy pease-pudding?'

'I should think so ! I get magnificent pennyworths at a shop in Cleveland Street, of a very rich quality indeed. Excellent faggots they have there, too. I'll give you a supper of them some night before you go.'

Biffen rose to enthusiasm in the contemplation of these dainties. He ate his bread and dripping with knife and fork; this always made the fare seem more substantial.

'Is it very cold out?' he asked, rising from the table. 'Need I put my overcoat on?'

This overcoat, purchased second-hand three years ago, hung on a door-nail. Comparative ease of circumstances had restored to the realist his ordinary indoor garment – a morning coat of the cloth called diagonal, rather large for him, but in better pre-servation than the other articles of his attire.

Reardon judging the overcoat necessary, his friend carefully brushed it and drew it on with a caution which probably had reference to starting seams. Then he put into the pocket his pipe, his pouch, his tobacco-stopper, and his matches, murmuring to himself a Greek iambic line which had come into his head *apropos* of nothing obvious.

'Go out,' he said, 'and then I'll extinguish the lamp. Mind the second step down, as usual.'

They issued into Clipstone Street, turned northward, crossed Euston Road, and came into Albany Street, where, in a house of decent exterior, Mr Whelpdale had his present abode. A girl who opened the door requested them to walk up to the topmost storey.

A cheery voice called to them from within the room at which they knocked. This lodging spoke more distinctly of civilisation than that inhabited by Biffen; it contained the minimum supply of furniture needed to give it somewhat the appearance of a study, but the articles were in good condition. One end of the room was concealed by a chintz curtain; scrutiny would have discovered behind the draping the essential equipments of a bed-chamber.

Mr Whelpdale sat by the fire, smoking a cigar. He was a plain-featured but graceful and refined-looking man of thirty, with wavy chestnut hair and a trimmed beard which became him well. At present he wore a dressing-gown and was without collar.

'Welcome, gents both!' he cried facetiously. 'Ages since I saw you, Reardon. I've been reading your new book. Uncommonly good things in it here and there – uncommonly good.'

Whelpdale had the weakness of being unable to tell a disagreeable truth, and a tendency to flattery which had always made Reardon rather uncomfortable in his society. Though there was no need whatever of his mentioning 'Margaret Home,' he preferred to frame smooth fictions rather than keep a silence which might be construed as unfavourable criticism.

'In the last volume,' he went on, 'I think there are one or two things as good as you ever did; I do indeed.'

Reardon made no acknowledgment of these remarks. They irritated him, for he knew their insincerity. Biffen, understanding his friend's silence, struck in on another subject.

'Who is this lady of whom you write to me?'

'Ah, quite a story! I'm going to be married, Reardon. A serious marriage. Light your pipes, and I'll tell you all about it. Startled you, I suppose, Biffen? Unlikely news, eh? Some people would call it a rash step, I dare say. We shall just take another room in this house, that's all. I think I can count upon an income of a couple of guineas a week, and I have plans without end that are pretty sure to bring in coin.'

Reardon did not care to smoke, but Biffen lit his pipe and waited with grave interest for the romantic narrative. Whenever he heard of a poor man's persuading a woman to share his poverty he was eager of details; perchance he himself might yet have that heavenly good fortune.

'Well,' began Whelpdale, crossing his legs and watching a wreath he had just puffed from the cigar, 'you know all about my literary advisership. The business goes on reasonably well. I'm going to extend it in ways I'll explain to you presently. About six weeks ago I received a letter from a lady who referred to my advertisements, and said she had the manuscript of a novel which she would like to offer for my opinion. Two publishers had refused it, but one with complimentary phrases, and she hoped it mightn't be impossible to put the thing into acceptable shape. Of course I wrote optimistically and the manuscript was sent to me. Well, it wasn't actually bad – by Jove! you should have seen some of the things I have been asked to recommend to publishers! It wasn't hopelessly bad by any means, and I gave serious thought to it. After exchange of several letters I asked the authoress to come and see me, that we might save postage-stamps and talk things over. She hadn't given me her address: I had to direct to a stationer's in Bayswater. She agreed to come, and did come. I had formed a sort of idea, but of course I was quite wrong. Imagine my excitement when there came in a very beautiful girl, a tremendously interesting girl, about one-and-twenty – just the kind of girl that most strongly appeals to me; dark, pale, rather consumptive-looking, slender – no, there's no describing her; there really isn't! You must wait till you see her.'

'I hope the consumption was only a figure of speech,' remarked Biffen in his grave way.

'Oh, there's nothing serious the matter, I think. A slight cough, poor girl –'

'The deuce!' interjected Reardon.

'Oh, nothing, nothing! It'll be all right. Well, now, of course

we talked over the story – in good earnest, you know. Little by
little I induced her to speak of herself – this, after she'd come two
or three times – and she told me lamentable things. She was absolutely alone in London, and hadn't had sufficient food for
weeks; had sold all she could of her clothing; and so on. Her
home was in Birmingham; she had been driven away by the
brutality of a step-mother; a friend lent her a few pounds, and
she came to London with an unfinished novel. Well, you know,
this kind of thing would be enough to make me soft-hearted to
any girl, let alone one who, to begin with, was absolutely my
ideal. When she began to express a fear that I was giving too
much time to her, that she wouldn't be able to pay my fees, and
so on, I could restrain myself no longer. On the spot I asked her
to marry me. I didn't practise any deception, mind. I told her I
was a poor devil who had failed as a realistic novelist and was
earning bread in haphazard ways and I explained frankly that I
thought we might carry on various kinds of business together :
she might go on with her novel-writing, and – so on. But she was
frightened; I had been too abrupt. That's a fault of mine, you
know; but I was so confoundedly afraid of losing her. And I
told her as much, plainly.'

Biffen smiled.

'This would be exciting,' he said, 'if we didn't know the end of
the story.'

'Yes. Pity I didn't keep it a secret. Well, she wouldn't say yes,
but I could see that she didn't absolutely say no. "In any case," I
said, "you'll let me see you often? Fees be hanged ! I'll work day
and night for you. I'll do my utmost to get your novel accepted."
And I implored her to let me lend her a little money. It was very
difficult to persuade her, but at last she accepted a few shillings. I
could see in her face that she was hungry. Just imagine ! A beautiful girl absolutely hungry : it drove me frantic ! But that was a
great point gained. After that we saw each other almost every
day, and at last – she consented ! Did indeed ! I can hardly believe it yet. We shall be married in a fortnight's time.'

'I congratulate you,' said Reardon.

'So do I,' sighed Biffen.

'The day before yesterday she went to Birmingham to see her
father and tell him all about the affair. I agreed with her it was as

well; the old fellow isn't badly off, and he may forgive her for running away, though he's under his wife's thumb, it appears. I had a note yesterday. She had gone to a friend's house for the first day. I hoped to have heard again this morning – must tomorrow, in any case. I live, as you may imagine, in wild excitement. Of course, if the old man stumps up a wedding-present, all the better. But I don't care; we'll make a living somehow. What do you think I'm writing just now? An author's Guide. You know the kind of thing; they sell splendidly. Of course I shall make it a good advertisement of my business. Then I have a splendid idea. I'm going to advertise: "Novel-writing taught in ten lessons!" What do you think of that? No swindle; not a bit of it. I am quite capable of giving the ordinary man or woman ten very useful lessons. I've been working out the scheme; it would amuse you vastly, Reardon. The first lesson deals with the question of subjects, local colour – that kind of thing. I gravely advise people, if they possibly can, to write of the wealthy middle class; that's the popular subject, you know. Lords and ladies are all very well, but the real thing to take is a story about people who have no titles, but live in good Philistine style. I urge study of horsey matters especially; that's very important. You must be well up, too, in military grades, know about Sandhurst, and so on. Boating is an important topic. You see? Oh, I shall make a great thing of this. I shall teach my wife carefully, and then let her advertise lessons to girls; they'll prefer coming to a woman, you know.'

Biffen leant back and laughed noisily.

'How much shall you charge for the course?' asked Reardon.

'That'll depend. I shan't refuse a guinea or two; but some people may be made to pay five, perhaps.'

Someone knocked at the door, and a voice said:

'A letter for you, Mr Whelpdale.'

He started up, and came back into the room with face illuminated.

'Yes, it's from Birmingham; posted this morning. Look what an exquisite hand she writes!'

He tore open the envelope. In delicacy Reardon and Biffen averted their eyes. There was silence for a minute, then a strange ejaculation from Whelpdale caused his friends to look up at him.

He had gone pale, and was frowning at the sheets of paper which trembled in his hand.

'No bad news, I hope?' Biffen ventured to say.

Whelpdale let himself sink into a chair.

'Now if this isn't too bad!' he exclaimed in a thick voice. 'If this isn't monstrously unkind! I never heard anything so gross as this – never!'

The two waited, trying not to smile.

'She writes – that she has met an old lover – in Birmingham – that it was with him she had quarrelled – not with her father at all – that she ran away to annoy him and frighten him – that she has made it up again, and they're going to be married!'

He let the sheet fall, and looked so utterly woebegone that his friends at once exerted themselves to offer such consolation as the case admitted of. Reardon thought better of Whelpdale for this emotion; he had not believed him capable of it.

'It isn't a case of vulgar cheating!' cried the forsaken one presently. 'Don't go away thinking that. She writes in real distress and penitence – she does indeed. Oh, the devil! Why did I let her go to Birmingham? A fortnight more, and I should have had her safe. But it's just like my luck. Do you know that this is the third time I've been engaged to be married? – no, by Jove, the fourth! And every time the girl has got out of it at the last moment. What an unlucky beast I am! A girl who was positively my ideal! I haven't even a photograph of her to show you; but you'd be astonished at her face. Why, in the devil's name, did I let her go to Birmingham?'

The visitors had risen. They felt uncomfortable, for it seemed as if Whelpdale might find vent for his distress in tears.

'We had better leave you,' suggested Biffen. 'It's very hard – it is indeed.'

'Look here! Read the letter for yourselves! Do!'

They declined, and begged him not to insist.

'But I want you to see what kind of girl she is. It isn't a case of farcical deceiving – not a bit of it! She implores me to forgive her, and blames herself no end. Just my luck! The third – no, the fourth time, by Jove! Never was such an unlucky fellow with women. It's because I'm so damnably poor; that's it, of course!'

Reardon and his companion succeeded at length in getting

away, though not till they had heard the virtues and beauty of the vanished girl described again and again in much detail. Both were in a state of depression as they left the house.

'What think you of this story?' asked Biffen. 'Is this possible in a woman of any merit?'

'Anything is possible in a woman,' Reardon replied, harshly.

They walked in silence as far as Portland Road Station. There, with an assurance that he would come to a garret-supper before leaving London, Reardon parted from his friend and turned westward.

As soon as he had entered, Amy's voice called to him.

'Here's a letter from Jedwood, Edwin!'

He stepped into the study.

'It came just after you went out, and it has been all I could do to resist the temptation to open it.'

'Why shouldn't you have opened it?' said her husband, carelessly.

He tried to do so himself, but his shaking hand thwarted him at first. Succeeding at length, he found a letter in the publisher's own writing, and the first word that caught his attention was 'regret.' With an angry effort to command himself he ran through the communication, then held it out to Amy.

She read, and her countenance fell. Mr Jedwood regretted that the story offered to him did not seem likely to please the particular public to whom his series of one-volume novels made appeal. He hoped it would be understood that, in declining, he by no means expressed an adverse judgment on the story itself &c.

'It doesn't surprise me,' said Reardon. 'I believe he is quite right. The thing is too empty to please the better kind of readers, yet not vulgar enough to please the worse.'

'But you'll try someone else?'

'I don't think it's much use.'

They sat opposite each other, and kept silence. Jedwood's letter slipped from Amy's lap to the ground.

'So,' said Reardon, presently, 'I don't see how our plan is to be carried out.'

'Oh, it *must* be!'

'But how?'

'You'll get seven or eight pounds from *The Wayside*. And — hadn't we better sell the furniture, instead of —'

His look checked her.

'It seems to me, Amy, that your one desire is to get away from me, on whatever terms.'

'Don't begin that over again!' she exclaimed, fretfully. 'If you don't believe what I say —'

They were both in a state of intolerable nervous tension. Their voices quivered, and their eyes had an unnatural brightness.

'If we sell the furniture,' pursued Reardon, 'that means you'll never come back to me. You wish to save yourself and the child from the hard life that seems to be before us.'

'Yes, I do; but not by deserting you. I want you to go and work for us all, so that we may live more happily before long. Oh, how wretched this is!'

She burst into hysterical weeping. But Reardon, instead of attempting to soothe her, went into the next room, where he sat for a long time in the dark. When he returned Amy was calm again; her face expressed a cold misery.

'Where did you go this morning?' he asked, as if wishing to talk of common things.

'I told you. I went to buy those things for Willie.'

'Oh yes.'

There was a silence.

'Biffen passed you in Tottenham Court Road,' he added.

'I didn't see him.'

'No; he said you didn't.'

'Perhaps,' said Amy, 'it was just when I was speaking to Mr Milvain.'

'You met Milvain?'

'Yes.'

'Why didn't you tell me?'

'I'm sure I don't know. I can't mention every trifle that happens.'

'No, of course not.'

Amy closed her eyes, as if in weariness, and for a minute or two Reardon observed her countenance.

'So you think we had better sell the furniture?'

'I shall say nothing more about it. You must do as seems best to you, Edwin.'

'Are you going to see your mother tomorrow?'

'Yes. I thought you would like to come too.'

'No; there's no good in my going.'

He again rose, and that night they talked no more of their difficulties, though on the morrow (Sunday) it would be necessary to decide their course in every detail.

Chapter 17

THE PARTING

AMY did not go to church. Before her marriage she had done so as a mere matter of course, accompanying her mother, but Reardon's attitude with regard to the popular religion speedily became her own; she let the subject lapse from her mind, and cared neither to defend nor to attack where dogma was concerned. She had no sympathies with mysticism; her nature was strongly practical, with something of zeal for intellectual attainment superadded.

This Sunday morning she was very busy with domestic minutiæ. Reardon noticed what looked like preparations for packing, and being as little disposed for conversation as his wife, he went out and walked for a couple of hours in the Hampstead region. Dinner over, Amy at once made ready for her journey to Westbourne Park.

'Then you won't come?' she said to her husband.

'No. I shall see your mother before I go away, but I don't care to till you have settled everything.'

It was half a year since he had met Mrs Yule. She never came to their dwelling, and Reardon could not bring himself to visit her.

'You had very much rather we didn't sell the furniture?' Amy asked.

'Ask your mother's opinion. That shall decide.'

'There'll be the expense of moving it, you know. Unless money comes from *The Wayside*, you'll only have two or three pounds left.'

Reardon made no reply. He was overcome by the bitterness of shame.

'I shall say, then,' pursued Amy, who spoke with averted face, 'that I am to go there for good on Tuesday? I mean, of course, for the summer months.'

'I suppose so.'

Then he turned suddenly upon her.

'Do you really imagine that at the end of the summer I shall be a rich man? What do you mean by talking in this way? If the furniture is sold to supply me with a few pounds for the present, what prospect is there that I shall be able to buy new?'

'How can we look forward at all?' replied Amy. 'It has come to the question of how we are to subsist. I thought you would rather get money in this way than borrow of mother – when she has the expense of keeping me and Willie.'

'You are right,' muttered Reardon. 'Do as you think best.'

Amy was in her most practical mood, and would not linger for purposeless talk. A few minutes, and Reardon was left alone.

He stood before his bookshelves and began to pick out the volumes which he would take away with him. Just a few, the indispensable companions of a bookish man who still clings to life – his Homer, his Shakespeare –

The rest must be sold. He would get rid of them to-morrow morning. All together they might bring him a couple of sovereigns.

Then his clothing. Amy had fulfilled all the domestic duties of a wife; his wardrobe was in as good a state as circumstances allowed. But there was no object in burdening himself with winter garments, for, if he lived through the summer at all, he would be able to repurchase such few poor things as were needful; at present he could only think of how to get together a few coins. So he made a heap of such things as might be sold.

The furniture? If it must go, the price could scarcely be more than ten or twelve pounds; well, perhaps fifteen. To be sure, in this way his summer's living would be abundantly provided for.

He thought of Biffen enviously. Biffen, if need be, could support life on three or four shillings a week, happy in the thought that no mortal had a claim upon him. If he starved to death – well, many another lonely man has come to that end. If he preferred to kill himself, who would be distressed? Spoilt child of fortune!

The bells of St Marylebone began to clang for afternoon service. In the idleness of dull pain his thoughts followed their summons, and he marvelled that there were people who could imagine it a duty or find it a solace to go and sit in that twilight church and listen to the droning of prayers. He thought of the wretched millions of mankind to whom life is so barren that they must needs believe in a recompense beyond the grave. For that he neither looked nor longed. The bitterness of his lot was that this world might be a sufficing paradise to him if only he could clutch a poor little share of current coin. He had won the world's greatest prize – a woman's love – but could not retain it because his pockets were empty.

That he should fail to make a great name, this was grievous disappointment to Amy, but this alone would not have estranged her. It was the dread and shame of penury that made her heart cold to him. And he could not in his conscience scorn her for being thus affected by the vulgar circumstances of life; only a few supreme natures stand unshaken under such a trial, and though his love of Amy was still passionate, he knew that her place was among a certain class of women, and not on the isolated pinnacle where he had at first visioned her. It was entirely natural that she shrank at the test of squalid suffering. A little money, and he could have rested secure in her love, for then he would have been able to keep ever before her the best qualities of his heart and brain. Upon him, too, penury had its debasing effect; as he now presented himself he was not a man to be admired or loved. It was all simple and intelligible enough – a situation that would be misread only by shallow idealism.

Worst of all, she was attracted by Jasper Milvain's energy and promise of success. He had no ignoble suspicions of Amy, but it was impossible for him not to see that she habitually contrasted the young journalist, who laughingly made his way among men, with her grave, dispirited husband, who was not even capable of holding such position as he had gained. She enjoyed Milvain's conversation, it put her into a good humour; she liked him personally, and there could be no doubt that she had observed a jealous tendency in Reardon's attitude to his former friend – always a harmful suggestion to a woman. Formerly she had appreciated her husband's superiority; she had smiled at Milvain's commoner stamp of mind and character. But tedious repetition of failure had outwearied her, and now she saw Milvain in the sunshine of progress, dwelt upon the worldly advantages of gifts and a temperament such as his. Again, simple and intelligible enough.

Living apart from her husband, she could not be expected to forswear society, and doubtless she would see Milvain pretty often. He called occasionally at Mrs Yule's, and would not do so less often when he knew that Amy was to be met there. There would be chance encounters like that of yesterday, of which she had chosen to keep silence.

A dark fear began to shadow him. In yielding thus passively to stress of circumstances, was he not exposing his wife to a danger which outweighed all the ills of poverty? As one to whom she was inestimably dear, was he right in allowing her to leave him, if only for a few months? He knew very well that a man of strong character would never have entertained this project. He had got into the way of thinking of himself as too weak to struggle against the obstacles on which Amy insisted, and of looking for safety in retreat; but what was to be the end of this weakness if the summer did not at all advance him? He knew better than Amy could how unlikely it was that he should recover the energies of his mind in so short a time and under such circumstances; only the feeble man's temptation to postpone effort had made him consent to this step, and now that he was all but beyond turning back, the perils of which he had thought too little forced themselves upon his mind.

He rose in anguish, and stood looking about him as if aid might somewhere be visible.

Presently there was a knock at the front door, and on opening he beheld the vivacious Mr Carter. This gentleman had only made two or three calls here since Reardon's marriage; his appearance was a surprise.

'I hear you are leaving town for a time,' he exclaimed. 'Edith told me yesterday, so I thought I'd look you up.'

He was in spring costume, and exhaled fresh odours. The contrast between his prosperous animation and Reardon's broken-spirited quietness could not have been more striking.

'Going away for your health, they tell me. You've been working too hard, you know. You mustn't overdo it. And where do you think of going to?'

'It isn't at all certain that I shall go,' Reardon replied. 'I thought of a few weeks – somewhere at the seaside.'

'I advise you to go north,' went on Carter cheerily. 'You want a tonic, you know. Get up into Scotland and do some boating and fishing – that kind of thing. You'd come back a new man. Edith and I had a turn up there last year, you know; it did me heaps of good.'

'Oh, I don't think I should go so far as that.'

'But that's just what you want – a regular change, something bracing. You don't look at all well, that's the fact. A winter in London tries any man – it does me, I know. I've been seedy myself these last few weeks. Edith wants me to take her over to Paris at the end of this month, and I think it isn't a bad idea; but I'm so confoundedly busy. In the autumn we shall go to Norway, I think; it seems to be the right thing to do nowadays. Why shouldn't you have a run over to Norway? They say it can be done very cheaply; the steamers take you for next to nothing.'

He talked on with the joyous satisfaction of a man whose income is assured, and whose future teems with a succession of lively holidays. Reardon could make no answer to such suggestions; he sat with a fixed smile on his face.

'Have you heard,' said Carter, presently, 'that we're opening a branch of the hospital in the City Road?'

'No; I hadn't heard of it.'

'It'll only be for out-patients. Open three mornings and three evenings alternately.'

'Who'll represent you there?'

'I shall look in now and then, of course; there'll be a clerk, like at the old place.'

He talked of the matter in detail – of the doctors who would attend, and of certain new arrangements to be tried.

'Have you engaged the clerk?' Reardon asked.

'Not yet. I think I know a man who'll suit me, though.'

'You wouldn't be disposed to give me the chance?'

Reardon spoke huskily, and ended with a broken laugh.

'You're rather above my figure nowadays, old man!' exclaimed Carter, joining in what he considered the jest.

'Shall you pay a pound a week?'

'Twenty-five shillings. It'll have to be a man who can be trusted to take money from the paying patients.'

'Well, I am serious. Will you give me the place?'

Carter gazed at him, and checked another laugh.

'What the deuce do you mean?'

'The fact is,' Reardon replied, 'I want variety of occupation. I can't stick at writing for more than a month or two at a time. It's because I have tried to do so that – well, practically, I have broken down. If you will give me this clerkship, it will relieve me from the necessity of perpetually writing novels; I shall be better for it in every way. You know that I'm equal to the job; you can trust me; and I dare say I shall be more useful than most clerks you could get.'

It was done, most happily done, on the first impulse. A minute more of pause, and he could not have faced the humiliation. His face burned, his tongue was parched.

'I'm floored!' cried Carter. 'I shouldn't have thought – but of course, if you really want it. I can hardly believe yet that you're serious, Reardon.'

'Why not? Will you promise me the work?'

'Well, yes.'

'When shall I have to begin?'

'The place 'll be opened to-morrow week. But how about your holiday?'

'Oh, let that stand over. It'll be holiday enough to occupy my-self in a new way. An old way, too; I shall enjoy it.'

He laughed merrily, relieved beyond measure at having come to what seemed an end of his difficulties. For half an hour they continued to talk over the affair.

'Well, it's a comical idea,' said Carter, as he took his leave, 'but you know your own business best.'

When Amy returned, Reardon allowed her to put the child to bed before he sought any conversation. She came at length and sat down in the study.

'Mother advises us not to sell the furniture,' were her first words.

'I'm glad of that, as I had quite made up my mind not to.'

There was a change in his way of speaking which she at once noticed.

'Have you thought of something?'

'Yes. Carter has been here, and he happened to mention that

they're opening an out-patient department of the hospital, in the City Road. He'll want someone to help him there. I asked for the post, and he promised it me.'

The last words were hurried, though he had resolved to speak with deliberation. No more feebleness; he had taken a decision, and would act upon it as became a responsible man.

'The post?' said Amy. 'What post?'

'In plain English, the clerkship. It'll be the same work as I used to have – registering patients, receiving their "letters," and so on. The pay is to be five-and-twenty shillings a week.'

Amy sat upright and looked steadily at him.

'Is this a joke?'

'Far from it, dear. It's a blessed deliverance.'

'You have asked Mr Carter to take you back as a clerk?'

'I have.'

'And you propose that we shall live on twenty-five shillings a week?'

'Oh no! I shall be engaged only three mornings in the week and three evenings. In my free time I shall do literary work, and no doubt I can earn fifty pounds a year by it – if I have your sympathy to help me. To-morrow I shall go and look for rooms some distance from here; in Islington, I think. We have been living far beyond our means; that must come to an end. We'll have no more keeping up of sham appearances. If I can make my way in literature, well and good; in that case our position and prospects will of course change. But for the present we are poor people, and must live in a poor way. If our friends like to come and see us, they must put aside all snobbishness, and take us as we are. If they prefer not to come, there'll be an excuse in our remoteness.'

Amy was stroking the back of her hand. After a long silence, she said in a very quiet, but very resolute tone:

'I shall not consent to this.'

'In that case, Amy, I must do without your consent. The rooms will be taken, and our furniture transferred to them.'

'To me that will make no difference,' returned his wife, in the same voice as before. 'I have decided – as you told me to – to go with Willie to mother's next Tuesday. You, of course, must do as you please. I should have thought a summer at the seaside

would have been more helpful to you; but if you prefer to live in
Islington –'

Reardon approached her, and laid a hand on her shoulder.

'Amy, are you my wife, or not?'

'I am certainly not the wife of a clerk who is paid so much a
week.'

He had foreseen a struggle, but without certainty of the form
Amy's opposition would take. For himself, he meant to be
gently resolute, calmly regardless of protest. But in a man to
whom such self-assertion is a matter of conscious effort, tremor
of the nerves will always interfere with the line of conduct he has
conceived in advance. Already Reardon had spoken with far more
bluntness than he proposed; involuntarily, his voice slipped
from earnest determination to the note of absolutism, and, as is
wont to be the case, the sound of these strange tones instigated
him to further utterances of the same kind. He lost control of
himself; Amy's last reply went through him like an electric
shock, and for the moment he was a mere husband defied by his
wife, the male stung to exertion of his brute force against the
physically weaker sex.

'However you regard me, you will do what I think fit. I shall
not argue with you. If I choose to take lodgings in Whitechapel,
there you will come and live.'

He met Amy's full look, and was conscious of that in it which
corresponded to his own brutality. She had become suddenly a
much older woman; her cheeks were tight drawn into thinness,
her lips were bloodlessly hard, there was an unknown furrow
along her forehead, and she glared like the animal that defends
itself with tooth and claw.

'Do as you think fit? Indeed!'

Could Amy's voice sound like that? Great Heaven! With just
such accent he had heard a wrangling woman retort upon her
husband at the street corner. Is there then no essential difference
between a woman of this world and one of that? Does the same
nature lie beneath such unlike surfaces?

He had but to do one thing: to seize her by the arm, drag her
up from the chair, dash her back again with all his force – there,
the transformation would be complete, they would stand towards
each other on the natural footing. With an added curse perhaps –

Instead of that, he choked, struggled for breath, and shed tears.

Amy turned scornfully away from him. Blows and a curse would have overawed her, at all events for the moment; she would have felt: 'Yes, he is a man, and I have put my destiny into his hands.' His tears moved her to a feeling cruelly exultant; they were the sign of her superiority. It was she who should have wept, and never in her life had she been further from such display of weakness.

This could not be the end, however, and she had no wish to terminate the scene. They stood for a minute without regarding each other, then Reardon faced to her.

'You refuse to live with me, then?'

'Yes, if this is the kind of life you offer me.'

'You would be more ashamed to share your husband's misfortunes than to declare to everyone that you had deserted him?'

'I shall "declare to everyone" the simple truth. You have the opportunity of making one more effort to save us from degradation. You refuse to take the trouble; you prefer to drag me down into a lower rank of life. I can't and won't consent to that. The disgrace is yours; it's fortunate for me that I have a decent home to go to.'

'Fortunate for you! – you make yourself unutterably contemptible. I have done nothing that justifies you in leaving me. It is for me to judge what I can do and what I can't. A good woman would see no degradation in what I ask of you. But to run away from me just because I am poorer than you ever thought I should be –'

He was incoherent. A thousand passionate things that he wished to say clashed together in his mind and confused his speech. Defeated in the attempt to act like a strong man, he could not yet recover standing-ground, knew not how to tone his utterances.

'Yes, of course, that's how you will put it,' said Amy. 'That's how you will represent me to your friends. My friends will see it in a different light.'

'They will regard you as a martyr?'

'No one shall make a martyr of me, you may be sure. I was unfortunate enough to marry a man who had no delicacy, no regard for my feelings. – I am not the first woman who has made a mistake of this kind.'

'No delicacy? No regard for your feelings? – Have I always utterly misunderstood you? Or has poverty changed you to a woman I can't recognise?'

He came nearer, and gazed desperately into her face. Not a muscle of it showed susceptibility to the old influences.

'Do you know, Amy,' he added in a lower voice, 'that if we part now, we part for ever?'

'I'm afraid that is only too likely.'

She moved aside.

'You mean that you wish it. You are weary of me, and care for nothing but how to make yourself free.'

'I shall argue no more. I am tired to death of it.'

'Then say nothing, but listen for the last time to my view of the position we have come to. When I consented to leave you for a time, to go away and try to work in solitude, I was foolish and even insincere, both to you and to myself. I knew that I was undertaking the impossible. It was just putting off the evil day, that was all – putting off the time when I should have to say plainly : "I can't live by literature, so I must look out for some other employment." I shouldn't have been so weak but that I knew how you would regard such a decision as that. I was afraid to tell the truth – afraid. Now, when Carter of a sudden put this opportunity before me, I saw all the absurdity of the arrangements we had made. It didn't take me a moment to make up my mind. Anything was to be chosen rather than a parting from you on false pretences, a ridiculous affectation of hope where there was no hope.'

He paused, and saw that his words had no effect upon her.

'And a grievous share of the fault lies with you, Amy. You remember very well when I first saw how dark the future was. I was driven even to say that we ought to change our mode of living; I asked you if you would be willing to leave this place and go into cheaper rooms. And you know what your answer was. Not a sign in you that you would stand by me if the worst came. I knew then what I had to look forward to, but I durst not believe it. I kept saying to myself : She loves me, and as soon as she really understands – That was all self-deception. If I had been a wise man, I should have spoken to you in a way you couldn't mistake. I should have told you that we were living recklessly, and that I had determined to alter it. I have no delicacy? No regard for your feelings? Oh, if I had had less ! I doubt whether you can even understand some of the considerations that weighed with me, and made me cowardly – though I once thought there was no refinement of sensibility that you couldn't enter into. Yes. I was absurd enough to say to myself : It will look as if I had consciously deceived her; she may suffer from the thought that I won her at all hazards, knowing that I should soon expose her to poverty and all sorts of humiliation. Impossible to speak of that again; I had to struggle desperately on, trying to hope. Oh ! if you knew –'

His voice gave way for an instant.

'I don't understand how you could be so thoughtless and heartless. You knew that I was almost mad with anxiety at times. Surely, any woman must have had the impulse to give what help was in her power. How could you hesitate? Had you no suspicion of what a relief and encouragement it would be to me, if you said : Yes, we must go and live in a simpler way? If only as a proof that you loved me, how I should have welcomed that ! You helped me in nothing. You threw all the responsibility upon me – always bearing in mind, I suppose, that there was a refuge for you. Even now, I despise myself for saying such things of you, though I know so bitterly that they are true. It takes a long time to see *you* as such a different woman from the one I worshipped. In passion, I can fling out violent words, but they don't yet answer to my actual feeling. It will be long enough yet before I *think* contemptuously of you. You know that when a light is suddenly extinguished, the image of it still shows before your eyes. But at last comes the darkness.'

Amy turned towards him once more.

'Instead of saying all this, you might be proving that I am wrong. Do so, and I will gladly confess it.'

'That you are wrong? I don't see your meaning.'

'You might prove that you are willing to do your utmost to save me from humiliation.'

'Amy, I *have* done my utmost. I have done more than you can imagine.'

'No. You have toiled on in illness and anxiety – I know that. But a chance is offered you now of working in a better way. Till that is tried, you have no right to give all up and try to drag me down with you.'

'I don't know how to answer. I have told you so often – You *can't* understand me!'

'I can! I can!' Her voice trembled for the first time. 'I know that you are so ready to give in to difficulties. Listen to me, and do as I bid you.' She spoke in the strangest tone of command. It was command, not exhortation, but there was no harshness in her voice. 'Go at once to Mr Carter. Tell him you have made a ludicrous mistake – in a fit of low spirits; anything you like to say. Tell him you of course couldn't dream of becoming his clerk. Tonight; at once! You understand me, Edwin? Go now, this moment.'

'Have you determined to see *how* weak I am? Do you wish to be able to despise me more completely still?'

'I am determined to be your friend, and to save you from yourself. Go at once! Leave all the rest to me. If I have let things take their course till now, it shan't be so in future. The responsibility shall be with *me*. Only do as I tell you.'

'You know it's impossible –'

'It is *not*! I will find money. No one shall be allowed to say that we are parting; no one has any such idea yet. You are going away for your health, just three summer months. I have been far more careful of appearances than you imagine, but you give me credit for so little. I will find the money you need, until you have written another book. I promise; I undertake it. Then I will find another home for us, of the proper kind. You shall have no trouble. You shall give yourself entirely to intellectual things. But Mr Carter must be told at once, before he can spread a report. If he has spoken, he must contradict what he has said.'

'But you amaze me, Amy. Do you mean to say that you look upon it as a veritable disgrace, my taking this clerkship?'

'I do. I can't help my nature. I am ashamed through and through that you should sink to this.'

'But everyone knows that I was a clerk once!'

'Very few people know it. And then that isn't the same thing. It doesn't matter what one has been in the past. Especially a literary man; everyone expects to hear that he was once poor. But to fall from the position you now have, and to take weekly wages – you surely can't know how people of my world regard that.'

'Of your world? I had thought your world was the same as mine, and knew nothing whatever of these imbecilities.'

'It is getting late. Go and see Mr Carter, and afterwards I will talk as much as you like.'

He might perhaps have yielded, but the unemphasised contempt in that last sentence was more than he could bear. It demonstrated to him more completely than set terms could have done what a paltry weakling he would appear in Amy's eyes if he took his hat down from the peg and set out to obey her orders.

'You are asking too much,' he said, with unexpected coldness. 'If my opinions are so valueless to you that you dismiss them like those of a troublesome child, I wonder you think it worth while to try and keep up appearances about me. It is very simple: make known to everyone that you are in no way connected with the disgrace I have brought upon myself. Put an advertisement in the newspapers to that effect, if you like – as men do about their wives' debts. I have chosen my part. I can't stultify myself to please you.'

She knew that this was final. His voice had the true ring of shame in revolt.

'Then go your way, and I will go mine!'

Amy left the room.

When Reardon went into the bedchamber an hour later, he unfolded a chair bedstead that stood there, threw some rugs upon it, and so lay down to pass the night. He did not close his eyes. Amy slept for an hour or two before dawn, and on waking she started up and looked anxiously about the room. But neither spoke.

There was a pretence of ordinary breakfast; the little servant necessitated that. When she saw her husband preparing to go out, Amy asked him to come into the study.

'How long shall you be away?' she asked, curtly.

'It is doubtful. I am going to look for rooms.'

'Then no doubt I shall be gone when you come back. There's no object, now, in my staying here till to-morrow.'

'As you please.'

'Do you wish Lizzie still to come?'

'No. Please to pay her wages and dismiss her. Here is some money.'

'I think you had better let me see to that.'

He flung the coin on to the table and opened the door. Amy stepped quickly forward, and closed it again.

'This is our good-bye, is it?' she asked, her eyes on the ground.

'As you wish it – yes.'

'You will remember that I have *not* wished it.'

'In that case, you have only to go with me to the new home.'

'I can't.'

'Then you have made your choice.'

She did not prevent his opening the door this time, and he passed out without looking at her.

His return was at three in the afternoon. Amy and the child were gone; the servant was gone. The table in the dining-room was spread as if for one person's meal.

He went into the bedroom. Amy's trunks had disappeared. The child's cot was covered over. In the study, he saw that the sovereign he had thrown on to the table still lay in the same place.

As it was a very cold day he lit a fire. Whilst it burnt up he sat reading a torn portion of a newspaper, and became quite interested in the report of a commercial meeting in the City, a thing he would never have glanced at under ordinary circumstances. The fragment fell at length from his hands; his head drooped; he sank into a troubled sleep.

About six he had tea, then began the packing of the few books that were to go with him, and of such other things as could be enclosed in box or portmanteau. After a couple of hours of this occupation he could no longer resist his weariness, so he went to bed. Before falling asleep he heard the two familiar clocks strike eight; this evening they were in unusual accord, and the querulous notes from the workhouse sounded between the deeper ones from St Marylebone. Reardon tried to remember when he had last observed this; the matter seemed to have a peculiar interest for him, and in dreams he worried himself with a grotesque speculation thence derived.

Chapter 18

THE OLD HOME

BEFORE her marriage Mrs Edmund Yule was one of seven motherless sisters who constituted the family of a dentist slenderly provided in the matter of income. The pinching and paring which was a chief employment of her energies in those early days had disagreeable effects upon a character disposed rather to generosity than the reverse; during her husband's lifetime she had enjoyed rather too eagerly all the good things which he put at her command, sometimes forgetting that a wife has duties as well as claims, and in her widowhood she indulged a pretentiousness and querulousness which were the natural, but not amiable, results of suddenly restricted circumstances.

Like the majority of London people, she occupied a house of which the rent absurdly exceeded the due proportion of her income, a pleasant foible turned to such good account by London landlords. Whereas she might have lived with a good deal of modest comfort, her existence was a perpetual effort to conceal the squalid background of what was meant for the eyes of her friends and neighbours. She kept only two servants, who were so ill paid and so relentlessly overworked that it was seldom they remained with her for more than three months. In dealings with other people whom she perforce employed she was often guilty of incredible meanness; as, for instance, when she obliged her half-starved dressmaker to purchase material for her, and then postponed payment alike for that and for the work itself to the last possible moment. This was not heartlessness in the strict sense of the word; the woman not only knew that her behaviour was shameful, she was in truth ashamed of it and sorry for her victims. But life was a battle. She must either crush or be crushed. With sufficient means, she would have defrauded no one, and would have behaved generously to many; with barely enough for her needs, she set her face and defied her feelings, inasmuch as she believed there was no choice.

She would shed tears over a pitiful story of want, and without shadow of hypocrisy. It was hard, it was cruel; such things oughtn't to be allowed in a world where there were so many rich people. The next day she would argue with her charwoman about halfpence, and end by paying the poor creature what she knew was inadequate and unjust. For the simplest reason: she hadn't more to give, without submitting to privations which she considered intolerable.

But whilst she could be a positive hyena to strangers, to those who were akin to her, and those of whom she was fond, her affectionate kindness was remarkable. One observes this peculiarity often enough; it reminds one how savage the social conflict is, in which those little groups of people stand serried against their common enemies; relentless to all others, among themselves only the more tender and zealous because of the ever-impending danger. No mother was ever more devoted. Her son, a gentleman of quite noteworthy selfishness, had board and lodging beneath her roof on nominal terms, and under no stress of pecuniary trouble had Mrs Yule called upon him to make the slightest sacrifice on her behalf. Her daughter she loved with profound tenderness, and had no will that was opposed to Amy's. And it was characteristic of her that her children were never allowed to understand of what baseness she often became guilty in the determination to support appearances. John Yule naturally suspected what went on behind the scenes; on one occasion – since Amy's marriage – he had involuntarily overheard a dialogue between his mother and a servant on the point of departing which made even him feel ashamed. But from Amy every paltriness and meanness had always been concealed with the utmost care; Mrs Yule did not scruple to lie heroically when in danger of being detected by her daughter.

Yet this energetic lady had no social ambitions that pointed above her own stratum. She did not aim at intimacy with her superiors; merely at superiority among her intimates. Her circle was not large, but in that circle she must be regarded with the respect due to a woman of refined tastes and personal distinction. Her little dinners might be of rare occurrence, but to be invited must be felt a privilege. 'Mrs Edmund Yule' must sound well on people's lips; never be the occasion of those peculiar smiles which she herself was rather fond of indulging at the mention of other people's names.

The question of Amy's marriage had been her constant thought from the time when the little girl shot into a woman grown. For Amy no common match, no acceptance of a husband merely for money or position. Few men who walked the earth were mates for Amy. But years went on, and the man of undeniable distinction did not yet present himself. Suitors offered, but Amy smiled coldly at their addresses, in private not seldom scornfully, and her mother, though growing anxious, approved. Then of a sudden appeared Edwin Reardon.

A literary man? Well, it was one mode of distinction. Happily, a novelist; novelists now and then had considerable social success. Mr Reardon, it was true, did not impress one as a man likely to push forward where the battle called for rude vigour, but Amy soon assured herself that he would have a reputation far other than that of the average successful story-teller. The best people would regard him; he would be welcomed in the penetralia of culture; superior persons would say: 'Oh, I don't read novels as a rule, but of course Mr Reardon's –' If that really were to be the case, all was well; for Mrs Yule could appreciate social and intellectual differences.

Alas! alas! What was the end of those shining anticipations?

First of all, Mrs Yule began to make less frequent mention of 'my son-in-law, Mr Edwin Reardon.' Next, she never uttered his name save when inquiries necessitated it. Then, the most intimate of her intimates received little hints which were not quite easy to interpret. 'Mr Reardon is growing so very eccentric – has an odd distaste for society – occupies himself with all sorts of out-of-the-way interests. No, I'm afraid we shan't have another of his novels for some time. I think he writes anonymously a good deal. And really, such curious eccentricities!' Many were the tears she wept after her depressing colloquies with Amy; and, as was to be expected, she thought severely of the cause of these sorrows. On the last occasion when he came to her house she received him with such extreme civility that Reardon thenceforth disliked her, whereas before he had only thought her a good-natured and silly woman.

Alas for Amy's marriage with a man of distinction! From step to step of descent, till here was downright catastrophe. Bitter enough in itself, but most lamentable with reference to the

friends of the family. How was it to be explained, this return of
Amy to her home for several months, whilst her husband was no
further away than Worthing? The bald, horrible truth – impossible! Yet Mr Milvain knew it, and the Carters must guess it.
What colour could be thrown upon such vulgar distress?

The worst was not yet. It declared itself this May morning,
when, quite unexpectedly, a cab drove up to the house, bringing
Amy and her child, and her trunks, and her band-boxes, and her
what-nots. From the dining-room window Mrs Yule was aware
of this arrival, and in a few moments she learnt the unspeakable
cause.

She burst into tears, genuine as ever woman shed.

'There's no use in that, mother,' said Amy, whose temper was
in a dangerous state. 'Nothing worse can happen, that's one consolation.'

'Oh, it's disgraceful! disgraceful!' sobbed Mrs Yule. 'What we
are to say I can *not* think.'

'I shall say nothing whatever. People can scarcely have the impertinence to ask us questions when we have shown that they are
unwelcome.'

'But there are some people I can't help giving some explanation to. My dear child, he is not in his right mind. I'm convinced
of it, there! He is *not* in his right mind.'

'That's nonsense, mother. He is as sane as I am.'

'But you have often said what strange things he says and does;
you know you have, Amy. That talking in his sleep; I've thought
a great deal of it since you told me about that. And – and so
many other things. My love, I shall give it to be understood that
he has become so very odd in his ways that –'

'I can't have that,' replied Amy with decision. 'Don't you see
that in that case I should be behaving very badly?'

'I can't see that at all. There are many reasons, as you know
very well, why one shouldn't live with a husband who is at all
suspected of mental derangement. You have done your utmost
for him. And this would be some sort of explanation, you know.
I am so convinced that there is truth in it, too.'

'Of course I can't prevent you from saying what you like,
but I think it would be very wrong to start a rumour of this
kind.'

There was less resolve in this utterance. Amy mused, and looked wretched.

'Come up to the drawing-room, dear,' said her mother, for they had held their conversation in the room nearest to the house-door. 'What a state your mind must be in! Oh dear! Oh dear!'

She was a slender, well-proportioned woman, still pretty in face, and dressed in a way that emphasised her abiding charms. Her voice had something of plaintiveness, and altogether she was of frailer type than her daughter.

'Is my room ready?' Amy inquired on the stairs.

'I'm sorry to say it isn't, dear, as I didn't expect you till to-morrow. But it shall be seen to immediately.'

This addition to the household was destined to cause grave difficulties with the domestic slaves. But Mrs Yule would prove equal to the occasion. On Amy's behalf she would have worked her servants till they perished of exhaustion before her eyes.

'Use my room for the present,' she added. 'I think the girl has finished up there. But wait here; I'll just go and see to things.'

'Things' were not quite satisfactory, as it proved. You should have heard the change that came in that sweetly plaintive voice when it addressed the luckless housemaid. It was not brutal; not at all. But so sharp, hard, unrelenting – the voice of the goddess Poverty herself perhaps sounds like that.

Mad? Was he to be spoken of in a low voice, and with finger pointing to the forehead? There was something ridiculous, as well as repugnant, in such a thought; but it kept possession of Amy's mind. She was brooding upon it when her mother came into the drawing-room.

'And he positively refused to carry out the former plan?'

'Refused. Said it was useless.'

'How could it be useless? There's something so unaccountable in his behaviour.'

'I don't think it unaccountable,' replied Amy. 'It's weak and selfish, that's all. He takes the first miserable employment that offers rather than face the hard work of writing another book.'

She was quite aware that this did not truly represent her

husband's position. But an uneasiness of conscience impelled her to harsh speech.

'But just fancy!' exclaimed her mother. 'What can he mean by asking you to go and live with him on twenty-five shillings a week? Upon my word, if his mind isn't disordered he must have made a deliberate plan to get rid of you.'

Amy shook her head.

'You mean,' asked Mrs Yule, 'that he really thinks it possible for all of you to be supported on those wages?'

The last word was chosen to express the utmost scorn.

'He talked of earning fifty pounds a year by writing.'

'Even then it could only make about a hundred a year. My dear child, it's one of two things: either he is out of his mind, or he has purposely cast you off.'

Amy laughed, thinking of her husband in the light of the latter alternative.

'There's no need to seek so far for explanations,' she said. 'He has failed, that's all; just like a man might fail in any other business. He can't write like he used to. It may be all the result of ill-health; I don't know. His last book, you see, is positively refused. He has made up his mind that there's nothing but poverty before him, and he can't understand why I should object to live like the wife of a working-man.'

'Well, I only know that he has placed you in an exceedingly difficult position. If he had gone away to Worthing for the summer we might have made it seem natural; people are always ready to allow literary men to do rather odd things – up to a certain point. We should have behaved as if there were nothing that called for explanation. But what are we to do now?'

Like her multitudinous kind, Mrs Yule lived only in the opinions of other people. What others would say was her ceaseless preoccupation. She had never conceived of life as something proper to the individual; independence in the directing of one's course seemed to her only possible in the case of very eccentric persons, or of such as were altogether out of society. Amy had advanced, intellectually, far beyond this standpoint, but lack of courage disabled her from acting upon her convictions.

'People must know the truth, I suppose,' she answered dispiritedly.

Now, confession of the truth was the last thing that would occur to Mrs Yule when social relations were concerned. Her whole existence was based on bold denial of actualities. And, as is natural in such persons, she had the ostrich instinct strongly developed; though very acute in the discovery of her friends' shams and lies, she deceived herself ludicrously in the matter of concealing her own embarrassments.

'But the fact is, my dear,' she answered, 'we don't know the truth ourselves. You had better let yourself be directed by me. It will be better, at first, if you see as few people as possible. I suppose you must say something or other to two or three of your own friends; if you take my advice you'll be rather mysterious. Let them think what they like; anything is better than to say plainly: "My husband can't support me, and he has gone to work as a clerk for weekly wages." Be mysterious, darling; depend upon it, that's the safest.'

The conversation was pursued, with brief intervals, all through the day. In the afternoon two ladies paid a call, but Amy kept out of sight. Between six and seven John Yule returned from his gentlemanly occupations. As he was generally in a touchy temper before dinner had soothed him, nothing was said to him of the latest developments of his sister's affairs until late in the evening; he was allowed to suppose that Reardon's departure for the seaside had taken place a day sooner than had been arranged.

Behind the dining-room was a comfortable little chamber set apart as John's sanctum; here he smoked and entertained his male friends, and contemplated the portraits of those female ones who would not have been altogether at their ease in Mrs Yule's drawing-room. Not long after dinner his mother and sister came to talk with him in this retreat.

With some nervousness Mrs Yule made known to him what had taken place. Amy, the while, stood by the table, and glanced over a magazine that she had picked up.

'Well, I see nothing to be surprised at,' was John's first remark. 'It was pretty certain he'd come to this. But what I want to know is, how long are we to be at the expense of supporting Amy and her youngster?'

This was practical, and just what Mrs Yule had expected from her son.

'We can't consider such things as that,' she replied. 'You don't wish, I suppose, that Amy should go and live in a back street at Islington, and be hungry every other day, and soon have no decent clothes?'

'I don't think Jack would be greatly distressed,' Amy put in quietly.

'This is a woman's way of talking,' replied John. 'I want to know what is to be the end of it all? I've no doubt it's uncommonly pleasant for Reardon to shift his responsibilities on to our shoulders. At this rate I think I shall get married, and live beyond my means until I can hold out no longer, and then hand my wife over to her relatives, with my compliments. It's about the coolest business that ever came under my notice.'

'But what is to be done?' asked Mrs Yule. 'It's no use talking sarcastically, John, or making yourself disagreeable.'

'We are not called upon to find a way out of the difficulty. The fact of the matter is, Reardon must get a decent berth. Somebody or other must pitch him into the kind of place that suits men who can do nothing in particular. Carter ought to be able to help, I should think.'

'You know very well,' said Amy, 'that places of that kind are not to be had for the asking. It may be years before any such opportunity offers.'

'Confound the fellow! Why the deuce doesn't he go on with his novel-writing? There's plenty of money to be made out of novels.'

'But he can't write, Jack. He has lost his talent.'

'That's all bosh, Amy. If a fellow has once got into the swing of it he can keep it up if he likes. He might write his two novels a year easily enough, just like twenty other men and women. Look here, I could do it myself if I weren't too lazy. And that's what's the matter with Reardon. He doesn't care to work.'

'I have thought that myself,' observed Mrs Yule. 'It really is too ridiculous to say that he couldn't write some kind of novels if he chose. Look at Miss Blunt's last book; why, anybody could have written that. I'm sure there isn't a thing in it I couldn't have imagined myself.'

'Well, all I want to know is, what's Amy going to do if things don't alter?'

'She shall never want a home as long as I have one to share with her.'

John's natural procedure, when beset by difficulties, was to find fault with everyone all round, himself maintaining a position of irresponsibility.

'It's all very well, mother, but when a girl gets married she takes her husband, I have always understood, for better or worse, just as a man takes his wife. To tell the truth, it seems to me Amy has put herself in the wrong. It's deuced unpleasant to go and live in back streets, and to go without dinner now and then, but girls mustn't marry if they're afraid to face these things.'

'Don't talk so monstrously, John!' exclaimed his mother. 'How could Amy possibly foresee such things? The case is quite an extraordinary one.'

'Not so uncommon, I assure you. Some one was telling me the other day of a married lady – well educated and blameless – who goes to work at a shop somewhere or other because her husband can't support her.'

'And you wish to see Amy working in a shop?'

'No, I can't say I do. I'm only telling you that her bad luck isn't unexampled. It's very fortunate for her that she has good-natured relatives.'

Amy had taken a seat apart. She sat with her head leaning on her hand.

'Why don't you go and see Reardon?' John asked of his mother.

'What would be the use? Perhaps he would tell me to mind my own business.'

'By jingo! precisely what you would be doing. I think you ought to see him and give him to understand that he's behaving in a confoundedly ungentlemanly way. Evidently he's the kind of fellow that wants stirring up. I've half a mind to go and see him myself. Where is this slum that he's gone to live in?'

'We don't know his address yet.'

'So long as it's not the kind of place where one would be afraid of catching a fever, I think it wouldn't be amiss for me to look him up.'

'You'll do no good by that,' said Amy, indifferently.

'Confound it! It's just because nobody does anything that things have come to this pass!'

The conversation was, of course, profitless. John could only return again and again to his assertion that Reardon must get 'a decent berth.' At length Amy left the room in weariness and disgust.

'I suppose they have quarrelled terrifically,' said her brother, as soon as she was gone.

'I am afraid so.'

'Well, you must do as you please. But it's confounded hard lines that you should have to keep her and the kid. You know I can't afford to contribute.'

'My dear, I haven't asked you to.'

'No, but you'll have the devil's own job to make ends meet; I know that well enough.'

'I shall manage somehow.'

'All right; you're a plucky woman, but it's too bad. – Reardon's a humbug, that's my opinion. I shall have a talk with Carter about him. I suppose he has transferred all their furniture to the slum?'

'He can't have removed yet. It was only this morning that he went to search for lodgings.'

'Oh, then I tell you what it is; I shall look in there the first thing to-morrow morning, and just talk to him in a fatherly way. You needn't say anything to Amy. But I see he's just the kind of fellow that, if everyone leaves him alone, he'll be content with Carter's five-and-twenty shillings for the rest of his life, and never trouble his head about how Amy is living.'

To this proposal Mrs Yule readily assented. On going upstairs she found that Amy had all but fallen asleep upon a settee in the drawing-room.

'You are quite worn out with your troubles,' she said. 'Go to bed, and have a good long sleep.'

'Yes, I will.'

The neat, fresh bedchamber seemed to Amy a delightful haven of rest. She turned the key in the door with an enjoyment of the privacy thus secured such as she had never known in her life; for in maidenhood safe solitude was a matter of course to her, and since marriage she had not passed a night alone. Willie was fast asleep in a little bed shadowed by her own. In an impulse of maternal love and gladness she bent over the child and covered his face with kisses too gentle to awaken him.

How clean and sweet everything was! It is often said, by people who are exquisitely ignorant of the matter, that cleanliness is a luxury within reach even of the poorest. Very far from that; only with the utmost difficulty, with wearisome exertion, with harassing sacrifice, can people who are pinched for money preserve a moderate purity in their persons and their surroundings. By painful degrees Amy had accustomed herself to compromises in this particular which in the early days of her married life would have seemed intensely disagreeable, if not revolting. A housewife who lives in the country, and has but a patch of back garden, or even a good-sized kitchen, can, if she thinks fit, take her place at the wash-tub and relieve her mind on laundry matters; but to the inhabitant of a miniature flat in the heart of London anything of that kind is out of the question. When Amy began to cut down her laundress's bill, she did it with a sense of degradation. One grows accustomed, however, to such unpleasant necessities, and already she had learnt what was the minimum of expenditure for one who is troubled with a lady's instincts.

No, no; cleanliness is a costly thing, and a troublesome thing when appliances and means have to be improvised. It was, in part, the understanding she had gained of this side of the life of poverty that made Amy shrink in dread from the still narrower lodgings to which Reardon invited her. She knew how subtly one's self-respect can be undermined by sordid conditions. The difference between the life of well-to-do educated people and that of the uneducated poor is not greater in visible details than in the minutiæ of privacy, and Amy must have submitted to an extraordinary change before it would have been possible for her to live at ease in the circumstances which satisfy a decent working-class woman. She was prepared for final parting from her husband rather than try to effect that change in herself.

She undressed at leisure, and stretched her limbs in the cold, soft, fragrant bed. A sigh of profound relief escaped her. How good it was to be alone!

And in a quarter of an hour she was sleeping as peacefully as the child who shared her room.

At breakfast in the morning she showed a bright, almost a happy face. It was long, long since she had enjoyed such a night's rest, so undisturbed with unwelcome thoughts on the threshold of sleep and on awaking. Her life was perhaps wrecked, but the thought of that did not press upon her; for the present she must enjoy her freedom. It was like a recovery of girlhood. There are few married women who would not, sooner or later, accept with joy the offer of some months of a maidenly liberty. Amy would not allow herself to think that her wedded life was at an end. With a woman's strange faculty of closing her eyes against facts that do not immediately concern her, she tasted the relief of the present and let the future lie unregarded. Reardon would get out of his difficulties sooner or later; somebody or other would help him; that was the dim background of her agreeable sensations.

He suffered, no doubt. But then it was just as well that he should. Suffering would perhaps impel him to effort. When he communicated to her his new address – he could scarcely neglect to do that – she would send a not unfriendly letter, and hint to him that now was his opportunity for writing a book, as good a book as those which formerly issued from his garret-solitude. If he found that literature was in truth a thing of the past with him, then he must exert himself to obtain a position worthy of an educated man. Yes, in this way she would write to him, without a word that could hurt or offend.

She ate an excellent breakfast, and made known her enjoyment of it.

'I am so glad!' replied her mother. 'You have been getting quite thin and pale.'

'Quite consumptive,' remarked John, looking up from his newspaper. 'Shall I make arrangements for a daily landau at the livery stables round here?'

'You can if you like,' replied his sister, 'it would do both mother and me good, and I have no doubt you could afford it quite well.'

'Oh indeed! You're a remarkable young woman, let me tell you. By-the-by, I suppose your husband is breakfasting on bread and water?'

'I hope not, and I don't think it very likely.'

'Jack, Jack!' interposed Mrs Yule, softly.

Her son resumed his paper, and at the end of the meal rose with an unwonted briskness to make his preparations for departure.

Chapter 19

THE PAST REVIVED

NOR would it be true to represent Edwin Reardon as rising to the new day wholly disconsolate. He too had slept unusually well, and with returning consciousness the sense of a burden removed was more instant than that of his loss and all the dreary circumstances attaching to it. He had no longer to fear the effects upon Amy of such a grievous change as from their home-like flat to the couple of rooms he had taken in Islington; for the moment, this relief helped him to bear the pain of all that had happened and the uneasiness which troubled him when he reflected that his wife was henceforth a charge to her mother.

Of course for the moment only. He had no sooner begun to move about, to prepare his breakfast (amid the relics of last evening's meal), to think of all the detestable work he had to do before to-morrow night, than his heart sank again. His position was well nigh as dolorous as that of any man who awoke that morning to the brutal realities of life. If only for the shame of it! How must they be speaking of him, Amy's relatives, and her friends? A novelist who couldn't write novels; a husband who couldn't support his wife and child; a literate who made eager application for illiterate work at paltry wages – how interesting it would all sound in humorous gossip! And what hope had he that things would ever be better with him?

Had he done well? Had he done wisely? Would it not have been better to have made that one last effort? There came before him a vision of quiet nooks beneath the Sussex cliffs, of the long lines of green breakers bursting into foam; he heard the wave-music, and tasted the briny freshness of the sea-breeze. Inspiration, after all, would perchance have come to him.

If Amy's love had but been of more enduring quality; if she had strengthened him for this last endeavour with the brave tenderness of an ideal wife! But he had seen such hateful things in her eyes. Her love was dead, and she regarded him as the man who had spoilt her hopes of happiness. It was only for her own sake that she urged him to strive on; let his be the toil, that hers might be the advantage if he succeeded.

'She would be glad if I were dead. She would be glad.'

He had the conviction of it. Oh yes, she would shed tears; they come so easily to women. But to have him dead and out of her way; to be saved from her anomalous position; to see once more a chance in life; she would welcome it.

But there was no time for brooding. To-day he had to sell all the things that were superfluous, and to make arrangements for the removal of his effects to-morrow. By Wednesday night, in accordance with his agreement, the flat must be free for the new occupier.

He had taken only two rooms, and fortunately as things were. Three would have cost more than he was likely to be able to afford for a long time. The rent of the two was to be six-and six-pence; and how if Amy had consented to come, could he have met the expenses of their living out of his weekly twenty-five shillings? How could he have pretended to do literary work in such cramped quarters, he who had never been able to write a line save in strict seclusion? In his despair he had faced the impossible. Amy had shown more wisdom, though in a spirit of unkindness.

Towards ten o'clock he was leaving the flat to go and find people who would purchase his books and old clothing and other superfluities; but before he could close the door behind him, an approaching step on the stairs caught his attention. He saw the shining silk hat of a well-equipped gentleman. It was John Yule.

'Ha! Good-morning!' John exclaimed, looking up. 'A minute or two and I should have been too late, I see.'

He spoke in quite a friendly way, and, on reaching the landing, shook hands.

'Are you obliged to go at once? Or could I have a word with you?'

'Come in.'

They entered the study, which was in some disorder; Reardon made no reference to circumstances, but offered a chair, and seated himself.

'Have a cigarette?' said Yule, holding out a box of them.

'No, thank you; I don't smoke so early.'

'Then I'll light one myself; it always makes talk easier to me. You're on the point of moving, I suppose?'

'Yes, I am.'

Reardon tried to speak in quite a simple way, with no admission of embarrassment. He was not successful, and to his visitor the tone seemed rather offensive.

'I suppose you'll let Amy know your new address?'

'Certainly. Why should I conceal it?'

'No, no; I didn't mean to suggest that. But you might be taking it for granted that – that the rupture was final, I thought.'

There had never been any intimacy between these two men. Reardon regarded his wife's brother as rather snobbish and disagreeably selfish; John Yule looked upon the novelist as a prig, and now of late as a shuffling, untrustworthy fellow. It appeared to John that his brother-in-law was assuming a manner wholly unjustifiable, and he had a difficulty in behaving to him with courtesy. Reardon, on the other hand, felt injured by the turn his visitor's remarks were taking, and began to resent the visit altogether.

'I take nothing for granted,' he said coldly. 'But I'm afraid nothing is to be gained by a discussion of our difficulties. The time for that is over.'

'I can't quite see that. It seems to me that the time has just come.'

'Please tell me, to begin with, do you come on Amy's behalf?'

'In a way, yes. She hasn't sent me, but my mother and I are so astonished at what is happening that it was necessary for one or other of us to see you.'

'I think it is all between Amy and myself.'

'Difficulties between husband and wife are generally best left to the people themselves, I know. But the fact is, there are peculiar circumstances in the present case. It can't be necessary for me to explain further.'

Reardon could find no suitable words of reply. He understood what Yule referred to, and began to feel the full extent of his humiliation.

'You mean, of course –' he began; but his tongue failed him.

'Well, we should really like to know how long it is proposed that Amy shall remain with her mother.'

John was perfectly self-possessed; it took much to disturb his equanimity. He smoked his cigarette, which was in an amber mouth-piece, and seemed to enjoy its flavour. Reardon found himself observing the perfection of the young man's boots and trousers.

'That depends entirely on my wife herself,' he replied mechanically.

'How so?'

'I offer her the best home I can.'

Reardon felt himself a poor, pitiful creature, and hated the well-dressed man who made him feel so.

'But really, Reardon,' began the other, uncrossing and recrossing his legs, 'do you tell me in seriousness that you expect Amy to live in such lodgings as you can afford on a pound a week?'

'I don't. I said that I had offered her the best home I could. I know it's impossible, of course.'

Either he must speak thus, or break into senseless wrath. It was hard to hold back the angry words that were on his lips, but he succeeded, and he was glad he had done so.

'Then it doesn't depend on Amy,' said John.

'I suppose not.'

'You see no reason, then, why she shouldn't live as at present for an indefinite time?'

To John, whose perspicacity was not remarkable, Reardon's changed tone conveyed simply an impression of bland impudence. He eyed his brother-in-law rather haughtily.

'I can only say,' returned the other, who is become wearily indifferent, 'that as soon as I can afford a decent home I shall give my wife the opportunity of returning to me.'

'But, pray, when is that likely to be?'

John had passed the bounds; his manner was too frankly contemptuous.

'I see no right you have to examine me in this fashion,' Reardon exclaimed. 'With Mrs Yule I should have done my best to be patient if she had asked these questions; but you are not justified in putting them, at all events not in this way.'

'I'm very sorry you speak like this, Reardon,' said the other, with calm insolence. 'It confirms unpleasant ideas, you know.'

'What do you mean?'

'Why, one can't help thinking that you are rather too much at your ease under the circumstances. It isn't exactly an everyday thing, you know, for a man's wife to be sent back to her own people –'

Reardon could not endure the sound of these words. He interrupted hotly.

'I can't discuss it with you. You are utterly unable to comprehend me and my position, utterly! It would be useless to defend myself. You must take whatever view seems to you the natural one.'

John, having finished his cigarette, rose.

'The natural view is an uncommonly disagreeable one,' he said. 'However, I have no intention of quarrelling with you. I'll only just say that, as I take a share in the expenses of my mother's house, this question decidedly concerns me; and I'll add that I think it ought to concern you a good deal more than it seems to.'

Reardon, ashamed already of his violence, paused upon these remarks.

'It shall,' he uttered at length, coldly. 'You have put it clearly enough to me, and you shan't have spoken in vain. Is there anything else you wish to say?'

'Thank you; I think not.'

They parted with distant civility, and Reardon closed the door behind his visitor.

He knew that his character was seen through a distorting medium by Amy's relatives, to some extent by Amy herself; but hitherto the reflection that this must always be the case when a man of his kind is judged by people of the world had strengthened him in defiance. An endeavour to explain himself would be maddeningly hopeless; even Amy did not understand aright the troubles through which his intellectual and moral nature was passing, and to speak of such experiences to Mrs Yule or to John would be equivalent to addressing them in alien tongues; he and they had no common criterion by reference to which he could make himself intelligible. The practical tone in which John had explained the opposing view of the situation made it impossible for him to proceed as he had purposed. Amy would never come to him in his poor lodgings; her mother, her brother, all her advisers would regard such a thing as out of the question. Very well; recognising this, he must also recognise his wife's claim upon him for material support. It was not in his power to supply her with means sufficient to live upon, but what he could afford she should have.

When he went out, it was with a different purpose from that of half an hour ago. After a short search in the direction of Edgware Road, he found a dealer in second-hand furniture, whom he requested to come as soon as possible to the flat on a matter of business. An hour later the man kept his appointment. Having brought him into the study, Reardon said:

'I wish to sell everything in this flat, with a few exceptions that I'll point out to you.'

'Very good, sir,' was the reply. 'Let's have a look through the rooms.'

That the price offered would be strictly a minimum Reardon knew well enough. The dealer was a rough and rather dirty fellow, with the distrustful glance which distinguishes his class. Men of Reardon's type, when hapless enough to be forced into vulgar commerce, are doubly at a disadvantage; not only their ignorance, but their sensitiveness, makes them ready victims of even the least subtle man of business. To deal on equal terms with a person you must be able to assert with calm confidence that you are not to be cheated; Reardon was too well aware that he would certainly be cheated, and shrank scornfully from the higgling of the market. Moreover, he was in a half-frenzied state of mind, and cared for little but to be done with the hateful details of this process of ruin.

He pencilled a list of the articles he must retain for his own use; it would of course be cheaper to take a bare room than furnished lodgings, and every penny he could save was of importance to him. The chair-bedstead, with necessary linen and blankets, a table, two chairs, a looking-glass – strictly the indispensable things; no need to complete the list. Then there were a few valuable wedding-presents, which belonged rather to Amy than to him; these he would get packed and send to Westbourne Park.

The dealer made his calculation, with many side-glances at the vendor.

'And what may you ask for the lot?'

'Please to make an offer.'

'Most of the things has had a good deal of wear –'

'I know, I know. Just let me hear what you will give.'

'Well, if you want a valuation, I say eighteen pound ten.'

It was more than Reardon had expected, though much less than a man who understood such affairs would have obtained.

'That's the most you can give?'

'Wouldn't pay me to give a sixpence more. You see –'

He began to point out defects, but Reardon cut him short.

'Can you take them away at once?'

'At wunst? Would two o'clock do?'

'Yes, it would.'

'And might you want these other things takin' anywheres?'

'Yes, but not till to-morrow. They have to go to Islington. What would you do it for?'

This bargain also was completed, and the dealer went his way. Thereupon Reardon set to work to dispose of his books; by half-past one he had sold them for a couple of guineas. At two came the cart that was to take away the furniture, and at four o'clock nothing remained in the flat save what had to be removed on the morrow.

The next thing to be done was to go to Islington, forfeit a week's rent for the two rooms he had taken, and find a single room at the lowest possible cost. On the way, he entered an eating-house and satisfied his hunger, for he had had nothing since breakfast. It took him a couple of hours to discover the ideal garret; it was found at length in a narrow little by-way running out of Upper Street. The rent was half a crown a week.

At seven o'clock he sat down in what once was called his study, and wrote the following letter:

'Enclosed in this envelope you will find twenty pounds. I have been reminded that your relatives will be at the expense of your support; it seemed best to me to sell the furniture, and now I send you all the money I can spare at present. You will receive to-morrow a box containing several things I did not feel justified in selling. As soon as I begin to have my payment from Carter, half of it shall be sent to you every week. My address is: 5 Manville Street, Upper Street, Islington. – EDWIN REARDON.'

He enclosed the money, in notes and gold, and addressed the envelope to his wife. She must receive it this very night, and he knew not how to insure that save by delivering it himself. So he went to Westbourne Park by train, and walked to Mrs Yule's house. At this hour the family were probably at dinner; yes, the window of the dining-room showed lights within, whilst those of the drawing-room were in shadow. After a little hesitation he rang the servants' bell. When the door opened, he handed his letter to the girl, and requested that it might be given to Mrs Reardon as soon as possible. With one more hasty glance at the window – Amy was perhaps enjoying her unwonted comfort – he walked quickly away.

As he re-entered what had been his home, its bareness made his heart sink. An hour or two had sufficed for this devastation; nothing remained upon the uncarpeted floors but the needments he would carry with him into the wilderness, such few evidences of civilisation as the poorest cannot well dispense with. Anger, revolt, a sense of outraged love – all manner of confused passions had sustained him throughout this day of toil; now he had leisure to know how faint he was. He threw himself upon his chair-bedstead, and lay for more than an hour in torpor of body and mind.

But before he could sleep he must eat. Though it was cold, he could not exert himself to light a fire; there was some food still in the cupboard, and he consumed it in the fashion of a tired labourer, with the plate on his lap, using his fingers and a knife. What had he to do with delicacies?

He felt utterly alone in the world. Unless it were Biffen, what mortal would give him kindly welcome under any roof? These stripped rooms were symbolical of his life; losing money, he had lost everything. 'Be thankful that you exist, that these morsels of food are still granted you. Man has a right to nothing in this world that he cannot pay for. Did you imagine that love was an exception? Foolish idealist! Love is one of the first things to be frightened away by poverty. Go and live upon your twelve and sixpence a week, and on your memories of the past.'

In this room he had sat with Amy on their return from the wedding holiday. 'Shall you always love me as you do now?' – 'For ever! for ever!' – 'Even if I disappointed you? If I failed?' –

'How could that affect my love?' The voices seemed to be lingering still, in a sad, faint echo, so short a time it was since those
words were uttered.

His own fault. A man has no business to fail; least of all can he
expect others to have time to look back upon him or pity him if
he sink under the stress of conflict. Those behind will trample
over his body; they can't help it; they themselves are borne on-
wards by resistless pressure.

He slept for a few hours, then lay watching the light of dawn
as it revealed his desolation.

The morning's post brought him a large heavy envelope, the
aspect of which for a moment puzzled him. But he recognised
the handwriting, and understood. The editor of *The Wayside*,
in a pleasantly-written note, begged to return the paper on
Pliny's letters which had recently been submitted to him; he was
sorry it did not strike him as quite so interesting as the other
contributions from Reardon's pen.

This was a trifle. For the first time he received a rejected piece
of writing without distress; he even laughed at the artistic completeness of the situation. The money would have been welcome,
but on that very account he might have known it would not
come.

The cart that was to transfer his property to the room in
Islington arrived about mid-day. By that time he had dismissed
the last details of business in relation to the flat, and was free to
go back to the obscure world whence he had risen. He felt that
for two years and a half he had been a pretender. It was not
natural to him to live in the manner of people who enjoy an
assured income; he belonged to the class of casual wage-earners.
Back to obscurity!

Carrying a bag which contained a few things best kept in his
own care he went by train to King's Cross, and thence walked
up Pentonville Hill to Upper Street and his own little by-way.
Manville Street was not unreasonably squalid; the house in
which he had found a home was not alarming in its appearance,
and the woman who kept it had an honest face. Amy would have
shrunk in apprehension, but to one who had experience of London garrets this was a rather favourable specimen of its kind. The

door closed more satisfactorily than poor Biffen's, for instance, and there were not many of those knot-holes in the floor which gave admission to piercing little draughts; not a pane of the window was cracked, not one. A man might live here comfortably – could memory be destroyed.

'There's a letter come for you,' said the landlady as she admitted him. 'You'll find it on your mantel.'

He ascended hastily. The letter must be from Amy, as no one else knew his address. Yes, and its contents were these:

'As you have really sold the furniture, I shall accept half this money that you send. I must buy clothing for myself and Willie. But the other ten pounds I shall return to you as soon as possible. As for your offer of half what you are to receive from Mr Carter, that seems to me ridiculous; in any case, I cannot take it. If you seriously abandon all further hope from literature, I think it is your duty to make every effort to obtain a position suitable to a man of your education. – AMY REARDON.'

Doubtless Amy thought it was her duty to write in this way. Not a word of sympathy; he must understand that no one was to blame but himself, and that her hardships were equal to his own.

In the bag he had brought with him there were writing materials. Standing at the mantelpiece, he forthwith penned a reply to this letter:

'The money is for your support, as far as it will go. If it comes back to me I shall send it again. If you refuse to make use of it, you will have the kindness to put it aside and consider it as belonging to Willie. The other money of which I spoke will be sent to you once a month. As our concerns are no longer between us alone, I must protect myself against anyone who would be likely to accuse me of not giving you what I could afford. For your advice I thank you, but remember that in withdrawing from me your affection you have lost all right to offer me counsel.'

He went out and posted this at once.

By three o'clock the furniture of his room was arranged. He had not kept a carpet; that was luxury, and beyond his due. His score of volumes must rank upon the mantelpiece; his clothing must be kept in the trunk. Cups, plates, knives, forks, and spoons would lie in the little open cupboard, the lowest section of which was for his supply of coals. When everything was in order he drew water from a tap on the landing and washed himself; then, with his bag, went out to make purchases. A loaf of bread, butter, sugar, condensed milk; a remnant of tea he had brought with him. On returning, he lit as small a fire as possible, put on his kettle, and sat down to meditate.

How familiar it all was to him! And not unpleasant for it brought back the days when he had worked to such good purpose. It was like a restoration of youth.

Of Amy he would not think. Knowing his bitter misery, she could write to him in cold, hard words, without a touch even of womanly feeling. If ever they were to meet again, the advance must be from her side. He had no more tenderness for her until she strove to revive it.

Next morning he called at the hospital to see Carter. The secretary's peculiar look and smile seemed to betray a knowledge of what had been going on since Sunday, and his first words confirmed this impression of Reardon's.

'You have removed, I hear?'

'Yes; I had better give you my new address.'

Reardon's tone was meant to signify that further remark on the subject would be unwelcome. Musingly, Carter made a note of the address.

'You still wish to go on with this affair?'

'Certainly.'

'Come and have some lunch with me, then, and afterwards we'll go to the City Road and talk things over on the spot.'

The vivacious young man was not quite so genial as of wont, but he evidently strove to show that the renewal of their relations as employer and clerk would make no difference in the friendly intercourse which had since been established; the invitation to lunch evidently had this purpose.

'I suppose,' said Carter, when they were seated in a restaurant, 'you wouldn't object to anything better, if a chance turned up?'

'I should take it, to be sure.'

'But you don't want a job that would occupy all your time? You're going on with writing, of course?'

'Not for the present, I think.'

'Then you would like me to keep a look-out? I haven't anything in view – nothing whatever. But one hears of things sometimes.'

'I should be obliged to you if you could help me to anything satisfactory.'

Having brought himself to this admission, Reardon felt more at ease. To what purpose should he keep up transparent pretences? It was manifestly his duty to earn as much money as he could, in whatever way. Let the man of letters be forgotten; he was seeking for remunerative employment, just as if he had never written a line.

Amy did not return the ten pounds, and did not write again. So, presumably, she would accept the moiety of his earnings; he was glad of it. After paying half a crown for rent, there would be left ten shillings. Something like three pounds that still remained to him he would not reckon; this must be for casualties. Half a sovereign was enough for his needs; in the old times he had counted it a competency which put his mind quite at rest.

The day came, and he entered upon his duties in City Road. It needed but an hour or two, and all the intervening time was cancelled; he was back once more in the days of no reputation, a harmless clerk, a decent wage-earner.

Chapter 20

THE END OF WAITING

IT was more than a fortnight after Reardon's removal to Islington when Jasper Milvain heard for the first time of what had happened. He was coming down from the office of the *Will-o'-the-Wisp* one afternoon, after a talk with the editor concerning a paragraph in his last week's *causerie* which had been complained of as libellous, and which would probably lead to the 'case' so much desired by everyone connected with the paper, when someone descending from a higher storey of the building overtook him and laid a hand on his shoulder. He turned and saw Whelpdale.

'What brings you on these premises?' he asked as they shook hands.

'A man I know has just been made sub-editor of *Chat*, upstairs. He has half promised to let me do a column of answers to correspondents.'

'Cosmetics? Fashions? Cookery?'

'I'm not so versatile as all that, unfortunately. No, the general information column. "Will you be so good as to inform me, through the medium of your invaluable paper, what was the exact area devastated by the Great Fire of London?" – that kind of thing, you know. Hopburn – that's the fellow's name – tells me that his predecessor always called the paper *Chat-moss*, because of the frightful difficulty he had in filling it up each week. By-the-by, what a capital column that is of yours in *Will-o'-the-Wisp*. I know nothing like it in English journalism; upon my word I don't!'

'Glad you like it. Some people are less fervent in their admiration.'

Jasper recounted the affair which had just been under discussion in the office.

'It may cost a couple of thousands, but the advertisement is worth that, Patwin thinks. Barlow is delighted; he wouldn't mind paying double the money to make those people a laughing-stock for a week or two.'

They issued into the street, and walked on together; Milvain, with his keen eye and critical smile, unmistakably the modern young man who cultivates the art of success; his companion of a less pronounced type, but distinguished by a certain subtlety of countenance, a blending of the sentimental and the shrewd.

'Of course you know all about the Reardons?' said Whelpdale.

'Haven't seen or heard of them lately. What is it?'

'Then you don't know that they have parted?'

'Parted?'

'I only heard about it last night; Biffen told me. Reardon is doing clerk's work at a hospital somewhere in the East-end, and his wife has gone to live at her mother's house.'

'Ho, ho!' exclaimed Jasper, thoughtfully. 'Then the crash has come. Of course I knew it must be impending. I'm sorry for Reardon.'

'I'm sorry for his wife.'

'Trust you for thinking of women first, Whelpdale.'

'It's in an honourable way, my dear fellow. I'm a slave to women, true, but all in an honourable way. After that last adventure of mine most men would be savage and cynical, wouldn't they now? I'm nothing of the kind. I think no worse of women – not a bit. I reverence them as much as ever. There must be a good deal of magnanimity in me, don't you think?'

Jasper laughed unrestrainedly.

'But it's the simple truth,' pursued the other. 'You should have seen the letter I wrote to that girl at Birmingham – all charity and forgiveness. I meant it, every word of it. I shouldn't talk to everyone like this, you know; but it's as well to show a friend one's best qualities now and then.'

'Is Reardon still living at the old place?'

'No, no. They sold up everything and let the flat. He's in lodgings somewhere or other. I'm not quite intimate enough with him to go and see him under the circumstances. But I'm surprised you know nothing about it.'

'I haven't seen much of them this year. Reardon – well, I'm afraid he hasn't very much of the virtue you claim for yourself. It rather annoys him to see me going ahead.'

'Really? His character never struck me in that way.'

'You haven't come enough in contact with him. At all events,

I can't explain his change of manner in any other way. But I'm sorry for him; I am, indeed. At a hospital? I suppose Carter has given him the old job again?'

'Don't know. Biffen doesn't talk very freely about it; there's a good deal of delicacy in Biffen, you know. A thoroughly good-hearted fellow. And so is Reardon, I believe, though no doubt he has his weaknesses.'

'Oh, an excellent fellow! But weakness isn't the word. Why, I foresaw all this from the very beginning. The first hour's talk I ever had with him was enough to convince me that he'd never hold his own. But he really believed that the future was clear before him; he imagined he'd go on getting more and more for his books. An extraordinary thing that that girl had such faith in him!'

They parted soon after this, and Milvain went homeward, musing upon what he had heard. It was his purpose to spend the whole evening on some work which pressed for completion, but he found an unusual difficulty in settling to it. About eight o'clock he gave up the effort, arrayed himself in the costume of black and white, and journeyed to Westbourne Park, where his destination was the house of Mrs Edmund Yule. Of the servant who opened to him he inquired if Mrs Yule was at home, and received an answer in the affirmative.

'Any company with her?'

'A lady – Mrs Carter.'

'Then please to give my name, and ask if Mrs Yule can see me.'

He was speedily conducted to the drawing-room, where he found the lady of the house, her son, and Mrs Carter. For Mrs Reardon his eye sought in vain.

'I'm so glad you have come,' said Mrs Yule, in a confidential tone. 'I have been wishing to see you. Of course, you know of our sad trouble?'

'I have heard of it only to-day.'

'From Mr Reardon himself?'

'No; I haven't seen him.'

'I do wish you had! We should have been so anxious to know how he impressed you.'

'How he impressed me?'

'My mother has got hold of the notion,' put in John Yule, 'that he's not exactly *compos mentis*.[22] I'll admit that he went on in a queer sort of way the last time I saw him.'

'And my husband thinks he is rather strange,' remarked Mrs Carter.'

'He has gone back to the hospital, I understand –'

'To a new branch that has just been opened in the City Road,' replied Mrs Yule. 'And he's living in a dreadful place – one of the most shocking alleys in the worst part of Islington. I should have gone to see him, but I really feel afraid; they give me such an account of the place. And everyone agrees that he has such a very wild look, and speaks so strangely.'

'Between ourselves,' said John, 'there's no use in exaggerating. He's living in a vile hole, that's true, and Carter says he looks miserably ill, but of course he may be as sane as we are.'

Jasper listened to all this with no small astonishment.

'And Mrs Reardon?' he asked.

'I'm sorry to say she is far from well,' replied Mrs Yule. 'To-day she has been obliged to keep her room. You can imagine what a shock it has been to her. It came with such extraordinary suddenness. Without a word of warning, her husband announced that he had taken a clerkship and was going to remove immediately to the East-end. Fancy! And this when he had already arranged, as you know, to go to the south coast and write his next book under the influences of the sea air. He was anything but well; we all knew that, and we had all joined in advising him to spend the summer at the seaside. It seemed better that he should go alone; Mrs Reardon would, of course, have gone down for a few days now and then. And at a moment's notice everything is changed, and in such a dreadful way! I *cannot* believe that this is the behaviour of a sane man!'

Jasper understood that an explanation of the matter might have been given in much more homely terms; it was natural that Mrs Yule should leave out of sight the sufficient, but ignoble, cause of her son-in-law's behaviour.

'You see in what a painful position we are placed,' continued the euphemistic lady. 'It is so terrible even to hint that Mr Reardon is not responsible for his actions, yet how are we to explain to our friends this extraordinary state of things?'

'My husband is afraid Mr Reardon may fall seriously ill,' said Mrs Carter. 'And how dreadful ! In such a place as that !'

'It would be so kind of you to go and see him, Mr Milvain,' urged Mrs Yule. 'We should be so glad to hear what you think.'

'Certainly, I will go,' replied Jasper. 'Will you give me his address?'

He remained for an hour, and before his departure the subject was discussed with rather more frankness than at first; even the word 'money' was once or twice heard.

'Mr Carter has very kindly promised,' said Mrs Yule, 'to do his best to hear of some position that would be suitable. It seems a most shocking thing that a successful author should abandon his career in this deliberate way; who could have imagined anything of the kind two years ago? But it is clearly quite impossible for him to go on as at present – if there is really no reason for believing his mind disordered.'

A cab was summoned for Mrs Carter, and she took her leave, suppressing her native cheerfulness to the tone of the occasion. A minute or two after, Milvain left the house.

He had walked perhaps twenty yards, almost to the end of the silent street in which his friends' house was situated, when a man came round the corner and approached him. At once he recognised the figure, and in a moment he was face to face with Reardon. Both stopped. Jasper held out his hand, but the other did not seem to notice it.

'You are coming from Mrs Yule's?' said Reardon, with a strange smile.

By the gaslight his face showed pale and sunken, and he met Jasper's look with fixedness.

'Yes, I am. The fact is, I went there to hear of your address. Why haven't you let me know about all this?'

'You went to the flat?'

'No, I was told about you by Whelpdale.'

Reardon turned in the direction whence he had come, and began to walk slowly; Jasper kept beside him.

'I'm afraid there's something amiss between us, Reardon,' said the latter, just glancing at his companion.

'There's something amiss between me and everyone,' was the reply, in an unnatural voice.

'You look at things too gloomily. Am I detaining you, by-the-by? You were going –'

'Nowhere.'

'Then come to my rooms, and let us see if we can't talk more in the old way.'

'Your old way of talk isn't much to my taste, Milvain. It has cost me too much.'

Jasper gazed at him. Was there some foundation for Mrs Yule's seeming extravagance? This reply sounded so meaningless, and so unlike Reardon's manner of speech, that the younger man experienced a sudden alarm.

'Cost you too much? I don't understand you.'

They had turned into a broader thoroughfare, which, however, was little frequented at this hour. Reardon, his hands thrust into the pockets of a shabby overcoat and his head bent forward, went on at a slow pace, observant of nothing. For a moment or two he delayed reply, then said in an unsteady voice:

'Your way of talking has always been to glorify success, to insist upon it as the one end a man ought to keep in view. If you had talked so to me alone, it wouldn't have mattered. But there was generally someone else present. Your words had their effect; I can see that now. It's very much owing to you that I am deserted, now that there's no hope of my ever succeeding.'

Jasper's first impulse was to meet this accusation with indignant denial, but a sense of compassion prevailed. It was so painful to see the defeated man wandering at night near the house where his wife and child were comfortably sheltered; and the tone in which he spoke revealed such profound misery.

'That's a most astonishing thing to say,' Jasper replied. 'Of course I know nothing of what has passed between you and your wife, but I feel certain that I have no more to do with what has happened than any other of your acquaintances.'

'You may feel as certain as you will, but your words and your example have influenced my wife against me. You didn't intend that; I don't suppose it for a moment. It's my misfortune, that's all.'

'That I intended nothing of the kind, you need hardly say, I should think. But you are deceiving yourself in the strangest way. I'm afraid to speak plainly; I'm afraid of offending you. But can you recall something that I said about the time of your marriage? You didn't like it then, and certainly it won't be pleasant to you to remember it now. If you mean that your wife has grown unkind to you because you are unfortunate, there's no need to examine into other people's influence for an explanation of that.'

Reardon turned his face towards the speaker.

'Then you have always regarded my wife as a woman likely to fail me in time of need?'

'I don't care to answer a question put in that way. If we are no longer to talk with the old friendliness, it's far better we shouldn't discuss things such as this.'

'Well, practically you have answered. Of course I remember those words of yours that you refer to. Whether you were right or wrong doesn't affect what I say.'

He spoke with a dull doggedness, as though mental fatigue did not allow him to say more.

'It's impossible to argue against such a charge,' said Milvain. 'I am convinced it isn't true, and that's all I can answer. But perhaps you think this extraordinary influence of mine is still being used against you?'

'I know nothing about it,' Reardon replied, in the same unmodulated voice.

'Well, as I have told you, this was my first visit to Mrs Yule's since your wife has been there, and I didn't see her; she isn't very well, and keeps her room. I'm glad it happened so – that I didn't meet her. Henceforth I shall keep away from the family altogether, so long, at all events, as your wife remains with them. Of course I shan't tell anyone why; that would be impossible. But you shan't have to fear that I am decrying you. By Jove! an amiable figure you make of me!'

'I have said what I didn't wish to say, and what I oughtn't to have said. You must misunderstand me; I can't help it.'

Reardon had been walking for hours, and was, in truth, exhausted. He became mute. Jasper, whose misrepresentation was wilful, though not maliciously so, also fell into silence; he did not believe that his conversations with Amy had seriously affected the course of events, but he knew that he had often said things to her in private which would scarcely have fallen from his lips if her husband had been present – little depreciatory phrases, wrong rather in tone than in terms, which came of his irresistible desire to assume superiority whenever it was possible. He, too, was weak, but with quite another kind of weakness than Reardon's. His was the weakness of vanity, which sometimes leads a man to commit treacheries of which he would believe himself incapable. Self-accused, he took refuge in the pretence of misconception, which again was a betrayal of littleness.

They drew near to Westbourne Park Station.

'You are living a long way from here,' Jasper said, coldly. 'Are you going by train?'

'No. You said my wife was ill?'

'Oh, not ill. At least, I didn't understand that it was anything serious. Why don't you walk back to the house?'

'I must judge of my own affairs.'

'True; I beg your pardon. I take the train here, so I'll say good-night.'

They nodded to each other, but did not shake hands.

A day or two later, Milvain wrote to Mrs Yule, and told her that he had seen Reardon; he did not describe the circumstances under which the interview had taken place, but gave it as his opinion that Reardon was in a state of nervous illness, and made by suffering quite unlike himself. That he might be on the way to positive mental disease seemed likely enough. 'Unhappily, I myself can be of no use to him; he has not the same friendly feeling for me as he used to have. But it is very certain that those of his friends who have the power should exert themselves to raise him out of this fearful slough of despond. If he isn't effectually helped, there's no saying what may happen. One thing is certain, I think: he is past helping himself. Sane literary work cannot be expected from him. It seems a monstrous thing that so good a fellow, and one with such excellent brains too, should perish by the way when influential people would have no difficulty in restoring him to health and usefulness.'

All the months of summer went by. Jasper kept his word, and never visited Mrs Yule's house; but once in July he met that lady at the Carters', and heard then, what he knew from other sources, that the position of things was unchanged. In August, Mrs Yule spent a fortnight at the seaside, and Amy accompanied her. Milvain and his sisters accepted an invitation to visit friends at Wattleborough, and were out of town about three weeks, the last ten days being passed in the Isle of Wight; it was an extravagant holiday, but Dora had been ailing, and her brother declared that they would all work better for the change. Alfred Yule, with his wife and daughter, rusticated somewhere in Kent. Dora and Marian exchanged letters, and here is a passage from one written by the former :

'Jasper has shown himself in an unusually amiable light since we left town. I looked forward to this holiday with some misgivings, as I know by experience that it doesn't do for him and us to be too much together; he gets tired of our company, and then his selfishness − believe me, he has a good deal of it − comes out in a way we don't appreciate. But I have never known him so forbearing. To me he is particularly kind, on account of my headaches and general shakiness. It isn't impossible that this young man, if all goes well with him, may turn out far better than Maud and I ever expected. But things will have to go very well, if the improvement is to be permanent. I only hope he may make a lot of money before long. If this sounds rather gross to you, I can only say that Jasper's moral nature will never be safe as long as he is exposed to the risks of poverty. There are such people, you know. As a poor man, I wouldn't trust him out of my sight; with money, he will be a tolerable creature − as men go.'

Dora, no doubt, had her reasons for writing in this strain. She would not have made such remarks in conversation with her friend, but took the opportunity of being at a distance to communicate them in writing.

On their return, the two girls made good progress with the book they were manufacturing for Messrs Jolly and Monk, and early in October it was finished. Dora was now writing little things for The English Girl, and Maud had begun to review an occasional novel for an illustrated paper. In spite of their poor lodgings, they had been brought into social relations with Mrs Boston Wright and a few of her friends; their position was understood, and in accepting invitations they had no fear lest unwelcome people should pounce down upon them in their shabby little sitting-room. The younger sister cared little for society such as Jasper procured them; with Marian Yule for a companion she would have been quite content to spend her evenings at home. But Maud relished the introduction to strangers. She was admired, and knew it. Prudence could not restrain her from buying a handsomer dress than those she had brought from her country home, and it irked her sorely that she might not reconstruct all her equipment to rival the appearance of well-to-do girls whom she studied and envied. Her disadvantages, for the present, were insuperable. She had no one to chaperon her; she could not form intimacies because of her poverty. A rare invitation to luncheon, a permission to call at the sacred hour of small-talk – this was all she could hope for.

'I advise you to possess your soul in patience,' Jasper said to her, as they talked one day on the sea-shore. 'You are not to blame that you live without conventional protection, but it necessitates your being very careful. These people you are getting to know are not rigid about social observances, and they won't exactly despise you for poverty; all the same, their charity mustn't be tested too severely. Be very quiet for the present; let it be seen that you understand that your position isn't quite regular – I mean, of course, do so in a modest and nice way. As soon as ever it's possible, we'll arrange for you to live with someone who will preserve appearances. All this is contemptible, of course; but we belong to a contemptible society, and can't help ourselves. For Heaven's sake, don't spoil your chances by rashness; be content to wait a little, till some more money comes in.'

Midway in October, about half-past eight one evening, Jasper received an unexpected visit from Dora. He was in his sitting-room, smoking and reading a novel.

'Anything wrong?' he asked, as his sister entered.

'No; but I'm alone this evening, and I thought I would see if you were in.'

'Where's Maud, then?'

'She went to see the Lanes this afternoon, and Mrs Lane invited her to go to the Gaiety to-night; she said a friend whom she had invited couldn't come, and the ticket would be wasted. Maud went back to dine with them. She'll come home in a cab.'

'Why is Mrs Lane so affectionate all at once? Take your things off; I have nothing to do.'

'Miss Radway was going as well.'

'Who's Miss Radway?'

'Don't you know her? She's staying with the Lanes. Maud says she writes for *The West End*.'

'And will that fellow Lane be with them?'

'I think not.'

Jasper mused, contemplating the bowl of his pipe.

'I suppose she was in rare excitement?'

'Pretty well. She has wanted to go to the Gaiety for a long time. There's no harm, is there?'

Dora asked the question with that absent air which girls are wont to assume when they touch on doubtful subjects.

'Harm, no. Idiocy and lively music, that's all. It's too late, or I'd have taken you, for the joke of the thing. Confound it! she ought to have better dresses.'

'Oh, she looked very nice, in that best.'

'Pooh! But I don't care for her to be running about with the Lanes. Lane is too big a blackguard; it reflects upon his wife to a certain extent.'

They gossiped for half an hour, then a tap at the door interrupted them; it was the landlady.

'Mr Whelpdale has called to see you, sir. I mentioned as Miss Milvain was here, so he said he wouldn't come up unless you sent to ask him.'

Jasper smiled at Dora, and said in a low voice:

'What do you say? Shall he come up? He can behave himself.'

'Just as you please, Jasper.'

'Ask him to come up, Mrs Thompson, please.'

Mr Whelpdale presented himself. He entered with much more ceremony than when Milvain was alone; on his visage was a grave respectfulness, his step was light, his whole bearing expressed diffidence and pleasurable anticipation.

'My younger sister, Whelpdale,' said Jasper, with subdued amusement.

The dealer in literary advice made a bow which did him no discredit, and began to speak in a low, reverential tone not at all disagreeable to the ear. His breeding, in truth, had been that of a gentleman, and it was only of late years that he had fallen into the hungry region of New Grub Street.

'How's the "Manual" going off?' Milvain inquired.

'Excellently! We have sold nearly six hundred.'

'My sister is one of your readers. I believe she has studied the book with much conscientiousness.'

'Really? You have really read it, Miss Milvain?'

Dora assured him that she had, and his delight knew no bounds.

'It isn't all rubbish, by any means,' said Jasper, graciously. 'In the chapter on writing for magazines, there are one or two very good hints. What a pity you can't apply your own advice, Whelpdale!'

'Now that's horribly unkind of you!' protested the other. 'You might have spared me this evening. But unfortunately it's quite true, Miss Milvain. I point the way, but I haven't been able to travel it myself. You mustn't think I have never succeeded in getting things published; but I can't keep it up as a profession. Your brother is the successful man. A marvellous facility! I envy him. Few men at present writing have such talent.'

'Please don't make him more conceited than he naturally is,' interposed Dora.

'What news of Biffen?' asked Jasper, presently.

'He says he shall finish "Mr Bailey, Grocer," in about a month. He read me one of the later chapters the other night. It's really fine; most remarkable writing, it seems to me. It will be scandalous if he can't get it published; it will, indeed.'

'I do hope he may!' said Dora, laughing. 'I have heard so much of "Mr Bailey," that it will be a great disappointment if I am never to read it.'

'I'm afraid it would give you very little pleasure,' Whelpdale replied, hesitatingly. 'The matter is so very gross.'

'And the hero *grocer*!' shouted Jasper, mirthfully. 'Oh, but it's quite indecent; only rather depressing. The decently ignoble – or, the ignobly decent? Which is Biffen's formula? I saw him a week ago, and he looked hungrier than ever.'

'Ah, but poor Reardon! I passed him at King's Cross not long ago. He didn't see me – walks with his eyes on the ground always, – and I hadn't the courage to stop him. He's the ghost of his old self. He can't live long.'

Dora and her brother exchanged a glance. It was a long time since Jasper had spoken to his sisters about the Reardons; nowadays he seldom heard either of husband or wife.

The conversation that went on was so agreeable to Whelpdale, that he lost consciousness of time. It was past eleven o'clock when Jasper felt obliged to remind him.

'Dora, I think I must be taking you home.'

The visitor at once made ready for departure, and his leave-taking was as respectful as his entrance had been. Though he might not say what he thought, there was very legible upon his countenance a hope that he would again be privileged to meet Miss Dora Milvain.

'Not a bad fellow, in his way,' said Jasper, when Dora and he were alone again.

'Not at all.'

She had heard the story of Whelpdale's hapless wooing half a year ago, and her recollection of it explained the smile with which she spoke.

'Never get on, I'm afraid,' Jasper pursued. 'He has his allowance of twenty pounds a year, and makes perhaps fifty or sixty more. If I were in his position, I should go in for some kind of regular business; he has people who could help him. Good-natured fellow; but what's the use of that if you've no money?'

They set out together, and walked to the girl's lodgings. Dora was about to use her latch-key, but Jasper checked her.

'No. There's a light in the kitchen still; better knock, as we're so late.'

'But why?'

'Never mind; do as I tell you.'

The landlady admitted them, and Jasper spoke a word or two with her, explaining that he would wait until his elder sister's return; the darkness of the second-floor windows had shown that Maud was not yet back.

'What strange fancies you have!' remarked Dora, when they were upstairs.

'So have people in general, unfortunately.'

A letter lay on the table. It was addressed to Maud, and Dora recognised the handwriting as that of a Wattleborough friend.

'There must be some news here,' she said. 'Mrs Haynes wouldn't write unless she had something special to say.'

Just upon midnight, a cab drew up before the house. Dora

ran down to open the door to her sister, who came in with very bright eyes and more colour than usual on her cheeks.

'How late for you to be here!' she exclaimed, on entering the sitting-room and seeing Jasper.

'I shouldn't have felt comfortable till I knew that you were back all right.'

'What fear was there?'

She threw off her wraps, laughing.

'Well, have you enjoyed yourself?'

'Oh yes!' she replied, carelessly. 'This letter for me? What has Mrs Haynes got to say, I wonder?'

She opened the envelope, and began to glance hurriedly over the sheet of paper. Then her face changed.

'What do you think? Mr Yule is dead!'

Dora uttered an exclamation; Jasper displayed the keenest interest.

'He died yesterday – no, it would be the day before yesterday. He had a fit of some kind at a public meeting, was taken to the hospital because it was nearest, and died in a few hours. So *that* has come, at last! Now what'll be the result of it, I wonder?'

'When shall you be seeing Marian?' asked her brother.

'She might come to-morrow evening.'

'But won't she go to the funeral?' suggested Dora.

'Perhaps; there's no saying. I suppose her father will, at all events. The day before yesterday? Then the funeral will be on Saturday, I should think.'

'Ought I to write to Marian?' asked Dora.

'No; I wouldn't,' was Jasper's reply. 'Better wait till she lets you hear. That's sure to be soon. She may have gone to Wattleborough this afternoon, or be going to-morrow morning.'

The letter from Mrs Haynes was passed from hand to hand. 'Everybody feels sure,' it said, 'that a great deal of his money will be left for public purposes. The ground for the park being already purchased, he is sure to have made provision for carrying out his plans connected with it. But I hope your friends in London may benefit.'

It was some time before Jasper could put an end to the speculative conversation and betake himself homewards. And even on getting back to his lodgings he was little disposed to go to bed.

This event of John Yule's death had been constantly in his mind, but there was always a fear it might not happen for long enough; the sudden announcement excited him almost as much as if he were a relative of the deceased.

'Confound his public purposes!' was the thought upon which he at length slept.

Chapter 21

MR YULE LEAVES TOWN

SINCE the domestic incidents connected with that unpleasant review in *The Current*, the relations between Alfred Yule and his daughter had suffered a permanent change, though not in a degree noticeable by anyone but the two concerned. To all appearances, they worked together and conversed very much as they had been wont to do; but Marian was made to feel in many subtle ways that her father no longer had complete confidence in her, no longer took the same pleasure as formerly in the skill and conscientiousness of her work, and Yule on his side perceived too clearly that the girl was preoccupied with something other than her old wish to aid and satisfy him, that she had a new life of her own alien to, and in some respects irreconcilable with, the existence in which he desired to confirm her. There was no renewal of open disagreement, but their conversations frequently ended, by tacit mutual consent, at a point which threatened divergence; and in Yule's case every such warning was a cause of intense irritation. He feared to provoke Marian, and this fear was again a torture to his pride.

Beyond the fact that his daughter was in constant communication with the Miss Milvains, he knew, and could discover, nothing of the terms on which she stood with the girls' brother, and this ignorance was harder to bear than full assurance of a disagreeable fact would have been. That a man like Jasper Milvain, whose name was every now and then forced upon his notice as a rising periodicalist and a faithful henchman of the unspeakable Fadge – that a young fellow of such excellent prospects should seriously attach himself to a girl like Marian seemed to him highly improbable, save, indeed, for the one consideration, that Milvain, who assuredly had a very keen eye to chances, might regard the girl as a niece of old John Yule, and therefore worth holding in view until it was decided whether or not she would benefit by her uncle's decease. Fixed in his antipathy to the young man, he would not allow himself to admit any but a base motive on Milvain's side, if, indeed, Marian and Jasper were more to each other than slight acquaintances; and he persuaded himself that anxiety for the girl's welfare was at least as strong a motive with him as mere prejudice against the ally of Fadge, and, it might be, the reviewer of 'English Prose.' Milvain was quite capable of playing fast and loose with a girl, and Marian, owing to the peculiar circumstances of her position, would easily be misled by the pretence of a clever speculator.

That she had never spoken again about the review in *The Current* might receive several explanations. Perhaps she had not been able to convince herself either for or against Milvain's authorship; perhaps she had reason to suspect that the young man *was* the author; perhaps she merely shrank from reviving a discussion in which she might betray what she desired to keep secret. This last was the truth. Finding that her father did not recur to the subject, Marian concluded that he had found himself to be misinformed. But Yule, though he heard the original rumour denied by people whom in other matters he would have trusted, would not lay aside the doubt that flattered his prejudices. If Milvain were not the writer of the review, he very well might have been; and what certainty could be arrived at in matters of literary gossip?

There was an element of jealousy in the father's feeling. If he did not love Marian with all the warmth of which a parent is capable, at least he had more affection for her than for any other person, and of this he became strongly aware now that the girl seemed to be turning from him. If he lost Marian, he would indeed be a lonely man, for he considered his wife of no account. Intellectually again, he demanded an entire allegiance from his daughter; he could not bear to think that her zeal on his behalf was diminishing, that perhaps she was beginning to regard his work as futile and antiquated in comparison with that of the new generation. Yet this must needs be the result of frequent intercourse with such a man as Milvain. It seemed to him that he remarked it in her speech and manner, and at times he with difficulty restrained himself from a reproach or a sarcasm which would have led to trouble.

Had he been in the habit of dealing harshly with Marian, as with her mother, of course his position would have been simpler. But he had always respected her, and he feared to lose that measure of respect with which she repaid him. Already he had suffered in her esteem, perhaps more than he liked to think, and the increasing embitterment of his temper kept him always in danger of the conflict he dreaded. Marian was not like her mother; she could not submit to tyrannous usage. Warned of that, he did his utmost to avoid an outbreak of discord, constantly hoping that he might come to understand his daughter's position, and perhaps discover that his greatest fear was unfounded.

Twice in the course of the summer he inquired of his wife whether she knew anything about the Milvains. But Mrs Yule was not in Marian's confidence.

'I only know that she goes to see the young ladies, and that they do writing of some kind.'

'She never even mentions their brother to you?'

'Never. I haven't heard his name from her since she told me the Miss Milvains weren't coming here again.'

He was not sorry that Marian had taken the decision to keep her friends away from St Paul's Crescent, for it saved him a recurring annoyance; but, on the other hand, if they had continued to come, he would not have been thus completely in the dark as to her intercourse with Jasper; scraps of information must now and then have been gathered by his wife from the girls' talk.

Throughout the month of July, he suffered much from his wonted bilious attacks, and Mrs Yule had to endure a double share of his ill-temper, that which was naturally directed against her, and that of which Marian was the cause. In August things were slightly better; but with the return to labour came a renewal of Yule's sullenness and savageness. Sundry pieces of ill-luck of a professional kind – warnings, as he too well understood, that it was growing more and more difficult for him to hold his own against the new writers – exasperated his quarrel with destiny. The gloom of a cold and stormy September was doubly wretched in that house on the far borders of Camden Town, but in October the sun reappeared and it seemed to mollify the literary man's mood. Just when Mrs Yule and Marian began to hope that this long distemper must surely come to an end, there befell an incident which, at the best of times, would have occasioned misery, and which in the present juncture proved disastrous.

It was one morning about eleven. Yule was in his study; Marian was at the Museum; Mrs Yule had gone shopping. There came a sharp knock at the front door, and the servant, on opening, was confronted with a decently-dressed woman, who asked in a peremptory voice if Mrs Yule was at home.

'No? Then is Mr Yule?'

'Yes, mum, but I'm afraid he's busy.'

'I don't care! I must see him. Say that Mrs Goby wants to see him at once.'

The servant, not without apprehensions, delivered this message at the door of the study.

'Mrs Goby? Who is Mrs Goby?' exclaimed the man of letters, irate at the disturbance.

There sounded an answer out of the passage, for the visitor had followed close.

'I am Mrs Goby, of the 'Olloway Road, wife of Mr C. O. Goby, 'aberdasher. I just want to speak to you, Mr Yule, if you please, seeing that Mrs Yule isn't in.'

Yule started up in fury, and stared at the woman, to whom the servant had reluctantly given place.

'What business can you have with me? If you wish to see Mrs Yule, come again when she is at home.'

'No, Mr Yule, I will *not* come again!' cried the woman, red in the face. 'I thought I might have had respectable treatment here, at all events; but I see you're pretty much like your relations in the way of behaving to people, though you *do* wear better clothes, and – I s'pose – call yourself a gentleman. I *won't* come again, and you shall just hear what I've got to say.'

She closed the door violently, and stood in an attitude of robust defiance.

'What's all this about?' asked the enraged author, overcoming an impulse to take Mrs Goby by the shoulders and throw her out – though he might have found some difficulty in achieving this feat. 'Who are you? And why do you come here with your brawling?'

'I'm the respectable wife of a respectable man – that's who I am, Mr Yule, if you want to know. And I always thought Mrs

Yule was the same, from the dealings we've had with her at the shop, though not knowing any more of her, it's true, except that she lived in St Paul's Crezzent. And so she may be respectable, though I can't say as her husband behaves himself very much like what he pretends to be. But I can't say as much for her relations in Perker Street, 'Olloway, which I s'pose they're *your* relations as well, at least by marriage. And if they think they're going to insult me, and use their blackguard tongues –'

'What are you talking about?' shouted Yule, who was driven to frenzy by the mention of his wife's humble family. 'What have I to do with these people?'

'What have *you* to do with them? I s'pose they're your relations, ain't they? And I s'pose the girl Annie Rudd is your niece, ain't she? At least, she's your wife's niece, and that comes to the same thing, I've always understood, though I dare say a gentleman as has so many books about him can correct me if I've made a mistake.'

She looked scornfully, though also with some surprise, round the volumed walls.

'And what of this girl? Will you have the goodness to say what your business is?'

'Yes, I *will* have the goodness! I s'pose you know very well that I took your niece Annie Rudd as a domestic servant' – she repeated this precise definition – 'as a domestic servant, because Mrs Yule 'appened to arst me if I knew of a place for a girl of that kind, as hadn't been out before, but could be trusted to do her best to give satisfaction to a good mistress? I s'pose you know that?'

'I know nothing of the kind. What have I to do with servants?'

'Well, whether you've much to do with them or little, that's how it was. And nicely she's paid me out, has your niece, Miss Rudd. Of all the trouble I ever had with a girl! And now when she's run away back 'ome, and when I take the trouble to go arfter her, I'm to be insulted and abused as never was! Oh, they're a nice respectable family, those Rudds! Mrs Rudd – that's Mrs Yule's sister – what a nice, polite-spoken lady she is, to be sure! If I was to repeat the language – but there, I wouldn't lower myself. And I've been a brute of a mistress; I ill-use my servants, and I don't give 'em enough to eat, and I pay 'em worse

than any woman in London! That's what I've learnt about myself by going to Perker Street, 'Olloway. And when I come here to
ask Mrs Yule what she means by recommending such a creature,
from such a 'ome, I get insulted by her gentleman husband.'

Yule was livid with rage, but the extremity of his scorn withheld him from utterance of what he felt.

'As I said, all this has nothing to do with me. I will let
Mrs Yule know that you have called. I have no more time to
spare.'

Mrs Goby repeated at still greater length the details of her
grievance, but long before she had finished Yule was sitting again
at his desk in ostentatious disregard of her. Finally, the exasperated woman flung open the door, railed in a loud voice along the
passage, and left the house with an alarming crash.

It was not long before Mrs Yule returned. Before taking off her
things, she went down into the kitchen with certain purchases,
and there she learnt from the servant what had happened during
her absence. Fear and trembling possessed her – the sick, faint
dread always excited by her husband's wrath – but she felt
obliged to go at once to the study. The scene that took place
there was one of ignoble violence on Yule's part, and, on that of
his wife, of terrified self-accusation, changing at length to
dolorous resentment of the harshness with which she was treated.
When it was over, Yule took his hat and went out.

He did not return for the mid-day meal, and when Marian,
late in the afternoon, came back from the Museum, he was still
absent.

Not finding her mother in the parlour, Marian called at the
head of the kitchen stairs. The servant answered, saying that
Mrs Yule was up in her bedroom, and that she didn't seem well.
Marian at once went up and knocked at the bedroom door. In a
moment or two her mother came out, showing a face of tearful
misery.

'What is it, mother? What's the matter?'

They went into Marian's room, where Mrs Yule gave free
utterance to her lamentations.

'I can't put up with it, Marian! Your father's too hard with
me. I was wrong, I dare say, and I might have known what would
have come of it, but he couldn't speak to me worse if I did him

all the harm I could on purpose. It's all about Annie, because I found a place for her at Mrs Goby's, in the 'Olloway Road; and now Mrs Goby's been here and seen your father, and told him she's been insulted by the Rudds, because Annie went off home, and she went after her to make inquiries. And your father's in such a passion about it as never was. That woman Mrs Goby rushed into the study when he was working; it was this morning, when I happened to be out. And she throws all the blame on me for recommending her such a girl. And I did it for the best, that I did! Annie promised me faithfully she'd behave well, and never give me trouble, and she seemed thankful to me, because she wasn't happy at home. And now to think of her causing all this disturbance! I oughtn't to have done such a thing without speaking about it to your father; but you know how afraid I am to say a word to him about those people. And my sister's told me so often I ought to be ashamed of myself, never helping her and her children; she thinks I could do such a lot if I only liked. And now that I did try to do something, see what comes of it!'

Marian listened with a confusion of wretched feelings. But her sympathies were strongly with her mother; as well as she could understand the broken story, her father seemed to have no just cause for his pitiless rage, though such an occasion would be likely enough to bring out his worst faults.

'Is he in the study?' she asked.

'No; he went out at twelve o'clock, and he's never been back since. I feel as if I must do something; I can't bear with it, Marian. He tells me I'm the curse of his life – yes, he said that. I oughtn't to tell you, I know I oughtn't; but it's more than I can bear. I've always tried to do my best, but it gets harder and harder for me. But for me, he'd never be in these bad tempers; it's because he can't look at me without getting angry. He says I've kept him back all through his life; but for me, he might have been far better off than he is. It may be true; I've often enough thought it. But I can't bear to have it told me like that, and to see it in his face every time he looks at me. I shall have to do something. He'd be glad if only I was out of his way.'

'Father has no right to make you so unhappy,' said Marian. 'I can't see that you did anything blameworthy; it seems to me that it was your duty to try and help Annie, and if it turned out unfortunately, that can't be helped. You oughtn't to think so much of what father says in his anger; I believe he hardly knows what he does say. Don't take it so much to heart, mother.'

'I've tried my best, Marian,' sobbed the poor woman, who felt that even her child's sympathy could not be perfect, owing to the distance put between them by Marian's education and refined sensibilities. 'I've always thought it wasn't right to talk to you about such things, but he's been too hard with me to-day.'

'I think it was better you should tell me. It can't go on like this; I feel that just as you do. I must tell father that he is making our lives a burden to us.'

'Oh, you mustn't speak to him like that, Marian! I wouldn't for anything make unkindness between you and your father; that would be the worst thing I'd done yet. I'd rather go away and work for my own living than make trouble between you and him.'

'It isn't you who make trouble; it's father. I ought to have spoken to him before this; I had no right to stand by and see how much you suffered from his ill-temper.'

The longer they talked, the firmer grew Marian's resolve to front her father's tyrannous ill-humour, and in one way or another to change the intolerable state of things. She had been weak to hold her peace so long; at her age it was a simple duty to interfere when her mother was treated with such flagrant injustice. Her father's behaviour was unworthy of a thinking man, and he must be made to feel that.

Yule did not return. Dinner was delayed for half an hour, then Marian declared that they would wait no longer. The two made a sorry meal, and afterwards went together into the sitting-room. At eight o'clock they heard the front door open, and Yule's footstep in the passage. Marian rose.

'Don't speak till to-morrow!' whispered her mother, catching at the girl's arm. 'Let it be till to-morrow, Marian!'

'I *must* speak! We can't live in this terror.'

She reached the study just as her father was closing the door behind him. Yule, seeing her enter, glared with blood-shot eyes; shame and sullen anger were blended on his countenance.

'Will you tell me what is wrong, father?' Marian asked, in a voice which betrayed her nervous suffering, yet indicated the resolve with which she had come.

'I am not at all disposed to talk of the matter,' he replied, with the awkward rotundity of phrase which distinguished him in his worst humour. 'For information you had better go to Mrs Goby – or a person of some such name – in Holloway Road. I have nothing more to do with it.'

'It was very unfortunate that the woman came and troubled you about such things. But I can't see that mother was to blame; I don't think you ought to be so angry with her.'

It cost Marian a terrible effort to address her father in these terms. When he turned fiercely upon her, she shrank back and felt as if strength must fail her even to stand.

'You can't see that she was to blame? Isn't it entirely against my wish that she keeps up any intercourse with those low people? Am I to be exposed to insulting disturbance in my very study, because she chooses to introduce girls of bad character as servants to vulgar women?'

'I don't think Annie Rudd can be called a girl of bad character, and it was very natural that mother should try to do something for her. You have never actually forbidden her to see her relatives.'

'A thousand times I have given her to understand that I utterly disapproved of such association. She knew perfectly well that this girl was as likely as not to discredit her. If she had consulted me, I should at once have forbidden anything of the kind; she was aware of that. She kept it secret from me, knowing that it would excite my displeasure. I will not be drawn into such squalid affairs; I won't have my name spoken in such connection. Your mother has only herself to blame if I am angry with her.'

'Your anger goes beyond all bounds. At the very worst, mother behaved imprudently, and with a very good motive. It is cruel that you should make her suffer as she is doing.'

Marian was being strengthened to resist. Her blood grew hot; the sensation which once before had brought her to the verge of conflict with her father possessed her heart and brain.

'You are not a suitable judge of my behaviour,' replied Yule, severely.

'I am driven to speak. We can't go on living in this way, father.

For months our home has been almost ceaselessly wretched, because of the ill-temper you are always in. Mother and I must
defend ourselves; we can't bear it any longer. You must surely
feel how ridiculous it is to make such a thing as happened this
morning the excuse for violent anger. How can I help judging
your behaviour? When mother is brought to the point of saying
that she would rather leave home and everything than endure
her misery any longer, I should be wrong if I didn't speak to you.
Why are you so unkind? What serious cause has mother ever
given you?'

'I refuse to argue such questions with you.'

'Then you are very unjust. I am not a child, and there's nothing wrong in my asking you why home is made a place of misery,
instead of being what home ought to be.'

'You prove that you *are* a child, in asking for explanations
which ought to be clear enough to you.'

'You mean that mother is to blame for everything?'

'The subject is no fit one to be discussed between a father and
his daughter. If you cannot see the impropriety of it, be so good
as to go away and reflect, and leave me to my occupations.'

Marian came to a pause. But she knew that his rebuke was
mere unworthy evasion; she saw that her father could not meet
her look, and this perception of shame in him impelled her to
finish what she had begun.

'I will say nothing of mother, then, but speak only for myself.
I suffer too much from your unkindness; you ask too much endurance.'

'You mean that I exact too much work from you?' asked her
father, with a look which might have been directed to a recal-
citrant clerk.

'No. But that you make the conditions of my work too hard. I
live in constant fear of your anger.'

'Indeed? When did I last ill-use you, or threaten you?'

'I often think that threats, or even ill-usage, would be easier to
bear than an unchanging gloom which always seems on the point
of breaking into violence.'

'I am obliged to you for your criticism of my disposition and
manner, but unhappily I am too old to reform. Life has made me
what I am, and I should have thought that your knowledge of

what my life has been would have gone far to excuse a lack of cheerfulness in me.'

The irony of this laborious period was full of self-pity. His voice quavered at the close, and a tremor was noticeable in his stiff frame.

'It isn't lack of cheerfulness that I mean, father. That could never have brought me to speak like this.'

'If you wish me to admit that I am bad-tempered, surly, irritable – I make no difficulty about that. The charge is true enough. I can only ask you again : What are the circumstances that have ruined my temper? When you present yourself here with a general accusation of my behaviour, I am at a loss to understand what you ask of me, what you wish me to say or do. I must beg you to speak plainly. Are you suggesting that I should make provision for the support of you and your mother away from my intolerable proximity? My income is not large, as I think you are aware, but of course if a demand of this kind is seriously made, I must do my best to comply with it.'

'It hurts me very much that you can understand me no better than this.'

'I am sorry. I think we used to understand each other, but that was before you were subjected to the influence of strangers.'

In his perverse frame of mind he was ready to give utterance to any thought which confused the point at issue. This last allusion was suggested to him by a sudden pang of regret for the pain he was causing Marian; he defended himself against self-reproach by hinting at the true reason of much of his harshness.

'I am subjected to no influence that is hostile to you,' Marian replied.

'You may think that. But in such a matter it is very easy for you to deceive yourself.'

'Of course I know what you refer to, and I can assure you that I don't deceive myself.'

Yule flashed a searching glance at her.

'Can you deny that you are on terms of friendship with a – a person who would at any moment rejoice to injure me?'

'I am friendly with no such person. Will you say whom you are thinking of?'

'It would be useless. I have no wish to discuss a subject on which we should only disagree unprofitably.'

Marian kept silence for a moment, then said in a low, unsteady voice :

'It is perhaps because we never speak of that subject that we are so far from understanding each other. If you think that Mr Milvain is your enemy, that he would rejoice to injure you, you are grievously mistaken.'

'When I see a man in close alliance with my worst enemy, and looking to that enemy for favour, I am justified in thinking that he would injure me if the right kind of opportunity offered. One need not be very deeply read in human nature to have assurance of that.'

'But I know Mr Milvain !'

'You know him ?'

'Far better than you can, I am sure. You draw conclusions from general principles; but I know that they don't apply in this case.'

'I have no doubt you sincerely think so. I repeat, that nothing can be gained by such a discussion as this.'

'One thing I must tell you. There was no truth in your suspicion that Mr Milvain wrote that review in *The Current*. He assured me himself that he was not the writer, that he had nothing to do with it.'

Yule looked askance at her, and his face displayed solicitude, which soon passed, however, into a smile of sarcasm.

'The gentleman's word no doubt has weight with you.'

'Father, what do you mean?' broke from Marian, whose eyes of a sudden flashed stormily. 'Would Mr Milvain tell me a lie?'

'I shouldn't like to say that it is impossible,' replied her father in the same tone as before.

'But – what right have you to insult him so grossly?'

'I have every right, my dear child, to express an opinion about him or any other man, provided I do it honestly. I beg you not to strike attitudes and address me in the language of the stage. You insist on my speaking plainly, and I have spoken plainly. I warned you that we were not likely to agree on this topic.'

'Literary quarrels have made you incapable of judging honestly in things such as this. I wish I could have done for ever with the hateful profession that so poisons men's minds!'

'Believe me, my girl,' said her father, incisively, 'the simpler thing would be to hold aloof from such people as use the profession in a spirit of unalloyed selfishness, who seek only material advancement, and who, *whatever* connection they form, have nothing but self-interest in view.'

And he glared at her with much meaning. Marian – both had remained standing all through the dialogue – cast down her eyes and became lost in brooding.

'I speak with profound conviction,' pursued her father, 'and, however little you credit me with such a motive, out of desire to guard you against the dangers to which your inexperience is exposed. It is perhaps as well that you have afforded me this –'

There sounded at the house-door that duplicated double-knock which generally announces the bearer of a telegram. Yule interrupted himself, and stood in an attitude of waiting. The servant was heard to go along the passage, to open the door, and then return towards the study. Yes, it was a telegram. Such despatches rarely came to this house; Yule tore the envelope, read its contents, and stood with gaze fixed upon the slip of paper until the servant inquired if there was any reply for the boy to take with him.

'No reply.'

He slowly crumpled the envelope, and stepped aside to throw it into the paper-basket. The telegram he laid on his desk. Marian stood all the time with bent head; he now looked at her with an expression of meditative displeasure.

'I don't know that there's much good in resuming our conversation,' he said, in quite a changed tone, as if something of more importance had taken possession of his thoughts and had made him almost indifferent to the past dispute. 'But of course I am quite willing to hear anything you would still like to say.'

Marian had lost her vehemence. She was absent and melancholy.

'I can only ask you,' she replied, 'to try and make life less of a burden to us.'

'I shall have to leave town to-morrow for a few days; no doubt it will be some satisfaction to you to hear that.'

Marian's eyes turned involuntarily towards the telegram.

'As for your occupation in my absence,' he went on, in a hard tone which yet had something tremulous, emotional, making it quite different from the voice he had hitherto used, 'that will be entirely a matter for your own judgment. I have felt for some time that you assisted me with less good-will than formerly, and now that you have frankly admitted it, I shall of course have very little satisfaction in requesting your aid. I must leave it to you; consult your own inclination.'

It was resentful, but not savage; between the beginning and the end of his speech he softened to a sort of self-satisfied pathos.

'I can't pretend,' replied Marian, 'that I have as much pleasure in the work as I should have if your mood were gentler.'

'I am sorry. I might perhaps have made greater efforts to appear at ease when I was suffering.'

'Do you mean physical suffering?'

'Physical and mental. But that can't concern you. During my absence I will think of your reproof. I know that it is deserved, in some degree. If it is possible, you shall have less to complain of in future.'

He looked about the room, and at length seated himself; his eyes were fixed in a direction away from Marian.

'I suppose you had dinner somewhere?' Marian asked, after catching a glimpse of his worn, colourless face.

'Oh, I had a mouthful of something. It doesn't matter.'

It seemed as if he found some special pleasure in assuming this tone of martyrdom just now. At the same time he was becoming more absorbed in thought.

'Shall I have something brought up for you, father?'

'Something –? Oh no, no; on no account.'

He rose again impatiently, then approached his desk, and laid a hand on the telegram. Marian observed this movement, and examined his face; it was set in an expression of eagerness.

'You have nothing more to say then?' He turned sharply upon her.

'I feel that I haven't made you understand me, but I can say nothing more.'

'I understand you very well, too well. That you should misunderstand and mistrust me, I suppose, is natural. You are young and I am old. You are still full of hope, and I have been so often deceived and defeated that I *dare* not let a ray of hope enter my mind. Judge me; judge me as hardly as you like. My life has been one long bitter struggle, and if now – I say,' he began a new sentence, 'that only the hard side of life has been shown to me; small wonder if I have become hard myself. Desert me; go your own way, as the young always do. But bear in mind my warning. Remember the caution I have given you.'

He spoke in a strangely sudden agitation. The arm with which he leaned upon the table trembled violently. After a moment's pause he added, in a thick voice:

'Leave me. I will speak to you again in the morning.'

Impressed in a way she did not understand Marian at once obeyed, and rejoined her mother in the parlour. Mrs Yule gazed anxiously at her as she entered.

'Don't be afraid,' said Marian, with difficulty bringing herself to speak. 'I think it will be better.'

'Was that a telegram that came?' her mother inquired after a silence.

'Yes. I don't know where it was from. But father said he would have to leave town for a few days.'

They exchanged looks.

'Perhaps your uncle is very ill,' said the mother in a low voice.

'Perhaps so.'

The evening passed drearily. Fatigued with her emotions, Marian went early to bed; she even slept later than usual in the morning, and on descending she found her father already at the breakfast table. No greeting passed, and there was no conversation during the meal. Marian noticed that her mother kept glancing at her in a peculiarly grave way; but she felt ill and dejected, and could fix her thoughts on no subject. As he left the table Yule said to her:

'I want to speak to you for a moment. I shall be in the study.'

She joined him there very soon. He looked coldly at her, and said in a distant tone:

'The telegram last night was to tell me that your uncle is dead.'

'Dead!'

'He died of apoplexy, at a meeting in Wattleborough. I shall go down this morning, and of course remain till after the funeral. I see no necessity for your going, unless, of course, it is your desire to do so.'

'No; I should do as you wish.'

'I think you had better not go to the Museum whilst I am away. You will occupy yourself as you think fit.'

'I shall go on with the Harrington notes.'

'As you please. I don't know what mourning it would be decent for you to wear; you must consult with your mother about that. That is all I wished to say.'

His tone was dismissal. Marian had a struggle with herself, but she could find nothing to reply to his cold phrases. And an hour or two afterwards Yule left the house without leave-taking.

Soon after his departure there was a visitor's rat-tat at the door; it heralded Mrs Goby. In the interview which then took place Marian assisted her mother to bear the vigorous onslaughts of the haberdasher's wife. For more than two hours Mrs Goby related her grievances, against the fugitive servant, against Mrs Yule, against Mr Yule; meeting with no irritating opposition, she was able in this space of time to cool down to the temperature of normal intercourse, and when she went forth from the house again it was in a mood of dignified displeasure which she felt to be some recompense for the injuries of yesterday.

A result of this annoyance was to postpone conversation between mother and daughter on the subject of John Yule's death until a late hour of the afternoon. Marian was at work in the study, or endeavouring to work, for her thoughts would not fix themselves on the matter in hand for many minutes together, and Mrs Yule came in with more than her customary diffidence.

'Have you nearly done for to-day, dear?'

'Enough for the present, I think.'

She laid down her pen, and leant back in the chair.

'Marian, do you think your father will be rich?'

'I have no idea, mother. I suppose we shall know very soon.'

Her tone was dreamy. She seemed to herself to be speaking of something which scarcely at all concerned her, of vague possibilities which did not affect her habits of thought.

'If that happens,' continued Mrs Yule, in a low tone of distress, 'I don't know what I shall do.'

Marian looked at her questioningly.

'I can't wish that it mayn't happen,' her mother went on; 'I can't, for his sake and for yours; but I don't know what I shall do. He'd think me more in his way than ever. He'd wish to have a large house, and live in quite a different way; and how could I manage then? I couldn't show myself; he'd be too much ashamed of me. I shouldn't be in my place; even you'd feel ashamed of me.'

'You mustn't say that, mother. I have never given you cause to think that.'

'No, my dear, you haven't; but it would be only natural. I couldn't live the kind of life that you're fit for. I shall be nothing but a hindrance and a shame to both of you.'

'To me you would never be either hindrance or shame; be quite sure of that. And as for father, I am all but certain that, if he became rich, he would be a very much kinder man, a better man in every way. It is poverty that has made him worse than he naturally is; it has that effect on almost everybody. Money does harm, too, sometimes; but never, I think, to people who have a good heart and a strong mind. Father is naturally a warm-hearted man; riches would bring out all the best in him. He would be generous again, which he has almost forgotten how to be among all his disappointments and battlings. Don't be afraid of that change, but hope for it.'

Mrs Yule gave a troublous sigh, and for a few minutes pondered anxiously.

'I wasn't thinking so much about myself,' she said at length. 'It's the hindrance I should be to father. Just because of me, he mightn't be able to use his money as he'd wish. He'd always be feeling that if it wasn't for me things would be so much better for him and for you as well.'

'You must remember,' Marian replied, 'that at father's age people don't care to make such great changes. His home life, I feel sure, wouldn't be so very different from what it is now; he would prefer to use his money in starting a paper or magazine. I know that would be his first thought. If more acquaintances came to his house, what would that matter? It isn't as if he wished for fashionable society. They would be literary people, and why ever shouldn't you meet with them?'

'I've always been the reason why he couldn't have many friends.'

'That's a great mistake. If father ever said that, in his bad temper, he knew it wasn't the truth. The chief reason has always been his poverty. It costs money to entertain friends; time as well. Don't think in this anxious way, mother. If we are to be rich, it will be better for all of us.'

Marian had every reason for seeking to persuade herself that this was true. In her own heart there was a fear of how wealth might affect her father, but she could not bring herself to face the darker prospect. For her so much depended on that hope of a revival of generous feeling under sunny influences.

It was only after this conversation that she began to reflect on all the possible consequences of her uncle's death. As yet she had been too much disturbed to grasp as a reality the event to which she had often looked forward, though as to something still remote and of quite uncertain results. Perhaps at this moment, though she could not know it, the course of her life had undergone the most important change. Perhaps there was no more need for her to labour upon this 'article' she was manufacturing.

She did not think it probable that she herself would benefit directly by John Yule's will. There was no certainty that even her father would, for he and his brother had never been on cordial terms. But on the whole it seemed likely that he would inherit money enough to free him from the toil of writing for periodicals. He himself anticipated that. What else could be the meaning of those words in which (and it was before the arrival of the news) he had warned her against 'people who made connections only with self-interest in view'? This threw a sudden light upon her father's attitude towards Jasper Milvain. Evidently he thought that Jasper regarded her as a possible heiress, sooner or later. That suspicion was rankling in his mind; doubtless it intensified the prejudice which originated in literary animosity.

Was there any truth in his suspicion? She did not shrink from admitting that there might be. Jasper had from the first been so frank with her, had so often repeated that money was at present his chief need. If her father inherited substantial property, would it induce Jasper to declare himself more than her friend? She could view the possibility of that, and yet not for a moment be shaken in her love. It was plain that Jasper could not think of marrying until his position and prospects were greatly improved: practically, his sisters depended upon him. What folly it would be to draw back if circumstances led him to avow what hitherto he had so slightly disguised! She had the conviction that he valued her for her own sake; if the obstacle between them could only be removed, what matter how?

Would he be willing to abandon Clement Fadge, and come over to her father's side? If Yule were able to found a magazine?

Had she read or heard of a girl who went so far in concessions, Marian would have turned away, her delicacy offended. In her own case she could indulge to the utmost that practicality which colours a woman's thought even in mid-passion. The cold exhibition of ignoble scheming will repel many a woman who, for her own heart's desire, is capable of that same compromise with her strict sense of honour.

Marian wrote to Dora Milvain, telling her what had happened. But she refrained from visiting her friends.

Each night found her more restless, each morning less able to employ herself. She shut herself in the study merely to be alone with her thoughts, to be able to walk backwards and forwards, or sit for hours in feverish reverie. From her father came no news. Her mother was suffering dreadfully from suspense, and often had eyes red with weeping. Absorbed in her own hopes and fears, whilst every hour harassed her more intolerably, Marian was unable to play the part of an encourager; she had never known such exclusiveness of self-occupation.

Yule's return was unannounced. Early in the afternoon, when he had been absent five days, he entered the house, deposited his travelling-bag in the passage, and went upstairs. Marian had come out of the study just in time to see him up on the first landing; at the same moment Mrs Yule ascended from the kitchen.

'Wasn't that father?'

'Yes, he has gone up.'

'Did he say anything?'

Marian shook her head. They looked at the travelling-bag, then went into the parlour and waited in silence for more than a quarter of an hour. Yule's foot was heard on the stairs; he came down slowly, paused in the passage, entered the parlour with his usual grave, cold countenance.

Chapter 22

THE LEGATEES

EACH day Jasper came to inquire of his sisters if they had news from Wattleborough or from Marian Yule. He exhibited no impatience, spoke of the matter in a disinterested tone; still, he came daily.

One afternoon he found Dora working alone. Maud, he was told, had gone to lunch at Mrs Lane's.

'So soon again? She's getting very thick with those people. And why don't they ask you?'

'Maud has told them that I don't care to go out.'

'It's all very well, but she mustn't neglect her work. Did she write anything last night or this morning?'

Dora bit the end of her pen, and shook her head.

'Why not?'

'The invitation came about five o'clock, and it seemed to unsettle her.'

'Precisely. That's what I'm afraid of. She isn't the kind of girl to stick at work if people begin to send her invitations. But I tell you what it is, you must talk seriously to her; she has to get her living, you know. Mrs Lane and her set are not likely to be much use, that's the worst of it; they'll merely waste her time, and make her discontented.'

Her sister executed an elaborate bit of cross-hatching on some waste paper. Her lips were drawn together, and her brows wrinkled. At length she broke the silence by saying:

'Marian hasn't been yet.'

Jasper seemed to pay no attention; she looked up at him, and saw that he was in thought.

'Did you go to those people last night?' she inquired.

'Yes. By-the-by, Miss Rupert was there.'

He spoke as if the name would be familiar to his hearer, but Dora seemed at a loss.

'Who is Miss Rupert?'

'Didn't I tell you about her? I thought I did. Oh, I met her first of all at Barlow's, just after we got back from the seaside.

Rather an interesting girl. She's a daughter of Manton Rupert, the advertising agent. I want to get invited to their house; useful people, you know.'

'But is an advertising agent a gentleman?'

Jasper laughed.

'Do you think of him as a bill-poster? At all events he is enormously wealthy, and has a magnificent house at Chislehurst. The girl goes about with her step-mother. I call her a girl, but she must be nearly thirty, and Mrs Rupert looks only two or three years older. I had quite a long talk with her – Miss Rupert, I mean – last night. She told me she was going to stay next week with the Barlows, so I shall have a run out to Wimbledon one afternoon.'

Dora looked at him inquiringly.

'Just to see Miss Rupert?' she asked, meeting his eyes.

'To be sure. Why not?'

'Oh!' ejaculated his sister, as if the question did not concern her.

'She isn't exactly good-looking,' pursued Jasper, meditatively, with a quick glance at the listener, 'but fairly intellectual. Plays very well, and has a nice contralto voice; she sang that new thing of Tosti's [23] – what do you call it? I thought her rather masculine when I first saw her, but the impression wears off when one knows her better. She rather takes to me, I fancy.'

'But –' began Dora, after a minute's silence.

'But what?' inquired her brother with an air of interest.

'I don't quite understand you.'

'In general, or with reference to some particular?'

'What right have you to go to places just to see this Miss Rupert?'

'What *right*?' He laughed. 'I am a young man with my way to make. I can't afford to lose any opportunity. If Miss Rupert is so good as to take an interest in me, I have no objection. She's old enough to make friends for herself.'

'Oh, then you consider her simply a friend?'

'I shall see how things go on.'

'But, pray, do you consider yourself perfectly free?' asked Dora, with some indignation.

'Why shouldn't I?'

'Then I think you have been behaving very strangely.'

Jasper saw that she was in earnest. He stroked the back of his head and smiled at the wall.

'With regard to Marian, you mean?'

'Of course I do.'

'But Marian understands me perfectly. I have never for a moment tried to make her think that – well, to put it plainly, that I was in love with her. In all our conversations it has been my one object to afford her insight into my character, and to explain my position. She has no excuse whatever for misinterpreting me. And I feel assured that she has done nothing of the kind.'

'Very well, if you feel satisfied with yourself –'

'But come now, Dora; what's all this about? You are Marian's friend, and, of course, I don't wish you to say a word about *her*. But let me explain myself. I have occasionally walked part of the way home with Marian, when she and I have happened to go from here at the same time; now there was nothing whatever in our talk at such time that anyone mightn't have listened to. We are both intellectual people, and we talk in an intellectual way. You seem to have rather old-fashioned ideas – provincial ideas. A girl like Marian Yule claims the new privileges of woman; she would resent it if you supposed that she couldn't be friendly with a man without attributing "intentions" to him – to use the old word. We don't live in Wattleborough, where liberty is rendered impossible by the cackling of gossips.'

'No, but –'

'Well?'

'It seems to me rather strange, that's all. We had better not talk about it any more.'

'But I have only just begun to talk about it; I must try to make my position intelligible to you. Now, suppose – a quite impossible thing – that Marian inherited some twenty or thirty thousand pounds; I should forthwith ask her to be my wife.'

'Oh indeed!'

'I see no reason for sarcasm. It would be a most rational proceeding. I like her very much; but to marry her (supposing she would have me) without money would be a gross absurdity, simply spoiling my career, and leading to all sorts of discontents.'

'No one would suggest that you should marry as things are.'

'No; but please to bear in mind that to obtain money somehow or other – and I see no other way than by marriage – is necessary to me, and that with as little delay as possible. I am not at all likely to get a big editorship for some years to come, and I don't feel disposed to make myself prematurely old by toiling for a few hundreds per annum in the meantime. Now all this I have frankly and fully explained to Marian. I dare say she suspects what I should do if she came into possession of money; there's no harm in that. But she knows perfectly well that, as things are, we remain intellectual friends.'

'Then listen to me, Jasper. If we hear that Marian gets nothing from her uncle, you had better behave honestly, and let her see that you haven't as much interest in her as before.'

'That would be brutality.'

'It would be honest.'

'Well, no, it wouldn't. Strictly speaking, my interest in Marian wouldn't suffer at all. I should *know* that we could be nothing but friends, that's all. Hitherto I haven't known what might come to pass; I don't know yet. So far from following your advice, I shall let Marian understand that, if anything, I am more her friend than ever, seeing that henceforth there can be no ambiguities.'

'I can only tell you that Maud would agree with me in what I have been saying.'

'Then both of you have distorted views.'

'I think not. It's you who are unprincipled.'

'My dear girl, haven't I been showing you that no man could be more above-board, more straightforward?'

'You have been talking nonsense, Jasper.'

'Nonsense? Oh, this female lack of logic! Then my argument has been utterly thrown away. Now that's one of the things I like in Miss Rupert; she can follow an argument and see consequences. And for that matter so can Marian. I only wish it were possible to refer this question to her.'

There was a tap at the door. Dora called 'Come in!' and Marian herself appeared.

'What an odd thing!' exclaimed Jasper, lowering his voice. 'I was that moment saying I wished it were possible to refer a question to you.'

Dora reddened, and stood in an embarrassed attitude.

'It was the old dispute whether women in general are capable of logic. But pardon me, Miss Yule; I forget that you have been occupied with sad things since I last saw you.'

Dora led her to a chair, asking if her father had returned.

'Yes, he came back yesterday.'

Jasper and his sister could not think it likely that Marian had suffered much from grief at her uncle's death; practically John Yule was a stranger to her. Yet her face bore the signs of acute mental trouble, and it seemed as if some agitation made it difficult for her to speak. The awkward silence that fell upon the three was broken by Jasper, who expressed a regret that he was obliged to take his leave.

'Maud is becoming a young lady of society,' he said – just for the sake of saying something – as he moved towards the door. 'If she comes back whilst you are here, Miss Yule, warn her that that is the path of destruction for literary people.'

'You should bear that in mind yourself,' remarked Dora, with a significant look.

'Oh, I am cool-headed enough to make society serve my own ends.'

Marian turned her head with a sudden movement which was checked before she had quite looked round to him. The phrase he uttered last appeared to have affected her in some way; her eyes fell, and an expression of pain was on her brows for a moment.

'I can only stay a few minutes,' she said, bending with a faint smile towards Dora, as soon as they were alone. 'I have come on my way from the Museum.'

'Where you have tired yourself to death as usual, I can see.'

'No; I have done scarcely anything. I only pretended to read; my mind is too much troubled. Have you heard anything about my uncle's will?'

'Nothing whatever.'

'I thought it might have been spoken of in Wattleborough, and some friend might have written to you. But I suppose there has hardly been time for that. I shall surprise you very much. Father receives nothing, but I have a legacy of five thousand pounds.'

Dora kept her eyes down.

'Then – what do you think?' continued Marian. 'My cousin Amy has ten thousand pounds.'

'Good gracious! What a difference *that* will make!'

'Yes, indeed. And her brother John has six thousand. But nothing to their mother. There are a good many other legacies, but most of the property goes to the Wattleborough Park – "Yule Park" it will be called – and to the Volunteers, and things of that kind. They say he wasn't as rich as people thought.'

'Do you know what Miss Harrow gets?'

'She has the house for her life, and fifteen hundred pounds.'

'And your father nothing whatever?'

'Nothing. Not a penny. Oh, I am so grieved! I think it so unkind, so wrong. Amy and her brother to have sixteen thousand pounds and father nothing! I can't understand it. There was no unkind feeling between him and father. He knew what a hard life father has had. Doesn't it seem heartless?'

'What does your father say?'

'I think he feels the unkindness more than he does the disappointment; of course he must have expected something. He came into the room where mother and I were, and sat down, and began to tell us about the will just as if he were speaking to strangers about something he had read in the newspaper – that's the only way I can describe it. Then he got up and went away into the study. I waited a little, then went to him there; he was sitting at work, as if he hadn't been away from home at all. I tried to tell him how sorry I was, but I couldn't say anything. I began to cry foolishly. He spoke kindly to me, far more kindly than he has done for a long time; but he wouldn't talk about the will, and I had to go away and leave him. Poor mother, for all she was afraid that we were going to be rich, is broken-hearted at his disappointment.'

'Your mother was afraid?' said Dora.

'Because she thought herself unfitted for life in a large house, and feared we should think her in our way.' She smiled sadly. 'Poor mother! she is so humble and so good. I do hope that father will be kinder to her. But there's no telling yet what the result of this may be. I feel guilty when I stand before him.'

'But he must feel glad that you have five thousand pounds.'

Marian delayed her reply for a moment, her eyes down.

'Yes, perhaps he is glad of that.'

'Perhaps!'

'He can't help thinking, Dora, what use he could have made of it. It has always been his greatest wish to have a literary paper of his own – like *The Study*, you know. He would have used the money in that way, I am sure.'

'But, all the same, he ought to feel pleasure in your good fortune.'

Marian turned to another subject.

'Think of the Reardons; what a change all at once! What will they do, I wonder? Surely they won't continue to live apart?'

'We shall hear from Jasper.'

Whilst they were discussing the affairs of that branch of the family Maud returned. There was ill-humour on her handsome face, and she greeted Marian but coldly. Throwing off her hat and gloves and mantle she listened to the repeated story of John Yule's bequests.

'But why ever has Mrs Reardon so much more than anyone else?' she asked.

'We can only suppose it is because she was the favourite child of the brother he liked best. Yet at her wedding he gave her nothing, and spoke contemptuously of her for marrying a literary man.'

'Fortunate for her poor husband that her uncle was able to forgive her. I wonder what's the date of the will? Who knows but he may have rewarded her for quarrelling with Mr Reardon.'

This excited a laugh.

'I don't know when the will was made,' said Marian. 'And I don't know whether uncle had even heard of the Reardons' misfortunes. I suppose he must have done. My cousin John was at the funeral, but not my aunt. I think it most likely father and John didn't speak a word to each other. Fortunately the relatives were lost sight of in the great crowd of Wattleborough people; there was an enormous procession, of course.'

Maud kept glancing at her sister. The ill-humour had not altogether passed from her face, but it was now blended with reflectiveness.

A few moments more, and Marian had to hasten home. When she was gone the sisters looked at each other.

'Five thousand pounds,' murmured the elder. 'I suppose that is considered nothing.'

'I suppose so. – He was here when Marian came, but didn't stay.'

'Then you'll take him the news this evening?'

'Yes,' replied Dora. Then, after musing, 'He seemed annoyed that you were at the Lanes' again.'

Maud made a movement of indifference.

'What has been putting you out?'

'Things were rather stupid. Some people who were to have come didn't turn up. And – well, it doesn't matter.'

She rose and glanced at herself in the little oblong mirror over the mantelpiece.

'Did Jasper ever speak to you of a Miss Rupert?' asked Dora.

'Not that I remember.'

'What do you think? He told me in the calmest way that he didn't see why Marian should think of him as anything but the most ordinary friend – said he had never given her reason to think anything else.'

'Indeed! And Miss Rupert is someone who has the honour of his preference?'

'He says she is about thirty, and rather masculine, but a great heiress. Jasper is shameful!'

'What do you expect? I consider it is your duty to let Marian know *everything* he says. Otherwise you help to deceive her. He has no sense of honour in such things.'

Dora was so impatient to let her brother have the news that she left the house as soon as she had had tea on the chance of finding Jasper at home. She had not gone a dozen yards before she encountered him in person.

'I was afraid Marian might still be with you,' he said laughing. 'I should have asked the landlady. Well?'

'We can't stand talking here. You had better come in.'

He was in too much excitement to wait.

'Just tell me. What has she?'

Dora walked quickly towards the house, looking annoyed.

'Nothing at all? Then what has her father?'

'*He* has nothing,' replied his sister, 'and *she* has five thousand pounds.'

Jasper walked on with bent head. He said nothing more until he was upstairs in the sitting-room, where Maud greeted him carelessly.

'Mrs Reardon anything?'

Dora informed him.

'What?' he cried, incredulously. 'Ten thousand? You don't say so!'

He burst into uproarious laughter.

'So Reardon is rescued from the slum and the clerk's desk! Well, I'm glad: by Jove, I am. I should have liked it better if Marian had had the ten thousand and he the five, but it's an excellent joke. Perhaps the next thing will be that he'll refuse to have anything to do with his wife's money; that would be just like him.'

After amusing himself with this subject for a few minutes more, he turned to the window and stood there in silence.

'Are you going to have tea with us?' Dora inquired.

He did not seem to hear her. On a repetition of the inquiry, he answered absently:

'Yes, I may as well. Then I can go home and get to work.'

During the remainder of his stay he talked very little, and as Maud also was in an abstracted mood, tea passed almost in silence. On the point of departing he asked:

'When is Marian likely to come here again?'

'I haven't the least idea,' answered Dora.

He nodded, and went his way.

It was necessary for him to work at a magazine article which he had begun this morning, and on reaching home he spread out his papers in the usual business-like fashion. The subject out of which he was manufacturing 'copy' had its difficulties, and was not altogether congenial to him; this morning he had laboured with unwonted effort to produce about a page of manuscript, and now that he tried to resume the task his thoughts would not centre upon it. Jasper was too young to have thoroughly mastered the art of somnambulistic composition; to write, he was still obliged to give exclusive attention to the matter under treatment. Dr Johnson's saying,[24] that a man may write at any time if he will set himself doggedly to it, was often upon his lips, and had even been of help to him, as no doubt it has to many another

man obliged to compose amid distracting circumstances; but
the formula had no efficacy this evening. Twice or thrice he rose
from his chair, paced the room with a determined brow, and sat
down again with vigorous clutch of the pen; still he failed to
excogitate a single sentence that would serve his purpose.

'I must have it out with myself before I can do anything,' was
his thought as he finally abandoned the endeavour. 'I must make
up my mind.'

To this end he settled himself in an easy-chair and began to
smoke cigarettes. Some dozen of these aids to reflection only
made him so nervous that he could no longer remain alone. He
put on his hat and overcoat and went out – to find that it was
raining heavily. He returned for an umbrella, and before long
was walking aimlessly about the Strand, unable to make up his
mind whether to turn into a theatre or not. Instead of doing so,
he sought a certain upper room of a familiar restaurant, where
the day's papers were to be seen, and perchance an acquaintance
might be met. Only half a dozen men were there, reading and
smoking, and all were unknown to him. He drank a glass of lager
beer, skimmed the news of the evening, and again went out into
the bad weather.

After all it was better to go home. Everything he encountered
had an unsettling effect upon him, so that he was further than
ever from the decision at which he wished to arrive. In Mornington Road he came upon Whelpdale, who was walking slowly
under an umbrella.

'I've just called at your place.'

'All right; come back if you like.'

'But perhaps I shall waste your time?' said Whelpdale, with
unusual diffidence.

Reassured, he gladly returned to the house. Milvain acquainted
him with the fact of John Yule's death, and with its result so far
as it concerned the Reardons. They talked of how the couple
would probably behave under this decisive change of circumstances.

'Biffen professes to know nothing about Mrs Reardon,' said
Whelpdale. 'I suspect he keeps his knowledge to himself, out of
regard for Reardon. It wouldn't surprise me if they live apart for
a long time yet.'

'Not very likely. It was only want of money.'

'They're not at all suited to each other. Mrs Reardon no doubt repents her marriage bitterly, and I doubt whether Reardon cares much for his wife.'

'As there's no way of getting divorced they'll make the best of it. Ten thousand pounds produce about four hundred a year; it's enough to live on.'

'And be miserable on – if they no longer love each other.'

'You're such a sentimental fellow,' cried Jasper. 'I believe you seriously think that love – the sort of frenzy you understand by it – ought to endure throughout married life. How has a man come to your age with such primitive ideas?'

'Well, I don't know. Perhaps you err a little in the opposite direction.'

'I haven't much faith in marrying for love, as you know. What's more, I believe it's the very rarest thing for people to be in love with each other. Reardon and his wife perhaps were an instance; perhaps – I'm not quite sure about *her*. As a rule, marriage is the result of a mild preference, encouraged by circumstances, and deliberately heightened into strong sexual feeling. You, of all men, know well enough that the same kind of feeling could be produced for almost any woman who wasn't repulsive.'

'The same kind of feeling; but there's vast difference of degree.'

'To be sure. I think it's only a matter of degree. When it rises to the point of frenzy people may strictly be said to be in love; and, as I tell you, I think that comes to pass very rarely indeed. For my own part, I have no experience of it, and think I never shall have.'

'I can't say the same.'

They laughed.

'I dare say you have imagined yourself in love – or really been so for aught I know – a dozen times. How the deuce you can attach any importance to such feeling where marriage is concerned I don't understand.'

'Well, now,' said Whelpdale, 'I have never upheld the theory – at least not since I was sixteen – that a man can be in love only once, or that there is one particular woman if he misses whom he can never be happy. There may be thousands of women whom I could love with equal sincerity.'

'I object to the word "love" altogether. It has been vulgarised. Let us talk about compatibility. Now, I should say that, no doubt, and speaking scientifically, there is one particular woman supremely fitted to each man. I put aside consideration of circumstances; we know that circumstances will disturb any degree of abstract fitness. But in the nature of things there must be one woman whose nature is specially well adapted to harmonise with mine, or with yours. If there were any means of discovering this woman in each case, then I have no doubt it would be worth a man's utmost effort to do so, and any amount of erotic jubilation would be reasonable when the discovery was made. But the thing is impossible, and, what's more, we know what ridiculous fallibility people display when they imagine they have found the best substitute for that indiscoverable. This is what makes me impatient with sentimental talk about marriage. An educated man mustn't play so into the hands of ironic destiny. Let him think he *wants* to marry a woman; but don't let him exaggerate his feelings or idealise their nature.'

'There's a good deal in all that,' admitted Whelpdale, though discontentedly.

'There's more than a good deal; there's the last word on the subject. The days of romantic love are gone by. The scientific spirit has put an end to that kind of self-deception. Romantic love was inextricably blended with all sorts of superstitions – belief in personal immortality, in superior beings, in – all the rest of it. What we think of now is moral and intellectual and physical compatibility; I mean, if we are reasonable people.'

'And if we are not so unfortunate as to fall in love with an incompatible,' added Whelpdale, laughing.

'Well, that is a form of unreason – a blind desire which science could explain in each case. I rejoice that I am not subject to that form of epilepsy.'

'You positively never were in love?'

'As you understand it, never. But I have felt a very distinct preference.'

'Based on what you think compatibility?'

'Yes. Not strong enough to make me lose sight of prudence and advantage. No, not strong enough for that.'

He seemed to be reassuring himself.

'Then of course that can't be called love,' said Whelpdale.

'Perhaps not. But, as I told you, a preference of this kind can be heightened into emotion, if one chooses. In the case of which I am thinking it easily might be. And I think it very improbable indeed that I should repent it if anything led me to indulge such an impulse.'

Whelpdale smiled.

'This is very interesting. I hope it may lead to something.'

'I don't think it will. I am far more likely to marry some woman for whom I have no preference, but who can serve me materially.'

'I confess that amazes me. I know the value of money as well as you do, but I wouldn't marry a rich woman for whom I had no preference. By Jove, no !'

'Yes, yes. You are a consistent sentimentalist.'

'Doomed to perpetual disappointment,' said the other, looking disconsolately about the room.

'Courage, my boy ! I have every hope that I shall see you marry and repent.'

'I admit the danger of that. But shall I tell you something I have observed? Each woman I fall in love with is of a higher type than the one before.'

Jasper roared irreverently, and his companion looked hurt.

'But I am perfectly serious, I assure you. To go back only three or four years. There was the daughter of my landlady in Barham Street; well, a nice girl enough, but limited, decidedly limited. Next came that girl at the stationer's – you remember? She was distinctly an advance, both in mind and person. Then there was Miss Embleton; yes, I think she made again an advance. She had been at Bedford College, you know, and was really a girl of considerable attainments; morally, admirable. Afterwards –'

He paused.

'The maiden from Birmingham, wasn't it?' said Jasper, again exploding.

'Yes, it was. Well, I can't be quite sure. But in many respects that girl was my ideal; she really was.'

'As you once or twice told me at the time.'

'I really believe she would rank above Miss Embleton – at all events from my point of view. And that's everything, you know.

It's the effect a woman produces on one that has to be considered.'

'The next should be a paragon,' said Jasper.

'The next?'

Whelpdale again looked about the room, but added nothing, and fell into a long silence.

When left to himself Jasper walked about a little, then sat down at his writing-table, for he felt easier in mind, and fancied that he might still do a couple of hours' work before going to bed. He did in fact write half a dozen lines, but with the effort came back his former mood. Very soon the pen dropped, and he was once more in the throes of anxious mental debate.

He sat till after midnight, and when he went to his bedroom it was with a lingering step, which proved him still a prey to indecision.

Chapter 23

A PROPOSED INVESTMENT

ALFRED YULE'S behaviour under his disappointment seemed to prove that even for him the uses of adversity could be sweet. On the day after his return home he displayed a most unwonted mildness in such remarks as he addressed to his wife, and his bearing towards Marian was gravely gentle. At meals he conversed, or rather monologised, on literary topics, with occasionally one of his grim jokes, pointed for Marian's appreciation. He became aware that the girl had been overtaxing her strength of late and suggested a few weeks of recreation among new novels. The coldness and gloom which had possessed him when he made a formal announcement of the news appeared to have given way before the sympathy manifested by his wife and daughter; he was now sorrowful, but resigned.

He explained to Marian the exact nature of her legacy. It was to be paid out of her uncle's share in a wholesale stationery business, with which John Yule had been connected for the last twenty years, but from which he had not long ago withdrawn a large portion of his invested capital. This house was known as 'Tuberville & Co.,' a name which Marian now heard for the first time.

'I knew nothing of his association with them,' said her father. 'They tell me that seven or eight thousand pounds will be realised from that source; it seems a pity that the investment was not left to you intact. Whether there will be any delay in withdrawing the money I can't say.'

The executors were two old friends of the deceased, one of them a former partner in his paper-making concern.

On the evening of the second day, about an hour after dinner was over, Mr Hinks called at the house; as usual, he went into the study. Before long came a second visitor, Mr Quarmby, who joined Yule and Hinks. The three had all sat together for some time, when Marian, who happened to be coming down stairs, saw her father at the study door.

'Ask your mother to let us have some supper at a quarter to

ten,' he said urbanely. 'And come in, won't you? We are only gossiping.'

It had not often happened that Marian was invited to join parties of this kind.

'Do you wish me to come?' she asked.

'Yes, I should like you to, if you have nothing particular to do.'

Marian informed Mrs Yule that the visitors would have supper, and then went to the study. Mr Quarmby was smoking a pipe; Mr Hinks, who on grounds of economy had long since given up tobacco, sat with his hands in his trouser pockets, and his long, thin legs tucked beneath the chair; both rose and greeted Marian with more than ordinary warmth.

'Will you allow me five or six puffs?' asked Mr Quarmby, laying one hand on his ample stomach and elevating his pipe as if it were a glass of beaded liquor. 'I shall then have done.'

'As many more as you like,' Marian replied.

The easiest chair was placed for her, Mr Hinks hastening to perform this courtesy, and her father apprised her of the topic they were discussing.

'What's your view, Marian? Is there anything to be said for the establishment of a literary academy in England?'

Mr Quarmby beamed benevolently upon her, and Mr Hinks, his scraggy neck at full length, awaited her reply with a look of the most respectful attention.

'I really think we have quite enough literary quarrelling as it is,' the girl replied, casting down her eyes and smiling.

Mr Quarmby uttered a hollow chuckle, Mr Hinks laughed thinly and exclaimed, 'Very good indeed! Very good!' Yule affected to applaud with impartial smile.

'It wouldn't harmonise with the Anglo-Saxon spirit,' remarked Mr Hinks, with an air of diffident profundity.

Yule held forth on the subject for a few minutes in laboured phrases. Presently the conversation turned to periodicals, and the three men were unanimous in an opinion that no existing monthly or quarterly could be considered as representing the best literary opinion.

'We want,' remarked Mr Quarmby, 'we want a monthly review which shall deal exclusively with literature. The *Fortnightly*, the *Contemporary* – they are very well in their way, but then they are mere miscellanies. You will find one solid literary article amid a confused mass of politics and economics and general clap-trap.'

'Articles on the currency and railway statistics and views of evolution,' said Mr Hinks, with a look as if something were grating between his teeth.

'The quarterlies?' put in Yule. 'Well, the original idea of the quarterlies was that there are not enough important books published to occupy solid reviewers more than four times a year. That may be true, but then a literary monthly would include much more than professed reviews. Hinks's essays on the historical drama would have come out in it very well; or your "Spanish Poets," Quarmby.'

'I threw out the idea to Jedwood the other day,' said Mr Quarmby, 'and he seemed to nibble at it.'

'Yes, yes,' came from Yule; 'but Jedwood has so many irons in the fire. I doubt if he has the necessary capital at command just now. No doubt he's the man, if some capitalist would join him.'

'No enormous capital needed,' opined Mr Quarmby. 'The thing would pay its way almost from the first. It would take a place between the literary weeklies and the quarterlies. The former are too academic, the latter too massive, for multitudes of people who yet have strong literary tastes. Foreign publications should be liberally dealt with. But, as Hinks says, no meddling with the books that are no books – biblia abiblia; [25] nothing about essays on bimetallism and treatises for or against vaccination.'

Even here, in the freedom of a friend's study, he laughed his Reading-room laugh, folding both hands upon his expansive waistcoat.

'Fiction? I presume a serial of the better kind might be admitted?' said Yule.

'That would be advisable, no doubt. But strictly of the better kind.'

'Oh, strictly of the better kind,' chimed in Mr Hinks.

They pursued the discussion as if they were an editorial committee planning a review of which the first number was shortly to appear. It occupied them until Mrs Yule announced at the door that supper was ready.

During the meal Marian found herself the object of unusual

attention; her father troubled to inquire if the cut of cold beef
he sent her was to her taste, and kept an eye on her progress. Mr
Hinks talked to her in a tone of respectful sympathy, and Mr
Quarmby was paternally jovial when he addressed her. Mrs Yule
would have kept silence in her ordinary way, but this evening her
husband made several remarks which he had adapted to her
intellect, and even showed that a reply would be graciously
received.

Mother and daughter remained together when the men withdrew to their tobacco and toddy. Neither made allusion to the
wonderful change, but they talked more light-heartedly than for
a long time.

On the morrow Yule began by consulting Marian with regard
to the disposition of matter in an essay he was writing. What she
said he weighed carefully, and seemed to think that she had set his
doubts at rest.

'Poor old Hinks!' he said presently, with a sigh. 'Breaking up,
isn't he? He positively totters in his walk. I'm afraid he's the kind
of man to have a paralytic stroke; it wouldn't astonish me to hear
at any moment that he was lying helpless.'

'What ever would become of him in that case?'

'Goodness knows! One might ask the same of so many of us.
What would become of me, for instance, if I were incapable of
work?'

Marian could make no reply.

'There's something I'll just mention to you,' he went on in a
lowered tone, 'though I don't wish you to take it too seriously.
I'm beginning to have a little trouble with my eyes.'

She looked at him, startled.

'With your eyes?'

'Nothing, I hope; but – well, I think I shall see an oculist. One
doesn't care to face a prospect of failing sight, perhaps of cataract, or something of that kind; still, it's better to know the facts,
I should say.'

'By all means go to an oculist,' said Marian, earnestly.

'Don't disturb yourself about it. It may be nothing at all. But
in any case I must change my glasses.'

He rustled over some slips of manuscript, whilst Marian regarded him anxiously.

'Now, I appeal to you, Marian,' he continued : 'could I possibly save money out of an income that has never exceeded two hundred and fifty pounds, and often – I mean even in latter years – has been much less?'

'I don't see how you could.'

'In one way, of course, I have managed it. My life is insured for five hundred pounds. But that is no provision for possible disablement. If I could no longer earn money with my pen, what would become of me?'

Marian could have made an encouraging reply, but did not venture to utter her thoughts.

'Sit down,' said her father. 'You are not to work for a few days, and I myself shall be none the worse for a morning's rest. Poor old Hinks! I suppose we shall help him among us, somehow. Quarmby, of course, is comparatively flourishing. Well, we have been companions for a quarter of a century, we three. When I first met Quarmby I was a Grub Street gazetteer, and I think he was even poorer than I. A life of toil! A life of toil!'

'That it has been, indeed.'

'By-the-by' – he threw an arm over the back of his chair – 'what did you think of our imaginary review, the thing we were talking about last night?'

'There are so many periodicals,' replied Marian, doubtfully.

'So many? My dear child, if we live another ten years we shall see the number trebled.'

'Is it desirable?'

'That there should be such growth of periodicals? Well, from one point of view, no. No doubt they take up the time which some people would give to solid literature. But, on the other hand, there's a far greater number of people who would probably not read at all, but for the temptations of these short and new articles; and they may be induced to pass on to substantial works. Of course it all depends on the quality of the periodical matter you offer. Now, magazines like' – he named two or three of popular stamp – 'might very well be dispensed with, unless one regards them as an alternative to the talking of scandal or any other vicious result of total idleness. But such a monthly as we projected would be of distinct literary value. There can be no doubt that someone or other will shortly establish it.'

'I am afraid,' said Marian, 'I haven't so much sympathy with literary undertakings as you would like me to have.'

Money is a great fortifier of self-respect. Since she had become really conscious of her position as the owner of five thousand pounds, Marian spoke with a steadier voice, walked with firmer step; mentally she felt herself altogether a less dependent being. She might have confessed this lukewarmness towards literary enterprise in the anger which her father excited eight or nine days ago, but at that time she could not have uttered her opinion calmly, deliberately, as now. The smile which accompanied the words was also new; it signified deliverance from pupilage.

'I have felt that,' returned her father, after a slight pause to command his voice, that it might be suave instead of scornful. 'I greatly fear that I have made your life something of a martyr-dom –'

'Don't think I meant that, father. I am speaking only of the general question. I can't be quite so zealous as you are, that's all. I love books, but I could wish people were content for a while with those we already have.'

'My dear Marian, don't suppose that I am out of sympathy with you here. Alas! how much of my work has been mere drudgery, mere labouring for a livelihood! How gladly I would have spent much more of my time among the great authors, with no thought of making money of them! If I speak approvingly of a scheme for a new periodical, it is greatly because of my necessi-ties.'

He paused and looked at her. Marian returned the look.

'You would of course write for it,' she said.

'Marian, why shouldn't I edit it? Why shouldn't it be *your* property?'

'My property – ?'

She checked a laugh. There came into her mind a more dis-agreeable suspicion than she had ever entertained of her father. Was this the meaning of his softened behaviour? Was he capable of calculated hypocrisy? That did not seem consistent with his character, as she knew it.

'Let us talk it over,' said Yule. He was in visible agitation, and his voice shook. 'The idea may well startle you at first. It will seem to you that I propose to make away with your property before you have even come into possession of it.' He laughed. 'But, in fact, what I have in mind is merely an investment for your capital, and that an admirable one. Five thousand pounds at three per cent – one doesn't care to reckon on more – represents a hundred and fifty a year. Now, there can be very little doubt that, if it were invested in literary property such as I have in mind, it would bring you five times that interest, and before long perhaps much more. Of course I am now speaking in the roughest outline. I should have to get trustworthy advice; complete and detailed estimates would be submitted to you. At present I merely suggest to you this form of investment.'

He watched her face eagerly, greedily. When Marian's eyes rose to his he looked away.

'Then, of course,' she said, 'you don't expect me to give any decided answer.'

'Of course not – of course not. I merely put before you the chief advantages of such an investment. As I am a selfish old fellow, I'll talk about the benefit to myself first of all. I should be editor of the new review; I should draw a stipend sufficient to all my needs – quite content, at first, to take far less than another man would ask, and to progress with the advance of the periodical. This position would enable me to have done with mere drudgery; I should only write when I felt called to do so – when the spirit moved me.' Again he laughed, as though desirous of keeping his listener in good humour. 'My eyes would be greatly spared henceforth.'

He dwelt on that point, waiting its effect on Marian. As she said nothing he proceeded:

'And suppose I really were doomed to lose my sight in the course of a few years, am I wrong in thinking that the proprietor of this periodical would willingly grant a small annuity to the man who had firmly established it?'

'I see the force of all that,' said Marian; 'but it takes for granted that the periodical will be successful.'

'It does. In the hands of a publisher like Jedwood – a vigorous man of the new school – its success could scarcely be doubtful.'

'Do you think five thousand pounds would be enough to start such a review?'

'Well, I can say nothing definite on that point. For one thing, the coat must be made according to the cloth; expenditure can be largely controlled without endangering success. Then again, I think Jedwood would take a share in the venture. These are details. At present I only want to familiarise you with the thought that an investment of this sort will very probably offer itself to you.'

'It would be better if we called it a speculation,' said Marian, smiling uneasily.

Her one object at present was to oblige her father to understand that the suggestion by no means lured her. She could not tell him that what he proposed was out of the question, though as yet that was the light in which she saw it. His subtlety of approach had made her feel justified in dealing with him in a matter-of-fact way. He must see that she was not to be cajoled. Obviously, and in the nature of the case, he was urging a proposal in which he himself had all faith; but Marian knew his judgment was far from infallible. It mitigated her sense of behaving unkindly to reflect that in all likelihood this disposal of her money would be the worst possible for her own interests, and therefore for his. If, indeed, his dark forebodings were warranted, then upon her would fall the care of him, and the steadiness with which she faced that responsibility came from a hope of which she could not speak.

'Name it as you will,' returned her father, hardly suppressing a note of irritation. 'True, every commercial enterprise is a speculation. But let me ask you one question, and beg you to reply frankly. Do you distrust my ability to conduct this periodical?'

She did. She knew that he was not in touch with the interests of the day, and that all manner of considerations akin to the prime end of selling his review would make him an untrustworthy editor. But how could she tell him this?

'My opinion would be worthless,' she replied.

'If Jedwood were disposed to put confidence in me, you also would?'

'There's no need to talk of that now, father. Indeed, I can't say anything that would sound like a promise.'

He flashed a glance at her. Then she was more than doubtful?

'But you have no objection, Marian, to talk in a friendly way of a project that would mean so much to me?'

'But I am afraid to encourage you,' she replied, frankly. 'It is impossible for me to say whether I can do as you wish, or not.'

'Yes, yes; I perfectly understand that. Heaven forbid that I should regard you as a child to be led independently of your own views and wishes! With so large a sum of money at stake, it would be monstrous if I acted rashly, and tried to persuade you to do the same. The matter will have to be most gravely considered.'

'Yes.' She spoke mechanically.

'But if only it should come to something! You don't know what it would mean to me, Marian.'

'Yes, father; I know very well how you think and feel about it.'

'Do you?' he leaned forward, his features working under stress of emotion. 'If I could see myself the editor of an influential review, all my bygone toils and sufferings would be as nothing; I should rejoice in them as the steps to this triumph. *Meminisse juvabit*!²⁶ My dear, I am not a man fitted for subordinate places. My nature is framed for authority. The failure of all my undertakings rankles so in my heart that sometimes I feel capable of every brutality, every meanness, every hateful cruelty. To you I have behaved shamefully. Don't interrupt me, Marian. I have treated you abominably, my child, my dear daughter – and all the time with a full sense of what I was doing. That's the punishment of faults such as mine. I hate myself for every harsh word and angry look I have given you; at the time, I hated myself!'

'Father –'

'No, no; let me speak, Marian. You have forgiven me; I know it. You were always ready to forgive, dear. Can I ever forget that evening when I spoke like a brute, and you came afterwards and addressed me as if the wrong had been on your side? It burns in my memory. It wasn't I who spoke; it was the demon of failure, of humiliation. My enemies sit in triumph, and scorn at me; the thought of it is infuriating. Have I deserved this? Am I the inferior of – of those men who have succeeded and now try to trample on me? No! I am not! I have a better brain and a better heart!'

Listening to this strange outpouring, Marian more than for-
gave the hypocrisy of the last day or two. Nay, could it be called
hypocrisy? It was only his better self declared at the impulse of
a passionate hope.

'Why should you think so much of these troubles, father? Is it
such a great matter that narrow-minded people triumph over
you?'

'Narrow-minded?' He clutched at the word. 'You admit they
are that?'

'I feel very sure that Mr Fadge is.'

'Then you are not on his side against me?'

'How could you suppose such a thing?'

'Well, well; we won't talk of that. Perhaps it isn't a great
matter. No – from a philosophical point of view, such things are
unspeakably petty. But I am not much of a philosopher.' He
laughed, with a break in his voice. 'Defeat in life is defeat, after
all; and unmerited failure is a bitter curse. You see, I am not too
old to do something yet. My sight is failing, but I can take care of
it. If I had my own review, I would write every now and then a
critical paper in my very best style. You remember poor old
Hinks's note about me in his book? We laughed at it, but he
wasn't so far wrong. I have many of those qualities. A man is
conscious of his own merits, as well as of his defects. I have done
a few admirable things. You remember my paper on Lord Herbert of Cherbury? [27] No one ever wrote a more subtle piece of
criticism; but it was swept aside among the rubbish of the
magazines. And it's just because of my pungent phrases that I
have excited so much enmity. Wait! Wait! Let me have my own
review, and leisure, and satisfaction of mind – heavens! what I
will write! How I will scarify!'

'That is unworthy of you. How much better to ignore your
enemies! In such a position, I should carefully avoid every word
that betrayed personal feeling.'

'Well, well; you are of course right, my good girl. And I believe
I should do injustice to myself if I made you think that those
ignoble motives are the strongest in me. No; it isn't so. From my
boyhood I have had a passionate desire of literary fame, deep
down below all the surface faults of my character. The best of
my life has gone by, and it drives me to despair when I feel that

I have not gained the position due to me. There is only one way of doing this now, and that is by becoming the editor of an important periodical. Only in that way shall I succeed in forcing people to pay attention to my claims. Many a man goes to his grave unrecognised, just because he has never had a fair judgment. Nowadays it is the unscrupulous men of business who hold the attention of the public; they blow their trumpets so loudly that the voices of honest men have no chance of being heard.'

Marian was pained by the humility of his pleading with her – for what was all this but an endeavour to move her sympathies? – and by the necessity she was under of seeming to turn a deaf ear. She believed that there was some truth in his estimate of his own powers; though as an editor he would almost certainly fail, as a man of letters he had probably done far better work than some who had passed him by on their way to popularity. Circumstances might enable her to assist him, though not in the way he proposed. The worst of it was that she could not let him see what was in her mind. He must think that she was simply balancing her own satisfaction against his, when in truth she suffered from the conviction that to yield would be as unwise in regard to her father's future as it would be perilous to her own prospect of happiness.

'Shall we leave this to be talked of when the money has been paid over to me?' she said, after a silence.

'Yes. Don't suppose I wish to influence you by dwelling on my own hardships. That would be contemptible. I have only taken this opportunity of making myself better known to you. I don't readily talk of myself, and in general my real feelings are hidden by the faults of my temper. In suggesting how you could do me a great service, and at the same time reap advantage for yourself, I couldn't but remember how little reason you have to think kindly of me. But we will postpone further talk. You will think over what I have said?'

Marian promised that she would, and was glad to bring the conversation to an end.

When Sunday came, Yule inquired of his daughter if she had any engagement for the afternoon.

'Yes, I have,' she replied, with an effort to disguise her embarrassment.

'I'm sorry. I thought of asking you to come with me to Quarmby's. Shall you be away through the evening?'

'Till about nine o'clock, I think.'

'Ah! Never mind, never mind.'

He tried to dismiss the matter as if it were of no moment, but Marian saw the shadow that passed over his countenance. This was just after breakfast. For the remainder of the morning she did not meet him, and at the mid-day dinner he was silent, though he brought no book to the table with him, as he was wont to do when in his dark moods. Marian talked with her mother, doing her best to preserve the appearance of cheerfulness which was natural since the change in Yule's demeanour.

She chanced to meet her father in the passage just as she was going out. He smiled (it was more like a grin of pain) and nodded, but said nothing.

When the front door closed, he went into the parlour. Mrs Yule was reading, or, at all events, turning over a volume of an illustrated magazine.

'Where do you suppose she has gone?' he asked, in a voice which was only distant, not offensive.

'To the Miss Milvains, I believe,' Mrs Yule answered, looking aside.

'Did she tell you so?'

'No. We don't talk about it.'

He seated himself on the corner of a chair and bent forward, his chin in his hand.

'Has she said anything to you about the review?'

'Not a word.'

She glanced at him timidly, and turned a few pages of her book.

'I wanted her to come to Quarmby's, because there'll be a man there who is anxious that Jedwood should start a magazine, and it would be useful for her to hear practical opinions. There'd be no harm if you just spoke to her about it now and then. Of course if she has made up her mind to refuse me it's no use troubling myself any more. I should think you might find out what's really going on.'

Only dire stress of circumstances could have brought Alfred Yule to make distinct appeal for his wife's help. There was no underhand plotting between them to influence their daughter; Mrs Yule had as much desire for the happiness of her husband as for that of Marian, but she felt powerless to effect anything on either side.

'If she ever says anything, I'll let you know.'

'But it seems to me that you have a right to question her.'

'I can't do that, Alfred.'

'Unfortunately, there are a good many things you can't do.'

With that remark, familiar to his wife in substance, though the tone of it was less caustic than usual, he rose and sauntered from the room. He spent a gloomy hour in the study, then went off to join the literary circle at Mr Quarmby's.

Chapter 24

JASPER'S MAGNANIMITY

OCCASIONALLY Milvain met his sisters as they came out of church on Sunday morning, and walked home to have dinner with them. He did so to-day, though the sky was cheerless and a strong north-west wind made it anything but agreeable to wait about in open spaces.

'Are you going to Mrs Wright's this afternoon?' he asked, as they went on together.

'I thought of going,' replied Maud. 'Marian will be with Dora.'

'You ought both to go. You mustn't neglect that woman.'

He said nothing more just then, but when presently he was alone with Dora in the sitting-room for a few minutes, he turned with a peculiar smile and remarked quietly :

'I think you had better go with Maud this afternoon.'

'But I can't. I expect Marian at three.'

'That's just why I want you to go.'

She looked her surprise.

'I want to have a talk with Marian. We'll manage it in this way. At a quarter to three you two shall start, and as you go out you can tell the landlady that if Miss Yule comes she is to wait for you, as you won't be long. She'll come upstairs, and I shall be there. You see?'

Dora turned half away, disturbed a little, but not displeased.

'And what about Miss Rupert?' she asked.

'Oh, Miss Rupert may go to Jericho for all I care. I'm in a magnanimous mood.'

'Very, I've no doubt.'

'Well, you'll do this? One of the results of poverty, you see; one can't even have a private conversation with a friend without plotting to get the use of a room. But there shall be an end of this state of things.'

He nodded significantly. Thereupon Dora left the room to speak with her sister.

The device was put into execution, and Jasper saw his sisters depart knowing that they were not likely to return for some three hours. He seated himself comfortably by the fire and mused. Five minutes had hardly gone by when he looked at his watch, thinking Marian must be unpunctual. He was nervous, though he had believed himself secure against such weakness. His presence here with the purpose he had in his mind seemed to him distinctly a concession to impulses he ought to have controlled; but to this resolve he had come, and it was now too late to re-commence the arguments with himself. Too late? Well, not strictly so; he had committed himself to nothing; up to the last moment of freedom he could always –

That was doubtless Marian's knock at the front door. He jumped up, walked the length of the room, sat down on an-other chair, returned to his former seat. Then the door opened and Marian came in.

She was not surprised; the landlady had mentioned to her that Mr Milvain was upstairs, waiting the return of his sisters.

'I am to make Dora's excuses,' Jasper said. 'She begged you would forgive her – that you would wait.'

'Oh yes.'

'And you were to be sure to take off your hat,' he added in a laughing tone; 'and to let me put your umbrella in the corner – like that.'

He had always admired the shape of Marian's head, and the beauty of her short, soft, curly hair. As he watched her uncovering it, he was pleased with the grace of her arms and the pliancy of her slight figure.

'Which is usually your chair?'

'I'm sure I don't know.'

'When one goes to see a friend frequently, one gets into regular habits in these matters. In Biffen's garret I used to have the most uncomfortable chair it was ever my lot to sit upon; still, I came to feel an affection for it. At Reardon's I always had what was supposed to be the most luxurious seat, but it was too small for me, and I eyed it resentfully on sitting down and rising.'

'Have you any news about the Reardons?'

'Yes. I am told that Reardon has had the offer of a secretaryship to a boys' home, or something of the kind, at Croydon. But I suppose there'll be no need for him to think of that now.'

'Surely not!'

'Oh, there's no saying.'

'Why should he do work of that kind now?'

'Perhaps his wife will tell him that she wants her money all for herself.'

Marian laughed. It was very rarely that Jasper had heard her laugh at all, and never so spontaneously as this. He liked the music.

'You haven't a very good opinion of Mrs Reardon,' she said.

'She is a difficult person to judge. I never disliked her, by any means; but she was decidedly out of place as the wife of a struggling author. Perhaps I have been a little prejudiced against her since Reardon quarrelled with me on her account.'

Marian was astonished at this unlooked-for explanation of the rupture between Milvain and his friend. That they had not seen each other for some months she knew from Jasper himself, but no definite cause had been assigned.

'I may as well let you know all about it,' Milvain continued, seeing that he had disconcerted the girl, as he meant to. 'I met Reardon not long after they had parted, and he charged me with being in great part the cause of his troubles.'

The listener did not raise her eyes.

'You would never imagine what my fault was. Reardon declared that the tone of my conversation had been morally injurious to his wife. He said I was always glorifying worldly success, and that this had made her discontented with her lot. Sounds rather ludicrous, don't you think?'

'It was very strange.'

'Reardon was in desperate earnest, poor fellow. And, to tell you the truth, I fear there may have been something in his complaint. I told him at once that I should henceforth keep away from Mrs Edmund Yule's; and so I have done, with the result, of course, that they suppose I condemn Mrs Reardon's behaviour. The affair was a nuisance, but I had no choice, I think.'

'You say that perhaps your talk really was harmful to her?'

'It may have been, though such a danger never occurred to me.'

'Then Amy must be very weak-minded.'

'To be influenced by such a paltry fellow.'

'To be influenced by anyone in such a way.'

'You think the worse of me for this story?' Jasper asked.

'I don't quite understand it. How did you talk to her?'

'As I talk to everyone. You have heard me say the same things many a time. I simply declare my opinion that the end of literary work – unless one is a man of genius – is to secure comfort and repute. This doesn't seem to me very scandalous. But Mrs Reardon was perhaps too urgent in repeating such views to her husband. She saw that in my case they were likely to have solid results, and it was a misery to her that Reardon couldn't or wouldn't work in the same practical way.'

'It was very unfortunate.'

'And you are inclined to blame me?'

'No; because I am so sure that you only spoke in the way natural to you, without a thought of such consequences.'

Jasper smiled.

'That's precisely the truth. Nearly all men who have their way to make think as I do, but most feel obliged to adopt a false tone, to talk about literary conscientiousness, and so on. I simply say what I think, with no pretences. I should like to be conscientious, but it's a luxury I can't afford. I've told you all this often enough, you know.'

'Yes.'

'But it hasn't been morally injurious to you,' he said with a laugh.

'Not at all. Still I don't like it.'

Jasper was startled. He gazed at her. Ought he, then, to have dealt with her less frankly? Had he been mistaken in thinking that the unusual openness of his talk was attractive to her? She spoke with quite unaccustomed decision; indeed, he had noticed from her entrance that there was something unfamiliar in her way of conversing. She was so much more self-possessed than of wont, and did not seem to treat him with the same deference, the same subdual of her own personality.

'You don't like it?' he repeated calmly. 'It has become rather tiresome to you?'

'I feel sorry that you should always represent yourself in an unfavourable light.'

He was an acute man, but the self-confidence with which he

had entered upon this dialogue, his conviction that he had but to speak when he wished to receive assurance of Marian's devotion, prevented him from understanding the tone of independence she had suddenly adopted. With more modesty he would have felt more subtly at this juncture, would have divined that the girl had an exquisite pleasure in drawing back now that she saw him approaching her with unmistakable purpose, that she wished to be wooed in less off-hand fashion before confessing what was in her heart. For the moment he was disconcerted. Those last words of hers had a slight tone of superiority, the last thing he would have expected upon her lips.

'Yet I surely haven't always appeared so – to you?' he said.

'No, not always.'

'But you are in doubt concerning the real man?'

'I'm not sure that I understand you. You say that you do really think as you speak.'

'So I do. I think that there is no choice for a man who can't bear poverty. I have never said, though, that I had pleasure in mean necessities; I accept them because I can't help it.'

It was a delight to Marian to observe the anxiety with which he turned to self-defence. Never in her life had she felt this joy of holding a position of command. It was nothing to her that Jasper valued her more because of her money; impossible for it to be otherwise. Satisfied that he did value her, to begin with, for her own sake, she was very willing to accept money as her ally in the winning of his love. He scarcely loved her yet, as she understood the feeling, but she perceived her power over him, and passion taught her how to exert it.

'But you resign yourself very cheerfully to the necessity,' she said, looking at him with merely intellectual eyes.

'You had rather I lamented my fate in not being able to devote myself to nobly unremunerative work?'

There was a note of irony here. It caused her a tremor, but she held her position.

'That you never do so would make one think – but I won't speak unkindly.'

'That I neither care for good work nor am capable of it,' Jasper finished her sentence. 'I shouldn't have thought it would make *you* think so.'

Instead of replying she turned her look towards the door. There was a footstep on the stairs, but it passed.

'I thought it might be Dora,' she said.

'She won't be here for another couple of hours at least,' replied Jasper with a slight smile.

'But you said –?'

'I sent her to Mrs Boston Wright's that I might have an opportunity of talking to you. Will you forgive the stratagem?'

Marian resumed her former attitude, the faintest smile hovering about her lips.

'I'm glad there's plenty of time,' he continued. 'I begin to suspect that you have been misunderstanding me of late. I must set that right.'

'I don't think I have misunderstood you.'

'That may mean something very disagreeable. I know that some people whom I esteem have a very poor opinion of me, but I can't allow you to be one of them. What do I seem to you? What is the result on your mind of all our conversations?'

'I have already told you.'

'Not seriously. Do you believe I am capable of generous feeling?'

'To say no, would be to put you in the lowest class of men, and that a very small one.'

'Good! Then I am not among the basest. But that doesn't give me very distinguished claims upon your consideration. Whatever I am, I aim high in some of my ambitions.'

'Which of them?'

'For instance, I have been daring enough to hope that you might love me.'

Marian delayed for a moment, then said quietly:

'Why do you call that daring?'

'Because I have enough of old-fashioned thought to believe that a woman who is worthy of a man's love is higher than he, and condescends in giving herself to him.'

His voice was not convincing; the phrase did not sound natural on his lips. It was not thus that she had hoped to hear him speak. Whilst he expressed himself thus conventionally he did not love her as she desired to be loved.

'I don't hold that view,' she said.

'It doesn't surprise me. You are very reserved on all subjects, and we have never spoken of this, but of course I know that your thought is never commonplace. Hold what view you like of woman's position, that doesn't affect mine.'

'Is yours commonplace, then?'

'Desperately. Love is a very old and common thing, and I believe I love you in the old and common way. I think you beautiful, you seem to me womanly in the best sense, full of charm and sweetness. I know myself a coarse being in comparison. All this has been felt and said in the same way by men infinite in variety. Must I find some new expression before you can believe me?'

Marian kept silence.

'I know what you are thinking,' he said. 'The thought is as inevitable as my consciousness of it.'

For an instant she looked at him.

'Yes, you look the thought. Why have I not spoken to you in this way before? Why have I waited until you are obliged to suspect my sincerity?'

'My thought is not so easily read, then,' said Marian.

'To be sure it hasn't a gross form, but I know you wish – whatever your real feelings towards me – that I had spoken a fortnight ago. You would wish that of any man in my position, merely because it is painful to you to see a possible insincerity. Well, I am not insincere. I have thought of you as of no other woman for some time. But – yes, you shall have the plain, coarse truth, which is good in its way, no doubt. I was afraid to say that I loved you. You don't flinch; so far, so good. Now what harm is there in this confession? In the common course of things I shouldn't be in a position to marry for perhaps three or four years, and even then marriage would mean difficulties, restraints, obstacles. I have always dreaded the thought of marriage with a poor income. You remember?

> Love in a hut, with water and a crust,
> Is – Love forgive us! – cinders, ashes, dust.[28]

You know that is true.'

'Not always, I dare say.'

'But for the vast majority of mortals. There's the instance of the Reardons. They were in love with each other, if ever two people were; but poverty ruined everything. I am not in the confidence of either of them, but I feel sure each has wished the other dead. What else was to be expected? Should I have dared to take a wife in my present circumstances – a wife as poor as myself?'

'You will be in a much better position before long,' said Marian. 'If you loved me, why should you have been afraid to ask me to have confidence in your future?'

'It's all so uncertain. It may be another ten years before I can count on an income of five or six hundred pounds – if I have to struggle on in the common way.'

'But tell me, what is your aim in life? What do you understand by success?'

'Yes, I will tell you. My aim is to have easy command of all the pleasures desired by a cultivated man. I want to live among beautiful things, and never to be troubled by a thought of vulgar difficulties. I want to travel and enrich my mind in foreign countries. I want to associate on equal terms with refined and interesting people. I want to be known, to be familiarly referred to, to feel when I enter a room that people regard me with some curiosity.'

He looked steadily at her with bright eyes.

'And that's all?' asked Marian.

'That is very much. Perhaps you don't know how I suffer in feeling myself at a disadvantage. My instincts are strongly social, yet I can't be at my ease in society, simply because I can't do justice to myself. Want of money makes me the inferior of the people I talk with, though I might be superior to them in most things. I am ignorant in many ways, and merely because I am poor. Imagine my never having been out of England! It shames me when people talk familiarly of the Continent. So with regard to all manner of amusements and pursuits at home. Impossible for me to appear among my acquaintances at the theatre, at concerts. I am perpetually at a disadvantage; I haven't fair play. Suppose me possessed of money enough to live a full and active life for the next five years; why, at the end of that time my position would be secure. To him that hath shall be given – you know how universally true that is.'

'And yet,' came in a low voice from Marian, 'you say that you love me.'

'You mean that I speak as if no such thing as love existed. But you asked me what I understood by success. I am speaking of worldly things. Now suppose I had said to you: My one aim and desire in life is to win your love. Could you have believed me? Such phrases are always untrue; I don't know how it can give anyone pleasure to hear them. But if I say to you: All the satisfactions I have described would be immensely heightened if they were shared with a woman who loved me – there is the simple truth.'

Marian's heart sank. She did not want truth such as this; she would have preferred that he should utter the poor, common falsehoods. Hungry for passionate love, she heard with a sense of desolation all this calm reasoning. That Jasper was of cold temperament she had often feared; yet there was always the consoling thought that she did not see with perfect clearness into his nature. Now and then had come a flash, a hint of possibilities. She had looked forward with trembling eagerness to some sudden revelation; but it seemed as if he knew no word of the language which would have called such joyous response from her expectant soul.

'We have talked for a long time,' she said, turning her head as if his last words were of no significance. 'As Dora is not coming, I think I will go now.'

She rose, and went towards the chair on which lay her out-of-door things. At once Jasper stepped to her side.

'You will go without giving me any answer?'

'Answer? To what?'

'Will you be my wife?'

'It is too soon to ask me that.'

'Too soon? Haven't you known for months that I thought of you with far more than friendliness?'

'How was it possible I should know that? You have explained to me why you would not let your real feelings be understood.'

The reproach was merited, and not easy to be outfaced. He turned away for an instant, then with a sudden movement caught both her hands.

'Whatever I have done or said or thought in the past, that is of no account now. I love you, Marian. I want you to be my wife. I have never seen any other girl who impressed me as you did from the first. If I had been weak enough to try to win anyone but you, I should have known that I had turned aside from the path of my true happiness. Let us forget for a moment all our circumstances. I hold your hands, and look into your face, and say that I love you. Whatever answer you give, I love you!'

Till now her heart had only fluttered a little; it was a great part of her distress that the love she had so long nurtured seemed shrinking together into some far corner of her being whilst she listened to the discourses which prefaced Jasper's declaration. She was nervous, painfully self-conscious, touched with maidenly shame, but could not abandon herself to that delicious emotion which ought to have been the fulfilment of all her secret imaginings. Now at length there began a throbbing in her bosom. Keeping her face averted, her eyes cast down, she waited for a repetition of the note that was in that last 'I love you.' She felt a change in the hands that held hers – a warmth, a moist softness; it caused a shock through her veins.

He was trying to draw her nearer, but she kept at full arm's length and looked irresponsive.

'Marian?'

She wished to answer, but a spirit of perversity held her tongue.

'Marian, don't you love me? Or have I offended you by my way of speaking?'

Persisting, she at length withdrew her hands. Jasper's face expressed something like dismay.

'You have not offended me,' she said. 'But I am not sure that you don't deceive yourself in thinking, for the moment, that I am necessary to your happiness.'

The emotional current which had passed from her flesh to his whilst their hands were linked made him incapable of standing aloof from her. He saw that her face and neck were warmer hued, and her beauty became more desirable to him than ever yet.

'You are more to me than anything else in the compass of life!' he exclaimed, again pressing forward. 'I think of nothing but you – you yourself – my beautiful, gentle, thoughtful Marian!'

His arm captured her, and she did not resist. A sob, then a

strange little laugh, betrayed the passion that was at length unfolded in her.

'You do love me, Marian?'

'I love you.'

And there followed the antiphony of ardour that finds its first
utterance – a subdued music, often interrupted, ever returning
upon the same rich note.

Marian closed her eyes and abandoned herself to the luxury of
the dream. It was her first complete escape from the world of intellectual routine, her first taste of life. All the pedantry of her
daily toil slipped away like a cumbrous garment; she was clad
only in her womanhood. Once or twice a shudder of strange
self-consciousness went through her, and she felt guilty, im-
modest; but upon that sensation followed a surge of passionate
joy, obliterating memory and forethought.

'How shall I see you?' Jasper asked at length. 'Where can we
meet?'

It was a difficulty. The season no longer allowed lingerings
under the open sky, but Marian could not go to his lodgings, and
it seemed impossible for him to visit her at her home.

'Will your father persist in unfriendliness to me?'

She was only just beginning to reflect on all that was involved
in this new relation.

'I have no hope that he will change,' she said sadly.

'He will refuse to countenance your marriage?'

'I shall disappoint him and grieve him bitterly. He has asked
me to use my money in starting a new review.'

'Which he is to edit?'

'Yes. Do you think there would be any hope of its success?'

Jasper shook his head.

'Your father is not the man for that, Marian. I don't say it
disrespectfully; I mean that he doesn't seem to me to have that
kind of aptitude. It would be a disastrous speculation.'

'I felt that. Of course I can't think of it now.'

She smiled, raising her face to his.

'Don't trouble,' said Jasper. 'Wait a little, till I have made
myself independent of Fadge and a few other men, and your
father shall see how heartily I wish to be of use to him. He will
miss your help, I'm afraid?'

'Yes. I shall feel it a cruelty when I have to leave him. He has only just told me that his sight is beginning to fail. Oh, why didn't his brother leave him a little money? It was such unkindness! Surely he had a much better right than Amy, or than myself either. But literature has been a curse to father all his life. My uncle hated it, and I suppose that was why he left father nothing.'

'But how am I to see you often? That's the first question. I know what I shall do. I must take new lodgings, for the girls and myself, all in the same house. We must have two sitting-rooms; then you will come to my room without any difficulty. These astonishing proprieties are so easily satisfied after all.'

'You will really do that?'

'Yes. I shall go and look for rooms to-morrow. Then when you come you can always ask for Maud or Dora, you know. They will be very glad of a change to more respectable quarters.'

'I won't stay to see them now, Jasper,' said Marian, her thoughts turning to the girls.

'Very well. You are safe for another hour, but to make certain you shall go at a quarter to five. Your mother won't be against us?'

'Poor mother – no. But she won't dare to justify me before father.'

'I feel as if I should play a mean part in leaving it to you to tell your father. Marian, I will brave it out and go and see him.'

'Oh, it would be better not to.'

'Then I will write to him – such a letter as he can't possibly take in ill part.'

Marian pondered this proposal.

'You shall do that, Jasper, if you are willing. But not yet; presently.'

'You don't wish him to know at once?'

'We had better wait a little. You know,' she added laughing, 'that my legacy is only in name mine as yet. The will hasn't been proved. And then the money will have to be realised.'

She informed him of the details; Jasper listened with his eyes on the ground.

They were now sitting on chairs drawn close to each other. It was with a sense of relief that Jasper had passed from dithyrambs to conversation on practical points; Marian's excited sensitiveness could not but observe this, and she kept watching the motions of his countenance. At length he even let go her hand.

'You would prefer,' he said reflectively, 'that nothing should be said to your father until that business is finished?'

'If you consent to it.'

'Oh, I have no doubt it's as well.'

Her little phrase of self-subjection, and its tremulous tone, called for another answer than this. Jasper fell again into thought, and clearly it was thought of practical things.

'I think I must go now, Jasper,' she said.

'Must you? Well, if you had rather.'

He rose, though she was still seated. Marian moved a few steps away, but turned and approached him again.

'Do you really love me?' she asked, taking one of his hands and folding it between her own.

'I do indeed love you, Marian. Are you still doubtful?'

'You're not sorry that I must go?'

'But I am, dearest. I wish we could sit here undisturbed all through the evening.'

Her touch had the same effect as before. His blood warmed again, and he pressed her to his side, stroking her hair and kissing her forehead.

'Are you sorry I wear my hair short?' she asked, longing for more praise than he had bestowed on her.

'Sorry? It is perfect. Everything else seems vulgar compared with this way of yours. How strange you would look with plaits and that kind of thing!'

'I am so glad it pleases you.'

'There is nothing in you that doesn't please me, my thoughtful girl.'

'You called me that before. Do I seem so very thoughtful?'

'So grave, and sweetly reserved, and with eyes so full of meaning.'

She quivered with delight, her face hidden against his breast.

'I seem to be new-born, Jasper. Everything in the world is new to me, and I am strange to myself. I have never known an hour of happiness till now, and I can't believe yet that it has come to me.'

She at length attired herself, and they left the house together, of course not unobserved by the landlady. Jasper walked about half the way to St Paul's Crescent. It was arranged that he should address a letter for her to the care of his sisters; but in a day or two the change of lodgings would be effected.

When they had parted, Marian looked back. But Jasper was walking quickly away, his head bent, in profound meditation.

END OF THE SECOND VOLUME

NEW GRUB STREET

Volume 3

Chapter 25

A FRUITLESS MEETING

R E F U G E from despair is often found in the passion of self-pity
and that spirit of obstinate resistance which it engenders. In
certain natures the extreme of self-pity is intolerable, and leads
to self-destruction; but there are less fortunate beings whom the
vehemence of their revolt against fate strengthens to endure in
suffering. These latter are rather imaginative than passionate;
the stages of their woe impress them as the acts of a drama, which
they cannot bring themselves to cut short, so various are the
possibilities of its dark motive. The intellectual man who kills
himself is most often brought to that decision by conviction of
his insignificance; self-pity merges in self-scorn, and the humili-
ated soul is intolerant of existence. He who survives under like
conditions does so because misery magnifies him in his own
estimate.

It was by force of commiserating his own lot that Edwin
Reardon continued to live through the first month after his
parting from Amy. Once or twice a week, sometimes early in the
evening, sometimes at midnight or later, he haunted the street at
Westbourne Park where his wife was dwelling, and on each occasion he returned to his garret with a fortified sense of the injustice
to which he was submitted, of revolt against the circumstances
which had driven him into outer darkness, of bitterness against
his wife for saving her own comfort rather than share his down-
fall. At times he was not far from that state of sheer distraction
which Mrs Edmund Yule preferred to suppose that he had
reached. An extraordinary arrogance now and then possessed
him; he stood amid his poor surroundings with the sensations of
an outraged exile, and laughed aloud in furious contempt of all
who censured or pitied him.

On hearing from Jasper Milvain that Amy had fallen ill, or at
all events was suffering in health from what she had gone
through, he felt a momentary pang which all but determined him
to hasten to her side. The reaction was a feeling of distinct
pleasure that she had her share of pain, and even a hope that her

illness might become grave; he pictured himself summoned to
her sick-chamber, imagined her begging his forgiveness. But it
was not merely, nor in great part, a malicious satisfaction; he
succeeded in believing that Amy suffered because she still had a
remnant of love for him. As the days went by and he heard
nothing, disappointment and resentment occupied him. At
length he ceased to haunt the neighbourhood. His desires grew
sullen; he became fixed in the resolve to hold entirely apart and
doggedly await the issue.

At the end of each month he sent half the money he had
received from Carter, simply enclosing postal orders in an envelope addressed to his wife. The first two remittances were in no
way acknowledged; the third brought a short note from Amy:

'As you continue to send these sums of money, I had perhaps better let you know that I cannot use them for any purposes
of my own. Perhaps a sense of duty leads you to make this sacrifice, but I am afraid it is more likely that you wish to remind me
every month that you are undergoing privations, and to pain me
in this way. What you have sent I have deposited in the Post
Office Savings' Bank in Willie's name, and I shall continue to do
so. – A. R.'

For a day or two Reardon persevered in an intention of not
replying, but the desire to utter his turbid feelings became in the
end too strong. He wrote:

'I regard it as quite natural that you should put the worst
interpretation on whatever I do. As for my privations, I think
very little of them; they are a trifle in comparison with the
thought that I am forsaken just because my pocket is empty. And
I am far indeed from thinking that you can be pained by whatever I may undergo; that would suppose some generosity in your
nature.'

This was no sooner posted than he would gladly have recalled
it. He knew that it was undignified, that it contained as many
falsehoods as lines, and he was ashamed of himself for having
written so. But he could not pen a letter of retraction, and there
remained with him a new cause of exasperated wretchedness.

Excepting the people with whom he came in contact at the hospital, he had no society but that of Biffen. The realist visited him once a week, and this friendship grew closer than it had been in the time of Reardon's prosperity. Biffen was a man of so much natural delicacy, that there was a pleasure in imparting to him the details of private sorrow; though profoundly sympathetic, he did his best to oppose Reardon's harsher judgments of Amy, and herein he gave his friend a satisfaction which might not be avowed.

'I really do not see,' he exclaimed, as they sat in the garret one night of midsummer, 'how your wife would have *acted* otherwise. Of course I am quite unable to judge the attitude of her mind, but I think, I can't help thinking, from what I knew of her, that there has been strictly a misunderstanding between you. It was a hard and miserable thing that she should have to leave you for a time, and you couldn't face the necessity in a just spirit. Don't you think there's some truth in this way of looking at it?'

'As a woman, it was her part to soften the hateful necessity; she made it worse.'

'I'm not sure that you don't demand too much of her. Unhappily, I know little or nothing of delicately-bred women, but I have a suspicion that one oughtn't to expect heroism in them, any more than in the women of the lower classes. I think of women as creatures to be protected. Is a man justified in asking them to be stronger than himself?'

'Of course,' replied Reardon, 'there's no use in demanding more than a character is capable of. But I believed her of finer stuff. My bitterness comes of the disappointment.'

'I suppose there were faults of temper on both sides, and you saw at least only each other's weaknesses.'

'I saw the truth, which had always been disguised from me.'

Biffen persisted in looking doubtful, and in secret Reardon thanked him for it.

As the realist progressed with his novel, 'Mr Bailey, Grocer,' he read the chapters to Reardon, not only for his own satisfaction, but in great part because he hoped that this example of productivity might in the end encourage the listener to resume his own literary tasks. Reardon found much to criticise in his friend's work; it was noteworthy that he objected and condemned with much less hesitation than in his better days, for sensitive reticence is one of the virtues wont to be assailed by suffering, at all events in the weaker natures. Biffen purposely urged these discussions as far as possible, and doubtless they benefited Reardon for the time; but the defeated novelist could not be induced to undertake another practical illustration of his own views. Occasionally he had an impulse to plan a story, but an hour's turning it over in his mind sufficed to disgust him. His ideas seemed barren, vapid; it would have been impossible for him to write half a dozen pages, and the mere thought of a whole book overcame him with the dread of insurmountable difficulties, immeasurable toil.

In time, however, he was able to read. He had pleasure in contemplating the little collection of sterling books that alone remained to him from his library; the sight of many volumes would have been a weariness, but these few – when he was again able to think of books at all – were as friendly countenances. He could not read continuously, but sometimes he opened his Shakespeare, for instance, and dreamed over a page or two. From such glimpses there remained in his head a line or a short passage, which he kept repeating to himself wherever he went; generally some example of sweet or sonorous metre which had a soothing effect upon him.

With odd result on one occasion. He was walking in one of the back streets of Islington, and stopped idly to gaze into the window of some small shop. Standing thus, he forgot himself, and presently recited aloud:

> 'Cæsar, 'tis his schoolmaster:
> An argument that he is pluck'd, when hither
> He sends so poor a pinion of his wing,
> Which had superfluous kings for messengers
> Not many moons gone by.' [29]

The last two lines he uttered a second time, enjoying their magnificent sound, and then was brought back to consciousness by the loud mocking laugh of two men standing close by, who evidently looked upon him as a strayed lunatic.

He kept one suit of clothes for his hours of attendance at the hospital ; it was still decent, and with much care would remain so for a long time. That which he wore at home and in his street wanderings declared poverty at every point; it had been discarded before he left the old abode. In his present state of mind he cared nothing how disreputable he looked to passers-by. These seedy habiliments were the token of his degradation, and at times he regarded them (happening to see himself in a shop mirror) with pleasurable contempt. The same spirit often led him for a meal to the poorest of eating-houses, places where he rubbed elbows with ragged creatures who had somehow obtained the price of a cup of coffee and a slice of bread and butter. He liked to contrast himself with these comrades in misfortune. 'This is the rate at which the world esteems me; I am worth no better provision than this.' Or else, instead of emphasising the contrast, he defiantly took a place among the miserables of the nether world, and nursed hatred of all who were well-to-do.

One of these he desired to regard with gratitude, but found it difficult to support that feeling. Carter, the vivacious, though at first perfectly unembarrassed in his relations with the City Road clerk, gradually exhibited a change of demeanour. Reardon occasionally found the young man's eyes fixed upon him with a singular expression, and the secretary's talk, though still as a rule genial, was wont to suffer curious interruptions, during which he seemed to be musing on something Reardon had said, or on some point of his behaviour. The explanation of this was that Carter had begun to think there might be a foundation for Mrs Yule's hypothesis – that the novelist was not altogether in his sound senses. At first he scouted the idea, but as time went on it seemed to him that Reardon's countenance certainly had a gaunt wildness which suggested disagreeable things. Especially did he remark this after his return from an August holiday in Norway. On coming for the first time to the City Road branch he sat down and began to favour Reardon with a lively description of how he had enjoyed himself abroad; it never occurred to him that such talk was not likely to enspirit the man who had passed his August between the garret and the hospital, but he observed before long that his listener was glancing hither and thither in rather a strange way.

'You haven't been ill since I saw you?' he inquired.

'Oh no!'

'But you look as if you might have been. I say, we must manage for you to have a fortnight off, you know, this month.'

'I have no wish for it,' said Reardon. 'I'll imagine I have been to Norway. It has done me good to hear of your holiday.'

'I'm glad of that! but it isn't quite the same thing, you know, as having a run somewhere yourself.'

'Oh, much better! To enjoy myself may be mere selfishness, but to enjoy another's enjoyment is the purest satisfaction, good for body and soul. I am cultivating altruism.'

'What's that?'

'A highly rarefied form of happiness. The curious thing about it is that it won't grow unless you have just twice as much faith in it as is required for assent to the Athanasian Creed.'

'Oh!'

Carter went away more than puzzled. He told his wife that evening that Reardon had been talking to him in the most extra-ordinary fashion, no understanding a word he said.

All this time he was on the look-out for employment that would be more suitable to his unfortunate clerk. Whether slightly demented or not, Reardon gave no sign of inability to discharge his duties; he was conscientious as ever, and might, unless he changed greatly, be relied upon in positions of more responsibility than his present one. And at length, early in October, there came to the secretary's knowledge an opportunity with which he lost no time in acquainting Reardon. The latter repaired that evening to Clipstone Street, and climbed to Biffen's chamber. He entered with a cheerful look, and exclaimed:

'I have just invented a riddle; see if you can guess it. Why is a London lodging-house like the human body?'

Biffen looked with some concern at his friend, so unwonted was a sally of this kind.

'Why is a London lodging-house –? Haven't the least idea.'

'Because the brains are always at the top. Not bad, I think, eh?'

'Well, no; it'll pass. Distinctly professional though. The general public would fail to see the point, I'm afraid. But what has come to you?'

'Good tidings. Carter has offered me a place which will be a

decided improvement. A house found – or rooms, at all events –
and salary a hundred and fifty a year.'

'By Plutus! That's good hearing. Some duties attached, I
suppose?'

'I'm afraid that was inevitable, as things go. It's the secretaryship of a home for destitute boys at Croydon. The post is far
from a sinecure, Carter assures me. There's a great deal of purely
secretarial work, and there's a great deal of practical work, some of
it rather rough, I fancy. It seems doubtful whether I am exactly
the man. The present holder is a burly fellow over six feet high,
delighting in gymnastics, and rather fond of a fight now and then
when opportunity offers. But he is departing at Christmas –
going somewhere as a missionary; and I can have the place if I
choose.'

'As I suppose you do?'

'Yes. I shall try it, decidedly.'

Biffen waited a little, then asked:

'I suppose your wife will go with you?'

'There's no saying.'

Reardon tried to answer indifferently, but it could be seen that
he was agitated between hopes and fears.

'You'll ask her, at all events?'

'Oh yes,' was the half-absent reply.

'But surely there can be no doubt that she'll come. A hundred
and fifty a year, without rent to pay. Why, that's affluence!'

'The rooms I might occupy are in the home itself. Amy won't
take very readily to a dwelling of that kind. And Croydon isn't
the most inviting locality.'

'Close to delightful country.'

'Yes, yes; but Amy doesn't care about that.'

'You misjudge her, Reardon. You are too harsh. I implore
you not to lose the chance of setting all right again! If only you
could be put into my position for a moment, and then be offered
the companionship of such a wife as yours!'

Reardon listened with a face of lowering excitement.

'I should be perfectly within my rights,' he said sternly, 'if I
merely told her when I have taken the position, and let her ask
me to take her back – if she wishes.'

'You have changed a great deal this last year,' replied Biffen, shaking his head, 'a great deal. I hope to see you your old self again before long. I should have declared it impossible for you to become so rugged. Go and see your wife, there's a good fellow.'

'No; I shall write to her.'

'Go and see her, I beg you! No good ever came of letter-writing between two people who have misunderstood each other. Go to Westbourne Park to-morrow. And be reasonable; be more than reasonable. The happiness of your life depends on what you do now. Be content to forget whatever wrong has been done you. To think that a man should need persuading to win back such a wife!'

In truth, there needed little persuasion. Perverseness, one of the forms or issues of self-pity, made him strive against his desire, and caused him to adopt a tone of acerbity in excess of what he felt; but already he had made up his mind to see Amy. Even if this excuse had not presented itself, he must very soon have yielded to the longing for a sight of his wife's face which day by day increased among all the conflicting passions of which he was the victim. A month or two ago, when the summer sunshine made his confinement to the streets a daily torture, he convinced himself that there remained in him no trace of his love for Amy; there were moments when he thought of her with repugnance, as a cold, selfish woman, who had feigned affection when it seemed her interest to do so, but brutally declared her true self when there was no longer anything to be hoped from him. That was the self-deception of misery. Love, even passion, was still alive in the depths of his being; the animation with which he sped to his friend as soon as a new hope had risen was the best proof of his feeling.

He went home and wrote to Amy.

'I have a reason for wishing to see you. Will you have the kindness to appoint an hour on Sunday morning when I can speak with you in private? It must be understood that I shall see no one else.'

She would receive this by the first post to-morrow, Saturday, and doubtless would let him hear in reply some time in the afternoon. Impatience allowed him little sleep, and the next day was a long weariness of waiting. The evening he would have to spend at the hospital; if there came no reply before the time of his leaving home, he knew not how he should compel himself to the ordinary routine of work. Yet the hour came, and he had heard nothing. He was tempted to go at once to Westbourne Park, but reason prevailed with him. When he again entered the house, having walked at his utmost speed from the City Road, the letter lay waiting for him; it had been pushed beneath his door, and when he struck a match he found that one of his feet was upon the white envelope.

Amy wrote that she would be at home at eleven to-morrow morning. Not another word.

In all probability she knew of the offer that had been made to him; Mrs Carter would have told her. Was it of good or of ill omen that she wrote only these half-dozen words? Half through the night he plagued himself with suppositions, now thinking that her brevity promised a welcome, now that she wished to warn him against expecting anything but a cold, offended de- meanour. At seven he was dressed; two hours and a half had to be killed before he could start on his walk westward. He would have wandered about the streets, but it rained.

He had made himself as decent as possible in appearance, but he must necessarily seem an odd Sunday visitor at a house such as Mrs Yule's. His soft felt hat, never brushed for months, was a greyish green, and stained round the band with perspir- ation. His necktie was discoloured and worn. Coat and waistcoat might pass muster, but of the trousers the less said the better. One of his boots was patched, and both were all but heelless.

Very well; let her see him thus. Let her understand what it meant to live on twelve and sixpence a week.

Though it was cold and wet he could not put on his overcoat. Three years ago it had been a fairly good ulster; at present, the edges of the sleeves were frayed, two buttons were missing, and the original hue of the cloth was indeterminable.

At half-past nine he set out and struggled with his shabby umbrella against wind and rain. Down Pentonville Hill, up Euston Road, all along Marylebone Road, then north-westwards towards the point of his destination. It was a good six miles from the one house to the other, but he arrived before the appointed time, and had to stray about until the cessation of bell-clanging and the striking of clocks told him it was eleven. Then he presented himself at the familiar door.

On his asking for Mrs Reardon, he was at once admitted and led up to the drawing-room; the servant did not ask his name.

Then he waited for a minute or two, feeling himself a squalid wretch amid the dainty furniture. The door opened. Amy, in a simple but very becoming dress, approached to within a yard of him; after the first glance she had averted her eyes, and she did not offer to shake hands. He saw that his muddy and shapeless boots drew her attention.

'Do you know why I have come?' he asked.

He meant the tone to be conciliatory, but he could not command his voice, and it sounded rough, hostile.

'I think so,' Amy answered, seating herself gracefully. She would have spoken with less dignity but for that accent of his.

'The Carters have told you?'

'Yes; I have heard about it.'

There was no promise in her manner. She kept her face turned away, and Reardon saw its beautiful profile, hard and cold as though in marble.

'It doesn't interest you at all?'

'I am glad to hear that a better prospect offers for you.'

He did not sit down, and was holding his rusty hat behind his back.

'You speak as if it in no way concerned yourself. Is that what you wish me to understand?'

'Won't it be better if you tell me why you have come here? As you are resolved to find offence in whatever I say, I prefer to keep silence. Please to let me know why you have asked to see me.'

Reardon turned abruptly as if to leave her, but checked himself at a little distance.

Both had come to this meeting prepared for a renewal of amity, but in these first few moments each was so disagreeably impressed by the look and language of the other that a revulsion of feeling undid all the more hopeful effects of their long severance. On entering, Amy had meant to offer her hand, but the unexpected meanness of Reardon's aspect shocked and restrained her. All but every woman would have experienced that shrinking from the livery of poverty. Amy had but to reflect, and she understood that her husband could in no wise help this shabbiness; when he parted from her his wardrobe was already in a long-suffering condition, and how was he to have purchased new garments since then? None the less such attire degraded him in her eyes; it symbolized the melancholy decline which he had suffered intellectually. On Reardon his wife's elegance had the same repellent effect, though this would not have been the case but for the expression of her countenance. Had it been possible for them to remain together during the first five minutes without exchange of words, sympathies might have prevailed on both sides; the first speech uttered would most likely have harmonized with their gentler thoughts. But the mischief was done so speedily.

A man must indeed be graciously endowed if his personal appearance can defy the disadvantage of cheap modern clothing worn into shapelessness. Reardon had no such remarkable physique, and it was not wonderful that his wife felt ashamed of him. Strictly ashamed; he seemed to her a social inferior; the impression was so strong that it resisted all memory of his spiritual qualities. She might have anticipated this state of things, and have armed herself to encounter it, but somehow she had not done so. For more than five months she had been living among people who dressed well; the contrast was too suddenly forced upon her. She was especially susceptible in such matters, and had become none the less so under the demoralizing influence of her misfortunes. True, she soon began to feel ashamed of her shame, but that could not annihilate the natural feeling and its results.

'I don't love him. I can't love him.' Thus she spoke to herself, with immutable decision. She had been doubtful till now, but all doubt was at an end. Had Reardon been practical man enough to procure by hook or by crook a decent suit of clothes for this interview, that ridiculous trifle might have made all the difference in what was to result.

He turned again, and spoke with the harshness of a man who feels that he is despised and is determined to show an equal contempt.

'I came to ask you what you propose to do in case I go to Croydon.'

'I have no proposal to make whatever.'

'That means, then, that you are content to go on living here?'

'If I have no choice, I must make myself content.'

'But you have a choice.'

'None has yet been offered me.'

'Then I offer it now,' said Reardon, speaking less aggressively. 'I shall have a dwelling rent free, and a hundred and fifty pounds a year – perhaps it would be more in keeping with my station if I say that I shall have something less than three pounds a week. You can either accept from me half this money, as up to now, or come and take your place again as my wife. Please to decide what you will do.'

'I will let you know by letter in a few days.'

It seemed impossible to her to say she would return, yet a refusal to do so involved nothing less than separation for the rest of their lives. Postponement of decision was her only resource.

'I must know at once,' said Reardon.

'I can't answer at once.'

'If you don't, I shall understand you to mean that you refuse to come to me. You know the circumstances; there is no reason why you should consult with anyone else. You can answer me immediately if you will.'

'I don't wish to answer you immediately,' Amy replied, paling slightly.

'Then that decides it. When I leave you we are strangers to each other.'

Amy made a rapid study of his countenance. She had never entertained for a moment the supposition that his wits were unsettled, but none the less the constant recurrence of that idea in her mother's talk had subtly influenced her against her husband. It had confirmed her in thinking that his behaviour was inexcusable. And now it seemed to her that anyone might be justified in holding him demented, so reckless was his utterance. It was difficult to know him as the man who had loved her so devotedly, who was incapable of an unkind word or look.

'If that is what you prefer,' she said, 'there must be a formal separation. I can't trust my future to your caprice.'

'You mean it must be put into the hands of a lawyer.'

'Yes, I do.'

'That will be the best, no doubt.'

'Very well; I will speak with my friends about it.'

'Your friends!' he exclaimed bitterly. 'But for those friends of yours this would never have happened. I wish you had been alone in the world and penniless.'

'A kind wish, all things considered.'

'Yes, it is a kind wish. Then your marriage with me would have been binding; you would have known that my lot was yours, and the knowledge would have helped your weakness. I begin to see how much right there is on the side of those people who would keep women in subjection. You have been allowed to act with independence, and the result is that you have ruined my life and debased your own. If I had been strong enough to treat you as a child, and bid you follow me wherever my own fortunes led, it would have been as much better for you as for me. I was weak, and I suffer as all weak people do.'

'You think it was my duty to share such a home as you have at present?'

'You know it was. And if the choice had lain between that and earning your own livelihood you would have thought that even such a poor home might be made tolerable. There were possibilities in you of better things than will ever come out now.'

There followed a silence. Amy sat with her eyes gloomily fixed on the carpet; Reardon looked about the room, but saw nothing. He had thrown his hat into a chair, and his fingers worked nervously together behind his back.

'Will you tell me,' he said at length, 'how your position is regarded by these friends of yours? I don't mean your mother and brother, but the people who come to this house.'

'I have not asked such people for their opinion.'

'Still, I suppose some sort of explanation has been necessary in your intercourse with them. How have you represented your relations with me?'

'I can't see that that concerns you.'

'In a manner it does. Certainly it matters very little to me how I am thought of by people of this kind, but one doesn't like to be reviled without cause. Have you allowed it to be supposed that I have made life with me intolerable for you?'

'No, I have not. You insult me by asking the question, but as you don't seem to understand feelings of that kind I may as well answer you simply.'

'Then have you told them the truth? That I became so poor you couldn't live with me?'

'I have never said that in so many words, but no doubt it is understood. It must be known also that you refused to take the step which might have helped you out of your difficulties.'

'What step?'

She reminded him of his intention to spend half a year in working at the seaside.

'I had utterly forgotten it,' he returned with a mocking laugh. 'That shows how ridiculous such a thing would have been.'

'You are doing no literary work at all?' Amy asked.

'Do you imagine that I have the peace of mind necessary for anything of that sort?'

This was in a changed voice. It reminded her so strongly of her husband before his disasters that she could not frame a reply.

'Do you think I am able to occupy myself with the affairs of imaginary people?'

'I didn't necessarily mean fiction.'

'That I can forget myself, then, in the study of literature? – I wonder whether you really think of me like that. How, in Heaven's name, do you suppose I spend my leisure time?'

She made no answer.

'Do you think I take this calamity as light-heartedly as you do, Amy?'

'I am far from taking it light-heartedly.'

'Yet you are in good health. I see no sign that you have suffered.'

She kept silence. Her suffering had been slight enough, and chiefly due to considerations of social propriety; but she would not avow this, and did not like to make admission of it to herself. Before her friends she frequently affected to conceal a profound sorrow; but so long as her child was left to her she was in no danger of falling a victim to sentimental troubles.

'And certainly I can't believe it,' he continued, 'now you declare your wish to be formally separated from me.'

'I have declared no such wish.'

'Indeed you have. If you can hesitate a moment about returning to me when difficulties are at an end, that tells me you would prefer final separation.'

'I hesitate for this reason,' Amy said after reflecting. 'You are so greatly changed from what you used to be, that I think it doubtful if I could live with you.'

'Changed? – Yes, that is true I am afraid. But how do you think this change will affect my behaviour to you?'

'Remember how you have been speaking to me.'

'And you think I should treat you brutally if you came into my power?'

'Not brutally, in the ordinary sense of the word. But with faults of temper which I couldn't bear. I have my own faults. I can't behave as meekly as some women can.'

It was a small concession, but Reardon made much of it.

'Did my faults of temper give you any trouble during the first year of our married life?' he asked gently.

'No,' she admitted.

'They began to afflict you when I was so hard driven by difficulties that I needed all your sympathy, all your forbearance. Did I receive much of either from you, Amy?'

'I think you did – until you demanded impossible things of me.'

'It was always in your power to rule me. What pained me worst, and hardened me against you, was that I saw you didn't care to exert your influence. There was never a time when I could have resisted a word of yours spoken out of your love for me. But even then, I am afraid, you no longer loved me, and now –'

He broke off, and stood watching her face.

'Have you *any* love for me left?' burst from his lips, as if the words all but choked him in the utterance.

Amy tried to shape some evasive answer, but could say nothing.

'Is there ever so small a hope that I might win some love from you again?'

'If you wish me to come and live with you when you go to Croydon I will do so.'

'But that is not answering me, Amy.'

'It's all I can say.'

'Then you mean that you would sacrifice yourself out of –
what? Out of pity for me, let us say.'

'Do you wish to see Willie?' asked Amy, instead of replying.

'No. It is you I have come to see. The child is nothing to me,
compared with you. It is you, who loved me, who became my
wife – you only I care about. Tell me you will try to be as you
used to be. Give me only that hope, Amy; I will ask nothing
except that, now.'

'I can't say anything except that I will come to Croydon if you
wish it.'

'And reproach me always because you have to live in such a
place, away from your friends, without a hope of the social success which was your dearest ambition?'

Her practical denial that she loved him wrung this taunt from
his anguished heart. He repented the words as soon as they were
spoken.

'What is the good?' exclaimed Amy in irritation, rising and
moving away from him. 'How can I pretend that I look forward
to such a life with any hope?'

He stood in mute misery, inwardly cursing himself and his
fate.

'I have said I will come,' she continued, her voice shaken with
nervous tension. 'Ask me or not, as you please, when you are
ready to go there. I can't talk about it.'

'I shall not ask you,' he replied. 'I will have no woman slave
dragging out a weary life with me. Either you are my willing
wife, or you are nothing to me.'

'I am married to you, and that can't be undone. I repeat that I
shan't refuse to obey you. I shall say no more.'

She moved to a distance, and there seated herself, half turned
from him.

'I shall never ask you to come,' said Reardon, breaking a short
silence. 'If our married life is ever to begin again it must be of
your seeking. Come to me of your own will, and I shall never
reject you. But I will die in utter loneliness rather than ask you
again.'

He lingered a few moments, watching her; she did not move.
Then he took his hat, went in silence from the room, and left the
house.

It rained harder than before. As no trains were running at this hour, he walked in the direction where he would be likely to meet with an omnibus. But it was a long time before one passed which was any use to him. When he reached home he was in cheerless plight enough; to make things pleasanter, one of his boots had let in water abundantly.

'The first sore throat of the season, no doubt,' he muttered to himself.

Nor was he disappointed. By Tuesday the cold had firm grip of him. A day or two of influenza or sore throat always made him so weak that with difficulty he supported the least physical exertion; but at present he must go to his work at the hospital. Why stay at home? To what purpose spare himself? It was not as if life had any promise for him. He was a machine for earning so much money a week, and would at least give faithful work for his wages until the day of final breakdown.

But, midway in the week, Carter discovered how ill his clerk was.

'You ought to be in bed, my dear fellow, with gruel and mustard plasters and all the rest of it. Go home and take care of yourself – I insist upon it.'

Before leaving the office, Reardon wrote a few lines to Biffen, whom he had visited on the Monday. 'Come and see me if you can. I am down with a bad cold, and have to keep in for the rest of the week. All the same, I feel far more cheerful. Bring a new chapter of your exhilarating romance.'

Chapter 26

MARRIED WOMAN'S PROPERTY

ON her return from church that Sunday Mrs Edmund Yule was anxious to learn the result of the meeting between Amy and her husband. She hoped fervently that Amy's anomalous position would come to an end now that Reardon had the offer of something better than a mere clerkship. John Yule never ceased to grumble at his sister's permanence in the house, especially since he had learnt that the money sent by Reardon each month was not made use of; why it should not be applied for household expenses passed his understanding.

'It seems to me,' he remarked several times, 'that the fellow only does his bare duty in sending it. What is it to anyone else whether he lives on twelve shillings a week or twelve pence? It is his business to support his wife; if he can't do that, to contribute as much to her support as possible. Amy's scruples are all very fine, if she could afford them; it's very nice to pay for your delicacies of feeling out of other people's pockets.'

'There'll have to be a formal separation,' was the startling announcement with which Amy answered her mother's inquiry as to what had passed.

'A separation? But, my dear –!'

Mrs Yule could not express her disappointment and dismay.

'We couldn't live together; it's no use trying.'

'But at your age, Amy! How can you think of anything so shocking? And then, you know it will be impossible for him to make you a sufficient allowance.'

'I shall have to live as well as I can on the seventy-five pounds a year. If you can't afford to let me stay with you for that, I must go into cheap lodgings in the country, like poor Mrs Butcher did.'

This was wild talking for Amy. The interview had upset her, and for the rest of the day she kept apart in her own room. On the morrow Mrs Yule succeeded in eliciting a clear account of the conversation which had ended so hopelessly.

'I would rather spend the rest of my days in the workhouse

than beg him to take me back,' was Amy's final comment, uttered with the earnestness which her mother understood but too well.

'But you are *willing* to go back, dear?'

'I told him so.'

'Then you must leave this to me. The Carters will let us know how things go on, and when it seems to be time I must see Edwin myself.'

'I can't allow that. Anything you could say on your own account would be useless, and there is nothing to say from me.'

Mrs Yule kept her own counsel. She had a full month before her during which to consider the situation, but it was clear to her that these young people must be brought together again. Her estimate of Reardon's mental condition had undergone a sudden change from the moment when she heard that a respectable post was within his reach; she decided that he was 'strange,' but then all men of literary talent had marked singularities, and doubtless she had been too hasty in interpreting the peculiar features natural to a character such as his.

A few days' later arrived the news of their relative's death at Wattleborough.

This threw Mrs Yule into a commotion. At first she decided to accompany her son and be present at the funeral; after changing her mind twenty times, she determined not to go. John must send or bring back the news as soon as possible. That it would be of a nature sensibly to affect her own position, if not that of her children, she had little doubt; her husband had been the favourite brother of the deceased, and on that account there was no saying how handsome a legacy she might receive. She dreamt of houses in South Kensington, of social ambitions gratified even thus late.

On the morning after the funeral came a postcard announcing John's return by a certain train, but no scrap of news was added.

'Just like that irritating boy! We must go to the station to meet him. You'll come, won't you, Amy?'

Amy readily consented, for she too had hopes, though circumstances blurred them. Mother and daughter were walking about the platform half an hour before the train was due; their agitation would have been manifest to anyone observing them. When

at length the train rolled in and John was discovered, they
pressed eagerly upon him.

'Don't you excite yourself,' he said gruffly to his mother.
'There's no reason whatever.'

Mrs Yule glanced in dismay at Amy. They followed John to a
cab, and took places with him.

'Now don't be provoking, Jack. Just tell us at once.'

'By all means. You haven't a penny.'

'I haven't? You are joking, ridiculous boy!'

'Never felt less disposed to, I assure you.'

After staring out of the window for a minute or two, he at
length informed Amy of the extent to which she profited by her
uncle's decease, then made known what was bequeathed to himself. His temper grew worse every moment, and he replied savagely to each successive question concerning the other items of the
will.

'What have you to grumble about?' asked Amy, whose face was
exultant notwithstanding the drawbacks attaching to her good
fortune. 'If Uncle Alfred receives nothing at all, and mother has
nothing, you ought to think yourself very lucky.'

'It's very easy for you to say that, with your ten thousand.'

'But is it her own?' asked Mrs Yule. 'Is it for her separate
use?'

'Of course it is. She gets the benefit of last year's Married
Woman's Property Act.[30] The will was executed in January this
year, and I dare say the old curmudgeon destroyed a former one.'

'What a splendid Act of Parliament that is!' cried Amy. 'The
only one worth anything that I ever heard of.'

'But my dear –' began her mother, in a tone of protest. However, she reserved her comment for a more fitting time and place,
and merely said: 'I wonder whether he had heard what has been
going on?'

'Do you think he would have altered his will if he had?' asked
Amy with a smile of security.

'Why the deuce he should have left you so much in any case is
more than I can understand,' growled her brother. 'What's the
use to me of a paltry thousand or two? It isn't enough to invest;
isn't enough to do anything with.'

'You may depend upon it your cousin Marian thinks her five

thousand good for something,' said Mrs Yule. 'Who was at the funeral? Don't be so surly, Jack; tell us all about it. I'm sure if anyone has cause to be ill-tempered it's poor me.'

Thus they talked, amid the rattle of the cab-wheels. By when they reached home silence had fallen upon them, and each one was sufficiently occupied with private thoughts.

Mrs Yule's servants had a terrible time of it for the next few days. Too affectionate to turn her ill-temper against John and Amy, she relieved herself by severity to the domestic slaves, as an English matron is of course justified in doing. Her daughter's position caused her even more concern than before; she constantly lamented to herself: 'Oh, why didn't he die before she was married!' – in which case Amy would never have dreamt of wedding a penniless author. Amy declined to discuss the new aspect of things until twenty-four hours after John's return; then she said:

'I shall do nothing whatever until the money is paid to me. And what I shall do then I don't know.'

'You are sure to hear from Edwin,' opined Mrs Yule.

'I think not. He isn't the kind of man to behave in that way.'

'Then I suppose you are bound to take the first step?'

'That I shall never do.'

She said so, but the sudden happiness of finding herself wealthy was not without its softening effect on Amy's feelings. Generous impulses alternated with moods of discontent. The thought of her husband in his squalid lodgings tempted her to forget injuries and disillusions, and to play the part of a generous wife. It would be possible now for them to go abroad and spend a year or two in healthful travel; the result in Reardon's case might be wonderful. He might recover all the energy of his imagination, and resume his literary career from the point he had reached at the time of his marriage.

On the other hand, was it not more likely that he would lapse into a life of scholarly self-indulgence, such as he had often told her was his ideal? In that event, what tedium and regret lay before her! Ten thousand pounds sounded well, but what did it represent in reality? A poor four hundred a year, perhaps; mere decency of obscure existence, unless her husband could glorify it by winning fame. If he did nothing, she would be the wife of a man who had failed in literature. She would not be able to take a place in society. Life would be supported without struggle; nothing more to be hoped.

This view of the future possessed her strongly when, in the second day, she went to communicate her news to Mrs Carter. This amiable lady had now become what she always desired to be, Amy's intimate friend; they saw each other very frequently, and conversed of most things with much frankness. It was between eleven and twelve in the morning when Amy paid her visit, and she found Mrs Carter on the point of going out.

'I was coming to see you,' cried Edith. 'Why haven't you let me know of what has happened?'

'You have heard, I suppose?'

'Albert heard from your brother.'

'I supposed he would. And I haven't felt in the mood for talking about it, even with you.'

They went into Mrs Carter's boudoir, a tiny room full of such pretty things as can be purchased nowadays by anyone who has a few shillings to spare, and tolerable taste either of their own or at second-hand. Had she been left to her instincts, Edith would have surrounded herself with objects representing a much earlier stage of artistic development; but she was quick to imitate what fashion declared becoming. Her husband regarded her as a remarkable authority in all matters of personal or domestic ornamentation.

'And what are you going to do?' she inquired, examining Amy from head to foot, as if she thought that the inheritance of so substantial a sum must have produced visible changes in her friend.

'I am going to do nothing.'

'But surely you're not in low spirits?'

'What have I to rejoice about?'

They talked for a while before Amy brought herself to utter what she was thinking.

'Isn't it a most ridiculous thing that married people who both wish to separate can't do so and be quite free again?'

'I suppose it would lead to all sorts of troubles – don't you think?'

'So people say about every new step in civilisation. What would have been thought twenty years ago of a proposal to make all married women independent of their husbands in money matters? All sorts of absurd dangers were foreseen, no doubt. And it's the same now about divorce. In America people can get divorced if they don't suit each other – at all events in some of the States – and does any harm come of it? Just the opposite I should think.'

Edith mused. Such speculations were daring, but she had grown accustomed to think of Amy as an 'advanced' woman, and liked to imitate her in this respect.

'It does seem reasonable,' she murmured.

'The law ought to encourage such separations, instead of forbidding them,' Amy pursued. 'If a husband and wife find that they have made a mistake, what useless cruelty it is to condemn them to suffer the consequences for the whole of their lives!'

'I suppose it's to make people careful,' said Edith with a laugh.

'If so, we know that it has always failed, and always will fail; so the sooner such a profitless law is altered the better. Isn't there some society for getting that kind of reform? I would subscribe fifty pounds a year to help it. Wouldn't you?'

'Yes, if I had it to spare,' replied the other.

Then they both laughed, but Edith the more naturally.

'Not on my own account, you know,' she added.

'It's because women who are happily married can't and won't understand the position of those who are not that there's so much difficulty in reforming marriage laws.'

'But I understand you, Amy, and I grieve about you. What you are to do I can't think.'

'Oh, it's easy to see what I shall do. Of course I have no choice really. And I *ought* to have a choice; that's the hardship and the wrong of it. Perhaps if I had, I should find a sort of pleasure in sacrificing myself.'

There were some new novels on the table; Amy took up a volume presently, and glanced over a page or two.

'I don't know how you can go on reading that sort of stuff, book after book,' she exclaimed.

'Oh, but people say this last novel of Markland's is one of his best.'

'Best or worst, novels are all the same. Nothing but love, love, love; what silly nonsense it is! Why don't people write about the really important things of life? Some of the French novelists do; several of Balzac's, for instance. I have just been reading his "Cousin Pons," a terrible book, but I enjoyed it ever so much because it was nothing like a love story. What rubbish is printed about love!'

'I get rather tired of it sometimes,' admitted Edith with amusement.

'I should hope you do, indeed. What downright lies are accepted as indisputable! That about love being a woman's whole life; who believes it really? Love is the most insignificant thing in most women's lives. It occupies a few months, possibly a year or two, and even then I doubt if it is often the first consideration.'

Edith held her head aside, and pondered smilingly.

'I'm sure there's a great opportunity for some clever novelist who will never write about love at all.'

'But then it *does* come into life.'

'Yes, for a month or two, as I say. Think of the biographies of men and women; how many pages are devoted to their love affairs? Compare those books with novels which profess to be biographies, and you see how false such pictures are. Think of the very words "novel," "romance" – what do they mean but exaggeration of one bit of life?'

'That may be true. But why do people find the subject so interesting?'

'Because there is so little love in real life. That's the truth of it. Why do poor people care only for stories about the rich? The same principle.'

'How clever you are, Amy!'

'Am I? It's very nice to be told so. Perhaps I have some cleverness of a kind; but what use is it to me? My life is being wasted. I ought to have a place in the society of clever people. I was never meant to live quietly in the background. Oh, if I hadn't been in such a hurry, and so inexperienced!'

'Oh, I wanted to ask you,' said Edith, soon after this. 'Do you wish Albert to say anything about you – at the hospital?'

'There's no reason why he shouldn't.'

'You won't even write to say –?'

'I shall do nothing.'

Since the parting from her husband, there had proceeded in Amy a noticeable maturing of intellect. Probably the one thing was a consequence of the other. During that last year in the flat her mind was held captive by material cares, and this arrest of her natural development doubtless had much to do with the appearance of acerbity in a character which had displayed so much sweetness, so much womanly grace. Moreover, it was arrest at a critical point. When she fell in love with Edwin Reardon her mind had still to undergo the culture of circumstances; though a woman in years she had seen nothing of life but a few phases of artificial society, and her education had not progressed beyond the final school-girl stage. Submitting herself to Reardon's influence, she passed through what was a highly useful training of the intellect; but with the result that she became clearly conscious of the divergence between herself and her husband. In endeavouring to imbue her with his own literary tastes, Reardon instructed Amy as to the natural tendencies of her mind, which till then she had not clearly understood. When she ceased to read with the eyes of passion, most of the things which were Reardon's supreme interests lost their value for her. A sound intelligence enabled her to think and feel in many directions, but the special line of her growth lay apart from that in which the novelist and classical scholar had directed her.

When she found herself alone and independent, her mind acted like a spring when pressure is removed. After a few weeks of *désœuvrement* she obeyed the impulse to occupy herself with a kind of reading alien to Reardon's sympathies. The solid periodicals attracted her, and especially those articles which dealt with themes of social science. Anything that savoured of newness and boldness in philosophic thought had a charm for her palate. She read a good deal of that kind of literature which may be defined as specialism popularised; writing which addresses itself to educated, but not strictly studious, persons, and which forms the reservoir of conversation for society above the sphere of turf and west-endism. Thus, for instance, though she could not undertake the volumes of Herbert Spencer, she was intelligently acquainted with the tenor of their contents; and though she had never opened one of Darwin's books, her knowledge of his main theories and illustrations was respectable. She was becoming a typical woman of the new time, the woman who has developed concurrently with journalistic enterprise.

Not many days after that conversation with Edith Carter, she had occasion to visit Mudie's, for the new number of some periodical which contained an appetising title. As it was a sunny and warm day she walked to New Oxford Street from the nearest Metropolitan station. Whilst waiting at the library counter, she heard a familiar voice in her proximity; it was that of Jasper Milvain, who stood talking with a middle-aged lady. As Amy turned to look at him his eye met hers; clearly he had been aware of her. The review she desired was handed to her; she moved aside, and turned over the pages. Then Milvain walked up.

He was armed *cap-à-pie* in the fashions of suave society; no Bohemianism of garb or person, for Jasper knew he could not afford that kind of economy. On her part, Amy was much better dressed than usual, a costume suited to her position of bereaved heiress.

'What a time since we met!' said Jasper, taking her delicately gloved hand and looking into her face with his most effective smile.

'And why?' asked Amy.

'Indeed, I hardly know. I hope Mrs Yule is well?'

'Quite, thank you.'

It seemed as if he would draw back to let her pass, and so make an end of the colloquy. But Amy, though she moved forward, added a remark:

'I don't see your name in any of this month's magazines.'

'I have nothing signed this month. A short review in *The Current*, that's all.'

'But I suppose you write as much as ever?'

'Yes; but chiefly in weekly papers just now. You don't see the *Will-o'-the-Wisp*?'

'Oh yes. And I think I can generally recognise your hand.'

They issued from the library.

'Which way are you going?' Jasper inquired, with something more of the old freedom.

'I walked from Gower Street station, and I think, as it's so fine, I shall walk back again.'

He accompanied her. They turned up Museum Street, and

Amy, after a short silence, made inquiry concerning his sisters.

'I am sorry I saw them only once, but no doubt you thought it better to let the acquaintance end there.'

'I really didn't think of it in that way at all,' Jasper replied.

'We naturally understood it so, when you even ceased to call, yourself.'

'But don't you feel that there would have been a good deal of awkwardness in my coming to Mrs Yule's?'

'Seeing that you looked at things from my husband's point of view?'

'Oh, that's a mistake! I have only seen your husband once since he went to Islington.'

Amy gave him a look of surprise.

'You are not on friendly terms with him?'

'Well, we have drifted apart. For some reason he seemed to think that my companionship was not very profitable. So it was better, on the whole, that I should see neither you nor him.'

Amy was wondering whether he had heard of her legacy. He might have been informed by a Wattleborough correspondent, even if no one in London had told him.

'Do your sisters keep up their friendship with my cousin Marian?' she asked, quitting the previous difficult topic.

'Oh yes!' He smiled. 'They see a great deal of each other.'

'Then of course you have heard of my uncle's death?'

'Yes. I hope all your difficulties are now at an end.'

Amy delayed a moment, then said: 'I hope so,' without any emphasis.

'Do you think of spending this winter abroad?'

It was the nearest he could come to a question concerning the future of Amy and her husband.

'Everything is still quite uncertain. But tell me something about our old acquaintances. How does Mr Biffen get on?'

'I scarcely ever see him, but I think he pegs away at an interminable novel, which no one will publish when it's done. Whelpdale I meet occasionally.'

He talked of the latter's projects and achievements in a lively strain.

'Your own prospects continue to brighten, no doubt,' said Amy.

'I really think they do. Things go fairly well. And I have lately received a promise of very valuable help.'

'From whom?'

'A relative of yours.'

Amy turned to interrogate him with a look.

'A relative? You mean –?'

'Yes; Marian.'

They were passing Bedford Square. Amy glanced at the trees, now almost bare of foliage; then her eyes met Jasper's, and she smiled significantly.

'I should have thought your aim would have been far more ambitious,' she said, with distinct utterance.

'Marian and I have been engaged for some time – practically.'

'Indeed? I remember now how you once spoke of her. And you will be married soon?'

'Probably before the end of the year. I see that you are criticising my motives. I am quite prepared for that in everyone who knows me and the circumstances. But you must remember that I couldn't foresee anything of this kind. It enables us to marry sooner, that's all.'

'I am sure your motives are unassailable,' replied Amy, still with a smile. 'I imagined that you wouldn't marry for years, and then some distinguished person. This throws new light upon your character.'

'You thought me so desperately scheming and cold-blooded?'

'Oh dear no! But – well, to be sure, I can't say that I know Marian. I haven't seen her for years and years. She may be admirably suited to you.'

'Depend upon it, I think so.'

'She's likely to shine in society? She is a brilliant girl, full of tact and insight?'

'Scarcely all that, perhaps.'

He looked dubiously at his companion.

'Then you have abandoned your old ambitions?' Amy pursued.

'Not a bit of it. I am on the way to achieve them.'

'And Marian is the ideal wife to assist you?'

'From one point of view, yes. Pray, why all this ironic questioning?'

'Not ironic at all.'

'It sounded very much like it, and I know from of old that you have a tendency that way.'

'The news surprised me a little, I confess. But I see that I am in danger of offending you.'

'Let us wait another five years, and then I will ask your opinion as to the success of my marriage. I don't take a step of this kind without maturely considering it. Have I made many blunders as yet?'

'As yet, not that I know of.'

'Do I impress you as one likely to commit follies?'

'I had rather wait a little before answering that.'

'That is to say, you prefer to prophesy after the event. Very well, we shall see.'

In the length of Gower Street they talked of several other things less personal. By degrees the tone of their conversation had become what it was used to be, now and then almost confidential.

'You are still at the same lodgings?' asked Amy, as they drew near to the railway station.

'I moved yesterday, so that the girls and I could be under the same roof – until the next change.'

'You will let us know when that takes place?'

He promised, and with exchange of smiles which were something like a challenge they took leave of each other.

Chapter 27

THE LONELY MAN

A TOUCH of congestion in the right lung was a warning to Reardon that his half-year of insufficient food and general waste of strength would make the coming winter a hard time for him, worse probably than the last. Biffen, responding in person to the summons, found him in bed, waited upon by a gaunt, dry, sententious woman of sixty – not the landlady, but a lodger who was glad to earn one meal a day by any means that offered.

'It wouldn't be very nice to die here, would it?' said the sufferer, with a laugh which was cut short by a cough. 'One would like a comfortable room, at least. Why, I don't know. I dreamt last night that I was in a ship that had struck something and was going down; and it wasn't the thought of death that most disturbed me, but a horror of being plunged in the icy water. In fact, I have had just the same feeling on shipboard. I remember waking up midway between Corfu and Brindisi, on that shaky tub of a Greek boat; we were rolling a good deal, and I heard a sort of alarmed rush and shouting up on deck. It was so warm and comfortable in the berth, and I thought with intolerable horror of the possibility of sousing into the black depths.'

'Don't talk, my boy,' advised Biffen. 'Let me read you the new chapter of "Mr Bailey." It may induce a refreshing slumber.'

Reardon was away from his duties for a week; he returned to them with a feeling of extreme shakiness, an indisposition to exert himself, and a complete disregard of the course that events were taking. It was fortunate that he had kept aside that small store of money designed for emergencies; he was able to draw on it now to pay his doctor, and provide himself with better nourishment than usual. He purchased new boots, too, and some articles of warm clothing of which he stood in need – an alarming outlay.

A change had come over him; he was no longer rendered miserable by thoughts of Amy – seldom, indeed, turned his mind to her at all. His secretaryship at Croydon was a haven within view; the income of seventy-five pounds (the other half to go to his wife) would support him luxuriously, and for anything beyond that he seemed to care little. Next Sunday he was to go over to Croydon and see the institution.

One evening of calm weather he made his way to Clipstone Street and greeted his friend with more show of light-heartedness than he had been capable of for at least two years.

'I have been as nearly as possible a happy man all to-day,' he said, when his pipe was well lit. 'Partly the sunshine, I suppose. There's no saying if the mood will last, but if it does all is well with me. I regret nothing and wish for nothing.'

'A morbid state of mind,' was Biffen's opinion.

'No doubt of that, but I am content to be indebted to morbidness. One must have a rest from misery somehow. Another kind of man would have taken to drinking; that has tempted me now and then, I assure you. But I couldn't afford it. Did you ever feel tempted to drink merely for the sake of forgetting trouble?'

'Often enough. I have done it. I have deliberately spent a certain proportion of the money that ought to have gone for food in the cheapest kind of strong liquor.'

'Ha! that's interesting. But it never got the force of a habit you had to break?'

'No. Partly, I dare say, because I had the warning of poor Sykes before my eyes.'

'You never see that poor fellow?'

'Never. He must be dead, I think. He would die either in the hospital or the workhouse.'

'Well,' said Reardon, musing cheerfully, 'I shall never become a drunkard; I haven't that diathesis,[31] to use your expression. Doesn't it strike you that you and I are very respectable persons? We really have no vices. Put us on a social pedestal, and we should be shining lights of morality. I sometimes wonder at our inoffensiveness. Why don't we run amuck against law and order? Why, at the least, don't we become savage revolutionists, and harangue in Regent's Park of a Sunday?'

'Because we are passive beings, and were meant to enjoy life very quietly. As we can't enjoy, we just suffer quietly, that's all. By-the-by, I want to talk about a difficulty in one of the Fragments of Euripides. Did you ever go through the Fragments?'

This made a diversion for half an hour. Then Reardon returned to his former line of thought.

'As I was entering patients yesterday, there came up to the table a tall, good-looking, very quiet girl, poorly dressed, but as neat as could be. She gave me her name, then I asked "Occupation?" She said at once, "I'm unfortunate, sir." I couldn't help looking up at her in surprise; I had taken it for granted she was a dressmaker or something of the kind. And, do you know, I never felt so strong an impulse to shake hands to show sympathy, and even respect, in some way. I should have liked to say, "Why, I am unfortunate, too !" such a good, patient face she had.'

'I distrust such appearances,' said Biffen in his quality of realist.

'Well, so do I, as a rule. But in this case they were convincing. And there was no need whatever for her to make such a declaration; she might just as well have said anything else; it's the merest form. I shall always hear her voice saying, "I'm unfortunate, sir." She made me feel what a mistake it was for me to marry such a girl as Amy. I ought to have looked about for some simple, kind-hearted work-girl; [32] that was the kind of wife indicated for me by circumstances. If I had earned a hundred a year she would have thought we were well-to-do. I should have been an authority to her on everything under the sun – and above it. No ambition would have unsettled her. We should have lived in a couple of poor rooms somewhere, and – we should have loved each other.'

'What a shameless idealist you are !' said Biffen shaking his head. 'Let me sketch the true issue of such a marriage. To begin with, the girl would have married you in firm persuasion that you were a "gentleman" in temporary difficulties, and that before long you would have plenty of money to dispose of. Disappointed in this hope, she would have grown sharp-tempered, querulous, selfish. All your endeavours to make her understand you would only have resulted in widening the impassable gulf. She would have misconstrued your every sentence, found food for suspicion in every harmless joke, tormented you with the vulgarest forms of jealousy. The effect upon your nature would have been degrading. In the end, you must have abandoned every effort to raise her to your own level, and either have sunk to hers or made a rupture. Who doesn't know the story of such attempts? I myself, ten years ago, was on the point of committing such a folly, but, Heaven be praised! an accident saved me.'

'You never told me that story.'

'And don't care to now. I prefer to forget it.'

'Well, you can judge for yourself, but not for me. Of course I might have chosen the wrong girl, but I am supposing that I had been fortunate. In any case there would have been a much better chance than in the marriage that I made.'

'Your marriage was sensible enough, and a few years hence you will be a happy man again.'

'You seriously think Amy will come back to me?'

'Of course I do.'

'Upon my word, I don't know that I desire it.'

'Because you are in a strangely unhealthy state.'

'I rather think I regard the matter more sanely than ever yet. I am quite free from sexual bias. I can see that Amy was not my fit intellectual companion, and all emotion at the thought of her has gone from me. The word "love" is a weariness to me. If only our idiotic laws permitted us to break the legal bond, how glad both of us would be!'

'You are depressed and anæmic. Get yourself in flesh, and view things like a man of this world.'

'But don't you think it the best thing that can happen to a man if he outgrows passion?'

'In certain circumstances, no doubt.'

'In all and any. The best moments of life are those when we contemplate beauty in the purely artistic spirit – objectively. I have had such moments in Greece and Italy; times when I was a free spirit, utterly remote from the temptations and harassings of sexual emotion. What we call love is mere turmoil. Who wouldn't release himself from it for ever, if the possibility offered?'

'Oh, there's a good deal to be said for that, of course.'

Reardon's face was illumined with the glow of an exquisite memory.

'Haven't I told you,' he said, 'of that marvellous sunset at Athens? I was on the Pnyx; had been rambling about there the whole afternoon. For I dare say a couple of hours I had noticed a growing rift of light in the clouds to the west; it looked as if the dull day might have a rich ending. That rift grew broader and brighter – the only bit of light in the sky. On Parnes there were white strips of ragged mist, hanging very low; the same on Hymettus, and even the peak of Lycabettus was just hidden. Of a sudden, the sun's rays broke out. They showed themselves first in a strangely beautiful way, striking from behind the seaward hills through the pass that leads to Eleusis, and so gleaming on the nearer slopes of Aigaleos, making the clefts black and the rounded parts of the mountain wonderfully brilliant with golden colour. All the rest of the landscape, remember, was untouched with a ray of light. This lasted only a minute or two, then the sun itself sank into the open patch of sky and shot glory in every direction; broadening beams smote upwards over the dark clouds, and made them a lurid yellow. To the left of the sun, the gulf of Ægina was all golden mist, the islands floating in it vaguely. To the right, over black Salamis, lay delicate strips of pale blue – indescribably pale and delicate.'

'You remember it very clearly.'

'As if I saw it now! But wait. I turned eastward, and there to my astonishment was a magnificent rainbow, a perfect semicircle, stretching from the foot of Parnes to that of Hymettus, framing Athens and its hills, which grew brighter and brighter – the brightness for which there is no name among colours. Hymettus was of a soft misty warmth, a something tending to purple, its ridges marked by exquisitely soft and indefinite shadows, the rainbow coming right down in front. The Acropolis simply glowed and blazed. As the sun descended all these colours grew richer and warmer; for a moment the landscape was nearly crimson. Then suddenly the sun passed into the lower stratum of cloud, and the splendour died almost at once, except that there remained the northern half of the rainbow, which had become double. In the west, the clouds were still glorious for a time; there were two shaped like great expanded wings, edged with refulgence.'

'Stop!' cried Biffen, 'or I shall clutch you by the throat. I warned you before that I can't stand those reminiscences.'

'Live in hope. Scrape together twenty pounds, and go there, if you die of hunger afterwards.'

'I shall never have twenty shillings,' was the despondent answer.

'I feel sure you will sell "Mr Bailey."'

'It's kind of you to encourage me; but if "Mr Bailey" is ever sold I don't mind undertaking to eat my duplicate of the proofs.'

'But now, you remember what led me to that. What does a man care for any woman on earth when he is absorbed in contemplation of that kind?'

'But it is only one of life's satisfactions.'

'I am only maintaining that it is the best, and infinitely preferable to sexual emotion. It leaves, no doubt, no bitterness of any kind. Poverty can't rob me of those memories. I have lived in an ideal world that was not deceitful, a world which seems to me, when I recall it, beyond the human sphere, bathed in diviner light.'

It was four or five days after this that Reardon, on going to his work in City Road, found a note from Carter. It requested him to call at the main hospital at half-past eleven the next morning. He supposed the appointment had something to do with his business at Croydon, whither he had been in the mean time. Some unfavourable news, perhaps; any misfortune was likely.

He answered the summons punctually, and on entering the general office was requested by the clerk to wait in Mr Carter's private room; the secretary had not yet arrived. His waiting lasted some ten minutes, then the door opened and admitted, not Carter, but Mrs Edmund Yule.

Reardon stood up in perturbation. He was anything but prepared, or disposed, for an interview with this lady. She came towards him with hand extended and a countenance of suave friendliness.

'I doubted whether you would see me if I let you know,' she said. 'Forgive me this little bit of scheming, will you? I have something so very important to speak to you about.'

He said nothing, but kept a demeanour of courtesy.

'I think you haven't heard from Amy?' Mrs Yule asked.

'Not since I saw her.'

'And you don't know what has come to pass?'

'I have heard of nothing.'

'I am come to see you quite on my own responsibility, quite. I took Mr Carter into my confidence, but begged him not to let Mrs Carter know, lest she should tell Amy; I think he will keep his promise. It seemed to me that it was really my duty to do whatever I could in these sad, sad circumstances.'

Reardon listened respectfully, but without sign of feeling.

'I had better tell you at once that Amy's uncle at Wattleborough is dead, and that in his will he has bequeathed her ten thousand pounds.'

Mrs Yule watched the effect of this. For a moment none was visible, but she saw at length that Reardon's lips trembled and his eyebrows twitched.

'I am glad to hear of her good fortune,' he said distantly and in even tones.

'You will feel, I am sure,' continued his mother-in-law, 'that this must put an end to your most unhappy differences.'

'How can it have that result?'

'It puts you both in a very different position, does it not? But for your distressing circumstances, I am sure there would never have been such unpleasantness – never. Neither you nor Amy is the kind of person to take a pleasure in disagreement. Let me beg you to go and see her again. Everything is so different now. Amy has not the faintest idea that I have come to see you, and she mustn't on any account be told, for her worst fault is that sensitive pride of hers. And I'm sure you won't be offended, Edwin, if I say that you have very much the same failing. Between two such sensitive people differences might last a lifetime, unless one could be persuaded to take the first step. Do be generous! A woman is privileged to be a little obstinate, it is always said. Overlook the fault, and persuade her to let bygones be bygones.'

There was an involuntary affectedness in Mrs Yule's speech which repelled Reardon. He could not even put faith in her assurance that Amy knew nothing of this intercession. In any case it was extremely distasteful to him to discuss such matters with Mrs Yule.

'Under no circumstances could I do more than I already have done,' he replied. 'And after what you have told me, it is impossible for me to go and see her unless she expressly invites me.'

'Oh, if only you would overcome this sensitiveness!'

'It is not in my power to do so. My poverty, as you justly say, was the cause of our parting; but if Amy is no longer poor, that is very far from a reason why I should go to her as a suppliant for forgiveness.'

'But do consider the facts of the case, independently of feeling. I really think I don't go too far in saying that at least some – some provocation was given by you first of all. I am so very, very far from wishing to say anything disagreeable – I am sure you feel that – but wasn't there some little ground for complaint on Amy's part? Wasn't there, now?'

Reardon was tortured with nervousness. He wished to be alone, to think over what had happened, and Mrs Yule's urgent voice rasped upon his ears. Its very smoothness made it worse.

'There may have been ground for grief and concern,' he answered, 'but for complaint, no, I think not.'

'But I understand' – the voice sounded rather irritable now – 'that you positively reproached and upbraided her because she was reluctant to go and live in some very shocking place.'

'I may have lost my temper after Amy had shown – But I can't review our troubles in this way.'

'Am I to plead in vain?'

'I regret very much that I can't possibly do as you wish. It is all between Amy and myself. Interference by other people cannot do any good.'

'I am sorry you should use such a word as "interference,"' replied Mrs Yule, bridling a little. 'Very sorry, indeed. I confess it didn't occur to me that my good-will to you could be seen in that light.'

'Believe me that I didn't use the word offensively.'

'Then you refuse to take any step towards a restoration of good feeling?'

'I am obliged to, and Amy would understand perfectly why I say so.'

His earnestness was so unmistakable that Mrs Yule had no choice but to rise and bring the interview to an end. She commanded herself sufficiently to offer a regretful hand.

'I can only say that my daughter is very, very unfortunate.'

Reardon lingered a little after her departure, then left the hospital and walked at a rapid pace in no particular direction.

Ah! if this had happened in the first year of his marriage, what more blessed man than he would have walked the earth! But it came after irreparable harm. No amount of wealth could undo the ruin caused by poverty.

It was natural for him, as soon as he could think with deliberation, to turn towards his only friend. But on calling at the house in Clipstone Street he found the garret empty, and no one could tell him when its occupant was likely to be back. He left a note, and made his way back to Islington. The evening had to be spent at the hospital, but on his return Biffen sat waiting for him.

'You called about twelve, didn't you?' the visitor inquired.

'Half-past.'

'I was at the police-court. Odd thing — but it always happens so — that I should have spoken of Sykes the other night. Last night I came upon a crowd in Oxford Street, and the nucleus of it was no other than Sykes himself, very drunk and disorderly, in the grip of two policemen. Nothing could be done for him; I was useless as bail; he e'en had to sleep in the cell. But I went this morning to see what would become of him. Such a spectacle when they brought him forward! It was only five shillings fine, and to my astonishment he produced the money. I joined him outside — it required a little courage — and had a long talk with him. He's writing a London Letter for some provincial daily, and the first payment had thrown him off his balance.'

Reardon laughed gaily, and made inquiries about the eccentric gentleman. Only when the subject was exhausted did he speak of his own concerns, relating quietly what he had learnt from Mrs Yule. Biffen's eyes widened.

'So,' Reardon cried with exultation, 'there is the last burden off my mind! Henceforth I haven't a care! The only thing that still troubled me was my inability to give Amy enough to live upon. Now she is provided for *in secula seculorum*.[33] Isn't this grand news?'

'Decidedly. But if she is provided for, so are you.'

'Biffen, you know me better. Could I accept a farthing of her money? This has made our coming together again for ever impossible, unless – unless dead things can come to life. I know the value of money, but I can't take it from Amy.'

The other kept silence.

'No! But now everything is well. She has her child, and can devote herself to bringing the boy up. And I – but I shall be rich on my own account. A hundred and fifty a year; it would be a farce to offer Amy her share of it. By all the gods of Olympus, we will go to Greece together, you and I!'

'Pooh!'

'I swear it! Let me save for a couple of years, and then get a good month's holiday, or more if possible, and, as Pallas Athene liveth! we shall find ourselves at Marseilles, going aboard some boat of the Messageries. I can't believe yet that this is true. Come, we will have a supper to-night. Come out into Upper Street, and let us eat, drink, and be merry!'

'You are beside yourself. But never mind; let us rejoice by all means. There's every reason.'

'That poor girl! Now, at last, she'll be at ease.'

'Who?'

'Amy, of course! I'm delighted on her account. Ah! but if it had come a long time ago, in the happy days! Then she, too, would have gone to Greece, wouldn't she? Everything in life comes too soon or too late. What it would have meant for her and for me! She would never have hated me then, never. Biffen, am I base or contemptible? She thinks so. That's how poverty has served me. If you had seen her, how she looked at me, when we met the other day, you would understand well enough why I couldn't live with her now, not if she entreated me to. That would make me base if you like. Gods! how ashamed I should be if I yielded to such a temptation! And once –'

He had worked himself to such intensity of feeling that at length his voice choked and tears burst from his eyes.

'Come out, and let us have a walk,' said Biffen.

On leaving the house they found themselves in a thick fog, through which trickled drops of warm rain. Nevertheless, they pursued their purpose, and presently were seated in one of the boxes of a small coffee-shop. Their only companion in the place was a cab-driver, who had just finished a meal, and was now nodding into slumber over his plate and cup. Reardon ordered fried ham and eggs, the luxury of the poor, and when the attendant woman was gone away to execute the order, he burst into excited laughter.

'Here we sit, two literary men! How should we be regarded by –'

He named two or three of the successful novelists of the day.

'With what magnificent scorn they would turn from us and our squalid feast! They have never known struggle; not they. They are public-school men, University men, club men, society men. An income of less than three or four hundred a year is inconceivable to them; that seems the minimum for an educated man's support. It would be small-minded to think of them with rancour, but, by Apollo! I know that we should change places with them if the work we have done were justly weighed against theirs.'

'What does it matter? We are different types of intellectual workers. I think of them savagely now and then, but only when hunger gets a trifle too keen. Their work answers a demand; ours – or mine at all events – doesn't. They are in touch with the reading multitude; they have the sentiments of the respectable; they write for their class. Well, you had *your* circle of readers, and, if things hadn't gone against you, by this time you certainly could have counted on your three or four hundred a year.'

'It's unlikely that I should ever have got more than two hundred pounds for a book; and, to have kept at my best, I must have been content to publish once every two or three years. The position was untenable with no private income. And I must needs marry a wife of dainty instincts! What astounding impudence! No wonder Fate pitched me aside into the gutter.'

They ate their ham and eggs, and exhilarated themselves with a cup of chicory – called coffee. Then Biffen drew from the pocket of his venerable overcoat the volume of Euripides he had brought, and their talk turned once more to the land of the sun. Only when the coffee-shop was closed did they go forth again into the foggy street, and at the top of Pentonville Hill they stood for ten minutes debating a metrical effect in one of the Fragments.

Day after day Reardon went about with a fever upon him. By

evening his pulse was always rapid, and no extremity of weariness brought him a refreshing sleep. In conversation he seemed either depressed or excited, more often the latter. Save when attending to his duties at the hospital, he made no pretence of employing himself; if at home, he sat for hours without opening a book, and his walks, excepting when they led him to Clipstone Street, were aimless.

The hours of postal delivery found him waiting in an anguish of suspense. At eight o'clock each morning he stood by his window, listening for the postman's knock in the street. As it approached he went out to the head of the stairs, and if the knock sounded at the door of his house, he leaned over the banisters, trembling in expectation. But the letter was never for him. When his agitation had subsided he felt glad of the disappointment, and laughed and sang.

One day Carter appeared at the City Road establishment, and made an opportunity of speaking to his clerk in private.

'I suppose,' he said with a smile, 'they'll have to look out for someone else at Croydon?'

'By no means! The thing is settled. I go at Christmas.'

'You really mean that?'

'Undoubtedly.'

Seeing that Reardon was not disposed even to allude to private circumstances the secretary said no more, and went away convinced that misfortunes had turned the poor fellow's brain.

Wandering in the city, about this time, Reardon encountered his friend the realist.

'Would you like to meet Sykes?' asked Biffen. 'I am just going to see him.'

'Where does he live?'

'In some indiscoverable hole. To save fuel, he spends his mornings at some reading-rooms; the admission is only a penny, and there he can see all the papers and do his writing and enjoy a grateful temperature.'

They repaired to the haunt in question. A flight of stairs brought them to a small room in which were exposed the daily newspapers; another ascent, and they were in a room devoted to magazines, chess, and refreshments; yet another, and they reached the department of weekly publications; lastly, at the top of the house, they found a lavatory, and a chamber for the use of those who desired to write. The walls of this last retreat were of blue plaster and sloped inwards from the floor; along them stood school desks with benches, and in one place was suspended a ragged and dirty card announcing that paper and envelopes could be purchased downstairs. An enormous basket full of waste-paper, and a small stove, occupied two corners; ink blotches, satirical designs, and much scribbling in pen and pencil served for mural adornment. From the adjacent lavatory came sounds of splashing and spluttering, and the busy street far below sent up its confused noises.

Two persons only sat at the desks. One was a hunger-bitten, out-of-work clerk, evidently engaged in replying to advertisements; in front of him lay two or three finished letters, and on the ground at his feet were several crumpled sheets of note-paper, representing abortive essays in composition. The other man, also occupied with the pen, looked about forty years old, and was clad in a very rusty suit of tweeds; on the bench beside him lay a grey overcoat and a silk hat which had for some time been moulting. His face declared the habit to which he was a victim, but it had nothing repulsive in its lineaments and expression; on the contrary, it was pleasing, amiable, and rather quaint. At this moment no one would have doubted his sobriety. With coat-sleeve turned back, so as to give free play to his right hand and wrist, revealing meanwhile a flannel shirt of singular colour, and with his collar unbuttoned (he wore no tie) to leave his throat at ease as he bent myopically over the paper, he was writing at express speed, evidently in the full rush of the ardour of composition. The veins of his forehead were dilated, and his chin pushed forward in a way that made one think of a racing horse.

'Are you too busy to talk?' asked Biffen, going to his side.

'I am! Upon my soul I am!' exclaimed the other looking up in alarm. 'For the love of Heaven don't put me out! A quarter of an hour!'

'All right. I'll come up again.'

The friends went downstairs and turned over the papers.

'Now let's try him again,' said Biffen, when considerably more than the requested time had lapsed. They went up, and found Mr Sykes in an attitude of melancholy meditation. He had turned back his coat-sleeve, had buttoned his collar, and was eyeing the slips of completed manuscript. Biffen presented his companion, and Mr Sykes greeted the novelist with much geniality.

'What do you think this is?' he exclaimed, pointing to his work. 'The first instalment of my autobiography for the *Shropshire Weekly Herald*. Anonymous, of course, but strictly veracious, with the omission of sundry little personal failings which are nothing to the point. I call it "Through the Wilds of Literary London." An old friend of mine edits the *Herald*, and I'm indebted to him for the suggestion.'

His voice was a trifle husky, but he spoke like a man of education.

'Most people will take it for fiction. I wish I had inventive power enough to write fiction anything like it. I have published novels, Mr Reardon, but my experience in that branch of literature was peculiar – as I may say it has been in most others to which I have applied myself. My first stories were written for *The Young Lady's Favourite*, and most remarkable productions they were, I promise you. That was fifteen years ago, in the days of my versatility. I could throw off my supplemental novelette of fifteen thousand words without turning a hair, and immediately after it fall to, fresh as a daisy, on the "Illustrated History of the United States," which I was then doing for Edward Coghlan. But presently I thought myself too good for the *Favourite*; in an evil day I began to write three-volume novels, aiming at reputation. It wouldn't do. I persevered for five years, and made about five failures. Then I went back to Bowring. "Take me on again, old man, will you?" Bowring was a man of few words; he said, "Blaze away, my boy." And I tried to. But it was no use; I had got out of the style; my writing was too literary by a long chalk. For a whole year I deliberately strove to write badly, but Bowring was so pained with the feebleness of my efforts that at last he sternly bade me avoid his sight. "What the devil," he roared one day, "do you mean by sending me stories about men and women? You ought to know better than that, a fellow of your experience!" So I had to give it up, and there was an end of my career as a writer of fiction.'

He shook his head sadly.

'Biffen,' he continued, 'when I first made his acquaintance, had an idea of writing for the working classes; and what do you think he was going to offer them? Stories *about* the working classes! Nay, never hang your head for it, old boy; it was excusable in the days of your youth. Why, Mr Reardon, as no doubt you know well enough, nothing can induce working men or women to read stories that treat of their own world. They are the most consumed idealists in creation, especially the women. Again and again work-girls have said to me: "Oh, I don't like that book; it's nothing but real life."'

'It's the fault of women in general,' remarked Reardon.

'So it is, but it comes out with delicious *naïveté* in the working classes. Now, educated people like to read of scenes that are familiar to them, though I grant you that the picture must be idealised if you're to appeal to more than one in a thousand. The working classes detest anything that tries to represent their daily life. It isn't because that life is too painful; no, no; it's downright snobbishness. Dickens goes down only with the best of them, and then solely because of his strength in farce and his melodrama.'

Presently the three went out together, and had dinner at an *à la mode* beef shop. Mr Sykes ate little, but took copious libations of porter at twopence a pint. When the meal was over he grew taciturn.

'Can you walk westwards?' Biffen asked.

'I'm afraid not, afraid not. In fact I have an appointment at two – at Aldgate station.'

They parted from him.

'Now he'll go and soak till he's unconscious,' said Biffen. 'Poor fellow! Pity he ever earns anything at all. The workhouse would be better, I should think.'

'No, no! Let a man drink himself to death rather. I have a horror of the workhouse. Remember the clock at Marylebone I used to tell you about.'

'Unphilosophic. I don't think I should be unhappy in the workhouse. I should have a certain satisfaction in the thought that I had forced society to support me. And then the absolute freedom from care! Why, it's very much the same as being a man of independent fortune.'

It was about a week after this, midway in November, that there at length came to Manville Street a letter addressed in Amy's hand. It arrived at three one afternoon; Reardon heard the postman, but he had ceased to rush out on every such occasion, and to-day he was feeling ill. Lying upon the bed, he had just raised his head wearily when he became aware that someone was mounting to his room. He sprang up, his face and neck flushing.

This time Amy began 'Dear Edwin'; the sight of those words made his brain swim.

'You must, of course, have heard [she wrote] that my uncle John has left me ten thousand pounds. It has not yet come into my possession, and I had decided that I would not write to you till that happened, but perhaps you may altogether misunderstand my silence.

'If this money had come to me when you were struggling so hard to earn a living for us, we should never have spoken the words and thought the thoughts which now make it so difficult for me to write to you. What I wish to say is that, although the property is legally my own, I quite recognise that you have a right to share in it. Since we have lived apart you have sent me far more than you could really afford, believing it your duty to do so; now that things are so different I wish you, as well as myself, to benefit by the change.

'I said at our last meeting that I should be quite prepared to return to you if you took that position at Croydon. There is now no need for you to pursue a kind of work for which you are quite unfitted, and I repeat that I am willing to live with you as before. If you will tell me where you would like to make a new home I shall gladly agree. I do not think you would care to leave London permanently, and certainly I should not.

'Please to let me hear from you as soon as possible. In writing like this I feel that I have done what you expressed a wish that I should do. I have asked you to put an end to our separation, and I trust that I have not asked in vain.   'Yours always,
                                        'AMY REARDON.'

The letter fell from his hand. It was such a letter as he might have expected, but the beginning misled him, and as his agitation throbbed itself away he suffered an encroachment of despair which made him for a time unable to move or even think.

His reply, written by the dreary twilight which represented sunset, ran thus:

'Dear Amy, – I thank you for your letter, and I appreciate your motive in writing it. But if you feel that you have "done what I expressed a wish that you should do," you must have strangely misunderstood me.

'The only one thing that I *wished* was, that by some miracle your love for me might be revived. Can I persuade myself that this is the letter of a wife who desires to return to me because in her heart she loves me? If that is the truth you have been most unfortunate in trying to express yourself.

'You have written because it seemed your duty to do so. But, indeed, a sense of duty such as this is a mistaken one. You have no love for me, and where there is no love there is no mutual obligation in marriage. Perhaps you think that regard for social conventions will necessitate your living with me again. But have more courage; refuse to act falsehoods; tell society it is base and brutal, and that you prefer to live an honest life.

'I cannot share your wealth, dear. But as you have no longer need of my help – as we are now quite independent of each other – I shall cease to send the money which hitherto I have considered yours. In this way I shall have enough, and more than enough, for my necessities, so that you will never have to trouble yourself with the thought that I am suffering privations. At Christmas I go to Croydon, and I will then write to you again.

'For we may at all events be friendly. My mind is relieved from ceaseless anxiety on your account. I know now that you are safe from that accursed poverty which is to blame for all our sufferings. You I do not blame, though I have sometimes done so. My own experience teaches me how kindness can be embittered by misfortune. Some great and noble sorrow may have the effect of drawing hearts together, but to struggle against destitution, to be crushed by care about shillings and sixpences – that must always degrade.

'No other reply than this is possible, so I beg you not to write in this way again. Let me know if you go to live elsewhere. I hope Willie is well, and that his growth is still a delight and happiness to you.

                              'EDWIN REARDON.'

That one word 'dear,' occuring in the middle of the letter, gave him pause as he read the lines over. Should he not obliterate it, and even in such a way that Amy might see what he had done? His pen was dipped in the ink for that purpose, but after all he held his hand. Amy was still dear to him, say what he might, and if she noted the word – if she pondered over it –

A street gas-lamp prevented the room from becoming abso-lutely dark. When he had closed the envelope he lay down on his bed again, and watched the flickering yellowness upon the ceiling. He ought to have some tea before going to the hospital, but he cared so little for it that the trouble of boiling water was too great. The flickering light grew fainter; he understood at length that this was caused by fog that had begun to descend. The fog was his enemy; it would be wise to purchase a respirator if this hideous weather continued, for sometimes his throat burned, and there was a rasping in his chest which gave dis-agreeable admonition.

He fell asleep for half an hour, and on awaking he was feverish, as usual at this time of day. Well, it was time to go to his work. Ugh! That first mouthful of fog!

Chapter 28

INTERIM

THE rooms which Milvain had taken for himself and his sisters
were modest, but more expensive than their old quarters. As the
change was on his account he held himself responsible for the
extra outlay. But for his immediate prospects this step would
have been unwarrantable, as his earnings were only just sufficient
for his needs on the previous footing. He had resolved that his
marriage must take place before Christmas; till that event he
would draw when necessary upon the girls' little store, and then
repay them out of Marian's dowry.

'And what are we to do when you are married?' asked Dora.

The question was put on the first evening of their being all
under the same roof. The trio had had supper in the girls' sitting-
room, and it was a moment for frank conversation. Dora rejoiced
in the coming marriage; her brother had behaved honourably,
and Marian, she trusted, would be very happy, notwithstanding disagreement with her father, which seemed inevitable.
Maud was by no means so well pleased, though she endeavoured
to wear smiles. It looked to her as if Jasper had been guilty of a
kind of weakness not to be expected in him. Marian, as an individual, could not be considered an appropriate wife for such a
man with such a future; and as for her five thousand pounds,
that was ridiculous. Had it been ten – something can be made of
ten thousand; but a paltry five! Maud's ideas on such subjects
had notably expanded of late, and one of the results was that
she did not live so harmoniously with her sister as for the first
few months of their London career.

'I have been thinking a good deal about that,' replied Jasper
to the younger girl's question. He stood with his back to the fire
and smoked a cigarette. 'I thought at first of taking a flat; but
then a flat of the kind I should want would be twice the rent of a
large house. If we have a house with plenty of room in it you
might come and live with us after a time. At first I must find you
decent lodgings in our neighbourhood.'

'You show a good deal of generosity, Jasper,' said Maud, 'but pray remember that Marian isn't bringing you five thousand a year.'

'I regret to say that she isn't. What she brings me is five hundred a year for ten years – that's how I look at it. My own income will make it something between six or seven hundred at first, and before long probably more like a thousand. I am quite cool and collected. I understand exactly where I am, and where I am likely to be ten years hence. Marian's money is to be spent in obtaining a position for myself. At present I am spoken of as a "smart young fellow," and that kind of thing; but no one would offer me an editorship, or any other serious help. Wait till I show that I have helped myself, and hands will be stretched to me from every side. 'Tis the way of the world. I shall belong to a club; I shall give nice, quiet little dinners to selected people; I shall let it be understood by all and sundry that I have a social position. Thenceforth I am quite a different man, a man to be taken into account. And what will you bet me that I don't stand in the foremost rank of literary reputabilities ten years hence?'

'I doubt whether six or seven hundred a year will be enough for this.'

'If not, I am prepared to spend a thousand. Bless my soul! As if two or three years wouldn't suffice to draw out the mean qualities in the kind of people I am thinking of! I say ten, to leave myself a great margin.'

'Marian approves this?'

'I haven't distinctly spoken of it. But she approves whatever I think good.'

The girls laughed at his way of pronouncing this.

'And let us just suppose that you are so unfortunate as to fail?'

'There's no supposing it, unless, of course, I lose my health. I am not presuming on any wonderful development of powers. Such as I am now, I need only to be put on the little pedestal of a decent independence and plenty of people will point fingers of admiration at me. You don't fully appreciate this. Mind, it wouldn't do if I had no qualities. I *have* the qualities; they only need bringing into prominence. If I am an unknown man, and publish a wonderful book, it will make its way very slowly, or not at all. If I, become a known man, publish that very same book, its praise will echo over both hemispheres. I should be within the truth if I had said "a vastly inferior book," but I am in a bland mood at present. Suppose poor Reardon's novels had been published in the full light of reputation instead of in the struggling dawn which was never to become day, wouldn't they have been magnified by every critic? *You have to become famous before you can secure the attention which would give fame.*'

He delivered this apophthegm with emphasis, and repeated it in another form.

'You have to obtain reputation before you can get a fair hearing for that which would justify your repute. It's the old story of the French publisher who said to Dumas: "Make a name, and I'll publish anything you write." "But how the *diable*," cries the author, "am I to make a name if I can't get published?" If a man can't hit upon any other way of attracting attention, let him dance on his head in the middle of the street; after that he may hope to get consideration for his volume of poems. I am speaking of men who wish to win reputation before they are toothless. Of course if your work is strong, you can afford to wait, the probability is that half a dozen people will at last begin to shout that you have been monstrously neglected, as you have. But that happens when you are hoary and sapless, and when nothing under the sun delights you.'

He lit a new cigarette.

'Now I, my dear girls, am not a man who can afford to wait. First of all, my qualities are not of the kind which demand the recognition of posterity. My writing is for to-day, most distinctly hodiernal. It has no value save in reference to to-day. The question is: How can I get the eyes of men fixed upon me? The answer: By pretending I am quite independent of their gaze. I shall succeed, without any kind of doubt; and then I'll have a medal struck to celebrate the day of my marriage.'

But Jasper was not quite so well assured of the prudence of what he was about to do as he wished his sisters to believe. The impulse to which he had finally yielded still kept its force; indeed, was stronger than ever since the intimacy of lovers' dialogue had revealed to him more of Marian's heart and mind. Undeniably he was in love. Not passionately, not with the consuming desire which makes every motive seem paltry compared with its own satisfaction; but still quite sufficiently in love to have a great difficulty in pursuing his daily tasks. This did not still the voice which bade him remember all the opportunities and hopes he was throwing aside. Since the plighting of troth with Marian he had been over to Wimbledon, to the house of his friend and patron Mr Horace Barlow, and there he had again met with Miss Rupert. This lady had no power whatever over his emotions, but he felt assured that she regarded him with strong interest. When he imagined the possibility of contracting a marriage with Miss Rupert, who would make him at once a man of solid means, his head drooped, and he wondered at his precipitation. It had to be confessed that he was the victim of a vulgar weakness. He had declared himself not of the first order of progressive men.

The conversation with Amy Reardon did not tend to put his mind at rest. Amy was astonished at so indiscreet a step in a man of his calibre. Ah! if only Amy herself were free, with her ten thousand pounds to dispose of! She, he felt sure, did not view him with indifference. Was there not a touch of pique in the elaborate irony with which she had spoken of his choice? – But it was idle to look in that direction.

He was anxious on his sisters' account. They were clever girls, and with energy might before long earn a bare subsistence; but it began to be doubtful whether they would persevere in literary work. Maud, it was clear, had conceived hopes of quite another kind. Her intimacy with Mrs Lane was effecting a change in her habits, her dress, even her modes of speech. A few days after their establishment in the new lodgings, Jasper spoke seriously on this subject with the younger girl.

'I wonder whether you could satisfy my curiosity in a certain matter,' he said. 'Do you, by chance, know how much Maud gave for that new jacket in which I saw her yesterday?'

Dora was reluctant to answer.

'I don't think it was very much.'

'That is to say, it didn't cost twenty guineas. Well, I hope not. I notice, too, that she has been purchasing a new hat.'

'Oh, that was very inexpensive. She trimmed it herself.'

'Did she? Is there any particular, any quite special, reason for this expenditure?'

'I really can't say, Jasper.'

'That's ambiguous, you know. Perhaps it means you won't allow yourself to say?'

'No, Maud doesn't tell me about things of that kind.'

He took opportunities of investigating the matter, with the result that some ten days after he sought private colloquy with Maud herself. She had asked his opinion of a little paper she was going to send to a ladies' illustrated weekly, and he summoned her to his own room.

'I think this will do pretty well,' he said. 'There's rather too much thought in it, perhaps. Suppose you knock out one or two of the less obvious reflections, and substitute a wholesome commonplace? You'll have a better chance, I assure you.'

'But I shall make it worthless.'

'No; you'll probably make it worth a guinea or so. You must remember that the people who read women's papers are irritated, simply irritated, by anything that isn't glaringly obvious. They hate an unusual thought. The art of writing for such papers – indeed, for the public in general – is to express vulgar thought and feeling in a way that flatters the vulgar thinkers and feelers. Just abandon your mind to it, and then let me see it again.'

Maud took up the manuscript and glanced over it with a contemptuous smile. Having observed her for a moment, Jasper threw himself back in the chair and said, as if casually:

'I am told that Mr Dolomore is becoming a great friend of yours.'

The girl's face changed. She drew herself up, and looked away towards the window.

'I don't know that he is a "great" friend.'

'Still, he pays enough attention to you to excite remark.'

'Whose remark?'

'That of several people who go to Mrs Lane's.'

'I don't know any reason for it,' said Maud, coldly.

'Look here, Maud, you don't mind if I give you a friendly warning?'

She kept silence, with a look of superiority to all monition.

'Dolomore,' pursued her brother, 'is all very well in his way, but that way isn't yours. I believe he has a good deal of money, but he has neither brains nor principle. There's no harm in your observing the nature and habits of such individuals, but don't allow yourself to forget that they are altogether beneath you.'

'There's no need whatever for you to teach me self-respect,' replied the girl.

'I'm quite sure of that; but you are inexperienced. On the whole, I do rather wish that you would go less frequently to Mrs Lane's. It was rather an unfortunate choice of yours. Very much better if you could have got on a good footing with the Barnabys. If you are generally looked upon as belonging to the Lanes' set it will make it difficult for you to get in with the better people.'

Maud was not to be drawn into argument, and Jasper could only hope that his words would have some weight with her. The Mr Dolomore in question was a young man of rather offensive type – athletic, dandiacal, and half-educated. It astonished Jasper that his sister could tolerate such an empty creature for a moment; who has not felt the like surprise with regard to women's inclinations? He talked with Dora about it, but she was not in her sister's confidence.

'I think you ought to have some influence with her,' Jasper said.

'Maud won't allow anyone to interfere in – her private affairs.'

'It would be unfortunate if she made me quarrel with her.'

'Oh, surely there isn't any danger of that?'

'I don't know, she mustn't be obstinate.'

Jasper himself saw a good deal of miscellaneous society at this time. He could not work so persistently as usual, and with wise tactics he used the seasons of enforced leisure to extend his acquaintance. Marian and he were together twice a week, in the evening.

Of his old Bohemian associates he kept up intimate relations with one only, and that was Whelpdale. This was in a measure obligatory, for Whelpdale frequently came to see him, and it would have been difficult to repel a man who was always making known how highly he esteemed the privilege of Milvain's friendship, and whose company on the whole was agreeable enough. At the present juncture Whelpdale's cheery flattery was a distinct assistance; it helped to support Jasper in his

self-confidence, and to keep the brightest complexion on the prospect to which he had committed himself.

'Whelpdale is anxious to make Marian's acquaintance,' Jasper
said to his sisters one day. 'Shall we have him here to-morrow
evening?'

'Just as you like,' Maud replied.

'You won't object, Dora?'

'Oh no! I rather like Mr Whelpdale.'

'If I were to repeat that to him he'd go wild with delight. But
don't be afraid; I shan't. I'll ask him to come for an hour, and
trust to his discretion not to bore us by staying too long.'

A note was posted to Whelpdale; he was invited to present
himself at eight o'clock, by which time Marian would have
arrived. Jasper's room was to be the scene of the assembly, and
punctual to the minute the literary adviser appeared. He was
dressed with all the finish his wardrobe allowed, and his face
beamed with gratification; it was rapture to him to enter the
presence of these three girls, one of whom he had, *more suo*,[34]
held in romantic remembrance since his one meeting with her at
Jasper's old lodgings. His eyes melted with tenderness as he
approached Dora and saw her smile of gracious recognition.
By Maud he was profoundly impressed. Marian inspired him
with no awe, but he fully appreciated the charm of her features
and her modest gravity. After all, it was to Dora that his eyes
turned again most naturally. He thought her exquisite, and,
rather than be long without a glimpse of her, he contented himself with fixing his eyes on the hem of her dress and the boot-toe
that occasionally peeped from beneath it.

As was to be expected in such a circle, conversation soon turned
to the subject of literary struggles.

'I always feel it rather humiliating,' said Jasper, 'that I have
gone through no very serious hardships. It must be so gratifying
to say to young fellows who are just beginning: "Ah, I remember
when I was within an ace of starving to death," and then come
out with Grub Street reminiscences of the most appalling kind.
Unfortunately, I have always had enough to eat.'

'I haven't,' exclaimed Whelpdale. 'I have lived for five days on
a few cents' worth of pea-nuts in the States.'

'What are pea-nuts, Mr Whelpdale?' asked Dora.

Delighted with the question, Whelpdale described that undesirable species of food.

'It was in Troy,' he went on, 'Troy, N.Y. To think that a man should live on peanuts in a town called Troy!'

'Tell us those adventures,' cried Jasper. 'It's a long time since I heard them, and the girls will enjoy it vastly.'

Dora looked at him with such good-humoured interest that the traveller needed no further persuasion.

'It came to pass in those days,' [35] he began, 'that I inherited from my godfather a small, a very small, sum of money. I was making strenuous efforts to write for magazines, with absolutely no encouragement. As everybody was talking just then of the Centennial Exhibition at Philadelphia, I conceived the brilliant idea of crossing the Atlantic, in the hope that I might find valuable literary material at the Exhibition – or Exposition, as they called it – and elsewhere. I won't trouble you with an account of how I lived whilst I still had money; sufficient that no one would accept the articles I sent to England, and that at last I got into perilous straits. I went to New York, and thought of returning home, but the spirit of adventure was strong in me. "I'll go West," I said to myself. "There I am bound to find material." And go I did, taking an emigrant ticket to Chicago. It was December, and I should like you to imagine what a journey of a thousand miles by an emigrant train meant at that season. The cars were deadly cold, and what with that and the hardness of the seats I found it impossible to sleep; it reminded me of tortures I had read about; I thought my brain would have burst with the need of sleeping. At Cleveland, in Ohio, we had to wait several hours in the night; I left the station and wandered about till I found myself on the edge of a great cliff that looked over Lake Erie. A magnificent picture! Brilliant moonlight, and all the lake away to the horizon frozen and covered with snow. The clocks struck two as I stood there.'

He was interrupted by the entrance of a servant who brought coffee.

'Nothing could be more welcome,' cried Dora. 'Mr Whelpdale makes one feel quite chilly.'

There was laughter and chatting whilst Maud poured out the beverage. Then Whelpdale pursued his narrative.

'I reached Chicago with not quite five dollars in my pockets, and, with a courage which I now marvel at, I paid immediately four dollars and a half for a week's board and lodging. "Well," I said to myself, "for a week I am safe. If I earn nothing in that time, at least I shall owe nothing when I have to turn out into the streets." It was a rather dirty little boarding-house, in Wabash Avenue, and occupied, as I soon found, almost entirely by actors. There was no fireplace in my bedroom, and if there had been I couldn't have afforded a fire. But that mattered little; what I had to do was to set forth and discover some way of making money. Don't suppose that I was in a desperate state of mind; how it was, I don't quite know, but I felt decidedly cheerful. It was pleasant to be in this new region of the earth, and I went about the town like a tourist who has abundant resources.'

He sipped his coffee.

'I saw nothing for it but to apply at the office of some news-paper, and as I happened to light upon the biggest of them first of all, I put on a bold face, marched in, asked if I could see the editor. There was no difficulty whatever about this; I was told to ascend by means of the "elevator" to an upper storey, and there I walked into a comfortable little room where a youngish man sat smoking a cigar at a table covered with print and manu-script. I introduced myself, stated my business. "Can you give me work of any kind on your paper?" "Well, what experience have you had?" "None whatever." The editor smiled. "I'm very much afraid you would be no use to us. But what do you think you could do?" Well now, there was but one thing that by any possibility I could do. I asked him: "Do you publish any fic-tion – short stories?" "Yes, we're always glad of a short story, if it's good." This was a big daily paper; they have weekly supple-ments of all conceivable kinds of matter. "Well," I said, "if I write a story of English life, will you consider it?" "With pleasure." I left him, and went out as if my existence were henceforth provided for.'

He laughed heartily, and was joined by his hearers.

'It was a great thing to be permitted to write a story, but then – *what* story? I went down to the shore of Lake Michigan; walked there for half an hour in an icy wind. Then I looked for a stationer's shop, and laid out a few of my remaining cents in the purchase of pen, ink, and paper – my stock of all these things was at an end when I left New York. Then back to the boarding-house. Impossible to write in my bedroom, the temperature was below zero; there was no choice but to sit down in the common room, a place like the smoke-room of a poor commercial hotel in England. A dozen men were gathered about the fire, smoking, talking, quarrelling. Favourable conditions, you see, for literary effort. But the story had to be written, and write it I did, sitting there at the end of a deal table; I finished it in less than a couple of days, a good long story, enough to fill three columns of the huge paper. I stand amazed at my power of concentration as often as I think of it!'

'And was it accepted?' asked Dora.

'You shall hear. I took my manuscript to the editor, and he told me to come and see him again next morning. I didn't forget the appointment. As I entered he smiled in a very promising way, and said, "I think your story will do. I'll put it into the Saturday supplement. Call on Saturday morning and I'll re-munerate you." How well I remember that word "'remunerate"! I have had an affection for the word ever since. And remunerate me he did; scribbled something on a scrap of paper, which I presented to the cashier. The sum was eighteen dollars. Behold me saved!'

He sipped his coffee again.

'I have never come across an English editor who treated me with anything like that consideration and general kindliness. How the man had time, in his position, to see me so often, and do things in such a human way, I can't understand. Imagine any-one trying the same at the office of a London newspaper! To be-gin with, one couldn't see the editor at all. I shall always think with profound gratitude of that man with the peaked brown beard and pleasant smile.'

'But did the pea-nuts come after that?' inquired Dora.

'Alas! they did. For some months I supported myself in Chicago, writing for that same paper, and for others. But at length the flow of my inspiration was checked; I had written myself out. And I began to grow home-sick, wanted to get back to England. The result was that I found myself one day in New

York again, but without money enough to pay for a passage home. I tried to write one more story. But it happened, as I was looking over newspapers in a reading-room, that I saw one of my Chicago tales copied into a paper published at Troy. Now Troy was not very far off, and it occurred to me that, if I went there, the editor of this paper might be disposed to employ me, seeing he had a taste for my fiction. And I went, up the Hudson by steamboat. On landing at Troy I was as badly off as when I reached Chicago; I had less than a dollar. And the worst of it was I had come on a vain errand; the editor treated me with scant courtesy, and no work was to be got. I took a little room, paying for it day by day, and in the meantime I fed on those loathsome pea-nuts, buying a handful in the street now and then. And I assure you I looked starvation in the face.'

'What sort of a town is Troy?' asked Marian, speaking for the first time.

'Don't ask me. They make straw-hats there principally, and they sell pea-nuts. More I remember not.'

'But you *didn't* starve to death,' said Maud.

'No, I just didn't. I went one afternoon into a lawyer's office, thinking I might get some copying work, and there I found an odd-looking old man, sitting with an open Bible on his knees. He explained to me that he wasn't the lawyer; that the lawyer was away on business, and that he was just guarding the office. Well, could he help me? He meditated, and a thought occurred to him. "Go," he said, "to such and such a boarding-house, and ask for Mr Freeman Sterling. He is just starting on a business tour, and wants a young man to accompany him." I didn't dream of asking what the business was, but sped, as fast as my trembling limbs would carry me, to the address he had mentioned. I asked for Mr Freeman Sterling, and found him. He was a photographer, and his business at present was to go about getting orders for the reproducing of old portraits. A good-natured young fellow. He said he liked the look of me, and on the spot engaged me to assist him in a house-to-house visitation. He would pay for my board and lodging, and give me a commission on all orders I obtained. Forthwith I sat down to a "square meal," and ate – my conscience, how I ate !'

'You were not eminently successful in that pursuit, I think?' said Jasper.

'I don't think I got half a dozen orders. Yet that good Samaritan supported me for five or six weeks, whilst we travelled from Troy to Boston. It couldn't go on; I was ashamed of myself; at last I told him that we must part. Upon my word, I believe he would have paid my expenses for another month; why, I can't understand. But he had a vast respect for me because I had written in newspapers, and I do seriously think that he didn't like to tell me I was a useless fellow. We parted on the very best of terms in Boston.'

'And you again had recourse to pea-nuts?' asked Dora.

'Well, no. In the meantime I had written to someone in England, begging the loan of just enough money to enable me to get home. The money came a day after I had seen Sterling off by train.'

An hour and a half quickly passed, and Jasper, who wished to have a few minutes of Marian's company before it was time for her to go, cast a significant glance at his sisters. Dora said innocently:

'You wished me to tell you when it was half-past nine, Marian.'

And Marian rose. This was a signal Whelpdale could not disregard. Immediately he made ready for his own departure, and in less than five minutes was gone, his face at the last moment expressing blended delight and pain.

'Too good of you to have asked me to come,' he said with gratitude to Jasper, who went to the door with him. 'You are a happy man, by Jove! A happy man!'

When Jasper returned to the room his sisters had vanished. Marian stood by the fire. He drew near to her, took her hands, and repeated laughingly Whelpdale's last words.

'Is it true?' she asked.

'Tolerably true, I think.'

'Then I am as happy as you are.'

He released her hands, and moved a little apart.

'Marian, I have been thinking about that letter to your father. I had better get it written, don't you think?'

She gazed at him with troubled eyes.

'Perhaps you had. Though we said it might be delayed until –'

'Yes, I know. But I suspect you had rather I didn't wait any longer. Isn't that the truth?'

'Partly. Do just as you wish, Jasper.'

'I'll go and see him, if you like.'

'I am so afraid – No, writing will be better.'

'Very well. Then he shall have the letter to-morrow afternoon.'

'Don't let it come before the last post. I had so much rather not. Manage it, if you can.'

'Very well. Now go and say good-night to the girls. It's a vile night, and you must get home as soon as possible.'

She turned away, but again came towards him, murmuring:

'Just a word or two more.'

'About the letter?'

'No. You haven't said –'

He laughed.

'And you couldn't go away contentedly unless I repeated for the hundredth time that I love you?'

Marian searched his countenance.

'Do you think it foolish? I live only on those words.'

'Well, they are better than pea-nuts.'

'Oh don't ! I can't bear to –'

Jasper was unable to understand that such a jest sounded to her like profanity. She hid her face against him, and whispered the words that would have enraptured her had they but come from his lips. The young man found it pleasant enough to be worshipped, but he could not reply as she desired. A few phrases of tenderness, and his love-vocabulary was exhausted; he even grew weary when something more – the indefinite something – was vaguely required of him.

'You are a dear, good, tender-hearted girl,' he said, stroking her short, soft hair, which was exquisite to the hand. 'Now go and get ready.'

She left him, but stood for a few moments on the landing before going to the girls' room.

Chapter 29

CATASTROPHE

MARIAN had finished the rough draft of a paper on James Harrington,[36] author of 'Oceana.' Her father went through it by the midnight lamp, and the next morning made his comments. A black sky and sooty rain strengthened his inclination to sit by the study fire and talk at large in a tone of flattering benignity.

'Those paragraphs on the Rota Club strike me as singularly happy,' he said, tapping the manuscript with the mouthpiece of his pipe. 'Perhaps you might say a word or two more about Cyriac Skinner; one mustn't be too allusive with general readers, their ignorance is incredible. But there is so little to add to this paper – so little to alter – that I couldn't feel justified in sending it as my own work. I think it is altogether too good to appear anonymously. You must sign it, Marian, and have the credit that is due to you.'

'Oh, do you think it's worth while?' answered the girl, who was far from easy under this praise. Of late there had been too much of it; it made her regard her father with suspicions which increased her sense of trouble in keeping a momentous secret from him.

'Yes, yes; you had better sign it. I'll undertake there's no other girl of your age who could turn out such a piece of work. I think we may fairly say that your apprenticeship is at an end. Before long,' he smiled anxiously, 'I may be counting upon you as a valued contributor. And that reminds me; would you be disposed to call with me on the Jedwoods at their house next Sunday?'

Marian understood the intention that lay beneath this proposal. She saw that her father would not allow himself to seem discouraged by the silence she maintained on the great subject which awaited her decision. He was endeavouring gradually to involve her in his ambitions, to carry her forward by insensible steps. It pained her to observe the suppressed eagerness with which he looked for her reply.

'I will go if you wish, father, but I had rather not.'

'I feel sure you would like Mrs Jedwood. One has no great opinion of her novels, but she is a woman of some intellect. Let me book you for next Sunday; surely I have a claim to your companionship now and then.'

Marian kept silence. Yule puffed at his pipe, then said with a speculative air:

'I suppose it has never even occurred to you to try your hand at fiction?'

'I haven't the least inclination that way.'

'You would probably do something rather good if you tried. But I don't urge it. My own efforts in that line were a mistake, I'm disposed to think. Not that the things were worse than multitudes of books which nowadays go down with the many-headed. But I never quite knew what I wished to be at fiction. I wasn't content to write a mere narrative of the exciting kind, yet I couldn't hit upon subjects of intellectual cast that altogether satisfied me. Well, well; I have tried my hand at most kinds of literature. Assuredly I merit the title of man of letters.'

'You certainly do.'

'By-the-by, what should you think of that title for a review – Letters? It has never been used, so far as I know. I like the word "letters." How much better "a man of letters" than "a literary man"! And apropos of that, when was the word "literature" first used in our modern sense to signify a body of writing? In Johnson's day it was pretty much the equivalent of our "culture." You remember his saying, "It is surprising how little literature people have." His dictionary, I believe, defines the word as "learning, skill in letters" – nothing else.'

It was characteristic of Yule to dwell with gusto on little points such as this; he prosed for a quarter of an hour, with a pause every now and then whilst he kept his pipe alight.

'I think Letters wouldn't be amiss,' he said at length, returning to the suggestion which he wished to keep before Marian's mind. 'It would clearly indicate our scope. No articles on bimetallism, as Quarmby said – wasn't it Quarmby?'

He laughed idly.

'Yes, I must ask Jedwood how he likes the name.'

Though Marian feared the result, she was glad when Jasper

made up his mind to write to her father. Since it was determined that her money could not be devoted to establishing a review, the truth ought to be confessed before Yule had gone too far in nursing his dangerous hope. Without the support of her love and all the prospects connected with it, she would hardly have been capable of giving a distinct refusal when her reply could no longer be postponed; to hold the money merely for her own benefit would have seemed to her too selfish, however slight her faith in the project on which her father built so exultantly. When it was declared that she had accepted an offer of marriage, a sacrifice of that kind could no longer be expected of her. Opposition must direct itself against the choice she had made. It would be stern, perhaps relentless; but she felt able to face any extremity of wrath. Her nerves quivered, but in her heart was an exhaustless source of courage.

That a change had somehow come about in the girl Yule was aware. He observed her with the closest study day after day. Her health seemed to have improved; after a long spell of work she had not the air of despondent weariness which had sometimes irritated him, sometimes made him uneasy. She was more womanly in her bearing and speech, and exercised an independence, appropriate indeed to her years, but such as had not formerly declared itself. The question with her father was whether these things resulted simply from her consciousness of possessing what to her seemed wealth, or something else had happened of the nature that he dreaded. An alarming symptom was the increased attention she paid to her personal appearance; its indications were not at all prominent, but Yule, on the watch for such things, did not overlook them. True, this also might mean nothing but a sense of relief from narrow means; a girl would naturally adorn herself a little under the circumstances.

His doubts came to an end two days after that proposal of a title for the new review. As he sat in his study the servant brought him a letter delivered by the last evening post. The handwriting was unknown to him; the contents were these:

'DEAR MR YULE, – It is my desire to write to you with perfect frankness and as simply as I can on a subject which has the deepest interest for me, and which I trust you will consider in that spirit of kindness with which you received me when we first met at Finden.

'On the occasion of that meeting I had the happiness of being presented to Miss Yule. She was not totally a stranger to me; at that time I used to work pretty regularly in the Museum Reading-room, and there I had seen Miss Yule, had ventured to observe her at moments with a young man's attention, and had felt my interest aroused, though I did not know her name. To find her at Finden seemed to me a very unusual and delightful piece of good fortune. When I came back from my holiday I was conscious of a new purpose in life, a new desire and a new motive to help me on in my chosen career.

'My mother's death led to my sisters' coming to live in London. Already there had been friendly correspondence between Miss Yule and the two girls, and now that the opportunity offered they began to see each other frequently. As I was often at my sisters' lodgings it came about that I met Miss Yule there from time to time. In this way was confirmed my attachment to your daughter. The better I knew her, the more worthy I found her of reverence and love.

'Would it not have been natural for me to seek a renewal of the acquaintance with yourself which had begun in the country? Gladly I should have done so. Before my sisters' coming to London I did call one day at your house with the desire of seeing you, but unfortunately you were not at home. Very soon after that I learnt to my extreme regret that my connection with *The Current* and its editor would make any repetition of my visit very distasteful to you. I was conscious of nothing in my literary life that could justly offend you – and at this day I can say the same – but I shrank from the appearance of importunity, and for some months I was deeply distressed by the fear that what I most desired in life had become unattainable. My means were very slight; I had no choice but to take such work as offered, and mere chance had put me into a position which threatened ruin to the hope that you would some day regard me as a not unworthy suitor for your daughter's hand.

'Circumstances have led me to a step which at that time seemed impossible. Having discovered that Miss Yule returned the feeling I entertained for her, I have asked her to be my wife, and she has consented. It is now my hope that you will permit me to call upon you. Miss Yule is aware that I am writing this letter; will you not let her plead for me, seeing that only by an unhappy chance have I been kept aloof from you? Marian and I are equally desirous that you should approve our union; without that approval, indeed, something will be lacking to the happiness for which we hope.

       'Believe me to be sincerely yours,

                   'JASPER MILVAIN.'

Half an hour after reading this Yule was roused from a fit of the gloomiest brooding by Marian's entrance. She came towards him timidly, with pale countenance. He had glanced round to see who it was, but at once turned his head again.

'Will you forgive me for keeping this secret from you, father?'

'Forgive you?' he replied in a hard, deliberate voice. 'I assure you it is a matter of perfect indifference to me. You are long since of age, and I have no power whatever to prevent your falling a victim to any schemer who takes your fancy. It would be folly in me to discuss the question. I recognise your right to have as many secrets as may seem good to you. To talk of forgiveness is the merest affectation.'

'No, I spoke sincerely. If it had seemed possible I should gladly have let you know about this from the first. That would have been natural and right. But you know what prevented me.'

'I do. I will try to hope that even a sense of shame had something to do with it.'

'That had nothing to do with it,' said Marian, coldly. 'I have never had reason to feel ashamed.'

'Be it so. I trust you may never have reason to feel repentance. May I ask when you propose to be married?'

'I don't know when it will take place.'

'As soon, I suppose, as your uncle's executors have discharged a piece of business which is distinctly germane to the matter?'

'Perhaps.'

'Does your mother know?'

'I have just told her.'

'Very well, then it seems to me that there's nothing more to be said.'

'Do you refuse to see Mr Milvain?'

'Most decidedly I do. You will have the goodness to inform him that that is my reply to his letter.'

'I don't think that is the behaviour of a gentleman,' said Marian, her eyes beginning to gleam with resentment.

'I am obliged to you for your instruction.'

'Will you tell me, father, in plain words, why you dislike Mr Milvain?'

'I am not inclined to repeat what I have already fruitlessly told you. For the sake of a clear understanding, however, I will let you know the practical result of my dislike. From the day of your marriage with that man you are nothing to me. I shall distinctly forbid you to enter my house. You make your choice, and go your own way. I shall hope never to see your face again.'

Their eyes met, and the look of each seemed to fascinate the other.

'If you have made up your mind to that,' said Marian in a shaking voice, 'I can remain here no longer. Such words are senselessly cruel. To-morrow I shall leave the house.'

'I repeat that you are of age, and perfectly independent. It can be nothing to me how soon you go. You have given proof that I am of less than no account to you, and doubtless the sooner we cease to afflict each other the better.'

It seemed as if the effect of these conflicts with her father were to develop in Marian a vehemence of temper which at length matched that of which Yule was the victim. Her face, outlined to express a gentle gravity, was now haughtily passionate; nostrils and lips thrilled with wrath, and her eyes were magnificent in their dark fieriness.

'You shall not need to tell me that again,' she answered, and immediately left him.

She went into the sitting-room, where Mrs Yule was awaiting the result of the interview.

'Mother,' she said, with stern gentleness, 'this house can no longer be a home for me. I shall go away to-morrow, and live in lodgings until the time of my marriage.'

Mrs Yule uttered a cry of pain, and started up.

'Oh, don't do that, Marian! What has he said to you? Come

and talk to me, darling – tell me what he's said – don't look like that!'

She clung to the girl despairingly, terrified by a transformation she would have thought impossible.

'He says that if I marry Mr Milvain he hopes never to see my face again. I can't stay here. You shall come and see me, and we will be the same to each other as always. But father has treated me too unjustly. I can't live near him after this.'

'He doesn't mean it,' sobbed her mother. 'He says what he's sorry for as soon as the words are spoken. He loves you too much, my darling, to drive you away like that. It's his disappointment, Marian; that's all it is. He counted on it so much. I've heard him talk of it in his sleep; he made so sure that he was going to have that new magazine, and the disappointment makes him that he doesn't know what he's saying. Only wait and see; he'll tell you he didn't mean it, I know he will. Only leave him alone till he's had time to get over it. Do forgive him this once.'

'It's like a madman to talk in that way,' said the girl, releasing herself. 'Whatever his disappointment, I can't endure it. I have worked hard for him, very hard, ever since I was old enough, and he owes me some kindness, some respect. It would be different if he had the least reason for his hatred of Jasper. It is nothing but insensate prejudice, the result of his quarrels with other people. What right has he to insult me by representing my future husband as a scheming hypocrite?'

'My love, he has had so much to bear – it's made him so quick-tempered.'

'Then I am quick-tempered too, and the sooner we are apart the better, as he said himself.'

'Oh, but you have always been such a patient girl.'

'My patience is at an end when I am treated as if I had neither rights nor feelings. However wrong the choice I had made, this was not the way to behave to me. His disappointment? Is there a natural law, then, that a daughter must be sacrificed to her father? My husband will have as much need of that money as my father has, and he will be able to make far better use of it. It was wrong even to ask me to give my money away like that. I have a right to happiness, as well as other women.'

She was shaken with hysterical passion, the natural conse-

quence of this outbreak in a nature such as hers. Her mother, in
the meantime, grew stronger by force of profound love that at
length had found its opportunity of expression. Presently she
persuaded Marian to come upstairs with her, and before long the
overburdened breast was relieved by a flow of tears. But Marian's
purpose remained unshaken.

'It is impossible for us to see each other day after day,' she
said when calmer. 'He can't control his anger against me, and I
suffer too much when I am made to feel like this. I shall take a
lodging not far off, where you can see me often.'

'But you have no money, Marian,' replied Mrs Yule, miserably.

'No money? As if I couldn't borrow a few pounds until all my
own comes to me! Dora Milvain can lend me all I shall want;
it won't make the least difference to her. I must have my money
very soon now.'

At about half-past eleven Mrs Yule went downstairs, and
entered the study.

'If you are coming to speak about Marian,' said her husband,
turning upon her with savage eyes, 'you can save your breath. I
won't hear her name mentioned.'

She faltered, but overcame her weakness.

'You are driving her away from us, Alfred. It isn't right! Oh,
it isn't right!'

'If she didn't go I should, so understand that! And if I go,
you have seen the last of me. Make your choice, make your
choice!'

He had yielded himself to that perverse frenzy which impels a
man to acts and utterances most wildly at conflict with reason.
His sense of the monstrous irrationality to which he was committed completed what was begun in him by the bitterness of a
great frustration.

'If I wasn't a poor, helpless woman,' replied his wife, sinking
upon a chair and crying without raising her hands to her face,
'I'd go and live with her till she was married, and then make a
home for myself. But I haven't a penny, and I'm too old to earn
my own living; I should only be a burden to her.'

'That shall be no hindrance,' cried Yule. 'Go, by all means;
you shall have a sufficient allowance as long as I can continue
to work, and when I'm past that, your lot will be no harder than

mine. Your daughter had the chance of making provision for my old age, at no expense to herself. But that was asking too much of her. Go, by all means, and leave me to make what I can of the rest of my life; perhaps I may save a few years still from the curse brought upon me by my own folly.'

It was idle to address him. Mrs Yule went into the sitting-room, and there sat weeping for an hour. Then she extinguished the lights, and crept upstairs in silence.

Yule passed the night in the study. Towards morning he slept for an hour or two, just long enough to let the fire go out and to get thoroughly chilled. When he opened his eyes a muddy twilight had begun to show at the window; the sounds of a clapping door within the house, which had probably awakened him, made him aware that the servant was already up.

He drew up the blind. There seemed to be a frost, for the moisture of last night had all disappeared, and the yard upon which the window looked was unusually clean. With a glance at the black grate he extinguished his lamp, and went out into the passage. A few minutes' groping for his overcoat and hat, and he left the house.

His purpose was to warm himself with a vigorous walk, and at the same time to shake off, if possible, the nightmare of his rage and hopelessness. He had no distinct feeling with regard to his behaviour of the past evening; he neither justified nor condemned himself; he did not ask himself whether Marian would to-day leave her home, or if her mother would take him at his word and also depart. These seemed to be details which his brain was too weary to consider. But he wished to be away from the wretchedness of his house, and to let things go as they would whilst he was absent. As he closed the front door he felt as if he were escaping from an atmosphere that threatened to stifle him.

His steps directing themselves more by habit than with any deliberate choice, he walked towards Camden Road. When he had reached Camden Town railway-station he was attracted by a coffee-stall; a draught of the steaming liquid, no matter its quality, would help his blood to circulate. He laid down his penny, and first warmed his hands by holding them round the cup. Whilst standing thus he noticed that the objects at which he looked had a blurred appearance; his eyesight seemed to have become worse this morning. Only a result of his insufficient sleep perhaps. He took up a scrap of newspaper that lay on the stall; he could read it, but one of his eyes was certainly weaker than the other; trying to see with that one alone, he found that everything became misty.

He laughed, as if the threat of new calamity were an amusement in his present state of mind. And at the same moment his look encountered that of a man who had drawn near to him, a shabbily-dressed man of middle age, whose face did not correspond with his attire.

'Will you give me a cup of coffee?' asked the stranger, in a low voice and with a shame-faced manner. 'It would be a great kindness.'

The accent was that of good breeding. Yule hesitated in surprise for a moment, then said :

'Have one by all means. Would you care for anything to eat?'

'I am much obliged to you. I think I should be none the worse for one of those solid slices of bread and butter.'

The stall-keeper was just extinguishing his lights; the frosty sky showed a pale gleam of sunrise.

'Hard times, I'm afraid,' remarked Yule, as his beneficiary began to eat the luncheon with much appearance of grateful appetite.

'Very hard times.' He had a small, thin, colourless countenance, with large, pathetic eyes; a slight moustache and curly beard. His clothes were such as would be worn by some very poor clerk. 'I came here an hour ago,' he continued, 'with the hope of meeting an acquaintance who generally goes from this station at a certain time. I have missed him, and in doing so I missed what I had thought my one chance of a breakfast. When one has neither dined nor supped on the previous day, breakfast becomes a meal of some importance.'

'True. Take another slice.'

'I am greatly obliged to you.'

'Not at all. I have known hard times myself, and am likely to know worse.'

'I trust not. — This is the first time that I have positively begged. I should have been too much ashamed to beg of the kind

of men who are usually at these places; they certainly have no
money to spare. I was thinking of making an appeal at a baker's
shop, but it is very likely I should have been handed over to a
policeman. Indeed I don't know what I should have done; the
last point of endurance was almost reached. I have no clothes
but these I wear, and they are few enough for the season. Still, I
suppose the waistcoat must have gone.'

He did not talk like a beggar who is trying to excite compassion, but with a sort of detached curiosity concerning the difficulties of his position.

'You can find nothing to do?' said the man of letters.

'Positively nothing. By profession I am a surgeon, but it's a
long time since I practised. Fifteen years ago I was comfortably
established at Wakefield; I was married and had one child. But
my capital ran out, and my practice, never anything to boast of,
fell to nothing. I succeeded in getting a place as an assistant to a
man at Chester. We sold up, and started on the journey.'

He paused, looking at Yule in a strange way.

'What happened then?'

'You probably don't remember a railway accident that took
place near Crewe in that year – it was 1869? I and my wife
and child were alone in a carriage that was splintered. One
moment I was talking with them, in fairly good spirits, and my
wife was laughing at something I had said; the next, there were
two crushed, bleeding bodies at my feet. I had a broken arm, that
was all. Well, they were killed on the instant; they didn't suffer.
That has been my one consolation.'

Yule kept the silence of sympathy.

'I was in a lunatic asylum for more than a year after that,'
continued the man. 'Unhappily, I didn't lose my senses at the
moment; it took two or three weeks to bring me to that pass. But
I recovered, and there has been no return of the disease. Don't
suppose that I am still of unsound mind. There can be little
doubt that poverty will bring me to that again in the end; but as
yet I am perfectly sane. I have supported myself in various ways.
No, I don't drink; I see the question in your face. But I am
physically weak, and, to quote Mrs Gummidge,[37] "things go
contrary with me." There's no use lamenting; this breakfast has
helped me on, and I feel in much better spirits.'

'Your surgical knowledge is no use to you?'

The other shook his head and sighed.

'Did you ever give any special attention to diseases of the eyes?'

'Special, no. But of course I had some acquaintance with the subject.'

'Could you tell by examination whether a man was threatened with cataract, or anything of that kind?'

'I think I could.'

'I am speaking of myself.'

The stranger made a close scrutiny of Yule's face, and asked certain questions with reference to his visual sensations.

'I hardly like to propose it,' he said at length, 'but if you were willing to accompany me to a very poor room that I have not far from here, I could make the examination formally.'

'I will go with you.'

They turned away from the stall, and the ex-surgeon led into a by-street. Yule wondered at himself for caring to seek such a singular consultation, but he had a pressing desire to hear some opinion as to the state of his eyes. Whatever the stranger might tell him, he would afterwards have recourse to a man of recognised standing; but just now companionship of any kind was welcome, and the poor hungry fellow, with his dolorous life-story, had made appeal to his sympathies. To give money under guise of a fee would be better than merely offering alms.

'This is the house,' said his guide, pausing at a dirty door. 'It isn't inviting, but the people are honest, so far as I know. My room is at the top.'

'Lead on,' answered Yule.

In the room they entered was nothing noticeable; it was only the poorest possible kind of bedchamber, or all but the poorest possible. Daylight had now succeeded to dawn, yet the first thing the stranger did was to strike a match and light a candle.

'Will you kindly place yourself with your back to the window?' he said. 'I am going to apply what is called the catoptric test. You have probably heard of it?'

'My ignorance of scientific matters is fathomless.'

The other smiled, and at once offered a simple explanation of the term. By the appearance of the candle as it reflected itself in the patient's eye it was possible, he said, to decide whether cataract had taken hold upon the organ.

For a minute or two he conducted his experiment carefully, and Yule was at no loss to read the result upon his face.

'How long have you suspected that something was wrong?' the surgeon asked, as he put down the candle.

'For several months.'

'You haven't consulted anyone?'

'No one. I have kept putting it off. Just tell me what you have discovered.'

'The back of the right lens is affected beyond a doubt.'

'That means, I take it, that before very long I shall be practically blind?'

'I don't like to speak with an air of authority. After all I am only a surgeon who has bungled himself into pauperdom. You must see a competent man; that much I can tell you in all earnestness. Do you use your eyes much?'

'Fourteen hours a day, that's all.'

'H'm! You are a literary man, I think?'

'I am. My name is Alfred Yule.'

He had some faint hope that the name might be recognised; that would have gone far, for the moment, to counteract his trouble. But not even this poor satisfaction was to be granted him; to his hearer the name evidently conveyed nothing.

'See a competent man, Mr Yule. Science has advanced rapidly since the day when I was a student; I am only able to assure you of the existence of disease.'

They talked for half an hour, until both were shaking with cold. Then Yule thrust his hand into his pocket.

'You will of course allow me to offer such return as I am able,' he said. 'The information isn't pleasant, but I am glad to have it.'

He laid five shillings on the chest of drawers – there was no table. The stranger expressed his gratitude.

'My name is Duke,' he said, 'and I was christened Victor – possibly because I was doomed to defeat in life. I wish you could have associated the memory of me with happier circumstances.'

They shook hands, and Yule quitted the house.

He came out again by Camden Town station. The coffee-stall had disappeared; the traffic of the great highway was growing uproarious. Among all the strugglers for existence who rushed this way and that, Alfred Yule felt himself a man chosen for fate's heaviest infliction. He never questioned the accuracy of the stranger's judgment, and he hoped for no mitigation of the doom it threatened. His life was over – and wasted.

He might as well go home, and take his place meekly by the fireside. He was beaten. Soon to be a useless old man, a burden and annoyance to whosoever had pity on him.

It was a curious effect of the imagination that since coming into the open air again his eyesight seemed to be far worse than before. He irritated his nerves of vision by incessant tests, closing first one eye then the other, comparing his view of nearer objects with the appearance of others more remote, fancying an occasional pain – which could have had no connection with his disease. The literary projects which had stirred so actively in his mind twelve hours ago were become an insubstantial memory; to the one crushing blow had succeeded a second, which was fatal. He could hardly recall what special piece of work he had been engaged upon last night. His thoughts were such as if actual blindness had really fallen upon him.

At half-past eight he entered the house. Mrs Yule was standing at the foot of the stairs; she looked at him, then turned away towards the kitchen. He went upstairs. On coming down again he found breakfast ready as usual, and seated himself at the table. Two letters waited him there; he opened them.

When Mrs Yule came into the room a few moments later she was astonished by a burst of loud, mocking laughter from her husband, excited, as it appeared, by something he was reading.

'Is Marian up?' he asked, turning to her.

'Yes.'

'She is not coming to breakfast?'

'No.'

'Then just take that letter to her, and ask her to read it.'

Mrs Yule ascended to her daughter's bedroom. She knocked, was bidden enter, and found Marian packing clothes in a trunk. The girl looked as if she had been up all night; her eyes bore the traces of much weeping.

'He has come back, dear,' said Mrs Yule, in the low voice of apprehension, 'and he says you are to read this letter.'

Marian took the sheet, unfolded it, and read. As soon as she had reached the end she looked wildly at her mother, seemed to endeavour vainly to speak, then fell to the floor in unconsciousness. The mother was only just able to break the violence of her fall. Having snatched a pillow and placed it beneath Marian's head, she rushed to the door and called loudly for her husband, who in a moment appeared.

'What is it?' she cried to him. 'Look, she has fallen down in a faint. Why are you treating her like this?'

'Attend to her,' Yule replied roughly. 'I suppose you know better than I do what to do when a person faints.'

The swoon lasted for several minutes.

'What's in the letter?' asked Mrs Yule whilst chafing the lifeless hands.

'Her money's lost. The people who were to pay it have just failed.'

'She won't get anything?'

'Most likely nothing at all.'

The letter was a private communication from one of John Yule's executors. It seemed likely that the demand upon Turberville & Co. for an account of the deceased partner's share in their business had helped to bring about a crisis in affairs that were already unstable. Something might be recovered in the legal proceedings that would result, but there were circumstances which made the outlook very doubtful.

As Marian came to herself her father left the room. An hour afterwards Mrs Yule summoned him again to the girl's chamber; he went, and found Marian lying on the bed, looking like one who had been long ill.

'I wish to ask you a few questions,' she said, without raising herself. 'Must my legacy necessarily be paid out of that investment?'

'It must. Those are the terms of the will.'

'If nothing can be recovered from those people, I have no remedy?'

'None whatever that I can see.'

'But when a firm is bankrupt they generally pay some portion of their debts?'

'Sometimes. I know nothing of the case.'

'This of course happens to me,' Marian said, with intense bitterness. 'None of the other legatees will suffer, I suppose?'

'Someone must, but to a very small extent.'

'Of course. When shall I have direct information?'

'You can write to Mr Holden; you have his address.'

'Thank you. That's all.'

He was dismissed, and went quietly away.

Chapter 30

WAITING ON DESTINY

THROUGHOUT the day Marian kept her room. Her intention to leave the house was, of course, abandoned; she was the prisoner of fate. Mrs Yule would have tended her with unremitting devotion, but the girl desired to be alone. At times she lay in silent anguish; frequently her tears broke forth, and she sobbed until weariness overcame her. In the afternoon she wrote a letter to Mr Holden, begging that she might be kept constantly acquainted with the progress of things.

At five her mother brought tea.

'Wouldn't it be better if you went to bed now, Marian?' she suggested.

'To bed? But I am going out in an hour or two.'

'Oh, you can't, dear! It's so bitterly cold. It wouldn't be good for you.'

'I have to go out, mother, so we won't speak of it.'

It was not safe to reply. Mrs Yule sat down, and watched the girl raise the cup to her mouth with trembling hand.

'This won't make any difference to you – in the end, my darling,' the mother ventured to say at length, alluding for the first time to the effect of the catastrophe on Marian's immediate prospects.

'Of course not,' was the reply, in a tone of self-persuasion.

'Mr Milvain is sure to have plenty of money before long.'

'Yes.'

'You feel much better now, don't you?'

'Much. I am quite well again.'

At seven, Marian went out. Finding herself weaker than she had thought, she stopped an empty cab that presently passed her, and so drove to the Milvains' lodgings. In her agitation she inquired for Mr Milvain, instead of for Dora, as was her habit; it mattered very little, for the landlady and her servants were of course under no misconception regarding this young lady's visits. Jasper was at home, and working. He had but to look at Marian to see that something wretched had been going on at her home; naturally he supposed it the result of his letter to Mr Yule.

'Your father has been behaving brutally,' he said, holding her hands and gazing anxiously at her.

'There is something far worse than that, Jasper.'

'Worse?'

She threw off her outdoor things, then took the fatal letter from her pocket and handed it to him. Jasper gave a whistle of consternation, and looked vacantly from the paper to Marian's countenance.

'How the deuce comes this about?' he exclaimed. 'Why, wasn't your uncle aware of the state of things?'

'Perhaps he was. He may have known that the legacy was a mere form.'

'You are the only one affected?'

'So father says. It's sure to be the case.'

'This has upset you horribly, I can see. Sit down, Marian. When did the letter come?'

'This morning.'

'And you have been fretting over it all day. But come, we must keep up our courage; you may get something substantial out of the scoundrels still.'

Even whilst he spoke his eyes wandered absently. On the last word his voice failed, and he fell into abstraction. Marian's look was fixed upon him, and he became conscious of it. He tried to smile.

'What were you writing?' she asked, making involuntary diversion from the calamitous theme.

'Rubbish for the Will-o'-the-Wisp. Listen to this paragraph about English concert audiences.'

It was as necessary to him as to her to have a respite before the graver discussion began. He seized gladly the opportunity she offered, and read several pages of manuscript, slipping from one topic to another. To hear him one would have supposed that he was in his ordinary mood; he laughed at his own jokes and points.

'They'll have to pay me more,' was the remark with which he closed. 'I only wanted to make myself indispensable to them, and at the end of this year I shall feel pretty sure of that. They'll have to give me two guineas a column; by Jove! they will.'

'And you may hope for much more than that, mayn't you, before long?'

'Oh, I shall transfer myself to a better paper presently. It seems to me I must be stirring to some purpose.'

He gave her a significant look.

'What shall we do, Jasper?'

'Work and wait, I suppose.'

'There's something I must tell you. Father said I had better sign that Harrington article myself. If I do that, I shall have a right to the money, I think. It will at least be eight guineas. And why shouldn't I go on writing for myself – for us? You can help me to think of subjects.'

'First of all, what about my letter to your father? We are forgetting all about it.'

'He refused to answer.'

Marian avoided closer description of what had happened. It was partly that she felt ashamed of her father's unreasoning wrath, and feared lest Jasper's pride might receive an injury from which she in turn would suffer; partly that she was unwilling to pain her lover by making display of all she had undergone.

'Oh, he refused to reply! Surely that is extreme behaviour.'

What she dreaded seemed to be coming to pass. Jasper stood rather stiffly, and threw his head back.

'You know the reason, dear. That prejudice has entered into his very life. It is not you he dislikes; that is impossible. He thinks of you only as he would of anyone connected with Mr Fadge.'

'Well, well; it isn't a matter of much moment. But what I have in mind is this. Will it be possible for you, whilst living at home, to take a position of independence, and say that you are going to work for your own profit?'

'At least I might claim half the money I can earn. And I was thinking more of –'

'Of what?'

'When I am your wife, I may be able to help. I could earn thirty or forty pounds a year, I think. That would pay the rent of a small house.'

She spoke with shaken voice, her eyes fixed upon his face.

'But, my dear Marian, we surely oughtn't to think of marrying so long as expenses are so nicely fitted as all that?'

'No. I only meant –'

She faltered, and her tongue became silent as her heart sank.

'It simply means,' pursued Jasper, seating himself and crossing his legs, 'that I must move heaven and earth to improve my position. You know that my faith in myself is not small; there's no knowing what I might do if I used every effort. But, upon my word, I don't see much hope of our being able to marry for a year or two under the most favourable circumstances.'

'No; I quite understand that.'

'Can you promise to keep a little love for me all that time?' he asked with a constrained smile.

'You know me too well to fear.'

'I thought you seemed a little doubtful.'

His tone was not altogether that which makes banter pleasant between lovers. Marian looked at him fearfully. Was it possible for him in truth so to misunderstand her? He had never satisfied her heart's desire of infinite love; she never spoke with him but she was oppressed with the suspicion that his love was not as great as hers, and, worse still, that he did not wholly comprehend the self-surrender which she strove to make plain in every word.

'You don't say that seriously, Jasper?'

'But answer seriously.'

'How can you doubt that I would wait faithfully for you for years if it were necessary?'

'It mustn't be years, that's very certain. I think it preposterous for a man to hold a woman bound in that hopeless way.'

'But what question is there of holding me bound? Is love dependent on fixed engagements? Do you feel that, if we agreed to part, your love would be at once a thing of the past?'

'Why no, of course not.'

'Oh, but how coldly you speak, Jasper !'

She could not breathe a word which might be interpreted as fear lest the change of her circumstances should make a change in his feeling. Yet that was in her mind. The existence of such a fear meant, of course, that she did not entirely trust him, and viewed his character as something less than noble. Very seldom indeed is a woman free from such doubts, however absolute her love; and perhaps it is just as rare for a man to credit in his heart all the praises he speaks of his beloved. Passion is compatible with a great many of these imperfections of intellectual esteem. To see more clearly into Jasper's personality was, for Marian, to suffer the more intolerable dread lest she should lose him.

She went to his side. Her heart ached because, in her great misery, he had not fondled her and intoxicated her senses with loving words.

'How can I make you feel how much I love you?' she murmured.

'You mustn't be so literal, dearest. Women are so desperately matter-of-fact; it comes out even in their love-talk.'

Marian was not without perception of the irony of such an opinion on Jasper's lips.

'I am content for you to think so,' she said. 'There is only one fact in my life of any importance, and I can never lose sight of it.'

'Well now, we are quite sure of each other. Tell me plainly, do you think me capable of forsaking you because you have perhaps lost your money?'

The question made her wince. If delicacy had held *her* tongue, it had not control of *his*.

'How can I answer that better,' she said, 'than by saying I love you?'

It was no answer, and Jasper, though obtuse compared with her, understood that it was none. But the emotion which had prompted his words was genuine enough. Her touch, the perfume of her passion, had their exalting effect upon him. He felt in all sincerity that to forsake her would be a baseness, revenged by the loss of such a wife.

'There's an uphill fight before me, that's all,' he said, 'instead of the pretty smooth course I have been looking forward to. But I don't fear it, Marian. I'm not the fellow to be beaten. You shall be my wife, and you shall have as many luxuries as if you had brought me a fortune.'

'Luxuries! Oh, how childish you seem to think me!'

'Not a bit of it. Luxuries are a most important part of life. I had rather not live at all than never possess them. Let me give you a useful hint; if ever I seem to you to flag, just remind me of the difference between these lodgings and a richly furnished house. Just hint to me that So-and-so, the journalist, goes about in his carriage, and can give his wife a box at the theatre. Just ask me, casually, how I should like to run over to the Riviera when London fogs are thickest. You understand? That's the way to keep me at it like a steam-engine.'

'You are right. All those things enable one to live a better and fuller life. Oh, how cruel that I – that we are robbed in this way! You can have no idea how terrible a blow it was to me when I read that letter this morning.'

She was on the point of confessing that she had swooned, but something restrained her.

'Your father can hardly be sorry,' said Jasper.

'I think he speaks more harshly than he feels. The worst was, that until he got your letter he had kept hoping that I would let him have the money for a new review.'

'Well, for the present I prefer to believe that the money isn't all lost. If the blackguards pay ten shillings in the pound you will get two thousand five hundred out of them, and that's something. But how do you stand? Will your position be that of an ordinary creditor?'

'I am so ignorant. I know nothing of such things.'

'But of course your interests will be properly looked after. Put yourself in communication with this Mr Holden. I'll have a look into the law on the subject. Let us hope as long as we can. By Jove! There's no other way of facing it.'

'No, indeed.'

'Mrs Reardon and the rest of them are safe enough, I suppose?'

'Oh, no doubt.'

'Confound them! – It grows upon one. One doesn't take in the whole of such misfortune at once. We must hold on the last rag of hope, and in the meantime I'll half work myself to death. Are you going to see the girls?'

'Not to-night. You must tell them.'

'Dora will cry her eyes out. Upon my word, Maud 'll have to draw in her horns. I must frighten her into economy and hard work.'

He again lost himself in anxious reverie.

'Marian, couldn't you try your hand at fiction?'

She started, remembering that her father had put the same question so recently.

'I'm afraid I could do nothing worth doing.'

'That isn't exactly the question. Could you do anything that would sell? With very moderate success in fiction you might make three times as much as you ever will by magazine pot-boilers. A girl like you. Oh, you might manage, I should think.'

'A girl like me?'

'Well, I mean that love-scenes, and that kind of thing, would be very much in your line.'

Marian was not given to blushing; very few girls are, even on strong provocation. For the first time Jasper saw her cheeks colour deeply, and it was with anything but pleasure. His words were coarsely inconsiderate, and wounded her.

'I think that is not my work,' she said coldly, looking away.

'But surely there's no harm in my saying –' he paused in astonishment. 'I meant nothing that could offend you.'

'I know you didn't, Jasper. But you make me think that –'

'Don't be so literal again, my dear girl. Come here and forgive me.'

She did not approach, but only because the painful thought he had excited kept her to that spot.

'Come, Marian! Then I must come to you.'

He did so and held her in his arms.

'Try your hand at a novel, dear, if you can possibly make time. Put me in it, if you like, and make me an insensible masculine. The experiment is worth a try I'm certain. At all events do a few chapters, and let me see them. A chapter needn't take you more than a couple of hours I should think.'

Marian refrained from giving any promise. She seemed irresponsive to his caresses. That thought which at times gives trouble to all women of strong emotions was working in her: had she been too demonstrative, and made her love too cheap? Now that Jasper's love might be endangered, it behoved her to use any arts which nature prompted. And so, for once, he was not wholly satisfied with her, and at their parting he wondered what subtle change had affected her manner to him.

'Why didn't Marian come to speak a word?' said Dora, when her brother entered the girls' sitting-room about ten o'clock.

'You knew she was with me, then?'

'We heard her voice as she was going away.'

'She brought me some enspiriting news, and thought it better I should have the reporting of it to you.'

With brevity he made known what had befallen.

'Cheerful, isn't it? The kind of thing that strengthens one's trust in Providence.'

The girls were appalled. Maud, who was reading by the fireside, let her book fall to her lap; and knit her brows darkly.

'Then your marriage must be put off, of course?' said Dora.

'Well, I shouldn't be surprised if that were found necessary,' replied her brother caustically. He was able now to give vent to the feeling which in Marian's presence was suppressed, partly out of consideration for her, and partly owing to her influence.

'And shall we have to go back to our old lodgings again?' inquired Maud.

Jasper gave no answer, but kicked a footstool savagely out of his way and paced the room.

'Oh, do you think we need?' said Dora, with unusual protest against economy.

'Remember that it's a matter for your own consideration,' Jasper replied at length. 'You are living on your own resources, you know.'

Maud glanced at her sister, but Dora was preoccupied.

'Why do you prefer to stay here?' Jasper asked abruptly of the younger girl.

'It is so very much nicer,' she replied with some embarrassment.

He bit the ends of his moustache, and his eyes glared at the impalpable thwarting force that to imagination seemed to fill the air about him.

'A lesson against being over-hasty,' he muttered, again kicking the footstool.

'Did you make that considerate remark to Marian?' asked Maud.

'There would have been no harm if I had done. She knows that I shouldn't have been such an ass as to talk of marriage without the prospect of something to live upon.'

'I suppose she's wretched?' said Dora.

'What else can you expect?'

'And did you propose to release her from the burden of her engagement?' Maud inquired.

'It's a confounded pity that you're not rich, Maud,' replied her brother with an involuntary laugh. 'You would have a brilliant reputation for wit.'

He walked about and ejaculated splenetic phrases on the subject of his ill-luck.

'We are here, and here we must stay,' was the final expression of his mood. 'I have only one superstition that I know of, and that forbids me to take a step backward. If I went into poorer lodgings again I should feel it was inviting defeat. I shall stay as long as the position is tenable. Let us get on to Christmas, and then see how things look. Heavens! Suppose we had married, and after that lost the money!'

'You would have been no worse off than plenty of literary men,' said Dora.

'Perhaps not. But as I have made up my mind to be considerably better off than most literary men that reflection wouldn't console me much. Things are in status quo, that's all. I have to rely upon my own efforts. What's the time? Half-past ten; I can get two hours' work before going to bed.'

And nodding a good-night he left them.

When Marian entered the house and went upstairs, she was followed by her mother. On Mrs Yule's countenance there was a new distress; she had been crying recently.

'Have you seen him?' the mother asked.

'Yes. We have talked about it.'

'What does he wish you to do, dear?'

'There's nothing to be done except wait.'

'Father has been telling me something, Marian,' said Mrs Yule after a long silence. 'He says he is going to be blind. There's something the matter with his eyes, and he went to see someone about it this afternoon. He'll get worse and worse, until there has been an operation; and perhaps he'll never be able to use his eyes properly again.'

The girl listened in an attitude of despair.

'He has seen an oculist? – a really good doctor?'

'He says he went to one of the best.'

'And how did he speak to you?'

'He doesn't seem to care much what happens. He talked of going to the workhouse, and things like that. But it couldn't ever come to that, could it, Marian? Wouldn't somebody help him?'

'There's not much help to be expected in this world,' answered the girl.

Physical weariness brought her a few hours of oblivion as soon as she had lain down, but her sleep came to an end in the early morning, when the pressure of evil dreams forced her back to consciousness of real sorrows and cares. A fog-veiled sky added its weight to crush her spirit; at the hour when she usually rose it was still all but as dark as midnight. Her mother's voice at the door begged her to lie and rest until it grew lighter, and she willingly complied, feeling indeed scarcely capable of leaving her bed.

The thick black fog penetrated every corner of the house. It could be smelt and tasted. Such an atmosphere produces low-spirited languor even in the vigorous and hopeful; to those wasted by suffering it is the very reek of the bottomless pit, poisoning the soul. Her face colourless as the pillow, Marian lay neither sleeping nor awake in blank extremity of woe; tears now and then ran down her cheeks, and at times her body was shaken with a throe such as might result from anguish of the torture chamber.

Midway in the morning, when it was still necessary to use artificial light, she went down to the sitting-room. The course of household life had been thrown into confusion by the disasters of the last day or two; Mrs Yule, who occupied herself almost exclusively with questions of economy, cleanliness, and routine, had not the heart to pursue her round of duties, and this morning, though under normal circumstances she would have been busy in 'turning out' the dining-room, she moved aimlessly and despondently about the house, giving the servant contradictory orders and then blaming herself for her absent-mindedness. In the troubles of her husband and her daughter she had scarcely greater share – so far as active participation went – than if she had been only a faithful old housekeeper; she could only grieve and lament that such discord had come between the two whom she loved, and that in herself was no power even to solace their distresses. Marian found her standing in the passage, with a duster in one hand and a hearth-brush in the other.

'Your father has asked to see you when you come down,' Mrs Yule whispered.

'I'll go to him.'

Marian entered the study. Her father was not in his place at the writing-table, nor yet seated in the chair which he used when he had leisure to draw up to the fireside; he sat in front of one of the bookcases, bent forward as if seeking a volume, but his chin was propped upon his hand, and he had maintained this position for a long time. He did not immediately move. When he raised his head Marian saw that he looked older, and she noticed – or fancied she did – that there was some unfamiliar peculiarity about his eyes.

'I am obliged to you for coming,' he began with distant formality. 'Since I saw you last I have learnt something which makes a change in my position and prospects, and it is necessary to speak on the subject. I won't detain you more than a few minutes.'

He coughed, and seemed to consider his next words.

'Perhaps I needn't repeat what I have told your mother. You have learnt it from her, I dare say?'

'Yes, with much grief.'

'Thank you, but we will leave aside that aspect of the matter. For a few more months I may be able to pursue my ordinary work, but before long I shall certainly be disabled from earning my livelihood by literature. Whether this will in any way affect your own position I don't know. Will you have the goodness to tell me whether you still purpose leaving this house?'

'I have no means of doing so.'

'Is there any likelihood of your marriage taking place, let us say, within four months?'

'Only if the executors recover my money, or a large portion of it.'

'I understand. My reason for asking is this. My lease of this house terminates at the end of next March, and I shall certainly not be justified in renewing it. If you are able to provide for yourself in any way it will be sufficient for me to rent two rooms after that. This disease which affects my eyes may be only temporary; in due time an operation may render it possible for me to work again. In hope of that I shall probably have to borrow a sum of money on the security of my life insurance, though in the first instance I shall make the most of what I can get for the furniture of the house and a large part of my library; your mother and I could live at very slight expense in lodgings. If the disease prove irremediable, I must prepare myself for the worst. What I wish to say is, that it will be better if from to-day you consider yourself as working for your own subsistence. So long as I remain here this house is of course your home; there can be no question between us of trivial expenses. But it is right that you should understand what my prospects are. I shall soon have no home to offer you; you must look to your own efforts for support.'

'I am prepared to do that, father.'

'I think you will have no great difficulty in earning enough for yourself. I have done my best to train you in writing for the periodicals, and your natural abilities are considerable. If you marry, I wish you a happy life. The end of mine, of many long years of unremitting toil, is failure and destitution.'

Marian sobbed.

'That's all I had to say,' concluded her father, his voice tremulous with self-compassion. 'I will only beg that there may be no further profitless discussion between us. This room is open to you, as always, and I see no reason why we should not converse on subjects disconnected with our personal differences.'

'Is there no remedy for cataract in its early stages?' asked Marian.

'None. You can read up the subject for yourself at the British Museum. I prefer not to speak of it.'

'Will you let me be what help to you I can?'

'For the present the best you can do is to establish a connection for yourself with editors. Your name will be an assistance to you. My advice is, that you send your "Harrington" article forthwith to Trenchard, writing him a note. If you desire my help in the suggestion of new subjects, I will do my best to be of use.'

Marian withdrew. She went to the sitting-room, where an ochreous daylight was beginning to diffuse itself and to render the lamp superfluous. With the dissipation of the fog rain had set in; its splashing upon the muddy pavement was audible.

Mrs Yule, still with a duster in her hand, sat on the sofa. Marian took a place beside her. They talked in low, broken tones, and wept together over their miseries.

Chapter 31

A RESCUE AND A SUMMONS

THE chances are that you have neither understanding nor sympathy for men such as Edwin Reardon and Harold Biffen. They merely provoke you. They seem to you inert, flabby, weakly envious, foolishly obstinate, impiously mutinous, and many other things. You are made angrily contemptuous by their failure to get on; why don't they bestir themselves, push and bustle, welcome kicks so long as halfpence follow, make a place in the world's eye – in short, take a leaf from the book of Mr Jasper Milvain?

But try to imagine a personality wholly unfitted for the rough and tumble of the world's labour-market. From the familiar point of view these men were worthless; view them in possible relation to a humane order of society, and they are admirable citizens. Nothing is easier than to condemn a type of character which is unequal to the coarse demands of life as it suits the average man. These two were richly endowed with the kindly and the imaginative virtues; if fate threw them amid incongruous circumstances, is their endowment of less value? You scorn their passivity; but it was their nature and their merit to be passive. Gifted with independent means, each of them would have taken quite a different aspect in your eyes. The sum of their faults was their inability to earn money; but, indeed, that inability does not call for unmingled disdain.

It was very weak of Harold Biffen to come so near perishing of hunger as he did in the days when he was completing his novel. But he would have vastly preferred to eat and be satisfied had any method of obtaining food presented itself to him. He did not starve for the pleasure of the thing, I assure you. Pupils were difficult to get just now, and writing that he had sent to magazines had returned upon his hands. He pawned such of his possessions as he could spare, and he reduced his meals to the mimimum. Nor was he uncheerful in his cold garret and with his empty stomach, for 'Mr Bailey, Grocer,' drew steadily to an end.

He worked very slowly. The book would make perhaps two

volumes of ordinary novel size, but he had laboured over it for many months, patiently, affectionately, scrupulously. Each sentence was as good as he could make it, harmonious to the ear, with words of precious meaning skilfully set. Before sitting down to a chapter he planned it minutely in his mind; then he wrote a rough draft of it; then he elaborated the thing phrase by phrase. He had not thought of whether such toil would be recompensed in coin of the realm; nay, it was his conviction that, if with difficulty published, it could scarcely bring him money. The work must be significant, that was all he cared for. And he had no society of admiring friends to encourage him. Reardon understood the merit of the workmanship, but frankly owned that the book was repulsive to him. To the public it would be worse than repulsive – tedious, utterly uninteresting. No matter; it drew to its end.

The day of its completion was made memorable by an event decidedly more exciting, even to the author.

At eight o'clock in the evening there remained half a page to be written. Biffen had already worked about nine hours, and on breaking off to appease his hunger he doubted whether to finish to-night or to postpone the last lines till to-morrow. The discovery that only a small crust of bread lay in the cupboard decided him to write no more; he would have to go out to purchase a loaf, and that was disturbance.

But stay; had he enough money? He searched his pockets. Two pence and two farthings; no more.

You are probably not aware that at bakers' shops in the poor quarters the price of the half-quartern loaf varies sometimes from week to week. At present, as Biffen knew, it was two-pence three-farthings, a common figure. But Harold did not possess three farthings, only two. Reflecting, he remembered to have passed yesterday a shop where the bread was marked twopence halfpenny; it was a shop in a very obscure little street off Hampstead Road, some distance from Clipstone Street. Thither he must repair. He had only his hat and a muffler to put on, for again he was wearing his overcoat in default of the under one, and his ragged umbrella to take from the corner; so he went forth.

To his delight the twopence halfpenny announcement was still in the baker's window. He obtained a loaf, wrapped it in the piece of paper he had brought – small bakers decline to supply paper for this purpose – and strode joyously homeward again.

Having eaten, he looked longingly at his manuscript. But half a page more. Should he not finish it to-night? The temptation was irresistible. He sat down, wrought with unusual speed, and at half-past ten wrote with magnificent flourish 'The End.'

His fire was out and he had neither coals nor wood. But his feet were frozen into lifelessness. Impossible to go to bed like this; he must take another turn in the streets. It would suit his humour to ramble a while. Had it not been so late he would have gone to see Reardon, who expected the communication of this glorious news.

So again he locked his door. Half-way downstairs he stumbled over something or somebody in the dark.

'Who is that?' he cried.

The answer was a loud snore. Biffen went to the bottom of the house and called to the landlady.

'Mrs Willoughby! Who is asleep on the stairs?'

'Why, I 'spect it's Mr Briggs,' replied the woman, indulgently. 'Don't you mind him, Mr Biffen. There's no 'arm; he's only had a little too much. I'll go up an' make him go to bed as soon as I've got my 'ands clean.'

'The necessity for waiting till then isn't obvious,' remarked the realist with a chuckle, and went his way.

He walked at a sharp pace for more than an hour, and about midnight drew near to his own quarter again. He had just turned up by the Middlesex Hospital, and was at no great distance from Clipstone Street, when a yell and scamper caught his attention; a group of loafing blackguards on the opposite side of the way had suddenly broken up, and as they rushed off he heard the word 'Fire!' This was too common an occurrence to disturb his equanimity; he wondered absently in which street the fire might be, but trudged on without a thought of making investigation. Repeated yells and rushes, however, assailed his apathy. Two women came tearing by him, and he shouted to them: 'Where is it?'

'In Clipstone Street, they say,' one screamed back.

He could no longer be unconcerned. If in his own street the conflagration might be in the very house he inhabited, and in that case – He set off at a run. Ahead of him was a thickening throng, its position indicating the entrance to Clipstone Street. Soon he found his progress retarded; he had to dodge this way and that, to force progress, to guard himself against overthrows by the torrent of ruffiandom which always breaks forth at the cry of fire. He could now smell the smoke, and all at once a black volume of it, bursting from upper windows, alarmed his sight. At once he was aware that, if not his own dwelling, it must be one of those on either side that was in flames. As yet no engine had arrived, and straggling policemen were only just beginning to make their way to the scene of uproar. By dint of violent effort Biffen moved forward yard by yard. A tongue of flame which suddenly illumined the fronts of the houses put an end to his doubt.

'Let me get past!' he shouted to the gaping and swaying mass of people in front of him. 'I live there! I must go upstairs to save something!'

His educated accent moved attention. Repeating the demand again and again he succeeded in getting forward, and at length was near enough to see that people were dragging articles of furniture out on to the pavement.

'That you, Mr Biffen?' cried someone to him.

He recognised the face of a fellow-lodger.

'Is it possible to get up to my room?' broke frantically from his lips.

'You'll never get up there. It's that — Briggs' – the epithet was alliterative – 'as upset his — lamp, and I 'ope he'll — well get roasted to death.'

Biffen leaped on to the threshold, and crashed against Mrs Willoughby, the landlady, who was carrying a huge bundle of household linen.

'I told you to look after that drunken brute!' he said to her. 'Can I get upstairs?'

'What do I care whether you can or not!' the woman shrieked. 'My God! And all them new chairs as I bought – !'

He heard no more, but bounded over a confusion of obstacles and in a moment was on the landing of the first storey. Here he

encountered a man who had not lost his head, a stalwart
mechanic engaged in slipping clothes on to two little children.

'If somebody don't drag that fellow Briggs down he'll be dead,'
observed the man. 'He's layin' outside his door. I pulled him out,
but I can't do no more for him.'

Smoke grew thick on the staircase. Burning was as yet confined
to that front room on the second floor tenanted by Briggs the disastrous, but in all likelihood the ceiling was ablaze, and if so it
would be all but impossible for Biffen to gain his own chamber,
which was at the back on the floor above. No one was making an
attempt to extinguish the fire; personal safety and the rescue of
their possessions alone occupied the thoughts of such people as
were still in the house. Desperate with the dread of losing his
manuscript, his toil, his one hope, the realist scarcely stayed to
listen to a warning that the fumes were impassable; with head
bent he rushed up to the next landing. There lay Briggs, perchance already stifled, and through the open door Biffen had a
horrible vision of furnace fury. To go yet higher would have been
madness but for one encouragement : he knew that on his own
storey was a ladder giving access to a trap-door by which he
might issue on to the roof, whence escape to the adjacent houses
would be practicable. Again a leap forward !

In fact, not two minutes elapsed from his commencing the
ascent of the stairs to the moment when, all but fainting, he
thrust the key into his door and fell forward into purer air.   Fell,
for he was on his knees, and had begun to suffer from a sense of
failing power, a sick whirling of the brain, a terror of hideous
death. His manuscript was on the table, where he had left it after
regarding and handling it with joyful self-congratulation;
though it was pitch dark in the room, he could at once lay his
hand on the heap of paper. Now he had it; now it was jammed
tight under his left arm; now he was out again on the landing, in
smoke more deadly than ever.

He said to himself : 'If I cannot instantly break out by the
trap-door it's all over with me.' That the exit would open to a
vigorous thrust he knew, having amused himself not long ago
by going on to the roof. He touched the ladder, sprang upwards,
and felt the trap above him. But he could not push it back. 'I'm
a dead man,' flashed across his mind, 'and all for the sake of "Mr

Bailey, Grocer."' A frenzied effort, the last of which his muscles were capable, and the door yielded. His head was now through the aperture, and though the smoke swept up about him, that gasp of cold air gave him strength to throw himself on the flat portion of the roof that he had reached.

So for a minute or two he lay. Then he was able to stand, to survey his position, and to walk along by the parapet. He looked down upon the surging and shouting crowd in Clipstone Street, but could see it only at intervals, owing to the smoke that rolled from the front windows below him.

What he had now to do he understood perfectly. This roof was divided from those on either hand by a stack of chimneys; to get round the end of these stacks was impossible, or at all events too dangerous a feat unless it were the last resource, but by climbing to the apex of the slates he would be able to reach the chimney-pots, to drag himself up to them, and somehow to tumble over on to the safer side. To this undertaking he forthwith addressed himself. Without difficulty he reached the ridge: standing on it he found that only by stretching his arm to the utmost could he grip the top of a chimney-pot. Had he the strength necessary to raise himself by such a hold? And suppose the pot broke?

His life was still in danger; the increasing volumes of smoke warned him that in a few minutes the uppermost storey might be in flames. He took off his overcoat to allow himself more freedom of action; the manuscript, now an encumbrance, must precede him over the chimney-stack, and there was only one way of effecting that. With care he stowed the papers into the pockets of the coat; then he rolled the garment together, tied it up in its own sleeves, took a deliberate aim – and the bundle was for the present in safety.

Now for the gymnastic endeavour. Standing on tiptoe, he clutched the rim of the chimney-pot, and strove to raise himself. The hold was firm enough, but his arms were far too puny to per-form such work, even when death would be the penalty of failure. Too long he had lived on insufficient food and sat over the debili-tating desk. He swung this way and that, trying to throw one of his knees as high as the top of the brickwork, but there was no chance of his succeeding. Dropping on to the slates, he sat there in perturbation.

He must cry for help. In front it was scarcely possible to stand by the parapet, owing to the black clouds of smoke, now mingled with sparks; perchance he might attract the notice of some person either in the yards behind or at the back windows of other houses. The night was so obscure that he could not hope to be seen; voice alone must be depended upon, and there was no certainty that it would be heard far enough. Though he stood in his shirt-sleeves in a bitter wind no sense of cold affected him; his face was beaded with perspiration drawn forth by his futile struggle to climb. He let himself slide down the rear slope, and, holding by the end of the chimney brickwork, looked into the yards. At the same instant a face appeared to him – that of a man who was trying to obtain a glimpse of this roof from that of the next house by thrusting out his head beyond the block of chimneys.

'Hollo!' cried the stranger. 'What are you doing there?'

'Trying to escape, of course. Help me to get on to your roof.'

'By God! I expected to see the fire coming through already. Are you the — as upset his lamp an' fired the bloomin' 'ouse?'

'Not I! He's lying drunk on the stairs; dead by this time.'

'By God! I wouldn't have helped you if you'd been him. How are you coming round? Blest if I see! You'll break your bloomin' neck if you try this corner. You'll have to come over the chimneys; wait till I get a ladder.'

'And a rope,' shouted Biffen.

The man disappeared for five minutes. To Biffen it seemed half an hour; he felt, or imagined he felt, the slates getting hot beneath him, and the smoke was again catching his breath. But at length there was a shout from the top of the chimney-stack. The rescuer had seated himself on one of the pots, and was about to lower on Biffen's side a ladder which had enabled him to ascend from the other. Biffen planted the lowest rung very carefully on the ridge of the roof, climbed as lightly as possible, got a footing between two pots; the ladder was then pulled over, and both men descended in safety.

'Have you seen a coat lying about here?' was Biffen's first question. 'I threw mine over.'

'What did you do that for?'

'There are some valuable papers in the pockets.'

They searched in vain; on neither side of the roof was the coat discoverable.

'You must have pitched it into the street,' said the man.

This was a terrible blow; Biffen forgot his rescue from destruction in lament for the loss of his manuscript. He would have pursued the fruitless search, but his companion, who feared that the fire might spread to adjoining houses, insisted on his passing through the trap-door and descending the stairs.

'If the coat fell into the street,' Biffen said, when they were down on the ground floor, 'of course it's lost; it would be stolen at once. But may not it have fallen into your back yard?'

He was standing in the midst of a cluster of alarmed people, who stared at him in astonishment, for the reek through which he had fought his way had given him the aspect of a sweep. His suggestion prompted someone to run into the yard, with the result that a muddy bundle was brought in and exhibited to him.

'Is this your coat, Mister?'

'Heaven be thanked! That's it! There are valuable papers in the pockets.'

He unrolled the garment, felt to make sure that 'Mr Bailey' was safe, and finally put it on.

'Will anyone here let me sit down in a room and give me a drink of water?' he asked, feeling now as if he must drop with exhaustion.

The man who had rescued him performed this further kindness, and for half an hour, whilst tumult indescribable raged about him, Biffen sat recovering his strength. By that time the firemen were hard at work, but one floor of the burning house had already fallen through, and it was probable that nothing but the shell would be saved. After giving a full account of himself to the people among whom he had come, Harold declared his intention of departing; his need of repose was imperative, and he could not hope for it in this proximity to the fire. As he had no money, his only course was to inquire for a room at some house in the immediate neighbourhood, where the people would receive him in a charitable spirit.

With the aid of the police he passed to where the crowd was

thinner, and came out into Cleveland Street. Here most of the house-doors were open, and he made several applications for hospitality, but either his story was doubted or his grimy appearance predisposed people against him. At length, when again his strength was all but at an end, he made appeal to a policeman.

'Surely you can tell,' he protested, after explaining his position, 'that I don't want to cheat anybody. I shall have money to-morrow. If no one will take me in you must haul me on some charge to the police station; I shall have to lie down on the pavement in a minute.'

The officer recognised a man who was standing half-dressed on a threshold close by; he stepped up to him, and made representations which were successful. In a few minutes Biffen took possession of an underground room furnished as a bedchamber, which he agreed to rent for a week. His landlord was not ungracious, and went so far as to supply him with warm water, that he might in a measure cleanse himself. This operation rapidly performed, the hapless author flung himself into bed, and before long was fast asleep.

When he went upstairs about nine o'clock in the morning he discovered that his host kept an oil-shop.

'Lost everything, have you?' asked the man sympathetically.

'Everything, except the clothes I wear and some papers that I managed to save. All my books burnt!'

Biffen shook his head dolorously.

'Your account-books!' cried the dealer in oil. 'Dear, dear! – and what might your business be?'

The author corrected this misapprehension. In the end he was invited to break his fast, which he did right willingly. Then, with assurances that he would return before nightfall, he left the house. His steps were naturally first directed to Clipstone Street; the familiar abode was a gruesome ruin, still smoking. Neighbours informed him that Mr Briggs's body had been brought forth in a horrible condition; but this was the only loss of life that had happened.

Thence he struck eastward, and at eleven came to Manville Street, Islington. He found Reardon by the fireside, looking very ill, and speaking with hoarseness.

'Another cold?'

'It looks like it. I wish you would take the trouble to go and buy me some vermin-killer. That would suit my case.'

'Then what would suit mine? Behold me, undeniably a philosopher; in the literal sense of the words *omnia mea mecum porto*.' [38]

He recounted his adventures, and with such humorous vivacity that when he ceased the two laughed together as if nothing more amusing had ever been heard.

'Ah, but my books, my books!' exclaimed Biffen, with a genuine groan. 'And all my notes! At one fell swoop! If I didn't laugh, old friend, I should sit down and cry; indeed I should. All my classics, with years of scribbling in the margins! How am I to buy them again?'

'You rescued "Mr Bailey." He must repay you.'

Biffen had already laid the manuscript on the table; it was dirty and crumpled, but not to such an extent as to render copying necessary. Lovingly he smoothed the pages and set them in order, then he wrapped the whole in a piece of brown paper which Reardon supplied, and wrote upon it the address of a firm of publishers.

'Have you note-paper? I'll write to them; impossible to call in my present guise.'

Indeed his attire was more like that of a bankrupt costermonger than of a man of letters. Collar he had none, for the griminess of that he wore last night had necessitated its being thrown aside; round his throat was a dirty handkerchief. His coat had been brushed, but its recent experiences had brought it one stage nearer to that dissolution which must very soon be its fate. His grey trousers were now black, and his boots looked as if they had not been cleaned for weeks.

'Shall I say anything about the character of the book?' he asked, seating himself with pen and paper. 'Shall I hint that it deals with the ignobly decent?'

'Better let them form their own judgment,' replied Reardon, in his hoarse voice.

'Then I'll just say that I submit to them a novel of modern life, the scope of which is in some degree indicated by its title. Pity they can't know how nearly it became a holocaust, and that I risked my life to save it. If they're good enough to accept it I'll tell them the story. And now, Reardon, I'm ashamed of myself, but can you without inconvenience lend me ten shillings?'

'Easily.'

'I must write to two pupils, to inform them of my change of address – from garret to cellar. And I must ask help from my prosperous brother. He gives it me unreluctantly, I know, but I am always loath to apply to him. May I use your paper for these purposes?'

The brother of whom he spoke was employed in a house of business at Liverpool; the two had not met for years, but they corresponded, and were on terms such as Harold indicated. When he had finished his letters, and had received the half-sovereign from Reardon, he went his way to deposit the brown-paper parcel at the publishers'. The clerk who received it from his hands probably thought that the author might have chosen a more respectable messenger.

Two days later, early in the evening, the friends were again enjoying each other's company in Reardon's room. Both were invalids, for Biffen had of course caught a cold from his exposure in shirt-sleeves on the roof, and he was suffering from the shock to his nerves; but the thought that his novel was safe in the hands of publishers gave him energy to resist these influences. The absence of the pipe, for neither had any palate for tobacco at present, was the only external peculiarity of this meeting. There seemed no reason why they should not meet frequently before the parting which would come at Christmas; but Reardon was in a mood of profound sadness, and several times spoke as if already he were bidding his friend farewell.

'I find it difficult to think,' he said, 'that you will always struggle on in such an existence as this. To every man of metal there does come an opportunity, and it surely is time for yours to present itself. I have a superstitious faith in "Mr Bailey." If he leads you to triumph, don't altogether forget me.'

'Don't talk nonsense.'

'What ages it seems since that day when I saw you in the library at Hastings, and heard you ask in vain for my book! And how grateful I was to you! I wonder whether any mortal ever asks for my books nowadays? Some day, when I am well established at Croydon, you shall go to Mudie's, and make inquiry if my novels ever by chance leave the shelves and then you shall give me a true and faithful report of the answer you get. "He is quite forgotten," the attendant will say; be sure of it.'

'I think not.'

'To have had even a small reputation, and to have outlived it, is a sort of anticipation of death. The man Edwin Reardon, whose name was sometimes spoken in a tone of interest, is really and actually dead. And what remains of me is resigned to that. I have an odd fancy that it will make death itself easier; it is as if only half of me had now to die.'

Biffen tried to give a lighter turn to the gloomy subject.

'Thinking of my fiery adventure,' he said, in his tone of dry deliberation, 'I find it vastly amusing to picture you as a witness at the inquest if I had been choked and consumed. No doubt it would have been made known that I rushed upstairs to save some particular piece of property – several people heard me say so – and you alone would be able to conjecture what this was. Imagine the gaping wonderment of the coroner's jury! The *Daily Telegraph* would have made a leader out of me. "This poor man was so strangely deluded as to the value of a novel in manuscript which it appears he had just completed, that he positively sacrificed his life in the endeavour to rescue it from the flames." And the *Saturday* would have had a column of sneering jocosity on the irrepressibly sanguine temperament of authors. At all events, I should have had my day of fame.'

'But what an ignoble death it would have been!' he pursued. 'Perishing in the garret of a lodging-house which caught fire by the overturning of a drunkard's lamp! One would like to end otherwise.'

'Where would you wish to die?' asked Reardon, musingly.

'At home,' replied the other, with pathetic emphasis. 'I have never had a home since I was a boy, and am never likely to have one. But to die at home is an unreasoning hope I still cherish.'

'If you had never come to London, what would you have now been?'

'Almost certainly a schoolmaster in some small town. And one might be worse off than that, you know.'

'Yes, one might live peaceably enough in such a position. And I – I should be in an estate-agent's office, earning a sufficient salary, and most likely married to some unambitious country girl. I should have lived an intelligible life, instead of only trying to live, aiming at modes of life beyond my reach. My mistake was that of numberless men nowadays. Because I was conscious of brains, I thought that the only place for me was London. It's easy enough to understand this common delusion. We form our ideas of London from old literature; we think of London as if it were still the one centre of intellectual life; we think and talk like Chatterton.[39] But the truth is that intellectual men in our day do their best to keep away from London – when once they know the place. There are libraries everywhere; papers and magazines reach the north of Scotland as soon as they reach Brompton; it's only on rare occasions, for special kinds of work, that one is bound to live in London. And as for recreation, why, now that no English theatre exists, what is there in London that you can't enjoy in almost any part of England? At all events, a yearly visit of a week would be quite sufficient for all the special features of the town. London is only a huge shop, with an hotel on the upper storeys. To be sure, if you make it your artistic subject, that's a different thing. But neither you nor I would do that by deliberate choice.'

'I think not.'

'It's a huge misfortune, this will-o'-the-wisp attraction exercised by London on young men of brains. They come here to be degraded, or to perish, when their true sphere is a life of peaceful remoteness. The type of man capable of success in London is more or less callous and cynical. If I had the training of boys, I would teach them to think of London as the last place where life can be lived worthily.'

'And the place where you are most likely to die in squalid wretchedness.'

'The one happy result of my experiences,' said Reardon, 'is that they have cured me of ambition. What a miserable fellow I should be if I were still possessed with the desire to make a name! I can't even recall very clearly that state of mind. My strongest desire now is for peaceful obscurity. I am tired out; I want to rest for the remainder of my life.'

'You won't have much rest at Croydon.'

'Oh, it isn't impossible. My time will be wholly occupied in a round of all but mechanical duties, and I think that will be the best medicine for my mind. I shall read very little, and that only in the classics. I don't say that I shall always be content in such a position; in a few years perhaps something pleasanter will offer. But in the meantime it will do very well. Then there is our expedition to Greece to look forward to. I am quite in earnest about that. The year after next, if we are both alive, assuredly we go.'

'The year after next.' Biffen smiled dubiously.

'I have demonstrated to you mathematically that it is possible.'

'You have; but so are a great many other things that one does not dare to hope for.'

Someone knocked at the door, opened it, and said:

'Here's a telegram for you, Mr Reardon.'

The friends looked at each other, as if some fear had entered the minds of both. Reardon opened the despatch. It was from his wife, and ran thus:

'Willie is ill of diphtheria. Please come to us at once. I am staying with Mrs Carter at her mother's, at Brighton.'

The full address was given.

'You hadn't heard of her going there?' said Biffen when he had read the lines.

'No, I haven't seen Carter for several days, or perhaps he would have told me. Brighton, at this time of year? But I believe there's a fashionable "season" about now, isn't there? I suppose that would account for it.'

He spoke in a slighting tone, but showed increasing agitation.

'Of course you will go?'

'I must. Though I'm in no condition for making a journey.'

His friend examined him anxiously.

'Are you feverish at all this evening?'

Reardon held out a hand that the other might feel his pulse. The beat was rapid to begin with, and had been heightened since the arrival of the telegram.

'But go I must. The poor little fellow has no great place in my heart, but, when Amy sends for me, I must go. Perhaps things are at the worst.'

'When is there a train? Have you a time-table?'

Biffen was despatched to the nearest shop to purchase one, and in the meanwhile Reardon packed a few necessaries in a small travelling-bag, ancient and worn, but the object of his affection because it had accompanied him on his wanderings in the South. When Harold returned, his appearance excited Reardon's astonishment – he was white from head to foot.

'Snow?'

'It must have been falling heavily for an hour or more.'

'Can't be helped; I must go.'

The nearest station for departure was London Bridge, and the next train left at 7.20. By Reardon's watch it was now about five minutes to seven.

'I don't know whether it's possible,' he said, in confused hurry, 'but I must try. There isn't another train till ten past nine. Come with me to the station, Biffen.'

Both were ready. They rushed from the house, and sped through the soft, steady fall of snowflakes into Upper Street. Here they were several minutes before they found a disengaged cab. Questioning the driver, they learnt what they would have known very well already but for their excitement: impossible to get to London Bridge Station in a quarter of an hour.

'Better to go on, all the same,' was Reardon's opinion. 'If the snow gets deep I shall perhaps not be able to have a cab at all. But you had better not come; I forgot that you are as much out of sorts as I am.'

'How can you wait a couple of hours alone? In with you!'

'Diphtheria is pretty sure to be fatal to a child of that age, isn't it?' Reardon asked when they were speeding along City Road.

'I'm afraid there's much danger.'

'Why did she send?'

'What an absurd question! You seem to have got into a thoroughly morbid state of mind about her. Do be human, and put away your obstinate folly.'

'In my position you would have acted precisely as I have done. I have had no choice.'

'I might; but we have both of us too little practicality. The art of living is the art of compromise. We have no right to foster sensibilities, and conduct ourselves as if the world allowed of ideal relations; it leads to misery for others as well as ourselves. Genial coarseness is what it behoves men like you and me to cultivate. Your reply to your wife's last letter was preposterous. You ought to have gone to her of your own accord as soon as ever you heard she was rich; she would have thanked you for such common-sense disregard of delicacies. Let there be an end of this nonsense, I implore you!'

Reardon stared through the glass at the snow that fell thicker and thicker.

'What are we – you and I?' pursued the other. 'We have no belief in immortality; we are convinced that this life is all; we know that human happiness is the origin and end of all moral considerations. What right have we to make ourselves and others miserable for the sake of an obstinate idealism? It is our duty to make the best of circumstances. Why will you go cutting your loaf with a razor when you have a serviceable bread-knife?'

Still Reardon did not speak. The cab rolled on almost silently.

'You love your wife, and this summons she sends is proof that her thought turns to you as soon as she is in distress.'

'Perhaps she only thought it her duty to let the child's father know –'

'Perhaps – perhaps – perhaps!' cried Biffen, contemptuously. 'There goes the razor again! Take the plain, human construction of what happens. Ask yourself what the vulgar man would do, and do likewise; that's the only safe rule for you.'

They were both hoarse with too much talking, and for the last half of the drive neither spoke.

At the railway-station they ate and drank together, but with poor pretence of appetite. As long as possible they kept within the warmed rooms. Reardon was pale, and had anxious, restless eyes; he could not remain seated, though when he had walked about for a few minutes the trembling of his limbs obliged him to sink down. It was an unutterable relief to both when the moment of the train's starting approached.

They clasped hands warmly, and exchanged a few last requests and promises.

'Forgive my plain speech, old fellow,' said Biffen. 'Go and be happy!'

Then he stood alone on the platform, watching the red light on the last carriage as the train whirled away into darkness and storm.

Chapter 32

REARDON BECOMES PRACTICAL

REARDON had never been to Brighton, and of his own accord never would have gone; he was prejudiced against the place because its name has become suggestive of fashionable imbecility and the snobbishness which tries to model itself thereon; he knew that the town was a mere portion of London transferred to the sea-shore, and as he loved the strand and the breakers for their own sake, to think of them in such connection could be nothing but a trial of his temper. Something of this species of irritation affected him in the first part of his journey, and disturbed the mood of kindliness with which he was approaching Amy; but towards the end he forgot this in a growing desire to be beside his wife in her trouble. His impatience made the hour and a half seem interminable.

The fever which was upon him had increased. He coughed frequently; his breathing was difficult; though constantly moving, he felt as if, in the absence of excitement, his one wish would have been to lie down and abandon himself to lethargy. Two men who sat with him in the third-class carriage had spread a rug over their knees and amused themselves with playing cards for trifling sums of money; the sight of their foolish faces, the sound of their laughs, the talk they interchanged, exasperated him to the last point of endurance, but for all that he could not draw his attention from them. He seemed condemned by some spiritual tormentor to take an interest in their endless games, and to observe their visages until he knew every line with a hateful intimacy. One of the men had a moustache of unusual form; the ends curved upward with peculiar suddenness, and Reardon was constrained to speculate as to the mode of training by which this singularity had been produced. He could have shed tears of nervous distraction in his inability to turn his thoughts upon other things.

On alighting at his journey's end he was seized with a fit of shivering, an intense and sudden chill which made his teeth chatter. In an endeavour to overcome this he began to run towards the row of cabs, but his legs refused such exercise, and coughing compelled him to pause for breath. Still shaking, he threw himself into a vehicle and was driven to the address Amy had mentioned. The snow on the ground lay thick, but no more was falling.

Heedless of the direction which the cab took, he suffered his physical and mental unrest for another quarter of an hour, then a stoppage told him that the house was reached. On his way he had heard a clock strike eleven.

The door opened almost as soon as he had rung the bell. He mentioned his name, and the maid-servant conducted him to a drawing-room on the ground-floor. The house was quite a small one, but seemed to be well furnished. One lamp burned on the table, and the fire had sunk to a red glow. Saying that she would inform Mrs Reardon at once, the servant left him alone.

He placed his bag on the floor, took off his muffler, threw back his overcoat, and sat waiting. The overcoat was new, but the garments beneath it were his poorest, those he wore when sitting in his garret, for he had neither had time to change them, nor thought of doing so.

He heard no approaching footstep, but Amy came into the room in a way which showed that she had hastened downstairs. She looked at him, then drew near with both hands extended, and laid them on his shoulders, and kissed him. Reardon shook so violently that it was all he could do to remain standing; he seized one of her hands, and pressed it against his lips.

'How hot your breath is!' she said. 'And how you tremble! Are you ill?'

'A bad cold, that's all,' he answered thickly, and coughed. 'How is Willie?'

'In great danger. The doctor is coming again to-night; we thought that was his ring.'

'You didn't expect me to-night?'

'I couldn't feel sure whether you would come.'

'Why did you send for me, Amy? Because Willie was in danger, and you felt I ought to know about it?'

'Yes – and because I –'

She burst into tears. The display of emotion came very suddenly; her words had been spoken in a firm voice, and only the pained knitting of her brows had told what she was suffering.

'If Willie dies, what shall I do? Oh, what shall I do?' broke forth between her sobs.

Reardon took her in his arms, and laid his hand upon her head in the old loving way.

'Do you wish me to go up and see him, Amy?'

'Of course. But first, let me tell you why we are here. Edith – Mrs Carter – was coming to spend a week with her mother, and she pressed me to join her. I didn't really wish to; I was unhappy, and felt how impossible it was to go on always living away from you. Oh, that I had never come! Then Willie would have been as well as ever.'

'Tell me when and how it began.'

She explained briefly, then went on to tell of other circumstances.

'I have a nurse with me in the room. It's my own bedroom, and this house is so small it will be impossible to give you a bed here, Edwin. But there's an hotel only a few yards away.'

'Yes, yes; don't trouble about that.'

'But you look so ill – you are shaking so. Is it a cold you have had long?'

'Oh, my old habit; you remember. One cold after another, all through the accursed winter. What does that matter when you speak kindly to me once more? I had rather die now at your feet and see the old gentleness when you look at me, than live on estranged from you. No, don't kiss me, I believe these vile sore-throats are contagious.'

'But your lips are so hot and parched! And to think of your coming this journey, on such a night!'

'Good old Biffen came to the station with me. He was angry because I had kept away from you so long. Have you given me your heart again, Amy?'

'Oh, it has all been a wretched mistake! But we were so poor. Now all that is over; if only Willie can be saved to me! I am so anxious for the doctor's coming; the poor little child can hardly draw a breath. How cruel it is that such suffering should come upon a little creature who has never done or thought ill!'

'You are not the first, dearest, who has revolted against nature's cruelty.'

'Let us go up at once, Edwin. Leave your coat and things here. Mrs Winter – Edith's mother – is a very old lady; she has gone to bed. And I dare say you wouldn't care to see Mrs Carter to-night?'

'No, no! only you and Willie.'

'When the doctor comes hadn't you better ask his advice for yourself?'

'We shall see. Don't trouble about me.'

They went softly up to the first floor, and entered a bedroom. Fortunately the light here was very dim, or the nurse who sat by the child's bed must have wondered at the eccentricity with which her patient's father attired himself. Bending over the little sufferer, Reardon felt for the first time since Willie's birth a strong fatherly emotion; tears rushed to his eyes, and he almost crushed Amy's hand as he held it during the spasm of his intense feeling.

He sat here for a long time without speaking. The warmth of the chamber had the reverse of an assuaging effect upon his difficult breathing and his frequent short cough – it seemed to oppress and confuse his brain. He began to feel a pain in his right side, and could not sit upright on the chair.

Amy kept regarding him, without his being aware of it.

'Does your head ache?' she whispered.

He nodded, but did not speak.

'Oh, why doesn't the doctor come? I must send in a few minutes.'

But as soon as she had spoken a bell rang in the lower part of the house. Amy had no doubt that it announced the promised visit. She left the room, and in a minute or two returned with the medical man. When the examination of the child was over, Reardon requested a few words with the doctor in the room downstairs.

'I'll come back to you,' he whispered to Amy.

The two descended together, and entered the drawing-room.

'Is there any hope for the little fellow?' Reardon asked.

Yes, there was hope; a favourable turn might be expected.

'Now I wish to trouble you for a moment on my own account. I shouldn't be surprised if you tell me that I have congestion of the lungs.'

The doctor, a suave man of fifty, had been inspecting his interlocutor with curiosity. He now asked the necessary questions, and made an examination.

'Have you had any lung trouble before this?' he inquired gravely.

'Slight congestion of the right lung not many weeks ago.'

'I must order you to bed immediately. Why have you allowed your symptoms to go so far without –'

'I have just come down from London,' interrupted Reardon.

'Tut, tut, tut! To bed this moment, my dear sir! There is inflammation, and –'

'I can't have a bed in this house; there is no spare room. I must go to the nearest hotel.'

'Positively? Then let me take you. My carriage is at the door.'

'One thing – I beg you won't tell my wife that this is serious. Wait till she is out of her anxiety about the child.'

'You will need the services of a nurse. A most unfortunate thing that you are obliged to go to the hotel.'

'It can't be helped. If a nurse is necessary, I must engage one.'

He had the strange sensation of knowing that whatever was needful could be paid for; it relieved his mind immensely. To the rich, illness has none of the worst horrors only understood by the poor.

'Don't speak a word more than you can help,' said the doctor as he watched Reardon withdraw.

Amy stood on the lower stairs, and came down as soon as her husband showed himself.

'The doctor is good enough to take me in his carriage,' he whispered. 'It is better that I should go to bed, and get a good night's rest. I wish I could have sat with you, Amy.'

'Is it anything? You look worse than when you came, Edwin.'

'A feverish cold. Don't give it a thought, dearest. Go to Willie. Good-night!'

She threw her arms about him.

'I shall come to see you if you are not able to be here by nine in the morning,' she said, and added the name of the hotel to which he was to go.

At this establishment the doctor was well known. By midnight Reardon lay in a comfortable room, a huge cataplasm fixed upon him, and other needful arrangements made. A waiter had undertaken to visit him at intervals through the night, and the man of medicine promised to return as soon as possible after daybreak.

What sound was that, soft and continuous, remote, now clearer, now confusedly murmuring? He must have slept, but now he lay in sudden perfect consciousness, and that music fell upon his ears. Ah! of course it was the rising tide; he was near the divine sea.

The night-light enabled him to discern the principal objects in the room, and he let his eyes stray idly hither and thither. But this moment of peacefulness was brought to an end by a fit of coughing, and he became troubled, profoundly troubled, in mind. Was his illness really dangerous? He tried to draw a deep breath, but could not. He found that he could only lie on his right side with any ease. And with the effort of turning he exhausted himself; in the course of an hour or two all his strength had left him. Vague fears flitted harassingly through his thoughts. If he had inflammation of the lungs – that was a disease of which one might die, and speedily. Death? No, no, no; impossible at such a time as this, when Amy, his own dear wife, had come back to him, and had brought him that which would insure their happiness through all the years of a long life.

He was still quite a young man; there must be great reserves of strength in him. And he had the will to live, the prevailing will, the passionate all-conquering desire of happiness.

How he had alarmed himself! Why, now he was calmer again, and again could listen to the music of the breakers. Not all the folly and baseness that paraded along this strip of the shore could change the sea's eternal melody. In a day or two he would walk on the sands with Amy, somewhere quite out of sight of the repulsive town. But Willie was ill; he had forgotten that. Poor little boy! In future the child should be more to him; though never what the mother was, his own love, won again and for ever.

Again an interval of unconsciousness, brought to an end by that aching in his side. He breathed very quickly; could not help doing so. He had never felt so ill as this, never. Was it not near morning?

Then he dreamt. He was at Patras, was stepping into a boat to be rowed out to the steamer which would bear him away from Greece. A magnificent night, though at the end of December; a sky of deep blue, thick set with stars. No sound but the steady splash of the oars, or perhaps a voice from one of the many vessels that lay anchored in the harbour, each showing its lantern-gleams. The water was as deep a blue as the sky, and sparkled with reflected radiance.

And now he stood on deck in the light of early morning. Southward lay the Ionian Islands; he looked for Ithaca, and grieved that it had been passed in the hours of darkness. But the nearest point of the main shore was a rocky promontory; it reminded him that in these waters was fought the battle of Actium.

The glory vanished. He lay once more a sick man in a hired chamber, longing for the dull English dawn.

At eight o'clock came the doctor. He would allow only a word or two to be uttered, and his visit was brief. Reardon was chiefly anxious to have news of the child, but for this he would have to wait.

At ten Amy entered the bedroom. Reardon could not raise himself, but he stretched out his hand and took hers, and gazed eagerly at her. She must have been weeping, he felt sure of that, and there was an expression on her face such as he had never seen there.

'How is Willie?'

'Better, dear; much better.'

He still searched her face.

'Ought you to leave him?'

'Hush! You mustn't speak.'

Tears broke from her eyes, and Reardon had the conviction that the child was dead.

'The truth, Amy!'

She threw herself on her knees by the bedside, and pressed her wet cheek against his hand.

'I am come to nurse you, dear husband,' she said a moment after, standing up again and kissing his forehead. 'I have only you now.'

His heart sank, and for a moment so great a terror was upon him that he closed his eyes and seemed to pass into utter darkness. But those last words of hers repeated themselves in his mind, and at length they brought a deep solace. Poor little Willie had been the cause of the first coldness between him and Amy; her love for him had given place to a mother's love for the child. Now it would be as in the first days of their marriage; they would again be all in all to each other.

'You oughtn't to have come, feeling so ill,' she said to him. 'You should have let me know, dear.'

He smiled and kissed her hand.

'And you kept the truth from me last night, in kindness.'

She checked herself, knowing that agitation must be harmful to him. She had hoped to conceal the child's death, but the effort was too much for her overstrung nerves. And indeed it was only possible for her to remain an hour or two by this sick bed, for she was exhausted by her night of watching, and the sudden agony with which it had concluded. Shortly after Amy's departure, a professional nurse came to attend upon what the doctor had privately characterised as a very grave case.

By the evening its gravity was in no respect diminished. The sufferer had ceased to cough and to make restless movements, and had become lethargic; later, he spoke deliriously, or rather muttered, for his words were seldom intelligible. Amy had returned to the room at four o'clock, and remained till far into the night; she was physically exhausted, and could do little but sit in a chair by the bedside and shed silent tears, or gaze at vacancy in the woe of her sudden desolation. Telegrams had been exchanged with her mother, who was to arrive in Brighton to-morrow morning; the child's funeral would probably be on the third day from this.

When she rose to go away for the night, leaving the nurse in attendance, Reardon seemed to lie in a state of unconsciousness, but just as she was turning from the bed, he opened his eyes and pronounced her name.

'I am here, Edwin,' she answered, bending over him.

'Will you let Biffen know?' he said in low but very clear tones.

'That you are ill, dear? I will write at once, or telegraph, if you like. What is his address?'

He had closed his eyes again, and there came no reply. Amy repeated her question twice; she was turning from him in hopelessness when his voice became audible.

'I can't remember his new address. I know it, but I can't remember.'

She had to leave him thus.

The next day his breathing was so harassed that he had to be raised against pillows. But throughout the hours of daylight his mind was clear, and from time to time he whispered words of tenderness in reply to Amy's look. He never willingly relinquished her hand, and repeatedly he pressed it against his cheek or lips. Vainly he still endeavoured to recall his friend's address.

'Couldn't Mr Carter discover it for you?' Amy asked.

'Perhaps. You might try.'

She would have suggested applying to Jasper Milvain, but that name must not be mentioned. Whelpdale, also, would perchance know where Biffen lived, but Whelpdale's address he had also forgotten.

At night there were long periods of delirium; not mere confused muttering, but continuous talk which the listeners could follow perfectly.

For the most part the sufferer's mind was occupied with revival of the distress he had undergone whilst making those last efforts to write something worthy of himself. Amy's heart was wrung as she heard him living through that time of supreme misery – misery which she might have done so much to alleviate, had not selfish fears and irritated pride caused her to draw further and further from him. Hers was the kind of penitence which is forced by sheer stress of circumstances on a nature which resents any form of humiliation; she could not abandon herself to unreserved grief for what she had done or omitted, and the sense of this defect made a great part of her affliction. When her husband lay in mute lethargy, she thought only of her dead child, and mourned the loss; but his delirious utterances constrained her to break from that bitter-sweet preoccupation, to confuse her mourning with self-reproach and with fears.

Though unconsciously, he was addressing her: 'I can do no more, Amy. My brain seems to be worn out; I can't compose, I can't even think. Look! I have been sitting here for hours, and

I have done only that little bit, half a dozen lines. Such poor stuff too! I should burn it, only I can't afford. I *must* do my regular quantity every day, no matter what it is.'

The nurse, who was present when he talked in this way, looked at Amy for an explanation.

'My husband is an author,' Amy answered. 'Not long ago he was obliged to write when he was ill and ought to have been resting.'

'I always thought it must be hard work writing books,' said the nurse with a shake of her head.

'You don't understand me,' the voice pursued, dreadful as a voice always is when speaking independently of the will. 'You think I am only a poor creature, because I can do nothing better than this. If only I had money enough to rest for a year or two, you should see. Just because I have no money I must sink to this degradation. And I am losing you as well; you don't love me!'

He began to moan in anguish.

But a happy change presently came over his dreaming. He fell into animated description of his experiences in Greece and Italy, and after talking for a long time, he turned his head and said in a perfectly natural tone:

'Amy, do you know that Biffen and I are going to Greece?'

She believed he spoke consciously, and replied:

'You must take me with you, Edwin.'

He paid no attention to this remark, but went on with the same deceptive accent.

'He deserves a holiday after nearly getting burnt to death to save his novel. Imagine the old fellow plunging headlong into the flames to rescue his manuscript! Don't say that authors can't be heroic!'

And he laughed gaily.

Another morning broke. It was possible, said the doctors (a second had been summoned), that a crisis which drew near might bring the favourable turn; but Amy formed her own opinion from the way in which the nurse expressed herself. She felt sure that the gravest fears were entertained. Before noon Reardon awoke from what had seemed natural sleep – save for the rapid breathing – and of a sudden recollected the number of the house in Cleveland Street at which Biffen was now living. He uttered it without explanation. Amy at once conjectured his meaning, and as soon as her surmise was confirmed she despatched a telegram to her husband's friend.

That evening, as Amy was on the point of returning to the sick-room after having dined at her friend's house, it was announced that a gentleman named Biffen wished to see her. She found him in the dining-room, and, even amid her distress, it was a satisfaction to her that he presented a far more conventional appearance than in the old days. All the garments he wore, even his hat, gloves, and boots, were new; a surprising state of things, explained by the fact of his commercial brother having sent him a present of ten pounds, a practical expression of sympathy with him in his recent calamity. Biffen could not speak; he looked with alarm at Amy's pallid face. In a few words she told him of Reardon's condition.

'I feared this,' he replied under his breath. 'He was ill when I saw him off at London Bridge. But Willie is better, I trust?'

Amy tried to answer, but tears filled her eyes and her head dropped. Harold was overcome with a sense of fatality; grief and dread held him motionless.

They conversed brokenly for a few minutes, then left the house, Biffen carrying the hand-bag with which he had travelled hither. When they reached the hotel he waited apart until it was ascertained whether he could enter the sick-room. Amy rejoined him and said with a faint smile:

'He is conscious, and was very glad to hear that you had come. But don't let him try to speak much.'

The change that had come over his friend's countenance was to Harold, of course, far more gravely impressive than to those who had watched at the bedside. In the drawn features, large sunken eyes, thin and discoloured lips, it seemed to him that he read too surely the presage of doom. After holding the shrunken hand for a moment he was convulsed with an agonising sob, and had to turn away.

Amy saw that her husband wished to speak to her; she bent over him.

'Ask him to stay, dear. Give him a room in the hotel.'

'I will.'

Biffen sat down by the bedside, and remained for half an hour.

His friend inquired whether he had yet heard about the novel; the answer was a shake of the head. When he rose, Reardon signed to him to bend down, and whispered :

'It doesn't matter what happens; she is mine again.'

The next day was very cold, but a blue sky gleamed over land and sea. The drives and promenades were thronged with people in exuberant health and spirits. Biffen regarded this spectacle with resentful scorn; at another time it would have moved him merely to mirth, but not even the sound of the breakers when he had wandered as far as possible from human contact could help him to think with resignation of the injustice which triumphs so flagrantly in the destinies of men. Towards Amy he had no shadow of unkindness; the sight of her in tears had impressed him as profoundly, in another way, as that of his friend's wasted features. She and Reardon were again one, and his love for them both was stronger than any emotion of tenderness he had ever known.

In the afternoon he again sat by the bedside. Every symptom of the sufferer's condition pointed to an approaching end : a face that had grown cadaverous, livid lips, breath drawn in hurrying gasps. Harold despaired of another look of recognition. But as he sat with his forehead resting on his hand Amy touched him; Reardon had turned his face in their direction, and with a conscious gaze.

'I shall never go with you to Greece,' he said distinctly.

There was silence again. Biffen did not move his eyes from the deathly mask; in a minute or two he saw a smile soften its lineaments, and Reardon again spoke :

'How often you and I have quoted it ! – "We are such stuff as dreams are made on,"[40] and our –" '

The remaining words were indistinguishable, and, as if the effort of utterance had exhausted him, his eyes closed, and he sank into lethargy.

When he came down from his bedroom on the following morning, Biffen was informed that his friend had died between two and three o'clock. At the same time he received a note in which Amy requested him to come and see her late in the afternoon. He spent the day in a long walk along the eastward cliffs;

again the sun shone brilliantly, and the sea was flecked with foam upon its changing green and azure. It seemed to him that he had never before known solitude, even through all the years of his lonely and sad existence.

At sunset he obeyed Amy's summons. He found her calm, but with the signs of long weeping.

'At the last moment,' she said, 'he was able to speak to me, and you were mentioned. He wished you to have all that he has left in his room at Islington. When I come back to London, will you take me there and let me see the room just as when he lived in it? Let the people in the house know what has happened, and that I am responsible for whatever will be owing.'

Her resolve to behave composedly gave way as soon as Harold's broken voice had replied. Hysterical sobbing made further speech from her impossible, and Biffen, after holding her hand reverently for a moment, left her alone.

Chapter 33

THE SUNNY WAY

ON an evening of early summer, six months after the death of Edwin Reardon, Jasper of the facile pen was bending over his desk, writing rapidly by the warm western light which told that sunset was near. Not far from him sat his younger sister; she was reading, and the book in her hand bore the title, 'Mr Bailey, Grocer.'

'How will this do?' Jasper exclaimed, suddenly throwing down his pen.

And he read aloud a critical notice of the book with which Dora was occupied; a notice of the frankly eulogistic species, beginning with: 'It is seldom nowadays that the luckless reviewer of novels can draw the attention of the public to a new work which is at once powerful and original;' and ending: 'The word is a bold one, but we do not hesitate to pronounce this book a masterpiece.'

'Is that for *The Current*?' asked Dora, when he had finished.

'No, for *The West End*. Fadge won't allow any one but himself to be lauded in that style. I may as well do the notice for *The Current* now, as I've got my hand in.'

He turned to his desk again, and before daylight failed him had produced a piece of more cautious writing, very favourable on the whole, but with reserves and slight censures. This also he read to Dora.

'You wouldn't suspect they were written by the same man, eh?'

'No. You have changed the style very skilfully.'

'I doubt if they'll be much use. Most people will fling the book down with yawns before they're half through the first volume. If I knew a doctor who had many cases of insomnia in hand, I would recommend "Mr Bailey" to him as a specific.'

'Oh, but it is really clever, Jasper!'

'Not a doubt of it. I half believe what I have written. And if only we could get it mentioned in a leader or two, and so on, old Biffen's fame would be established with the better sort of readers. But he won't sell three hundred copies. I wonder whether Robertson would let me do a notice for his paper?'

'Biffen ought to be grateful to you, if he knew,' said Dora, laughing.

'Yet, now, there are people who would cry out that this kind of thing is disgraceful. It's nothing of the kind. Speaking seriously, we know that a really good book will more likely than not receive fair treatment from two or three reviewers; yes, but also more likely than not it will be swamped in the flood of literature that pours forth week after week, and won't have attention fixed long enough upon it to establish its repute. The struggle for existence among books is nowadays as severe as among men. If a writer has friends connected with the press, it is the plain duty of those friends to do their utmost to help him. What matter if they exaggerate, or even lie? The simple, sober truth has no chance whatever of being listened to, and it's only by volume of shouting that the ear of the public is held. What use is it to Biffen if his work struggled to slow recognition ten years hence? Besides, as I say, the growing flood of literature swamps everything but works of primary genius. If a clever and conscientious book does not spring to success at once, there's precious small chance that it will survive. Suppose it were possible for me to write a round dozen reviews of this book, in as many different papers, I would do it with satisfaction. Depend upon it, this kind of thing will be done on that scale before long. And it's quite natural. A man's friends must be helped, by whatever means, *quocunque modo*,[41] as Biffen himself would say.'

'I dare say he doesn't even think of you as a friend now.'

'Very likely not. It's ages since I saw him. But there's much magnanimity in my character, as I have often told you. It delights me to be generous, whenever I can afford it.'

Dusk was gathering about them. As they sat talking, there came a tap at the door, and the summons to enter was obeyed by Mr Whelpdale.

'I was passing,' he said in his respectful voice, 'and couldn't resist the temptation.'

Jasper struck a match and lit the lamp. In this clearer light Whelpdale was exhibited as a young man of greatly improved exterior; he wore a cream-coloured waistcoat, a necktie of subtle hue, and delicate gloves; prosperity breathed from his whole person. It was, in fact, only a moderate prosperity to which he had as yet attained, but the future beckoned to him flatteringly. Early in this year, his enterprise as 'literary adviser' had brought him in contact with a man of some pecuniary resources, who proposed to establish an agency for the convenience of authors who were not skilled in disposing of their productions to the best advantage. Under the name of Fleet & Co., this business was shortly set on foot, and Whelpdale's services were retained on satisfactory terms. The birth of the syndicate system had given new scope to literary agencies, and Mr Fleet was a man of keen eye for commercial opportunities.

'Well, have you read Biffen's book?' asked Jasper.

'Wonderful, isn't it? A work of genius, I am convinced. Ha! you have it there, Miss Dora. But I'm afraid it is hardly for you.'

'And why not, Mr Whelpdale?'

'You should only read of beautiful things, of happy lives. This book must depress you.'

'But why will you imagine me such a feeble-minded person?' asked Dora. 'You have so often spoken like this. I have really no ambition to be a doll of such superfine wax.'

The habitual flatterer looked deeply concerned.

'Pray forgive me!' he murmured humbly, leaning forward towards the girl with eyes which deprecated her displeasure. 'I am very far indeed from attributing weakness to you. It was only the natural, unreflecting impulse; one finds it so difficult to associate you, even as merely a reader, with such squalid scenes. The ignobly decent, as poor Biffen calls it, is so very far from that sphere in which you are naturally at home.'

There was some slight affectation in his language, but the tone attested sincere feeling. Jasper was watching him with half an eye, and glancing occasionally at Dora.

'No doubt,' said the latter, 'it's my story in *The English Girl* that inclines you to think me a goody-goody sort of young woman.'

'So far from that, Miss Dora, I was only waiting for an opportunity to tell you how exceedingly delighted I have been with the last two weeks' instalments. In all seriousness, I consider that story of yours the best thing of the kind that ever came under my notice. You seem to me to have discovered a new *genre*; such writing as this has surely never been offered to girls, and all the readers of the paper must be immensely grateful to you. I run eagerly to buy the paper each week; I assure you I do. The stationer thinks I purchase it for a sister, I suppose. But each section of the story seems to be better than the last. Mark the prophecy which I now make : when this tale is published in a volume its success will be great. You will be recognised, Miss Dora, as the new writer for modern English girls.'

The subject of this panegyric coloured a little and laughed. Unmistakably she was pleased.

'Look here, Whelpdale,' said Jasper, 'I can't have this; Dora's conceit, please to remember, is, to begin with, only a little less than my own, and you will make her unendurable. Her tale is well enough in its way, but then its way is a very humble one.'

'I deny it !' cried the other, excitedly. 'How can it be called a humble line of work to provide reading, which is at once intellectual and moving and exquisitely pure, for the most important part of the population – the educated and refined young people who are just passing from girlhood to womanhood?'

'The most important fiddlestick !'

'You are grossly irreverent, my dear Milvain. I cannot appeal to your sister, for she's too modest to rate her own sex at its true value, but the vast majority of thoughtful men would support me. You yourself do, though you affect this profane way of speaking. And we know,' he looked at Dora, 'that he wouldn't talk like this if Miss Yule were present.'

Jasper changed the topic of conversation, and presently Whelpdale was able to talk with more calmness. The young man, since his association with Fleet & Co., had become fertile in suggestions of literary enterprise, and at present he was occupied with a project of special hopefulness.

'I want to find a capitalist,' he said, 'who will get possession of that paper *Chat*, and transform it according to an idea I have in my head. The thing is doing very indifferently, but I am convinced it might be made splendid property, with a few changes in the way of conducting it.'

'The paper is rubbish,' remarked Jasper, 'and the kind of rubbish – oddly enough – which doesn't attract people.'

'Precisely, but the rubbish is capable of being made a very valuable article, if it were only handled properly. I have talked to the people about it again and again, but I can't get them to believe what I say. Now just listen to my notion. In the first place, I should slightly alter the name; only slightly, but that little alteration would in itself have an enormous effect. Instead of *Chat*, I should call it *Chit-Chat*!' [42]

Jasper exploded with mirth.

'That's brilliant!' he cried. 'A stroke of genius!'

'Are you serious? Or, are you making fun of me? I believe it is a stroke of genius. *Chat* doesn't attract any one, but *Chit-Chat* would sell like hot cakes, as they say in America. I know I am right; laugh as you will.'

'On the same principle,' cried Jasper, 'if *The Tatler* were changed to *Tittle-Tattle*, its circulation would be trebled.'

Whelpdale smote his knee in delight.

'An admirable idea! Many a true word uttered in joke, and this is an instance! *Tittle-Tattle* – a magnificent title; the very thing to catch the multitude.'

Dora was joining in the merriment, and for a minute or two nothing but bursts of laughter could be heard.

'Now do let me go on,' implored the man of projects, when the noise subsided. 'That's only one change, though a most important one. What I next propose is this: – I know you will laugh again, but I will demonstrate to you that I am right. No article in the paper is to measure more than two inches in length, and every inch must be broken into at least two paragraphs.'

'Superb!'

'But you are joking, Mr Whelpdale?' exclaimed Dora.

'No, I am perfectly serious. Let me explain my principle. I would have the paper address itself to the quarter-educated; that is to say, the great new generation that is being turned out by the Board schools, the young men and women who can just read, but are incapable of sustained attention. People of this kind want something to occupy them in trains, and on 'buses and trams. As a rule they care for no newspapers except the Sunday ones; what they want is the lightest and frothiest of chit-chatty information – bits of stories, bits of description, bits of scandal, bits of jokes, bits of statistics, bits of foolery. Am I not right? Everything must be very short, two inches at the utmost; their attention can't sustain itself beyond two inches. Even chat is too solid for them: they want chit-chat.'

Jasper had begun to listen seriously.

'There's something in this, Whelpdale,' he remarked.

'Ha! I have caught you?' cried the other delightedly. 'Of course there's something in it!'

'But –' began Dora, and checked herself.

'You were going to say –' Whelpdale bent towards her with deference.

'Surely these poor, silly people oughtn't to be encouraged in their weakness.'

Whelpdale's countenance fell. He looked ashamed of himself. But Jasper came speedily to the rescue.

'That's twaddle, Dora. Fools will be fools to the world's end. Answer a fool according to his folly; supply a simpleton with the reading he craves, if it will put money in your pocket. You have discouraged poor Whelpdale in one of the most notable projects of modern times.'

'I shall think no more of it,' said Whelpdale, gravely. 'You are right, Miss Dora.'

Again Jasper burst into merriment. His sister reddened, and looked uncomfortable. She began to speak timidly :

'You said this was for reading in trains and 'buses?'

Whelpdale caught at hope.

'Yes. And really, you know, it may be better at such times to read chit-chat than to be altogether vacant, or to talk unprofitably. I am not sure; I bow to your opinion unreservedly.'

'So long as they only read the paper at such times,' said Dora, still hesitating. 'One knows by experience that one really can't fix one's attention in travelling; even an article in a newspaper is often too long.'

'Exactly! And if *you* find it so, what must be the case with the mass of untaught people, the quarter-educated. It *might* encourage in more of them a taste for reading – don't you think?'

'It might,' assented Dora, musingly. 'And in that case you would be doing good!'

'Distinct good!'

They smiled joyfully at each other. Then Whelpdale turned to Jasper:

'You are convinced that there is something in this?'

'Seriously, I think there is. It would all depend on the skill of the fellows who put the thing together every week. There ought always to be one strongly sensational item – we won't call it article. For instance, you might display on a placard: "What the Queen eats!" or, "How Gladstone's collars are made!" – things of that kind.'

'To be sure, to be sure. And then, you know,' added Whelpdale, glancing anxiously at Dora, 'when people had been attracted by these devices, they would find a few things that were really profitable. We would give nicely written little accounts of exemplary careers, of heroic deeds, and so on. Of course nothing whatever that could be really demoralising – *cela va sans dire*. Well, what I was going to say was this: would you come with me to the office of *Chat*, and have a talk with my friend Lake, the sub-editor? I know your time is very valuable, but then you're often running into the *Will-o'-the-Wisp*, and *Chat* is just upstairs, you know.'

'What use should I be?'

'Oh, all the use in the world. Lake would pay most respectful attention to your opinion, though he thinks so little of mine. You are a man of note, I am nobody. I feel convinced that you could persuade the *Chat* people to adopt my idea, and they might be willing to give me a contingent share of contingent profits, if I had really shown them the way to a good thing.'

Jasper promised to think the matter over. Whilst their talk still ran on this subject, a packet that had come by post was brought into the room. Opening it, Milvain exclaimed:

'Ha! this is lucky. There's something here that may interest you, Whelpdale.'

'Proofs?'

'Yes. A paper I have written for *The Wayside*.' He looked at Dora, who smiled. 'How do you like the title? – "The Novels of Edwin Reardon!"'

'You don't say so!' cried the other. 'What a good-hearted fellow you are, Milvain! Now that's really a kind thing to have done. By Jove! I must shake hands with you; I must indeed! Poor Reardon! Poor old fellow!'

His eyes gleamed with moisture. Dora, observing this, looked at him so gently and sweetly that it was perhaps well he did not meet her eyes; the experience would have been altogether too much for him.

'It has been written for three months,' said Jasper, 'but we have held it over for a practical reason. When I was engaged upon it, I went to see Mortimer, and asked him if there was any chance of a new edition of Reardon's books. He had no idea the poor fellow was dead, and the news seemed really to affect him. He promised to consider whether it would be worth while trying a new issue, and before long I heard from him that he would bring out the two best books with a decent cover and so on, provided I could get my article on Reardon into one of the monthlies. This was soon settled. The editor of *The Wayside* answered at once, when I wrote to him, that he should be very glad to print what I proposed, as he had a real respect for Reardon. Next month the books will be out – "Neutral Ground," and "Hubert Reed." Mortimer said he was sure these were the only ones that would pay for themselves. But we shall see. He may alter his opinion when my article has been read.'

'Read it to us now, Jasper, will you?' asked Dora.

The request was supported by Whelpdale, and Jasper needed no pressing. He seated himself so that the lamp-light fell upon the pages, and read the article through. It was an excellent piece of writing (see *The Wayside*, June 1884), and in places touched with true emotion. Any intelligent reader would divine that the author had been personally acquainted with the man of whom he wrote, though the fact was nowhere stated. The praise was not exaggerated, yet all the best points of Reardon's work were admirably brought out. One who knew Jasper might reasonably have doubted, before reading this, whether he was capable of so worthily appreciating the nobler man.

'I never understood Reardon so well before,' declared Whelpdale, at the close. 'This is a good thing well done. It's something to be proud of, Miss Dora.'

'Yes, I feel that it is,' she replied.

'Mrs Reardon ought to be very grateful to you, Milvain. By-the-by, do you ever see her?'

'I have met her only once since his death – by chance.'

'Of course she will marry again. I wonder who'll be the fortunate man?'

'Fortunate, do you think?' asked Dora quietly, without looking at him.

'Oh, I spoke rather cynically, I'm afraid,' Whelpdale hastened to reply. 'I was thinking of her money. Indeed, I knew Mrs Reardon only very slightly.'

'I don't think you need regret it,' Dora remarked.

'Oh well, come, come!' put in her brother. 'We know very well that there was little enough blame on her side.'

'There was *great* blame!' Dora exclaimed. 'She behaved shamefully! I wouldn't speak to her; I wouldn't sit down in her company!'

'Bosh! What do you know about it? Wait till you are married to a man like Reardon, and reduced to utter penury.'

'Whoever my husband was, I would stand by him, if I starved to death!'

'If he ill-used you?'

'I am not talking of such cases. Mrs Reardon had never anything of the kind to fear. It was impossible for a man such as her husband to behave harshly. Her conduct was cowardly, faithless, unwomanly!'

'Trust one woman for thinking the worst of another,' observed Jasper with something like a sneer.

Dora gave him a look of strong disapproval; one might have suspected that brother and sister had before this fallen into disagreement on the delicate topic. Whelpdale felt obliged to interpose, and had of course no choice but to support the girl.

'I can only say,' he remarked with a smile, 'that Miss Dora takes a very noble point of view. One feels that a wife ought to be staunch. But it's so very unsafe to discuss matters in which one cannot know all the facts.'

'We know quite enough of the facts,' said Dora, with delightful pertinacity.

'Indeed, perhaps we do,' assented her slave. Then, turning to her brother, 'Well, once more I congratulate you. I shall talk of your article incessantly, as soon as it appears. And I shall pester every one of my acquaintances to buy Reardon's books – though it's no use to him, poor fellow. Still, he would have died more contentedly if he could have foreseen this. By-the-by, Biffen will be profoundly grateful to you, I'm sure.'

'I'm doing what I can for him, too. Run your eye over these slips.'

Whelpdale exhausted himself in terms of satisfaction.

'You deserve to get on, my dear fellow. In a few years you will be the Aristarchus of our literary world.'

When the visitor rose to depart, Jasper said he would walk a short distance with him. As soon as they had left the house, the future Aristarchus [43] made a confidential communication.

'It may interest you to know that my sister Maud is shortly to be married.'

'Indeed ! May I ask to whom?'

'A man you don't know. His name is Dolomore — a fellow in society.'

'Rich, then, I hope?'

'Tolerably well-to-do. I dare say he has three or four thousand a year !'

'Gracious heavens ! Why, that's magnificent.'

But Whelpdale did not look quite so much satisfaction as his words expressed.

'Is it to be soon?' he inquired.

'At the end of the season. Make no difference to Dora and me, of course.'

'Oh? Really? No difference at all? You will let me come and see you – both – just in the old way, Milvain?'

'Why the deuce shouldn't you?'

'To be sure, to be sure. By Jove ! I really don't know how I should get on if I couldn't look in of an evening now and then. I have got so much into the habit of it. And – I'm a lonely beggar, you know. I don't go into society, and really –'

He broke off, and Jasper began to speak of other things.

When Milvain re-entered the house, Dora had gone to her own sitting-room. It was not quite ten o'clock. Taking one set of the proofs of his 'Reardon' article, he put it into a large envelope; then he wrote a short letter, which began 'Dear Mrs Reardon,' and ended 'Very sincerely yours,' the communication itself being as follows :

'I venture to send you the proofs of a paper which is to appear in next month's *Wayside*, in the hope that it may seem to you not badly done, and that the reading of it may give you pleasure. If anything occurs to you which you would like me to add, or if you desire any omission, will you do me the kindness to let me know of it as soon as possible, and your suggestions shall at once be adopted. I am informed that the new edition of "On Neutral Ground" and "Hubert Reed" will be ready next month. Need I say how glad I am that my friend's work is not to be forgotten?'

This note he also put into the envelope, which he made ready for posting. Then he sat for a long time in profound thought.

Shortly after eleven his door opened, and Maud came in. She had been dining at Mrs Lane's. Her attire was still simple, but of quality which would have signified recklessness, but for the outlook whereof Jasper spoke to Whelpdale. The girl looked very beautiful. There was a flush of health and happiness on her cheek, and when she spoke it was in a voice that rang quite differently from her tones of a year ago; the pride which was natural to her had now a firm support; she moved and uttered herself in queenly fashion.

'Has anyone been?' she asked.

'Whelpdale.'

'Oh! I wanted to ask you, Jasper: do you think it wise to let him come quite so often?'

'There's a difficulty, you see. I can hardly tell him to sheer off. And he's really a decent fellow.'

'That may be. But – I think it's rather unwise. Things are changed. In a few months, Dora will be a good deal at my house, and will see all sorts of people.'

'Yes; but what if they are the kind of people she doesn't care anything about? You must remember, old girl, that her tastes are quite different from yours. I say nothing, but – perhaps it's as well they should be.'

'You say nothing, but you add an insult,' returned Maud, with a smile of superb disregard. 'We won't reopen the question.'

'Oh dear no! And, by-the-by, I have a letter from Dolomore. It came just after you left.'

'Well?'

'He is quite willing to settle upon you a third of his income from the collieries; he tells me it will represent between seven and eight hundred a year. I think it rather little, you know; but I congratulate myself on having got this out of him.'

'Don't speak in that unpleasant way ! It was only your abruptness that made any kind of difficulty.'

'I have my own opinion on that point, and I shall beg leave to keep it. Probably he will think me still more abrupt when I request, as I am now going to do, an interview with his solicitors.'

'Is that allowable?' asked Maud, anxiously. 'Can you do that with any decency?'

'If not, then I must do it with indecency. You will have the goodness to remember that if I don't look after your interests, no one else will. It's perhaps fortunate for you that I have a good deal of the man of business about me. Dolomore thought I was a dreamy, literary fellow. I don't say that he isn't entirely honest, but he shows something of a disposition to play the autocrat, and I by no means intend to let him. If you had a father, Dolomore would have to submit his affairs to examination. I stand to you *in loco parentis*, and I shall bate no jot of my rights.'

'But you can't say that his behaviour hasn't been perfectly straightforward.'

'I don't wish to. I think, on the whole, he has behaved more honourably than was to be expected of a man of his kind. But he must treat *me* with respect. My position in the world is greatly superior to his. And, by the gods ! I will be treated respectfully ! It wouldn't be amiss, Maud, if you just gave him a hint to that effect.'

'All I have to say is, Jasper, don't do me an irreparable injury. You might, without meaning it.'

'No fear whatever of it. I can behave as a gentleman, and I only expect Dolomore to do the same.'

The conversation lasted for a long time, and when he was again left alone Jasper again fell into a mood of thoughtfulness.

By a late post on the following day he received this letter:

'DEAR MR MILVAIN, — I have received the proofs, and have just read them; I hasten to thank you with all my heart. No suggestion of mine could possibly improve this article; it seems to me perfect in taste, in style, in matter. No one but you could have written this, for no one else understood Edwin so well, or had given such thought to his work. If he could but have known that such justice would be done to his memory! But he died believing that already he was utterly forgotten, that his books would never again be publicly spoken of. This was a cruel fate. I have shed tears over what you have written, but they were not only tears of bitterness; it cannot but be a consolation to me to think that, when the magazine appears, so many people will talk of Edwin and his books. I am deeply grateful to Mr Mortimer for having undertaken to republish those two novels; if you have an opportunity, will you do me the great kindness to thank him on my behalf? At the same time, I must remember that it was you who first spoke to him on this subject. You say that it gladdens you to think Edwin will not be forgotten, and I am very sure that the friendly office you have so admirably performed will in itself reward you more than any poor expression of gratitude from me. I write hurriedly, anxious to let you hear as soon as possible.

> 'Believe me, dear Mr Milvain,
> > 'Yours sincerely,
> > > 'AMY REARDON.'

Chapter 34

A CHECK

MARIAN was at work as usual in the Reading-room. She did her best, during the hours spent here, to convert herself into the literary machine which it was her hope would some day be invented for construction in a less sensitive material than human tissue. Her eyes seldom strayed beyond the limits of the desk; and if she had occasion to rise and go to the reference shelves, she looked at no one on the way. Yet she herself was occasionally an object of interested regard. Several readers were acquainted with the chief facts of her position; they knew that her father was now incapable of work, and was waiting till his diseased eyes should be ready for the operator; it was surmised, moreover, that a good deal depended upon the girl's literary exertions. Mr Quarmby and his gossips naturally took the darkest view of things; they were convinced that Alfred Yule could never recover his sight, and they had a dolorous satisfaction in relating the story of Marian's legacy. Of her relations with Jasper Milvain none of these persons had heard; Yule had never spoken of that matter to any one of his friends.

Jasper had to look in this morning for a hurried consultation of certain encyclopædic volumes, and it chanced that Marian was standing before the shelves to which his business led him. He saw her from a little distance, and paused; it seemed as if he would turn back; for a moment he wore a look of doubt and worry. But after all he proceeded. At the sound of his 'Good-morning,' Marian started – she was standing with an open book in hand, – and looked up with a gleam of joy on her face.

'I wanted to see you to-day,' she said, subduing her voice to the tone of ordinary conversation. 'I should have come this evening.'

'You wouldn't have found me at home. From five to seven I shall be frantically busy, and then I have to rush off to dine with some people.'

'I couldn't see you before five?'

'Is it something important?'

'Yes, it is.'

'I tell you what. If you could meet me at Gloucester Gate at four, then I shall be glad of half an hour in the park. But I mustn't talk now; I'm driven to my wits' end. Gloucester Gate, at four sharp. I don't think it'll rain.'

He dragged out a tome of the 'Britannica.' Marian nodded, and returned to her seat.

At the appointed hour she was waiting near the entrance of Regent's Park which Jasper had mentioned. Not long ago there had fallen a light shower, but the sky was clear again. At five minutes past four she still waited, and had begun to fear that the passing rain might have led Jasper to think she would not come. Another five minutes, and from a hansom that rattled hither at full speed, the familiar figure alighted.

'Do forgive me!' he exclaimed. 'I couldn't possibly get here before. Let us go to the right.'

They betook themselves to that tree-shadowed strip of the park which skirts the canal.

'I'm so afraid that you haven't really time,' said Marian, who was chilled and confused by this show of hurry. She regretted having made the appointment; it would have been much better to postpone what she had to say until Jasper was at leisure. Yet nowadays the hours of leisure seemed to come so rarely.

'If I get home at five, it'll be all right,' he replied. 'What have you to tell me, Marian?'

'We have heard about the money, at last.'

'Oh?' He avoided looking at her. 'And what's the upshot?'

'I shall have nearly fifteen hundred pounds.'

'So much as that? Well, that's better than nothing, isn't it?'

'Very much better.'

They walked on in silence. Marian stole a glance at her companion.

'I should have thought it a great deal,' she said presently, 'before I had begun to think of thousands.'

'Fifteen hundred. Well, it means fifty pounds a year, I suppose.'

He chewed the end of his moustache.

'Let us sit down on this bench. Fifteen hundred – h'm! And nothing more is to be hoped for?'

'Nothing. I should have thought men would wish to pay their debts, even after they had been bankrupt; but they tell us we can't expect anything more from these people.'

'You are thinking of Walter Scott, and that kind of thing' – Jasper laughed. 'Oh, that's quite unbusinesslike; it would be setting a pernicious example nowadays. Well, and what's to be done?'

Marian had no answer for such a question. The tone of it was a new stab to her heart, which had suffered so many during the past half year.

'Now, I'll ask you frankly,' Jasper went on, 'and I know you will reply in the same spirit: would it be wise for us to marry on this money?'

'On this money?'

She looked into his face with painful earnestness.

'You mean,' he said, 'that it can't be spared for that purpose?'

What she really meant was uncertain even to herself. She had wished to hear how Jasper would receive the news, and thereby to direct her own course. Had he welcomed it as offering a possibility of their marriage, that would have gladdened her, though it would then have been necessary to show him all the difficulties by which she was beset; for some time they had not spoken of her father's position, and Jasper seemed willing to forget all about that complication of their troubles. But marriage did not occur to him, and he was evidently quite prepared to hear that she could no longer regard this money as her own to be freely disposed of. This was on one side a relief, but on the other it confirmed her fears. She would rather have heard him plead with her to neglect her parents for the sake of being his wife. Love excuses everything, and his selfishness would have been easily lost sight of in the assurance that he still desired her.

'You say,' she replied, with bent head, 'that it would bring us fifty pounds a year. If another fifty were added to that, my father and mother would be supported in case the worst comes. I might earn fifty pounds.'

'You wish me to understand, Marian, that I mustn't expect that you will bring me anything when we are married.'

His tone was that of acquiescence; not by any means of displeasure. He spoke as if desirous of saying for her something she found a difficulty in saying for herself.

'Jasper, it is so hard for me! So hard for me! How could I help remembering what you told me when I promised to be your wife?'

'I spoke the truth rather brutally,' he replied, in a kind voice. 'Let all that be unsaid, forgotten. We are in quite a different position now. Be open with me, Marian; surely you can trust my common sense and good feeling. Put aside all thought of things I have said, and don't be restrained by any fear lest you should seem to me unwomanly – you can't be that. What is your own wish? What do you really wish to do, now that there is no uncertainty calling for postponements?'

Marian raised her eyes, and was about to speak as she regarded him; but with the first accent her look fell.

'I wish to be your wife.'

He waited, thinking and struggling with himself.

'Yet you feel that it would be heartless to take and use this money for our own purposes?'

'What is to become of my parents, Jasper?'

'But then you admit that the fifteen hundred pounds won't support them. You talk of earning fifty pounds a year for them.'

'Need I cease to write, dear, if we were married? Wouldn't you let me help them?'

'But, my dear girl, you are taking for granted that we shall have enough for ourselves.'

'I didn't really mean at once,' she explained hurriedly. 'In a short time – in a year. You are getting on so well. You will soon have a sufficient income, I am sure.'

Jasper rose.

'Let us walk as far as the next seat. Don't speak. I have something to think about.'

Moving on beside him, she slipped her hand softly within his arm; but Jasper did not put the arm into position to support hers, and her hand fell again, dropped suddenly. They reached another bench, and again became seated.

'It comes to this, Marian,' he said, with portentous gravity. 'Support you, I could – I have little doubt of that. Maud is provided for, and Dora can make a living for herself. I could support you and leave you free to give your parents whatever you can earn by your own work. But –'

He paused significantly. It was his wish that Marian should supply the consequence, but she did not speak.

'Very well,' he exclaimed. 'Then when are we to be married?'

The tone of resignation was too marked. Jasper was not good as a comedian; he lacked subtlety.

'We must wait,' fell from Marian's lips, in the whisper of despair.

'Wait? But how long?' he inquired, dispassionately.

'Do you wish to be freed from your engagement, Jasper?'

He was not strong enough to reply with a plain 'Yes,' and so have done with his perplexities. He feared the girl's face, and he feared his own subsequent emotions.

'Don't talk in that way, Marian. The question is simply this: Are we to wait a year, or are we to wait five years? In a year's time, I shall probably be able to have a small house somewhere out in the suburbs. If we are married then, I shall be happy enough with so good a wife, but my career will take a different shape. I shall just throw overboard certain of my ambitions, and work steadily on at earning a livelihood. If we wait five years, I may perhaps have obtained an editorship, and in that case I should of course have all sorts of better things to offer you.'

'But, dear, why shouldn't you get an editorship all the same if you are married?'

'I have explained to you several times that success of that kind is not compatible with a small house in the suburbs and all the ties of a narrow income. As a bachelor, I can go about freely, make acquaintances, dine at people's houses, perhaps entertain a useful friend now and then – and so on. It is not merit that succeeds in my line; it is merit *plus* opportunity. Marrying now, I cut myself off from opportunity, that's all.'

She kept silence.

'Decide my fate for me, Marian,' he pursued, magnanimously. 'Let us make up our minds and do what we decide to do. Indeed, it doesn't concern me so much as yourself. Are you content to lead a simple, unambitious life? Or should you prefer your husband to be a man of some distinction?'

'I know so well what your own wish is. But to wait for years – you will cease to love me, and will only think of me as a hindrance in your way.'

'Well now, when I said five years, of course I took a round number. Three – two *might* make all the difference to me.'

'Let it be just as you wish. I can bear anything rather than lose your love.'

'You feel, then, that it will decidedly be wise not to marry whilst we are still so poor?'

'Yes; whatever you are convinced of is right.'

He again rose, and looked at his watch.

'Jasper, you don't think that I have behaved selfishly in wishing to let my father have the money?'

'I should have been greatly surprised if you hadn't wished it. I certainly can't imagine you saying: "Oh, let them do as best they can!" That would have been selfish with a vengeance.'

'Now you are speaking kindly! Must you go, Jasper?'

'I must indeed. Two hours' work I am bound to get before seven o'clock.'

'And I have been making it harder for you, by disturbing your mind.'

'No, no; it's all right now. I shall go at it with all the more energy, now we have come to a decision.'

'Dora has asked me to go to Kew on Sunday. Shall you be able to come, dear?'

'By Jove, no! I have three engagements on Sunday afternoon. I'll try and keep the Sunday after; I will indeed.'

'What are the engagements?' she asked timidly.

As they walked back towards Gloucester Gate, he answered her question, showing how unpardonable it would be to neglect the people concerned. Then they parted, Jasper going off at a smart pace homewards.

Marian turned down Park Street, and proceeded for some distance along Camden Road. The house in which she and her parents now lived was not quite so far away as St Paul's Crescent; they rented four rooms, one of which had to serve both as Alfred Yule's sitting-room and for the gatherings of the family at meals. Mrs Yule generally sat in the kitchen, and Marian used her bedroom as a study. About half the collection of books had been sold; those that remained were still a respectable library, almost covering the walls of the room where their disconsolate possessor passed his mournful days.

He could read for a few hours a day, but only large type, and fear of consequences kept him well within the limit of such indulgence laid down by his advisers. Though he inwardly spoke as if his case were hopeless, Yule was very far from having resigned himself to this conviction; indeed, the prospect of spending his latter years in darkness and idleness was too dreadful to him to be accepted so long as a glimmer of hope remained. He saw no reason why the customary operation should not restore him to his old pursuits, and he would have borne it ill if his wife or daughter had ever ceased to oppose the despair which it pleased him to affect.

On the whole, he was noticeably patient. At the time of their removal to these lodgings, seeing that Marian prepared herself to share the change as a matter of course, he let her do as she would without comment; nor had he since spoken to her on the subject which had proved so dangerous. Confidence between them there was none; Yule addressed his daughter in a grave, cold, civil tone, and Marian replied gently, but without tenderness. For Mrs Yule the disaster to the family was distinctly a gain; she could not but mourn her husband's affliction, yet he no longer visited her with the fury or contemptuous impatience of former days. Doubtless the fact of needing so much tendance had its softening influence on the man; he could not turn brutally upon his wife when every hour of the day afforded him some proof of her absolute devotion. Of course his open-air exercise was still unhindered, and in this season of the returning sun he walked a great deal, decidedly to the advantage of his general health – which again must have been a source of benefit to his temper. Of evenings, Marian sometimes read to him. He never requested this, but he did not reject the kindness.

This afternoon Marian found her father examining a volume of prints which had been lent him by Mr Quarmby. The table was laid for dinner (owing to Marian's frequent absence at the Museum, no change had been made in the order of meals) and Yule sat by the window, his book propped on a second chair. A whiteness in his eyes showed how the disease was progressing, but his face had a more wholesome colour than a year ago.

'Mr Hinks and Mr Gorbutt inquired very kindly after you to-day,' said the girl, as she seated herself.

'Oh, is Hinks out again?'

'Yes, but he looks very ill.'

They conversed of such matters until Mrs Yule – now her own servant – brought in the dinner. After the meal, Marian was in her bedroom for about an hour; then she went to her father, who sat in idleness, smoking.

'What is your mother doing?' he asked, as she entered.

'Some needlework.'

'I had perhaps better say' – he spoke rather stiffly, and with averted face – 'that I make no exclusive claim to the use of this room. As I can no longer pretend to study, it would be idle to keep up the show of privacy that mustn't be disturbed. Perhaps you will mention to your mother that she is quite at liberty to sit here whenever she chooses.'

It was characteristic of him that he should wish to deliver this permission by proxy. But Marian understood how much was implied in such an announcement.

'I will tell mother,' she said. 'But at this moment I wished to speak to you privately. How would you advise me to invest my money?'

Yule looked surprised, and answered with cold dignity.

'It is strange that you should put such a question to me. I should have supposed your interests were in the hands of – of some competent person.'

'This will be my private affair, father. I wish to get as high a rate of interest as I safely can.'

'I really must decline to advise, or interfere in any way. But, as you have introduced this subject, I may as well put a question which is connected with it. Could you give me any idea as to how long you are likely to remain with us?'

'At least a year,' was the answer, 'and very likely much longer.'

'Am I to understand, then, that your marriage is indefinitely postponed?'

'Yes, father.'

'And will you tell me why?'

'I can only say that it has seemed better – to both of us.'

Yule detected the sorrowful emotion she was endeavouring to suppress. His conception of Milvain's character made it easy for him to form a just surmise as to the reasons for this postponement; he was gratified to think that Marian might learn how rightly he had judged her wooer, and an involuntary pity for the girl did not prevent his hoping that the detestable alliance was doomed. With difficulty he refrained from smiling.

'I will make no comment on that,' he remarked, with a certain emphasis. 'But do you imply that this investment of which you speak is to be solely for your own advantage?'

'For mine, and for yours and mother's.'

There was a silence of a minute or two. As yet it had not been necessary to take any steps for raising money, but a few months more would see the family without resources, save those provided by Marian, who, without discussion, had been simply setting aside what she received for her work.

'You must be well aware,' said Yule at length, 'that I cannot consent to benefit by any such offer. When it is necessary, I shall borrow on the security of –'

'Why should you do that, father?' Marian interrupted. 'My money is yours. If you refuse it as a gift, then why may not I lend to you as well as a stranger? Repay me when your eyes are restored. For the present, all our anxieties are at an end. We can live very well until you are able to write again.'

For his sake she put it in his way. Supposing him never able to earn anything, then indeed would come a time of hardship; but she could not contemplate that. The worst would only befall them in case she was forsaken by Jasper, and if that happened all else would be of little account.

'This has come upon me as a surprise,' said Yule, in his most reserved tone. 'I can give no definite reply; I must think of it.'

'Should you like me to ask mother to bring her sewing here now?' asked Marian, rising.

'Yes, you may do so.'

In this way the awkwardness of the situation was overcome, and when Marian next had occasion to speak of money matters no serious objection was offered to her proposal.

Dora Milvain of course learnt what had come to pass; to

anticipate criticism, her brother imparted to her the decision at which Marian and he had arrived. She reflected with an air of discontent.

'So you are quite satisfied,' was her question at length, 'that Marian should toil to support her parents as well as herself?'

'Can I help it?'

'I shall think very ill of you if you don't marry her in a year at latest.'

'I tell you, Marian has made a deliberate choice. She understands me perfectly, and is quite satisfied with my projects. You will have the kindness, Dora, not to disturb her faith in me.'

'I agree to that; and in return I shall let you know when she begins to suffer from hunger. It won't be very long till then, you may be sure. How do you suppose three people are going to live on a hundred a year? And it's very doubtful indeed whether Marian can earn as much as fifty pounds. Never mind; I shall let you know when she is beginning to starve, and doubtless that will amuse you.'

At the end of July Maud was married. Between Mr Dolomore and Jasper existed no superfluous kindness, each resenting the other's self-sufficiency; but Jasper, when once satisfied of his proposed brother-in-law's straightforwardness, was careful not to give offence to a man who might some day serve him. Provided this marriage resulted in moderate happiness to Maud, it was undoubtedly a magnificent stroke of luck. Mrs Lane, the lady who has so often been casually mentioned, took upon herself those offices in connection with the ceremony which the bride's mother is wont to perform; at her house was held the wedding-breakfast, and such other absurdities of usage as recommend themselves to Society. Dora of course played the part of a bridesmaid, and Jasper went through his duties with the suave seriousness of a man who has convinced himself that he cannot afford to despise anything that the world sanctions.

About the same time occurred another event which was to have more importance for this aspiring little family than could as yet be foreseen. Whelpdale's noteworthy idea triumphed; the weekly paper called Chat was thoroughly transformed, and appeared as Chit-Chat. From the first number, the success of the enterprise was beyond doubt; in a month's time all England was ringing with the fame of this noble new development of journalism; the proprietor saw his way to a solid fortune, and other men who had money to embark began to scheme imitative publications. It was clear that the quarter-educated would soon be abundantly provided with literature to their taste.

Whelpdale's exultation was unbounded, but in the fifth week of the life of *Chit-Chat* something happened which threatened to overturn his sober reason. Jasper was walking along the Strand one afternoon, when he saw his ingenious friend approaching him in a manner scarcely to be accounted for, unless Whelpdale's abstemiousness had for once given way before convivial invitation. The young man's hat was on the back of his head and his coat flew wildly as he rushed forwards with perspiring face and glaring eyes. He would have passed without observing Jasper, had not the latter called to him; then he turned round, laughed insanely, grasped his acquaintance by the wrists, and drew him aside into a court.

'What do you think?' he panted. 'What do you think has happened?'

'Not what one would suppose, I hope. You seem to have gone mad.'

'I've got Lake's place on *Chit-Chat*!' cried the other hoarsely. 'Two hundred and fifty a year! Lake and the editor quarrelled – pummelled each other – neither know nor care what it was about. My fortune's made!'

'You're a modest man,' remarked Jasper, smiling.

'Certainly I am. I have always admitted it. But remember that there's my connection with Fleet as well; no need to give that up. Presently I shall be making a clear six hundred, my dear sir! A clear six hundred, if a penny!'

'Satisfactory, so far.'

'But you must remember that I'm not a big gun, like you! Why, my dear Milvain, a year ago I should have thought an income of two hundred a glorious competence. I don't aim at such things as are fit for you. You won't be content till you have thousands; of course I know that. But I'm a humble fellow. Yet no; by Jingo, I'm not! In one way I'm not – I must confess it.'

'In what instance are you arrogant?'

'I can't tell you – not yet; this is neither time nor place. I say, when will you dine with me? I shall give a dinner to half a dozen of my acquaintances somewhere or other. Poor old Biffen must come. When can you dine?'

'Give me a week's notice, and I'll fit it in.'

That dinner came duly off. On the day that followed, Jasper and Dora left town for their holiday; they went to the Channel Islands, and spent more than half of the three weeks they had allowed themselves in Sark. Passing over from Guernsey to that island, they were amused to see a copy of *Chit-Chat* in the hands of an obese and well-dressed man.

'Is *he* one of the quarter-educated?' asked Dora, laughing.

'Not in Whelpdale's sense of the word. But, strictly speaking, no doubt he is. The quarter-educated constitute a very large class indeed; how large, the huge success of that paper is demonstrating. I'll write to Whelpdale and let him know that his benefaction has extended even to Sark.'

This letter was written, and in a few days there came a reply.

'Why, the fellow has written to you as well!' exclaimed Jasper, taking up a second letter; both were on the table of their sitting-room when they came to their lodgings for lunch. 'That's his hand.'

'It looks like it.'

Dora hummed an air as she regarded the envelope, then she took it away with her to her room upstairs.

'What had he to say?' Jasper inquired, when she came down again and seated herself at the table.

'Oh, a friendly letter. What does he say to you?'

Dora had never looked so animated and fresh of colour since leaving London; her brother remarked this, and was glad to think that the air of the Channel should be doing her so much good. He read Whelpdale's letter aloud; it was facetious, but oddly respectful.

'The reverence that fellow has for me is astonishing,' he observed with a laugh. 'The queer thing is it increases the better he knows me.'

Dora laughed for five minutes.

'Oh, what a splendid epigram!' she exclaimed. 'It is indeed a queer thing, Jasper! Did you mean that to be a good joke, or was it better still by coming out unintentionally?'

'You are in remarkable spirits, old girl. By-the-by, would you mind letting me see that letter of yours?'

He held out his hand.

'I left it upstairs,' Dora replied carelessly.

'Rather presumptuous in him, it seems to me.'

'Oh, he writes quite as respectfully to me as he does to you,' she returned, with a peculiar smile.

'But what business has he to write at all? It's confounded impertinence, now I come to think of it. I shall give him a hint to remember his position.'

Dora could not be quite sure whether he spoke seriously or not. As both of them had begun to eat with an excellent appetite, a few moments were allowed to pass before the girl again spoke.

'His position is as good as ours,' she said at length.

'As good as ours? The "sub." of a paltry rag like *Chit-Chat*, and assistant to a literary agency!'

'He makes considerably more money than we do.'

'Money! What's money?'

Dora was again mirthful.

'Oh, of course money is nothing! *We* write for honour and glory. Don't forget to insist on that when you reprove Mr Whelpdale; no doubt it will impress him.'

Late in the evening of that day, when the brother and sister had strolled by moonlight up to the windmill which occupies the highest point of Sark, and as they stood looking upon the pale expanse of sea, dotted with the gleam of lighthouses near and far, Dora broke the silence to say quietly:

'I may as well tell you that Mr Whelpdale wants to know if I will marry him.'

'The deuce he does!' cried Jasper, with a start. 'If I didn't half suspect something of that kind! What astounding impudence!'

'You seriously think so?'

'Well, don't you? You hardly know him, to begin with. And then – oh, confound it!'

'Very well, I'll tell him that his impudence astonishes me.'

'You will?'

'Certainly. Of course in civil terms. But don't let this make any difference between you and him. Just pretend to know nothing about it; no harm is done.'

'You are speaking in earnest?'

'Quite. He has written in a very proper way, and there's no reason whatever to disturb our friendliness with him. I have a right to give directions in a matter like this, and you'll please to obey them.'

Before going to bed Dora wrote a letter to Mr Whelpdale, not, indeed, accepting his offer forthwith, but conveying to him with much gracefulness an unmistakable encouragement to persevere. This was posted on the morrow, and its writer continued to benefit most remarkably by the sun and breezes and rock-scrambling of Sark.

Soon after their return to London, Dora had the satisfaction of paying the first visit to her sister at the Dolomores' house in Ovington Square. Maud was established in the midst of luxuries, and talked with laughing scorn of the days when she inhabited Grub Street; her literary tastes were henceforth to serve as merely a note of distinction, an added grace which made evident her superiority to the well attired and smooth-tongued people among whom she was content to shine. On the one hand, she had contact with the world of fashionable literature, on the other with that of fashionable ignorance. Mrs Lane's house was a meeting-point of the two spheres.

'I shan't be there very often,' remarked Jasper, as Dora and he discussed their sister's magnificence. 'That's all very well in its way, but I aim at something higher.'

'So do I,' Dora replied.

'I'm very glad to hear that. I confess it seemed to me that you were rather too cordial with Whelpdale yesterday.'

'One must behave civilly. Mr Whelpdale quite understands me.'

'You are sure of that? He didn't seem quite so gloomy as he ought to have been.'

'The success of Chit-Chat keeps him in good spirits.'

It was perhaps a week after this that Mrs Dolomore came quite unexpectedly to the house by Regent's Park, as early as eleven o'clock in the morning. She had a long talk in private with Dora. Jasper was not at home; when he returned towards evening, Dora came to his room with a countenance which disconcerted him.

'Is it true,' she asked abruptly, standing before him with her hands strained together, 'that you have been representing yourself as no longer engaged to Marian?'

'Who has told you so?'

'That doesn't matter. I have heard it, and I want to know from you that it is false.'

Jasper thrust his hands into his pockets and walked apart.

'I can take no notice,' he said with indifference, 'of anonymous gossip.'

'Well, then, I will tell you how I have heard. Maud came this morning, and told me that Mrs Betterton had been asking her about it. Mrs Betterton had heard from Mrs Lane.'

'From Mrs Lane? And from who did *she* hear, pray?'

'That I don't know. Is it true or not?'

'I have never told anyone that my engagement was at an end,' replied Jasper, deliberately.

The girl met his eyes.

'Then I was right,' she said. 'Of course I told Maud that it was impossible to believe this for a moment. But how has it come to be said?'

'You might as well ask me how any lie gets into circulation among people of that sort. I have told you the truth, and there's an end of it.'

Dora lingered for a while, but left the room without saying anything more.

She sat up late, mostly engaged in thinking, though at times an open book was in her hand. It was nearly half-past twelve when a very light rap at the door caused her to start. She called, and Jasper came in.

'Why are you still up?' he asked, avoiding her look as he moved forward and took a leaning attitude behind an easy-chair.

'Oh, I don't know. Do you want anything?'

There was a pause; then Jasper said in an unsteady voice:

'I am not given to lying, Dora, and I feel confoundedly uncomfortable about what I said to you early this evening. I didn't lie in the ordinary sense; it's true enough that I have never told anyone that my engagement was at an end. But I have acted as if it were, and it's better I should tell you.'

His sister gazed at him with indignation.

'You have acted as if you were free?'

'Yes. I have proposed to Miss Rupert. How Mrs Lane and that lot have come to know anything about this I don't understand. I am not aware of any connecting link between them and the Ruperts, or the Barlows either. Perhaps there are none; most likely the rumour has no foundation in their knowledge. Still, it is better that I should have told you. Miss Rupert has never heard that I was engaged, nor have her friends the Barlows – at least I don't see how they could have done. She may have told Mrs Barlow of my proposal – probably would; and this *may* somehow have got round to those other people. But Maud didn't make any mention of Miss Rupert, did she?'

Dora replied with a cold negative.

'Well, there's the state of things. It isn't pleasant, but that's what I have done.'

'Do you mean that Miss Rupert has accepted you?'

'No. I wrote to her. She answered that she was going to Germany for a few weeks, and that I should have her reply whilst she was away. I am waiting.'

'But what name is to be given to behaviour such as this?'

'Listen: didn't you know perfectly well that this must be the end of it?'

'Do you suppose I thought you utterly shameless and cruel beyond words?'

'I suppose I am both. It was a moment of desperate temptation though. I had dined at the Ruperts' – you remember – and it seemed to me there was no mistaking the girl's manner.'

'Don't call her a girl!' broke in Dora, scornfully. 'You say she is several years older than yourself.'

'Well, at all events, she's intellectual, and very rich. I yielded to the temptation.'

'And deserted Marian just when she has most need of help and consolation? It's frightful!'

Jasper moved to another chair and sat down. He was much perturbed.

'Look here, Dora, I regret it; I do, indeed. And, what's more, if that woman refuses me – as it's more than likely she will – I will go to Marian and ask her to marry me at once. I promise that.'

His sister made a movement of contemptuous impatience.

'And if the woman *doesn't* refuse you?'

'Then I can't help it. But there's one thing more I will say. Whether I marry Marian or Miss Rupert, I sacrifice my strongest feelings – in the one case to a sense of duty, in the other to worldly advantage. I was an idiot to write that letter, for I knew at the time that there was a woman who is far more to me than Miss Rupert and all her money – a woman I might, perhaps, marry. Don't ask any questions; I shall not answer them. As I have said so much, I wished you to understand my position fully. You know the promise I have made. Don't say anything to Marian; if I am left free I shall marry her as soon as possible.'

And so he left the room.

For a fortnight and more he remained in uncertainty. His life was very uncomfortable, for Dora would only speak to him when necessity compelled her; and there were two meetings with Marian, at which he had to act his part as well as he could. At length came the expected letter. Very nicely expressed, very friendly, very complimentary, but – a refusal.

He handed it to Dora across the breakfast-table, saying with a pinched smile:

'Now you can look cheerful again. I am doomed.'

Chapter 35

FEVER AND REST

MILVAIN'S skilful efforts notwithstanding, 'Mr Bailey, Grocer,' had no success. By two publishers the book had been declined; the firm which brought it out offered the author half profits and fifteen pounds on account, greatly to Harold Biffen's satisfaction. But reviewers in general were either angry or coldly contemptuous. 'Let Mr Biffen bear in mind,' said one of these sages, 'that a novelist's first duty is to tell a story.' 'Mr Biffen,' wrote another, 'seems not to understand that a work of art must before everything else afford amusement.' 'A pretentious book of the *genre ennuyant*,' was the brief comment of a Society journal. A weekly of high standing began its short notice in a rage : 'Here is another of those intolerable productions for which we are indebted to the spirit of grovelling realism. This author, let it be said, is never offensive, but then one must go on to describe his work by a succession of negatives; it is never interesting, never profitable, never –' and the rest. The eulogy in *The West End* had a few timid echoes. That in *The Current* would have secured more imitators, but unfortunately it appeared when most of the reviewing had already been done. And, as Jasper truly said, only a concurrence of powerful testimonials could have compelled any number of people to affect an interest in this book. 'The first duty of a novelist is to tell a story :' the perpetual repetition of this phrase is a warning to all men who propose drawing from the life. Biffen only offered a slice of biography, and it was found to lack flavour.

He wrote to Mrs Reardon : 'I cannot thank you enough for this very kind letter about my book; I value it more than I should the praises of all the reviewers in existence. You have understood my aim. Few people will do that, and very few indeed could express it with such clear conciseness.'

If Amy had but contented herself with a civil acknowledgment of the volumes he sent her ! She thought it a kindness to write to him so appreciatively, to exaggerate her approval. The poor fellow was so lonely. Yes, but his loneliness only became intolerable when a beautiful woman had smiled upon him, and so forced him to dream perpetually of that supreme joy of life which to him was forbidden.

It was a fatal day, that on which Amy put herself under his guidance to visit Reardon's poor room at Islington. In the old times, Harold had been wont to regard his friend's wife as the perfect woman; seldom in his life had he enjoyed female society, and when he first met Amy it was years since he had spoken with any woman above the rank of a lodging-house keeper or a needle-plier. Her beauty seemed to him of a very high order, and her mental endowments filled him with an exquisite delight, not to be appreciated by men who have never been in his position. When the rupture came between Amy and her husband, Harold could not believe that she was in any way to blame; held to Reardon by strong friendship, he yet accused him of injustice to Amy. And what he saw of her at Brighton confirmed him in this judgment. When he accompanied her to Manville Street, he allowed her, of course, to remain alone in the room where Reardon had lived; but Amy presently summoned him, and asked him questions. Every tear she shed watered a growth of passionate tenderness in the solitary man's heart. Parting from her at length, he went to hide his face in darkness and think of her – think of her.

A fatal day. There was an end of all his peace, all his capacity for labour, his patient endurance of penury. Once, when he was about three-and-twenty, he had been in love with a girl of gentle nature and fair intelligence; on account of his poverty, he could not even hope that his love might be returned, and he went away to bear the misery as best he might. Since then the life he had led precluded the forming of such attachments; it would never have been possible for him to support a wife of however humble origin. At intervals he felt the full weight of his loneliness, but there were happily long periods during which his Greek studies and his efforts in realistic fiction made him indifferent to the curse laid upon him. But after that hour of intimate speech with Amy, he never again knew rest of mind or heart.

Accepting what Reardon had bequeathed to him, he removed the books and furniture to a room in that part of the town which he had found most convenient for his singular tutorial pursuits. The winter did not pass without days of all but starvation, but in

March he received his fifteen pounds for 'Mr Bailey,' and this was a fortune, putting him beyond the reach of hunger for full six months. Not long after that he yielded to a temptation that haunted him day and night, and went to call upon Amy, who was still living with her mother at Westbourne Park. When he entered the drawing-room Amy was sitting there alone; she rose with an exclamation of frank pleasure.

'I have often thought of you lately, Mr Biffen. How kind to come and see me!'

He could scarcely speak; her beauty, as she stood before him in the graceful black dress, was anguish to his excited nerves, and her voice was so cruel in its conventional warmth. When he looked at her eyes, he remembered how their brightness had been dimmed with tears, and the sorrow he had shared with her seemed to make him more than an ordinary friend. When he told her of his success with the publishers, she was delighted.

'Oh, when is it to come out? I shall watch the advertisements so anxiously.'

'Will you allow me to send you a copy, Mrs Reardon?'

'Can you really spare one?'

Of the half-dozen he would receive, he scarcely knew how to dispose of three. And Amy expressed her gratitude in the most charming way. She had gained much in point of manner during the past twelve months; her ten thousand pounds inspired her with the confidence necessary to a perfect demeanour. That slight hardness which was wont to be perceptible in her tone had altogether passed away; she seemed to be cultivating flexibility of voice.

Mrs Yule came in, and was all graciousness. Then two callers presented themselves. Biffen's pleasure was at an end as soon as he had to adapt himself to polite dialogue; he escaped as speedily as possible.

He was not the kind of man that deceives himself as to his own aspect in the eyes of others. Be as kind as she might, Amy could not set him strutting Malvolio-wise; she viewed him as a poor devil who often had to pawn his coat – a man of parts who would never get on in the world – a friend to be thought of kindly because her dead husband had valued him. Nothing more than that; he understood perfectly the limits of her feeling. But this could not put restraint upon the emotion with which he received any most trifling utterance of kindness from her. He did not think of what was, but of what, under changed circumstances, might be. To encourage such fantasy was the idlest self-torment, but he had gone too far in this form of indulgence. He became the slave of his inflamed imagination.

In that letter with which he replied to her praises of his book, perchance he had allowed himself to speak too much as he thought. He wrote in reckless delight, and did not wait for the prudence of a later hour. When it was past recall, he would gladly have softened many of the expressions the letter contained. 'I value it more than the praises of all the reviewers in existence' – would Amy be offended at that? 'Yours in gratitude and reverence,' he had signed himself – the kind of phrase that comes naturally to a passionate man, when he would fain say more than he dares. To what purpose this half-revelation? Unless, indeed, he wished to learn once and for ever, by the gentlest of repulses, that his homage was only welcome so long as it kept well within conventional terms.

He passed a month of distracted idleness, until there came a day when the need to see Amy was so imperative that it mastered every consideration. He donned his best clothes, and about four o'clock presented himself at Mrs Yule's house. By ill-luck there happened to be at least half a dozen callers in the drawing-room; the strappado would have been preferable, in his eyes, to such an ordeal as this. Moreover, he was convinced that both Amy and her mother received him with far less cordiality than on the last occasion. He had expected it, but he bit his lips till the blood came. What business had he among people of this kind? No doubt the visitors wondered at his comparative shabbiness, and asked themselves how he ventured to make a call without the regulation chimney-pot hat. It was a wretched and foolish mistake.

Ten minutes saw him in the street again, vowing that he would never approach Amy more. Not that he found fault with her; the blame was entirely his own.

He lived on the third floor of a house in Goodge Street, above a baker's shop. The bequest of Reardon's furniture was a great advantage to him, as he had only to pay rent for a bare room; the books, too, came as a godsend, since the destruction of his own. He had now only one pupil, and was not exerting himself to find others; his old enemy had forsaken him.

For the failure of his book he cared nothing. It was no more than he anticipated. The work was done – the best he was capable of – and this satisfied him.

It was doubtful whether he loved Amy, in the true sense of exclusive desire. She represented for him all that is lovely in womanhood; to his starved soul and senses she was woman, the complement of his frustrate being. Circumstance had made her the means of exciting in him that natural force which had hither-to either been dormant or had yielded to the resolute will.

Companionless, inert, he suffered the tortures which are so ludicrous and contemptible to the happily married. Life was barren to him, and would soon grow hateful; only in sleep could he cast off the unchanging thoughts and desires which made all else meaningless. And rightly meaningless; he revolted against the unnatural constraints forbidding him to complete his man-hood. By what fatality was he alone of men withheld from the winning of a woman's love?

He could not bear to walk the streets where the faces of beauti-ful women would encounter him. When he must needs leave the house, he went about in the poor, narrow ways, where only spec-tacles of coarseness, and want, and toil would be presented to him. Yet even here he was too often reminded that the poverty-stricken of the class to which poverty is natural were not con-demned to endure in solitude. Only he who belonged to no class, who was rejected alike by his fellows in privation and by his equals in intellect, must die without having known the touch of a loving woman's hand.

The summer went by, and he was unconscious of its warmth and light. How his days passed he could not have said.

One evening in early autumn, as he stood before the book-stall at the end of Goodge Street, a familiar voice accosted him. It was Whelpdale's. A month or two ago he had stubbornly refused an invitation to dine with Whelpdale and other acquaintants – you remember what the occasion was – and since then the prosperous young man had not crossed his path.

'I've something to tell you,' said the assailer, taking hold of his arm. 'I'm in a tremendous state of mind, and want someone to share my delight. You can walk a short way, I hope? Not too busy with some new book?'

Biffen gave no answer, but went whither he was led.

'You *are* writing a new book, I suppose? Don't be discouraged, old fellow. "Mr Bailey" will have his day yet; I know men who consider it an undoubted work of genius. What's the next to deal with?'

'I haven't decided yet,' replied Harold, merely to avoid argument. He spoke so seldom that the sound of his own voice was strange to him.

'Thinking over it, I suppose, in your usual solid way. Don't be hurried. But I must tell you of this affair of mine. You know Dora Milvain; I have asked her to marry me, and, by the Powers! she has given me an encouraging answer! Not an actual yes, but encouraging! She's away in the Channel Islands, and I wrote –'

He talked on for a quarter of an hour. Then, with a sudden movement, the listener freed himself.

'I can't go any farther,' he said hoarsely. 'Good-bye!'

Whelpdale was disconcerted.

'I have been boring you. That's a confounded fault of mine; I know it.'

Biffen had waved his hand, and was gone.

A week or two more would see him at the end of his money. He had no lessons now, and could not write; from his novel nothing was to be expected. He might apply again to his brother, but such dependence was unjust and unworthy. And why should he struggle to preserve a life which had no prospect but of misery?

It was in the hours following his encounter with Whelpdale that he first knew the actual desire of death, the simple longing for extinction. One must go far in suffering before the innate will-to-live is thus truly overcome; weariness of bodily anguish may induce this perversion of the instincts; less often, that despair of suppressed emotion which had fallen upon Harold. Through the night he kept his thoughts fixed on death in its aspect of repose, of eternal oblivion. And herein he had found solace.

The next night it was the same. Moving about among common needs and occupations, he knew not a moment's cessation of heart-ache, but when he lay down in the darkness a hopeful summons whispered to him. Night, which had been the worst season of his pain, had now grown friendly; it came as an anticipation of the sleep that is everlasting.

A few more days, and he was possessed by a calm of spirit such as he had never known. His resolve was taken, not in a moment of supreme conflict, but as the result of a subtle process by which his imagination had become in love with death. Turning from contemplation of life's one rapture, he looked with the same intensity of desire to a state that had neither fear nor hope.

One afternoon he went to the Museum Reading-room, and was busy for a few minutes in consultation of a volume which he took from the shelves of medical literature. On his way homeward he entered two or three chemists' shops. Something of which he had need could be procured only in very small quantities; but repetition of his demand in different places supplied him sufficiently. When he reached his room, he emptied the contents of sundry little bottles into one larger, and put this in his pocket. Then he wrote rather a long letter, addressed to his brother at Liverpool.

It had been a beautiful day, and there wanted still a couple of hours before the warm, golden sunlight would disappear. Harold stood and looked round his room. As always, it presented a neat, orderly aspect, but his eye caught sight of a volume which stood upside down, and this fault – particularly hateful to a bookish man – he rectified. He put his blotting-pad square on the table, closed the lid of the inkstand, arranged his pens. Then he took his hat and stick, locked the door behind him, and went downstairs. At the foot he spoke to his landlady, and told her that he should not return that night. As soon as possible after leaving the house he posted his letter.

His direction was westward; walking at a steady, purposeful pace, with cheery countenance and eyes that gave sign of pleasure as often as they turned to the sun-smitten clouds, he struck across Kensington Gardens, and then on towards Fulham, where he crossed the Thames to Putney. The sun was just setting; he paused a few moments on the bridge, watching the river with a quiet smile, and enjoying the splendour of the sky. Up Putney

Hill he walked slowly; when he reached the top it was growing dark, but an unwonted effect in the atmosphere caused him to turn and look to the east. An exclamation escaped his lips, for there before him was the new-risen moon, a perfect globe, vast and red. He gazed at it for a long time.

When the daylight had entirely passed, he went forward on to the heath, and rambled, as if idly, to a secluded part, where trees and bushes made a deep shadow under the full moon. It was still quite warm, and scarcely a breath of air moved among the reddening leaves.

Sure at length that he was remote from all observation, he pressed into a little copse, and there reclined on the grass, leaning against the stem of a tree. The moon was now hidden from him, but by looking upward he could see its light upon a long, faint cloud, and the blue of the placid sky. His mood was one of ineffable peace. Only thoughts of beautiful things came into his mind; he had reverted to an earlier period of life, when as yet no mission of literary realism had been imposed upon him, and when his passions were still soothed by natural hope. The memory of his friend Reardon was strongly present with him, but of Amy he thought only as of that star which had just come into his vision above the edge of dark foliage – beautiful, but infinitely remote.

Recalling Reardon's voice, it brought to him those last words whispered by his dying companion. He remembered them now:

> We are such stuff
> As dreams are made on, and our little life
> Is rounded with a sleep.

Chapter 36

JASPER'S DELICATE CASE

ONLY when he received Miss Rupert's amiably-worded refusal to become his wife was Jasper aware how firmly he had counted on her accepting him. He told Dora with sincerity that his proposal was a piece of foolishness; so far from having any regard for Miss Rupert, he felt towards her with something of antipathy, and at the same time he was conscious of ardent emotions, if not love, for another woman who would be no bad match even from the commercial point of view. Yet so strong was the effect upon him of contemplating a large fortune, that, in despite of reason and desire, he lived in eager expectation of the word which should make him rich. And for several hours after his disappointment he could not overcome the impression of calamity.

A part of that impression was due to the engagement which he must now fulfil. He had pledged his word to ask Marian to marry him without further delay. To shuffle out of this duty would make him too ignoble even in his own eyes. Its discharge meant, as he had expressed it, that he was 'doomed'; he would deliberately be committing the very error always so flagrant to him in the case of other men who had crippled themselves by early marriage with a penniless woman. But events had enmeshed him; circumstances had proved fatal. Because, in his salad days, he dallied with a girl who had indeed many charms, step by step he had come to the necessity of sacrificing his prospects to that raw attachment. And, to make it more irritating, this happened just when the way began to be much clearer before him.

Unable to think of work, he left the house and wandered gloomily about Regent's Park. For the first time in his recollection the confidence which was wont to inspirit him gave way to an attack of sullen discontent. He felt himself ill-used by destiny, and therefore by Marian, who was fate's instrument. It was not in his nature that this mood should last long, but it revealed to him those darker possibilities which his egoism would develop if it came seriously into conflict with overmastering misfortune.

A hope, a craven hope, insinuated itself into the cracks of his infirm resolve. He would not examine it, but conscious of its existence he was able to go home in somewhat better spirits.

He wrote to Marian. If possible she was to meet him at half-past nine next morning at Gloucester Gate. He had reasons for wishing this interview to take place on neutral ground.

Early in the afternoon, when he was trying to do some work, there arrived a letter which he opened with impatient hand; the writing was Mrs Reardon's, and he could not guess what she had to communicate.

'DEAR MR MILVAIN, – I am distressed beyond measure to read in this morning's newspaper that poor Mr Biffen has put an end to his life. Doubtless you can obtain more details than are given in this bare report of the discovery of his body. Will you let me hear, or come and see me?'

He read and was astonished. Absorbed in his own affairs, he had not opened the newspaper to-day; it lay folded on a chair. Hastily he ran his eye over the columns, and found at length a short paragraph which stated that the body of a man who had evidently committed suicide by taking poison had been found on Putney Heath; that papers in his pockets identified him as one Harold Biffen, lately resident in Goodge Street, Tottenham Court Road; and that an inquest would be held, &c. He went to Dora's room, and told her of the event, but without mentioning the letter which had brought it under his notice.

'I suppose there was no alternative between that and starvation. I scarcely thought of Biffen as likely to kill himself. If Reardon had done it, I shouldn't have felt the least surprise.'

'Mr Whelpdale will be bringing us information, no doubt,' said Dora, who, as she spoke, thought more of that gentleman's visit than of the event that was to occasion it.

'Really, one can't grieve. There seemed no possibility of his ever earning enough to live decently upon. But why the deuce did he go all the way out there? Consideration for the people in whose house he lived, I dare say; Biffen had a good deal of native delicacy.'

Dora felt a secret wish that someone else possessed more of that desirable quality.

Leaving her, Jasper made a rapid, though careful, toilet, and was presently on his way to Westbourne Park. It was his hope that he should reach Mrs Yule's house before any ordinary afternoon caller could arrive; and so he did. He had not been here since that evening when he encountered Reardon on the road and heard his reproaches. To his great satisfaction, Amy was alone in the drawing-room; he held her hand a trifle longer than was necessary, and returned more earnestly the look of interest with which she regarded him.

'I was ignorant of this affair when your letter came,' he began, 'and I set out immediately to see you.'

'I hoped you would bring me some news. What can have driven the poor man to such extremity?'

'Poverty, I can only suppose. But I will see Whelpdale. I hadn't come across Biffen for a long time.'

'Was he still so very poor?' asked Amy, compassionately.

'I'm afraid so. His book failed utterly.'

'Oh, if I had imagined him still in such distress, surely I might have done something to help him!' – So often the regretful remark of one's friends, when one has been permitted to perish.

With Amy's sorrow was mingled a suggestion of tenderness which came of her knowledge that the dead man had worshipped her. Perchance his death was in part attributable to that hopeless love.

'He sent me a copy of his novel,' she said, 'and I saw him once or twice after that. But he was much better dressed than in former days, and I thought –'

Having this subject to converse upon put the two more quickly at ease than could otherwise have been the case. Jasper was closely observant of the young widow; her finished graces made a strong appeal to his admiration, and even in some degree awed him. He saw that her beauty had matured, and it was more distinctly than ever of the type to which he paid reverence. Amy might take a foremost place among brilliant women. At a dinner-table, in grand toilet, she would be superb; at polite receptions people would whisper: 'Who is that?'

Biffen fell out of the dialogue.

'It grieved me very much,' said Amy, 'to hear of the misfortune that befell my cousin.'

'The legacy affair? Why, yes, it was a pity. Especially now that her father is threatened with blindness.'

'Is it so serious? I heard indirectly that he had something the matter with his eyes, but I didn't know –'

'They may be able to operate before long, and perhaps it will be successful. But in the meantime Marian has to do his work.'

'This explains the – the delay?' fell from Amy's lips, as she smiled.

Jasper moved uncomfortably. It was a voluntary gesture.

'The whole situation explains it,' he replied, with some show of impulsiveness. 'I am very much afraid Marian is tied during her father's life.'

'Indeed? But there is her mother.'

'No companion for her father, as I think you know. Even if Mr Yule recovers his sight, it is not at all likely that he will be able to work as before. Our difficulties are so grave that –'

He paused, and let his hand fall despondently.

'I hope it isn't affecting your work – your progress?'

'To some extent, necessarily. I have a good deal of will, you remember, and what I have set my mind upon, no doubt, I shall some day achieve. But – one makes mistakes.'

There was silence.

'The last three years,' he continued, 'have made no slight difference in my position. Recall where I stood when you first knew me. I have done something since then, I think, and by my own steady effort.'

'Indeed, you have.'

'Just now I am in need of a little encouragement. You don't notice any falling off in my work recently?'

'No, indeed.'

'Do you see my things in *The Current* and so on, generally?'

'I don't think I miss many of your articles. Sometimes I believe I have detected you when there was no signature.'

'And Dora has been doing well. Her story in that girls' paper has attracted attention. It's a great deal to have my mind at rest about both the girls. But I can't pretend to be in very good spirits.' He rose. 'Well, I must try to find out something more about poor Biffen.'

'Oh, you are not going yet, Mr Milvain?'

'Not, assuredly, because I wish to. But I have work to do.' He stepped aside, but came back as if on an impulse. 'May I ask you for your advice in a very delicate matter?'

Amy was a little disturbed, but she collected herself and smiled in a way that reminded Jasper of his walk with her along Gower Street.

'Let me hear what it is.'

He sat down again, and bent forward.

'If Marian insists that it is her duty to remain with her father, am I justified or not in freely consenting to that?'

'I scarcely understand. Has Marian expressed a wish to devote herself in that way?'

'Not distinctly. But I suspect that her conscience points to it. I am in serious doubt. On the one hand,' he explained in a tone of candour, 'who will not blame me if our engagement terminates in circumstances such as these? On the other – you are aware, by-the-by, that her father objects in the strongest way to this marriage?'

'No, I didn't know that.'

'He will neither see me nor hear of me. Merely because of my connection with Fadge. Think of that poor girl thus situated. And I could so easily put her at rest by renouncing all claim upon her.'

'I surmise that – that you yourself would also be put at rest by such a decision?'

'Don't look at me with that ironical smile,' he pleaded. 'What you have said is true. And really, why should I not be glad of it? I couldn't go about declaring that I was heart-broken, in any event; I must be content for people to judge me according to their disposition, and judgments are pretty sure to be unfavourable. What can I do? In either case I must to a certain extent be in the wrong. To tell the truth, I was wrong from the first.'

There was a slight movement about Amy's lips as these words were uttered : she kept her eyes down, and waited before replying.

'The case is too delicate, I fear, for my advice.'

'Yes, I feel it; and perhaps I oughtn't to have spoken of it at all. Well, I'll go back to my scribbling. I am so very glad to have seen you again.'

'It was good of you to take the trouble to come – whilst you have so much on your mind.'

Again Jasper held the white, soft hand for a superfluous moment.

The next morning it was he who had to wait at the rendez-vous; he was pacing the pathway at least ten minutes before the appointed time. When Marian joined him, she was panting from a hurried walk, and this affected Jasper disagreeably; he thought of Amy Reardon's air of repose, and how impossible it would be for that refined person to fall into such disorder. He observed, too, with more disgust than usual, the signs in Marian's attire of encroaching poverty – her unsatisfactory gloves, her mantle out of fashion. Yet for such feelings he reproached himself, and the reproach made him angry.

They walked together in the same direction as when they met here before. Marian could not mistake the air of restless trouble on her companion's smooth countenance. She had divined that there was some grave reason for this summons, and the panting with which she had approached was half caused by the anxious beats of her heart. Jasper's long silence again was ominous. He began abruptly:

'You've heard that Harold Biffen has committed suicide?'

'No!' she replied, looking shocked.

'Poisoned himself. You'll find something about it in to-day's *Telegraph*.'

He gave her such details as he had obtained, then added:

'There are two of my companions fallen in the battle. I ought to think myself a lucky fellow, Marian. What?'

'You are better fitted to fight your way, Jasper.'

'More of a brute, you mean.'

'You know very well I don't. You have more energy and more intellect.'

'Well, it remains to be seen how I shall come out when I am weighted with graver cares than I have yet known.'

She looked at him inquiringly, but said nothing.

'I have made up my mind about our affairs,' he went on pre-cisely. 'Marian, if ever we are to be married, it must be now.'

The words were so unexpected that they brought a flush to her cheeks and neck.

'Now?'

'Yes. Will you marry me, and let us take our chance?'

Her heart throbbed, violently.

'You don't mean at once, Jasper? You would wait until I know what father's fate is to be?'

'Well, now, there's the point. You feel yourself indispensable to your father at present?'

'Not indispensable, but – wouldn't it seem very unkind? I should be so afraid of the effect upon his health, Jasper. So much depends, we are told, upon his general state of mind and body. It would be dreadful if I were the cause of –'

She paused, and looked up at him touchingly.

'I understand that. But let us face our position. Suppose the operation is successful; your father will certainly not be able to use his eyes much for a long time, if ever; and perhaps he would miss you as much then as now. Suppose he does *not* regain his sight; could you then leave him?'

'Dear, I can't feel it would be my duty to renounce you because my father had become blind. And if he can see pretty well, I don't think I need remain with him.'

'Has one thing occurred to you? Will he consent to receive an allowance from a person whose name is Mrs Milvain?'

'I can't be sure,' she replied, much troubled.

'And if he obstinately refuses – what then? What is before him?'

Marian's head sank, and she stood still.

'Why have you changed your mind so, Jasper?' she inquired at length.

'Because I have decided that the indefinitely long engagement would be unjust to you – and to myself. Such engagements are always dangerous; sometimes they deprave the character of the man or woman.'

She listened anxiously and reflected.

'Everything,' he went on, 'would be simple enough but for your domestic difficulties. As I have said, there is the very serious doubt whether your father would accept money from you when you are my wife. Then again, shall we be able to afford such an allowance?'

'I thought you felt sure of that?'

'I'm not very sure of anything, to tell the truth. I am harassed. I can't get on with my work.'

'I am very, very sorry.'

'It isn't your fault, Marian, and – Well, then, there's only one thing to do. Let us wait, at all events, till your father has undergone the operation. Whichever the result, you say your own position will be the same.'

'Except, Jasper, that if father is helpless, I *must* find means of assuring his support.'

'In other words, if you can't do that as my wife, you must remain Marian Yule.'

After a silence, Marian regarded him steadily.

'You see only the difficulties in our way,' she said, in a colder voice. 'They are many, I know. Do you think them insurmountable?'

'Upon my word, they almost seem so,' Jasper exclaimed distractedly.

'They were not so great when we spoke of marriage a few years hence.'

'A few years!' he echoed, in a cheerless voice. 'That is just what I have decided is impossible. Marian, you shall have the plain truth. I can trust your faith, but I can't trust my own. I will marry you now, but – years hence – how can I tell what may happen? I don't trust myself.'

'You say you "will" marry me now; that sounds as if you had made up your mind to a sacrifice.'

'I didn't mean that. To face difficulties, yes.'

Whilst they spoke, the sky had grown dark with a heavy cloud, and now spots of rain began to fall. Jasper looked about him in annoyance as he felt the moisture, but Marian did not seem aware of it.

'But shall you face them willingly?'

'I am not a man to repine and grumble. Put up your umbrella, Marian.'

'What do I care for a drop of rain,' she exclaimed with passionate sadness, 'when all my life is at stake! How am I to understand you? Every word you speak seems intended to dishearten me. Do you no longer love me? Why need you conceal it, if that is the truth? Is that what you mean by saying you distrust yourself? If you do so, there must be reason for it in the present. Could I distrust *myself*? Can I force myself in any manner to believe that I shall ever cease to love you?'

Jasper opened his umbrella.

'We must see each other again, Marian. We can't stand and talk in the rain – confound it! Cursed climate, where you can never be sure of a clear sky for five minutes!'

'I *can't* go till you have spoken more plainly, Jasper! How am I to live an hour in such uncertainty as this? Do you love me or not? Do you wish me to be your wife, or are you sacrificing yourself?'

'I do wish it!' Her emotion had an effect upon him, and his voice trembled. 'But I can't answer for myself – no, not for a year. And how are we to marry now,. in face of all these –'

'What can I do? What can I do?' she sobbed. 'Oh, if I were but heartless to everyone but you! If I could give you my money, and leave my father and mother to their fate! Perhaps some could do that. There is no natural law that a child should surrender everything for her parents. You know so much more of the world than I do; can't you advise me? Is there no way of providing for my father?'

'Good God! This is frightful, Marian. I can't stand it. Live as you are doing. Let us wait and see.'

'At the cost of losing you?'

'I will be faithful to you!'

'And your voice says you promise it out of pity.'

He had made a pretence of holding his umbrella over her, but Marian turned away and walked to a little distance, and stood beneath the shelter of a great tree, her face averted from him. Moving to follow, he saw that her frame was shaken with soundless sobbing. When his footsteps came close to her, she again looked at him.

'I know now,' she said, 'how foolish it is when they talk of love being unselfish. In what can there be more selfishness? I feel as if I could hold you to your promise at any cost, though you have made me understand that you regard our engagement as your great misfortune. I have felt it for weeks – oh, for months! But I couldn't say a word that would seem to invite such misery as this. You don't love me, Jasper, and that's an end of everything. I should be shamed if I married you.'

'Whether I love you or not, I feel as if no sacrifice would be too great that would bring you the happiness you deserve.'

'Deserve!' she repeated bitterly. 'Why do I deserve it? Because I long for it with all my heart and soul? There's no such thing as deserving. Happiness or misery come to us by fate.'

'Is it in my power to make you happy?'

'No; because it isn't in your power to call dead love to life again. I think perhaps you never loved me. Jasper, I could give my right hand if you had said you loved me before – I can't put it into words; it sounds too base, and I don't wish to imply that you behaved basely. But if you had said you loved me before that, I should have it always to remember.'

'You will do me no wrong if you charge me with baseness,' he replied gloomily. 'If I believe anything, I believe that I did love you. But I knew myself, and I should never have betrayed what I felt, if for once in my life I could have been honourable.'

The rain pattered on the leaves and the grass, and still the sky darkened.

'This is wretchedness to both of us,' Jasper added. 'Let us part now, Marian. Let me see you again.'

'I can't see you again. What can you say to me more than you have said now? I should feel like a beggar coming to you. I must try and keep some little self-respect, if I am to live at all.'

'Then let me help you to think of me with indifference. Remember me as a man who disregarded priceless love such as yours to go and make himself a proud position among fools and knaves – indeed that's what it comes to. It is you who reject me, and rightly. One who is so much at the mercy of a vulgar ambition as I am, is no fit husband for you. Soon enough you would thoroughly despise me, and though I should know it was merited, my perverse pride would revolt against it. Many a time I have tried to regard life practically as I am able to do theoretically, but it always ends in hypocrisy. It is men of my kind who succeed; the conscientious, and those who really have a high ideal, either perish or struggle on in neglect.'

Marian had overcome her excess of emotion.

'There is no need to disparage yourself,' she said. 'What can be simpler than the truth? You loved me, or thought you did, and now you love me no longer. It is a thing that happens every day, either in man or woman, and all that honour demands is the courage to confess the truth. Why didn't you tell me as soon as you knew that I was burdensome to you?'

'Marian, will you do this? – will you let our engagement last for another six months, but without our meeting during that time?'

'But to what purpose?'

'Then we would see each other again, and both would be able to speak calmly, and we should both know with certainty what course we ought to pursue.'

'That seems to me childish. It is easy for you to contemplate months of postponement. There must be an end now; I can bear it no longer.'

The rain fell unceasingly, and with it began to mingle an autumnal mist. Jasper delayed a moment, then asked calmly :

'Are you going to the Museum?'

'Yes.'

'Go home again for this morning, Marian. You can't work –'

'I must; and I have no time to lose. Good-bye !'

She gave him her hand. They looked at each other for an instant, then Marian left the shelter of the tree, opened her umbrella, and walked quickly away. Jasper did not watch her; he had the face of a man who is suffering a severe humiliation.

A few hours later he told Dora what had come to pass, and without extenuation of his own conduct. His sister said very little, for she recognised genuine suffering in his tones and aspect. But when it was over, she sat down and wrote to Marian.

'I feel far more disposed to congratulate you than to regret what has happened. Now that there is no necessity for silence, I will tell you something which will help you to see Jasper in his true light. A few weeks ago he actually proposed to a woman for whom he does not pretend to have the slightest affection, but who is very rich, and who seemed likely to be foolish enough to marry him. Yesterday morning he received her final answer – a refusal. I am not sure that I was right in keeping this a secret from you, but I might have done harm by interfering. You will understand (though surely you need no fresh proof) how utterly unworthy he is of you. You cannot, I am sure you cannot, re-

gard it as a misfortune that all is over between you. Dearest
Marian, do not cease to think of me as your friend because my
brother has disgraced himself. If you can't see me, at least let us
write to each other. You are the only friend I have of my own
sex, and I could not bear to lose you.'

And much more of the same tenor.

Several days passed before there came a reply. It was written
with undisturbed kindness of feeling, but in a few words.

'For the present we cannot see each other, but I am very far
from wishing that our friendship should come to an end. I must
only ask that you will write to me without the least reference to
these troubles; tell me always about yourself, and be sure that
you cannot tell me too much. I hope you may soon be able to
send me the news which was foreshadowed in our last talk –
though "foreshadowed" is a wrong word to use of coming happiness, isn't it? That paper I sent to Mr Trenchard is accepted,
and I shall be glad to have your criticism when it comes out;
don't spare my style, which needs a great deal of chastening. I
have been thinking: couldn't you use your holiday in Sark for a
story? To judge from your letters, you could make an excellent
background of word-painting.'

Dora sighed, and shook her little head, and thought of her
brother with unspeakable disdain.

Chapter 37

REWARDS

WHEN the fitting moment arrived, Alfred Yule underwent an operation for cataract, and it was believed at first that the result would be favourable. This hope had but short duration; though the utmost prudence was exercised, evil symptoms declared themselves, and in a few months' time all prospect of restoring his vision was at an end. Anxiety, then the fatal assurance, undermined his health; with blindness, there fell upon him the debility of premature old age.

The position of the family was desperate. Marian had suffered much all the winter from attacks of nervous disorder, and by no effort of will could she produce enough literary work to supplement adequately the income derived from her fifteen hundred pounds. In the summer of 1885 things were at the worst; Marian saw no alternative but to draw upon her capital, and so relieve the present at the expense of the future. She had a mournful warning before her eyes in the case of poor Hinks and his wife, who were now kept from the workhouse only by charity. But at this juncture the rescuer appeared. Mr Quarmby and certain of his friends were already making a subscription for the Yules' benefit, when one of their number – Mr Jedwood, the publisher – came forward with a proposal which relieved the minds of all concerned. Mr Jedwood had a brother who was the director of a public library in a provincial town, and by this means he was enabled to offer Marian Yule a place as assistant in that institution; she would receive seventy-five pounds a year, and thus, adding her own income, would be able to put her parents beyond the reach of want. The family at once removed from London, and the name of Yule was no longer met with in periodical literature.

By an interesting coincidence, it was on the day of this departure that there appeared a number of *The West End* in which the place of honour, that of the week's Celebrity, was occupied by Clement Fadge. A coloured portrait of this illustrious man challenged the admiration of all who had literary tastes, and two columns of panegyric recorded his career for the encouragement of aspiring youth. This article, of course unsigned, came from the pen of Jasper Milvain.

It was only by indirect channels that Jasper learnt how Marian and her parents had been provided for. Dora's correspondence with her friend soon languished; in the nature of things this could not but happen; and about the time when Alfred Yule became totally blind the girls ceased to hear anything of each other. An event which came to pass in the spring sorely tempted Dora to write, but out of good feeling she refrained.

For it was then that she at length decided to change her name for that of Whelpdale. Jasper could not quite reconcile himself to this condescension; in various discourses he pointed out to his sister how much higher she might look if she would only have a little patience.

'Whelpdale will never be a man of any note. A good fellow, I admit, but *borné* in all senses. Let me impress upon you, my dear girl, that I have a future before me, and that there is no reason – with your charm of person and mind – why you should not marry brilliantly. Whelpdale can give you a decent home, I admit, but as regards society he will be a drag upon you.'

'It happens, Jasper, that I have promised to marry him,' replied Dora, in a significant tone.

'Well, I regret it, but – you are of course your own mistress. I shall make no unpleasantness. I don't dislike Whelpdale, and I shall remain on friendly terms with him.'

'That is very kind of you,' said his sister suavely.

Whelpdale was frantic with exultation. When the day of the wedding had been settled, he rushed into Jasper's study and fairly shed tears before he could command his voice.

'There is no mortal on the surface of the globe one-tenth so happy as I am!' he gasped. 'I can't believe it! Why in the name of sense and justice have I been suffered to attain this blessedness? Think of the days when I all but starved in my Albany Street garret, scarcely better off than poor, dear old Biffen! Why should I have come to this, and Biffen have poisoned himself in despair? He was a thousand times a better and cleverer fellow than I. And poor old Reardon, dead in misery! Could I for a moment compare with him?'

'My dear fellow,' said Jasper, calmly, 'compose yourself and be logical. In the first place, success has nothing whatever to do with moral deserts; and then, both Reardon and Biffen were hopelessly unpractical. In such an admirable social order as ours, they were bound to go to the dogs. Let us be sorry for them, but let us recognise *causas rerum*,[44] as Biffen would have said. You have exercised ingenuity and perseverance; you have your reward.'

'And when I think that I might have married fatally on thirteen or fourteen different occasions. By-the-by, I implore you never to tell Dora those stories about me. I should lose all her respect. Do you remember the girl from Birmingham?' He laughed wildly. 'Heaven be praised that she threw me over! Eternal gratitude to all and sundry of the girls who have plunged me into wretchedness!'

'I admit that you have run the gauntlet, and that you have had marvellous escapes. But be good enough to leave me alone for the present. I must finish this review by mid-day.'

'Only one word. I don't know how to thank Dora, how to express my infinite sense of her goodness. Will you try to do so for me? You can speak to her with calmness. Will you tell her what I have said to you?'

'Oh, certainly. — I should recommend a cooling draught of some kind. Look in at a chemist's as you walk on.'

The heavens did not fall before the marriage-day, and the wedded pair betook themselves for a few weeks to the Continent. They had been back again and established in their house at Earl's Court for a month, when one morning about twelve o'clock Jasper dropped in, as though casually. Dora was writing; she had no thought of entirely abandoning literature, and had in hand at present a very pretty tale which would probably appear in *The English Girl*. Her boudoir, in which she sat, could not well have been daintier and more appropriate to the charming characteristics of its mistress. Mrs Whelpdale affected no literary slovenliness; she was dressed in light colours, and looked so lovely that even Jasper paused on the threshold with a smile of admiration.

'Upon my word,' he exclaimed, 'I am proud of my sisters! What did you think of Maud last night? Wasn't she superb?'

'She certainly did look very well. But I doubt if she's very happy.'

'That is her own look out; I told her plainly enough my opinion of Dolomore. But she was in such a tremendous hurry.'

'You are detestable, Jasper! Is it inconceivable to you that a man or woman should be disinterested when they marry?'

'By no means.'

'Maud didn't marry for money any more than I did.'

'You remember the Northern Farmer:[45] "Doän't thou marry for money, but go where money is." An admirable piece of advice. Well, Maud made a mistake, let us say. Dolomore is a clown, and now she knows it. Why, if she had waited, she might have married one of the leading men of the day. She is fit to be a duchess, as far as appearance goes; but I was never snobbish. I care very little about titles; what I look to is intellectual distinction.'

'Combined with financial success.'

'Why, that is what distinction means.' He looked round the room with a smile. 'You are not uncomfortable here, old girl. I wish mother could have lived till now.'

'I wish it very, very often,' Dora replied in a moved voice.

'We haven't done badly, drawbacks considered. Now you may speak of money as scornfully as you like; but suppose you had married a man who could only keep you in lodgings? How would life look to you?'

'Who ever disputed the value of money? But there are things one mustn't sacrifice to gain it.'

'I suppose so. Well, I have some news for you, Dora. I am thinking of following your example.'

Dora's face changed to grave anticipation.

'And who is it?'

'Amy Reardon.'

His sister turned away, with a look of intense annoyance.

'You see, I am disinterested myself,' he went on. 'I might find a wife who had wealth and social standing. But I choose Amy deliberately.'

'An abominable choice!'

'No; an excellent choice. I have never yet met a woman so well fitted to aid me in my career. She has a trifling sum of money, which will be useful for the next year or two –'

'What has she done with the rest of it, then?'

'Oh, the ten thousand is intact, but it can't be seriously spoken of. It will keep up appearances till I get my editorship and so on. We shall be married early in August, I think. I want to ask you if you will go and see her.'

'On no account! I couldn't be civil to her.'

Jasper's brows blackened.

'This is idiotic prejudice, Dora. I think I have some claim upon you; I have shown some kindness –'

'You have, and I am not ungrateful. But I dislike Mrs Reardon, and I couldn't bring myself to be friendly with her.'

'You don't know her.'

'Too well. You yourself have taught me to know her. Don't compel me to say what I think of her.'

'She is beautiful, and high-minded, and warm-hearted. I don't know a womanly quality that she doesn't possess. You will offend me most seriously if you speak a word against her.'

'Then I will be silent. But you must never ask me to meet her.'

'Never?'

'Never!'

'Then we shall quarrel. I haven't deserved this, Dora. If you refuse to meet my wife on terms of decent friendliness, there's no more intercourse between your house and mine. You have to choose. Persist in this fatuous obstinacy, and I have done with you!'

'So be it!'

'That is your final answer?'

Dora, who was now as angry as he, gave a short affirmative, and Jasper at once left her.

But it was very unlikely that things should rest at this pass. The brother and sister were bound by a strong mutual affection, and Whelpdale was not long in effecting a compromise.

'My dear wife,' he exclaimed, in despair at the threatened calamity, 'you are right, a thousand times, but it's impossible for you to be on ill terms with Jasper. There's no need for you to see much of Mrs Reardon –'

'I hate her! She killed her husband; I am sure of it.'

'My darling!'

'I mean by her base conduct. She is a cold, cruel, unprincipled creature! Jasper makes himself more than ever contemptible by marrying her.'

All the same, in less than three weeks Mrs Whelpdale had called upon Amy, and the call was returned. The two women were perfectly conscious of reciprocal dislike, but they smothered the feeling beneath conventional suavities. Jasper was not backward in making known his gratitude for Dora's concession, and indeed it became clear to all his intimates that this marriage would be by no means one of mere interest; the man was in love at last, if he had never been before.

Let lapse the ensuing twelve months, and come to an evening at the end of July, 1886. Mr and Mrs Milvain are entertaining a small and select party of friends at dinner. Their house in Bayswater is neither large nor internally magnificent, but it will do very well for the temporary sojourn of a young man of letters who has much greater things in confident expectation, who is a good deal talked of, who can gather clever and worthy people at his table, and whose matchless wife would attract men of taste to a very much poorer abode.

Jasper had changed considerably in appearance since that last holiday that he spent in his mother's house at Finden. At present he would have been taken for five-and-thirty, though only in his twenty-ninth year; his hair was noticeably thinning; his moustache had grown heavier; a wrinkle or two showed beneath his eyes; his voice was softer, yet firmer. It goes without saying that his evening uniform lacked no point of perfection, and somehow it suggested a more elaborate care than that of other men in the room. He laughed frequently, and with a throwing back of the head which seemed to express a spirit of triumph.

Amy looked her years to the full, but her type of beauty, as you know, was independent of youthfulness. That suspicion of masculinity observable in her when she became Reardon's wife impressed one now only as the consummate grace of a perfectly-built woman. You saw that at forty, at fifty, she would be one of the stateliest of dames. When she bent her head towards the person with whom she spoke, it was an act of queenly favour. Her words were uttered with just enough deliberation to give them the value of an opinion; she smiled with a delicious shade of irony; her glance intimated that nothing could be too subtle for her understanding.

The guests numbered six, and no one of them was insignificant. Two of the men were about Jasper's age, and they had already made their mark in literature; the third was a novelist of circulating fame, spirally crescent. The three of the stronger sex were excellent modern types, with sweet lips attuned to epigram, and good broad brows.

The novelist at one point put an interesting question to Amy.

'Is it true that Fadge is leaving *The Current?*'

'It is rumoured, I believe.'

'Going to one of the quarterlies, they say,' remarked a lady. 'He is getting terribly autocratic. Have you heard the delightful story of his telling Mr Rowland to persevere, as his last work was one of considerable promise?'

Mr Rowland was a man who had made a merited reputation when Fadge was still on the lower rungs of journalism. Amy smiled and told another anecdote of the great editor. Whilst speaking, she caught her husband's eye, and perhaps this was the reason why her story, at the close, seemed rather amiably pointless – not a common fault when she narrated.

When the ladies had withdrawn, one of the younger men, in a conversation about a certain magazine, remarked:

'Thomas always maintains that it was killed by that solemn old stager, Alfred Yule. By the way, he is dead himself, I hear.'

Jasper bent forward.

'Alfred Yule is dead?'

'So Jedwood told me this morning. He died in the country somewhere, blind and fallen on evil days,[46] poor old fellow.'

All the guests were ignorant of any tie of kindred between their host and the man spoken of.

'I believe,' said the novelist, 'that he had a clever daughter who used to do all the work he signed. That used to be a current bit of scandal in Fadge's circle.'

'Oh, there was much exaggeration in that,' remarked Jasper, blandly. 'His daughter assisted him, doubtless, but in quite a legitimate way. One used to see her at the Museum.'

The subject was dropped.

An hour and a half later, when the last stranger had taken his leave, Jasper examined two or three letters which had arrived since dinner-time and were lying on the hall table. With one of them open in his hand, he suddenly sprang up the stairs and leaped, rather than stepped, into the drawing-room. Amy was reading an evening paper.

'Look at this!' he cried, holding the letter to her.

It was a communication from the publishers who owned *The Current*; they stated that the editorship of that review would shortly be resigned by Mr Fadge, and they inquired whether Milvain would feel disposed to assume the vacant chair.

Amy sprang up and threw her arms about her husband's neck, uttering a cry of delight.

'So soon! Oh, this is great! this is glorious!'

'Do you think this would have been offered to me but for the spacious life we have led of late? Never! Was I right in my calculations, Amy?'

'Did I ever doubt it?'

He returned her embrace ardently, and gazed into her eyes with profound tenderness.

'Doesn't the future brighten?'

'It has been very bright to me, Jasper, since I became your wife.'

'And I owe my fortune to you, dear girl. Now the way is smooth!'

They placed themselves on a settee, Jasper with an arm about his wife's waist, as if they were newly plighted lovers. When they had talked for a long time, Milvain said in a changed tone:

'I am told that your uncle is dead.'

He mentioned how the news had reached him.

'I must make inquiries to-morrow. I suppose there will be a notice in *The Study*, and some of the other papers. I hope somebody will make it an opportunity to have a hit at that ruffian Fadge. By-the-by, it doesn't much matter now how you speak of Fadge; but I was a trifle anxious when I heard your story at dinner.'

'Oh, you can afford to be more independent. – What are you thinking about?'

'Nothing.'

'Why do you look sad? – Yes, I know, I know. I'll try to forgive you.'

'I can't help thinking at times of the poor girl, Amy. Life will be easier for her now, with only her mother to support. Someone spoke of her this evening, and repeated Fadge's lie that she used to do all her father's writing.'

'She was capable of doing it. I must seem to you rather a poor-brained woman in comparison. Isn't it true?'

'My dearest, you are a perfect woman, and poor Marian was only a clever school-girl. Do you know, I never could help imagining that she had ink-stains on her fingers. Heaven forbid that I should say it unkindly! It was touching to me at the time, for I knew how fearfully hard she worked.'

'She nearly ruined your life; remember that.'

Jasper was silent.

'You will never confess it, and that is a fault in you.'

'She loved me, Amy.'

'Perhaps! as a school-girl loves. But you never loved *her*.'

'No.'

Amy examined his face as he spoke.

'Her image is very faint before me,' Jasper pursued, 'and soon I shall scarcely be able to recall it. Yes, you are right; she nearly ruined me. And in more senses than one. Poverty and struggle, under such circumstances, would have made me a detestable creature. As it is, I am not such a bad fellow, Amy.'

She laughed, and caressed his cheek.

'No, I am far from a bad fellow. I feel kindly to everyone who deserves it. I like to be generous, in word and deed. Trust me, there's many a man who would like to be generous, but is made despicably mean by necessity. What a true sentence that is of Landor's.[47] "It has been repeated often enough that vice leads to misery; will no man declare that misery leads to vice?" I have much of the weakness that might become viciousness, but I am now far from the possibility of being vicious. Of course there are men, like Fadge, who seem only to grow meaner the more prosperous they are; but these are exceptions. Happiness is the nurse of virtue.'

'And independence the root of happiness.'

'True. "The glorious privilege of being independent" – yes, Burns understood the matter.[48] Go to the piano, dear, and play me something. If I don't mind, I shall fall into Whelpdale's vein, and talk about my "blessedness." Ha! isn't the world a glorious place?'

'For rich people.'

'Yes, for rich people. How I pity the poor devils! – Play any-thing. Better still if you will sing, my nightingale!'

So Amy first played, and then sang, and Jasper lay back in dreamy bliss.

NOTES

1. p.37. *He got a hundred pounds for "On Neutral Ground"*: Gissing published his first novel, *Workers in the Dawn* (1880), at his own expense. He received £30 for *The Unclassed* (1884), £15 for *Isabel Clarendon* (1886), and £100 for *Demas* (1886). For *New Grub Street* itself he received £150.

2. p.37. *must take either a work-girl or an heiress*. Gissing was much preoccupied with this question whilst writing *New Grub Street*; on 25 October 1890, he wrote to Eduard Bertz: 'I have made the acquaintance of a work-girl who will perhaps come to live with me when I leave this place at Christmas'. This was Edith Underwood, whom he married in February 1891.

3. p.46. *the valley of the shadow of books*. This phrase alludes to the 23rd Psalm: 'Yea, though I walk through the valley of the shadow of death, I will fear no evil'.

4. p.54. *training of the body*. Such notions were in the air at the time; see, for instance, Skepsey's idea of the 'regeneration of the English race by boxing' in Meredith's *One of Our Conquerors*, which appeared in the same year as *New Grub Street* (1891).

5. p.55. *Carlyle*. The reference may be to a passage in Carlyle's Inaugural Address as Rector of Edinburgh University: 'It would be much safer and better for many a reader that he had no concern with books at all. There is a number, a frightfully increasing number, of books that are decidedly, to the readers of them, not useful'. (I am indebted to Mr Ioan Williams for pointing this out to me).

6. p.58. *Some lines of Tennyson*. These lines come, not from the *Idylls*, but from one of the songs in *The Princess*, IV, 106.

7. p.68. *Elkanah Settle* (1648–1724) rivalled Dryden's popularity as a dramatist, and was satirized by Dryden as Doeg in the second part of *Absalom and Achitophel*. Settle published *Absalom Senior, or Achitophel Transpros'd* in 1682. Alfred Yule, in attacking Fadge, gets the title wrong himself.

8. p.69. *Cottle's poem*. Joseph Cottle (1770–1853), poet, bookseller, publisher, and friend of Coleridge, published *Malvern Hills: A Poem* in 1798.

9. p.88. *Tottenham Court Road*. Gissing had lodgings in this area when he first lived in London in 1878.

10. p.92. *half profits*. This method of publishing was used, as an

alternative to the outright sale by an author of his copyright, throughout the Victorian period, but was never very popular:
'In theory the half-profit contract should have identified the interests of author and publisher more closely than any other kind of arrangement. In actual practice it was distrusted by authors. As early as 1840 the author of a manual for young writers declared, 'By the last-named arrangement [profit-sharing] I must inform the inexperienced author that, except in extraordinary circumstances, *he will never receive one penny.*' One reason for this distrust was the too frequent lack of a definite understanding between the parties about the rendering of accounts.' Royal A. Gettmann, *A Victorian Publisher*, Cambridge, 1961, pp.105–106.

11. p.104. *merum sel*: 'pure salt', or true wit.

12. p.106. '*There is a tide*', From *Julius Caesar*, IV, iii:
There is a tide in the affairs of men,
Which taken at the flood, leads on to fortune.

13. p.122. *hinken*: to limp or hobble.

14. p.158. *Gets a royalty*. Towards the end of the nineteenth century the royalty system came to supersede the outright purchase of copyright, or the half-profits method. Gettmann records that it was first used by the house of Bentley in 1885. See *A Victorian Publisher*, pp.115–118.

15. p.179. *took the name of the chief female character*. As Gissing had done with *Isabel Clarendon* in 1886.

16. pp.181. *Mudie's*. The most celebrated of the London circulating libraries, founded by Charles Edward Mudie in 1840; it was exceedingly powerful in upholding conventional standards of literary taste.

17. p.187. *Diogenes Laertius*. He lived in the second or third century A.D., and was chiefly famous for the *Lives of the Philosophers*, in ten books.

18. p.203. *Noscitur ex sociis*: 'a man is known by the company he keeps'.

19. p.222. '*a kind of fighting*'. From *Hamlet*, V, 2:
In my heart there was a kind of fighting
That would not let me sleep.

20. p.235. *Coleridge*. James Gillman was a medical practitioner, in whose house at Highgate Coleridge lived from 1816 until his death.

21. p.235. *opera omnia*: all the works.

22. p.297. *compos mentis*: of sound mind.

23. p.330. *Tosti's*. The Italian song-writer, Francesco Tosti (1846–

1916), lived in England and established a great reputation as a writer of drawing-room ballads.

24. p.337. *Dr Johnson's saying.* Recorded in Boswell's *Life*, entry for March 1760.

25. p.345. *biblia abiblia*: books that are no books.

26. p.351. *Meminisse juvabit!* Yule's tag comes from Virgil, *Aeneid*, I, 203: *Forsan et haec olim meminisse juvabit*: Perhaps one day this too will be pleasant to remember.

27. p.352. *Lord Herbert of Cherbury* (1583–1648), elder brother of George Herbert, was philosopher, historian and poet.

28. p.362. *Love in a hut* ... The couplet comes from Keats, *Lamia*, II, 1.

29. p.376. *Caesar, 'tis his schoolmaster* ... : from *Antony and Cleopatra*, III, 12.

30. p.392. *Married Woman's Property Act.* This act came into force at the beginning of 1883, and abolished the traditional system whereby all a woman's property passed to her husband on her marriage. It meant that a married woman could own property and carry on a business in her own right, and was an important step towards female emancipation.

31. p.403. *diathesis*: constitutional predisposition, habit.

32. p.404. *some simple, kind-hearted work-girl.* See note to page 37.

33. p.410. *in secula seculorum*: world without end, for ever and ever.

34. p.426. *more suo*: in his own way.

35. p.427. Whelpdale's narrative recapitulates some of Gissing's own experiences in America in 1876–7.

36. p.433. *James Harrington* (1611–77), published *Oceana*, a utopian romance in 1656. He founded the Rota Club in 1659 for the advocacy of republican ideas. Cyriac Skinner, pupil and friend of Milton, was a member of the Club.

37. p.443. *Mrs Gummidge.* A character in *David Copperfield*.

38. p.471. *omnia mea mecum porto*: I carry all my possessions with me.

39. p.474. *Chatterton.* The celebrated boy poet and forger. He came to London from Bristol in 1770, at the age of eighteen, and committed suicide in the same year.

40. p.490. '*We are such stuff as dreams are made on* ...' From *The Tempest*, IV, 1.

41. p.493. *quocunque modo*: in whatever manner.

42. p.496. *Chit-Chat.* The magazine Whelpdale is describing patently refers to George Newnes's highly successful *Tit-Bits*, and

to Alfred Harmsworth's imitation of it, *Answers*, both launched in the eighties.

43. p.501. *Aristarchus.* Celebrated grammarian and critic of Alexandria, c. 150 B.C., who revised the text of the *Iliad* and *Odyssey*.

44. p.544. *causas rerum*: the causes of things.

45. p.545. *Northern Farmer.* A poem by Tennyson, written in Lincolnshire dialect.

46. p.548. *fallen on evil days.* Milvain is alluding to a passage in *Paradise Lost*, VII, in which the blind Milton laments his fate:

> More safe I sing with mortal voice, unchanged
> To hoarse or mute, though fall'n on evil days,
> On evil days though fall'n, and evil tongues.

47. p.450. *Landor's.* I have not been able to trace this quotation, although there is a similar sentiment expressed in Volume I of *Imaginary Conversations* ('Lord Brooke and Sir Philip Sidney'): 'Goodness does not more certainly make men happy, than happiness makes them good'.

48. p.450. *Burns understood the matter.* The reference is to 'Epistle to a Young Friend':

> To catch Dame Fortune's golden smile,
> Assiduous wait upon her;
> And gather gear by ev'ry wile
> That's justify'd by Honor:
> Not for to hide it in a hedge,
> Nor for a train-attendant;
> But for the glorious privilege
> Of being independent.

MORE ABOUT PENGUINS

Penguin Book News, which appears every month, contains details of all the new books issued by Penguins as they are published. Every four months it is supplemented by *Penguins in Print,* which is a complete list of all books published by Penguins which are in print. (There are nearly three thousand of these.)

A specimen copy of *Penguin Book News* will be sent to you free on request, and you can become a subscriber at 3s. for a year's issues (with the complete lists). Just write to Dept EP, Penguin Books Ltd, Harmondsworth, Middlesex, enclosing a cheque or postal order, and your name will be added to the mailing list.

Note: *Penguin Book News* and *Penguins in Print* are not available in the U.S.A. or Canada.